THE NASHVILLE FURY SERIES

CHELLE SLOAN

CWR PUBLISHING, LLC

OFF THE RECORD

NASHVILLE FURY: BOOK 1

1

SADIE

ATTACH.

Save.

Send.

I drum my manicured fingertips along the top of my makeshift desk as I impatiently wait for my computer to give me the signal that the longest workday of my life is officially over.

Sent.

"Done!" I shout as I throw my arms in the air in celebration. I'm sure I even let out a high-pitched "woo hoo!" for good measure. I would never consider myself a "woo-hoo girl" by any means. That's how excited I am that this day, and this football season, is finally over.

I wait for a reaction from someone. Anyone. But I get nothing. Not a clap. Not a "thatta-girl." Not even a sarcastic "It's about damn time."

I look around the empty press box and realize that yet again I'm the last one left working. Oh well. I don't even care. All I care about is that after seventeen agonizing weeks, this horrific, historic-for-all-the-wrong-reasons season of the Nashville Fury is officially in the books.

God, that was painful.

Not the stories I wrote. Those, if I do say so myself, were some of the best I've ever written. There's never a shortage of topics to write about when you're trying to figure out why a team that has made the playoffs every year all of a sudden can't figure out how to win. Why can't the defense tackle? Why can't the offense score? Why hasn't anyone been fired?

This is why the fans turn to me. They need answers. I provide them. Even if it means I'm the one turning out the lights in the press box after every game.

"About time you're done. You make the rest of us look bad when you work that hard."

I jump at the sound of Tommy's voice, but my look of scorn quickly morphs into a smile. You can't be mad when Tommy Reese is giving you shit.

"Maybe you should get on my level, old man. Can't let the young girl beat you."

Tommy is the most veteran reporter in the group of ten of us who cover the Fury on a regular basis. He's the only reporter who has covered the team for every game of their twenty-year existence and has sources so deep in the organization that the team owner doesn't even know where he gets his intel. He also smokes more cigarettes than the Marlboro Man and hasn't had a drop of liquor in a decade. And despite working for the rival newspaper in town, he quickly became my unofficial protector when I got assigned to cover the Fury two years ago.

"You don't get to play the girl card and you know it," he says as I begin to pack up my laptop and notes. "I told you that shit wasn't going to work on me when you got the job, and it's not going to work now. Let's go. You deserve a drink. The rest of the guys are waiting."

And that's what I love about Tommy. He doesn't care that I'm only twenty-seven. He doesn't care about my gender. I'm a reporter to him. Plain and simple.

It caused a lot of waves around town when I got this job. Not only was I a woman, but I was also the youngest by more than a decade. It was assumed because of my age that I didn't know anything. Add in that I have lady parts. Well, that obviously meant I had slept with someone to get here. At least, that was the chatter I heard when the rest of the reporters didn't think I was listening.

I did neither of those things. I worked my ass off and earned this spot fair and square. After two years of covering the Fury, that kind of talk has simmered. Mostly.

Occasionally, I'll get a fan who doesn't agree with me. Instead of just saying "I respectfully disagree," I'll get called a bitch who doesn't know a thing about football. Earlier this year I broke a story about a rookie getting a DUI, and I heard a reporter ask who I fucked to get the scoop.

Joke's on him. The only action of the sexual variety I'm seeing is from my good friend Ted.

He's my vibrator. He's great. Actually, he's more than great and he doesn't care if I haven't shaved in days.

"Gentlemen, the lady is finally gracing us with her presence!"

I laugh and take a little bow as my fellow reporters clap when I enter the media break room, which is down the hall from the press box. Now *this* is the reaction I was looking for ten minutes ago.

"Why, thank you, gentlemen. Your sarcasm doesn't go unnoticed," I say, putting down my oversized purse that carries my life inside it. Mary Poppins would be jealous of this thing. "Please tell me you left at least one beer for the lady."

"We left you two because you are such an overachiever," says Joe, one of the national writers. I take a seat next to him and twist open the ice-cold goodness. "What were you writing anyway? We were done an hour ago."

Joe has a fair point. Today's loss capped off a 2-14 season for the Fury, the worst, by far, in the team's history. The only thing to celebrate was that it was over, which is what I and the rest of the reporters are doing now. After the end of each season, the reporters traditionally hang around and have a celebratory, end-of-the-season beer, compliments of the team. After watching the horrible football that we were forced to endure this year, these beers were the least they could give us. They should have thrown in a pizza for good measure.

"I filed a story to have ready to go for when they fire Bancroft," I say, taking a pull from my beer bottle. "This way, when they do fire him, I don't have to rush to write a story."

I get a "what the fuck are you talking about" look from every man in the room. This isn't the first time I've been on the receiving end of this look. My guess is that it won't be the last.

"They aren't firing him. No way in hell," Joe says. "His contract is too big. And it was just one bad season. No one gets fired for one bad year."

I shrug my shoulders and sit back, not ready to fight with him or any other reporter about whether or not the offensive coordinator, Nick Bancroft, is about to be fired after the worst offensive season in Fury history.

"Plus," Joe continues, apparently not done with trying to flex his knowledge. "They're going to draft that hotshot quarterback from Clemson, and Bancroft will get his chance at redemption. None of us need to worry. We won't have to worry about football until the spring, and we can finally take the vacations our wives planned for us now. I, for one, am looking forward to ringing in the new year on a beach."

The conversation pivots to the trips they are taking, a few leaving as early as tomorrow. Many are on their way to family-friendly destinations such as Disney, or a beach house in the Carolinas. As for me? My annual singles' vacation isn't until June, and it was picked by closing my eyes and pointing to a map.

The winner? San Francisco. The Golden Gate Bridge, Alcatraz, and anything else my heart desires. That's the joy of being single. I can do anything I want, and I don't have to answer to anyone.

And that is not at all depressing. That's at least what I keep telling myself. Most days I believe it.

Buzz. Buzz. Buzz.

The sound of my cell phone breaks me from my thoughts. And it's not just my phone going off with alerts. Every cell phone in the room is buzzing or chirping.

We all grab our phones, which are never too far out of reach, and check what just came through. An email. From the Fury.

Subject: Media release: Nashville Fury, Offensive Coordinator Nick Bancroft part ways

The synchronized mutters of "oh fuck" and "you have got to be shitting me" are heard from around the room. The guys scramble to turn their laptops back on, text their wives that they won't be home any time soon, and to cancel their vacation plans.

Me? I sit back, kick my feet up on the table, and smile as I finish my beer, knowing my June vacation plans are fully intact.

The story I just got made fun of for writing? It was for this reason. As my fellow reporters are frantically typing away, my story is already written and filed with my editor. As I pick up my phone and head to the website for *The Nashville Banner*, my story is already live with the esteemed honor of being the first to report.

I worked smart. I was first. And if I have anything to say about it, I will be breaking the story when the team makes the new hire, whoever he is.

Sadie: 1.

Rest of the reporters: 0.

2

____

HUNTER

"I'LL TAKE A MEDIUM COFFEE, two creams. To go. Thank you, darlin'."

The young girl behind the counter blushes and almost drops my change when she hands me back the bills that I promptly put in her tip jar. I give her one more smile before walking to the other side of the counter to wait for my drink—a smile that earns me another blush.

She's cute. A bit young, and I say that sincerely being only twenty-eight myself. I wonder if she's a regular worker here? Would I see her all the time if the Fury hire me?

I step away from the counter and take a look around the quaint sandwich and coffee shop that sits across the street from the Fury's training facility. I like it. There's country music playing in the background, but it's not blaring. There are some people having lunch together. Some have headphones on and are furiously typing on their laptops. I have a perfect view of my potential new office from the booth seating at the windows. I can picture it now, picking up a cup of coffee before heading to practice, or coming over here to grab lunch with the other coaches to strategize for the next game.

The best part? No one is staring at me. No one is whispering. No one knows who I am.

I can't lie, it's been a while since something like that happened.

I like it. A lot.

I don't remember a time in my life when I wasn't recognized. Growing up, I was the son of Bo McAvoy—the best quarterback to ever play collegiately at Alabama. When you grow up in Birmingham, that makes you sports royalty.

When I announced that I was carrying on the family tradition for the Crimson Tide, I couldn't go anywhere without a camera being in my face. The media created the narrative that I was going to be the second coming of my father.

However, I never lived up to that hype. My dad led his team to four championships, won two Heisman Trophies and was the top draft pick when he turned pro. He went on to have a ten-year pro career, retired in his prime and was inducted into the Hall of Fame on the first ballot.

Me? I was a good quarterback, but I wasn't great. What I lacked in my play-making ability, I made up for with my brains. I'm what you call "football smart." I love strategizing Xs and Os. Designing plays. Outsmarting the guys across the sideline. It excites me more than throwing a touchdown ever did. So, after my last play at Alabama, which included lifting up my only national championship trophy, I transitioned my life from playing to coaching.

Much to my father's dismay.

I've been called a coaching prodigy. The talking heads on sports radio think that I'm the future of what a professional coach will look like. If I'm hired by the Fury, I will be the youngest offensive coordinator in league history.

All of that doesn't mean a thing to Bo McAvoy, though. I'm not a professional football player, therefore I am nothing.

I can't let his voice in my head today. Not when the biggest interview of my life is happening in an hour.

"Thanks. I don't think I tell you this enough, but you are the MVP of my life." The sound of a female voice grabs my attention. I look over to the counter and realize it is coming from a pretty brunette placing an order. "Oh! And good luck with your show tonight. I'm doing my best to make it."

I don't know why the sound of this conversation breaks me from my thoughts, but it does. I also don't know why I'm intrigued by a mundane conversation.

"You don't have to come. I know you're busy."

"Nonsense," the customer says, waving the comment away. "You keep me caffeinated every day. The least I can do is come and watch you perform."

I'm now officially eavesdropping. Yet, I can't seem to find it in myself to stop. If I'm being real, I couldn't care less about the conversation. What has me intrigued is that I can't stop staring at the profile of the brunette.

A brunette who is now looking at me.

I hurry and turn away, not wanting to come across as some sort of creep. Though, I can't help but sneak another look as she walks toward me to wait for her order. If she sees me looking again, she doesn't notice. And for that I'm grateful because I now have a direct view.

She's shorter than I am, which doesn't say much considering I'm six foot three. Her small frame is housing a set of curves I want to get lost in. I've never been a fan of women who resemble sticks, and this girl is anything but that.

She's not one of those overdone sorority girls I would see at Alabama. She looks… real. Her hair is on top of her head in one of those messy buns that I only know the name of because of my younger sister. Her black-rimmed glasses don't hide her hazel eyes. I don't think she has an ounce of makeup on her face either.

She's gorgeous. My physical type in every way. That's not even taking into account the smile I saw her give a few minutes ago. It's a smile that would make men spill war secrets.

If I knew I was getting this job, I would be striking up a conversation with this woman immediately. Maybe even asking her out for dinner. Definitely getting her number. It has been years since I was in a relationship. When you're a coach who is still earning his stripes, you are told you won't be at the same place for very long, so don't get comfortable. I've never had an apartment lease longer than a year. I haven't had a girlfriend since college. What's the point in trying to date when you know you can't offer them anything long term? Plus, I've needed to focus on my career. I'm not going to climb the professional football coaching ladder by wasting time on relationships that will likely not go anywhere.

But if I'm hired in Nashville, all of that changes.

"Excuse me? Hunter?"

The sound of my name snaps me out of my trance. Apparently, a beautiful smile and an amazing ass render me stupid.

"Yes?" I say, hoping to cover up my obvious staring.

"Are you Hunter?"

I try not to, but I let out a disappointed sigh. I knew it was too good to be true that no one would recognize me. It might not be Alabama, or Houston, where I'm currently coaching, but I'm still Hunter McAvoy.

"I am. Are you a football fan?"

She lets out an almost evil laugh. "Not even a little bit."

It's my turn to give her a perplexed look. "Then how did you know my name?"

She glances at the counter, then back to me. "Because they're calling out an order for Hunter, and you are the only one here without a drink in his hand. Besides me. And I know my name isn't Hunter."

As soon as she's done putting me in my place, I hear the call, "Medium coffee for Hunter!"

I let out a nervous laugh. "Sorry. I don't know where my head went."

She gives me a side-eye, but luckily doesn't call me on my shit. "No worries. Though I'm afraid you're missing out on the greatness that is Sandwich City by only getting a coffee."

She's making conversation with me. I like it. I grab my coffee off the counter and turn my focus directly back to her. "It's my first time here. I wanted to play it safe. What should I have gotten? You know, since I'm missing out."

She thinks about it for a second, one eyebrow raising slightly over her glasses. "I know it's called Sandwich City, but I'm a sucker for their wraps. I pretty much live on them. I highly recommend the chicken Caesar. Though they do serve good coffee, so you didn't completely strike out."

The worker doesn't even call out her name when her order is ready. She tells him thanks, grabs her tray—a wrap and drink on it— and starts walking toward an open table.

I follow her like a lost puppy. I realize she hasn't invited me, but I'm not ready for this conversation to be over. Though I should leave. I should be taking this time to prepare for the interview that could change the course of my career. I should not be flirting with a woman whose name I don't even know, much less whose name I'll never learn if I don't get this job because I'll never see her again.

"What's so good about the chicken Caesar?" I say, taking a seat across from her.

"Make yourself comfortable," she says with a hint of teasing in her voice.

"I don't mind if I do."

We both stare at each other for a few seconds. I can tell she's trying to figure me out. Me? I'm wondering if her eyes have flecks of gold in them, or if I'm imagining things being blinded by her beauty.

"It's the dressing," she says, breaking the silence.

"The dressing?"

"Yes. You asked what was so good about the chicken Caesar." She shakes her head and laughs a little. Likely at the fact that I can't seem to remember what I'm saying around her. "It's the dressing. I don't know what they put in it, and they won't tell me. I've decided it's crack. It's delicious and I crave it daily."

I want to think of something witty to say. Something smooth. Something that will make her smile at me like she did the barista earlier. For the life of me, I can't think of anything. Instead, I just stare at her like a fucking idiot.

This isn't me. I'm charming. Or so I've been told. I was raised to be a southern gentleman. You wouldn't know it now with the way I'm acting around… Shit. I still don't know her name.

"I hope I'll be back to try it." My words come out shakier than I'd like, but hell, at least I'm speaking. "I'm sorry. I didn't catch your name?"

She gives me a knowing smile. "Because I didn't tell you."

Interesting. Is she playing hard to get? "That's not fair. You know mine."

"Who said I planned on playing fair?"

I laugh, loving how confident she is in her words. "You're right. Thank you for the wrap recommendation."

"In town on business?" she asks, fishing a laptop out of the biggest purse I have ever seen.

"An interview." Though, right now, her question makes me feel like the interview has already started.

"Interesting," she says, now booting up her laptop that is covered in stickers. "Well, if you end up getting the job, I highly recommend this place. I eat here almost every day."

"Do you live nearby?"

"Not really," she says, though she isn't looking at me. She's typing something furiously on her laptop. Message received. She's more interested in her laptop than a conversation with me. "My work is just nearby, which means I'm here a lot."

I want to ask her what she does for a living. I want to know her damn name. I want to know a lot of things about this beautiful woman who didn't kick me away from her table. But my Smartwatch vibrates, notifying me it's time for me to head over to the Fury's front offices.

"As much as I would love to stay and chat, and believe me, I would, I have to get going," I say, though I make no immediate attempt to stand up.

She finishes typing and looks up at me, giving me a smile that is a combination of devious and beautiful. Holy hell, am I getting mixed signals from this woman.

"Good luck on your interview. Maybe we'll see each other around again."

"Do I get to know your name?" I ask, finally standing up and grabbing my coffee.

"You'll know it soon enough." Her words are followed by that knowing smile before she focuses back on her laptop. I let my gaze hang on her for a few extra seconds before I turn to leave, wondering what her words mean.

As soon as I step out into the cool air of January in Nashville, I feel my phone vibrate in my pocket. I fish it out, wondering who is texting me. My family knows not to bother me today until I call them. Same with the few friends I've told about this.

I don't see a text alert. Rather, it's a notification that I get when a new story is written about me and is posted on the Internet.

Huh. That's weird.

I know for a fact that no one from Houston leaked that I was here. Nashville is also keeping a tight lid on candidates. Firing Bancroft was a gutsy move on their part. He has been bashing them to every media outlet that will listen to him. They know they have to get this hire right.

When I open my phone, I see the article clear as day:

"Hunter McAvoy in Nashville; interviewing for offensive coordinator job"

How in the hell did this get out?

I hurry and read the story, making sure what is written is at least accurate. On a quick glance, nothing seems out of place or completely erroneous.

I scroll back up to the top of the article, wondering who this reporter is. I'll have to keep my eye out for him if I get the job. He has to have some good sources if he was able to break this story when only a few people know I'm in town.

Except when I get back to the top and see the picture of the reporter, it's definitely not a him. I'm greeted by a photo of a beautiful, smiling brunette next to the name Sadie Benson. Her hair isn't up on top of her head in this photo, though, but a familiar pair of hazel eyes are looking at me.

As I look back inside the deli, that same set of eyes are now filled with mischief as Sadie gives me a little wave before closing her laptop.

3

———

SADIE

"GOOD REPORTING, Sadie! You kicked that story's ass."

I smile at Bill, one of the copy editors and a self-proclaimed Fury fanatic, as I walk into the newsroom of *The Banner*. "Thanks. I appreciate that. How've you been?"

"Not as good as you. Is there a story about Hunter McAvoy that you *haven't* broken? Huge scoops! What do you think about him? Is he the guy? Is it a good hire?"

What I want to say is that Hunter McAvoy is a brilliant offensive football mind and a great hire. I predict that under his coaching and guidance, the Fury will be back in the playoffs as soon as this year.

I also want to say that he's the hottest man I've ever seen in real life, and I don't know how I'm going to function at my job when I have to look at him all the time.

In preparation, I've already bought extra batteries for Ted.

My cheeks flush just thinking about his dark blond hair and his perfectly built frame. The man might not have played football for a few years, but you'd never know that based off of his physique. I know this because I interviewed him once in college. I doubt he remembers me. I was in a pool of a dozen other reporters, though I did ask one semi-memorable question. But you don't forget seeing a man like Hunter. No matter how many years have passed.

That was also the first time I noticed his smile. Back then it was a camera-ready one. One that every newspaper in the country wanted to put on the front page. The one I got at Sandwich City? It was the same, but different. More genuine. Still devastating.

For a few seconds when he sat down with me, I wondered what it would be like if I wasn't a reporter. I let myself pretend, just for a second, that I was a normal, twenty-something having an impromptu lunch with a good-looking guy. I might not be the most experienced when it comes to men and relationships, but I could tell Hunter was flirting with me.

Which is a whole other new feeling for me. Men don't flirt with me. I'm not what you'd call your classic beauty. I'm a reformed tomboy who has a few extra curves, and who tolerates the bare minimum of makeup. I'm not the girl guys like Hunter McAvoy have lunch with.

Though, I'd be a liar if I said I didn't like the idea of it.

It had been a very long time since a man flirted with me. Yes, guys with their keyboard courage hit on me on Twitter (not the best place to try to shoot your shot). In real life? Men who approach me are few and far between.

Sitting with Hunter, Pretend Me wanted to flirt back. She wanted to continue listening to his southern accent and let our impromptu lunch turn into an impromptu afternoon. Pretend Me might have even gone as far as to slyly offer him my phone number in hopes that he'd call me for another meal, only this time planned.

Then I remembered I was a reporter. And he was interviewing for a job for the team I cover. Just the thought of that was like an ice-cold bath to my thoughts and fantasies.

Not that they have completely gone away. Talking to Bill right now? I'm the definition of cool, calm, and unaffected by Hunter McAvoy. To myself when I'm at home with Ted? Not so much.

"We'll see how he fits with the team," I say, remembering that Bill had asked me a question. And now that I've been thinking about

Hunter for more than five seconds, I really want this conversation to be over before the coloring on my cheeks gives me away. "Have you seen John? I have a meeting with him."

"He's in the editors' meeting. Do you think they are going to draft that Clemson quarterback?"

I smile because Bill always has to sneak in one more Fury question. "They'd be stupid not to. I'll talk to you later."

I wave to a few other reporters as I head to my boss's office and take a seat at my usual spot on his raggedy couch. It has seen better days. There is a spring cutting into my back, and the cushions are down to their final threads. I don't care though. All of my best brainstorming has been done sitting here while John sits at his desk. Why mess with things now when I've been on the best professional roll of my career?

I might have downplayed my excitement to Bill, but I have been kicking ass on all things related to the hiring of Hunter McAvoy.

Seeing him at Sandwich City was sheer luck. The fact that he told me he was in town for an interview was the gift I didn't ask for, but I wasn't about to turn it down. Should I have told him who I was? Maybe. Do I regret writing the story? Not one bit.

A week after his interview, he was hired. Again, I was first on the story thanks to my source inside the Fury front office.

I've really been kicking ass and taking names lately.

"There's our girl!" John says as he comes into his office. "I just left a meeting where every editor praised you up and down for the work you've been doing. You're impressing a lot of people, Benson."

I shrug off the compliment. I've never been good at taking them. Especially from John. "Thanks. It was my first coaching search, so I wanted to do a good job."

John sits down at his desk, propping his feet up on the corner like he always does. "Good job? You've been doing a great job. You're a good reporter, Sadie. I've always known that about you. But since you started working the Fury beat? You've excelled. I'm proud of you."

I smile and say thanks, almost embarrassed by the praise. John is the only boss I've ever known. He gave me a shot at a sports internship during my sophomore year of college. I worked for him each summer, and when I graduated from Tennessee, he hired me to cover high school sports. I did that for three years before I was promoted to cover the Fury. He gave me my first real chance in the big leagues. I don't want to let him down.

"So, what story do you want next?" I ask, getting my notebook ready to jot down the story ideas.

"I want you to get the one-on-one with him."

I look up from my notebook and give John a questioning look. Which I hope covers the blush that is trying to creep through as he mentions the thought of me and Hunter one-on-one.

And now, thinking about not blushing is making me blush. Because oh, the things I'd love for Hunter McAvoy to do to me one-on-one.

Shit. Bad thoughts, Sadie. Bad, dirty thoughts!

Quick. Think of unsexy things.

Dentures.

Burps.

Opossums.

Phew. That was a close one.

"The one-on-one?" My voice comes out still a little too high-pitched, but John doesn't seem to notice. "Don't they always give that interview to Tommy?"

The Fury is famous, at least famous among the reporters, for giving only one exclusive interview to a reporter of their choosing when a new coach or executive is hired. And "of their choosing" always means Tommy.

"Yes, they have in the past. But I don't want you to give up on it." John moves his feet off his desk to assume his serious pose. Which for him is his hands clasped together, elbows on his desk. "You have been doing good work, Sadie. Actually, it's great work. If you continue doing what you're doing, you could be getting a call from the Mothership."

If I gave John a questioning look before when he brought up the one-on-one, I am straight-up looking at him like he's an alien now.

The Mothership is what we call our national news outlet, *US Daily*. It's the largest newspaper in the country. If you get a job there, you've made it.

"*US Daily*? What are you talking about? You know they only hire reporters who have covered teams for at least ten years. Plus, they already have a woman on staff. You know sports departments can't have too much estrogen walking around freely or they crumble."

He laughs, knowing that even though I'm joking, I'm mostly right. "It's just whispers right now, but there could be an opening. I know the national editors have been impressed with your work. Landing the one-on-one with McAvoy would be a big win for you."

John and I finish up our meeting, strategize for the next month of coverage, and he makes me promise on his coveted stack of classic *Sports Illustrated* magazines that I will not only take my vacation to San Francisco in June, but that I won't fight him on taking a week off after the Super Bowl, which is in two weeks.

His reasoning? I work too much and taking time off between the Super Bowl and the draft won't kill me.

I try to process everything as I take my short walk back to my apartment from *The Banner*. Is John right? Could a national job be on the horizon for me? Can I afford to take time off if I could seriously be hired at *US Daily*?

Being a national football writer is something I've dreamed of since I started reading *US Daily* as a kid. My dad used to save the sports page for me every Sunday, and we would talk about every story. We would dissect every word. That's what I get for being the daughter of a high school English teacher who is also a sports freak. It was what we did together.

It's why being a sports reporter is the only thing I've ever wanted to be. I dreamed of the day that my name would grace the pages of *US Daily.* I knew it wouldn't be easy. It's not. It's a demanding job. I'm always on call. There's no room for a personal life. There's barely time to cook a meal, let alone schedule one with someone else. I don't care, though. I love it. It's who I am. I can't imagine doing anything else with my life.

It's why my apartment is small and barely decorated. It's why I haven't had a real relationship since college. It's why I can't cook more than a pot of spaghetti.

None of that matters when my goals are within reach.

And they are. I just need to keep my eye on the prize.

No complications.

No distractions.

Especially ones that come in the form of a sexy and charming coach.

4

HUNTER

The question comes from an intern, and I resist the urge to tell him to not call me Mr. McAvoy. Mr. McAvoy is my father—who couldn't be bothered to come to Nashville for my introductory press conference, which is set to start at any minute.

"Ready as I'll ever be."

My tone is more confident than what I'm feeling inside, which doesn't make any sense. It's not because I'm nervous to face a group of reporters. I couldn't give a shit about them.

Well, that's mostly true.

I don't remember a time when I wasn't being followed by a reporter or a camera. The first time I was interviewed was when I was eight. He wanted to know where I planned to play college football. At the college football national championship game, I was flooded with no less than one hundred cameras during a three-hour media day. One time a reporter followed me around a grocery store.

The headline read:

"What does Hunter McAvoy eat for breakfast? You won't believe his cereal choice."

It was Cheerios. Not even the flavored kind, the plain ol' original. That must have been a very slow news day.

So, when I say I don't care about the media, I really don't. They have been the annoying rock in the bottom of my shoe for most of my life. From my experience, they are all about getting the story by any means possible. If they have to elaborate, they will. If they have to twist your words for a good headline, they will do it without thinking twice.

Then there are the reporters who just have to flash you a pretty smile, and you unknowingly become the unnamed source in your own story.

I really should have been more upset after Sadie wrote the article spilling the secret that I was in town for my interview. The Fury freaked out that my name leaked, and Houston wasn't all too happy about the news getting out, either.

As much as I wanted to hate it, and her, I had to admit she did nothing wrong. The article was accurate. In fact, everything I've read of hers since I was hired has been good. I generally don't read much of what is written about me—I found over the years it was mostly half-truths or straight-up lies—but I couldn't help but read what the girl who has been on my mind since I first saw her had to say.

She's smart. She writes well. She knows her football. I haven't met many good reporters, but she seems to fit that bill.

And it has nothing to do with the fact that I can still hear her laugh. Or that her ass has been the subject of my dreams since our first encounter.

The sound of a door opening breaks me from my thoughts as Paul, the head of media relations, waves me into the interview room. I don't even get the chance to smooth my tie one more time before the flashes of cameras start going off from every direction. Somehow, I find my focus and make my way to the table where I'll be seated next to Jimbo Gordon, the Fury's veteran head coach.

If my dad is a legend as a player, the same can be said for Jimbo Gordon as a head coach. He won three championship rings before coming to Nashville, and up until this year, he led the Fury to the playoffs every season. He's also in his late seventies, and he says to anyone who will listen that the only way he's retiring from coaching is if he's taken off the field in a body bag. Now *that* would be a headline.

I reach my hand out to shake Coach Gordon's, pausing and turning to give the photographers what they want: a grip-and-grin photo of the elder statesman head coach, and his bright, shiny, young offensive coordinator.

As I stand posed with a smile plastered on my face, I can't help but look around the room. I tell myself it's to familiarize myself with the setup of reporters, but I know deep down there is only one reporter I'm looking for. In the back are the video guys, pointing their cameras at me. There are the photographers in front on the floor, trying to get different angles of a standard handshake. Sitting in the middle of the room are a flock of reporters, all a bunch of middle-aged white men who look like they have never missed a meal.

My eyes make their way to the front row of seats… and there she is. Sadie is furiously typing away on a familiar-looking laptop. I don't normally notice things like laptops, but then again, not many women have a sticker on theirs that says, "Not Today, Satan." I also can't help but notice that her hair is exactly how it was when we first met.

I wonder what it looks like down over her shoulders? Or what it would look like fanned out across my pillow?

Coach Gordon gives my hand a final squeeze, signaling for me to take a seat and, even if he doesn't know it, to drag my mind out of the gutter.

Paul prepared me for how this would go, and now, twenty minutes in, everything has gone to script. Coach Gordon began the press conference with a statement about me and why I'm a good fit for the Fury. After that, it was my turn to recite the speech that I rehearsed so much over the past two days, I could say it in my sleep.

The second I was done talking, hands from the reporters flew into the air, which is exactly what Paul said would happen. Each question thrown at me was a little more asinine than the last.

"How does it feel knowing you are the youngest offensive coordinator in league history?"

"What's it like being Bo McAvoy's son?"

"What did your dad say about you getting this job?"

"Does it bother you that half of your players are older than you?"

"Talk about why you think you're experienced enough to have this job."

I hate when reporters say, "talk about." It's not a question. It's a demand.

As the press conference rolls along, I answer every question, each one more remedial than the last. Finally, there are no more hands in the air.

"Any last questions?" Paul asks, and I secretly hope no one says anything. That is, until I see a hand from the front row go up.

"Hunter. Sadie Benson from *The Banner*. Having not been a coordinator before, you have no prior track record of what kind of offensive scheme you plan on running. Do you have an offensive plan in mind that will be implemented no matter what? Or will you wait and tailor your offense around whoever the team drafts to be the next quarterback?"

I have to blink a few times as the question settles in my brain. That wasn't an easy question. That wasn't a standard press conference question. That was a thought-through, intelligent, football-minded question. And it came from the mouth of a woman who has done nothing but surprise me since the moment she told me my coffee was ready.

"Great question, Sadie. You're right. There isn't film on how I've run offenses in the past. Having been a quarterback, though, I understand that offenses run better when your signal caller is comfortable. Whoever our next quarterback will be, this offense will play to his strengths. No matter who is under center, I will look at the personnel at my disposal and put together the best offense I can around the pieces I have."

As soon as my answer is complete, Paul closes the press conference, reminding reporters that he'll be in touch with them when draft prep begins.

As the reporters file out, I take a sip of my water, trying to calm myself down. I don't know what it says about me that just the sound of a beautiful woman asking me football questions turns me on so much that I need an extra minute before I stand up.

My reaction to Sadie is inappropriate on so many levels, especially in public and when cameras are present.

For starters, I'm a coach. She's the media. There are clear lines that have been drawn between coaches and reporters for years. It's defined and respected. The two don't intermingle. They aren't friends. They for sure don't date.

Plus, I might have told myself the day I met Sadie that I could see myself asking her out, but at the end of the day, I'm focused on my career. I'm not here for a relationship. I'm here to make my mark on the coaching world. I'm here to show that I might be young, but I am going to be damn good at this job. I'm going to lead the Fury back to the playoffs, and if I have my say so, to a championship.

I'm here to show everyone that I'm not just Bo McAvoy's son. That I am my own man.

None of that will happen if I let myself be distracted. Especially by the likes of Sadie Benson.

"Sadie. Can you come back here? Hunter. Do you have another minute?"

Paul's request takes me by surprise, and from the look on Sadie's face as she turns back toward us, the same can be said for her. Hell, I didn't even know he was right beside me.

"I don't know if you two have officially met. Hunter, this is Sadie Benson. She covers the team for *The Nashville Banner*."

I don't know how she wants to play this, and I sure as hell don't want to give away that my dick has just now calmed down from her question during the press conference, so I choose the nonchalant route. "Nice to officially meet you."

"Likewise," she says, giving me a cordial smile, clearly picking up on tone and choice of words. "Congratulations on the position."

She extends her hand to shake mine, which I gladly accept. I'm not going to think about how smooth her skin feels against mine, or that I have to fight the urge not to run my thumb across the top of her knuckles.

"Hunter, I wanted to introduce Sadie to you because she will be spending one day with you, one-on-one, for an exclusive interview. Sadie, congratulations, the one-on-one is yours."

I drop Sadie's hand like it's on fire from Paul's words. Paul has unloaded a lot of information on me since it was formally announced that I was hired, but I'm sure I would have remembered the possibility of Sadie getting a one-on-one interview with me. And as I take a glance at Sadie, the look on her face is just as shocked as mine. Though I doubt it's for the same reason—unless she's also trying to figure out how to navigate an entire day with her without getting hard.

"Sadie, do you have any ideas of where you'd like this?" Paul continues, clearly not realizing the inadvertent bomb he dropped on me. "The setting can be of your choosing, as long as Hunter is comfortable."

Comfortable? Paul is worried about my comfort? Does he not realize that if this woman is talking football to me for hours on end that I will not be able to walk for a week? That sure as shit is not comfortable.

Fuck. I need to get these thoughts under control. She's a reporter. I'm a coach. Yes, she's attractive. Yes, a woman talking football to me is apparently my sexual kryptonite. But this isn't the first, or last, time I will be interviewed by her. I can't let my attraction get the best of me every time we are in the same room. If I do, then this will be a very long season.

With a lot of cold showers.

"I'd like to interview him with his family in Birmingham."

The words "family" and "Birmingham" snap me out of my thoughts. That cold shower I was contemplating not even a minute ago? She might as well have dumped an entire ice bath over my head.

Of course, she would want to interview my dad. Figures. This proves that despite my attraction toward her, she's just like every other reporter I've encountered. It's not about me as my own man. It's about how my dad has influenced my life. Or how he molded me into the coach I am today.

The answer? He didn't.

But I can't say that. No one knows that the relationship between me and my father is cordial on a good day. So I do what I've done my entire life when a reporter has wanted to interview me and the great Bo McAvoy.

I suck it up.

"Sounds great. Pick a day next week and we can head to Birmingham."

5

____

SADIE

"DID you pack extra batteries for your recorder?"

"Yes, Dad."

"And your laptop charger? You know you tend to forget that."

"Already double-checked for it."

"And the pepper spray? You still carry that, right?"

"Yes, I still carry it. Though I doubt I will need it."

He's silent for a moment, and even though this is a normal phone conversation, I can feel him giving me his dad stare through his wire-rimmed glasses. It's the stare that screams, "I don't care how many times I've asked you, I'm going to always ask you, so deal with it."

"You will be alone in a car with a man you barely know," he says, breaking the silence. "A lot can happen on a three-hour drive."

"It's two hours and forty-five minutes."

My attempt at a joke falls short on my father. I can hear the exasperated breath he lets out. I'm quite familiar with the sound. If I had to put money on it, he has his head tilted back, asking for some sort of celestial guidance in regard to my sarcastic humor.

"Don't get sassy with me, young lady. You know Helen and I worry about you. And you wouldn't have to hear all of my dad warnings if you didn't require these packing phone calls."

I smile at my dad's words as I toss my notebook and pen into my purse. I don't know if the word "require" is the best word to use, but our phone calls while I'm packing have become a tradition for us. It started when I was in college. I was so nervous before my first out-of-town assignment that I was sure I was going to forget something. So, I called my dad and stepmom to start naming off things I might need. Had I not called them, I would have forgotten important things like my hairbrush, my computer charger, and toothpaste.

Since then, I've called my dad to help me pack before every out-of-town assignment. Yes, this is only a short drive to Birmingham—we'll go down and come back in the same day—but it felt weird to not call my dad as I prepared for Hunter to pick me up. It's tradition, after all. And you don't break tradition.

That's at least what I tell myself as I toss my extra phone charger into my purse. I refuse to admit that I need my dad as a buffer to keep my thoughts away from the fact that I'll be alone in a car for two hours and forty-five minutes with Hunter McAvoy.

I can do this. I can be strong. I won't even need my random gross things to keep my mind out of the gutter.

The day is straightforward. Hunter insisted on driving to Birmingham, and during the car ride, he agreed to allow me to ask him some initial interview questions. That will make the drive go by in a snap. We'll then arrive at his parents' house, where I'll interview his mom and dad about their son's accomplishments. Readers love good family anecdotes. The photographer we hired out of Birmingham will take some photos to accompany the article, and before I know it, we'll be heading back toward Music City.

Easy, right? What could go wrong?

Nothing. Nothing will go wrong. That is, as long as Hunter doesn't look at me like he did the first day we met. And as long as he doesn't smile. And as long as I don't feel a spark like I did when we shook hands at the press conference.

As long as none of those things happen, or anything else that makes me think about him naked, then everything will go off without a hitch.

BeepBeep! Beep! Beep! BeepBeep! Beeeeeeeeeep!

"When do you plan to change that alarm sound?" My dad asks as the alert on my watch goes off, telling me it's time to go downstairs and meet Hunter. "That is, without a doubt, the most annoying sound in the world."

"Never. I've never missed a reminder because of it. I have a system. You remind me of everything I need, and the alarm tells me it's time to go. It's fool-proof."

"Whatever you need to tell yourself, slugger."

I smile at the old nickname my dad gave me when I was six. Who knew me wanting to play baseball would lead to a nickname carried on years later? "I have to go downstairs and meet Hunter. I'll text you when I'm back in town tonight."

"Be safe, Sadie. I love you."

"Love you, too, Dad."

I hang up the phone and grab my oversized purse before locking up my apartment and heading down to the street level. My apartment might be convenient to both the stadium and the newspaper, but street parking is horrible for guests, which is why I told Hunter I'd meet him out front at nine a.m.

As soon as I exit my building, I notice a newer-model, sleek, red pickup truck parked against the curb. Even though the windows are slightly tinted, I can see Hunter clear as day. I'm immediately drawn to his profile, the strong cut of his jawline, and even though I can only see a little bit of him, he definitely is something nice to look at in the morning.

Stop it, Sadie! Right the fuck now!

Pimples.

Body odor.

Toenail clippings.

I've got a combined five-and-a-half hours of being alone with him. Maybe I didn't think this thing completely through. I take one long breath before opening up the truck door, doing my best to level my voice so I don't come across sounding like a teenage girl who is being picked up by the most popular boy in school. "Hi. Thanks for picking me up."

"You ready?"

The shortness in his tone takes me off guard. That, and he didn't even look my way or acknowledge me when I got in the truck. Not a glance. Not even a side-eye. I'm not saying that he had to look at me like he did when we first met, I'd actually prefer it if he didn't, but a glance or a nod of the head would have been nice.

I wonder what crawled up his ass this morning?

"Sure," I say, a bit defeated at how this trip is beginning. "Let's go."

The car ride is deathly silent as we make our way out of Nashville. The radio isn't even on. It's an uncomfortable silence that I was not mentally prepared for.

"Do you mind if I ask you a few of the questions I had planned?" I say, getting my recorder and notebook out of my purse.

"Fine."

Well, if that isn't a welcoming invitation for a personal and forthright interview, I don't know what is.

"Do you remember the first time you thought to yourself, 'I want to be a coach'?"

"Not really."

I blink a few times. Really? That's his answer? If the temperature in the cab of his truck was icy before, it's downright frigid now.

I attempt to rephrase the question. "You don't? Not even an old play you drew up on a notebook in elementary school?"

My attempt at being more conversational falls on deaf ears. He doesn't answer. He keeps his focus strictly on the road.

I try to ask a few more questions. They run from the basic "What is your favorite part of coaching?" to the complex "What do you think is the best offense to run in this age of football?" All of my questions come with one- to three-word answers, and a pissy tone thrown in for good measure.

I should be happy about this. Well, not the interview. His quotes that are barely sentences won't do shit for my article. But him being cold to me is exactly what I need to keep my mind out of the gutter and focused on the article. This is what today is about. Today is not about how his demeanor makes me sad and confused. It's about the story, only the story.

This is what I keep telling myself as we cross the Tennessee border into Alabama. I keep telling myself that all the way to Birmingham.

And when we pull into his parents' driveway, I almost believe it.

6

HUNTER

I REMEMBER the first time I realized that as long as my last name was McAvoy, I'd always be Bo's son, first and foremost. That no matter what I did, my accomplishments would always be tied back to him.

I was seven years old.

I had just thrown my first touchdown in Pop Warner football. I was so excited. I saw my receiver wide open, and before I knew it, he was running into the end zone.

It was one of the best moments of my life.

That was until my coach said words that I'll never forget: *"It was just like your daddy threw that ball."*

I remember being confused. I was pretty sure it was a compliment. At least, in my coach's eyes, it was. But my dad didn't throw the touchdown. I did. It was at that moment I realized that every touchdown I threw for the rest of my life… every decision that involved a football… would all be somehow tied back to Bo.

Later, I figured out that everything I did was never good enough for him. If I threw for 150 yards in a game, he would tell me why it should have been 160. When I was the number two quarterback recruit in the country in high school, all I heard for months was what I did wrong to not be number one.

That is why I became a perfectionist. Maybe if I got it perfect, it would be good enough for my dad.

Little did I know that was a losing battle.

"Did Hunter always want to play football? Was he born with a football in his hand?"

Sadie's question brings me back to the present. We've been in Birmingham for a few hours, and she's been interviewing my parents for half of that time—though I've barely been paying attention. I tried to listen to a couple of her questions, but every time I did, it was some sort of question revolving around football and my childhood. I've been around one too many interviews to know that she's trying to see where the earliest Bo McAvoy comparisons can be found.

And here I thought she was different. I should have known better. I let a beautiful smile and a great ass cloud my judgment.

"In Alabama, every little boy is born with a football in his hand," my mom, Francine, says, a smile on her face from ear to ear. She never gets tired of saying that I was a 'Bama boy since day one. "When a boy is born in this state, the hospital asks you if you're an Alabama or an Auburn fan so they can dress him accordingly. It's the most precious thing. I bet I have pictures somewhere I can show you."

"I'll hold you to that," Sadie says, giving my mom the smile I'm all too familiar with. It's the one that sucked me in that first day I met her. "Was there ever a chance he wouldn't play college for Alabama?"

"He thought he could go somewhere else," my father says gruffly from his chair. "Then he came to his senses."

Dad's curt tone sucks the air out of the room almost instantly. I can see my mom's shoulders grow tense. My blood turns cold as I stand next to the fireplace in my childhood living room, remembering the one time I asked if we could visit another campus that wasn't in Tuscaloosa. That wasn't one of the best memories of my teenage years, but it's definitely one of the ones that's most memorable, and not in a good way. It was the worst argument we ever had.

I didn't win.

I give Sadie credit, though, she doesn't flinch. She simply turns the page of her notebook and continues to ask more questions about my childhood and early football career, my mother all too happy to answer everything she wants to know about her first born's football successes.

This is the first time I've really allowed myself to look at her today. I was purposely a dick to her this morning. I was hoping that if I kept answering her questions with barely there answers, she'd just be quiet. She held out much longer than I thought she would.

From the second she suggested coming here, all I could think about was that she was like every other reporter. She might be asking some easy questions now, but I'm just waiting for the "so, does your dad help you draw up plays?" question. Because it happens all the damn time.

The answer: hell no. And he never will. The man might be in the Hall of Fame, but he couldn't design an offensive game plan if a gun was held to his head.

Now that I'm allowing myself to look at her, I realize everything I missed today. She's wearing a loose blouse and a fitted pair of pants. I bet if I would have let myself look at her this morning, the ass that has been haunting my dreams would have been showcased in the best way. Her hair is on top of her head in what I've now come to know as the signature Sadie look. Her face has more makeup on it than I've seen her wear before, but it's not overdone.

It's perfect. She's perfect. Well, she would be if she wasn't a reporter. Figures, the one woman who has made me think about anything other than football in years is the one person I can't have.

"This question is for each of you," I hear Sadie ask my parents. "What was your proudest moment of Hunter during his football career? Playing or coaching."

Oh, this ought to be good...

"I have so many," my mom begins as I walk over and take a seat next to her. "There are so many of his playing days that I'll always cherish. I couldn't name just one. As a parent, though, I think my proudest moment was when he told us that he knew what he wanted to do with his future. His eyes lit up when he talked about becoming a coach. He was so excited about it. And as a parent, that's what you want. That something, or someone, that will make our child's eyes light up, and we know then and there that they are ready to be set free. He was becoming his own man, and I'm very proud of the man he is today."

I might have dated the head cheerleader in high school, but without a doubt, my number-one fan, always and forever, will be my mother. Want to talk about the stereotypical football mom? Francine McAvoy is it, hands down. She never missed a game when I was a player. Since I turned to coaching, she has called me after every game to tell me good job, or to give me a pep talk if we lost. And don't get me started on her wardrobe. If you want to know where I'm coaching, all you have to do is look at what colors my mom is wearing on any given day and go from there. Today? She's decked out in red and black with gold jewelry. She's a combination of a southern belle and a Fury superfan.

My dad, on the other hand? He might have been there physically when I played, but he was never there emotionally. While my mother was cheering her loudest, he was silently judging me. Hell, he still is. Only now he doesn't make his critiques silent.

"That's great," Sadie says, bringing me back to the present conversation. "How about you, Mr. McAvoy? What was a proud papa moment for you?"

I appreciate Sadie trying to use some humor to ease the tension. Too bad for her it won't work.

"Easy. His National Championship win at Alabama."

Sadie waits for him to elaborate, but he doesn't, so she continues. "Why that moment?"

"I knew by then he wasn't heading for the league. He had already made his choice to go into coaching. Which is a fine profession. You know, for those who can't hack it as a player. Helps that he's a McAvoy. And I'm proud of him for getting hired in Nashville. But there's nothing like being the guy on the field holding up the trophy. That moment was the only time he was going to get to do that."

The answer shouldn't surprise or anger me, but it does. Hearing his words, spoken to a reporter no less, makes my blood both boil and turn cold at the same time. I don't know if I want to storm out of the room, or stare at him in shock that he would say that out loud.

"He could lead the Fury, or one day his own team, to a championship," Sadie says, making direct eye contact with my father. "I'm fairly certain those coaches get to hoist up a trophy. Or did I misinterpret pictures that I've seen after every championship game?"

"It's not the same," my dad fires back.

"It's not?" she asks, now leaning forward in her chair. Is she about to go toe to toe with Bo McAvoy? By the defiant look in her eyes, she absolutely is. She's staring right at him, daring him to look away. Begging him to tell her she's wrong.

Holy hell.

"Well, I think it is," Sadie continues. "Not like I'll ever have the chance to do it. Us reporters don't know much, I guess. Except I do know that if Hunter led the Fury to the championship this year, he would be the youngest coordinator in league history to win a championship. And if he did, hypothetically speaking, lift that trophy, it would be one hell of an accomplishment. One that a father might be proud of. But I digress. I'd like to now ask you about what you think of Hunter's play-calling, Mr. McAvoy? Could you run his offense, or is it too advanced from when you played all those years ago?"

Sadie's words stun me. I'd have to check, but I think my jaw is on the ground.

That. Was. Amazing.

She defended me. No reporter has ever gone after my dad like that. And asking him if he could run my offense? Fuck. I know for a damn fact that is the first time anyone has asked him that. Usually, they are all about kissing his ass.

But not Sadie. Not by a longshot.

I now replay every question I heard her ask today. They were all about me. Not about what my dad might have taught me. Not about how his career influenced mine.

She wanted to know about *me*. As a person and a coach. How my younger days shaped who I am today. How they think I will do in

Nashville. Trying to see if my mom kept any early plays that I might have drawn up as a kid.

I feel like an absolute asshole. I assumed Sadie's motives for this interview weren't pure. I treated her like shit because I couldn't fathom any other reason for why she would want to come to Birmingham to interview my family. Everyone has always used me for a story. I thought she was the same.

Yet I should have known that she would be different.

She's been different from the first time I laid eyes on her.

7

———

SADIE

The only thing keeping me from jumping out of my seat at Hunter's words is the seatbelt across my shoulders and the computer on my lap.

We've been on the road for nearly an hour, and just like the ride down to Birmingham, he has been silent since we left his parents' house.

Until now. And I don't know how to respond to him.

I want to be mad at him. I want to slam my computer shut and ask what the hell I did that warranted the silent treatment all day.

I also want to hug him, because I have a feeling his mood has everything to do with his father, and this whole day is my fault, as it was my suggestion to go to Birmingham.

I also want to jump his bones, because even with him being all grouchy and angry, he still gives me butterflies in the best and worst ways every time I look at him.

Basically, I want to scream in frustration because I'm feeling a lot of things right now that I most definitely shouldn't be feeling when it comes to Hunter McAvoy.

"Are you apologizing for giving me the silent treatment for most of the day? Or are you apologizing to me and hoping I pass it on to the photographer after you bit his head off for suggesting you play catch with your dad?"

"When you put it like that, I guess both," Hunter says apologetically, though he still hasn't looked at me.

"I'll pass your words of overwhelming sympathy on to the photographer."

My words are laced in sarcasm. I don't care. Mad is the emotion that wants to win right now, but it's really hard when I let my eyes wander over to the driver's seat. As he lets out another sigh, this one I'm guessing of frustration, he switches his hands around that he's driving with, putting his right hand on top of the wheel.

This shouldn't be sexy. Driving a truck should not be sexy. Yet, Hunter makes it sexy. Even when I'm pissed at him for the way he acted today, I can't help but have ridiculously dirty thoughts about this man.

Dentist appointments.

Boogers.

Granny panties.

It's not just the dirty thoughts that are making my head a confusing place to be right now. Behind his anger and prickliness, I saw a side of Hunter I didn't expect to see today, a vulnerable one. He probably doesn't think I noticed. When his dad was passive-aggressively talking shit about his profession, I caught a glimpse of Hunter sitting next to his mom. He looked defeated. Sad. Angry.

My heart broke for him.

How long has he been dealing with this? My guess would be way before I showed up on their doorstep. Seeing that exposed side to Hunter added another layer to my conflicting feelings. Now he just wasn't an attractive man driving a sexy truck who gives me butterflies when he smiles at me. He is a man who is trying to use every weapon in his arsenal to prove to his doubters—aka his father—that he was capable. That he could be the best at his craft, that he would excel, no matter what.

I know that feeling all too well.

"I'm truly sorry, Sadie. I've been acting like an ass all day, and you've been taking the brunt of it."

I turn slightly to face him, and for the first time today, Hunter takes his eyes off the road to catch a glimpse of me. "Can I ask why you were Captain Grouchypants today?"

"Captain Grouchypants?" he asks as the smallest hint of a smile breaks through.

"I said what I said."

He lets out a soft laugh. "Off the record?"

If there is such a thing as a "safe word" for journalists, it's "off the record." When a reporter hears that, all things stop. Notebooks get put down. Recorders are turned off. Cameras stop rolling. In my case right now? I power down my laptop and promptly put it and my phone in my purse.

"Off the record," I say, reassuring him I'm not recording this.

"Sorry. It's not that I don't trust you—"

Hunter's words come out shaky. It's almost as if he's nervous, which is the first time that has happened since we've met. He has always been so calm and collected. Well, when he wasn't being an asshole. I have a feeling I'm right, though. He has been fidgety since he broke the silence. My point is proven when he shifts his driving arm again, putting the left arm back on top of the steering wheel, leaving his right arm resting against the center console.

"Hunter," I say, gently putting my hand on his forearm. I don't know why I'm doing this. It's completely inappropriate. But I want him to know that right now I'm a safe space. "You have no reason to trust me. I'm a reporter you met less than a month ago who wasn't exactly forthcoming on my identity when we met. I get it. No offense taken. But you can talk to me. Off the record."

He nods before taking a deep breath. If he feels my hand on his arm, he doesn't acknowledge it. I also don't let go.

"If you couldn't tell, my dad and I don't have the best relationship."

"I noticed."

I feel him tense underneath my touch. "You did?"

"I interview and read people for a living," I begin, giving his arm a reassuring yet gentle squeeze, hoping to calm his nerves. "Choice of words is key into figuring out what people really mean. They might say the right things, but *how* they say them mean just as much. Or sometimes it's what they don't say that speaks the loudest."

"You picked up on some things?" he asks, his voice again shaky.

I could tell from the first question I asked that Bo McAvoy's relationship with his son was strained, at best. While his mom couldn't wait to show me the endless amount of photo albums of young Hunter, his dad only watched from afar. And the way he answered questions about Hunter's coaching career? You would have thought he invented football, and the only reason his son was a coach was because of his last name.

That was the moment I knew, at least partly, why Hunter was on edge all day. I honestly don't blame him.

"Many," I say, regret in my voice for having seen behind the curtain that is the McAvoy family.

"Are you going to write about them?"

Hunter's question is laced with concern. I let out a frustrated sigh, because I honestly don't know the answer. "What we are talking about now? No. I gave you my word that this was off the record. Now, what he said at the house? I don't know yet. I have to use a few things. But I promise, whatever I write, I won't show the world what I saw today."

Hunter nods, I hope he understands the situation I'm in. I shouldn't have even promised him that. If I wrote a story that Bo McAvoy didn't approve of his son's career, and that he was a jackass to his flesh and blood, it would make national headlines. The job at *US Daily* would be in the bag.

I'm breaking about ten different, unwritten reporter rules by telling him I wouldn't write about how Bo treated him. I should care, but I don't. Their relationship is a private matter. I'm not about to be the one who airs that dirty laundry to the world.

Even though it would make my career. If I would have known that an interview in Birmingham would reveal all of this, I wouldn't have asked for it.

"When you said that you wanted to come to Birmingham for the interview, I assumed you were like every other reporter. That you were only using me to get an interview with my dad."

And there it is. The final piece of the grouchy Hunter puzzle. And while I should be offended that he thought I was using him to get an interview with the great Bo McAvoy, I'm not. I don't blame him. He barely knows me. When every reporter has only ever used him to get to his dad, why would he think I was different?

Little does he know, I am different. At least, I strive to be. Every article by every other reporter written about Hunter in some way, shape, or form circles back to his dad. I knew this going in. However, I wanted to know about young Hunter. What drove him? What made him want to be a coach? Who better to ask that to than the people who raised him?

Or so I thought. Here I was just trying to be different, and I released a can of worms that I didn't realize was about to bust open.

"That's why you didn't speak to me this morning?" I ask cautiously, even though I think I know my answer.

He nods. "I'm sorry to have assumed that about you."

"I'm sorry you've been interviewed by shitty reporters your whole life."

This makes him laugh. "I should have known you would be different."

"And what makes you say that?"

He gives another glance my way, and his eyebrow goes up a little. "Isn't it obvious?"

I let out an exasperated sigh and fall back into my seat, my hand finally moving from his arm. "Are you really playing the girl card right now? I thought you were better than that, McAvoy."

"Now look who's doing the assuming," he says with a small smile. And dammit. The butterflies are back. "You're different because you're a different kind of reporter. I read the things you wrote about me when I was first hired. You're talented. You ask different questions. You take different angles to stories. It makes you stand out. You're damn good at your job, Sadie Benson. I'm sorry I assumed you were using me. It won't happen again."

Some girls get giddy when a boy tells them they are beautiful. Some get excited when a guy will send a "good morning" text.

Me? Compliment my writing or my job, and I will be putty in your hands.

Hunter saying that I am damn good at my job? Holy fuckballs, Ted better be ready for tonight.

It takes all the strength I possess in my five-foot-five frame to not squeal like a schoolgirl. I'm also doing my best not to clench my legs together because… yeah. All those feelings from earlier? They are now manifesting into one main one.

A crush. I am officially crushing on Hunter McAvoy.

"Thank you." It's all I trust myself to say. Luckily, I say it without my voice going into a high-range octave.

"You're welcome."

He smiles, and this time our silence is of the comfortable variety. Before I know it, he is pulling up to my apartment complex. This started as the longest car ride in the history of ever. Now I don't want it to end.

I don't have a reason to stay in his truck, though. I can't ask him upstairs for a drink. Hell, I can't even pretend that I have too much to carry and I need a second set of hands.

This is where our day ends. Even as rocky as it was, I'm not ready for it to be over.

Snapping me out of that thought is the cool Nashville air. I didn't even realize Hunter got out of the truck, let alone that he walked around to open the door for me.

"Well, aren't you the gentleman?" I say, gathering my purse and stepping down from my seat.

"My mom would have smacked me today if she knew how I treated you this morning," he says, a hint of embarrassment in his words. "Figured I could at least make up for it now."

I smile as I step onto the sidewalk. "Thank you for today."

He gives me a confused look. "Really? Even after this morning? And… well, most of the day?"

My hand reaches out again for his forearm. I don't know why I keep doing this. It's like my fingers have a mind of their own, and all they want to do is reassure him through my touch. I should pull away. I don't. Even after our eyes make contact, my fingers stay connected to his skin. As I look at him, all I see is a mixture of confusion, want, and something that I can't identify passing through his eyes.

I'm sure mine are the same.

"Even after all of that," I continue. "You really have a lot to be proud of, Hunter. Don't let his words bring you down. You are an incredible man. It's too bad he chooses not to see it."

My words hang in the air, and Hunter doesn't reply. Instead, he takes his free hand and places it on top of mine, giving my fingers a gentle squeeze that sends a wave of sensation through my entire body.

When Hunter broke the silence earlier, it legitimately shocked me. But this? This is downright terrifying.

Because I've never felt anything like this in my entire life.

"Thank you, Sadie. That means a lot."

His voice is so sincere I don't know how to respond. All I know is that I'm standing in the middle of a Nashville sidewalk, all but holding hands with Hunter.

This is bad. This is very, very bad.

"I should probably go upstairs," I say, my voice weak.

He gives my hand one more squeeze before he releases it. I immediately let go of his arm. "I guess I'll see you around."

I nod and dig my keys out of my purse, my eyes focused on finding the damn things. They are definitely avoiding Hunter's gaze. It's too much. Too intense.

All of this is too intense.

I eventually find them and give him a small wave as I make my way to my door, though I feel his eyes on me the entire time. I don't dare turn around. I don't trust myself or what I would do if I did. All I want to do is go upstairs, drop my purse, kick off my shoes, take a cold shower, or find Ted, whichever is closer.

However, Hunter doesn't make that possible. At least, not yet.

"Hey, Sadie."

I hesitantly look back over my shoulder. He's standing right where I left him. The look in his eyes is still too much for me to handle.

"Yeah?"

"You thanked me for today, but I didn't get a chance to thank you."

Does he not remember what happened today? "And what do you need to thank me for?"

I have noticed a lot of smiles on Hunter in the short time I've known him. There is the camera smile he used at his press conference. There was the fake one he used today around his dad. There was even the flirty one he gave me when we first met.

But this one? This smile, the small one that goes a little higher on the right, might be the most genuine one I have ever seen.

"For being you. Because you're pretty amazing."

And with that, Hunter gets in his truck and leaves me standing outside my door, my jaw slacked and my emotions all over the place.

Screw the shower. I need to find Ted.

8

———

SADIE

THERE ARE a lot of things I'm good at. Hell, I'd even venture to say I'm borderline great at them.

I'm a hard worker. I'm organized. I'm a good friend, though I choose to keep my circle small. I call my dad at least three times a week and visit him and my stepmom every Monday night for dinner.

The things I'm not good at? Well, those are easy to spot. And I don't deny them.

I'm a horrible cook. I'm even worse when it comes to decorating my living space. I can't sing to save my life. And I'm really, really bad at taking days off.

Like extraordinarily bad.

It stems back to early in my career. I took a day off, turned off my phone and said that I was unplugging for the day. When I turned it back on six hours later, I realized that I missed a story on a high school coach getting fired for inappropriate relations with a student.

I never turned my phone off again. Not even now as I head west on I-40 toward Memphis for a boss-mandated week of relaxation.

The Super Bowl has come and gone. I've reported on everything I can about Hunter being hired. To call the story about him and his family a success would be an understatement. According to John, it was the most clicked-on sports story in *Banner* history. And that's without me writing about how his dad is a passive-aggressive jackass.

With nothing pressing left to write about, I packed my bags—with my father's over-the-phone guidance, of course—and picked up an abundance of road snacks before hitting the road to Memphis. My plans are to take in the atmosphere of Beale Street, visit the National Civil Rights Museum, and eat my weight in barbeque.

And not think about Hunter.

That's my mini-vacation to-do list. Maybe this won't be so bad after all.

My stepmom was adamant that this was not a real vacation. Her justification? I wasn't leaving the state. She couldn't wrap her head around the fact that I have a week off and I'm only going two-hundred-miles west.

She's also never had Memphis barbeque, so I didn't argue with her. I assured her that I was taking my annual solo trip in June to San Francisco still, and this was just a small getaway to recharge my batteries. I left out the part where John all but forced me to get out of town for a bit.

She seemed to like that answer. My dad, on the other hand, completely understood my motives and put in a to-go order from our favorite barbeque restaurant.

He gets me. Helen, though she has made a lot of strides over the years, has never been able to figure me out. Which is fine. I'm not mad. I'm a tomboy, book nerd who loved sports for the games and not the boys who played them. She and my stepsister Bethany are the definition of girly-girls with their fashionable clothes, perfect makeup, and never a hair out of place.

Having a tomboy for a stepdaughter was not what she signed up for when she and my dad got married my sophomore year of high school. But over the years, we seem to have found a comfortable balance. One year, she asked me to teach her the basics of football so she could watch it with my dad. Which he loved. In return, she showed me how great regular manicures can be. Especially for someone who has to look at her fingers every day while typing.

I take a quick look down at my fresh manicure—I went with a deep blue color this time—before checking the GPS to make sure I'm still on the quickest route. This was another reason I chose to come to Memphis. It was a quick and easy drive, but it was far enough away that I could separate myself for a few minutes from real life.

Or, more specifically? From all thoughts involving Hunter McAvoy.

I haven't seen the man in two weeks, and I can still feel the weight of his gaze on me as he dropped me off at my apartment building. I can still see his smile. I can still feel his skin under mine as I tried to give him comfort. I can still hear the sincerity in his voice when he told me "thank you."

It's been a good thing that I haven't had to see him again after our trip to Birmingham. I needed that time to pull myself together on all things related to that man.

If it was just a physical attraction, that would be one thing. I could handle being sexually attracted to a man I couldn't have. But it wasn't. Now at night, rather than just fantasizing about his body, I'm thinking about how he made me feel that first day we met at the shop. I'm thinking about how much I admire his determination to prove his father wrong. I'm thinking about how when we were standing outside my apartment building, it was like we were the only two people in Nashville.

This is bad. It's so very, very bad.

If I'm reacting this way now, how am I going to handle the season? With him being the offensive coordinator, I don't have to interview him every day. But it will be a lot. And if my heart and my body can't get on the same page as my brain that this man is off-limits, then I need to figure out a lot more grotesque things to think about.

Or buy stock in batteries.

Why did he have to be literally everything I want in a man? He's gorgeous. He's funny. He's charming. He loves football. He loves his family. Yes, even despite his issues with his dad, there is love there. And the way he looked at his mom when she praised him? You can't fake that.

The man is perfect. And he is so off-limits, it isn't even funny. Figures. The first man who has made me want to date in years is a man whom I can't even pretend to consider.

I laugh to myself as signs for Memphis tell me I'm about forty miles away. Even if we could date—and that's going under the assumption that he also wants to date me—what would that even be like?

For weeks I've not allowed myself to go down this mental road. I knew it wouldn't do any good, so why even entertain the idea? But now? With nothing to do and a half hour left in my drive, I let myself fantasize.

Some girls might picture the perfect date as a fancy dinner. In Nashville, a popular date-night activity is catching a live band or getting drinks at the latest up-and-coming restaurant. Or so I've been told by some of the other female news reporters I occasionally grab drinks with. But for me? The perfect date is a night spent at home.

That's where I imagine Hunter. Relaxing on my couch after we enjoy our dinner. I'm cleaning up the take-out boxes, because obviously I didn't cook. I ask him if he wants a drink, which he takes me up on, and when I go to take it to him, he grabs my wrist and pulls me down on the couch so I'm sitting across his lap. The drink spills a little, but neither of us care. How can I when my body is touching his? He takes the drink from my hand, puts it down on the table, and guides me so I'm now straddling him. Our eyes lock, and there's no denying the fire we're holding for each other. In my fantasy, he wants me just as much as I want him. His fingertips are slowly grazing up and down my sides, and even though this is only in my head, just the thought of it sends goose bumps down my spine.

My hands are wrapped around his neck, softly playing with the spot where his hair meets his nape, and I can't help myself. I lean in for the kiss. He doesn't stop me. In my mind, this isn't our first kiss. This kiss is familiar. Hot and sweet. Slow but intense. Promising of more later.

Knock-knock-knock.

The sound of a tap against my car window brings me back to the present. Actually, it scares the shit out of me. Somehow, someway, I managed to steer my car to my hotel in downtown Memphis while fantasizing about me and Hunter making out on my couch.

Nose hair.

Road kill.

Skunks.

I roll down my window, hopeful that my three gross images have calmed me down enough to be able to think straight.

"Hi. Sorry about that."

"No problem, ma'am," the valet says. "Are you checking in?"

I nod and retrieve my bags from my car and hand my keys off to the very nice young man who did not call me out for sitting in my car like a loon for God knows how long reveling in my dirty thoughts. If just those thoughts of Hunter can make me forget reality, then I absolutely, without a doubt, need to push these feelings to the far, far recesses of my mind.

With a little shake of my head, clearing away any last thoughts of kissing on my couch, I make my way into the Memphis hotel. I've stayed here plenty of times before. To the left is a seating area. The center is open for comers and goers. To the right is the check-in desk, which is where I make my way.

I take two steps before I nearly fall on my face.

No. It can't be. What are the odds?

I shake my head again, hoping that my mind is playing a dirty, dirty trick on me. Because that's the only logical explanation I can think of as to why Hunter McAvoy is standing at the check-in counter at the same hotel I'm staying at in Memphis.

Mucus.

Dirty diapers.

Chia pets.

9

———————

HUNTER

"GIVE US ONE SECOND, Mr. McAvoy, and we'll get you into a room."

I bite back a snarky response to the "one second" part of the front desk clerk's statement. Nothing about this check-in process has been one second. Instead, I paste a smile on my face and wait not so patiently for my key card.

I'd like to think that I'm an even-keeled guy. I generally don't get bothered when things inconvenience me. But right now? When I'm running on fumes and have been in five states in seven days while scouting more than twenty players? Yeah… right now I'm bothered.

All I want is a hot shower and a bed.

The draft is in two months, and from now until then, it's my job, along with the other coaches, to make sure we have scouted every player we could possibly draft. Especially because we have the number-one pick.

That pick won't define our draft. It's who we take in the later rounds that will help build our future. And for the past week, I've been touring colleges from Florida to California and everywhere in between trying to find those hidden gems.

I thought I was done scouting for the week. I was set to fly home to Nashville from Missouri when I got a call from a former teammate who coaches at Memphis. He told me he had a guy I *had* to see. That he was a game changer. As much as I wanted to be back in Nashville, and to finally get some use out of the king-size bed that I have barely used, I figured there wasn't any harm in one more stop.

I'll see him tomorrow. Today I need sleep. And a shower. And eventually food.

Except right now, none of those things are happening because "one second" has actually turned into "twenty minutes."

"I'm sorry, Mr. McAvoy, this is taking longer than expected," the front desk clerk says with a smile that screams "I hope he doesn't bite my head off." "We're trying to get a room ready for you, it will just be another minute."

"Take your time." I mean for the words to come out pleasant, but I can hear the bite to my tone. And by her reaction, I did, in fact, snap at her. I feel bad for my behavior. She's just doing her job. I'm the one who walked in without a reservation demanding a room. Apparently, when I don't get sleep, I'm a bit crabby. And by a bit, I mean a lot.

I turn away from the desk—mostly so I don't accidentally give this poor girl a death glare—and I'm struck stupid by a sight that I did not expect to see outside of the Nashville city limits.

My mood instantly lightens.

And by the look on Sadie's face, seeing me is just as much of a surprise. That and the fact that she nearly tripped over her feet when our eyes made contact.

The reaction makes me laugh. I haven't seen Sadie since I dropped her off after our trip to Birmingham. That doesn't mean I haven't thought about her, though.

I have. A lot. More than I'm willing to admit out loud. And most of the ways I have thought about her are not appropriate for polite conversation. Not that I can actually share my feelings about Sadie to anyone. She's my forbidden fruit. The apple I want to taste but I know I can't have.

"Hunter?" she says, now standing behind me at the front desk. "What are you doing in Memphis?"

"I could ask you the same thing," I say, my tone much more pleasant than it was just a few minutes ago.

"I know deflection when I hear it," she says, her words teasing. "I know you've been out scouting all week."

"Stalking me now?"

"Ha! You wish," she says, all but rolling her eyes as she steps up to the counter to hand her credit card and license to another hotel staff member. "It's my job to know what the team I'm covering is up to at all times. That includes coaches."

"And what is it I'm doing?"

She doesn't answer for a second, instead keeping me waiting as she goes through her check-in process. I don't mind, though. It gives me the chance to take in her profile. Her rounded nose is the perfect size for her face. Her cheeks are the slightest shade of pink, but I don't think it's from makeup. The spot where her neck meets her shoulders is begging for my lips to be on them. And then there is the ass that I haven't been able to stop thinking about since I first laid eyes on her. The whole, gorgeous package.

"You've been out scouting all week," she says, breaking me from my trance. "If I heard right, you started in Florida, ended up in Texas and California, before making stops in Colorado and Missouri, before landing back here. This stop wasn't planned, but if I'd have to guess, I'd put money on the fact that you're here to check out the Memphis running back I've been hearing buzz about."

I shouldn't be shocked anymore by Sadie and the things she knows. I should also know by now that whenever she talks football to me, I'm a fucking goner. Yet, hearing her recite exactly everything I've done over the past week sends an unexpected wave of excitement through my body.

It also makes me say things I shouldn't—or normally wouldn't—to a reporter.

"Have dinner with me tonight."

My request, which comes off more like a demand, catches her off guard. I don't blame her. Hell, I said it and I'm still not sure where it came from.

"Have dinner with you?"

I can do two things right now. I can wave it off and make it seem like a joke. Or I can own it. I can ask her again and ignore every red flag that is popping up in my brain right now telling me why having dinner with Sadie Benson is a horrible idea.

Fuck the red flags.

"Yes. Have dinner with me." I ignore her silence and take a step closer to her. I'm not close enough that I can touch her, but I can smell the faintest scent of something floral coming from her body. All that does is make me want this to happen even more. I want to be closer to her. I want to wake up tomorrow smelling that on my skin. "Unless you have plans?"

I see her swallow heavily, clearly not knowing how to respond. In the time that I've spent thinking about her, most of that has been wondering if she felt what I did. Did she have even an inkling of the attraction that I had toward her? When we met at Sandwich City, I knew it was one-sided. During our drive to Birmingham, I thought there might be times when she was feeling what I felt.

Then, she put her hand on my arm. And I was confident there was a chance.

Right now? Watching how my invite has made her cheeks flush? How she has been looking at everyone and everything but me since I mentioned dinner? Now I know.

She's feeling this too.

"Sadie? Do you have plans tonight?"

She finally meets my gaze before shaking her head. "No. No plans."

"Then have dinner with me."

She doesn't say anything again, but this time she doesn't stop looking at me. Which is good. I can see her weighing every part of this in her eyes.

"Just dinner?"

I nod and give her a reassuring smile. "Just dinner."

"On or off the record?"

And there it is. The million-dollar question. Or, if I'm reading this code right, she's asking without uttering the words, "Is this, or is this not, a date?"

"Off the record." I take another step forward, wanting to make sure I'm as clear as I can be. "Tonight, I don't want to talk about football. I don't want to talk about our jobs. I just want to have dinner with a beautiful woman whom I haven't been able to stop thinking about since the moment I laid eyes on her. I want to explore the streets of Memphis with her. I want to get lost in a conversation where we both wonder where the night went. What do you say?"

"Sir! Your room is ready! Mr. McAvoy! Your room is ready!"

I hear the woman calling for me. I don't care. Minutes ago I was fuming, wondering what took her so long. Now I wish she would have taken a few minutes longer. I'm not leaving Sadie's space until I have my answer. Luckily, she doesn't make me wait much longer.

"Yes. I'll have dinner with you. Off the record."

Her words come out in almost a whisper, but I hear them clear as day. Even more, I hear the meaning behind them.

Tonight isn't Coach McAvoy and Reporter Benson.

Tonight is Hunter and Sadie.

And I really, really like that play.

10

———

SADIE

I'VE FANTASIZED about a lot of things when it comes to Hunter. And yes, most of them have been of the sexual variety.

Sue me. The man is a football coach who could simultaneously pose for a *GQ* cover. *Cosmo* named him one of their most eligible bachelors. He is *that* good looking.

There was the obvious daydream in my car today that left me so discombobulated I autopiloted my way to Memphis.

There have also been the times when I'm alone in my apartment with Ted an arm's reach away. Those fantasies consist of me wondering what it would feel like for his weight to be on top of me. And what it would be like to wake up in his arms. They were blissful thoughts until I realized that Ted could only do so much.

After Birmingham my fantasies became less sexual and more... intimate. They morphed into thoughts of us holding hands, cuddling on the couch or watching football together. And somehow, those thoughts seemed more scandalous than any sexual scenario I could dream up. I pushed aside thoughts that I was probably not his type or that I was imagining the way he looked at me. These were my fantasies. And I was going to bask in them.

Yet somehow, in all the times I thought about me and Hunter

together, I never thought about what a first date would look like. In all the seconds and minutes and hours that Hunter has overtaken my thoughts, I never gave any thought to what I'd wear to make his jaw drop a little. I never debated where we would go. I never thought about the gazillion butterflies that were bound to be in my stomach at just the thought of him coming to pick me up for a night out.

I might have never thought about where we'd go, but even if I were to be given a hundred guesses, I never would have chosen this. A casual Memphis barbeque restaurant sharing a plate of pork nachos while we laugh about the most embarrassing moments of our childhood.

The conversation is easy. The company is wonderful.

The butterflies in my stomach are setting up permanent residence.

They started as soon as I heard the knock on the hotel room door. Oh hell, who am I kidding? They started the second we walked away from each other at the check-in desk after he asked me to dinner. They slowly increased as I looked through every piece of clothing I packed to find something to wear tonight before I settled on leggings and an off-the-shoulder, light blue sweater. They multiplied by a trillion when I opened my door to see him standing in front of me in dark jeans and a navy sweater over a white, button-down shirt.

The count of butterflies hovered somewhere around fifty gazillion when he put his hand on the small of my back as we entered the elevator to head to the lobby. They haven't lessened since we sat down at our table. At this point, I don't think they will.

Especially if he keeps looking at me like he is right now—like he's trying to see through to my soul.

If I wasn't so enamored by this man, it would be unnerving.

"Favorite television show?"

I laugh at his question. Only because before this he asked me my favorite movie and what kind of music I liked to listen to. "Are you the reporter now?"

He shrugs before taking a sip of his beer, a small smile gracing his face. "You're always the one asking the questions. I figured it was my turn."

"I have never once asked you what your favorite television show is," I say, hoping my tone comes off flirty. That's what I'm going for, at least. It's been a while since I've actively tried to flirt with a man on a date.

Even though I know I shouldn't be.

"No. But you should have. No reporter has ever asked me about my favorite television shows," he says, reaching across the table to take my hand in his. One at a time, he laces our fingers together. A slow but deliberate process that I can't help but stare at.

And there go the butterflies again.

"I thought we weren't talking about work tonight?" My voice coming out a bit rough. I can't help it. The man is messing with every one of my senses right now. Because yes, I can smell the woodsy scent of his cologne across the table.

He slowly brings my hand to his mouth. I'm sure I'm staring, but I can't make myself look away as he places the softest kiss on my hand before putting my hand back on the table.

"You're right. No work talk," he says, a devilish grin passing over his face. "Unless you're dying to know what my favorite television show is. You *would* be the first reporter to ever ask that."

It's like he knows that even out on a date, I can't resist the chance for a scoop. Even if it's not a real interview.

"Fine," I say with a half-defeated sigh. "What's your favorite television show, Hunter?"

He flashes me a smile that screams nothing but mischief. "I think you should guess."

"That's not how an interview works, Coach McAvoy."

My words have the desired effect. His eyes get a little fire in them as he leans closer to me. "Maybe I like throwing you off of your game."

Oh, holy hell. The butterflies now are compounded by the pulsing in my lady parts. He has now taken my hand back in his and it's... It's too much. I can't think. I can barely breathe. That's the only reason I can fathom why I say the first television show that pops into my head.

"*SportsCenter.*"

He drops my hand and clutches his hand over his heart, mocking that I've somehow stabbed him with my words. "Wow. That hurts. You think that there is nothing more to me than football or sports?"

I shake my head, partly to shake off the embarrassment, and the other part to try and get my wits back. "*SportsCenter* is a perfectly fine guess."

"For a frat boy."

"Weren't you in a fraternity at Alabama?"

"That's beside the point," he says, taking my hand back in his. And just like that, my brain is getting scrambled again. "I'll have you know that I'm a very cultured man. My television choices are of high quality and have been applauded as some of the greatest television shows in history."

Now it's my turn to give him the questioning eyebrow. "Oh, really? Then tell me, oh cultured and sophisticated one, what is your favorite show that is among the best in history?"

He doesn't answer for a second. It's not an uncomfortable silence. It's more like a buildup. An anticipation.

I'm here for it.

"Friday Night Lights."

It's another second again before both of us start laughing uncontrollably.

"You did all of that buildup just to tell me your favorite television show is about a high school football team?"

He shrugs, but gives me a smile in return. It's that sly smile. It's the one where it signals that he's telling me a secret. The smile that says this is a part of him that only a few people get to know.

It's my favorite.

"It was too much fun not to."

Before I can respond, our main dishes are brought out to us. Not knowing what we wanted, we decided to split a big plate of meats and sides. It looks like we're feeding the entire Fury team.

We keep our word to avoid interview questions for the rest of dinner. We share stories of our childhood and families. Well, I did. I tell him about how my mom died when I was five, and how for a while it was just me and my dad until he married Helen. He doesn't dive deep into the family well, and I don't blame him. He does tell me a story about one Halloween when he dressed up as a cheerleader and his sister, Whitley, was the football player.

Now that's the photo I wish his mom would have shown me in Birmingham.

The conversation is easy and flowing. Before I know it, he has paid our bill and we are walking hand in hand toward Beale Street, still talking about everything and anything. It's a bit chilly for Memphis in February, but I don't mind. I'm not ready for this night to be over.

"I can't believe I'm out with a Tennessee graduate," he says, giving a shiver as if he said something that tasted horrible on his tongue. "Please tell me you don't own twenty pieces of orange checkerboard clothing."

"I do not, but even if I did, it's better than that houndstooth your school insists on claiming for itself," I say, giving his shoulder a nudge. "You think I like being seen in public with a 'Bama man? I have a reputation to uphold, ya know."

"Your reputation?" he asks, pulling me around so I'm now standing in front of him, our bodies just inches away from each other. "I'm one of the most famous men to ever graduate from my school. How would it look if someone saw me out with *you*?"

I know we're teasing each other about our schools being rivals, but his words are laced in a double meaning that we are both deeply aware of. I'm now looking up at him, my hand still in his. I feel like I'm short of breath, but it's not because of the chilly air or the walk. It's because being this close to Hunter is physically taking my breath away.

"Are you okay?" he asks, but instead of taking a step back, he takes a half a step closer.

I look down because his gaze is too much for me to handle. "What are we doing?"

My words come out as a whisper, and for a second, I wonder if I actually said them out loud. Especially because Hunter doesn't answer right away. When I've convinced myself I only said those words in my head, he takes my chin in his free hand, tilting my head up to look into his eyes.

"I don't know, Sadie. All I know is that I can't *not* touch you. I need to hold your hand. I needed to know what it would be like walking next to you like you were mine to have."

"We shouldn't be doing this."

My breathy words are the truth, but they taste like a lie as they pass through my lips. The sensation of my hand in Hunter's feels right. The way he is looking at me right now? Like I'm the most beautiful thing he has ever seen? No other man has ever looked at me like that. No man has made me feel as feminine and as wanted as I do right now.

How can something that feels so right and natural be so wrong?

"Sadie?" Hunter's words are soft, and even though we are on a busy street in the middle of Memphis, I can hear them like it's the only sound around us.

"Yes?"

"I know we shouldn't be doing this. But if I don't kiss you right now, it will be the biggest regret of my life."

Then he does. Before I can object, before I can utter again why this is a horrible idea, Hunter leans down and presses his lips against mine. In the middle of Beale Street, with strangers walking past us, with jazz music filling the air, Hunter gives me the best first kiss of my life.

And it is better than any fantasy I have ever had.

11

HUNTER

IF SOMEONE WERE HOLDING a gun to my head right now and demanded to know what Sadie's lips tasted like, I would not be able to tell them.

What I do know is that whatever flavor they are, it's my new favorite. I also know that at this moment, there is nothing better in the world than kissing Sadie. Feeling her so close to me is making me feel more than I ever have in my entire life. And that includes winning a National Championship.

I also know that at this moment, Sadie Benson absolutely owns every part of me.

Our kiss started soft. When our lips first met, they were hesitant. That lasted all of three seconds before my mouth opened, and hers followed soon after. We are still kissing, and I'm sure it's bordering on indecent for a public audience, but I don't care. I can't make myself stop.

I never want to stop kissing her.

Unfortunately, I don't have that luxury as a body slams into me from behind, nearly knocking me over and taking Sadie down in the process.

"Get a fucking room, you two!" the man yells at us, stumbling away.

"Watch it, asshole!" I scream.

I'm about ready to chase this guy down when I feel Sadie's hand on my chest. I look down, and all I see are the most mesmerizing pair of hazel eyes looking up at me. "He's not worth it. Plus, I don't think making out on Beale Street is really the best idea."

I study her face, worried I'll see regret. I'm thankful when I don't. Instead, I see Sadie smiling up at me, her eyes sparkling. Her lips are plump from our kiss, and her cheeks are flushed. Her hair is a bit wild, and I can't stop staring at it. It's the first time I've seen it down, and it just adds to her beauty.

She's never looked more radiant.

"I think making out on Beale Street is a great idea," I say, wrapping my hands around her waist to bring her flush to me. "In fact, I think we should do it again."

I lean in for the kiss, but this time she stops me, putting two fingers on my lips. But it's not a rejection. The smile on her face is a dead giveaway.

"I have a better idea."

I gently kiss her fingers before taking her hand in mine. "And what do you suggest?"

"We dance."

"Dance?"

She nods. "What? Does Hunter McAvoy not dance?"

I don't. I hate dancing. One of the reasons I wasn't a great quarterback is because of my lead feet. But for Sadie? Who is looking at me right now with hope and want in her eyes? I'll do the fucking Macarena to keep that look on her face.

I lean down and kiss her forehead. "Don't hold it against me if I step on your feet."

She laughs, looping her arms around my neck. "I promise. Just listen to the music and sway with me."

The music she's referring to is coming from a saxophone player about five feet from where we are standing. I can't pinpoint the song he's playing, but I know I've heard it before. And I know now every time I hear it, I will remember this moment. The moment that a girl who bewitched me from the second I met her made me dance with her on the streets in Memphis.

My hands instinctively go to the small of her back, and I bring her close to me. Our chests are touching as she places her head right over my heart. It's beating out of control and I know she can feel it. The only reason I'm not embarrassed is because I can feel her heart as well, and it's matching pace with mine.

I don't know how long we dance. I don't know if people have been walking around us. Hell, for all I know, we have thirty cell phones pointing at us right now. There could be a hundred and I wouldn't care. I'm oblivious to my surroundings. With Sadie in my arms, I feel invincible. Alive. Like nothing can be better than this moment, right here, right now.

Sadie says something, but I can't hear it. Between the music and the fact that her face is buried in my shirt, her mouth is covered.

I lean down so she can hear me. "What was that, gorgeous?"

She lifts her head off my chest. And then I see it. A small tear sliding down her cheek. "This isn't fair."

I take my thumb and gently wipe the tear away. "What isn't fair?"

She takes a breath. Our swaying nearly comes to a standstill. "This. Us. Hunter… this has been the best night of my life. You… me… I think… I think there is something here between us. I don't know if it's just me who feels it but—"

"No," I say, cutting her off, squeezing her to me a little tighter. "I feel it too, Sadie. I feel it in my bones. I can't stop thinking about you. I haven't been able to stop thinking about you since the coffee shop."

"I can't either. But you know we can't, right? This… tonight… it can't happen again."

I hear the words she's saying. I know she's trying to protect our careers. Careers we have both worked fucking hard to get. Our professions—coaches and reporters—aren't supposed to be friends, let alone lovers.

But she's right. And I fucking hate it.

For the first time in my life, I hate my job. I hate this situation. I hate fucking everything.

"You're probably right," I say, resigned and despising the words as they come out of my mouth.

"I know I am," she says, the sadness clear in her voice.

Despite our words, neither of us let go. We embrace each other a little tighter, swaying some more to the sounds of Memphis.

And then the song stops.

We take it as our cue to leave. We link our fingers together and walk slowly back to the hotel. Neither of us say a word. We don't need to. We are soaking in this moment and this night, knowing it can't happen again.

I want to hesitate when we approach the front of the hotel. I want something to delay us so I get just a few more minutes with her. I don't want to take her to her room. I know the second we stand in front of that door that it's the end. It will be over before we even had a chance to start.

I don't get my way, though. We make our way onto the elevator and it goes directly to her floor. We both slowly step out of the car, our hands still locked.

"I meant what I said," Sadie says, looking up at me with sad eyes as we approach her door. "Tonight was the best night of my life."

"Mine too," I say, brushing my fingers along the side of her face. She leans into my touch, and I soak up every second that I can feel her skin against mine.

"Can I ask you for one thing?"

Her words are soft, but I hear them clear as day. "Anything." And I mean it. I'll give her literally anything she asks for right now.

"I'm probably stupid for asking this. It will probably make it worse. But can I have one more—"

I don't give her a chance to finish the sentence. My lips are on hers in an instant, and I kiss her with everything I have. There is so much that needs to be said through this kiss, and I know this is the only moment I have to say it.

It's a kiss that screams what we could have been. It's a kiss to let her know how much tonight has meant to me. It's a kiss I want her to know I will never forget, and I hope she doesn't either.

When our lips part, I see the tears forming again, and I know now what I have to do. The hardest thing I've ever had to do in my life.

I have to let her go.

"Good night, gorgeous," I say, placing one last kiss on her forehead.

"Good night, Hunter."

I stand and watch as she fishes her key card out of her purse. With sad eyes that look back at me one more time, she unlocks her door and walks inside her room.

I watch as she shuts the door, and I stand there for an extra moment. I know she's not going to open it up. But I can't leave just yet.

Yet, I know I have to walk away.

12

SADIE

THE MONTH of March can suck a big fat one.

Work is tedious and slow. It's more than a month away from the draft. I write stories every day on players the Fury will likely choose—including the obvious, first-overall pick, quarterback Bryce Donald. Those stories don't take me long to write though, so most of my days are spent realizing how little I have to look forward to in my life.

I realize this every year when my work life is slow. For some reason, this year it's hitting a little harder.

I'm not admitting to myself why that is.

I go to the gym occasionally. I've met up with a few friends from the paper for dinner and drinks. And like clockwork, every Monday night, I'm at my dad's house for my weekly dinner with him, Helen, and Bethany, which is where I'm at tonight.

Want to know what also happens like clockwork? Every day I wake up and miss Hunter.

I know it's ridiculous. And silly. And totally not like me. I can't help it. The man got under my skin that night in Memphis more than any man ever has.

Before Memphis, I could safely say I had a crush on Hunter. After

Memphis, I can safely say that if circumstances were different, I'd be trying not to fall too hard, too fast.

I'm officially, and regretfully, smitten.

How can I not be? He's hot as hell, funny, loves football, loves his mom, makes me smile like I've never smiled before and laugh until my stomach hurts. Add to it that he didn't make me feel self-conscious when I suggested ordering our weight in barbecue. In fact, he added more to the order to make sure we could try them all.

Then he kissed me. Then, he held me in his arms as we danced in the middle of Beale Street. And then he soothed me when my emotions became too much for me to handle. I hated crying in front of him. I'm not a crier. I didn't want to, but I couldn't help it. The man makes me feel things I didn't know I could.

I got a taste of what being with Hunter is like. And I can't let myself have another bite.

"Only one thing can make someone look like that, and that's a man," Bethany says as she catches me staring off into space as I help prep Monday-night dinner. "Spill it, sis."

I want to laugh at her calling me sis, but I don't. Yes, we are stepsisters. But our relationship has never been a close one, let alone close enough to think of each other as real sisters.

We went to the same high school, so we knew of each other when our parents started dating when we were freshmen. We weren't friends, though. Our interests and friends were polar opposite. I was a tomboy and worked for the school newspaper. She was a cheerleader whose afterschool activity was boys. I didn't own a piece of makeup, and she loved all things glitter. My tomboy ways may have slightly faded over the years, but her love of all things pink and pretty has not.

And she still loves the boys.

To this day we have very little in common. She hates sports. She loves fashion and makeup, and is a successful cosmetologist at a hip Nashville salon. She's blonde where I'm brunette. She's tiny where I have plenty of curves. We couldn't be more different if we tried.

The only thing we have ever had in common is our bad luck in the dating department. Mine I have always blamed on my job and lack of time to try to date. Hers is because, well, she has absolutely horrible taste in men.

"There's nothing to spill," I say as I move the chopped cucumbers to the salad bowl.

"I call bullshit on that," she says, mixing the salad for me as I add the last of the vegetables. "It actually surprises me. I've never seen you with that look on your face. Now me? I see that face in the mirror monthly."

"Is it really only monthly?"

She lets out a sigh of defeat. "Maybe more like weekly, but that's not the point. Come on. *Please!* You can tell me. Plus, it will make me feel better that I'm not the only one depressed and single."

I let out a chuckle because I am depressed and single. And until Hunter came along, I was never that person. My job was my only focus. I figured that if I met someone and he fit in with my life and job, then great. But otherwise, I was fine living the solo life.

Funny how your mentality changes in such a short amount of time.

Though I'm not about to tell Bethany that.

"I'm not depressed."

She tilts her head and gives me a look that screams that she's not buying it. "Really? You're not? There's no man who is keeping you up at night? No man who is driving you wild and you don't know why?"

"Nope," I say, a little too much emphasis on the *ope*. "I have no clue what you're talking about."

I hurry and move around the kitchen island, trying to find something, anything, else to chop or prep. Anything to get me out of this conversation.

"I think you do," Bethany says as she takes a seat at the island, watching me act like a lunatic. "I don't know why you won't tell me. It's not like I'll even know who you're talking about."

Now that is true. She doesn't even know what the Fury is, let alone who Hunter is. She wouldn't know a professional football coach if he was standing in front of her. I don't even know if she realizes there is a football team in Nashville.

I have wanted to talk to someone, anyone, about this. I thought if maybe I talked about Hunter, it might help dull the ache in my chest that has been there every day since I woke up in that hotel in Memphis the morning after our date. But all of my friends are in the newspaper business. I don't want them to look at me differently when I say that I committed the female sports reporter cardinal sin—falling for a coach.

But Bethany wouldn't look at me differently. Actually, my stepsister might be just the person I need right now.

"Fine," I begin, letting out a defeated breath. "Yes, I met someone. Yes, I like him. But nothing can happen between us because he's off-limits. End of story."

I find a green pepper to cut and start furiously chopping, hoping that now that I've said it out loud, I'll suddenly feel better.

I don't.

"What do you mean, he's off-limits? Is he married?"

That's her first guess? Who does she take me for?

"No, he's not married."

"Seeing someone?"

"No."

"Gay?"

I laugh. "If he is, then he has a funny way of showing it."

Her lips raise in a smile. "Is that because things have happened between the two of you that confirms the fact that he doesn't play for the other team?"

I can't help but laugh at Bethany, who is being very animated now describing what she assumes happened. "Yes. Something happened. And before you ask, no, we did not sleep together."

"But you want to."

Do I want to? *DO I WANT TO?* Fuck yes, I want to. I wanted to that night. I wanted to invite him into my hotel room and have a night so amazing that Memphis would have become my favorite city on the planet. I wanted to wake up in his arms and do it all over again. I wanted him to stay with me for the week and have the best vacation of my life.

Instead, I woke up alone with puffy eyes from crying all night. I then spent the next three days trying to enjoy the sights of Memphis, only to find myself missing him a little more each minute. I ended up cutting my stay short and hiding in my apartment for the rest of the week.

"Yes, I wanted to."

"So why is this man off-limits?"

"Because…" I take a breath, fortifying myself to say the words I need to. "Because he's a coach. For the team I cover. It's the definition of 'frowned upon.'"

"So?" Bethany says, giving me a confused look. "You're both adults. If he likes you and you like him, I don't see what the big deal is? It's not like you work for the same company."

How can I make her understand this?

"The big deal is that when you're a female who covers football for your job, many people assume that you don't know what you're talking about. That the only way you could possibly know about football, or get the scoop on a story, is that you're fucking someone to get it. So, imagine if people, namely my employer, found out that I was sleeping with a coach. That I was sharing a bed with a man whose employer tells him that reporters are not your friends, that in fact, they are the enemy, and that they will do anything to get a story. That is why we can't be together."

I see the moment it all clicks for Bethany, and before I know it, she's standing behind me at the island, her arms wrapped around my shoulders. And I don't know why, maybe it's the combination of her gesture and my admission, but I can't hold it in anymore.

My tears are slow as they fall down my face, and neither of us say anything for a long minute. We just stand there, letting my admission hang in the air.

"I'm sorry, Sadie. That fucking sucks."

I let out a laugh between the tears. Because she nailed it. Right on the nose.

"Yeah, it does. But what is there to do?"

The question is rhetorical. She and I both know it. What can I do?

Neither of us are about to give up our careers. We're not about to let some feelings, compounded by one amazing night, get in the way of those.

Bethany gives me one more squeeze. "Sadie, I've known you for a long time. In all those years, I've never seen this look on your face. I know the situation feels impossible. And it might be, I don't know. But I do know that you shouldn't give up on it yet. Because if there was a man who put that look on my face? I'd hold on to him and never let go."

And with that Bethany takes the salad off the counter and leaves me standing in the kitchen, wondering what the hell I've got myself into.

13

HUNTER

"ARE YOU GOING TO ORDER? The menu isn't that complicated. Pick a damn sandwich and let's go."

I hear the words coming from Davis, my wide receivers' coach, but his nagging isn't making me order any faster. The only thing I can see on the Sandwich City menu is "chicken Caesar wrap." Which makes me think of Sadie.

At least today I made it until noon before she took over my thoughts. Usually it happens the second I wake up.

"I'll have the chicken Caesar wrap with fries. And a sweet tea."

"Fucking finally," he mumbles. I choose to ignore the comment as I hand my credit card to the cashier before we make our way to the other side of the counter to wait for our to-go order.

Out of habit, I can't help but look around the café, hoping I'll see a brunette with hair on top of her head staring into a computer. I do this every time I come here. And every time, I'm disappointed.

Even more so today.

This isn't the first time I've been to Sandwich City since we first met, but it is the first time since our night in Memphis. And as soon as I looked up at the chalkboard menu over the cash register, the first thing that caught my eye is that damn wrap.

I can't even get lunch without thinking about her.

"Seriously, I didn't realize lunch was such a big decision," Davis says as he turns around to face the café. From his vantage point, he can see every table. Not that I know this from experience.

"Am I not allowed to weigh my options?" I ask, wondering why the delay in my lunch order is such a big deal.

Davis turns back toward me, giving a shrug to my words. "I'm just saying, if it took you ten minutes to figure out lunch, what the hell is going to happen on draft night?"

I ball up the wrapper of my straw and throw it at him, which he easily ducks away from. I know he's saying it in jest, but the dig hits the mark.

Draft night is a pressure-cooker. The team only has a few minutes to make each selection. Luckily, I'm not the one who will be making the Fury's picks on draft night. That job is for Coach Gordon and Neil, our general manager. It is my job to present to them the best offensive players to consider. That's a big responsibility. One I don't take lightly.

Which is why I've been working Davis and the rest of my offensive coaches to the bone over the last few weeks. We've been pulling long hours at the facility scouting players and coming up with draft scenarios. It's what we need to do to make sure we have the best draft class possible.

It also helps that working long hours means less time I have to let my mind wander back to that night in Memphis, or how Sadie's lips felt against mine.

It has been three weeks since that night. Three. Long. Fucking. Weeks. I would have thought by now I wouldn't feel like this anymore. I wouldn't feel like a part of me is missing because we made the smart decision not to be together. Instead, it just gets a little worse every day.

"Oh shit," Davis says as he slaps my shoulder. "Isn't that the reporter chick from the paper? Fuck, she is fine as hell."

My head snaps to the door as soon as the words leave Davis's mouth.

Fuck, I've missed her. I know that sounds ridiculous, but I have. I realize our relationship stopped before it even had a chance to start. It's not like I went from talking to her every day to nothing. We never had a texting stage. We never even had a dating stage. But I recognize possibility when it's in front of me. And the possibilities with Sadie were endless. They made me hopeful.

Now all they do is make me wonder what I did in my twenty-eight years to have my perfect woman put in front of me, only for me not to be able to have her.

"I keep wondering when it will be my turn for an interview," Davis says, his words pulling me back to the present. "Maybe I should go to talk to her. Ask her if she wants a little one-on-one time."

"Shut the fuck up," I snap, my harsh reply taking him off guard. "You will not speak to her. Especially not like a horny fucking teenager."

Davis holds his hands up in surrender, realizing that I'm not kidding. "Damn, man. Sorry. Didn't realize you called dibs."

Is that how this is coming off? That I'm calling dibs? Fuck, that can't happen.

"I'm not calling dibs," I say, trying to get my tone under control. "I would just like it if you, as a member of my staff, would act like an adult and not a pubescent boy looking at his first *Playboy*. She's a reporter trying to do her job. She doesn't need assholes like you treating her like a piece of meat."

My words get through to Davis, who mutters an apology. Luckily, Sadie was likely too far away to have heard what he said. Thank God.

How do I know that? Because since Davis announced her arrival, I haven't taken my eyes off of her for more than a second.

And she hasn't looked at me once.

She's dressed more casually than the last time I saw her. Her hair is back up on the top of her head, and her glasses are perched on her nose. She looks almost exactly how she did the first time I saw her in this very place.

She took my breath away then, and she's doing it again now.

What is it about this woman that makes me absolutely insane?

"Order for Hunter!"

The sound of my name gets Sadie's attention, and before I can look away, her eyes find mine. At first, there's shock. I don't blame her for that one. I might have looked around the café to find her when we got here, but I still would have been surprised if she was, in fact, here.

When the shock went away, the next emotion that passed through her eyes about broke my fucking heart. It was sadness. It was only there for a second before she looked away. But I saw it. I recognized it. I see it in my eyes every fucking day.

She's hurting just as much as I am.

I know I've been an intolerable bastard since I came back from Memphis. If that look she gave me is a glimpse of what she's feeling, then I'd bet she's equally as miserable as I have been.

Why does it have to be like this? How in the world is this fair to either of us? Why in the world do we have to suffer because of some unwritten rule that our professions have latched on to? We are responsible adults. We can keep our professional and personal lives separate.

Well, that I'm not sure about. But I know for Sadie I'd be willing to try. Hell, I'd do about anything right now just to have a chance to see where this goes.

And just like that, a plan forms in my head.

This could completely blow up in my face.

This could be the worst decision I've made in a very, very long time.

But it's worth the risk.

"Order for Hunter! Going once! Going twice!"

I grab the to-go bags and hand them to Davis. "You go. I'll meet you back there."

He takes the bags awkwardly, not expecting me to pass them to him. "Why?"

Shit. Why am I?

"I'm going to talk to Sadie and make sure your voice didn't carry." That explanation was the first thing I could think of, even though it's a loose excuse. "Last thing I need is to have to tell HR to expect a phone call from a reporter about inappropriate comments being said about her."

His face goes white, and shit, I almost feel bad about that. But I don't because I need him out of here. And fast.

"Okay. Sorry if I caused any trouble."

I watch him leave the café and cross the street before I make my way over to Sadie. If she sees me coming, she doesn't show it. She's already typing at rapid speed, her eyes not leaving the computer.

"Is this seat taken?"

She doesn't move at the sound of my voice. In fact, she doesn't react at all.

"Fancy seeing you here."

Again, nothing. Though, this time I take her silence as a green light and sit across from her.

"What are you working on? Trying to write another story about me without me knowing?"

My questions don't get a verbal response, but at least this time I see the corner of her lip rise slightly.

And there it is. My opening.

"How about I give you a scoop?"

Her eyes snap up to mine. It was like dangling a piece of meat in front of a tiger.

"What kind of scoop?"

I curl my finger at her, asking her to come closer so I can whisper. "We're trading our first pick to Denver for a sack of potatoes, some bubble gum, and a player to be named later."

Before the joke is even out of my mouth, she balls up a napkin and throws it at me.

"You play dirty, McAvoy. You know I hear the word scoop and I forget all my senses."

I laugh, because that was way too easy. "I don't play as dirty as you do. You have to give me credit. You're talking to me, at least."

This makes her laugh and a smile adorns her face. In this moment, all the depression I have felt over the last three weeks fades away.

"Fine," she says with a playful huff. "I'm talking to you. Hello, Hunter. How are you today?"

"Much better now that you're here."

I flash her a flirtatious smile which earns me an exaggerated eye roll. "Really? That's what you're going with? You're not much of a player, ya know. You can do better than that, McAvoy."

She makes the motion to go back to her writing, but before she can, I grab her wrist. Not hard, but enough to send a shock through my body. And by the look in her eye, she felt it too.

It's the same shock that passes through us every time we touch. That can't be a coincidence, right?

"You play dirty, McAvoy," she says quietly, her eyes glancing quickly around to see if anyone is looking at us. She might have repeated her words from earlier, but this time I can hear the different meaning in them. Just with this one touch, we are both transported back to that night on Beale Street. Just one touch is reminding us both of how good we feel when we are together.

"Not as dirty as you, Benson," I say, still not letting go of her wrist.

"And how is that?"

I decide to slightly change the course of this conversation. "The first day we met, you said that you weren't a football fan. You tricked me."

She shrugs away from my hold and leans forward on her elbows, the smile on her face nothing but mischievous as my goal of lightening the mood works. "I didn't lie. I'm not a fan. I have to be unbiased as a reporter. You just assumed what the meaning of my words meant."

I also lean forward, matching her position. "Touché. Still, I feel as if you owe me."

Her eyebrow quirks up. "I owe you? If anything, you owe me. You were quite the grump that day in Birmingham. And frankly, I don't think I'm over it."

I hear the humor in her voice, even though I know I was a complete asshole to her that day. "You're right. The least I can do is cook you dinner to make up for it."

"Dinner? Hunter… we—"

I look around, making sure that no one here knows us. Or, at least, me. I know this might be my only chance to say this, and I don't want to mess this up.

"Sadie, I've been a miserable bastard since Memphis," I say, taking her hands in mine. "That night… I can't stop thinking about it. I can't stop thinking about you."

I know now that I was right earlier about the look in her eyes. It was sadness. It's the same look she's giving me now.

"I can't stop thinking about you either."

"Then why are we doing this to ourselves?" I ask, my voice rising just a bit out of the frustration of the situation.

"You know why, Hunter. The Fury would freak out on you. And me? Might as well throw the Scarlet A on me now if word got out that I was dating a coach."

"Who says it has to get out?"

My words shock her. Her eyes go wide and her jaw drops a little. Honestly? They shock me a bit, too. I don't want to hide this. I want to be free to go to lunch with my girlfriend and hold her hand and sneak a kiss across the table. But if hiding us is what I need to do to see her again, then I'm willing to do it.

"Are you saying what I think you're saying?"

I take a breath, giving her hands another squeeze. "Come over for dinner. We'll talk. We'll figure this out. Just don't make me go another night wondering what could have been."

I don't know how long we sit in silence. It's probably only a few seconds, but I swear it could have been a few hours. I know what I'm asking for is risky. Both of us could lose our jobs over this.

I also know she's worth the risk.

I start to wonder if I was smart in asking her to take this chance. That is, until I hear four amazing words from her beautiful lips.

"Send me your address."

14

SADIE

WHAT THE FUCK am I doing?

What the fuck am I doing?

What in the actual ever-loving fuck am I doing?

Dinner? With Hunter? That he made himself with his own hands? Hands that I know feel amazing when they touch me?

I can't have dinner with Hunter. At his home. Alone. Unsupervised.

Nope. This is such a bad idea. Like the worst idea in the history of bad ideas.

I'll jump him. I will see him in his home looking sexy as hell, and I will want to climb him like a fucking tree. A girl only has so much willpower, and I know I used every ounce of it that night in Memphis.

> Sadie: Tell me again why I'm here?

I had this same freak out while I was getting ready, so I called Bethany for a pep talk. Her words were enough to get me out of my apartment, but apparently not strong enough to get me out of my car. Hence my needing a few more words of encouragement.

Bethany: Because as much as you want to talk yourself out of this, you know you want to go. You like him. And that's OK. Get out of your head. Enjoy the night. Text me tomorrow with all the naughty deets!

I toss my phone into my purse and take another deep breath.

I can't do this. What made me think I could do this? What spell did he have me under today when I agreed to this?

That's it. He must be some sort of wizard or something. That's the only logical explanation I can think of as to why I'm now sitting in my parked car outside his condo for a date. And not any kind of date. A date where he's cooking me dinner while likely looking all handsome and stuff. And since we're at his home, he's probably going to be casual and comfortable and all sorts of tempting.

Which means I'll want to have sex with him. More than once.

And that is such a bad idea. A really tempting, horribly bad, idea.

Maybe I'll be able to resist him. Maybe when I walk inside, I'll see behind the veil that is handsome, charming, funny, sweet Hunter. Maybe he's really an asshole. Maybe his cooking will suck, and I'll have to leave on account of food poisoning. Maybe his condo will look like he lives in a frat house. Maybe there will be no furniture except for a lawn chair in the living room and a television propped up by a milk crate with a gaming system loaded with every Madden game ever made. Hell, maybe he doesn't even have a bed frame.

Guys without bed frames are douches.

As I continue to wage a war inside my brain, a knock against my car window scares the daylights out of me. So much so I almost hit my head on the top of my car from the shock.

I look to my left and see Hunter, who is laughing hysterically at me.

"Not funny," I say in mock anger as I partly open my door.

"I beg to differ. My only regret is not videoing your reaction."

I let out a huff and turn to grab my purse and the six-pack I bought that is sitting in my passenger seat. "Why did you feel the need to come out and scare the bejesus out of me?"

With a gorgeous smile and his southern manners, he opens the door for me the rest of the way as I slide out of my car. Before I know it, he's guiding me toward his condo with his hand on the small of my back, his thumb gently rubbing up and down on the outside of my blouse.

Morning breath.

Vomit.

The word moist.

"At first it was cute watching you have an internal debate with yourself about whether or not you should come in," he says as we step inside. "But the longer you sat there, the more I was worried you were going to start your car back up and go home. And I couldn't let that happen, so I decided to come out and make sure you didn't run away. The scaring you part was just an added comedic bonus."

"Well, it wasn't very nice."

He takes the beer from my hand and puts it on a small table in his foyer. I really want to keep pretending to be mad at him. But I know I can't keep it up. And by the look on his face when he turns back to me, he knows it too.

He takes my chin in his fingers, gently tilting my face up to look at him. He uses his other hand to thread our fingers together.

I didn't realize how much I missed his touch until right now.

Well, that's a lie.

"I'm sorry," he says, gently rubbing his thumb over the top of my hand. "I didn't mean to scare you."

"Well, you did." My words come out breathy, though I don't mean for them to. I can't seem to control my voice, or my body, when I'm around this man. Especially when he is looking at me like he is right now, his eyes full of desire and want.

"How can I make it up to you?"

"I'm sure you can think of something."

"Let's see if this does the trick."

His lips meet mine in the softest of kisses. But he doesn't go in for another one, or one more intense. Rather, he lets his lips trail to the corner of my mouth. To my cheek. To my jaw. To my neck.

"That… that's working."

He chuckles before working his way back up to my lips, giving them one last kiss. This one longer than the first before he backs away.

"All better?" he asks softly.

I nod because right now, I can't find my words.

"Are you still thinking about leaving?"

"I was never going to leave," I admit, my voice still low as I try to regain my composure. Even though I know this is a bad idea, and I can think of a million reasons why I should leave, I'm not.

I can't. I don't want to. Tonight I want to just be a woman who has dinner with a man who makes her feel beautiful on the inside and out. I want a Memphis Part Two.

Fuck our jobs. Fuck the stereotypes. Fuck it all.

Tonight I'm choosing me.

Tonight I'm choosing Hunter.

***

"WAIT! THAT REPORTER WAS YOU?"

I laugh before taking a sip of the beer I brought over. "One and the same."

"Why didn't you say anything before? You were a legend in our locker room for months!"

I set my beer down on the patio table. The one strategically placed between me and Hunter. "And when would it have been a good time to slip it into conversation? It's not like I can just randomly say, 'Hey, do you remember the reporter who asked your college coach an innocent question about his thoughts on paying college athletes? And do you remember the rant he went on that went viral? Guess what. That was me.'"

We fall into laughter as we enjoy the beautiful night on his patio. It is an unusually warm March night, so we decided to take advantage of it after we ate dinner.

Which was delicious. It was simple, grilled chicken with a honey mustard glaze, roasted vegetables, and baked potatoes, but the fact that he went to the trouble to cook it made it that much more special.

Which is another reason why I need a table between us. All of those possibilities that I concocted in my head about being able to resist him? He has tossed a flamethrower to every single one.

His cooking was delicious. His house is decorated perfectly to fit his style. A lot of black, white, and grays, with pops of blue scattered. He showed off his office, which was decorated with football memorabilia in every available space. His bathroom is immaculately clean.

And I might have even snuck into his bedroom to check for a bed frame. He has one. Because, of course, he does.

Then there is him. The man is more beautiful on the inside than the out. Which says a lot. I know how he made me feel in Memphis. And part of me wondered if I built that up in my head because of some magical night where the stars aligned and I danced with a prince on Beale Street.

I didn't build it up. In fact, he's more than I remembered. We haven't had a lag in conversation all night. Even now, as we tiptoe around conversations about our jobs, it still doesn't feel wrong. I know it should. But it doesn't.

I. Am. So. Screwed.

"Well, you should have said something," Hunter says, pulling me back to the present. "It would have broken up some of those asinine questions I got at my opening press conference."

I give him a sideways glance. "You better not be talking about my question."

"Of course not," Hunter says, getting up to move to the seat next to me. Shit. No more table between us. That point is emphasized as I get a hint of his woodsy cologne. "Yours was the only question that actually made me think. I like it when I have to think of an answer."

"Oh, really," I say, sitting up as I tilt my body toward his. I don't know why I do this. It's like I have this pull to him when he's near me. "I'll have to remember that the next time we're at a press conference."

We fall into a comfortable silence—the first of the night—as he reaches for my hands. Hands that I willingly let him hold.

"See, we can do this," Hunter says.

"Hunter..."

"Just listen," he says, bringing his lips to my knuckles for a kiss. Damn, that was a dirty move. "I think there are certain things we can agree on."

"And that would be?"

"Why, I'm glad you asked. I have a plan." The smile on his face right now is mischievous. All I want to do is lean over and kiss that look off of him. "I'm attracted to you. And, for the sake of speeding this conversation along, I'm going on the assumption that you find me attractive as well."

"Sure. We'll go with that," I tease.

"We'll deal with that comment later," he says, picking up on my flirty tone. "We are two consenting adults who are attracted to each other. Bonus, we both enjoy spending time together. Would I be right on those two points?"

I nod. No sake in arguing with the obvious.

"Knowing those factors, and knowing that we are two determined individuals who have never let a little roadblock get in their way, it would be silly for us to not continue to do something that brings both of us happiness."

"What about—"

His finger is on my lips before I can get the next sentence out. "Our jobs. Yes, that is the elephant in the room. The Fury would be less than happy to find out that I'm spending my free time with someone who shouldn't know all the team's dirty secrets."

"And my job would rather not have to question me about whether or not I got information in a non-ethical way from my boyfriend."

"Boyfriend, huh? I like the sound of that," he says teasingly.

I give his arm a playful slap. "Let's get back to the point."

"Fine, but you can't take that word back. I like it and I'm keeping it." He gives my hand one more kiss before he continues. "I don't like this idea, but I can't think of anything else, so I'm just going to say it.

What if we start seeing each other and see where this goes, but keep it between us? We owe it to ourselves to find out if this is just attraction, or if what we're feeling could be for real. But while we do that, we don't tell anyone. No one needs to know."

I let his words marinate as I replay them in my head. I know he's right. Our jobs, at least right now, cannot find out if we were to pursue this. But lying to everyone? Our families? Friends? That part doesn't sit well with me. At all.

"I hate being a dirty little secret."

"No, gorgeous," he says, scooping me so I'm now sitting on his lap. I hate that immediately I feel more at ease being in his arms. I don't want to feel this way. But apparently my body already knows what my head isn't ready to admit. "You aren't my dirty secret. God, I wish I could shout from the rooftops right now that I had dinner tonight with a woman who has had me in knots since the moment I laid eyes on her. I want to call my mom and tell her that you're my girl and I'm bringing you to dinner this Sunday. I don't like the situation. At all. But if we can do this, say for six months, and show both the Fury and *The Banner* that we can have this relationship, and keep our professional lives separate, then they have nothing to worry about."

Can we do that? Six months? Six months would be for a good portion of the upcoming season. If we can make it a season with me doing my job, Hunter doing his, and nothing happening, then neither one of our jobs could object. Well, they could. But at least now we'd have proof we can keep personal and professional lines drawn.

I have never been so torn about a decision. Everything he said is right. Can we do it? Can we keep something this big to ourselves for that long?

The alternative of not trying this is not having him in my life at all, save for the occasional interview. I then think about leaving here tonight. I think about never getting to kiss him again. I think about one day him finding a woman he wants to date, and I'll have to come to terms with the fact that she gets to feel his lips against hers.

The thought terrifies me.

"Six months," I repeat, knowing that we need to make this a clear ground rule.

"Six months. It will be no time at all. What do you say? Take a chance on us?"

He circles his arms around my waist, pulling me even closer to him before kissing my hair. I knew I was saying yes before this gesture. But right now, at this moment, somehow I know for a fact that even though there are a million reasons not to do this, I would be an idiot to walk away from Hunter.

"Let's do it."

The smile on his face is instant and infectious. "Really?"

I nod, a smile slowly forming across my face. "Really."

He doesn't say another word. Instead, he does the most perfect thing.

He kisses me like I've never been kissed before.

15

———

HUNTER

That's the only word that I can think of as my lips find Sadie's. After months of wanting and wishing, of almost having then having to let her go, I can finally say that Sadie is mine.

Well, I can't say it out loud. I know we have to keep this quiet.

That doesn't change the fact that this woman is officially mine.

Kissing her on my patio might not be the best idea right now. I do have neighbors who I'm sure aren't counting on a show. But I can't seem to move from this spot. Her body feels too right as she molds herself to me. Her lips feel too good. And honestly? I'm afraid if I stop kissing her she'll decide that she doesn't want to be in a relationship where she has to hide. Or she realizes that dating me is too big of a risk.

If I keep kissing her, she can't change her mind. I'll just have to never stop kissing her.

No arguments here.

"Hunter," she says breathlessly.

"Less talking." My mouth travels from her lips to her neck. God, it tastes so sweet. The floral scent she wears is taking over my senses. "More kissing."

She giggles. "We should move this inside."

I unbutton the top two buttons of her blouse, giving me more skin to explore. "I'm not done kissing you yet."

She brings her head back upright, cutting off my access to her neck. I dislike that immediately.

"I wasn't done kissing there."

My pout is immediately erased when I see the seductive smile come across her face. She moves closer to my ear, and just when I think she's about to start doing some exploring of her own, she does one better.

"If we go inside right now, I'll let you kiss me wherever you want."

I don't even let her walk. As soon as the words leave her mouth I have her scooped up in my arms and I'm carrying her inside.

"Hunter!" she shrieks, the happiness in her tone unmistakable. "At least turn off the lights."

I groan and turn around, but I don't put her down. Nope. I quite like carrying Sadie through my condo.

I hurry up and flip off the patio and kitchen lights. Anything else I'll deal with later. I have much more important things to attend to right now.

Like getting Sadie into my bedroom.

Then getting naked.

In that order.

"You know I could have walked," she says between giggles as I place her down on my king-size bed.

"I know you could have. Consider it my first act as your boyfriend," I say as I look down at her while I kick off my shoes and socks.

There have been many nights where I've imagined what Sadie would look like in my bed. Never in my wildest dreams did she look as breathtaking as she does right now. Her hair is fanned across my pillows, the light blue of the comforter contrasts with the dark brown of her hair. Her eyes are filled with desire and passion. She's still dressed, but I can see the curves of her body. I'm nearly salivating at the thought of having her naked underneath me.

I lower myself next to her and immediately my lips are on hers. It's like she's a magnet. Whenever I'm in proximity of her, I have to touch her in some way.

I know that's not good for the fact that we have to keep this a secret. But for right now… for tonight… I'm taking full advantage that I can kiss and touch her wherever I like.

Because she's mine.

"I thought I said we'd circle back to the boyfriend label," she says a bit breathlessly, her hips writhing as my mouth continues to explore her skin.

"I'll make you a deal," I say after kissing her one more time. "If I can make you come with just my mouth, right now, then I'm officially your boyfriend."

Her eyes shine with excitement. "And if you don't?"

"I'll just have to keep trying until I do."

I begin my exploration down her body, my lips finding a new place to kiss with each inch. I finish unbuttoning her shirt as I place kisses on the tops of her breasts.

Note to self, come back and explore more here later.

When her shirt is off, I leave a trail of kisses across her stomach. Her skin is smooth, and now that her shirt is fanned open, I can see every one of her luscious curves.

Another note to self, worship her curves at a later time.

I continue kissing her stomach as I work her pants down, taking the lace that I feel underneath them down as well. I take one second to look back up at her, and when our gazes meet… fuck… the heat that I'm seeing in her hazel eyes only propels me on.

"Lie back, gorgeous. I have to taste you."

I place a kiss on her thighs, and the smell of her sex is making me insane with want. I leave soft kisses on either side, working my way toward the center, and when I get there, I can see that she's already wet for me. I've been hard for her since we were on the patio. The sight of this? My cock is now solid steel.

"Wet for me already?" I ask, my tongue slowly beginning to work her center.

She doesn't answer. She just grinds her hips into my face, and fuck, that only makes me harder.

I'm done talking. I work my tongue over her clit, rotating between sucking, licking, and flicking, which is driving her mad by the way her body is moving on my bed, her hands clutching the comforter like she needs to ground herself.

Just driving her insane isn't my goal. My goal is to make my girl see stars. To make her know that after tonight, there will be no other man who will ever make her feel the way I can.

"Hunter… please… I'm so close."

Her words light a fire in me. I insert two fingers, which sends her hips off the bed. I place a hand over her stomach, grounding her to me. I don't know where she thinks she's going, but I'm not done yet.

I work my fingers as my tongue continues to feast on the sweetest treat it has ever tasted. And then, with one crook of my finger, I feel her still. And then I hear the hottest sound I have ever heard.

"Hunter!"

Sadie explodes on my fingers, and I'm pretty sure on my deathbed I will remember this experience. I slowly bring her down, her legs shaking as her orgasm releases.

I place one more kiss on her pussy before I get up to fetch a warm washcloth to clean her up. When I get back to my room, Sadie is in the same position as I left her, looking spent and satisfied.

"Are you okay?" I ask, taking the washcloth to her center.

"I am more than okay… boyfriend."

I look up to find Sadie smiling back at me. I wish I had a camera right now to capture this moment. She's sitting up on her elbows, her blouse open, a white lace bra the only thing covering her. Her hair is a mess, her lips are swollen from our kisses, and she looks sated and satisfied.

In short? She's the most beautiful thing I have ever seen.

And she's not going anywhere because she's all mine.

16

SADIE

Hunter's words are soft and right next to my ear, and the feel of his breath against my skin makes me squirm. I swear I don't mean to rub my ass on his dick. His very hard, very alert dick that is currently giving me the best wake-up call in the history of wake-up calls.

"Good morning, yourself," I say, rolling over on my back. Hunter is propped up on one elbow, and from this angle, half of his body is over mine. It doesn't take long for him to lean down and kiss me. A kiss I willingly accept.

If this is how I'm now woken up each morning, I could quickly get used to this.

Just the thought of that brings everything from last night back into focus.

Admitting that we both feel something for the other.

Agreeing to give this a shot.

Hunter making me come with his mouth. Holy shit, that was the best orgasm of my life.

I expected that to lead to sex. In my limited experience with men, that's how things went. Either the guy or the girl did a little foreplay, and then the sex happened. Orgasms were *to be determined* for the woman. Orgasms were always a must for the man.

But not last night. Instead of Hunter wanting his, all he did was hold me. We didn't talk about all the "what ifs." I fell asleep in his arms, the rhythmic rise and fall of his chest lulling me to sleep. At least for one night, we had a bubble around us. A bubble where we didn't have to think about the repercussions that could happen with our relationship. A bubble where we didn't have to hide our feelings for each other.

Last night was just about being together.

And it was incredible.

As soon as his lips release mine, I feel the bubble burst. And by the look in his eyes, he does too.

"We need to figure this out," I say, my voice low and a bit sad.

"I know," he says, giving me one more kiss at the corner of my mouth. "But can we at least do it with coffee?"

"If we don't do it over coffee, there will be no relationship to have. I need caffeine, boyfriend."

This makes him smile. "I'd hate to upset my girlfriend one day in. Let's go."

I stay in bed as Hunter puts on joggers and a T-shirt. I let him leave the room before I get out of bed and find one of his T-shirts to slip on. It hangs down to my mid-thigh and is in no way sexy. At least, I don't think so.

When I walk into Hunter's kitchen his eyes turn to fire. The look he is giving me right now, one of appreciation and desire, is thrilling. The smile on his face is downright dirty.

I wonder what his thoughts on kitchen sex are?

"What are you smiling at?" I say, taking a seat on one of the barstools around his island.

"Well, a few things," he says, placing a cup of coffee in front of me. "First, I really, really, like you wearing my T-shirts, and I think that should be your standard-issue clothing when you are over here. But before that, I remembered something from last night."

"I remember a lot of things from last night," I say, smiling over my cup as I take a sip.

"You better," he says, taking a seat across the island from me. "What I was remembering was when we went upstairs to my bedroom. My door was open. I didn't realize it last night because, well, let's just say I was focused on very specific things. But for some reason this morning, I remembered that I thought I had shut my door before you came over. Do you have any idea how that happened?"

Fuck. I am so busted.

"I don't know what you speak of," I say, though I'm looking everywhere but at him. I could tell in his tone he's not mad. In fact, I know he's teasing me. But if I admit this, then I admit a level of crazy I'm not sure I'm ready for him to know about.

"I think you do."

I finally make eye contact, and the smile on his face, the small one that says he knows my secret, melts me on the spot.

Dammit. This man is going to have me eating out of the palm of his hand with just one look.

"Fine," I say, taking a breath before admitting this. "I might have snuck a peek to see if you were hiding anything."

Hunter laughs, which is good. At least right now my act of crazy is still amusing. "Like a dead body or something?"

"No. I wanted to see if you had a bed frame."

His look turns to confusion. "A bed frame?"

I let out a sigh. Here it goes.

"You're perfect. In every way. You probably even work at soup kitchens in the offseason. I was trying to find one way you weren't. So, before dinner, when I went to use the bathroom, I might have taken a quick look inside your room. I was *really* hoping you didn't have a bed frame to prove that there is SOMETHING wrong with you."

His laugh is instant and takes over his body. And I must admit, now that I said it out loud, it is funny. Crazy. But funny.

"Well," he says, getting up from his stool to walk around the island so we are now on the same side. "There is something wrong with me."

I turn to watch him walk toward me, which is exactly what he wanted. His hands are now on both sides of me, clutching on to the island, caging me in between him.

"And what is that?" I say as I look up at him.

"I haven't kissed you in way too long."

"Well." My voice is breathless as I loop my hands around his neck. "We better remedy that."

***

"WE REALLY NEED TO TALK."

This is the first time I've had a chance to voice that thought. Hunter has been otherwise keeping my lips occupied for most of the morning. Our kissing went from the kitchen to the living room. And though we frustratingly stayed clothed, I can think of a lot worse ways of starting my day than by making out with Hunter McAvoy.

"Do we really need to?"

At least, that's what I think he says. It came out mumbled as his head was buried between my boobs.

"Yes," I say, lifting his head up. His mouth is in a pout and… damn, this man is freaking adorable. "If we're going to do this, we can't just wing it."

"Fine," he says, sitting up to face me on his couch. "I think our first rule is that you spend the night as much as possible."

"And how do you see that working?" I don't hate the idea, I'm just curious.

"Well, it would be a lot like last night. You come here. We eat dinner. You sleep here. At some point we get naked. You wake up naked with me. Done and done. What's next on the list?"

I laugh, loving the simplicity of his answer, even if I have much bigger things on my mind. "Hunter, be serious."

He takes my hand in his, and already his touch calms my nerves. "You tell me what you're concerned about, and we'll figure out how we handle it."

I take in a breath, which gives me a second to decide what I want to talk about first. "Well, actually, the first thing did have to do with… seeing each other. My apartment is within walking distance of *The Banner*. And the parking sucks. There is a very good chance someone could see you if you came to my apartment."

"Fine. You'll come here, then."

"Is it safe?"

He nods. "As far as I know, no one from the team lives around here. Most of the players live downtown, and the rest of the coaches are in the suburbs. See. I figured out our first problem and you didn't even know it."

This makes me laugh. "Okay. Next problem, Mr. I Have It All Figured Out. You know we can't go out on dates like a normal couple. We can't go downtown just to catch some music. We can't chance being seen. Are you okay with that?"

"That does suck," he says, giving the tops of my knuckle a brush with his thumb. "That just means I'll have to get creative on date nights. And it also means a lot more being naked."

All I can do is laugh because this man has an answer for everything. We agreed that we needed to try to keep our distance from each other when we were both at the Fury facility, at least for now, as to not accidentally give off any weird vibes. We agreed that in the times we do have to see each other at work, we need to be as casual as possible. And, just in case we left our phones anywhere or in plain sight, our numbers are now saved as "boyfriend" and "girlfriend."

His choice. He's very excited about this title, obviously.

We even set ground rules for the nights that I might have to bring work home with me. Simply, he can't comment on anything I'm working on. To make things fair, he said he would make sure to keep game plans under lock and key, so I didn't get an inside look at what the Fury might be planning for their next opponent.

"See! This is simple," Hunter says, moving closer as he wraps his arm around my shoulder. "We should write the handbook on having a secret relationship."

"Don't get too excited there. We haven't dealt with one major topic."

"And that is?"

"Our families."

And with that one word, I can tell that I have let the wind out of Hunter's sails. So, I move a little closer to him, hoping that I can soothe his worries as he's done for me so much already.

"I don't want to lie to my family," I say, my fingers playing with the fabric of his T-shirt. "I've never held back anything from my dad. I'm a little nervous to tell him, but I don't want to lie either."

He kisses my hair, and in some way, I think it comforts him as much as it does me. "I don't want you to lie to them. You do whatever makes you feel comfortable."

"I also don't want to make you uncomfortable. We're in this together."

He lifts my chin so we're now looking at each other. "I know my family dynamic is completely different than yours. If you can trust your family and you feel it's safe, then tell them. Hell, I'll come over for dinner. I'll meet your dad and win him over. I just don't want you to think that if I don't tell my family, it's because I'm ashamed of you. And if it were just my mom and Whitley, then I'd be calling them now and telling them all about you. But Bo... I don't know how he'll react. He'll probably tell me that dating a reporter is just one more dumb move that I've made in my life. And I don't... I can't... he doesn't get to tell me anything about this."

I place a kiss on his chest, hating that he has to deal with that.

"Is there anything else?" Hunter asks.

"Yes, there's one more thing."

"What is it?"

I lift my head up, then promptly straddle him on his couch. "It's been a long time since you've kissed me."

17

———

SADIE

I KNEW at some point by dating Hunter that there would be a time when we would be at one another's houses, both of us doing work.

More specifically, both of us doing work while trying not to look at what the other one is doing.

I just didn't think it would happen so soon. Yet, this is how we have been every night for the past week.

We're three days away from the draft, which means both of us have been fairly busy. Well, Hunter more so than me. I've been writing two to three stories a day about guys they could possibly pick. I've also written every story I possibly could on Bryce Donald, the quarterback whom they would be idiots to not pick first overall. Not that I know this from Hunter. We have been keeping our word and not talking about what we are working on.

I sit on the sectional and work diligently on my laptop. He has created his space on his dining room table. That's his zone. He has been poring over draft videos and scouting reports, even after he and the coaches leave the facility for the night. It's like he's making it his personal mission to know the life story of every player in the draft.

Want to know what he doesn't know? What it's like to have sex with me.

We've been together for one month. One month since we said that we'd give it a try.

In that one month, we've learned a lot about each other. He has learned that I can't cook a thing. He's made it his mission to teach me how to make grilled cheese. I burned the first two attempts, so it's not looking good. We figured out that we like the same pizza toppings, which is quite convenient on the nights that I ruin dinner. I've learned that he has never seen an episode of *Game of Thrones*. We're now in a serious binge of that.

However, he doesn't know if I like to be on the top or the bottom. I don't know if he's a rough or gentle lover.

Why haven't we had sex yet? I have my theories, though I haven't asked him. Because… well, how do you ask your boyfriend why he doesn't want to have sex with you *without* seeming desperate?

So, I wait. And wonder. And continue to write my stories on his couch while he talks to himself about draft scenarios at his dining table.

"You okay over there?" I ask, his grumbles getting louder.

"I'm just trying to go through different scenarios for the second round."

I could have guessed that. That's all he's been doing for the past two days.

ALL he's been doing.

I'm usually never this horny. Hell, it's been years since I've even had sex. But just a few orgasms from Hunter now have me all sorts of hot and bothered.

"You should take a break," I say, my eyes still focused on my story. "You've been working all day. You're not solving the draft puzzle tonight."

I hear him let out a sigh, and he comes over to the sectional where he promptly moves my computer to the coffee table and puts his head on my lap.

"Maybe I wasn't done writing?" I say teasingly, my fingers beginning to play with his hair.

This must be having a good effect on him because he nuzzles deeper into my leg. It's like he's a cat. "You were."

"How do you know that?"

"Because when you're writing on a deadline, you always bite your bottom lip because you're concentrating. When you are trying to work ahead, you are much more relaxed."

I smile and lean down to place a kiss on his head.

"I didn't realize you were paying that much attention to me." What man notices those little things? Especially one who I thought was so in his zone that he barely realized I was even here?

He gives my leg a small kiss. "I notice everything about you."

Well, not everything. Or else he'd realize that I'm going out of my mind for him.

"You think very loudly," he comments, though he's still not looking up at me. "What's going through that brain of yours?"

"I'm sorry. Was my thinking getting in the way of your draft strategizing? Or was I slacking on the head rub."

"Ha ha. You've got jokes," he says, rolling over so now he's looking up at me. "What's on your mind, gorgeous?"

Can I just tell him? Is it that easy? He was honest with me when he said we should give this a try. The least I can do is give him the same courtesy.

"Just say it, Sadie."

I take in a deep breath. Here goes nothing. "Are you not attracted to me?"

This makes him sit straight up. "Are you out of your mind? Why would you think that? I'm borderline obsessed with you."

"Because…" I let my words trail, because damn, this is hard to say. "Why haven't you tried to have sex with me?"

I don't know what response I was expecting from such an intimate and vulnerable question. What I wasn't expecting, laughter.

But that's what he does. The asshole laughs.

"This isn't funny."

This only makes him laugh some more. "Oh, baby. If you only knew."

Now I'm just pissed. "Care to enlighten me since I'm *clearly* not in on the joke?"

Hunter moves toward me and somehow scoops me up off the couch and sets me so I am sitting across his lap.

"First off, if you don't know this by now, I think you are perfect in every way. Which makes me hate this all that much more that I can't give you a normal relationship," he begins, his fingers softly stroking the side of my face. "We don't get to date. We are cocooned in this bubble. So I didn't want to rush the sex. I wanted to give us time to get to know each other and get a handle on our normal, because nothing that we do will be conventional. I thought if we waited, at least that was something normal I could give you. Looking back, I should have told you my grand plan. I'm still getting used to this boyfriend thing. I'm sorry."

"Well, I guess that makes sense," I say, my voice just above a whisper.

"Sadie," he says, his lips now just a few inches from mine. "I want you every second of every day. There is not a minute that goes by that I don't wish I knew how it felt to be inside you. I just want to make sure we don't rush into anything."

I close the distance between us, fusing our lips together. As soon as I open my mouth, he slips his tongue inside. We've mastered this. If there were awards to win for kissing, we'd take first place every time.

But I want more. And now I know, so does he.

"Take me to bed, Hunter."

He doesn't waste a second. Much like he did that first night, Hunter carries me up to his room. Only this time I don't object.

My mouth is on his neck as he takes the steps two at a time. They only leave his skin when he places me down on his comforter. He immediately joins me in bed. Our lips find their way back to each other as our hands are frantically trying to unbutton and remove every piece of clothing we have on.

"I am so sorry I kept us waiting," he says as his lips travel down to my breasts.

"No. Don't apologize." I mean it. His admission made my heart melt a little more for this man. "But don't make me wait anymore."

And he doesn't. He rolls to the side of the bed and takes a condom out of his bedside table. He doesn't take long to cover himself and find his way back to me.

"I'll never make you wait again."

Then he enters me.

And it was absolutely worth the wait.

18
____

HUNTER

AND WITH THE *first pick of the draft, the Nashville Fury select... Bryce Donald, quarterback, Clemson.*

As the words leave the commissioner's mouth, our draft room goes absolutely insane. Grown men jump out of their chairs and start hugging the first person near them. Manly, back-slapping hugs, of course. We're a professional football team, after all.

Though, we've known Bryce was our top pick from the moment I stepped foot into the Fury facility four months ago, hearing it being said out loud, in front of thousands of fans and millions of people watching at home, makes it official.

This is the player who's going to turn the franchise around. And as the offensive coordinator, it's my job to make sure that happens.

"We got our guy," Coach Gordon says to me, adding in a backslap for good measure.

"Hell yeah, we did," I say, excitement pouring out of me. "Now we need to nail the next six rounds."

"From your mouth to God's ears, son."

The only round that happens tonight is the first—the league and the television broadcast determine that. Since we had the first pick and we don't plan on making any trades, our night is technically over.

Yes, we have some assistants keeping an eye on things to make sure nothing gets crazy and to see which players are selected, but for the most part, the heavy lifting is done for the night.

"When do you have to go in for interviews?" I ask Coach Gordon. I'm genuinely curious. It has nothing to do with me wondering when he's going to see my secret girlfriend.

A secret girlfriend who gave me a good luck blow job before I had to leave for the facility today.

She's the fucking best.

"In a few minutes. Which is why I came over here. Do you mind coming in with me?"

My body goes still at his request. "Me? You want me to come with you? For the interviews?"

I'm shocked. Reporters rarely want to talk to coordinators, which was another reason why Sadie and I have been hopeful this can work. We figured we could make it through a few interviews during the season and keep our cool.

Apparently, we are testing that theory earlier than we both thought.

"Is there another Hunter McAvoy? Yes you. The Mob thinks it's a story that a new offensive coordinator gets a bright new shiny quarterback to play with in his first season. Or some shit like that."

The Mob is the nickname that Coach Gordon has for the reporter pool. He's not a fan of the media. At all. And that's actually putting it lightly. One time he said that they were a waste of space on Earth and didn't deserve to share the same air as the rest of humanity. I don't even want to imagine what his reaction would be if he found out about me and Sadie.

"Well, we'd hate to have an angry mob on our hands. Just let me know when it's time."

This is fine. Everything is fine. I'll run to the bathroom, splash a little bit of cold water on my face and get my head right. It's just a few questions. About a player I've been scouting and talking to every day for the past two months.

Questions asked by your secret girlfriend.

Yup. Everything is fine.

Coach Gordon gives me a slap on the back, which might be just as effective as the cold splash of water. "No time like the present. Let's go and get this over with."

"Now? As in, right now?" I almost choke on my words. Can't the man give me five minutes?

Coach Gordon gives me a questioning look. "You have somewhere else to be?"

I give my head a shake because he's going to realize something is up.

Get your fucking shit together, Hunter.

"No, sir. Let's do this."

We head to the interview room where we held my introductory press conference. Paul is there to meet us, and when he opens the door, the sight in front of me is much different than what I remember from January.

There aren't as many reporters this time. Now it's just the local group. The television cameras are still in the back. A few photographers are on the floor in the front. The group of middle-aged men are again congregated in the middle of the seating area.

And then I look to the front row and there she is. My girl. Typing away like her life depends on it.

I can't help but smile. She's in her element. Yes, she's sexy and kind and funny and makes me feel like I can conquer the world. But she's also independent and determined and motivated and that's just as sexy as anything else.

Except for the time she wore my old college football jersey to bed. That shit was fucking hot.

"Drafting Bryce Donald put that smile on your face?"

The comment comes from one of the male reporters, and I'm immediately reminded that I'm here to do my job, not to drool over my girlfriend.

Game face on, McAvoy. Don't fuck this up.

"For sure," I say, plastering on my camera-ready smile. "You draft one of the highest-rated quarterback prospects in years and see what kind of smile is on your face."

My banter works, and the middle-aged men laugh at my response. Sadie, though, doesn't look up from her computer. Even though we don't make eye contact, I see a slight smile break through as she shakes her head like I told the worst dad joke she's ever heard.

Before I can make eye contact with her, Coach Gordon and I take our seats, and the questions start coming at us like rapid fire. Most are about Bryce. Some are about what we plan to do over the next two days of the draft. Most are basic questions that anyone who has been interviewed can see coming a mile away. And yet again, Sadie hasn't asked anything.

"Last question."

Sadie raises her hand and Paul calls on her. I wonder what she has up her sleeve?

"Coach Gordon, you have never had a rookie quarterback start on any team you've coached during your career. Are you confident that Bryce could be the first, or are you looking to pick up a veteran in free agency to allow him a year to learn?"

And I'm hard.

I could be on my deathbed, knowing all the knowledge I'll ever know on this Earth, and I will still not know the answer as to why when Sadie Benson talks football, I get hornier than a virgin on prom night.

I have no clue how Coach Gordon answers Sadie's question. As soon as the words left her mouth, all I heard was Charlie Brown's teacher from all the *Peanuts* specials talking. Somehow, by the grace of God, I do hear her question to me.

"Coach McAvoy, what do you think? Could he start in the opener? Do you think Bryce is the future of this franchise?"

Coach McAvoy.

Holy hell, why does that turn me on so much?

Focus, Hunter. Focus!

"We wouldn't have drafted him if we didn't think he was the future of our franchise," I say, my eyes meeting hers. I give her credit, she's keeping her game face on better than I am. Or so I'd guess. "Bryce is a more than capable quarterback and if he does the right things and works hard, the job could be his this season."

Sadie nods her head, signaling that she has the answer she was looking for, but I'm not done.

"The future doesn't have to wait. The future can start right now. Tonight is the beginning of a new era of Fury football."

Her eyes are now locked on mine in a questioning look. If I had to guess what she was trying to convey to me, it would be something along the lines of, "you've answered my question, now shut the hell up."

But I don't. I need to say the next words. I need to tell her this. "Will it take work? Yes. Will it have some highs and lows? Yes. But tonight we made a choice, and every choice we make this weekend will affect our future. We will stand by those choices because they are what we think is best for our team and for our future. We can't wait to see what comes next."

I don't know where that speech came from. It's like looking at her in this room made me see everything that I have in front of me. My job. Our relationship. The future. For the first time in my life, I have everything I've ever wanted, as well as a few things I didn't know I needed.

I stand up from the table and steal one more glance at her before Paul escorts me out. She's not looking at me, so I can stare at her an extra second. And I don't know what she's saying, but I swear I see her talking to herself.

Did she just mouth the word diarrhea?

19

SADIE

DIARRHEA.

Socks with sandals.

Bleu cheese.

Those things aren't even disgusting enough for me to shake away the butterflies that Hunter's speech just gave me.

And I fucking hate bleu cheese.

Never in a million years when I asked him that question did I expect a monologue that not only had to do with the Fury, but also our relationship. At first, I thought I might be reading too much into it. No way, during the first time that we had to be in the same room together around people whom we have to hide our relationship from, would he do that.

Oh, but he did. When our eyes met, I knew I wasn't imagining it. His gaze was locked on me. It's like there wasn't another person in the room.

And as much as it freaked me out, it also sent a feeling through my body that I hope never goes away when it comes to Hunter.

When he was done, I couldn't look at him. I had to avert my eyes because I didn't trust myself. I had to whisper to myself three massively grotesque things, or else I was likely to follow Hunter back to his office and jump him.

As soon as it was appropriate, I bolted out of my seat and made a beeline for the reporter's work room at the Fury's facility. I hurry and get to my chair at my workstation and take three deep breaths as I sit down.

Holy hell, that was intense.

I allow myself a minute to gather my thoughts before I start writing. I have to. It's the only way I'll be able to concentrate.

I take those minutes to look around the other workstations in the pressroom. The Fury added a workspace for the reporters a few years ago when they did a remodel. We all have our own areas that they insisted we decorate to make us feel more comfortable. Which is nice of them. I'm here more than I'm ever at my desk at *The Banner*.

The decorations are what I'd assume to be typical for a group of sports writers. Some have pictures of their wives and kids displayed. Others have bobbleheads or an assortment of sports memorabilia. Me? There's a picture of me and Dad at a UT game. There's one of me, Dad, Helen, and Bethany at Christmas. There's no picture of a significant other. Not that I ever had one to hang up.

And even now that I do, I can't.

With that sobering thought, I open my phone, meaning to go to the voice recording app that I use to record press conferences. I do this with every intention of beginning to transcribe the interviews. Instead, my finger clicks to my photos.

Staring back at me is the last photo I took.

One of me and Hunter from last night.

The draft is a very long, very tiresome, grind for the both of us. All either of us wanted to do was relax before the insanity of the draft began. For us, that meant Chinese delivery and a few episodes of *Game of Thrones*. At some point, we found ourselves lying on the couch, his arms wrapped around me with my back to his front. I love that position. Every time he holds me like that, I feel... cherished. Safe. Dare I say loved.

So, I grabbed my phone and snapped a picture of us. Us cuddling, me feeling cherished.

I could stare at this picture all day. We look so content. Like we don't have a care in the world. Like we aren't keeping a secret that could ruin both of us.

I swipe to the next photo. We're in the same position, but this time Hunter is kissing my cheek as I laugh. What the picture doesn't show is that he started tickling me after he realized I took the first picture.

I look back up at my empty desk area and let out a sad sigh. I would love nothing more than to print these out and hang them at my workstation. That's what people in relationships do, right? I know I can't, though. I know it's foolish to even fantasize about it. It can't happen, so why waste time and energy even thinking about it? We still have at least five months before we can even think about telling people about us.

That doesn't stop me from wanting it.

"Earth to Sadie! Yoo-hoo! You there?"

I almost drop my phone at the sound of Tommy shouting in front of me. I scramble to lock my phone and quickly put it face down next to my computer.

"Jesus Christ, you scared me," I say as my hand covers my heart.

He laughs. "You were staring at your phone like it was hypnotizing you. Do we need to have a talk about screen time?"

"Ha ha, old man," I say, quickly rebooting my laptop back to life, hoping that avoids any suspicion of what I was doing. "You can talk to me about screen time when you finally figure out how to download an app by yourself."

Tommy waves off my comeback, and we both turn to get to work.

Phew. That was close.

"I wonder who they're picking tomorrow?" someone says out loud as I begin working on my next story. "Larry, you get any inside information?"

"Well, it could go a few ways," Larry begins, a smugness to his voice. It makes my skin crawl. "I think they'll try to draft that receiver from Oregon. And you know, when I was talking to the coaching staff last week, they all but told me that if Cole Campbell wasn't drafted, that he was their guy."

A snort comes out of my mouth before I can hold it back. I *really* didn't want to be in this conversation—I just wanted to get my work done and go home, but apparently my lack of self-control is making that impossible.

"Why are you laughing, Benson?" Larry says in a challenging way. "You don't think they'll try to get Campbell? They would be stupid not to. You *do* know who Cole Campbell is, right? Or do you need me to fill you in?"

Larry has never been a fan of mine. In fairness, it's not me, specifically. It's my gender. He's one of those old-school, *women belong in the kitchen and not the locker room* kind of guys. One of his favorite things to do is to try to call me out on something I don't know.

He has never succeeded.

And tonight is not the night he does.

Not today, Satan.

"Yes, I know who Cole Campbell is," I say, turning to face him and the rest of the reporters who are now staring at us like this is a duel straight out of the Wild West. "I don't think anyone in here needs me to read his bio, but in case anyone forgot, he's a six-foot-eight offensive lineman who has played with, and protected Bryce Donald since they played Pop Warner football together in Ohio. They have been on the same team since they were six years old. The only reason he did not go in the first round is because he had an off-season knee surgery that pushed him back to a second-day pick. So, therefore, it would absolutely be idiotic to *not* draft the player who knows your new franchise quarterback better than any person on the planet. And I knew *all* of that information, and I didn't have a meeting with the coaches last week. It must feel *really good* being in the know like that, Larry. Really, it was a good scoop on your part. I one day hope to be as good of a reporter as you."

Larry's face turns beet red, and I hear snickers from the other guys as I put my earbuds in and get to work.

Another day, another idiot I had to prove myself to.

Maybe one day it won't be like this. Today is not that day.

I'm just about to get in a groove on this story when I feel my cell phone vibrate next to me. I flip it over and quickly look around to make sure no one is peeking over my shoulder when I read this.

> Boyfriend: You are so fucking hot.

I can't help but laugh at his out-of-the-blue text. I mean, I'll never get tired of Hunter saying that to me, but why now? The press conference has been over for almost an hour now. If he was going to text me, I figured it would be right after.

> Girlfriend: And what do I owe this text message to?

> Boyfriend: I had to walk past the workroom, and I heard you dropping the hammer on Larry. I fucking love it when you talk football. Instead of sexting, you should just talk football to me, bonus points if there's a boob picture that accompanies the text.

I let out a laugh, but quickly catch myself. As I take a look around, it seems that everyone has headphones in and is busy typing away. Thank God.

> Girlfriend: I'll keep that in mind next time I need to seduce you.

> Boyfriend: I doubt you'll ever need to try and seduce me. Your beauty does it every time I see you.

Was that cheesy? Yes. Does it give me the butterflies in my stomach that I've now coined it the Hunter McAvoy Feeling? Also, yes.

> Girlfriend: You need to stop texting me. I'm smiling so big someone might notice.

> Boyfriend: Who knew me making you smile was a bad thing? I like making you smile. It's a great honor as the boyfriend to make you smile.

> Girlfriend: It's not. It's just… never mind. Don't you have players to draft or something?

> Boyfriend: You know not until tomorrow. But fine. I get it. You have to work, and me texting you makes you think of inappropriate things. I'll stop texting you. =)

> Girlfriend: Thank you. Talk to you later. <3

I'm just about to put my phone down when another message comes through.

> Boyfriend: Wait! I need to tell you something first.

I have no idea what I'm waiting on. I thought he was going to send another reply right away, but he doesn't. It's almost a full minute before I get his next one.

> Boyfriend: I hate that you had to defend yourself to that asshole, but I've never been prouder of you. Keep kicking ass, gorgeous. <3

My smile is so big now that I'm sure someone is bound to notice. But I don't care.

That Hunter McAvoy Feeling is too big to suppress.

20

HUNTER

"IS THAT IT?"

I regret the question as soon as it leaves my mouth. I think we're done. But the way I worded the question leaves room for Coach Gordon to say, "no, there's more to do."

I'm sure there is more to do. I just hope it can wait until tomorrow. My body and brain are drained. I feel like I haven't left the Fury facility in days.

The draft started Thursday and ended Saturday. It's now Sunday, and the entire day has been spent making offers to undrafted players we want to invite to training camp. That's almost as grueling as the draft process.

The last four days have been a blur of adrenaline and exhaustion. It was all worth it, though, because we fucking nailed it. Every analyst on all the major television networks are saying we knocked the draft out of the park, highlighted by drafting Bryce Donald and Cole Campbell. Our team is better today than it was earlier in the week. We are already being predicted to go back to the playoffs.

This week was a rush like I'd never experienced. But now it's over and my body is crashing. All I want is to go home, order a pizza, and curl up on the couch with my girl.

"Nah. Get out of here, McAvoy," Coach Gordon says, waving me off. "You've done good work this week, son. A lot of what we did this week was because of you."

His praise hits me square in the gut. I shouldn't react like this. It was just a few words from a superior to an employee. But when you grow up and never hear words like that, they take on a whole new meaning when you hear them.

"Thanks, Coach. Just doing my job," I say, hoping to sound nonchalant at his praise as I gather up my tablet and notebooks. "I'll see you tomorrow."

If he says anything else, I don't hear it. Before I'm even out the door, I have my cell phone out, hitting dial on Sadie's number.

"Yeah."

Sadie's greeting takes me off guard. I didn't expect her to gush over the sound of my voice, but a little more than a mumbled syllable would have been nice.

"Nice to talk to you too."

I hear her let out a sigh as I open the door to my truck.

"I'm sorry. That probably sounded bitchy."

"Not very. Just a little. I'm sure I can find ways for you to make it up to me."

Usually my playful banter makes her laugh, but this time, nothing.

Oh shit. Did I do something wrong? If I did, I'd like to know what. I've barely talked to her since the draft started. We've exchanged a few texts, but that was it. We were both going to be so busy we decided to not spend the night with each other so we didn't have to coordinate our schedules.

"Is everything okay?" I ask.

"Yeah," she says, sounding defeated. "The website crashed at the paper. I had two stories I had saved in the system that are now gone. The one time I don't back them up to my computer, this happens."

"I'm sorry," I say, backing my truck out of the Fury's parking lot. "What can I do?"

"Nothing, unfortunately." I hear her fingers typing away between her words. "It also means I probably won't make it over tonight. I have at least another hour of work left, and I'm too exhausted to even think about going anywhere after that."

I check the time on my dashboard. It's just past seven o'clock.

"When was the last time you ate?" I ask her, developing a plan as I drive away.

"What time is it?"

"Seven."

"I had a bagel sometime before noon."

Well, that's unacceptable. So is the thought of not seeing Sadie tonight.

"All right, here's the plan. Text me your building code. I'll be over in an hour."

"Hunter, someone might—"

"No. Don't finish that sentence. Just do what you're told. Keep writing and I'm going to make everything better."

I don't know how, but I know she's smiling now. "You're a bossy boyfriend."

"I am. And I don't like it when my girlfriend is grumpy. Get your work done. I'll see you soon."

"GET IN HERE, YOU BEAUTIFUL MAN."

Now that's the greeting I was looking for when I called earlier. I lean down to kiss her, but I'm not fast enough. She has already stolen the pizza box from my hands, leaving me standing alone with my lips puckered at her doorway.

"It's good to see you too."

She puts the pizza box down and quickly makes her way back toward me, jumping into my arms. My hands immediately cup her ass as I hold her close as we kiss each other like we haven't seen each other in years, rather than just a few days.

God, I've missed her.

I know we haven't been dating long, but I'm already used to her sleeping next to me. The last three nights just felt... off. I reached over the first night to bring her back into my arms and she wasn't there. My bed felt empty.

It wasn't just the lack of sex or sleeping arrangements. I missed talking to her. I missed the way she does a little dance each morning when she's brushing her teeth. I miss how she always tucks her head into my shoulder when we get into bed, but always rolls away after five minutes to get into her sleep position.

Fuck... I've got it bad.

"That's much better," I say, giving her one more kiss as she slides down my body.

"I'm sorry. I'm moody when I'm hangry."

"Noted," I say, closing the door behind me. "Did you get all your work done?"

She grabs plates out of the cupboard as I join her in the kitchen, my arms instinctively going around her waist. "I just hit send on my last one. Thank you for coming over here. I know my apartment isn't the best... but—"

I lean down and place a kiss on her cheek. "It's fine. I know your apartment is close to your work and someone could see me, but it's Sunday night. I doubt anyone saw me come in. Plus, I have been curious about where you live."

"It's not much," she says, wiggling out of my hold to grab us each a beer before escorting me to her living room. "It's small, but it's just me. And I'm barely here. Doesn't make sense to spend money on a big place for it to go to waste."

She's not wrong, though I won't say that out loud. Her space is small. I'm fairly certain her entire apartment is the first floor of my condo. But it's not the size of the space that has me curious. It's the fact that I'm the one who just moved to Nashville, but she's the one who looks like she just moved in.

There are barely any photos. A few on her refrigerator. One on her TV stand. The furniture is nice, but sparse. There are no decorations or anything that gives her apartment life.

Hell, even I have accent pillows. I mean, my sister, Whitley, made me get them, but still.

"Go ahead. Ask it," she says as we take a seat on her couch.

"What?"

Was I that transparent?

"I can see the wheels in your brain turning. If I had to guess, you're probably saying to yourself, 'Damn. She was checking to see if I had a bed frame and she doesn't even have coasters.'"

Well, shit. I guess I am.

"This has nothing to do with the bed frame," I say, kicking off my shoes. "You just didn't strike me as a girl who would have a barely decorated apartment. I'm not judging. It just surprised me."

She takes a bite of her pizza before answering. "I have my reasons."

"I'd love to hear them."

I realize now how much about Sadie I still don't know. I know what side of the bed she likes to sleep on. I know her Chinese food order. I know the spot to kiss when I want to make her squirm. It's things like this, though, me here tonight, in her space, going behind the curtain, that is still foreign territory to me.

"If you didn't know by now, I'm a bit of a workaholic," she begins.

"Yes, I do," I say, taking a second to brush my fingers down the line of her face. "It's a very attractive quality."

She laughs. "Well, you are the first guy to ever think that. It's why I don't date. I tried a few times, but none of them could handle my irregular hours, or the fact that I'm always on call, so none of them proceeded to the level of 'want to come over.' As for friends, I have a few, other reporters, but none of them ever come over here. I'll go to their houses or we'll meet for dinner or drinks. It's just me and my job. And this apartment works for that. I have my desk. And a spot at my kitchen counter. That's all I need. The other stuff isn't necessary."

She tries to say that last part with bravado, but I'm not buying it. I doubt she talks about this often, or to anyone, and I love the fact that she trusts me with this part of her. I could break the silence, but I'm not going to. Instead, I tuck a loose strand of hair behind her ear, hoping that my touch eases her nerves.

"I guess I just never felt the need to decorate for just myself," she continues, her voice now a bit more somber. "When it's just me and my laptop, what's the point? Until tonight, it's not like I had anyone to impress."

I hear the sadness in her voice, and then it hits me. Did she say what I just think she did? "Are you telling me that I'm the first person to be in your apartment?"

She nods and a bitter laugh comes out. "Pathetic, right? I've lived in Nashville for five years and you are my first house guest. Only tonight did it even hit me that maybe I should have a plant, or coasters, or... I don't know, a basic Live, Laugh, Love sign or something."

The way she says those words breaks my heart a little. This girl is so strong on the outside. She'll go toe to toe with doubters and Internet trolls all day. She'll work her ass off to prove her worth to everyone she can. She has given so much of herself to be the best reporter she can be, that she doesn't know who she is when she's *not* doing that. I know a few decorations isn't a big deal on a grand scale, but it's just one of I'm sure a dozen ways she's put herself on the back burner in the name of her career.

Well, that ends tonight, if I have my way.

"Come here," I say, putting down my plate so I can bring her in my arms. She immediately melts against my chest. "You know you aren't pathetic, right? I could come up with a hundred words to describe you, and that one wouldn't even cross my mind."

She shrugs. "I'm twenty-seven years old and I don't have coasters. Are you sure this is what you want out of a girlfriend?"

I lift her chin so she's looking at me. I know she's trying to use humor to deflect, but I'm not having that. "I couldn't give two shits about your coasters. In fact, until tonight, I've never had so many conversations about coasters. I just want you to be happy. If you want plants and decorations, then tomorrow we go shopping. If you want to keep your place like this, then that is your right. But don't think you have to do this to impress me. You impress me every day."

She gives me a small smile. "Well, that's good. I'd hate for this to end because I've never been to HomeGoods."

I laugh and kiss her forehead. "I do have one important question, though."

"What's that?"

"How is your bedroom decorated?"

She smiles and slowly stands up while taking my hand. "Let me show you."

21

———

SADIE

IT WAS the hair tuck behind the ear.

That's what did me in. That's what made all my rational decision making go away. That's the only reason I can come up with that I spilled all of that emotional baggage onto Hunter's lap. I can't believe I told him all that. I've never admitted my loneliness to anyone. That in the process of advancing my career, I put myself second in every facet of my life.

Then, he brought me onto his lap. At that moment, I knew he was the one I was supposed to admit that to. That he was supposed to be the first person ever to be in my apartment. That he was supposed to be the first person to see my bedroom.

That he is supposed to be the first person to have me in my bed.

I lead Hunter out of my living room and take the ten steps required to get to my bedroom. By step nine, Hunter's mouth is already on the back of my neck, gently kissing the exposed skin as his arms wrap around my waist.

"You could have at least waited until I stopped walking," I say, though I'm not really mad about the journey his lips are taking.

He doesn't say anything, instead mumbling something that I think sounded like "didn't want to."

I don't stop him. His mouth feels too good on me. His hands are now working their way up my front until they reach my breasts. He takes one in each hand, kneading them as he continues to spread kisses around my neck and shoulders.

"God, I've missed you," I say breathlessly. And I have. Who knew you could get so used to someone in such a short amount of time? Not seeing him these past few days has been torture. But our days were insanely long. It was the responsible decision to make.

Now I'm ready to make up for lost time.

"Well, then, we should reacquaint ourselves," he says as he slowly walks me the rest of the way into my room.

He lets go just long enough for me to turn around, and before I know it, he has me lying on my bed.

My room is dark, save for the light coming in through the hallway. It's just enough so I can see him. The square line of his jaw. The fire in his blue eyes. The smile that promises dirty and amazing things are about to happen.

Hunter slowly begins taking off his shirt, his broad chest now on display for me. His body is built like he still plays football. His pecs and abs make it clear he never misses a workout. His arms are perfectly defined, and all I want to do is grab on to his biceps as he enters me. He unzips his pants, his hard cock straining against his boxer briefs.

"See something you like?" he says, moving next to me on the bed. "Or has it been so long that you forgot how hard you make me?"

I want to say something sexy. I want to speak dirty, dirty things to this man because he brings out a sexual side of me I didn't know I had. But I don't say anything. I raise to my knees and take off my shirt, thankful I didn't wear the plain white cotton bra today.

"Fuck, Sadie," Hunter says, moving his hand down to his cock.

His words spur me on. I sit back and begin taking down my leggings. I don't know if I'm giving Hunter the show he gave me, but considering somehow his briefs are off and he is full-on stroking himself while he watches me, I think I'm doing a fine job.

Next comes my black lace panties, and finally, the matching bra. I'm back kneeling on the bed, naked and on display for Hunter.

"I need you." Those are the only words he says as he falls into bed with me. I don't know how he does it, but in one motion, I'm underneath him and his mouth is on me in a million places. His kisses are wet and hungry, and my body has never felt more alive.

He settles in on one of my breasts, sucking it so hard I'm sure it will leave a bruise, but I don't care. It's only fitting that he leaves a mark on me. He left a mark on me the first day we met.

He switches sides, but now his hand has made its way to my center. He pushes in one finger, and while it feels amazing, it's not enough. I need him. All of him.

"Hunter… more," I say as my hips rotate against his hand, my orgasm is building, begging to be released.

He doesn't make me wait. He rolls away for the three seconds it takes to grab a condom and is back kneeling on my bed before I blink. My legs are on both sides of him, my center wet and open for whatever he wants to give me. Our eyes stay locked as he covers himself, and holy hell, this is the hottest moment of my life.

"Do you know what it does to me knowing that I'm the first one to have you in this bed?" Hunter asks with an intensity in his voice I didn't know he had.

"You're the only one."

"Say it again."

"You're the only one."

My breathy words are barely out of my mouth before Hunter is entering me, his chest falling onto mine as he pushes in and out of me. Our lips find each other, and for I don't know how long, all we are is a mixture of thrusts, kisses, and touches. We're so close in this moment; I don't know where I end and he begins.

His mouth is back on my neck, leaving sloppy kisses as he moves in and out of me. I wrap my legs around his ass, and the slight change of position is exactly what I need.

"Yes, Hunter. Right there. More."

My words spur him on. Before I know it, he has one of my legs on his shoulder and… oh fuck me, does that feel good.

"I'm… I'm not going to last."

I don't mean my words to come out as a challenge, but that's how he takes it as he buries himself deeper. In one thrust, I come undone, my body quaking from my head to my toes.

"Sadie! Fuck!"

Hunter follows right behind me. He drops my leg as he spills himself into the condom. Before I know it, he's collapsing on top of me.

I don't know how long we lie there. I don't care either. I love the feeling of his weight on top of me. I don't feel smothered or confined. I feel treasured and safe.

And there's another word I could add to what I'm feeling that I'm not ready to admit yet.

22

———————

HUNTER

"I CAN'T BELIEVE you didn't buy the decorative bowl," I say, dropping the shopping bags on the floor of her apartment.

She shoots daggers at me as she puts down her bags and keys. Because yes, to make it in one trip from her car, we both had to have our arms full of the newly purchased home décor and kitchen gadgets. "One, never say the words 'decorative bowl' again. It just sounds weird. Two, I'm not rolling in the cash like some of us who signed a huge contract because they are some big shot coordinator. And three, I *refuse* to pay twenty-five dollars for a bowl to sit on my counter."

"But it would go so well next to your new Instant Pot," I say, trying to lighten the mood with a bit of teasing. "Or, you could have put it next to your new wine rack. For the wine you don't drink."

A new set of eye daggers hit me. "I'm trying to become an adult. Which, by the way, this is *all* your fault. I was perfectly fine being a barely functioning adult until you strutted in here with your perfectly decorated condo and matching dishes and snarky comments."

I want to laugh at her rant, but I know that will just earn me another death glare. Instead, I walk over to her in her kitchen and wrap her in my arms. I lean down for a kiss, which she resists at first.

But not for long. Within seconds, her head is against my chest and we are standing in her kitchen, surrounded by bags from Target.

"You know I don't care about this stuff," I say softly, hoping to put her at ease. "You also know that I had nothing to do with decorating my condo. That was all my mother and sister."

She looks up and gives me a pouty look. I kiss that away immediately.

Today's shopping trip was brought on by what was meant to be a harmless joke. A little playful banter, if you will.

Since the draft is over and I only have limited meetings, we've been able to spend most nights together. Last night, we were at my condo, laying on the couch watching television, when she shivered. So, I did what any good boyfriend would do. I reached behind me and grabbed a blanket that I have laying on the top of my couch and covered her up.

I should have stopped there. She was happy and snuggling into me. Her ass was doing that wiggle against my dick that makes me hard every time.

Then, I had to open up my mouth. This is where I know I made the mistake.

"What do you do when you're on your couch at your apartment and you get cold?"

She turns her head to look up at me, like she didn't understand the question. "I get up and get a blanket."

I wrinkle my nose at her response. "That seems like so much work. If you had a blanket that you used for decoration and warmth, you wouldn't need to get up. It would be right there. But we know that you don't have that because you are anti-decorations."

She withheld sex last night. And dragged me to Target today, where she bought every item in the home goods section. The Target an hour outside of Nashville to give us a better chance of not being recognized.

I understand all of her decisions.

We bought blankets. And an area rug. And curtains. And decorative pillows.

And yes, we bought coasters.

She didn't stop there. At one point I think she became a woman possessed. I believe I heard the words, "if I'm going to be a fucking adult, I'm going to do it right." Next thing I know, we were in the kitchen department buying things that she can learn to cook with.

Every day being with Sadie I learn something new. Today's lesson: when she does something, she doesn't half-ass it.

Not one bit.

"I know you were teasing about the blanket. And the bowl," she says, her fingers now playing with the hair on the back of my neck. "But you were right. I've avoided all of that stuff for too long. I don't want to be embarrassed or self-conscious when you come over. Heck, maybe I'll even invite my family over. Now I won't have to worry about Bethany wanting to decorate my apartment in glitter."

I kiss her on the nose. "We should probably start putting this stuff away."

She leans up and gives me one more peck on the cheek. "Sounds good. You can start by hanging the curtain rods for me, and I'll start organizing the kitchen."

The next half hour is so... domestic. Easy. I don't have much experience with adult relationships... the last time I had a serious girlfriend was in college, but I'd have to guess that spending a Saturday shopping for household items and hanging curtain rods is about as domestic as you can get.

This is how it's been for Sadie and me. Well, not the shopping. But the easiness of everything. We spend nearly every night together. We both know once the season starts in July, our time together will be minimal, at best. So, we are taking every moment we can to be together over the next few months.

"Do you want to stay here for dinner tonight?" she asks from the kitchen. "Since your car isn't here and no one saw you come in, it's safe to stay here tonight."

At that moment, my phone rings with a FaceTime request. I tell her that's fine, and I put down the curtain to pick up my phone and answer it, not bothering to see who it is.

That's the second bad decision I've made in the last twenty-four hours.

"Hunter Michael. Now, son, I know you are busy coaching and getting those boys into shape and I am so proud of you but how dare you not call me all week! I am your mother for goodness' sake!"

"Hey, Mom!" I say nervously and a little louder than my normal tone. I take a second to look across the apartment to Sadie, whose face has gone a very bright shade of white.

Shit. I shouldn't have answered, even though I would have had to hear about it from her later. It would have been one thing if it was a phone call, but my mom helped me move into my Nashville condo. Just one look at the exposed brick in Sadie's apartment, and she'll know I'm not at home.

Fuck, fuck, fuck.

"How are you?" I say quickly, trying to find a non-discreet angle, if that's possible.

"I'm fine. Your sister is trying to send me to an early grave, but that's nothing new." Just when I think I'm in the clear, she starts looking around, tilting her head and the phone screen like she'll be able to see more if she moves a little more to the right.

"Where are you, Hunter? That doesn't look like your house."

"I'm at Davis's place," I say, again a bit too loudly. "He needed some help moving furniture."

I take that second to look up at Sadie. I wish I hadn't. All I see is the sadness on her face before she walks into her bedroom, shutting the door behind her.

Fuck. I hate being the one who put that look on her face. I hate that I can't tell my mom about us. Don't get me wrong, I could. She'd be ecstatic. She'd probably start planning our wedding.

But if I tell my mom, then Dad finds out. And like everything else in my life, I know he'd have an opinion. I'm sure he will have plenty to say when he finds out I'm dating the reporter who told him he was basically too old to run my offense.

Yeah, that would go over swimmingly.

So, I lie to my mom. She talks for a few minutes, and I answer when appropriate. She tells me that she and Dad have secured season tickets for the Fury's home games next year, and that she wants to make a visit before the season starts.

Finally, we say our goodbyes, and before I've even hung up, I'm making my way to Sadie's bedroom. What I see when I open the door breaks my damn heart.

She's sitting in the middle of her bed, holding a pillow against her chest. She's looking away from the door toward her window, but I don't think she's looking at anything. As I sit next to her, that's when I see a tear falling down her face.

"Sadie." My voice is hoarse as I bring her into my arms. "I'm so fucking sorry."

"It's okay." Her voice sounds anything but okay. "I understand. Not like I've told my family yet. But I haven't had to lie to them, either."

For the next few minutes, I just hold her. She has let go of the pillow and she has wrapped her arms around mine as we slowly rock back and forth.

"I hate lying to her," I say. And it's the truth.

"I know. And I get why you have to. It just..." her voice trails off for a second. When I hear her swallow, I then realize it is because she's holding back tears. "It just sucks, Hunter."

Silence falls back on us again. This isn't the first time we've been in this situation. But it is the first time we've actually talked about it.

A few weeks ago, there was a black-tie dinner for advertisers and season ticket holders. I had to go and schmooze. She was there covering the event. I was there in a custom-made suit, and she was standing off to the side in her everyday clothes. I tried to be very specific with who I talked to that night, but out of nowhere, the team owner came up to me, making sure to introduce me to his daughter. His daughter who is twenty-five and was just offered a modeling contract. I had to play nice and talk to her. The whole time I could feel Sadie's eyes on me.

By the time I ended the conversation, the reporters were gone. I tried texting her, but she wouldn't respond. The second I could leave, I hurried back to my condo. Luckily, she still came over. When I found her in my bed she was asleep. Though I'm pretty sure she had been crying. I didn't want to wake her up, so I just laid next to her and brought her into my arms.

The next morning we pretended like nothing happened.

"You know I wish I could tell everyone about you," I say, squeezing her a little tighter into me.

"I know. When we decided to do this, six months didn't feel like that long. It's barely been two, and I feel like it's never going to end."

Damn. When she says it like that, it does make it seem more daunting.

The two months we have spent together have been amazing. But we've been secluded. We have been so worried about being noticed, that every date night is spent at my house. Besides Memphis, we've never been on an actual date.

That ends now.

"Can you do me a favor?"

She looks back over her shoulder at me. "What's that?"

"Can you put on a sexy dress and be ready at seven?"

Her eyebrow lifts up, which I can't blame her for. "And why is that?"

I lean down and give her a quick kiss before I get off her bed. "Because I'm taking my girlfriend on a date."

23

SADIE

I HAVE NEVER BEEN MORE focused on anything in my entire life.

"Baby, you look so sexy in that skirt. I wish I could just take you home and bend you over my bed. You know I love taking you from behind."

Unsweet tea.

Ear wax.

The smell of a locker room after a game.

I ignore Hunter's words. I know he's just trying to get in my head. He thinks if he keeps talking about sexy things that he will distract me from my target.

Not a chance in hell, McAvoy.

I take three steps and slowly bring the ball back behind me, and after another two I heave it forward, saying a silent prayer as my bowling ball rolls down the alley.

I swear I watch it play out in slow motion. I also hear Hunter behind me trying to will the ball into the gutter with just the sound of his voice.

After what feels like hours, my ball finally connects with the pins, knocking all ten down one by glorious one.

Strike.

Game.

Set.

Match.

"Woohoo!" I can't help but let out a little cry of celebration as I do a little shimmy back to where Hunter is sitting.

"You cheated," he says, looking up at the scoreboard to make sure that the computer did the math right. "There's no way in hell you beat me."

I take a seat across his lap, wrapping my arms around his neck. "Is someone a sore loser? Or does someone not like getting beat by his *girlfriend?*"

The look he gives me is priceless, and I can't help but let out a loud laugh. It's a mix of mock anger, real confusion, and a little bit of hurt pride. Poor baby.

"What are you laughing at?" His pouty question makes me laugh even harder.

"You. Your face." I can barely get the words out. This man really is pouting because he lost to me. "I need a picture. I need to document this moment."

I slide off of Hunter's lap to retrieve my phone from my purse. That's right. I left my phone in my purse. I wasn't letting any distractions get in the way of our first official date as a couple.

This is uncharted territory for me. I put my work aside to enjoy life.

Life with my boyfriend.

When Hunter suggested date night, I knew he was trying to make me feel better. I hated the way I reacted when his mom called, but I couldn't help it. Another example of my emotions being too big for me to handle when it comes to Hunter.

The second that he showed up at my door, dressed in dark jeans and a fitted polo, I forgot about the events that led up to this moment. My boyfriend was picking me up for a date. And I was not about to let anything ruin it.

Not only was it our first date, but it was the most cliché first date ever. Dinner and bowling. Honestly, though? It was perfect. He found a restaurant just outside of the Nashville city limits, hoping that it would give us a little more anonymity, before a night of bowling.

It is casual. And fun. And everything I needed.

"I still can't believe you didn't tell me you were a junior bowling champion," Hunter grumbles as I make my way back to his lap, cell phone in hand. "That would have been good information to know."

"You didn't ask," I say, bringing up the camera and setting the timer. "Now smile and say, 'My girlfriend just kicked my ass!'"

He does no such thing. His lips attack my neck, making me shriek. My body is thrashing on his lap as I try to break away, which just makes his hold on me that much stronger. The bowling alley only has about ten people in it right now, so I'm sure we are causing quite the scene. I'm not even paying attention to the camera when I hear it go off.

"Hunter," I say, trying to catch my breath. "Hunter, stop!"

He puts one more sloppy kiss on my cheek before I bring my phone up to look at the picture. It wasn't the one I was going for.

It's better.

I'm laughing. And smiling. And enjoying this impromptu moment with the man I adore.

As for Hunter? The camera caught the one moment his lips weren't buried in my neck. It caught the moment when he's looking at me with… is that love? If it is, until now I wasn't sure what it looked like. But for some reason, that's the only word that comes to mind. I don't know if I'm right, but if he looked at me like that every day for the rest of our lives, I wouldn't be mad.

All in all, this is the perfect picture.

One I can't help but make the new background of my phone. Why not? I'm not going to be around any of the other reporters for a few more months. I spend most of my free time with Hunter these days. Why can't I?

So, I do. It's scary how sometimes the smallest things can be the most freeing.

"Do you want one more game for redemption? Or have you had enough ass kicking for the night?"

He goes in for one more neck kiss before moving me off his lap to take off his rental shoes. "My ego has had enough. Plus, I've been watching you bowl all night in a dress. There's only so much a man can take, woman. I've had enough torture."

"Hey, that last part is your fault," I say, sitting back down to take off the hideous bowling lane shoes as Hunter returns our balls to the racks. "I was just following your directions."

"Yes you did," Hunter says, holding his arm out for me so I'm able to slip right into his embrace. We walk side by side to the counter to return our shoes when he leans down and whispers in my ear, "I wonder if you'll follow directions tonight when I tell you to come for me."

I don't even have a second to be turned on by his words, because before I know it, he's pinching my side and tickling my waist. The action makes me laugh obnoxiously loud, which then Hunter takes advantage of. He brings me into his side a little tighter before placing a kiss on my hair.

With all of this flirting and dirty talk, I need this man to get me home. Immediately.

"Oh my God! You're Hunter McAvoy! Babe! Look! He's a Fury coach!"

Hunter and I freeze when we hear the words. I'm not shocked that he was noticed, considering who he is, it makes sense. All I can do is hope the man doesn't recognize me. I know the chances are slim, but they are still there. My picture is in the newspaper and online so I'm not anonymous.

"Hey, man. How are you tonight?" Hunter asks in a polite tone as we place our shoes up on the counter.

"I'm great. Just great," the man is bouncing on his toes like he's meeting Santa on Christmas Eve. "I'm a big fan. Also, a 'Bama fan. Roll Tide."

Hunter smiles his fake-polite smile. It's the one the media gets most of the time. It's like the fake smile you give a relative on Christmas Day when they get you a shitty present. "Roll Tide. Have a good night."

"Wait! Can I have your autograph?"

Hunter looks down at me, and I give him a small nod that it's okay. It's not like there are a slew of people here. It's a guy who hasn't looked at me once because he is all but drooling over Hunter. And by the looks of it, an annoyed wife or girlfriend who can't believe her man is fan-boying over a football coach like he's in a boy band.

"Sure. No problem." Hunter asks the bowling alley worker for a pen and paper and begins signing the small piece of paper.

"Sorry about that," the girlfriend/wife says to me. "As soon as he saw you two, he was freaking out so much I told him just to suck it up and say hello. I'm sorry if we're ruining your night."

I shake my head. "It's no problem. We were on our way out. The alley is yours."

"He is a big fan of yours too."

My eyes go wide at her words. "Excuse me?"

She leans a little closer, her words a little lower. "I know you're Sadie Benson. I've read your stuff for years. So does my jackass of a husband. But he's too starstruck to realize right now who you are. Please, don't take offense."

I'm speechless. Completely and utterly speechless.

"I'm… it's… we're…"

"It's none of my business," she says, now averting her eyes as to not draw attention to us. "All I see here are two adults spending a fun night together at a bowling alley. Who am I to judge anything about that?"

I feel the wetness pooling in my eyes, which is ridiculous. "Thank you. I appreciate that."

She gives me a nod and a smile. "No worries. Now get your man out of here before mine tries to kidnap him."

I turn back to Hunter, who is handing his autograph to the fan. "Here you go. Have a good night."

"Thanks, man! You, too!"

We hurry to Hunter's truck, not saying a word until we're back on the road.

"That was close," Hunter says, giving my hand a squeeze as we make our way back to his condo.

It was close. Too close.

That woman didn't care. Unfortunately, though, she is one of the rare people who won't.

"So, I guess that was our first and last public date within an hour of the Nashville city limits," I say. We got lucky this time. I doubt we'll get lucky again.

Hunter brings my hand to his mouth, and I know it's to soothe my anxiety. "I'm sorry, Sadie."

"It's not your fault. We knew this could happen."

He lets out a defeated sigh. "I wish we could go somewhere where no one would recognize us."

"And where in the continental United States can Hunter McAvoy go without being recognized?"

"I doubt people would know me out West. They hate the SEC. And they don't like to acknowledge any pro teams on the wrong side of the Rockies."

I laugh, but then get an idea.

Can I?

Is it too soon?

What if he says no?

What if he says yes?

"What's going on in that brain of yours?"

I have no idea how he knows my wheels are turning as he has both eyes on the road.

"Just an idea. But it's stupid."

This gets his attention. "No idea you could have is stupid. Lay it on me."

I take a big breath for courage. Because I can't believe I'm about to ask this.

"Next month I had a vacation scheduled in San Francisco. What if... would you like to... I was thinking maybe..."

In a case of perfect timing, we come up to a red light, which allows

Hunter to turn to me. And when he does, I'm greeted with the best and brightest of all of the Hunter McAvoy smiles.

"Are you asking me to go on vacation with you?"

"That depends."

"On what?"

"If you're saying yes."

This earns me a laugh. "Oh, Sadie. Don't you know?"

I quirk an eyebrow at him. "Know what?"

He leans down and gives me a quick kiss before the light turns green. "You could ask me to go to the moon with you and I'd do it. I'm crazy about you. Let's go to San Francisco."

24

———

SADIE

"TOOTHBRUSH?"

I laugh because my father is nothing but predictable. That is always his first reminder. "Got it."

"Tennis shoes because you'll be walking a lot?"

"Packed before anything else."

"Did you remember to get your sunglasses out of your car?"

That reminder comes from Helen. They love doing these reminders on speakerphone. "I put them in my purse last night."

"How about your laptop charger?"

"I'm not taking it, so I don't need the charger."

My admission stuns Dad and Helen silent. It was the same reaction John had when I told him. I've never gone on a vacation, or any trip, without my laptop. I've always been scared that something would happen, and I'd need to jump online to write a story.

Not this trip. This trip I'm determined to enjoy the moments, enjoy the scenery, and enjoy time with Hunter.

That means breaking news can wait.

I never thought I'd say those words out loud.

"I… I don't know what to say." Dad finally finds his words after at least a minute of silence. "What made you decide that? I mean, I'm happy. Don't get me wrong. I've always said you work too much. It's just... I never thought I'd see the day."

Me neither, Dad. Me neither.

I look down at my open suitcase and notice the clothes that are not generally packed for one of my trips. Dad would never think to ask if I have packed these things.

New bikini? *Check.*

New lingerie? *Check.*

New dress that I've been promised by Bethany will make Hunter's eyes pop out of his head? *Check.*

Ted, because I had a very dirty fantasy about using that with Hunter? *Double check.*

These are definitely *not* my normal vacation items. And ones that he *definitely* does not need to know about. I wouldn't have told him about those items regardless of whether he knew about me and Hunter or not.

Which he doesn't.

Because I've been too scared to tell him. I know I said I didn't want to lie to him, but the thought of telling him has been worse, so I haven't said anything. The only person who knows is Bethany.

"Well, I for one am glad that you are leaving work behind," Helen says, breaking the silence. "Though, I still hate the thought of you going around that big city all alone."

"I'll be fine," I say, trying to figure out a way to turn this conversation. I wish I could tell them I won't be alone. That for the first time in my life, I'm looking forward to a vacation. That I'm thrilled that I'm leaving my laptop behind because I'm going on a vacation with my boyfriend who I am head over heels for.

But I can't. Not yet. Maybe when I get back from San Francisco. And even then, it's not a conversation you have over the phone. If I'm telling Dad and Helen that I'm not only seeing someone, but it's Hunter, that needs to be an in-person conversation.

Preferably with beer.

I'm barely listening to the list that my dad and Helen are saying when I hear the door to my apartment open and shut. I take a quick glance at my watch and realize that Hunter is a half-hour early to pick me up.

He pops his head inside my bedroom door, and I hold a finger up. The last thing I need him to do is announce his presence as I'm on the phone with my dad.

I thought that was the universal signal for "give me a minute." Apparently, Hunter either doesn't know that or doesn't care, because before I know it, he's inside my bedroom with his arms wrapped around my stomach, placing quiet kisses on the back of my neck.

Fuck, that feels good.

"Sadie! Are you listening to me? You know I'm not helping you pack for my own benefit!"

My dad's words break me from the spell that Hunter was trying to put me under. "Sorry. I was distracted. I was… zipping my suitcase."

"Zipping your suitcase distracts you?"

I reluctantly nudge Hunter away from my body so I can actually zip my suitcase and not make me out to be a bigger liar to my father than I already am.

"I had other things on my mind. Sorry. But thanks for helping me pack as always. But it's time for me to go."

"No, it's not," Helen says. "Your plane doesn't leave for another three hours and your alarm didn't go off. I would know the sound of that blasted thing anywhere."

"I…" Shit. I have no idea what to say. I'm breaking under the pressure. I can still feel Hunter behind me and all I can think about is if we have time for a quickie before we leave for the airport.

"Sadie? Is everything okay?"

"I have to go to the bathroom!" I say a little too loudly. "You know. Hate to do that in the airport. Better to do it now."

If there is any way to kill a mood, it's talking about bathroom usage. Because as soon as the words leave my mouth, I feel Hunter step away from me. When I turn to look at him, all I hear are gasps of air as Hunter is trying not to break into a fit of laughter. His face is beet red, and he looks like he's about to explode.

I don't care. It's his fault that he's early and got me all hot and bothered.

"That's smart. Have a safe trip, slugger," Dad says. "Bring us back something fun."

"You know I will. Love you both."

I have barely hung up the phone when Hunter's laugh erupts from his body.

"This is not funny," I say, tossing a pillow at him that he successfully dodges.

"Oh, but it was. You should have seen your face."

I lean over to zip my carry-on while Hunter continues to laugh at what he must think is the world's funniest joke. "This is all your fault. If you weren't early, then I wouldn't have had to lie."

Still laughing, he sits down on my bed next to my suitcase. "If I wasn't early, then I wouldn't have time to do this."

He brings me in for a kiss, and before I know it, I'm straddling his lap and my arms are looped around his neck.

I figured after three months I'd be tired of kissing Hunter whenever I can. That couldn't be further from the truth. Each time we kiss, it's a new experience. I fall for him a little bit more every time our lips touch.

And each time we kiss, I fall closer and closer to that L-word that I never thought I'd say.

He breaks the kiss first, but not before giving me a small peck on the corner of my lips. "See now why I came over early? We have a long flight, and I'm not going to get to do that for hours."

I check my watch. We still have three hours before our flight takes off. And it only takes twenty minutes to get to the airport.

"Do we have time for anything else?" I ask, my hips rotating on his lap for emphasis.

His eyes go a shade darker at my question. "It's like you can read my mind."

25
____

HUNTER

Sadie doesn't even laugh at my horrible Sean Connery impression as she collapses onto the bed. "How long are you going to be saying that?"

I plop down next to her, completely spent from our day touring the famous prison. "At least for the rest of the trip. And probably every time I look at the pictures from today."

I take out my phone and flip through the pictures. We've been the definition of tourists this week. We've been to the Golden Gate Bridge and Fisherman's Wharf. We rode the cable cars and walked through the streets of San Francisco. Today we toured Alcatraz, and tomorrow we are on a mission to find the house from the opening of the television show *Full House*. She thinks she's "dragging" me to find it. Little does she know my childhood crush was D.J. Tanner.

Tonight I made reservations at a Michelin-star restaurant that I have been told will change my life and will make me never want to order a steak from another restaurant ever again.

We are living our best vacation life. And we've been able to do it without feeling guilty or having to hide.

"We're going to fall asleep if we keep lying here," I say drowsily.

"Is that a bad thing?" she says, snuggling next to me.

I kiss the top of her head because no, a nap does not sound bad. Except I am bound and determined to see her in the dress that she's been hiding from me all week.

"You take a nap. I'm jumping in the shower," I say, kissing her cheek before I get up. "Unless you want to join me?"

She shakes her head, further burrowing it into the bed. "Can't move. Too sleepy."

I laugh and make my way into the bathroom. I don't blame her. We are on day five of seven, and we've been running ourselves ragged, determined to do and see everything we wanted on this trip.

We've caught the attractions. We've eaten everything in sight. We've drunk to our heart's content. We've lounged at the pool. And each night, we end up back in this bed and make love until we pass out.

And yes, we make love. Calling it sex anymore feels wrong.

As I step into the hot shower, I let that thought pass over my mind. It does feel wrong to call it sex. It's so much more than that. Honestly, it was never just sex with us. From the first kiss, I knew it was something more with Sadie.

I didn't admit it to myself then, but I knew I was in denial. And as the days continue, I know I can't deny it for much longer.

I'm in love with this woman.

I'm not exactly sure when it happened, but somewhere along the way I fell in love with Sadie Benson.

I take that back. I know exactly the moment it happened. It happened on Beale Street.

This week getting to be together, not having to hide ourselves from the public, has been freeing. I didn't realize how much of a bubble we were staying in while living in Nashville until we got to experience complete freedom to be ourselves. To be a couple who is slowly falling in love with each other.

Well, I am. I hope she is as well.

I don't linger in the shower because I'm way too eager to climb back into bed and take a nap with Sadie before our reservations tonight. However, when I step out of the shower, I hear her talking to someone. She's obviously on the phone because I only hear one voice.

"It better be very important if you're calling me on a vacation that you said I wasn't allowed to work on."

Silence.

"Are you serious?"

Longer silence.

"And you couldn't wait to tell me this until I got back? You know I'm going to freak out until then."

Another round of silence.

"Thanks, John. I appreciate this. I'll call you when I'm back in town and we can talk more. Thanks. Bye."

I wait a second before stepping out of the bathroom. Immediately, I can tell Sadie is in her brain in some far-off place that's not our hotel room in San Francisco.

"Who was that?" I ask, sitting across from her on the bed.

"John. My boss. He… he had some news for me."

"Good news?" I ask, taking her hand in mine.

She nods. "A few months ago, he told me there was a possibility of a job opening at *US Daily.* But then it was just a rumor. Turns out that the job is real. And they want me to interview for it."

Shit. I'm not even in the media and I know that *US Daily* is a big deal. When I was at Alabama, they were the only ones to get access that no other media outlet got. They are the top dogs.

"Sadie. That's amazing."

"It would be," she says, a smile finally coming through. "I've always wanted to work for them. Your goal is to one day coach your own team? Mine is to work for *US Daily.*"

My heart is swelling with pride right now. I've witnessed firsthand how hard she works. She absolutely deserves this chance.

I can't help but think about what this means for us. She wouldn't be covering the Fury anymore, which would be a good thing. But if they make her a national writer, does she have to move? Is that better or worse for us? Am I selfish for thinking like that?

"You know you make fun of me for thinking out loud, but you do the same thing," she says, her smile teasing. "What's going on in that brain, McAvoy?"

I let out a small laugh. "One of these days I'm going to be able to hide an emotion from you."

She shakes her head. "Today isn't that day. Spill it."

"I'm just curious, what would happen if you got the job?"

"I can ask the same thing about you."

This takes me off guard. "What do you mean?"

She takes her free hand in mine. "Hunter, I'm not naïve enough to think that you will be coaching in Nashville forever. If things go well in a few years, teams will be calling you to be a head coach. Maybe that's in Nashville? Maybe it isn't. I knew that when we started this. And as for me? I'm not sure where they will want me. A few of the national writers live wherever they'd like. A few they have asked to move to certain parts of the country to make travel easier. I won't know anything until I talk to them. And even if they like me, I'd probably not get it. I feel like I'm one major breaking news story away from them seriously considering me. And stories like that don't come around every day."

I let her words sink in. She's right. Here I am freaking out about her job when I'm the one who could be moving sooner rather than later. Just because I'm a coordinator now doesn't mean I'm setting down permanent roots. If a team calls me next year offering me a head coaching job, especially if and when we make the playoffs, there's a very good chance I will take it.

And where would that leave me and Sadie? If she gets the *US Daily* job, feasibly, she could come with me. If she doesn't, well, then I guess we cross that bridge when we get there.

"You know we don't have to figure out everything right now."

Her words are soft and put me a little more at ease. "You're right. But we should celebrate."

This gets me a smile, followed quickly by a yawn. "Can we take a nap first? John woke me up and I'm not about to fall asleep face-first in my steak tonight."

I laugh as we move under the sheets, cuddling together for a mid-afternoon nap.

Well, she takes a nap. I can't help but think about all of the scenarios for the future.

And there isn't one I can think of that doesn't have Sadie by my side.

26

HUNTER

I NOW KNOW why Sadie was hiding this particular dress from me all week.

She knew that if I saw her in it, we wouldn't have left the hotel.

She knows me too well.

When she stepped into the sitting area of our suite, I just stared at her. She looked stunning. Her hair was down and styled with soft curls. Her makeup was bolder than I had ever seen it, making her hazel eyes even brighter. She's also wearing red lipstick, which is a first for her. As soon as I saw that, all I could think of was a ring of red around my cock later.

And that dress? I want to write a thank-you card to whoever designed it. Because they had to have done it with Sadie in mind.

The black fabric clings to every one of her curves. There isn't an ounce of cleavage showing, yet the dress is so tight that it's making my mouth water when I look at her full tits pressing against the fabric. And her ass? Kill me right fucking now.

I wanted to punch every man who tried to get a glimpse of her as we walked through the restaurant. I almost slapped our waiter who stared a bit too long when he was delivering our drinks. And now that our meals are done? All I want to do is get her back to our room and slowly peel that dress off of her.

"You're staring again," she says before taking a sip of her cocktail.

"I can't help it. You're a vision."

I know it probably sounded cheesy leaving my tongue, but I can't think of any other words.

"If I knew doing my hair and makeup would get this kind of reaction from you, I would have done it a lot sooner."

She sets her glass down and I take her hand from across the table. "You know that I couldn't give two shits whether you were wearing makeup or not, right? And hell, I can spot you easier when your hair is on the top of your head."

This makes her laugh a little, but the heaviness isn't gone yet. "I know you don't care. Which kind of shocked me at first. I figured you'd be one of those football guys who was used to having the hot girl on his arm with the perfect makeup and perfect outfit. It's kind of why I was surprised when you flirted with me that first day."

"So you noticed I was flirting." I move my eyebrows up and down to try to make her laugh. It works a little. "That first day I saw you, it was like a punch in the gut. I couldn't take my eyes off you. And I remember thinking to myself how gorgeous you were without a drop of makeup on. I remember wishing that I would get this job so I could move to Nashville and take you out to dinner. Little did I know that you would turn my world upside down that day."

Now that gets me a real smile. "You turned my world upside down, too, McAvoy."

Our waiter breaks the moment by coming back and giving me the check; I give him my credit card immediately. I need to get her back to the hotel. I need to worship her body. I need to show her she is the only woman I will ever want.

"What are you staring at?" she asks as we stand to leave the restaurant. "Do I have something on me?"

I grab her hand and pull her into me. I don't care if we have an audience. I need to kiss her.

And I do.

It's hard and fast and leaves her breathless.

"I'm staring at you. Only you. Now, let's go back to the room so I can remind you how much you drive me fucking crazy."

TELLING Sadie that she drives me crazy may not have been my best idea.

She has been taking my words quite literally from the moment we stepped out of the restaurant and into our Uber.

She sat flush against me in the back seat, her hand resting on my thigh. Her touch alone was enough to make me hard. Every time I squirmed a bit to adjust myself, for the sheer fact that my cock was beginning to feel uncomfortable, the vixen moved her hand up.

By the time we stepped onto the elevator, I was hard as stone for her. Unfortunately, we weren't the only ones in the car, so I couldn't kiss her the way I wanted to. Instead, she decided to take that opportunity to stand in front of me, slowly moving her ass back and forth over my dick.

She was teasing me in the best possible way.

Now it's payback.

"Bed. Now," I demand the second we walk into our hotel suite.

"I didn't know you could get so caveman," she says as she makes her way back to the bedroom. "I kind of like it."

"Oh, you do? Then you're going to love what I have in mind," I say, pulling her into my arms. I don't ask for permission. I don't go in slowly. I take her mouth, claiming it as mine. Because it is. I kiss her hard and rough, because if there is one thing she needs to know at the end of tonight, it's that no other woman brings this out in me.

Only Sadie.

We stumble to the bed, ungracefully falling onto the soft mattress. We're a mess of lips and limbs and it's perfect. Our hands are grabbing at clothes, doing our best to shed them as quickly as possible. I think I heard a tear. I don't know if it was her clothing or mine.

This is wild. Insane. Crazy.

It's fitting. We're crazy about each other. We're crazy for each other.

I release her lips only because I have more skin that I need to taste. I don't know what kind of perfume she wore tonight, but it's new and intoxicating, and I'm determined to lick it off of wherever I taste it.

"Mmm." Her moan only spurs me on, and I take one of her tits into my mouth, letting my other hand travel down to her center.

"Fuck, baby. You're fucking soaked."

"Only for you, Hunter. Only for you."

Damn right only for me.

My mouth switches to the other, and Sadie's hands are now in my hair, pulling me farther into her chest. Holy hell, this woman... she's just as unhinged right now as I am.

"Hunter... suitcase."

Did I hear her right?

"Whatever you need can wait."

I continue where I left off before she lifts me off of her. "In my suitcase is my vibrator. I thought we could..."

Holy. Fucking. Hell.

"Don't move an inch," I say, giving her nipple one last suck before I nearly sprint to her suitcase. First, she hid the dress from me all week. Now I find out she's had this gem stowed away?

This woman is going to be the death of me.

Vibrator in hand, I make my way back to the bed. I allow myself a moment to take her in. Her eyes are dark and full of heat. Her lipstick is smeared, and her hair is wild. I love seeing her like this. She's so deliberate in everything else she does. But with me? With me, she lets herself be free.

"See something you like?" She parts her legs for me as her hand travels down to her center.

"A few things."

I flip on her toy and I can feel it hum in my hand.

"Where do you want this?" I'm unable to hide the lust in my voice. This is turning me on so fucking much.

"On my pussy," she says.

She's already so turned on, the words barely come out of her mouth. I move to stand next to her and lower the toy to her center. I barely touch her, and her hips shoot off of the bed.

"Yes. Fuck, yes."

God, this is hot. Watching her come undone like this? I can't help but start stroking myself. I move the vibrator slowly over her folds, keeping a close eye on what movements make her moan more than others. But that's not enough for me. I let go of my cock and lean down, taking her tit into my mouth.

"Oh God, Hunter. I… I'm not going to be able to last."

As much as I love seeing her come unraveled like this, she's coming on my cock. There are no other alternatives tonight. I flip the vibrator off and toss it to the bed as I climb on top of her.

"Fuck. Condom." I forgot to grab it out of my pants. I start to roll off of her when she puts a hand on my arm, stopping me.

"I'm safe. And clean. I want to feel all of you, Hunter."

Fuccccck.

"Are you sure?" We've always used a condom. *I've* always used a condom.

"Yes, Hunter. Will you?"

The fact that she even has to ask me that is absurd. This woman could tell me to rob the hotel right now and I would.

I lean down and press another kiss to her lips. "I'll give you anything you want."

And with one thrust, I'm inside her. And holy fuck, I have never felt anything better in my entire life.

She's hot and wet and tight and fucking perfect.

My pace starts as slow and intentional. It's like my body knows I'll want to memorize every minute of this. Sadie and I have been together countless times, but this, this is different. This is… love.

I fucking love this woman.

"More, Hunter. I need you to move."

She doesn't have to ask me twice. I slowly begin to increase my speed, and Sadie meets me thrust for thrust. Our pace soon becomes frantic. Her arms are gripping my biceps like she needs an anchor to hold on to.

"Hunter, I'm close. Make me come, Hunter."

I'll never get tired of hearing those words.

I take her legs over my arms, tilting her hips up just enough to hit the spot I know she loves. The scream that comes out of her mouth is enough to send me over the edge, and all at once, I feel her contract around me as I let myself explode inside her.

I'm breathless as I fall on the bed next to her, doing my best to keep my weight off of her. But I crave her touch. I need to feel her body on me.

"That…" she says, her words barely able to come out of her mouth.

"Yeah," I say, kissing her neck as I slowly pull myself out of her. "That."

She pushes a piece of sweaty hair off of my forehead. "Is it always supposed to be like that?"

I take her hand, placing a kiss on her palm.

"No, gorgeous. That's just because it's us."

27

———

SADIE

"ARE you sure you're okay? We don't have to do this. You can drop me off then turn around and—"

Hunter turns down the volume of the radio and gives me a quick *you have got to be kidding me* look as we make our way through the suburbs of Nashville on our way to my dad's house.

I don't blame the look, though. I'd probably give it to me too. I've asked that question in some form no less than thirty times today.

"For the last time, because according to my GPS we are five minutes away, I'm excited to meet your dad. And Helen and Bethany. You know I *have* met parents before, right? I'm not a complete boyfriend virgin. Parents love me."

He's right. I'm being ridiculous. I know they will love him. I can't think of a better guy to bring home to meet my family than Hunter. And considering he's the first guy I've ever brought home, not counting random prom dates in high school, I have nothing to worry about.

At least, I hope.

I knew after we got back from San Francisco that I wanted to figure out how to tell them. I knew they'd be overjoyed about me dating someone. I just didn't know how they'd react to it being

Hunter. At least, my dad. Helen would probably be like Bethany and not understand the true significance of this. But my dad would.

And that's what I was most afraid of.

So, I weighed my options of how to tell them. At one point I considered just randomly showing up at the house with him and yelling, "Surprise!" and letting the cards fall where they may. I also considered the opposite, never telling them.

Both had solid points in the pro column.

Then, I got back from San Francisco. And little did I know that Helen would back me into a corner so much that I had no choice but to admit the secret.

"Why didn't you post any pictures?" Helen asks at the first Monday night dinner after my return. "I was looking on your Instagram every day hoping to see your trip, and I didn't see anything! After dinner you need to show me."

"Oh..." I don't know what to say. Shit. I didn't post anything because every picture was of me and Hunter together. "I just didn't want to publicize where I was. And I really didn't take that many."

She scrunches her nose at me, so I quickly look away. If I make eye contact with her, I might break. This doesn't stop her from wondering out loud.

"Well, that makes no sense. You posted pictures from Memphis. And last year when you went to Savannah. What was different this year? And if you didn't take pictures from the Golden Gate Bridge, I don't even know why you went."

"Mom, give her a break," Bethany chimes in while simultaneously reaching for the potatoes. "Maybe she wanted some privacy. Or maybe she met a guy and had a wild tryst and they never left the hotel room."

I shoot Bethany a look because she knows that Hunter was with me. Why is she stirring the pot? I thought she was on my side. The evil grin she's giving me right now means she knows EXACTLY what she is doing.

"I'd rather not hear about that if she did," Dad says, taking the potatoes from Bethany.

"Nonsense. We'd know if Sadie was seeing someone. Or if she met someone. She wouldn't hide that from us. Now would you, Sadie?"

That's when I make my mistake. I look up from methodically placing

*roast beef on my plate to two sets of eyes looking at me in curiosity. The other
set is all of a sudden very interested in her dinner.*

And then I break.

*"I've been secretly dating a coach of the Fury for three months and we
went on vacation together!"*

I crumbled at the guilt. I'd be a horrible CIA agent, handing over
all the nation's secrets with just a side eye and a few cupcake
questions.

So, I told them. Well, not everything. I told them that for the past
three months I had been seeing Hunter. I told them that I hadn't told
anyone due to the nature of our jobs, hoping that would smooth over
my secret keeping. Bethany pretended this was new information.
Helen was so excited she all but demanded I bring Hunter to the next
Monday dinner.

My dad didn't say anything. And he hasn't since I left their house
last week.

"Hey, you okay?" Hunter asks, and I realize then that I was so
zoned out that we are now in the driveway of my childhood home.

"Yeah," I say, giving my head a little shake. "I'm fine."

Hunter reaches for my hand and brings it to his lips. I don't know
why this relaxes me so much, but whenever he does it, an instant
sense of calm overtakes me.

He pins me with his stare. I feel like I'm about to get a pep talk like
he'd give one of his players.

"The hard part is over. They know about us. You played defense
and got me the ball. Now it's my job to make them fall in love with
me. I got this, gorgeous. Don't worry about anything."

Hunter gets out of the truck and I put my phone in my purse as I
wait for him to open the door for me. I've learned my lesson over the
past few months. I am not, under any circumstances, to open my own
door.

At first, I thought it was ridiculous. Now, I kind of love it.

Hunter takes my hand as I step down from his truck and doesn't
let go as we make our way up the driveway. Before we are even on the

front porch, the door opens, and standing there are Helen and my dad.

The smile on Helen's face is one I've never seen on her before. Not even on her and my dad's wedding day.

My dad, on the other hand? I wouldn't necessarily call his expression a smile. It's more like a grimace. It's stern. What I would expect him to give his class of English students if they all failed a test.

Hunter gives my hand one more squeeze before he drops it to put his hand on the small of my back, leading me up the few stairs to the door.

"Hi, Dad. Helen. This is Hunter."

"Mr. Benson. Mrs. Benson, it's a pleasure to meet you," Hunter says, extending his hand.

"Hunter. It's nice to meet you. I'm Mike Benson," my dad says, meeting his hand for a shake. "Come inside. We have a lot to talk about."

I LOST MY BOYFRIEND TONIGHT.

I never had a chance. Really, I should have known this would happen.

"What do you mean, the Alabama-Auburn rivalry is better? Tennessee-Alabama is a tradition that you can literally set your calendar for every year!"

"Mr. Benson, while I appreciate your passion about the discussion, take it from a man who *played* in the rivalries. There is nothing like an Iron Bowl when the season is on the line. I'm sorry."

"What did I tell you about calling me Mr. Benson. It's Mike. And fine, that game does have more meaning being at the end of the season. But let's talk about the Peyton Manning years. Now *those* were some classic games."

This is all I hear from the back patio as my dad and Hunter continue to argue and debate the ranking of college football rivalries.

Honestly, there hasn't been a football topic they *haven't* discussed.

Once Dad got Hunter in his clutches, he was a goner. That is, after Dad let it be known that he was "willing to look past" me dating an Alabama graduate.

Apparently, *that* was what gave Dad pause last week. Not that he's a coach. Not that I felt the need to sneak around. It's the fact that he went to the school that my dad considers his college football enemy.

I shouldn't be surprised. This is the South and college football.

But he loves him. I can tell. Which makes my heart so full it could burst.

"And to think you were worried," Helen says as she passes me a dish to load into the dishwasher. We are both staring out the back window, watching the two men we love have a friendly argument about uniform combinations.

Because yes, I'm in love with Hunter McAvoy.

It's been on the tip of my tongue for a while now. I almost said it in San Francisco. Now that I see Hunter interacting with my family like this, I don't know how long I'm going to be able to keep it in.

I can only hope that he feels the same way.

"I wasn't worried," I fib. "I wasn't worried at all."

"That's some bull crap, and you know it. You only told us because you got busted," Bethany whispers, bringing in the last of the serving platters from the dining room.

She's right. I didn't want to tell them. Who could blame me? We have to worry about what the Fury and *The Banner* will think when we tell them. I really have to worry about my reputation to my readers and the fans.

It just made sense in my head to lump my family in with the rest of those people.

But they don't care who Hunter is. All they care about is that Hunter treats me right and that I'm happy.

He does. And I am.

"He's a very nice young man," Helen says, handing me a pan to load.

"He's very nice to look at too," Bethany adds, her eyebrows going up and down.

"Bethany! Be nice."

"I am! I'm complimenting my stepsister on her hunk of a boyfriend, and I'm using this opportunity to ask if he has any single friends. Or maybe a brother who doesn't fall too far from the family tree, or maybe a family friend who is clinging onto a branch with biceps the same shape as Hunter's?"

I laugh, closing the dishwasher. "Only a sister, so sorry on that one. And… well, I haven't met any of his friends. Because we have to keep things a secret, not many people know. In fact, besides a random couple at the bowling alley, you three are the first to know."

This causes the mood to turn somber. I told them that Hunter and I weren't telling people about our relationship, but I don't think they truly realized to what extent that meant.

"Are you okay with that?" Helen asks, concern heavy in her voice.

Am I? At first, I was. It was nice getting to know Hunter and figuring out the dynamics of our relationship without having outside interference. Now that we are a few months in? There are times I wish we could be a normal couple. I wish I could ask him if he has anyone to set Bethany up with. I wish we could be more open.

But this is our reality. Training camp starts in a few weeks, and before we know it, the season will be upon us. We only have a few more months to go.

"I have to be," I say, unable to hold in the honesty. "It's only for a few more months. The reward will be worth it."

As the words leave my mouth, Hunter and Dad open the screen door and make their way back inside.

"Slugger, your boyfriend here thinks he knows more pro football facts than I do. Tell him that he might be a big, hotshot coach, but when it comes to random factoids, no one will beat me."

I can't help but laugh at Dad's bravado as I walk over to stand next to Hunter, who promptly puts his arm around my shoulders to bring me to his side as he places a kiss to my temple.

"Sorry, babe. Dad here has made it his life's mission to remember every small fact he can. I think he's got you."

"I refuse to believe this," Hunter says. "Next time we come over, Sadie will quiz us. Twenty bucks says I'll win."

"You're on. And make it fifty, that's how confident I am that I'll smoke you," Dad says, reaching his hand out to shake Hunter's.

I don't know why, but this small gesture makes tears well in my eyes.

I really need to get this crying thing under control.

One hour and one more football debate later, Hunter and I begin saying our goodbyes. There are only five of us so I didn't think it would take long. However, I didn't count on Bethany cornering Hunter about his single friends.

"That's a good one you got there," Dad says as he brings me in for a hug.

"I was so nervous to tell you all," I admit, squeezing him a little tighter. "I'm sorry I didn't. Please know I wanted to."

He kisses me on the top of my head like he did when I was little. I can't believe I was hesitant to tell him. This is the man who told me I could do and be anything I wanted. He let me fall so I could learn to get back up. He supported me in every decision I have ever made.

I should have known this was going to be no different.

"I know you did, slugger. And I know what's on the line for you," he says, releasing me from the hug but keeping his arm around my shoulder. "I also know that you wouldn't have even started this if you didn't think he was worth it. And he is."

If I had any reservations about Hunter before, with my dad's words, they all disappear.

28

HUNTER

I SHOULD BE WORRIED.

Okay. I am worried.

Why is Sadie's car in my driveway?

Don't get me wrong, she is welcome over whenever she wants. It's why I gave her a key. However, she has never once used it. She said she felt uncomfortable being at my place without me there.

So why tonight?

When I talked to her earlier today, I told her I'd be home a little after six, which she then promptly said she'd be over by seven. Our plan was to spend the night relaxing since training camp opens tomorrow.

Also known as the time of the year where our relationship is going to be put through tests we have yet to face.

Both of our jobs are about to go from zero to sixty, literally overnight. And we know this. I'll be trying to install a new offense with players who have never worked with me before. She's working her ass off knowing that the *US Daily* job could be hers.

It's a busy time for both of us. And we know what that means.

Less time together. Less time being us.

Neither of us has said it, but we both know it.

Tonight is supposed to be our last night of normal. We had plans to order in, throw on our latest Netflix binge, and just spend the night wrapped in each other's arms.

So Sadie beating me here has my spidey senses on alert.

They perk up even more when I walk into my condo to hear music playing and the smell of spaghetti sauce tickling my nose.

What is she up to?

I drop my keys and wallet on my front table and make my way back to the kitchen. If she heard me, she hasn't acknowledged me yet. Which is good. That gives me a chance to take her in.

She's wearing black leggings and a tank top that hugs all of her curves. Her hair is on the top of her head as always. I've learned that I like her hair up like that, it gives me a view of the line where her neck meets her shoulders. I love putting my mouth on the spot that sends shivers down her spine.

She has music connected to the speaker in the kitchen, and she's dancing back and forth. Nothing big, just swaying her hips to the sound. And then I get a glimpse of what she's doing.

Spaghetti noodles are in water on the stove, just waiting to be cooked. There's a pot of sauce next to it based on the smell. She's chopping vegetables and placing them into a salad bowl.

Holy shit. Sadie Benson is cooking for me. More importantly, Sadie Benson is cooking and it's not burning.

The gesture hits me square in the heart. This woman doesn't cook for herself. Well, not since the failed attempts at grilled cheese. She returned half of the kitchen items we bought as she came to terms that she was not meant to be a cook.

But here she is. In my home, cooking us dinner for two. The gesture might not be grand in size, but in meaning? There isn't one bigger.

I fucking love this woman so damn much.

Without saying a word, I walk into my kitchen and slip my arms around her waist. She jumps a bit, but as my lips kiss her neck, she melts into me like she always does.

"You scared me," she says, putting her arms around mine to squeeze a little tighter.

"I could say the same thing about you. I didn't know what to think when I saw your car in the driveway."

I turn her around, and her hands immediately go around my neck. "I hope it's okay. I wanted to surprise you."

I kiss her nose, because I know if I kiss her lips I won't stop. "I loved seeing your car here. You didn't have to do this all for me."

"I wanted to. I thought it would be nice since this is probably our last date night for a while."

"You know we will see each other when the season starts."

She lets out a small sigh. "I know. But it won't be the same. It'll be a lot of late nights and long days. Which is why I wanted one more special night. It doesn't get much more special than me cooking."

We both laugh, knowing no truer words have been spoken. "It smells amazing"

"You have to thank Helen for this one. She talked me through everything."

"I'll have to make sure to thank her at the next dinner," I say in a low tone, the intimacy of the moment getting to me.

At that moment, the song on the speaker changes. It's slow. Familiar.

Where have I heard this?

I instinctively pull Sadie closer to me, taking her hand in mine, my other brings her in close to me so her head can lay on my chest. Slowly, our bodies start swaying with the song.

Like a lightning bolt it hits me.

This is the song.

The song that we danced to on Beale Street.

The song that was playing the moment I knew that I had something special right in my arms.

The song that was playing the first time I knew I could love this woman forever.

"It's our song," she says in a whisper.

"It is. You know I couldn't remember the words that night."

"It's Elvis," she says, and even though I can't see her, I can feel her smile against me. "How can you not remember Elvis?"

I lean down and place my lips on her hair as I let the words of the song run through me.

Words about fools rushing in. Words about not being able to help but falling in love.

"I love you."

She raises her head off my chest, her hazel eyes finding mine.

"What did you just say?"

I can't help but smile before leaning down and kissing her. Nothing deep. Just a soft kiss to let her know that yes, I did just say that.

And no, I don't regret it.

"I love you, Sadie Benson. I think I loved you the first time we danced to this song. You're strong, and kind, and smart, and funny, and I thank my lucky stars every day that you came into my life."

"You haven't tried the spaghetti sauce yet."

"Woman, let me finish," I say, giving her hips a squeeze, which makes her laugh. Of course, she would throw in a joke right now. "I love you. I know it's probably too soon, but things are about to get crazy and I just wanted to let you know that—"

"I love you too," she says, cutting me off. "I love the man you are. I love the man you want to be. I love every single thing about you, Hunter McAvoy."

What else is there to say? Nothing. Which is why I scoop her up into my arms and take her to my bedroom.

The sauce can wait.

Making love to Sadie can't.

29

SADIE

"KNOCK-KNOCK! YOO-HOO? BOYFRIEND? ANYONE HOME?"

I'm surprised when I don't get an answer. His truck is in the driveway and he's not outside. He was the one who texted me to come over tonight and to pick up the pizza he ordered.

I have the pizza. I even picked up a six-pack of beer that he likes.

Now I just need to find him.

I check all the rooms in his condo, this time not feeling like a creep like I did that first night when I was checking out if he had a bed frame or not, but I can't find him. I shoot him a text, wondering where he is before settling on the sectional with my laptop. I figured he would have to work a bit tonight, so I brought my computer as well to get some work done.

The second week of training camp has ended. I don't even need two hands to keep track of how many times I've talked to Hunter. It's even less when you count how many times we've spent the night with each other.

To say that the official start of the season has been a rude awakening for us is an understatement. I knew it would be hard, but I didn't think it would be like this.

He is at the Fury facility from morning until night. I'm there every day as well, but not as long as him. This is an important part of the season for him. This is the first time he really gets to work with his players and install his offense. I know how much pressure he is putting on himself. I know how hard he has been working.

Which is why I have been giving him his space and not freaking out when he says that I should stay at my place because he won't be home until late. I want to make sure he has all the space he needs to get his feet under him as the season begins. I want him to excel. He is so determined to be the best, and I'm going to do everything possible to help him get there.

Even if that means I'm pushed to the back seat for a while.

Most days I at least get to physically see him. Though that comes from the limited viewing the media has of practices. And every time I catch a glimpse of him, it takes all my willpower not to stare at him the whole time.

The few times I have allowed myself to watch him, I have an overwhelming sense of pride in my heart. He's in his element. He's firm with his players, but you can tell there is a respect there. He knows what he wants, and he's not afraid to get his hands dirty and show the players what he means.

And if I must say, no man should make basketball shorts and a T-shirt look that good.

Today was a day off for the team, so there was no reason for the media to go to the facility. That doesn't mean the coaches got the day off. Needless to say, it was a pleasant surprise when Hunter texted me asking me to come over and to pick up pizza on the way.

Which makes it even more strange that he isn't home. Why would he have texted me? And why is his truck here, but he isn't?

I check my phone and see no reply, so I boot up my computer and throw my earbuds in. Today's mission: find the best stories I've ever written and send them to *US Daily* while jamming out to some Boyband Radio.

I exchanged emails with the editor, and they want to have a phone interview with me next week. They also want me to send them what I feel are my best stories. They also specifically asked for everything that I wrote about Hunter to see how I reported his hiring.

I can't help but smile as I go back and read all of those early stories. Then he was just a coach, a good-looking coach whom I had a reluctant crush on, but a coach, nonetheless. How funny that in such a short amount of time he has become so much a part of my life.

He's not just a part of my life. He's the love of my life. I don't know how I know that, I just do. I don't know what will happen in the future. I don't know if we'll survive this season, and I don't know what will happen when we are finally able to tell people about us. But I do know that even if this crumbles and fails, that when I'm eighty years old, I'll look back at these months with Hunter and smile because they happened.

"Dude! I have never seen your place. Plus, I have to take a piss. I'll be five minutes."

"Can't you hold—"

Hunter's voice is cut off when Davis, one of the Fury coaches, comes bursting through the front door. We're both frozen when we catch sight of each other. I'm sure he wasn't expecting me, and I sure as hell wasn't expecting him.

"Whoa! What are you doing here? Did you break in or something?"

His confused eyes look back and forth from me to Hunter. What he sees on both of our faces are looks of straight guilt.

We have been officially busted.

"I… I need to take a piss… so I'm…"

"Up the stairs. First door on the right," Hunter instructs, a resignation to his voice.

Davis gives me one more confused look before making his way up the stairs. Before I can say anything, Hunter is on the couch next to me, taking my hands in his.

"I'm so sorry," he says, bringing my knuckles to his lips. "I just got home and texted you when he messaged that he was on his way over and he needed my help with something back at the facility. I said I'd drive, but he was apparently not far from here. I couldn't think quick enough to make an excuse. And then I forgot my phone in my bedroom. I plugged it in to charge. I am so sorry, Sadie."

I don't even have the chance to respond before Davis is coming back down the stairs, his eyes glued to us on the couch.

"Davis—" Hunter says, but he holds up his hands, effectively cutting Hunter off.

"I won't say anything," he says, making sure to make eye contact with both of us. "As long as you both promise me that nothing shady is going on, I'll keep my mouth shut. This is none of my business. But I must say, everything now makes a hell of a lot more sense."

I nod in thanks, though I'm confused by that last part. Before I can ask what he means, Hunter is leading him out of the condo. I don't know what else he says. I think I hear something about "calling dibs" and Hunter giving him a slap on the back of the head as they step out of the condo.

I put my computer away and fall back onto the cushions of Hunter's sectional. I knew at some point we'd be found out. I just never thought it would be like this.

"So that happened," Hunter says, collapsing next to me. His head goes immediately to my lap. The man has a thing for me playing with his hair. Especially when he's on edge.

"What was that about calling dibs?" I ask, trying to lighten the mood. Hunter laughs, so mission accomplished.

"He was with me the day I saw you at Sandwich City after Memphis. Let's just say I didn't react well when he said that you were hot."

This makes me laugh. "So, you called dibs?"

He nuzzles into my lap a little more. "More or less."

We sit there for a few minutes in complete silence. For a second, I think I've put him to sleep. It wouldn't be the first time he's fallen asleep on my lap when I'm playing with his hair. Then, he speaks, and his words nearly break my heart.

"I've missed you so damn much."

I lean down and place a kiss on his head. "I've missed you too."

"I don't like you not sleeping here. I know why you haven't, but that doesn't mean I have to like it. I feel like we never talk. Or see each other. I fucking hate it."

I let out a sigh. I haven't liked it either. "I know you've had long days. I just don't want to be in the way. So I haven't wanted to bother you."

This makes him sit up. "I've been a miserable bastard to my coaches and players, and it's because I have to see you almost every day, and know that I didn't get to kiss you that morning. Our days have been long, and at first I thought it would be best if some nights we stayed apart, but I was wrong. Dead wrong. I don't care if I've been working for thirty-six straight hours, I need to see you when I get home. Hell, if you started moving your stuff in here, I would be over the moon."

My eyes go wide. "You… you want me to move in?"

He gives me a shrug, and for the first time in God knows how long, I'm greeted by my favorite small smile. "I know we can't right now. We have to wait until we're free to be out in the open. But I just want to let you know that if you were here every day, and a few of your clothes happened to make their way over here, I wouldn't be upset."

I can't help myself anymore. I adjust myself so I'm straddling him because I need to feel as much of him as possible against me. I bring our lips together, and as soon as they connect, I feel like I'm home. That the weirdness of the past two weeks was just another milestone and building block in our relationship.

Hunter eventually breaks our kiss, but his hands don't leave my body. "Promise me no more staying away when we are in Nashville. I know when we're on the road we'll need to keep our distance. But if we are here, it doesn't matter how long our days have been, or how early we have to be up in the morning, from now on we are beginning and ending each day together."

"Promise," I say, leaning down and giving him one kiss. "Did you really call dibs on me?"

"Hell yeah, I did," he says as he stands up, still holding me so my legs wrap around his body. "And I'd do it all over again."

30

____

HUNTER

"IT'S his first game as a pro. You need to give him some breathing room. He's a fucking rookie, Hunter."

Davis's words run through me as I slam my now-empty beer can down on the small patio outside my hotel room in Miami. I unceremoniously toss it on the ground, joining the now five other empty cans.

All from me.

"I know he's a fucking rookie," I say, cracking open another beer. "It doesn't give him the excuse to forget how to throw a damn pass. Or to act like he doesn't give a fuck."

I should be quieter. It's nearing midnight. I don't know if the Fury has every room on this floor booked or not.

I can't find it in me to care, though.

We had our first preseason game tonight.

We got our asses beat.

And when I say we, I mean the offense.

I've never felt like such a failure in my life.

The offense completely crumbled. Bryce Donald, our quarterback of the future, was a deer in headlights. He didn't complete one pass. It was like he wasn't even in the same stadium as the rest of us. Every play we ran was a failure. Luckily, we went into the game only planning to play our starters in the first quarter. That was the only thing that stopped the bleeding.

I didn't speak to anyone after the game. I immediately came to my hotel room and planned on sulking here, alone, until Davis showed up with a case of beer. Thankfully, I don't have to put on a brave or happy face around Sadie. She's staying at a different hotel, and I know she's still working.

Just as well. I'm shit company tonight. And I don't want her to see me like this.

"Why are you taking this so hard?" Davis asks. "It's the first preseason game. Everyone knows preseason games don't mean shit."

"Because we are not where we need to be as an offense, and tonight proved it."

I had a sinking feeling in my gut for the past few weeks that what I was trying to do with the Fury wasn't working. Practices have been horrible. The defense was kicking our ass every day during intra-squad scrimmages. But I wasn't letting it get to me. I was a new coach, and these guys had never worked with me before. It was going to take some time for us to hit our stride.

Tonight was a rude awakening and confirmed every doubt I was having. Was I too tough? Was I not tough enough? Was my offense too complex? Was I not a good coach or teacher?

Every time I let my mind go down these rabbit holes, I only hear one voice in the back of my mind fueling my doubt. And his voice is getting louder with each passing day.

"All tonight proved was that we still have work to do," Davis says as I hear my message alert go off from my phone inside my hotel suite.

I walk through the patio doors and grab my phone off the charger to see a text from Sadie.

Girlfriend: I'm on my way back to my hotel. I'll call you in an hour if that's OK?

Boyfriend: Great.

I know my response is short, but I'm worried that between my piss-poor attitude and the fact that I'm drunk will lead to a text message I might regret. Still, just seeing her name on my phone slightly brightens my mood as I take back my seat on the patio, phone in hand.

"Remind me to thank Sadie next time I see her. At least now I know how to get you out of a mental spiral," Davis jokes. "How's that going?"

His question is sincere. It also catches me off guard. That's not an uncommon question for friends to ask one another. But because no one knew about me and Sadie, no one has ever asked me that.

"She's great," I say, my tone a little lighter now that I'm not talking about football. "It's been a little hard since the season started, but we're getting by. Thanks again by the way for not saying anything to anyone about us. It's… it's complicated."

"No problem, man." My phone starts ringing in my hand, and Davis slaps my shoulder as he stands. "I'm sure that's her. Take the call. Try to forget about tonight. We'll get back to the drawing board when we're back in Nashville."

I swipe the phone to answer as Davis leaves the room, not even looking down to see who called. "I thought you weren't calling me for another hour, gorgeous."

"I'm ignoring the gorgeous comment. And you're lucky I didn't call you the second that putrid excuse for a game was over."

Fucking wonderful.

I lean down and grab another beer out of the case that Davis left. That's the only way I will get through this phone call with my father.

"To what do I owe the pleasure, Dad?"

"Don't get salty with me, Hunter. I wouldn't be calling you if it wasn't clear that you need my help."

His help! He has got to be fucking kidding me.

"Your help? Your help! What in God's name makes you think that I want, or need, your help?"

"Hunter, don't be stubborn." His voice is stern, like he's lecturing me when he was teaching me how to drive. "You clearly need some help. Your players looked horrible tonight. Now, I don't know why you insist on running that convoluted offense, but I think if you simplify it down…"

I tune him out. I have no clue what he's saying, and I honestly don't give a flying fuck. My entire life my father has believed that he is God's gift to football. Don't get me wrong, in his day, he was great. One of the best. I'll never argue about why he's in the Hall of Fame.

But he still thinks it's the late 1980s. Defenses were slower then. Offenses didn't need to have so many plays to be successful. He has never understood that the game has evolved over the countless decades since he was last on the field.

I really don't want to listen to him, but the last words he says catches my attention. "…and I don't understand why you think you have to reinvent the wheel with offenses. Just run the ball on first and second down, and then pass it on third. It's not that hard, Hunter. Back in my day, that's all I had to do, and look where it got me. I'm in the Hall of Fame. You keep this up, and you'll be unemployed by your bye week."

That's it. I'm about to fucking lose it.

"Shut the fuck up, Dad. Just shut… the fuck… up."

"Excuse me? Don't use that tone with me, Hunter."

"No. You don't get to call and tell me how to do my job." I'm now standing on the patio, pacing back and forth. I feel it. Years of rage and anger are about to bubble over. "Did my team have a bad night tonight? Yes. I won't argue with you on that. And if you ever *once* showed an interest or supported me in my career, then *maybe* I'd let you give me advice. But every time I hear you bash my profession, or bash my offenses, it's just another reminder of how bitter you are. That forward-thinking coaches like me, and new offenses, were the reason you had to retire early. You knew you couldn't hang. You knew you couldn't handle it. You were a coward. You were a damn coward and you quit. Well, guess what, Dad? You don't get to take that anger out on me."

Silence is heavy on the line. I have never in my life talked to my dad that way. Hell, the whole part of him retiring early and being a coward, I don't even know where that came from. I've thought about that from time to time, but it was always just my conspiracy theory as to why he retired in the prime of his career.

Now it's out there in the open. And I can't take it back.

I don't want to take it back either.

"Well, I think you've said all there is to say," he says, a defeat to his voice I've never heard before. "Call your mother soon. She misses you."

Click.

I stare at the phone, still in shock about what just transpired. The game tonight. Bryce's performance. My dad. Everything is spinning out of control right now.

I just unleashed years of pent-up anger at my dad, but he's right. Something isn't working in the offense. And I don't know how to fix it. What if he's right? What if I'm not cut out for this? What if I am a failure?

I feel the doubt starting to slowly seep into my veins.

I shake my head, trying to snap myself out of this. Giving into these feelings of doubt means he wins. I won't let that happen. Then I take my phone and bring back up the last text I received.

Boyfriend: Are you back at your hotel yet?

Girlfriend: Halfway. Why?

Boyfriend: I had a blowup with Bo.

Girlfriend: I'll be right there.

I know this is risky. Someone could see her coming into the hotel. At this point, I don't care. Let them find out.

I need calm. I need my center.

I need Sadie.

31

SADIE

> Girlfriend: I'll probably come over to your place around six, if that works?

> Boyfriend: I won't be home till late. Probably past ten. Maybe best if you stay at your place tonight. I'm sorry.

> Girlfriend: OK. Miss you. <3

AND LIKE I PREDICTED, no response. No I miss you too. No I love you.

Nothing.

The sad thing is that I'm not shocked by this. This isn't the first time this kind of message exchange has happened since we returned from Miami. Or what I like to call, our last good night.

That was five weeks ago.

I hate that I associate that night with good when it was horrible for Hunter. The fight with his dad shook him in ways he wasn't ready for. I'll never admit I saw this, but he fell asleep crying on my lap.

My heart broke for him.

But we were together. We were a team.

Since he came back, he's been a man possessed trying to turn this offense around. And he's on a solo mission to do so. He tried easing up on the playbook. He tried adding new plays. He tried becoming a straight asshole to the players. He tried being their friend.

Nothing has worked.

We're now two weeks into the regular season, and the Fury has yet to win. Or even score a touchdown.

The offense has been putrid. Bryce can't figure out how to run the offense. Nothing is gelling. And Hunter is taking the brunt of it from the media.

Including me.

And here lies the other component of why my boyfriend has been avoiding me. Yes, he promised me during preseason that we would spend every night together. But would you want to share a bed with a woman who is writing daily articles about how bad your offense is? I wouldn't want to see me either.

Funny how I never thought about this scenario when we started dating. It's my job as a reporter to talk about why things are or aren't working with a team. I did it last year leading up to Bancroft getting fired. I had to speculate daily on his job security and his future. I pulled no punches. I told it like it was.

I never thought I'd have to do that with Hunter. Especially this early into his season. Every time I write a story about "what's wrong with Hunter McAvoy's offense" it kills me a little inside.

I know Hunter's text about being there late isn't a lie or a cop out. The Fury staff has been pulling all-nighters trying to figure out what's wrong. I give them credit; they aren't just waiting for the ship to right itself. That means I've been spending many nights alone.

And many nights wondering if Hunter and I will survive this.

I can't do this another night. I'm driving myself crazy with "what ifs." What if Hunter breaks up with me because of a story I write? What if the Fury has to fire Hunter this season and he has to move? What if I get fired because I let my feelings for Hunter get in the way of my reporting?

"AAAAAHHHHHHHHH!" I scream to no one, because I can't hold it in anymore.

I grab my phone off the charger and bring up my contacts. I need to talk to someone or I might go insane.

"Hello? Sadie?"

"Bethany, are you busy?"

"No. I'm just finishing up at the shop. Is everything okay? You sound upset."

"I…" I push back the tears. Damn Hunter McAvoy for turning me into a crier. "I'm going crazy and I might cry and I'm freaking out."

"I'll be there in an hour. Do you have wine?"

"You know I'm not a wine drinker." I pause to try and get a glimpse of something from the view in my living room. Boom. There it is.

"I have tequila."

"Even better. Call for pizza. I'll bring ice cream."

Fifty-eight minutes later, Bethany is standing in my apartment with three different kinds of ice cream and a bag full of limes.

"You're my hero," I say as I grab plates for the pizza that was delivered. "I hope you didn't have plans tonight."

She gives me a wave of her hand as she puts away the ice cream. "Not a one. I was with my last client when you texted, and I really didn't want to eat alone tonight. This worked out for everyone."

We load our plates and grab a drink before heading into my living room. I can't help but notice Bethany looking around, taking in every inch of my space.

"Your place is great," she says, taking a seat on one end of my couch. "I can't believe this is the first time I've been over here. I love this area rug."

I give her a sad smile, because now I'm reminded of Hunter and our shopping excursion to decorate my apartment. He picked this rug out.

"Oh gosh, what did I say?" She immediately puts her pizza down on the coffee table. "Sadie, talk to me. I've never seen you this upset."

I give my head a shake, determined not to cry. What is there to cry about? It's not like we are broken up. I just miss my boyfriend. That's all.

Right?

"Things with Hunter… well… they haven't been great as of late."

"Did you two break up?"

I shake my head. "No. At least, I don't think so. The season has been rough on him and it's kind of spilling over to us."

"Talk to me about it."

And I do. I spill everything. When my word vomit is over, I expect to see an *I told you so look* on Bethany's face. Hell, that's how I'd be looking at me.

Instead, I see my stepsister looking at me with kindness. Sympathy. There is not an ounce of judgment in her eyes. Even as she hands me a tissue, because at some point in this story, I started crying my eyes out.

Right here, right now, I've never been so thankful for my dad marrying Helen.

"Girl. I didn't realize this was going to get so heavy," Bethany says, standing up from the couch. "Be right back. Don't move."

I don't even look to see what she's doing. Before I know it, she has returned to the couch with two shot glasses, the bottle of tequila, and a cut-up lime.

"Here. We should have done this before we started."

I laugh but do what she says. I sling back the shot and suck on the lime. The tequila burns down my throat.

It's exactly what I needed.

"Thanks," I say, wiping my mouth with the tissue. "I'm a mess."

"Girl, if you weren't a mess right now, I'd wonder if there was something wrong with you."

I can't help but laugh. "I don't want to lose him, Bethany. I love him."

She takes my hand and gives it a squeeze. "I know, sis. I know."

32

———————

HUNTER

"WHAT IN THE fuck is this shit?"

I didn't know my voice could reach this level, and I'm sure everyone in the Fury facility heard me. Hell, everyone in the metro Nashville limits heard me. Paul physically flinches at my outburst. Though my reaction shouldn't surprise him. If he didn't want me to react like this, then he shouldn't have shown me this morning's edition of *The Banner* with a huge headline:

Too much to handle? Hunter McAvoy in over his head as Fury offensive coordinator

You would think that if my girlfriend was writing an article wondering if the Fury made the right decision to hire me, that she would have given me some fucking notice.

Yes, that would require us speaking to each other more than a couple of times a week. We haven't spent the night with each other in… fuck, I don't know how long it's been. Most nights I don't even go home, choosing to sleep on my office couch. But still, a little bit of a heads-up would have been nice. Glad to know she has so much confidence in me. Though, based on the past few weeks of her articles, this shouldn't have been a shock. The woman has been busting my balls every day in her paper.

Though she's not wrong. Every word she's saying is right. Doesn't mean I have to like it.

"Did you know she was writing this?" I ask Paul as steam comes out of my ears. At least that's what it feels like.

He shakes his head. "The reporters don't exactly give me a daily rundown of what stories they are writing, Hunter. I just wanted you to see it before you have your weekly press conference."

Fuck me.

Of course, that's today. Just my luck. Not only do I have to answer questions about "am I in over my head," I have to do it looking at Sadie, who apparently thinks that I'm not cut out for this job.

Fucking great.

A rational person would understand where she's coming from. Right now, I am anything but rational. I'm pissed, confused, and frustrated. And it gets worse every day.

The beginning of this season has been awful. Things didn't get better after Miami. In fact, they got worse. We are now three games into the season, and we just scored our first touchdown last week. I've had to bench Bryce because he was just not getting it. The veteran backup has been doing all right, but he's not built for the offense that I built specifically for my first overall pick, quarterback prodigy.

Things are going downhill quick. I can't seem to make it stop.

Trying to figure out what the hell I'm doing wrong has been plaguing my mind every second of every day. I've been a bastard to be around, which is why I haven't seen Sadie. I can't be around her right now. Hell, I can't be around anyone. I need to figure this out.

If today's article is any indication, it's probably best I've kept her at arm's length. If she thinks I'm in over my head, I can only imagine what she would think if she saw me every night poring over plays and game film, trying to figure out where I've gone wrong.

She'd see that I'm struggling. That I'm lost. That I'm exactly what Bo thinks I am—not good enough and who only made it this far in life because of my last name.

"How much time do I have until I have to face The Mob?"

Paul checks his watch. "Less time than you'd like."

"Now?"

"Unfortunately. Let's get it over with."

"HUNTER, what's going on with the offense?"

"Is Bryce a bust?"

"Have you felt overwhelmed with the position?"

The questions are coming at me faster than I can answer them. As soon as I get the words out for one, another asshole reporter is throwing something else at me.

Except Sadie. Like always, she hasn't asked me a thing yet. She's probably waiting until the end, like always.

I wish she'd just ask. It would be better just to get it over with. Then I can hear in her voice how much of a failure she thinks I am.

I've never doubted my abilities so much like I have the past few months. Before, I had little voices in my head telling me I wasn't good enough, or that I was only getting jobs because of who my dad was. But I always shut those voices up by proving the doubters, and my father, wrong.

Those voices are getting louder. So loud that I can barely think anymore. And I didn't realize it, but they all sound like him.

"You're only coaching because you knew you couldn't hack it as a player."

"Why are you running this play?"

"Coaches are the guys who weren't good enough to make it."

"At least you won one championship."

I'm about to go down a long road of self-doubt when I hear her voice, though I don't have any idea what Sadie just asked.

"I'm sorry. Can you repeat the question?" I ask.

For the first time today, I allow myself to look at her. I feel like I haven't seen her in weeks. Months. She's still my beautiful girl. She's wearing her glasses today and, as always, her hair is on the top of her head. To anyone else, she probably looks fine.

I can see more. She looks… sad. Tired.

That's probably my fault as well.

I've never been so angry at a person, yet also want to take their pain away.

I love her, but I want to scream at her.

Right now, I can't do any of those things.

"My question is regarding Bryce," Sadie says, before clearing her throat. "Could his performance be a mental block stemming from a personal matter? Or has the transition to the pros been too much for him to handle?"

Too much for him to handle.

That was the headline on her fucking article today.

"It's funny… the phrase too much to handle," I begin, trying to keep the sarcasm and snark out of my voice. "You never know when you're going to be ready to handle something. All the signs could point to 'you're ready.' You could cross every t and dot every i to prepare for it. You could think of one thousand scenarios and think you have an answer for all of them. Everything could seem to be in perfect alignment. Then, BAM! Something happens. Maybe it's the reality of being in a live game. Maybe it's an injury. Maybe it's just something that you forgot to take into consideration. No matter what, though, that doesn't mean you give up on that person. We aren't giving up on Bryce. We aren't giving up on the season. This isn't too much for anyone to handle. We just have to figure out how to get the pieces back in order."

My words hang in the air as Paul dismisses the reporters. I know I probably said too much. It's all the truth.

It's true about Bryce. I'm not giving up on him.

The same can be said for me and Sadie. We thought we could handle this relationship. We thought we had a perfect game plan. Turns out we didn't.

And also, like Bryce, I'm not ready to give up on her. On us.

But we can't keep going on like this.

"Benson!" I yell, which causes all of the reporters who are exiting the room to look back at me in confusion. Coaches never directly address reporters. "Can I have a word with you?"

She doesn't say anything as she turns around to walk back toward me, but I can see the mix of emotion in her eyes. I'm sure it's exactly how mine look right now as well. Paul has left, thank God, and by the time Sadie reaches me, we're the only two in the interview room.

"Nice article today," I say, my sarcasm thick.

"Just doing my job," she replies matter-of-factly.

I let out a sigh and pinch the bridge of my nose because I want to yell at her. I want to kiss her. I want to scream at her. I want to break down in front of her and confess that I'm overwhelmed and confused. I want to fuck her over this chair.

But I can't do any of that.

"I'm coming over tonight. We need to talk."

She looks around quickly, making sure no one can hear. "You can't come over. It's a weekday. Someone might see you."

I lean in close. So close that if someone were to walk in right now, they might think I was kissing her.

If only.

"I don't give a flying fuck if anyone sees me. We have shit to figure out. Off the record."

33

SADIE

HUNTER DOESN'T EVEN KNOCK.

I didn't know what time to expect him. It's not like we've been seeing much of each other lately, and even before then, some nights were later than others. All I know is that I've been on pins and needles since I got home today.

Is he coming over to break up with me? I wouldn't blame him. I'd break up with me too for the story I wrote in today's paper.

I hated it. I didn't write the headline, that's my editor's job, but it's not like it was wrong or misleading. I did question whether or not he was in over his head. Because it's a logical question to ask, and I would have speculated it had it been any other coach. I can't show favorable treatment.

I cried as soon as I hit send on the article. I cried more than I ever have in my entire life. Every word I wrote broke another piece inside me.

I nearly didn't go to the Fury facility today. I have never taken a sick day, and I almost did. I wanted to hide in my bedroom and not have to see Hunter's face. When I came face-to-face with him, it made the pain come right back.

Normally, I'd stay and write at the facility after a press conference.

I couldn't today. I couldn't be in the same building as him. I came back to my apartment. I don't even remember what I wrote. I've been on autopilot as I sat and stewed, waiting for Hunter to get here.

And now that he is, I have no idea what to think. Because he's not empty-handed.

"What in the world?"

Hunter doesn't acknowledge my question. Instead, he walks right to my kitchen counter and sets down a box of pizza, another to-go box which smells like chicken wings, and a six-pack of beer.

Is he feeding me before dumping me? I don't know whether to be happy or sad about that.

"I didn't know if you had eaten. We have a lot of shit to figure out, and I'm not trying to do it if you're hangry."

I don't know whether to be touched because he was thinking of me, or angry because he thought I couldn't have a rational discussion without food. He's not wrong… but still. Ouch.

I don't say a word as he fishes paper plates out of my cabinet and pulls out two beers before setting the rest of the bottles in the refrigerator.

"Here," he says. "Fix a plate."

I stare at the plate, then back up at him, my anger and frustration beginning to take over. "Are you fucking kidding me right now? We have barely spoken in weeks, and all you can say to me is 'fix a plate'?"

"What would you rather have me say?"

Is he… is he serious? What would I rather have him say?

Does he really need to fucking ask that?

"I would rather you say, 'Sadie, I'm an asshole for shutting you out.' I'd rather you say, 'Sadie, we need to end this because I can't be with someone who writes negative things about me.' Hell, I'd even rather you say, 'Let's tell everyone about us and rip the fucking Band-Aid off.' But in no universe do I want you to tell me to fix a goddamn plate when I have no idea where we stand!"

My breathing is heavy because damn, that felt really good. It's not nearly everything I have to tell Hunter tonight. Or make him tell me. But getting out that anger… yeah. That was needed.

When my breathing slows down, I take a look at Hunter. I expected him to yell back. I expected him to have some sort of rebuttal.

I didn't expect him to be standing in my kitchen looking like I just killed his puppy.

"You want to break up?"

I let out a shriek of frustration as I march back to my living room and sit down. He's been here five minutes and I already have a headache.

"No. I do not want to break up with you. But I don't want to keep going on like this. We aren't in a good spot, Hunter. And the longer you shut me out, the worse it will get."

He leaves his plate and beer in the kitchen before coming to sit by me. He immediately takes my hand in his. God, I have missed his touch.

"You're right. I have been shutting you out. And for that, I'm sorry. I promised you that no matter how tough things got, we would begin and end our days with each other, and I haven't kept that promise."

"You haven't." My words come out more defeated than I mean them to, but it's like right now, all the emotions and frustration of the past few weeks are crashing down on me.

"I knew this job would be tough. But I never expected this," he says, not looking at me, but brushing his thumb over my hand, I'm guessing needing the contact. "I've never not succeeded in something. Even the people who said I only got certain things because I was Bo's son, I was able to prove them wrong. Then, this season happens. My self-doubt came creeping in. All I could hear was my dad in my head telling me that I'd never make it."

I inch a little closer to him because while he never said this out loud, I had a sinking suspicion that Bo had a large part to do with this.

"I needed to fix it. I needed to prove to everyone that I could do this. So I cut myself off. I cut you off. But what has that gotten me? An offense that isn't getting any better, and a pissed-off girlfriend who writes articles about me doubting whether or not I should have been hired."

"In my defense, I would have written that about you even if we weren't dating. That wasn't because I was a scorned woman. That's because I'm a reporter and I have to write the story. No matter what. That's my job, Hunter, to report the news. You knew that when we got together."

He collapses back into my couch, letting out the most defeated sigh I've ever heard.

"I didn't mean to insinuate you wrote that because you were angry at me. Fuck, I can't even apologize correctly."

I shift my legs underneath me, which puts me an inch or two closer to Hunter. "If it counts for anything, I thought you'd come over here and just start screaming at me. The food threw me for a loop."

"Why would you think that?"

"Because of how you spoke to me today after the press conference. You were quite pissed."

He sits back up, his head now in his hands as his elbows rest on his knees. "I was. I'm not going to lie, I still am."

This I was expecting. This I'm ready for. "I'm not apologizing for doing my job, Hunter."

"And you shouldn't have to," he says, now looking back my way. "I don't want you to. I might not like it, but I don't blame you for what you wrote."

"You don't?"

He shakes his head. "I don't. I can *not* like it and also understand it all at once. When I saw you, Paul had just shown me the headline. It set me off. That's why I was angry before the interviews. And that's why I snapped at you afterward."

"So, what changed? Why were you spitting fire earlier, and then just a few hours later you bring me pizza?"

He turns back to me, now taking both of my hands in his. I can't help but look directly into his eyes. Earlier today I saw rage. Now? Now, I'm seeing remorse.

"The question you asked me today, that's what."

"I'm not following."

"You asked me about Bryce's headspace. The kid has more talent in his pinkie than I ever had. But you were right, there is something not right with him. So, I pulled him aside today and asked if he was okay. And not just physically. He didn't say much, but I feel like we had a breakthrough. And then I thought, maybe that's my problem? Maybe my problem is in my head as well. I was letting the voices of doubt get the best of me, and it was affecting everything around me. And not just my job. It was affecting my relationship with you. I don't know if I would have gotten there had you not pushed me along."

I look away, the compliment too much to take. "All I did was ask a question."

"No, gorgeous," he says, bringing my hands to his lips. "There's a good chance you saved the season."

He leans forward in search of my lips. I don't deny him.

It's been too long. I missed the feel of his mouth on me. I missed the feeling of his weight on me.

I missed him.

The rest of the night is a blur of kisses, apologies, agreements, and more kisses. Yes, we eat the pizza. Yes, we have amazing makeup sex.

In between all of that, Hunter and I agree that we can't let things fester. He now knows he can come to me if something is weighing on his mind, and he needs me to be a girlfriend and not a reporter. I promise him that if I'm going to tell Fury fans everywhere that he's doing a shitty job, that I'll give him a warning. We also come to the decision that after the bye week in New Orleans, we are getting away for a few days. Just the two of us.

And that night, after way too many nights apart, we end the day together. Just as promised.

34

———

SADIE

Boyfriend: I miss you.

Girlfriend: You just saw me two hours ago. And I'm literally down the hall from you.

Boyfriend: This isn't my fault. It's yours. You can't wake me up the way you did today and not expect me to miss you.

Girlfriend: I just wanted to make sure you had something to remember me by since I won't see you for a few days. <3

Boyfriend: Mission accomplished. And what are you still doing here? Didn't the rest of The Mob go home?

Girlfriend: 1. You know I hate it when you call it that. 2. Yes, the rest of them went home. I'm just trying to get ahead so I don't have to work tomorrow. Plus, I have time to kill before I meet Bethany tonight for dinner.

Boyfriend: I'd like to eat you for dinner.

Girlfriend: Behave. <3

I CAN'T HELP but smile reading Hunter's texts. Though, in my defense, all I seem to do lately is smile.

Since our heart-to-heart last week, everything seems to have gotten back on track.

Our relationship as well as the Fury's season.

After starting off 0-4, the team pulled out its first win. Bryce was put back in as starter, and he looked like a whole new quarterback. The offense set a franchise record in points scored in a game, and Bryce was named the league's rookie of the week.

No one could believe it. Hell, I think Hunter was even a little shocked at the one-eighty.

It's like everything is now right again with the world.

As for me and Hunter? Things are better than ever. I feel like we're back to the Sadie and Hunter of before the season. I can't wait to steal a few days away with him in New Orleans after this week's game.

Boyfriend: I don't like behaving. When do I get to see you again?

Girlfriend: Well, let's see. It's Friday. You leave with the team later this afternoon. I won't be in town until Saturday night, but unless you have another blowup with your father, I don't think we should chance me coming to the team hotel. Which, unfortunately, means you have to wait until Sunday night to see me.

Boyfriend: What I got from that is all I have to do is text Bo, have a fight, and you'll come over? I can do that. I mean, I haven't talked to him since Miami. I'm sure I've done plenty since then to irritate him.

Girlfriend: Don't pick a fight. You'll survive. See you Sunday. Love you.

Boyfriend: Love you more.

"Why are you smiling like a lunatic?" Tommy asks from over my shoulder, scaring the shit out of me. I hurry up and click off of the text message app and set my phone down. Just one more second, and he would have seen my background picture that is clearly me and Hunter.

"None of your business, old man," I say. "I didn't realize anyone else was still working today."

"You would have if you hadn't been glued to your phone for the last fifteen minutes. If I didn't know better, I'd think you were texting your boyfriend."

My face goes white. My blood goes cold.

Does Tommy know? No. He couldn't. Could he?

"What do you mean?" I say hurriedly, turning back to my computer so I don't have to make eye contact with him.

Tommy takes a seat next to me. "It means you have the look on your face that my teenage daughter does every time her punk-ass boyfriend messages her."

"You calling me a teenager? Come on, Tommy. You can do better than that."

"You know that's not what I meant. Quit trying to deflect," he says.

I am. And I'm not being very good about it. I can tell him I'm dating someone, right? I just won't give names. At least then I'm not lying to him and I don't have to continue to look like I got caught with my hand in the cookie jar.

"Fine. I'm seeing someone. There. You happy?"

He leans back in his chair with a satisfied smile. "Yes. I am. And I'm happy for you. This business will kill you, and any semblance of a personal life, if you let it. Just ask my ex-wife. I've been worried about you. I know you put a lot of hours into your job. I'm glad you're realizing there is a world outside of reporting football."

I let Tommy's words sink in. He's right. For so many years, I didn't think I could have a relationship and a successful career. And I loved my job. I wasn't giving that up. So I just told myself that I didn't need love to be happy.

But my laptop doesn't keep me warm at night. One text from

Hunter telling me that he loves me makes me feel a million times better than a random fan on Twitter telling me that he liked a story I wrote.

I love my job. I really do.

But I love Hunter more.

"Thanks, Tommy," I say, all of a sudden feeling very emotional. "He's a good guy."

"I hope I can meet him sometime."

Me, too, Tommy. Me, too.

"I mean, if you're still here, then I think I should come get a goodbye kiss."

Oh. Shit.

Fuck. Fuck. Fuckety-fuck.

I hear Hunter walking through the pressroom, each step getting closer to my desk area. You can't see my work station from the doorway. He has no idea that Tommy is sitting next to me as he makes his intentions to kiss me known.

He has no idea that he unintentionally just outed us. And not to family or friends.

To a man who has the ability to end this for us.

As soon as he rounds the corner, it's as if time stops. I'm staring at Hunter. Hunter is staring at Tommy. And Tommy? He's looking back and forth between us as he's slowly putting together the puzzle pieces.

"I can explain!" I blurt out at the same time as Hunter shouts, "That's not what I meant!"

If we didn't look guilty before, we do now.

Tommy turns to Hunter. "Have you given her any information that you shouldn't have?"

His tone is firm. Probably the most firm I've ever heard Tommy speak. It's almost like if my dad were asking Hunter what his intentions were with me.

"No, sir, I have not," Hunter replies.

Tommy turns back to face me. I was ready to see disappointment in his eyes. But his expression is blank, and I think that might be worse. Now I don't know what to think.

"Sadie, I would ask you if you've given him favorable treatment, but considering you all but said he might not be ready for this job just a few weeks ago, I can see you're not pulling any punches."

I laugh under my breath. "No. No favorable treatment. We've been careful."

Hunter closes the distance between us, and before I know it, he's next to me, reaching for my hand. "I know what you're probably thinking. And you're probably right on most of it. But this? It's not just a fling. I love her. She loves me. We know what's on the line for both of us."

Tommy weighs Hunter's words, and at this moment, I am so glad that Hunter's hand is keeping me grounded.

"Is he the one who was making you smile?" Tommy asks me.

I nod. "He was. He does. This isn't casual, Tommy. I love him. I also understand if you need to write about this. I'd never ask you to sit on a story."

I hate having to say that, but it's true. I know I'd at least consider writing about it. I don't know if I would, but I'd think about it.

Tommy shakes his head. "I'm not about to start writing sports gossip. As long as this stays fair. The second I see either one of you pulling punches on the other, or if she gets information I know came from you, I'm telling both of your superiors."

I nod. "I understand."

Tommy eyes Hunter again. "McAvoy."

Hunter straightens himself. "Yes, sir?"

Tommy puts his hand on Hunter's shoulder and gives it a squeeze. "Off the record. If you hurt this girl, you'll need to find a new job. You won't want to face The Mob if you do."

This makes Hunter laugh. "Yes, sir. And I don't plan on it."

Tommy seems satisfied with that answer. "I'm leaving now. You two do whatever you were going to do when I wasn't supposed to be here. See you both in New Orleans."

Hunter and I both let out huge breaths the second Tommy leaves the room.

"I am so sorry," he says, taking my other hand in his. "I had no clue he was here."

I shrug. "I know you didn't know. It was bound to happen sooner or later."

We both lean in, our foreheads now touching. We stand like that for more than a few minutes, letting everything process.

"I think I was more scared of him than your dad," Hunter says, which makes me laugh.

"I think I was more scared for his reaction than my dad's." And that's the truth. I just didn't realize it until the second Hunter walked into the room.

"Can we trust him?" Hunter's question is legitimate. He doesn't know Tommy like I do. To him, he's just another reporter. To me? He might be one of my rivals, but he's also a good friend.

"We can. But we need to be more careful."

"No more sneaking in for a kiss goodbye," Hunter says, crossing his heart with his fingers. "I promise."

"What kiss? There hasn't been any kiss."

My words light a spark in Hunter's eyes as he closes the distance between us, bringing our lips together. Considering that we are doing it in a space that is hugely forbidden and fraught with danger, the intensity is amplified in ways I wasn't expecting.

"What time is your flight?" I ask, my finger stroking down the front of his shirt.

"I don't have to be at the airport for another two hours."

I turn away from him and quickly pack up my laptop. "Then we better get a move on so I can tell you goodbye properly."

35

———————

HUNTER

I look back over my shoulder to Sadie, who is getting ready in our en suite bathroom in our hotel in New Orleans. "Weird in a good way I hope."

She shrugs, exiting the bathroom in nothing but her white lace bra and panties, her hair styled and makeup done. I swallow the lump in my throat because damn, that's a sight I could never get tired of seeing.

I don't get to see her like this often. Sadie isn't a frills kind of woman. Don't get me wrong, I love her exactly how she is. I fell in love with the girl who throws her hair on top of her head and forgets most mornings to put on makeup.

But getting to see this side of Sadie? It's like a gift. A gift I plan on cherishing, then unwrapping later.

"Yes, weird in a good way. We've barely gone on any real dates. A double date feels so scandalous," she says before slipping on a dress that takes my breath away. It's simple, and it hugs every one of her curves. The navy material in contrast to the white lingerie underneath it is doing things for me.

And for my dick.

I stand up and force myself to quit watching her get dressed. If I keep doing this, we are never leaving the room, and that bra and panty set will be wrecked.

"Brady and Kendra can't wait to meet you. Plus, we get to indulge in authentic New Orleans cuisine on his tab."

When Sadie and I decided to stay behind in New Orleans after yesterday's game—a game in which we kicked ass and took names, giving us two wins in a row—I got a hold of my old college roommate. Marcus Brady is a New Orleans boy through and through. He and his brother grew up in one of the worst parishes in the city. His family was homeless for a few months after Katrina. He and his brother were determined not to just be another statistic. So, they came up with a plan. Marcus went to Alabama on a football scholarship and got his business degree. His brother went to culinary school. Now we are about to eat at his critically reviewed restaurant right off the French Quarter.

We understood each other in college. We might have come from two completely different backgrounds and upbringings, but we knew what it was like for playing football to not be our end game. He followed his heart. He understood when I followed mine. He was my biggest supporter when I declared that I was pursuing a coaching career and not turning pro.

"I heard his restaurant is amazing," Sadie said, walking over to me so I can zip the back of her dress.

"Not as amazing as you look tonight," I say, placing a soft kiss on her shoulder after I finish helping with her dress.

"That was cheesy, even for you, McAvoy," she teases.

"I speak only truths," I say, turning her around to face me. "Now, let's get out of here before I take this dress back off and fuck you senseless."

"HOW IN THE hell are you dating the reporter who asked Coach the question to end all questions, and you are *just now* telling me this!"

We made it halfway through dinner before I dropped that fun fact. That story has officially won Sadie over in Brady's eyes.

Not that she needed it.

As soon as we arrived, I knew tonight was going to be amazing. She and Brady's wife, Kendra, hit it off immediately. I believe at some point during the night when we were catching up on former teammates, the two of them were sharing social media information.

The dinner was excellent. The company was better. All in all, this has been a perfect night.

A perfect, normal night.

I look over at Sadie, who is now engrossed in Kendra's photos of their dog, and all I can do is smile. I can't wait until we can tell the world about us. I can't wait until I can take her out on the town regularly, not just when we are away from the prying eyes of Nashville.

I want to give her normal. I want to give her everything. I want to give her anything she asks for.

"All right, boys, it's time for you to talk about us as we go to the ladies' room," Kendra announces.

"Who said we were going to talk about you?"

She leans over and gives Brady a kiss on the cheek. "Because I know you, Marcus. We'll be at least ten minutes. Enjoy your man time."

Sadie gives me a small wave as she and Kendra link arms and walk away from the table.

"You got it bad, bro."

I look over at Marcus, not realizing I was so transparent. "Is it that obvious?"

Marcus chuckles as he takes a sip of his drink. "I've known you too many years, McAvoy. I've never seen you look at a woman like that. And the fact that you're willing to put your career on the line for her speaks volumes."

"She's worth it," I say matter-of-factly.

I wasn't about to lie to Marcus in regard to who Sadie is. He was shocked, to say the least. He knows from my college days that I was never a huge fan of the media. He promised that he wouldn't treat her any differently tonight, and he has kept his word.

"She seems good for you," he continues. "How does it work between you two? Do you just not talk about your jobs?"

"There is more to me than football. Give me some credit."

His eyebrow quirks up, clearly seeing through my attempt at bullshit. "Since the moment I met you freshman year, all you've wanted to do is coach. You had more notebooks for plays you drew up than for your schoolwork. You would talk for hours about plays and strategies. Even to the girls you dated for five seconds. So, you're going to sit here and tell me you and Sadie don't talk about football or work at all?"

Well, shit. He's not wrong. But I deflect.

"We have much more important things to do other than talk football."

I wag my eyebrows for emphasis. The answer is that I want to talk to Sadie about my day. She is likely the one woman on the planet who would get just as excited as I do about cracking the code to an opposition's defense.

But we can't. That's the line neither of us can cross.

"Fine. You don't want to answer that. But riddle me this, McAvoy, when Gordon retires and you become the head coach of the Fury, how will that work between you two? Are you *not* going to tell the woman you clearly love that you are up for a promotion?"

Brady's words stun me. I don't think I blink for a solid minute.

I mean, I've thought about that possibility. Gordon isn't getting any younger, and his contract is up after next season. If I have success, it could very well happen that I'm promoted to head coach.

"You haven't thought about that, have you?" Brady asks, breaking me out of my shock.

"I honestly haven't. Not in detail anyway. No one has talked about it, and I've had enough on my plate trying to fix this offense. I'll cross that bridge when it happens."

"You better figure it out soon. I saw Gordon's press conference last week. The man looks old. It could be your turn before you know it."

"Whose turn is it for what?" Kendra says as she and Sadie make their way back to the table. I didn't even see them coming.

"I was just saying that Hunter's boss looks to be only a few steps away from the grave. Our man could be the youngest head coach in football history."

I shoot Brady a glare as I slip my arm around Sadie's shoulders.

"What?" Brady asks. "I'm not exactly giving your girl top-secret information."

I turn to look at Sadie as Brady and Kendra shift away from football conversation to ordering dessert. And from what it sounds like, they are ordering the entire menu.

"You know he was just joking, right?" I ask, making sure she understands that it's not happening.

"Was he joking that Gordon is old? Because if he's actually only twenty-two, then that's the story I need to write."

I laugh, appreciating her deflective humor. "No one has talked to me about a job. Gordon isn't retiring anytime soon. He was just talking in hypotheticals."

Sadie doesn't respond right away, instead leaning a little closer, kissing my cheek. "Don't worry, Hunter. It's off the record. And not a thing. Your conversation, and Brady's imagination, are safe with me."

Everyone at the table falls into an easy conversation but me. I can't get Brady's words out of my head.

When Gordon does decide to retire, which will be after next season, at the earliest, Sadie and I would be out in the public by then. I'd be able to talk to her about the promotion then, right? I mean, this is the woman I can see myself spending the rest of my life with. I'd have to be able to talk to her about my future job.

I can't think about that now. That's a problem to think about a long time in the future.

36

HUNTER

I'M NOT one of those coaches who circles games on calendars. Every game is important. Every win is one more step to the playoffs.

However, I circled this game from the moment the schedule came out.

We hosted Cincinnati. Also known as Nick Bancroft's new team.

And we won. Correction. We kicked his fucking ass.

I've never met the man. However, that hasn't stopped him from spewing lies and bullshit to anyone who will listen about his firing from the Fury from the moment he was let go. And lies about why they hired me.

He was crying that he was unjustly fired. That he didn't get a fair shake and his firing "came out of nowhere." He even threw out that the only reason I was hired was because the owner of the Fury was an Alabama graduate, and he was doing a favor for my dad. He even insinuated that my dad financially bribed the owner to hire me.

Those words meant war. After I heard that, I grabbed the red Sharpie out of my desk drawer and put a huge circle around this game.

I didn't have to motivate my players much for this week. The returning players hated him. They were more than happy to see him fired and wanted to stick it to him just as bad as I did.

Add all of that up, and it meant a big win for the Fury: 48-13.

More importantly? That's now five wins in a row.

That's right. After starting off the season 0-4, we are now 5-4, and all signs are pointing up. The offense has clicked. Bryce is making a case to be the Rookie of the Year. The defense is playing amazing. Everything is fucking fantastic.

"Helluva game plan, Hunter," Coach Gordon says to me, giving me a slap on the back as I make my way out of the locker room to the coaches' offices. "I still can't believe the turnaround we've made."

"You and me both, sir."

My words aren't meant to be humble. I still have no fucking clue how everything turned around. I'm not about to look a gift horse in the mouth, though.

"Are you on your way to the press conference?" I ask, knowing that the reporters' room is just a few steps away.

"Yeah." Irritation laced in his one word. "They wanted to interview Bancroft since it's the first time he's been back. They had to grab him right off the field because they thought he'd duck out if they didn't."

"I'd love to be a fly on the wall to hear what shit he's telling them."

"Let's go listen," Gordon says, nodding his head toward the interview room.

"Really?"

"Hell yeah. That man was a fucking cancer in our locker room. If he's spreading lies about me in front of The Mob, I at least want to know what he's saying so I know how to respond."

The man is devious and smart. It's probably why he's as successful as he is.

We make our way to the interview room and stand in the open doorway, which is in the back. We have a clear view of the interview room without drawing attention to ourselves. I am staring at Bancroft, who is trying to feed lines of bullshit to The Mob.

The room is smaller than the one at the practice facility. The reporters are a little more jammed together. I take a quick look around for Sadie, who, like always, is sitting up front. I can't help but smile watching her in action. Luckily, Coach Gordon doesn't notice my reaction as I watch my girlfriend raise her hand to ask the next question.

I hope she rips Bancroft a new asshole.

"Coach Bancroft, you were quoted as saying that you weren't given proper warning about being fired. Can you clarify those comments, specifically the part where an employer is supposed to give an employee they plan to terminate a warning that they are, in fact, being let go?"

That's my girl.

Sadie's question, like every one she asks, is with intent and has thought behind it. And I can see by the look in Bancroft's eyes he has not missed her line of questioning.

"Oh, Benson. It's been a while since I've been on the receiving end of one of your close-the-press-conference questions. I wish I could say I missed them."

"And I wish I could say I miss you not answering them. So, I must ask, is that your answer?"

His eyes fill with anger at Sadie's snarky response. "No, Benson. My answer is that after all the years I put into this team, all the years I spent making this franchise a name around the league, I was let go without so much of a hint of a notice. There weren't even talks of them looking to get rid of me. That's not good business. I thought this franchise was better than that."

"Follow up, please." Sadie doesn't even wait for Paul to tell her yes. "The team had its worst offensive year in history last year. Are you saying that as the offensive coordinator, that a performance like that wasn't a fireable offense?"

Bancroft's face is now a shade of red I didn't know existed. "I'm saying that good football business gives someone the chance to turn it around."

"Are you accusing the Fury of bad or malicious business practices?"

"I'm saying that they did bad business and then brought in the owner's golden boy to replace me. That is all. Are we done yet, Benson?"

"Damn, Benson is giving Bancroft the business," Gordon whispers as we watch Sadie and Bancroft stare each other down. "That woman is a damn shark."

She is, which is what has me nervous right now. Especially when she asks her next question.

"No. I have one more question," Sadie begins. "Would you have been able to turn it around? You have said that good business would have allowed you the chance to right the ship. Hypothetically speaking, if you were to have stayed employed, would you have been able to do what the Fury has been doing the past five games?"

I see the moment that Bancroft loses it. And there is nothing anyone can do to stop it.

"Do I think I would have been able to turn it around? Could I win with an offense led by a prodigy quarterback? Anyone can. What McAvoy is doing right now is nothing special, and I'm tired of everyone thinking he's God's fucking gift to offenses. You've asked a lot of idiotic questions over the years, Benson, but this is the dumbest. Which shouldn't surprise me since everyone knows you were a token hire. You don't know shit about football, and it's clear you still don't. I can't believe you still have a job. Who are you fucking these days for your information? It's McAvoy, isn't it? Yeah, I heard you two have a thing going on. He the one you getting on your knees for these days for the scoop?"

I don't even remember bursting into the room. I don't remember grabbing Bancroft by the shirt and pulling him away from the podium to punch him. I don't remember Paul or Coach Gordon pulling me off of him. I don't remember the cameras flashing.

I do remember yelling at him to not say a fucking word about her or I'll do a lot worse than break his nose.

And I remember the second my eyes lock on to Sadie. She looks shocked. Afraid. Confused. Angry. Sad.

And then it hits me.

We are no longer a secret.

37

SADIE

I'M NEVER SUPPOSED to be the story.

Yet here I am, the talk of professional football.

You can't pick up a newspaper, turn on the television or the radio without hearing someone talk about what happened between me, Hunter, and Bancroft.

Nick Bancroft loses cool over questions from *Banner* reporter

Nick Bancroft fired after inappropriate remarks to *Banner* reporter

Hunter McAvoy comes to defense of *Banner* reporter

Love in the air? Hunter McAvoy and *Banner* reporter rumored to be in relationship

Pictures emerge of Hunter McAvoy, *Banner* reporter together on romantic getaway

Pro football's most eligible bachelor off the market?

Funny how my name is never mentioned in the headline. That doesn't mean I've been anonymous in this. My picture is everywhere. The story was all over the Internet immediately. It's not every day a coach goes on a tirade against a reporter and another coach attacks him for said tirade.

As for the pictures of me and Hunter in New Orleans? I can't prove it, but I have a feeling Nick Bancroft has everything to do with those even existing. It's no secret he has been trying to smear Hunter's name since the day he replaced him. Do I think he leaked them personally to the gossip sites? No. The timing doesn't fit. But I'll go to my grave saying he hired someone to follow Hunter to try and tarnish his image and that person knows a payday when they see one.

The fact that I was with him was icing on the cake.

Rat bastard.

Bancroft was probably holding on to those photos until the perfect time to try and get Hunter fired. Maybe he was waiting until after this game?

Even if this wasn't how he planned on it, he still might get his wish.

We're outed. Busted. And now all we can do is let the chips fall where they may.

My phone hasn't stopped ringing since everything went down yesterday. Even as I'm sitting on the well-worn couch in John's office, I can feel it vibrating with some sort of alert every five seconds.

I read some of the stories and comments. Some have been in defense of me and Hunter. Others have now speculated that the only way I've been able to do my job is because I was sleeping with a coach. I didn't point out that I was doing this job long before Hunter was hired, but the haters don't want to hear that.

And those weren't even the worst. There were ones calling me names. There were the trolls saying this is why women shouldn't be allowed in locker rooms. In one day I've created a media shit storm about reporter and coach relations and women covering male sports.

God, has it only been a day? It feels like so much longer. Probably because I didn't sleep. I couldn't. I was too shook by everything. And I haven't talked to Hunter. I think that's what's killing me the most.

Is he okay? Does he still have a job? Are they forcing him to pick between me and the Fury? All of those are possibilities.

They are the same for me.

I've been waiting, okay, fine, hiding, in John's office for the past hour. He's talking with his bosses about how to "handle" the situation.

Who knew a few hard questions would send Bancroft off like that? Who knew Hunter was listening? Who knew that in just a few seconds my life would be flipped upside down?

"I've told you for years to make sure you have a work-life balance. This was not what I meant," John's words hit hard as he walks into his office, taking a seat behind his desk.

I can't even look at him yet. My head is in my hands, staring at the floor. "This wasn't supposed to happen this way."

"How was it supposed to happen, Sadie? Tell me how in the world this was supposed to happen where everyone came out smelling like fucking roses."

I nearly flinch at John's tone. Though it's deserving, this is the first time he has ever raised his voice to me.

I finally look up at him. All I see is anger and disappointment in his eyes. "We planned on coming forward at the end of the season. We figured that if we made it through a football season without our relationship affecting our performances, then neither you nor the Fury could object. Was it optimistic and probably a little foolish? Yes. But we both agreed it was worth a shot."

"Worth a shot? Me trying a different ice cream flavor is worth a shot. You don't do something that could jeopardize everything you've worked for because it's *worth a shot.*"

"It's more than that," I say, his words making this situation seem so black-and-white when it's not.

"Please, tell me, Sadie. Please tell me how it is more than you two being reckless with both of your jobs."

"Because I love him." His eyes go wide at my declaration. "Because for the first time in my life I didn't want to work twenty hours a day. Because even if you fire me right now, I know that I'm going to be okay because I have him in my life."

John is speechless. I don't blame him. I'm speechless, and I said those words. But they are all true.

I realized them before. I knew all of that in my head, but I never admitted it out loud. Hunter showed me that I'm not just my job. I'm more than just a reporter. He showed me there was more to life than breaking news and writing about football. He showed me what it was like to have a partner who supports you and wants you to succeed, and isn't jealous of the time you don't spend with him.

He showed me what true love is.

"How long have you two been together?" John asks.

"Before the draft."

My answer makes him give me a curious look. "You're meaning to tell me that you were dating Hunter McAvoy at the same time that you wrote that he might not be cut out for the job and that he was in over his head?"

I can't help but laugh. "Yeah. He didn't take too kindly to that one."

Now it's John's turn to laugh. "I bet not."

We're back to being silent. I have no idea which way this will go. There is one huge elephant sitting in this room, and I have to address it before I explode.

"Am I fired?"

"Before I can answer that. I have to ask you a few questions."

I take a big swallow. "Anything."

"Has he given you information as an unnamed source?"

I shake my head. "No. We have a strict rule that neither of us talks about work in front of the other. My sources with the team are in the front office, not on the coaching staff."

"Would you be willing to allow another reporter to interview him on days when he gives his press conferences, to make sure that we aren't accused of unfair treatment."

I nod my head. "Yes. I would like to be in the room, though, in case I need anything for future stories."

"That's fine. As long as you promise me from here on out that you will not use any privileged information, or that if there is a conflict of interest, you come to me immediately. With that, I see no reason to fire you. However, at the end of the season we need to reevaluate things and your position."

The sigh of relief I let out could be heard throughout the city. "Thank you, John. And for what it's worth, I'm sorry I lied. I hated it. I just didn't see another way."

He gives me a sympathetic nod. "As your boss, I'm sorry you had to lie to me as well. This could have gone very different, but I appreciate that both of you were cautious and thought about this fully. Also, as your boss, I would highly consider you pursuing the *US Daily* job. You wouldn't be covering the Fury every day, which means that it won't be a conflict of interest for you two to stay together."

He's right. The *US Daily* position is a national job. I'd be writing in-depth, investigative stories around the league. I haven't heard from them in a few weeks since my phone interview.

That's not even taking into account the events of the past day. Who knows if they would even consider hiring me now? Who would want to hire the reporter who just made national headlines for having a romantic relationship with a coach?

Maybe I shot myself in the foot for a chance at *US Daily*. Or maybe I could write such a big story they would have no choice but to hire me. Scandal or not.

I stand up from the couch, suddenly feeling more relieved. "Thanks, John. I appreciate… well, everything."

He holds up a finger, signaling me to stop. "You didn't let me finish. That was me as your boss. Now, as your friend and a man who has known you a long time, I'm happy for you. I was really worried that you were going to become one of the statistics that this industry is known for producing."

"What kind of statistic?" I ask, genuinely curious.

"The kind that works themselves to death because they feel they have to, then before they know it, their whole life has gone by and they haven't lived it. You deserve to live your life, Sadie. And if it's with Hunter, then he's a lucky guy."

38

HUNTER

Girlfriend: I'm still employed. How about you?

Boyfriend: Let's put it this way, it worked to my benefit that we're on a winning streak.

Girlfriend: Can I come over?

Boyfriend: Please do.

Girlfriend: Pizza and beer?

Boyfriend: Add breadsticks and whiskey.

Girlfriend: See you soon. I love you.

Boyfriend: I love you more.

I STEP into my condo and re-read her text messages, making sure I read what I did.

Thank God she's okay.

I grab a bottle of water before collapsing on the couch as a wave of relief rushes through me. If Sadie wasn't on her way over, I'd fall asleep right here. Instead, I force myself to keep my eyes open as the last twenty-four hours plays on repeat.

"About time you got home."

"What the fuck?" I can't help but scream as I jump off of my couch only to see my mother coming out of my bathroom. "How? What? Why are you here?"

"I saw your press conference today," she says, making her way to sit next to me. "I wanted to make sure you were all right. I also wanted to yell at you for having a girlfriend and neglecting to tell me about her."

This ought to be good.

I straighten myself while simultaneously preparing myself for what's about to come. My mom's interrogation is about to be ten-times worse than the one I got from the team.

"You didn't bring Bo along to read me the riot act?"

In a move I have never seen Francine McAvoy do in my twenty-eight years, she rolls her eyes at the mention of my father.

"Let's put it this way, your father is on my list. We were driving back to Birmingham last night after the game when we heard the story come across the radio. I didn't care for what he had to say about you and Sadie, and I let him know that. I also wasn't very pleased with him after the argument I heard you two had, but I figured you two would make up in due time. But if he ever wants to be allowed to sleep in his bed again, then he better get his head out of his ass when it comes to you. I dropped him off, told him to get his mind right, and that I was going back to Nashville to see my baby and the woman he felt he needed to hide from me."

My eyes grow wide before I let out a laugh that comes straight from my gut. "You're making him sleep on the couch because of me and Sadie?"

"Darn right I am. He started spewing some nonsense about you and my future daughter-in-law, and how it wasn't right and that both of you were not thinking with the right parts of your body. I told him what I thought of that, and that until he pulled his head out of his ass, he can make himself comfy in his study."

There's a lot I want detail about, but there's one part I can't glaze over. "Did you say future daughter-in-law?"

She smiles. It's the kind of smile that only a mother can wear when she knows something her child has yet to realize. "Yes, Hunter. My future daughter-in-law. I don't know much about modern datin', but I doubt you'd punch another man if this girl was… what do the kids call it? Friends with benefits?"

I nearly spit out my water. "What do you know about friends with benefits?"

"Oh, Hunter," she says, waving off my comment like I just said something ridiculous. "I know things. I watch TikToks."

That's a conversation for another day.

"Back to you and Sadie," she says, folding her hands across her lap. "Are you two okay? What did the Fury say?"

I take the next ten minutes to fill my mother in on everything I wasn't allowed to talk about at the press conference the Fury made me do today in response to my "altercation" with Bancroft. The press conference where I had to pretend to be sorry for punching that asshole. I gave a statement, answered two questions—both from Tommy because he is the only one I trusted—and left. I know they wanted more. They wanted the sordid details of Sadie's and my relationship.

That wasn't about to happen.

After Gordon and a few of the security guards dragged me off of Bancroft, I was immediately taken back to Neil, the general manager's, office. There I was greeted by Neil, Coach Gordon, and Mr. Henderson, the owner of the Fury. Though greeted makes it sound like they were happy to see me.

They were not.

I knew at that point there was nothing to hide. I felt bad telling them everything without talking to Sadie first, but I didn't have a choice.

All three of them were angry when I told them that Sadie and I had been seeing each other for months. They were both equal parts mad that I was, because none of them trust reporters, and also that it was a secret, because they were blindsided by this. However, there is nothing in any rule book or in my contract that says Sadie and I can't have a relationship. Therefore, they can't fire me.

They also can't take away Sadie's press credentials or access, which I was relieved to hear. I assured them that I have not given Sadie insider information. Even though I didn't give them much reason to, they took me on my word that I hadn't. Coach Gordon even laughed about the fact that she wrote an article saying I was in over my head. When I left, they made me promise that I would give Sadie no inside information or tips, and that they would be monitoring her stories closely to make sure it stayed the case.

"So, everything is okay?" my mom asks, making sure she didn't miss anything.

"Except for the fact that I have a bruised hand, will likely have to pay a fine to the league for attacking Bancroft and my bosses aren't super trusting of me right now, yeah. Everything worked out."

"That makes me so happy," Mom says, standing up to take my empty bottle of water to the kitchen. "I would have hated for you two to have ended things. What about a spring wedding? That's a good time of the year for both of you. Right?"

"Slow down," I say, following her to the kitchen where she is now wiping down my counter that doesn't need cleaning. "How do you know that Sadie is the one for me? I've never talked to you about her. You met her once, and that was before we were dating. Please tell me how you've come to this conclusion based on the limited knowledge you have of my relationship."

She stops and gives me that knowing smile again. "I told you, I watched the press conference today. What aren't you getting?"

I stare at her in confusion. "I don't understand how watching a press conference equates to you knowing that Sadie and I are going to get married."

She takes a few steps toward me and puts her hand over mine. She used to do this when I came to her after Bo and I had a fight. It always made me feel like everything would be okay. "When I watched you talk about her today, you had that look in your eye. I've only seen you have that look once in your life, and that's when you told me and your daddy that you wanted to become a coach. You were so sure of yourself. You knew it was it for you. That's what I saw today, Hunter. You know it's her. You know she's the one. And now that you don't have to hide anything, maybe you two can really start your lives together."

As if on cue, Sadie comes walking into my condo, pizza and booze in hand.

"Oh! Mrs. McAvoy! I-I didn't know you'd be here."

Sadie barely has a chance to put down the supplies before my mom nearly tackles her in a hug.

"My sweet girl. I knew you were special the day we met," Mom says, and if I had to guess, she's fighting back tears right now. "Be good to my boy. And when he messes up, because he's a man and he will, don't hesitate to call me. Lord knows I have years of experience with his father."

This makes us both laugh. "I will. Thank you, Mrs. McAvoy."

"Oh no. There will be none of that," Mom says, grabbing her purse off the counter. "Mrs. McAvoy was my mother-in-law. Dreadful woman. God rest her soul. You will call me Francine or Mom."

I make my way over to Sadie, bringing her into my side. "Thank you… Francine. I hope we didn't upset you by not telling you. It was… complicated."

"I understand," Mom says, giving me a kiss on the cheek before doing the same to Sadie. "It doesn't mean I like it. But I understand. That just means you two owe me a visit. I get you for a whole day. And a weekend when the season is over. And breakfast tomorrow."

My mom wraps Sadie in one more hug and gives me a kiss on the cheek before she makes her way out of my condo and to her hotel where she'll be staying tonight.

"Sorry about that," I say, wrapping my arms around her waist. "I had no idea she was here."

"It's fine," she says, her arms looping around my neck. "I'm glad we got to see her. Now she knows. Now there's no more hiding."

She's right. Now that my family and our jobs know, we are completely free. No more hiding. No more sneaking around.

"We're free," I say, though I didn't mean for it to play out that way.

"We are."

"What do you want to do first? Date night? Movie? Want to go downtown and see some music? You name it and it's yours."

She doesn't respond. Instead, she leans up and kisses me.

"I want you to make love to me. I want you to make me forget the past few days happened. I want to get lost in you."

I don't hesitate. I sweep her up in my arms, ready to make both of us forget the past two days. "That I can do."

39

———

SADIE

I'VE GOTTEN USED to Hunter carrying me to his room. In fact, I now look forward to it.

Especially tonight. After the last two days, I need to feel as close to him as possible. I need to feel myself pressed against his chest. And if I'm reading his body language right, he needs this too.

Typically when he carries me to bed, he sets me down, strips himself, strips me, then we fall into each other's arms.

This is why I'm confused as to what is happening. Instead of going up the stairs, Hunter is making his way outside to his patio.

"Where are we going?"

"Trust me, gorgeous."

The weather is reasonably warm for October. That's not the problem. The problem is that Hunter lives in a condo development. With neighbors.

"Hunter..." I want to ask what he's thinking, but my brain is immediately scattered when I feel his mouth on my neck.

He doesn't respond. Instead, he lifts my shirt over my head. The October air hits my skin and sends chills up my spine. They don't last long. My body is rushed with heat when Hunter's mouth moves to kissing the tops of my breasts, his cock growing harder against my center.

"Don't worry. My neighbors are gone for the week," Hunter says before switching his mouth to the other side. "It's just you and me out here. And we don't have to hide anymore. From anyone."

Now it all makes sense. Before we had to stay inside. We were essentially trapped. Now it doesn't matter who sees us. Let them. We have nothing more to be afraid of.

We're Sadie and Hunter. And we don't give a damn who knows about us.

That thought spurs me on, and before I know it, I'm slinking down off of his lap onto my knees.

"Sadie... baby... you don't have to."

"Shh," I say, unzipping Hunter's pants. "I want to. And like you said, we aren't hiding."

I lick my lips as his cock springs free. It's already hard and it's begging for me to take it into my mouth. I give him one slow lick from base to tip before circling my tongue around his crown.

"You're killing me, gorgeous. Fucking killing me."

I slowly take every inch of him into my mouth, which makes Hunter groan so loud I'd bet the condo three units down heard him. He doesn't care. Neither do I. I begin going up and down on his shaft, my tongue circling him as I go. I'm using one hand to cover where my mouth isn't, and my other hand is quickly taken in his. His hips are moving into my mouth as if he has no control over his movements.

Every time I do this to Hunter, he has to touch me in some way. Sometimes it's my hair. He'll take it in his hand and work me up and down on him. Sometimes he'll take my fingers and slowly kiss them one by one.

This time Hunter has decided to give my chest special attention. He has edged my cups down, letting my breasts spill out. As I work his cock in and out of my mouth, he flicks my nipples, which sends immediate shocks to my center.

"Baby, I'm not going to last long if you keep that up," he says, his breath ragged.

"Neither am I," I say, his movements in conjunction with what I'm doing to him are too much for my brain, and my body, to handle.

"Stand up, baby. Stand up right now."

I don't argue. I slowly get to my feet, and as soon as I'm upright, Hunter is peeling my pants and panties down to my ankles before shoving his jeans down just enough to allow him some movement.

He doesn't say another word. Instead, he takes my hand and pulls me toward him. Our lips find each other as if there are magnets pulling us in. My legs immediately go to either side of his, and I slowly lower myself onto him.

We both let out a loud moan of pleasure as he fills me. I will never get tired of this. This feeling of being claimed. This feeling of being wanted. This feeling of being loved.

Hunter's hips begin to move in a slow rhythm, and my hips are answering to his every thrust. This will never go down as the most comfortable place we've had sex—that award will forever belong to the hotel we stayed at in New Orleans—but this night will live in my memory forever.

We made it. Months of hiding and lying are over. We don't need to watch who we are around when we text. We don't have to use code names. We can just be us.

And right here, on Hunter's patio, is us at our best.

"You're mine, Sadie," Hunter says into my neck, his strong arms holding me tightly against him as his thrusts begin to pick up speed. "Forever."

"Forever."

My words come out in a whisper before I let out a gasp. Hunter is hitting a spot in me I didn't know existed, and without warning, my center is clenching him as I'm ready to explode.

"Fuck, Sadie!"

I hold off just long enough so Hunter comes with me. We sit there for a long time. He's grown soft, but he's still inside me, and neither of us are in a rush to move.

We don't have to be in a rush at all now. We can go at our own pace. We can go as fast or as slow as we want.

We have all the time in the world. And to think, just a few months ago we were sitting on this same porch, deciding to give this a shot.

Now I can't imagine my life if I would have said no.

"I love you, Sadie. I love you so damn much."

I look up at Hunter and see nothing but love in his eyes. Is this always how it's going to be? God, I hope so.

Now that we're free, I can't wait to start truly living everyday with this man.

"I love you, too, Hunter. More than I can ever say."

40

HUNTER

HOLY HELL.

We're going to make the playoffs.

There's less than a month left in the regular season—four games, to be exact—and we'd have to lose all four to not be in the postseason. Considering the teams we are playing are at the bottom of the league, I like our chances.

I kick my feet up on my desk and let out the most peaceful sigh of contentment. Everything in my life is just about perfect. Sadie and I are amazing. We decided that after the season she's moving into my condo. We even talked about getting a dog.

As for things with the Fury? I couldn't be happier with how this season has gone. Yes, it started off rough. But honestly, I think it made us better. It made us work harder. If Bryce doesn't win Rookie of the Year, it will be a shock. I have no fears about being fired at the end of the season, and I'm happy to let this wave ride for as long as it will go.

Hopefully, that's to a championship game.

"Oh good, you're still here."

I turn toward my door as Coach Gordon stands in the frame. "Yup. I was getting ahead for the next few days of practice."

"You don't need to do that," he says, batting my words away with this hand. "We're playing Pittsburgh. Come on. Walk with me."

I grab my phone from my desk and join Coach Gordon. Sadie should be texting me any minute to let me know that she and Bethany are done with their girls' day, which means it's my cue to grab Davis and meet them for drinks.

Yes. We're going on a double date with Bethany and Davis. The most girly-girl I have ever met, paired with the guy who most days acts like he's still eighteen.

I don't know how I let her talk me into this. Well, I do. She was naked. I do most things she tells me to do when she's naked.

We pass by Coach Gordon's office and continue walking toward the executives' offices. You only come here if you're getting hired or fired.

"Wipe that scared look off your face," Coach Gordon says, obviously figuring out that I've turned an interesting shade of white. "You aren't in trouble. At least, not yet."

He lets out an evil laugh at his joke, which does not ease my mind whatsoever.

He stops in front of the general manager's office and signals me to take a step inside. I've been here twice. Once during my interview, and once when I had to explain to him how I was not giving my girlfriend inside information.

When I step inside, it's not just Neil. Paul is in the room, as well as Mr. Henderson, the Fury's owner. Quickly exiting the room is Neil's secretary. I think her name is Tina? Tonya?

"Hunter, glad you could join us," Mr. Henderson says. "Please, take a seat."

I look anxiously around the room as I sit at a small conference table in the corner of Neil's office. "Am I in some sort of trouble?"

Mr. Henderson shakes his head. "Not in the least. We wanted to bring you in today because what you have done with the offense this year is something to be commended. Especially with a rookie quarterback."

"Thank you," I say, feeling a little more confident in his words. "It wasn't easy at first. It took a lot of work. I'm glad it's paying off. For all of us."

"How you handled and came back from that early stuff was impressive, Hunter. As well as the media circus that came after the Bancroft situation. Not many coaches would have been able to navigate those waters. Not only did you survive them, you thrived after."

Neil's words are setting off little warning bells in my head. I've had small conversations with Coach Gordon and Neil about the turnaround. At this point, it's almost old news. And they've never brought up Bancroft. So why now?

"Put him out of his misery, Neil. Just tell him already before he throws up on your fancy carpet."

I look at Coach Gordon and then back to Neil. Then from Neil to Mr. Henderson. "Tell me what?"

"Coach Gordon is retiring at the end of this season. And we are hoping that you will want to take over and be the next head coach of the Nashville Fury."

Everything in the room stops. I play the words over and over in my head. Coach Gordon was right. I might vomit.

"I thought you had another year on your contract?" I ask Coach Gordon, because this was the last thing I was expecting.

"Technically, I do," he says, looking very nonchalant for a man who helped drop the biggest bomb on me of my life. "But there is wording in my contract that I can back out at any time with enough notice. That's the beauty of being as old as I am. My wife doesn't want to wait another year for me to be done. Something about grandkids and she's tired of spending weekends alone."

"This is why we brought you on, Hunter," Mr. Henderson adds. "We knew that you could do this, and you've proven yourself, son. None of us can think of a better man to guide the Fury into the future."

I'm stunned. I have no clue what to say.

My head is spinning.

I'm the man for the future of the Fury?

Yes, we've had success this year. I just didn't expect a head coaching offer to be on my radar for at least another two years, at the earliest. I figured teams would want to see how I developed players and offenses for at least another couple of seasons.

"What questions do you have for us," Neil asks. "And don't say none. I see the wheels in your head working overtime."

I give my head a shake, because I don't know what to ask first.

"Would I be able to still call the offensive plays?"

Neil nods. "If that's what you want to do. Yes. All play calling and coaching personnel decisions are yours. You and I will work together on player personnel."

I nod, liking that answer. "Who knows about this?"

"Just the men in this room," Coach Gordon says. "And we need it to stay that way until the season is over. Is that clear, Hunter? No one can know. Do you understand what we are saying?"

And there it is. The stern warning that I can't tell Sadie. Which I hate. Aren't you supposed to be able to tell the woman you love about an amazing job opportunity? Aren't you supposed to be able to bask in this glory with the person you love?

This is just a cruel reminder that we might be known to the public, but we still are who we are.

"I understand. I won't say a word."

"Good," Neil says. "We've emailed you preliminary contract details. Just a starting point. Send them to your agent. When the season is over, we'll circle back."

"Thank you," I say, standing up and extending my hand to shake all of theirs. "I'll definitely consider it."

"As you should," Mr. Henderson says. "It's not every day a person gets the chance to become the youngest head coach in professional football history. And an Alabama man, no less. Roll Tide!"

I hear polite laughter from the others, but I can't react. My head is spinning. This came out of nowhere, and I'm not sure how to process it.

A vibration from my pocket pulls me from my thoughts. I grab my cell phone to find a text from Sadie saying she and Bethany are ready to meet me and Davis for drinks.

Great. Just great. How am I supposed to plaster on a happy face when I'm also weighing the biggest decision of my life?

41

SADIE

I CAN'T BELIEVE the messages I'm reading right now. Luckily, I'm sitting down as Bethany is trying on yet another dress for our double date tonight.

> T: Girl, Hunter just went into Neil's office with Gordon. Henderson is here too. Paul followed them in, but he looked confused AF. Per usual.

> Sadie: What's going on? Was it on his schedule?

> T: It wasn't. But it seems important if they are all in there. Let me go listen. BRB.

I have to wait for twenty minutes to pass before Tara responds to me. Tara, as in Neil's secretary. Tara, as in my inside source for all things Fury-related.

She knows everything. And Neil is too dumb to realize she does.

Neil is a good general manager. He's apparently a shitty boss, which is why Tara doesn't mind tipping me off when big things are coming down the pike. She's the one who told me about Hunter being hired. Every scoop I've had is because of her, and all because her boss doesn't like to close his door to meetings. I learned quickly the best people for sources in this business aren't the men who run the show, it's the women who hold everything together.

I made friends with Tara on the first day I was assigned to cover the Fury. I bought her a coffee and a donut. We've been tight ever since. And she's never once given me bad information.

> T: GIRL. You aren't gonna believe this shit.

> Sadie: Just tell me! You're killing me.

> T: Gordon is retiring at the end of the season. They want Hunter to be the next head coach. They basically offered him the job. He didn't say yes yet. They aren't saying anything until Hunter makes a decision.

> Sadie: Are you positive? You heard them offer Hunter the head coach job?

> T: I swear on a dozen donuts and my nana's grave that's what I heard. Girl, your man is about to become the head coach of the Fury. Shit, I hear movement. GTG.

"How does this one look? Does it scream, 'I'll eventually put out, but not tonight'?" Bethany asks me, taking my attention away from the news that is burning a hole through my phone.

"Looks great. Totally only half slutty," I say, barely looking at her, hoping my fake enthusiasm comes through.

"Perfect." She bounces back to the dressing room, and I turn my attention back to the messages.

This news is huge. Astronomical.

Jimbo Gordon retiring is the end of an era in football. He's one of the last of his generation. If Hunter accepts the job, which I don't see why he wouldn't, he would become the youngest head coach in pro football history.

The girlfriend in me wants to scream and jump up and down in excitement.

The reporter in me wants to start making phone calls.

No one will see this coming. Gordon has another year left on his contract. How is this even happening? I highly doubt that Tommy, or any of the other writers, are even thinking this is a possibility. I know I didn't when Brady casually brought it up at dinner in New Orleans. And it was so far out there I honestly didn't even think about it again until right now.

That was a hypothetical. This is real life.

I want to run home and start writing. I want to research Gordon's contract and start making calls.

That's what the old Sadie would do. If this were a normal date with some random guy off a dating app, I'd be texting him and canceling to write the story that will make my career.

But I can't. For one, if I canceled, it would devastate Bethany. Once I showed her a picture of Davis, she has not stopped talking about tonight.

Then, there's Hunter. I'm sure he would be suspicious if not only did I cancel, but that I also chose to stay at my apartment for no known reason. I've worked on stories at his condo, but I can't write a story about him while he's sitting twenty feet from me. Plus, I have to tell John. There is a clear conflict of interest, so he will have to put another reporter on this with me to make sure we have all of our bases covered.

None of that can happen until tomorrow. So date night lives on.

"Did you text the guys?" Bethany asks, stepping out of the dressing room donning her new dress and carrying a bag that I'm assuming has her old clothes in it. "I am ready to date."

I take my phone out and send a quick text to Hunter, letting him know we're on our way.

The story will have to wait.

I DON'T KNOW what the point of a double date is when the other couple doesn't acknowledge your existence.

We decided to meet at a bar downtown that has a fun patio and Giant Jenga. What better way for two people to be set up than to have to team up in a battle of skill?

That was the plan. I didn't think they would hit it off so well that an hour into our night they would be cozied up at the bar, every signal pointing to the fact that they are going home together.

Likely soon.

So much for the "I won't put out yet" dress.

Normally, I'd be happy for Bethany. She's had her fair share of dating disappointments. Even if Davis only proves to be a good time for tonight, this girl could use a little fun.

Only problem? With the two of them looking at each other like they want to swallow each other whole, it has left me and Hunter by ourselves.

He has a secret. He doesn't know I know the secret. I can't say that I know the secret.

It's… uncomfortable. Awkward. And it's never uncomfortable with me and Hunter. Yet I'm afraid if I start talking, then somehow I'll spill that I know about his meeting today. I really needed Bethany and Davis to help ease the discomfort.

However, they are too busy eye fucking each other to help me out.

"That seems to be going well," Hunter says, nodding toward Bethany and Davis.

"Yup. We sure know how to match them. Maybe that could be our side hustle. We start a matchmaking business."

Hunter chuckles before taking a sip of his beer. "McAvoy Matchmakers. It has a ring to it."

I quirk an eyebrow. "What about McAvoy and Benson? Where's my credit?"

Hunter smiles and leans a little closer to me. "My hope is that one day your last name will be McAvoy. Problem solved."

My eyes bug out of my head. Marriage? Hunter is thinking about marriage?

"I… you… I… huh?"

This is why I write for a living and don't speak.

Hunter softly laughs, inching closer to me. Still not as close as Bethany and Davis are, who at last glance have no regard that they are in a public place.

"If you didn't know it by now, I'm kind of in love with you," he begins, taking my hand in his. "I've been thinking about the future a lot lately. And every time I do, you're there. I know we don't need to rush it. But I wanted you to know that I'm thinking about it."

I grab my beer and take a healthy drink. Not because the thought of spending the rest of my life with Hunter makes me nervous. But because knowing the information I now know, that he doesn't know I know, makes things very… unknowing.

Hunter will be in Nashville for the foreseeable future. I would also like to be in Nashville. My family is here. My friends are here. It's a no-brainer.

However, if *US Daily* says they want to hire me, but they need me to move to the West Coast, would I turn it down? I used to think that nothing would stop me from turning down a job with them. If they wanted me to cover hockey on the moon I would do it.

Now? Now I'm not sure.

"Sadie?" Hunter says, snapping his fingers in front of my face. "Are you there? Did I freak you out that much? I didn't think you'd be so stunned at the fact that I would one day like to marry you."

"No. Sorry," I say, giving my head a shake. "It just caught me off guard. That's all. I feel like for months everything was so slow, and now because we don't have to hide, it's going warp speed. At first I was worrying about being caught, now I get to wonder if I'll still write under Sadie Benson or Sadie McAvoy."

Wow, that word vomit wasn't a total lie.

"It's fine," he says. "I'm just going on record that one day, even if it doesn't say McAvoy in the newspaper, you'll be a McAvoy to me."

"Sounds good to me," I say, leaning in for a kiss, hoping that will take any attention away from my reaction.

The second our lips touch, Hunter's phone vibrates on our table. He opens up the message app and shows me a text from Davis.

Davis: Come to the bar. They won't let me put drinks on your tab without you.

Hunter groans and all I can do is laugh. "Do you need anything?"

"Sure. Another beer. I'll hold down the fort."

Hunter sets his phone down and makes his way over to the bar. I follow his path and Bethany gives me an enthusiastic thumbs-up. I return the gesture, sincerely happy for her that she's having a good time.

At least one of us is.

42

HUNTER

"I'LL TAKE the chicken Caesar wrap with fries and a sweet tea."

"Coming right up, Hunter."

I smile and drop my tip in the jar before making my way to the other side of the counter to wait for my food. Yes, I'm now on a first-name basis with the staff at Sandwich City.

I can't help but let out a laugh as I lean against the counter. It's been nearly a year since I first walked into this shop. Eleven months, to be exact. On that day, I was hoping that my life was about to change.

It did. In more ways than I even thought possible.

Now I smile because I know it is.

I've told the Fury that I'll accept the position when Coach Gordon decides to retire. He and I had a long chat after our impromptu meeting. He plans on telling the team after the final regular-season game this week. We'll alert the media then.

That's the only part I hate. I hate that Sadie is going to find out that I'm getting the job of my dreams from a press release rather than from me.

Not telling her has been killing me. Every night I want to tell her. I want to be able to share my excitement with her.

But I can't. I know I can't.

And it fucking sucks.

I trust her. I trust her with my life. Hell, the first purchase I plan to make after getting promoted is to buy an engagement ring.

I don't want to put her in a difficult situation. If I told her, she'd feel obligated to report it. She has to. It's her job. And for her to do her job means I might not get mine.

No way they'd promote me if I leaked this information out. So here I am, beating myself up every day that I'm keeping a life-changing secret from the love of my life.

"Hunter! Your order is ready!"

I turn back to the counter and take my to-go bag, needing to head back to the Fury facility. It's Monday, which is strategy day for Coach Gordon, me, and our defensive coordinator. One more week of the regular season, and then it's playoff time.

The chill of Nashville in December hits me as soon as I step outside. It might be the South, but damn, it's cold right now. I reach into my pocket to grab my hat when I feel my phone vibrate from my back pocket. I have no clue if it's a text or a story alert, so I let it go.

The story alerts have been happening like crazy these days. Luckily, all in a good way. Even the national writers are starting to see that my offense is not only innovative, but they've dubbed my system "the offense of the future."

Suck on that, Dad.

I still haven't spoken to him since our blowup at the beginning of the season. He won't apologize first, and like hell if I will. They both come to the games. I can see their season ticket seats from the sideline, but neither stay to talk to me after. When I do talk to Mom, she tries to tell me that he wants to reach out. He also could have just told her that so she'd let him sleep upstairs again.

When I get back to the facility, I'm not prepared for the audience in my office. But standing, and looking angry as hell, are Coach Gordon and Neil.

"Sorry, guys. If I knew you were coming by, I would have ordered for the group."

"Have you seen the latest article in *The Banner?*" Neil asks, clearly not amused by my attempt at a joke.

"I haven't. Then again, the only thing I've read in the last hour is the Sandwich City menu."

Again, my joke falls flat. "What's going on? Why does everyone look like they are ready to punch something?"

"Sadie knows."

I have to blink a few times at Coach Gordon's words.

Sadie knows?

"How? What? I'm confused."

"Check your phone," Neil says, which I do.

If I had checked the notification that I got ten minutes ago, it would have shown me a story from *The Banner,* with a headline that clearly reads:

Hunter McAvoy to be named Fury head coach when Jimbo Gordon retires

What the fuck?

How does she know?

"I'm giving you one chance to tell the truth, Hunter," Neil says, his eyes spitting fire. "Did you tell Sadie after we explicitly told you not to? If you lie to us, you're done."

I shake my head, still confused at everything. "No. I haven't said a word. Hell, I haven't even told my parents. I swear I'm telling the truth. She didn't get this from me."

"Fuck!" Neil yells, nearly pulling his hair out as he paces around my office. "How does she fucking find out these things! I swear to God when I find out who is giving her this information their ass is fired!"

Chaos ensues with everyone running around trying to figure out what fire to put out. I'm just standing there stunned.

How in the hell did she know? No one knew. Five people knew, and none of them would have leaked it. I've been careful around her. I haven't said a word. Hell, if anything, I've been overly quiet.

Where could she have found this out?

Was this from New Orleans? Could this all have stemmed from the conversation that night at dinner with Brady and Kendra? She said she knew what Brady said was off the record. Hell, at that point it was a hypothetical. That doesn't mean though that the idea couldn't have been planted in her head.

Even if that's the case, there is more. There are more pieces to this puzzle. I just don't know what they are.

My phone buzzes again, this time with an email alert. Out of habit, I swipe open the app, and then I see it. Clear as day.

The contract.

No. She wouldn't. Would she? Would Sadie go through my phone?

I want to believe she wouldn't, but right now I can't figure out a better explanation. I leave my phone out around her all the time. She knows my passcode. She would have had plenty of chances to snoop through team emails, just looking to see if she could come up with anything.

"Fucking hell!" Neil yells as he grabs his phone. "Now *US Daily* wants a comment. Fuck. Your little girlfriend has fucked everything up. We were supposed to do this on our terms. Now this is what we're going to be dealing with all week."

Neil stomps out of my office to take the phone call, and I'm left frozen in place.

US Daily. Her job. This was her ticket.

She told me she needed one more big story to lock it down. Well, you don't get much bigger than breaking the news about the hiring of the youngest coach in football history whom you just happen to be in a relationship with.

She used me. She used me for the scoop of a lifetime.

"Your girl really did a number on us, McAvoy. A real fucking number."

Coach Gordon turns and leaves my office. I'm left standing behind my desk, ready to punch something.

Sadie fooled me once, thinking she was different. She might not have used me to get to Bo, but she sure as hell used me for herself.

And that's much worse.

43

———

SADIE

HUNTER HASN'T CALLED.

He hasn't messaged.

He hasn't said a thing.

And I have a feeling I know what's coming.

I hope I'm wrong, but I don't think I am.

I'm about to lose the only man I've ever loved because of a story I wrote.

I knew the consequences when I told John I had this information. I volunteered to pass it to another reporter. While he was happy that I offered that, he made the decision that he and I would work on the story together. I had the sources, and he could be on the calls with me to make sure that everything was on the up-and-up.

I also had thoughts about keeping my mouth shut. I could have pretended Tara never told me that information, and I could have found out when everyone else did. Or worse, after another reporter would have broke it. But if it ever came to light that I knew this information and didn't write about it, I could kiss my career goodbye.

I look at the clock in Hunter's kitchen, and it's nearly eight o'clock. My story has been online for four hours now, and he still isn't home. I grab one of his sweatshirts and head out to his patio. As soon as I step outside, my teeth start chattering. Yet this is exactly what I need.

I need to be wrapped in Hunter's scent, in the spot where we decided to give this a try. I need to be in the spot where we knew we were worth the risk and pray that everything is going to be okay.

I picked my job over Hunter. I know this. But the more I thought about it, the more I knew I had to report it. Plus, it's a positive. Hunter is getting his dream job. He's getting to stay in Nashville. One might think this would be cause for celebration. But I threw the Fury for a loop. Tara told me that Neil's head was about to explode when he saw the headline. The one thing about professional sports teams is that they like to control the narrative. They want to tell the story in their words, to their fans, on their time frame.

I fucked that all up.

And now, I fucked up everything with Hunter in the process.

I knew he would be upset. But I didn't think it would be *this* bad. I figured we would have a fight about me writing stories about him and not telling him. A little argument which would lead to some makeup sex.

Which is why the longer he stays away, the more worried I am that we won't survive this.

I don't know how long I sit outside, but I know the instant that Hunter comes through the door. Even out here on the patio, the air shifts. And not in a good way.

I take a deep breath before I stand up and make my way back inside. Part of me hoped that Hunter would be standing in the kitchen, pizza and beer in his hands, ready to talk this out rationally. Like we did before when I was expecting a fight.

Now? All I see on his face is hurt and anger.

"I understand you're probably mad, but I can explain—"

The laugh he lets out is downright bone-chilling. It's colder than the air I just walked in from. It sounds nothing like the Hunter I've come to know and love.

"Explain? What would *you* like to start with, Sadie? Because I have no fucking clue where to even begin."

I take a breath. "I'm sorry I didn't tell you that I was writing the sto—"

"That's what you think your biggest fault is?" he begins, furiously pacing back and forth. "Out of everything that you set in motion from the second you decided to report this story, you not telling me about it is your biggest regret? I always thought you were smart, but right now, I'm not impressed."

"What are you talking about?" I shake my head, because he's not making sense. "I wrote a story that shocked you. Yes, I know that it's not ideal. I know I said I'd give you a heads-up when I wrote stories about you, but I couldn't on this one. What I don't understand is why you're this upset about it? You got the job of your dreams! You should be elated!"

"Because you fucking used me for the story!" He stops in front of me and I can see nothing but rage in his eyes. I stare at him in shock. That's what he thinks? "You used your access to me for your own personal benefit! That is the one thing we promised each other we would never do! When did you do it? When I was asleep? When I was in the shower?"

"Hunter, I would never do that. I don't even know what you think I did! How did I use you?"

"My emails! My emails, Sadie. I know you went through them. That's the only way you could have found out about the promotion is if you saw the contract that was emailed to me. Five people knew about it and guess what, you were not one of them. I thought you were better than that, but apparently not. This is what I get for letting the enemy into my bed."

"Fuck you, Hunter," I say, my anger now coming to a boiling point. I could understand him being upset that I reported the story. But accusing me of going through his personal property for a scoop? It's like he doesn't even know me. "Did you ever think for one minute that maybe I did my job and used my sources when I was tipped off about the story? That I reported it without having to use my boyfriend?"

"Who are your sources then? Tell me. Clear everything up right now. Because the five people who knew sure as hell weren't the ones."

"I can't."

"You can't?"

I straighten my stance. "I don't care how much you are pissed at me. I don't care that you think I'm a shitty human right now. I will never name sources. Not for you. Not for anyone."

Hunter looks at me in shock. "You're telling me that you would rather protect your source than save our relationship?"

What? Are we...? Is he...?

"Hunter. It's not like that. It doesn't have to be like that."

"No Sadie. It is. It's exactly like that. Either you're picking me or you're picking your job. That's what this comes down to. But hey, at least now we're both going to get the jobs we wanted. I'm sure *US Daily* will be calling you soon. Glad I could help with that. Next time, though, you don't need to fuck me for a story."

He didn't...

No...

He wouldn't have...

I can't believe those words just came out of his mouth.

"That is the lowest fucking thing you could have ever said to me, Hunter McAvoy. I know you're pissed. I get it. But if you think for one second that I used you for a chance at that job, then you don't know me at all."

All the bastard does is shrug. "Everyone uses me, Sadie. Reporters have used me for years. You're just joining the club."

"I'm not justifying that statement with a response." My voice is starting to falter as the tears well in my eyes. But I'll be damned if I start crying in front of this man. "I was doing my job. I was tipped off about a story. I reported it. My boss had to watch over my shoulder every step of the way to make sure I *wasn't* using you. That's my job, Hunter. You knew what you were getting into with me when we got together."

"You're right, I did." His voice is somewhere between sarcastic and resigned. "You told me up front that you were a reporter first. I did this to myself. And I knew you were good. Hell, that first day you wrote about me right in front of my face and I didn't even know! What kind of idiot am I? How did I not think it would come to this?"

I want to scream. I want to hit something.

More than anything, I want to cry.

I can't be here anymore. I can't be in the same room with him.

I rip his sweatshirt off, thankful I kept a T-shirt on underneath. I don't want anything of his touching me right now. I grab my keys and purse and march toward his door.

"You thought I was different?" I say as I open his door. "I thought you were different too. I thought you were the one man who wouldn't think that I had to fuck my way to a story. Turns out we were both wrong."

I slam the door shut behind me and all but sprint to my car. I can't hold back my tears for another second.

I cry the whole way home.

I cry all night.

I cry the next day.

And it turns out Hunter was right. *US Daily* offered me the job.

Then, I cried some more.

44

SADIE

FOR THE FIRST time in my entire career, I called out sick on a game day.

I couldn't do it. I couldn't be in the same space as Hunter. Yes, he would be coaching and I'd be working and I don't even see him on most game days. But just the thought of knowing that he was there was too much for me to handle.

So I did what any girl going through a breakup does. I ordered pizza and breadsticks, called Bethany to bring over ice cream and booze, and I put on my rattiest pair of sweatpants.

At least, I think this is what people going through breakups do. All of my relationships never made it past two weeks. They never required this kind of therapy.

The worst part? I don't know if we broke up. The words were never said.

It sure as hell felt like it, though.

Neither of us has reached out. No texts or phone calls. I did all of my work from home this week. John sent another reporter to the press conference the Fury had to have because of me breaking the news about Hunter taking over for Gordon.

Today when I started to get ready, I just started crying. I thought all the tears were gone. I've been crying for six days.

I texted John to tell him to send someone else. Then, I texted Bethany asking her to come over.

I hate myself right now. I really do. I'm not this girl. I don't cry over men. I don't cry because I put my job first.

Yet, here I am, curled up in a blanket on my couch, not remembering the last time I showered.

I thought I was stronger than this. I've survived haters telling me I couldn't do my job. I've stood up to Internet bullies who thought they could hide behind a username and tell me that I'm shit at my job and to get my fat ass back in the kitchen.

What I couldn't survive was Hunter looking at me like I was a stranger. Or that I used him to get ahead.

That's what broke me.

"Oh God. This is worse than I thought."

I don't acknowledge Bethany as she walks into my apartment. I'm really glad I gave her my building code so I didn't have to get up to let her in.

That would have required effort. I don't have that in me today.

"Sadie… Oh, sis," she says, moving my legs onto her lap as she sits down on my couch. "Why didn't you call me sooner? I would have come over. At least… maybe I could have done some dishes."

I peek over my blanket to see what she's talking about. I don't know whether or not she means the stack of cups on my coffee table, or the pile of dishes in my sink.

"You know before I met Hunter I didn't have any real dishes?"

"What did you use to eat?"

"Paper plates. Plastic cups. I didn't see the point in having nice things for just me. Now it's just me again, and now I have to do the fucking dishes."

I know I'm rambling and making zero sense. But these are the thoughts that go through my brain these days.

"Is that why you have a pile of pillows in the corner?" Bethany asks, as I assume she now sees the pile of throw pillows, curtains, and every other knickknack that I bought the day Hunter and I went apartment shopping.

"They reminded me of him," I say, not able to hold the sadness back. "Why does it still hurt, Bethany? Why does it hurt? I want it to stop hurting."

She pulls me up and immediately brings me into her arms. And I just cry. And not a pretty cry. I'm straight ugly crying on my stepsister's shoulder.

If there is one good thing that has come from all of this, it's that Bethany and I are now close. I used to laugh when she called me sis. I don't anymore. We might not be related by blood. We might not have one single thing in common. But she's my sister.

And I couldn't do this without her right now.

"What can I do?" she asks, stroking my hair. "We have food. We have booze. I've never committed a crime before, but if that's what's needed, we can do that."

I let out a laugh, which comes out as a hiccup between my tears. "I really should shower. I'm a mess."

"Oh, thank you, Jesus. I didn't want to be the one to say it."

Bethany gives me a squeeze before she lets go of me. She stands up and holds out her hands to help me off the couch.

"You shower. I'll start cleaning up the kitchen. Then we get sloppy drunk on a Sunday and complain about men."

"SINCE WHEN DO YOU WATCH FOOTBALL?"

Bethany turns to me like a deer in headlights. "I don't know what you mean. I watch the Fury every Sunday. It's great to have on when I'm cleaning."

I eye her suspiciously as she turns her attention back to a dish that doesn't look like it needs washing.

"Okay, Miss Fury fan. Name a player. Any player. Doesn't even have to still be on the team. If you can do that, then I'll drop this conversation."

Bethany doesn't say anything for a minute. "Oh! There's that guy. He throws the football. He plays for the Fury."

"Does this player have a name?" I ask as I reach for a slice of pizza.

She bites her lip as I can visibly see the level of concentration on her face. "Starts with… a *B*? Bobby? Brian? Bryce! His name is Bryce! I win!"

This makes me laugh, which feels nice. It's been a long time since I did that.

"Fine. You win," I say, grabbing a glass to start making myself a drink. "I won't ask if you are watching the Fury game to maybe get a glance at a certain coach."

Bethany's face begins to blush at the mention of Davis. "I don't know what you're talking about. Plus, I'm not here to talk about me and my Fury coach. Today is about yours."

"A-ha! So you're saying there is a Fury coach who is yours?"

She swats a dish towel at me and we can't keep our laughter in. This feels nice. Normal. The shower did wonders for me. I only feel like I want to kind of cry.

That's what I call an improvement.

We gather our food and beverages of choice and make our way back out to the living room. The Fury game is still on the television, and the sight that I see as soon as I sit down threatens to tear my heart in two.

The camera pans to Hunter on the sidelines, and it takes everything in me not to start crying again.

I've never really got to watch him coach. From my angle in the press box, I can only see his back, and he's too far away.

Right now, I can take him all in. He's bent over, his hands on his knees, and he's watching as Bryce calls the play. The television goes back to the action of the game, and I want to scream to put the camera back on him. I wasn't done looking at him.

I wasn't done loving him yet either.

"I heard you got the job at *US Daily*?" Bethany asks, breaking our silence.

"Yeah. I got it." My words are the opposite of how they should sound when someone gets the job of their dreams.

"You have to be so excited. Your dad was gushing at dinner the other night. He told me and Mom about all the mornings y'all would read the paper together. Which is adorable. I'm so happy for you."

All I can do is shrug. "Thanks. But I haven't accepted it yet."

"What!" Bethany shrieks, nearly dropping her pizza. "What do you mean, you haven't accepted it."

"It means what it means. They called me. I said thanks, but that I needed a few days to think it over. They told me to call them Monday."

I look over to Bethany who is staring at me like I'm growing horns out of my head. "I'll admit that I've never been super smart, but you're going to have to help me out with this. You're telling me that you were offered your dream job. The job that you earned by giving up all forms of a social or personal life. You worked your butt off for years, got that job, and you didn't accept it on the spot?"

Well, when she puts it like that.

"It didn't feel right," I say. It's now my turn to not make eye contact.

"It didn't feel right because the job isn't what you thought it would be? Or it didn't feel right because of Hunter?"

For being the girl who says all the time that she isn't the smart one, she sure does get it right when it comes to my life crises.

"The job is perfect," I admit. "They said I could stay in Nashville. Or if I wanted to move, I could do that as well. I would be writing more in-depth and investigative pieces and not covering just one team. They also know about Hunter and that our relationship wouldn't be a problem. Not that it will be a problem anymore."

"So what *is* the problem?"

"The problem is that I'll always know that my dream job came at the price of my chance at love. And I don't know if I can live with that for the rest of my life."

Surprisingly, I don't cry after saying that out loud. I want to. I feel the heat burn behind my eyes.

But I don't. Instead, I stare at the television with my head on Bethany's shoulder and wonder what the hell I'm going to do with my life.

Likely without Hunter in it.

45

HUNTER

"WELL, McAvoy. We did it. We fucking did it."

Coach Gordon tosses me a beer as we each take a seat in his office. Him behind his desk. Me on the couch next to it.

Soon this office will be mine. At this time next year I'll be the one seated behind the desk passing out beers to my coaches. Hopefully, as we are making our way to the playoffs.

"We did, sir. I can't believe we did it. Thank you for everything this season. It was a true team effort." Even though we made the playoffs a few weeks ago, it still hasn't hit me that we went from the worst team in the league, to a favorite to win the championship.

"You know, son, it was at this time last year that I was sitting with Bancroft, wondering whether or not to boot his ass."

I nod but don't speak. I've always wondered how that conversation went down, especially now knowing what kind of hot head Bancroft is like.

"I was going to keep him," Coach Gordon begins, telling the story like he's remembering stories back from the war. "Part of me said that it was one bad season and the man deserved another chance. He was right in that aspect. He had done a lot for us on the field. Off the field, he was a mean motherfucker with a horrible temper. How no one ever wrote about that before his blowup is beyond me."

I shake my head but edge myself a little closer. It's like I'm listening to a ghost story around a campfire.

"I suggested that maybe he bring in some help to run the offense. I brought up your name. I knew you had a bright future ahead of you and selfishly I wanted you on my staff."

Wow. I didn't know this.

"I'm assuming he didn't take too well to that?"

Coach Gordon shakes his head. "Not at all. The man lost it. He went into a rage. You think he was bad a few weeks ago? You should have seen him then. He trashed my office. Started yelling profanities. Was blaming everyone but himself on why the offense was so bad. Told me that the media, specifically Sadie, got in my head. We had to call security on him and have him escorted from the facilities."

Holy shit. "How did none of this ever leak out?"

"The media were taking part in their end of the season beers that we give them. The timing was lucky."

Wow. I never knew any of this. Everything makes much more sense now though. Why he was so hellbent about bashing me in the media. About why Sadie's questions set him off.

Sadie.

I haven't thought about her much today. And like always, at first I miss her. Then I remember what she did, and the anger boils back up in me.

After Sadie's initial story went viral, instead of prepping for this week's game, almost all of my time was spent fielding phone calls or doing interviews about becoming the youngest head coach in league history. Luckily, Davis was able to handle all the game prep for me. The man is really making a case to replace me as offensive coordinator.

Coach Gordon has been ribbing me all week, telling me I better get used to doing all of those interviews. "That's half the damn job. At least you have a pretty face for the camera," he joked after a day when I did four different television spots back-to-back.

He has now found humor in the situation. Neil and Mr. Henderson are both still upset that Sadie found out and have made it their mission to find the mole, though no one is talking.

Probably because a mole doesn't exist.

She didn't have a source. She used me. Plain and simple.

"Your girl wasn't here today," Coach Gordon says. "It was weird not seeing her when I looked into the front row. It was some pimply face kid."

This takes me by surprise. "She wasn't?" That's odd. Sadie one time told me how she prided herself on never taking a sick day. She boasted that her personal record was working forty-three consecutive days without a day off.

"Nope, an intern filled in for her," Paul says, entering the office. "Got a call from her boss before the game to make sure we had a credential for him."

My first thought is to wonder if she's all right. The second thought is to kick my own ass for having that thought.

"That girl, she might have been a pain in our ass this week, but she wipes the floor with those guys," Coach Gordon says. I have to do a double-take because I'd bet this is the most positive thing he's ever said about someone in The Mob. "Don't you ever tell her this, but I look forward to her questions. The ones the guys ask me my granddaughter could answer, and she can't talk yet."

I don't say that I won't tell her that, because I'll likely never talk to her again. I don't say that he's right.

I just don't say anything.

"I know I can't ask her, but I would love to know who her source is here," Paul says, inviting himself to take a seat next to me. "The scoops and tips she gets are almost impressive, if it didn't make my life hell."

I quirk an eyebrow. Source my ass. "How do you know she has a source? No one knows who it is. Maybe she doesn't have one."

"Oh, she has one. We just can't figure out who," Paul says. "Reporters will never give up their sources. But it's the only plausible explanation. Either she has a mole or she somehow figured out how to plant listening devices around the facility. Two years ago, she had just taken the job, and she called me to confirm that a player was getting traded. I hadn't even heard about the trade yet. I had to go ask Neil. The only people who knew at that time were Neil and Gordon. She's doing this shit all the time. One day, I'll figure out how she's getting her info."

Fuck.

"Hunter? Why does it look like you saw a ghost, all the while wanting to vomit?"

I ignore Coach's comment. "Paul, can you tell me exactly what Sadie asked from you before she wrote the story?"

"She called me the day after we offered you the job requesting Coach Gordon's contract, which she has every right to do. I thought something might be up then because of the timing, but then I didn't hear from her after. So I chalked it up to coincidence. Then, at the beginning of this week, she came back asking if it was true that you were taking over next season as head coach. She asked about the clause in Coach Gordon's contract letting him retire early and that if I could confirm you were his replacement. I had to confirm it because though I hate that she got it first, it would have been worse for us if I lied to her."

"Did she say anything about my contract?"

Paul shakes his head. "No. It's funny you mention that. She asked if I could give her contract specifics, but I declined, saying that it was still being negotiated. I was actually surprised that there were no suspected contract numbers in her initial story. That means her source isn't anyone in legal. Or that she saw a copy of your contract. Hell, I even thought for a minute she saw the contract we emailed you, but clearly that wasn't it. Which is why I say she has to have a spy."

Fuck. Fuck. Fuck.

I was so angry at Sadie the other night; I didn't even listen to her. She tried to tell me all of this. She tried to tell me she reported the story straight-up. That she didn't go through my phone or email. I just didn't want to listen.

"Paul, is The Mob still here?" I say, shooting up from Coach Gordon's couch.

"Yeah. Why?"

"Tell them there's a press conference tomorrow morning. Tell them all if they help me, they can each get a one-on-one with me after the season. And call Sadie. Make sure she's here. I have an apology I need to make."

46

SADIE

I HAVE ABSOLUTELY no clue what I'm doing here. Or what any of us are doing here.

I also have no clue as to why there is a single red rose on my normal chair in the Fury's press conference room.

Mondays are usually off for the team and media. Unless there is a big announcement. I honestly can't figure out why Paul called me last night to make sure that I was here this morning for a press conference. Especially since I let the cat out of the bag in terms of the big announcement last week.

Everything looks normal. The reporters are milling around waiting for the press conference to start. The videographers from the television stations are setting up their cameras.

The only difference? No one is looking at me.

In fact, if I had to guess, everyone is blatantly ignoring me.

Case in point? Tommy just walked right by me and didn't say a word.

"Tommy!" I say, walking a little faster to catch up with him. "What's going on?"

"I don't know," he says, though he's doing everything he can not to look me in the eye. "I know just as much as you do."

While I find that hard to believe, I don't press him. Paul walks into the room, signaling for all of us to take our seats.

I do, moving the rose to the seat next to me.

I begin to take out my laptop and recorder when I feel him in the room. I don't even have to look up to know he's there. I dig in my purse for as long as possible for nothing in particular. Anything to distract me from having to come back to the present where Hunter is a mere ten feet away from me.

When I do muster the courage to look up, my breath hitches. My cheeks are turning about six shades of pink. I'm glad I don't have to talk right now because I don't know what I would say.

Hunter is more handsome than I remember.

He's dressed in a full suit. Jacket, tie, and if I had to guess, a vest underneath. He wore a suit like this in New Orleans. We missed our dinner reservation that night.

Bad breath.

The smell of cat pee.

Liver.

God, it hurts to see him. I thought I hurt last week, but that's nothing compared to being in the same room with him. It's probably a good thing that I'll be working for *US Daily* next season. I'm not sure I could endure this kind of suffering every week.

Our eyes make contact, and for the millionth time in the past week, I have to fight back tears. I'm sure he can see the sadness in my eyes. The only thing consoling me right now is that there is sadness in his, too.

"Thank you all for coming," Hunter begins. "I'm sure you are all wondering why we dragged you out of bed this morning. To show my appreciation, I made sure Paul brought donuts."

The guys laugh but I don't.

Why is Hunter talking? He's not the coach yet. Unless Gordon died and no one told me, there is no reason for Hunter to be speaking to the media right now.

"The reason I gathered everyone here today is because I have something I need to say. And it needs to be on the record. What better way to do that than in front of a room full of reporters?"

He pauses and looks directly at me. Those six shades of pink earlier? They are now ten shades of red.

"When I was first hired by the Fury, a smart person told me that the choice of words was key to figuring out what people really meant. Last week, after the news broke about me becoming the next head coach of the Fury, I said things to a very important person to me that spoke quite loudly. They were mean, hateful, and born out of rage. And for that, I will be forever sorry."

I'm not typing a single word. I don't think I've blinked or even taken a breath.

Did Hunter really call a press conference to apologize to me?

No. That's ridiculous. I'm reading too much into this.

But then he pins his eyes back on me, and I don't know how to react.

"No matter what I've done in my life, I wanted to be the best. I wanted to be the best son. I wanted to be the best football player. I wanted to be the best coach. Over the past nine months, I wanted to be the best partner to a woman I didn't deserve. Most of those have happened. As we know, I was never going to be the best football player."

He pauses for effect, which works because these guys are eating out of the palm of his hand. Me? I'm waiting for a shoe to drop.

"I've tried to be a good son. Sometimes I do better than others. After a rough start to the season, I think I became a good coach. My efforts were rewarded with a promotion. It's a job I will not take lightly. I will always strive to be the best coach I can be. And every one of you can hold me to that every time I step up to this podium."

He pauses again, but this time, his eyes train on me. "What I have failed at is being the best partner. I think I had my moments. But when the going got tough, I failed. I assumed things without trying to validate facts. I let past experiences dictate my reactions. And the worst part? I lost my best friend in the process. Because, Sadie

Benson, you're not just the woman I'm madly in love with, but you're the best person in my life."

And there they go. The tears. They are falling. I can't stop them.

And the butterflies. Fuck, those damn butterflies are back.

Hunter steps away from the podium and makes his way over so he is standing right in front of me. He picks up the rose and extends his hand for mine. I give it to him without question as he pulls me up to stand in front of him.

I'm too close to him now. I can smell his cologne. It's the same cologne that drew me to him all those months ago. His blue eyes are trying to see through my soul like they did in Memphis. I want to look away, but I can't.

I don't think I ever could.

"Sadie, there aren't enough words or enough press conferences to tell you how sorry I am. I was an idiot. The things I said to you… I'm ashamed they left my mouth. Please, don't ever tell my mother that I said those things."

I laugh at his joke, which helps the tears for all of two seconds. "You are a damn good reporter. The best one in this room. Sorry, guys, but you know it's true. You scooped me on my own story not once, but twice. I should have never doubted you as a reporter. And I should have never doubted you as my partner. My best friend. The love of my life. Please, Sadie. Forgive me?"

The room goes silent. This is as quiet as it's ever been in here. I'm sure if I took a second to look around, I'd see a bunch of middle-aged men leaning forward on their seat in response. I know I'd be.

Instead, I'm standing in front of Hunter and I can't form words. I want to forgive him. I want to jump in his arms right now and kiss the hell out of him.

Can I do it that easily? Can I forgive the pain and hurt he caused me just because of one grand gesture?

"Sadie, what's your answer?" someone asks.

"Sadie, what did he say that was so horrifying?" another person, I believe Joe, asks.

"Sadie, have you already moved on and that's why you're keeping Hunter here waiting?" Tommy asks.

This makes me laugh. "No comment to the last two questions."

"What about the first?"

I give a small smile to the men who have become my peers before looking back up at Hunter. "I forgive you. And that's on the record."

Hunter doesn't waste a second before bringing me in for a kiss that I'd guarantee will be on every sports page and gossip column tomorrow.

I hate being the story.

Right now, I don't mind it.

47

HUNTER

"WHY DID he hand it off? He's an idiot for not running a pass play."

"Did he think he had them fooled! Princess over here knew he was doing that! And she's only watching the game for the commercials."

"Excuse me. I take offense to that. But you're right. I totally did. And I totally am."

All I can do is smile and laugh as Sadie, Davis, and Bethany each give their commentary about the championship game that's currently playing on the flat-screen television in my living room. Somehow, I drew the short straw to go get another round of drinks.

I don't mind. I don't even mind that I'm not coaching in the game that every football coach wants to be in.

No. Tonight it feels right watching the game in sweatpants in Nashville.

The Fury's playoff run lasted two games. The next day, Coach Gordon officially stepped down as the Fury's head coach and I was promoted. I moved into his office, put together my coaching staff, which included promoting Davis to offensive coordinator and hiring Tara, Neil's former secretary to come work for me. Neil is still the general manager, but Sadie suggested that I see if Tara wanted a change of professional scenery. She also said it would be a good idea that if I didn't want things to get out to the press, to treat Tara right. And to buy her donuts.

That's how Sadie revealed her source to me without ever saying the words.

More importantly, Sadie and I are better than ever. After the makeshift press conference, which made national headlines and even got me an interview with *Cosmo* about grand gestures, we had a long talk. A few parts got tense. A few parts were sad. In the end, we're stronger than ever.

We're now officially living together. She has been slowly moving her things over to my condo, including her decorative pillows and coasters, which she now says she can't imagine ever parting with.

With the league season over after tonight, we'll both have some downtime, so we decided to take a trip to Memphis at the end of the month to celebrate our sort of one-year anniversary.

I hope I come back being able to call her my fiancée.

"What did I miss?" I ask, handing drinks off and taking my place back on my sectional next to Sadie. I also can't help but notice how far apart Davis and Bethany are sitting tonight.

Definitely not as cozy as they were at the bar a few months ago.

"You missed the worst play call in championship game history," Davis says, his eyes never leaving the television.

"That true?" I whisper to Sadie, who has snuggled her way into my side.

"Yup. Shit play call. They had to punt after it. Made no sense."

I still get hard when Sadie talks about football. I don't know if that will ever change. But getting to watch it with her while we debate strategy and comment on plays? I sport a hard-on the entire game.

"Halftime!" Davis yells, standing up. "Time to refill the plate."

"I'll come with you," Bethany says a little too eagerly. Which Sadie doesn't let slide.

"I thought you wanted to watch the halftime show?"

"I'll watch it on Facebook later."

The two of them make their way back to the kitchen, and all we can do is laugh. They are not sly. At all.

"Why are they sitting on opposite ends of the room when it's clear they're still sleeping together?"

Sadie stands up to stretch, and the sweatshirt she's wearing comes up just enough to give me a peek of some skin. Which gives me all sorts of ideas.

"Because they're ridiculous and swear it was just a one-time thing."

That sounds like Davis. "I'm glad we were never a one-time thing," I say, standing up and taking Sadie's hand in mine as I make my way to the patio.

"Where are we going," she asks.

I pull the patio door open and signal for her to go outside. "Consider it our own halftime show."

I sit down and bring her to my lap. It's chilly for February, but neither of us care. She naturally puts her legs over mine and snuggles in close to me. Whenever we need to reconnect, or if things are feeling off, or if we just want a minute to breathe, this is where we come. It's like our reset button.

Tonight, I don't need a reset. I just need her alone for a few minutes. And I know if I take her to bed, we won't be watching the rest of the game.

"Are you ready to start your job tomorrow?" I ask, running the tip of my nose up and down her neck.

"Is it weird I'm nervous?"

I place a kiss right under her ear, which causes her to shiver against me. "I don't think so. This is a big deal, and you want to do well. I know I was nervous as hell at the first press conference."

Sadie shoots me a look that screams "I don't believe you."

"What? It's true!"

"Hunter Michael McAvoy, you're going to sit here and tell me that you, the man who can wrap a room full of reporters around his pinky by just smiling, the man who used the press to win me back, were nervous when you were officially introduced by the Fury?"

Sadie found out my middle name the last time we went to Birmingham. She now uses it every chance she gets.

Yes. We've been to Birmingham. Yes, I've spoken to my father.

And in a shocking turn of events, he congratulated me on being named the Fury's head coach. He and Mom even came to my press conference after Gordon officially retired.

Are we best friends yet? Not by a long shot. Maybe one day we'll get there.

"I was. I must have smoothed down my tie ten times before I walked out there. I think the intern thought I was going to pass out."

She studies me for a second, probably deciding whether or not to try to catch me in a line of bullshit. "Fine. I'll bite. Why were you nervous?"

"Because," I say, giving her a quick kiss before I continue, "I knew you'd be there."

I've come to expect a playful slap when I dish out my overly cheesy comments to her, even though they are all the truth. This time, though, Sadie surprises me.

She twists herself so she's now straddling me and brings my mouth to hers for a kiss that could heat all of Nashville.

My hands slide around her back and down to her ass. I remember when I first saw her, and this was the first thing I noticed. Such a guy move.

It didn't take long for me to notice the rest of her. And not just her physical features, which are stunning, and I'm in love with every inch of her.

I love her for her heart. I love her for her humor. I love her for the fact that she never lets me settle for less. I love her for her determination.

I just love her.

"Gorgeous," I reluctantly say as I pull away from her lips. "As much as I would love to keep doing this. And you know I have no problem with patio sex. We probably should get back inside. We do have guests."

She turns back to look through the patio door.

"They left."

I crane my neck to look over her shoulder. "How do you know?"

"Davis's keys were on the coffee table. They aren't now."

Without another word, I stand up and carry Sadie back inside. Her laugh follows us in as I shut the door and make our way straight to my bedroom.

The game can wait.

Sadie can't.

EPILOGUE
SADIE

FIVE YEARS LATER

I SWEAR I didn't used to be a crier.

Before Hunter and I started dating, I barely shed a tear.

These days I cry at everything.

That's also Hunter's fault.

I cry at dog food commercials. One time I cried when the new cashier at Sandwich City told me to have a nice day.

That's what happens when you're six-months' pregnant.

Tonight, though, I'd like to think that I'd be crying whether or not I was preggo.

I don't even try to contain the tears as I stand off to the side of the stage next to my dad, Helen, Bethany and her daughter, and my in-laws as we watch the league commissioner hand the championship trophy to Hunter, who led the Nashville Fury to its first championship in team history.

My man, my husband, the father of my children, got to hoist his trophy.

And I couldn't be prouder.

"Look at him up there," Francine says, giving my hand a squeeze. "I'm just… I'm just so proud of him."

"We all are," Bo says as he holds Camden, our two-year-old son. "Do you see your daddy up there? Wave to Daddy!"

If you would have told me five years ago that Bo McAvoy would be having a proud father moment as his son, a coach, held up the league championship trophy, I'd tell you that you were crazy. I'd then ask you what you were smoking if you added that he was doing it as a proud grandpa.

I'm sorry. Pappy. He prefers Pappy.

A lot has changed with Bo over the years. After Hunter was named head coach, the two of them finally sat down and let out years of pent-up emotions. Granted, Francine and I might have tricked them into having this discussion by locking them in a room, but nonetheless, it happened. And we are all better for it. Hunter has slowly learned that some things Bo says are indeed helpful, and Bo has become better at expressing his advice to not sounding like a criticism.

That is when he's not too busy being Pappy. That man loves his grandson more than anything in this world. He tells me on a weekly basis that Camden will one day play for Alabama and continue the McAvoy lineage. I tell him that Camden will do what he wants and carve his own path.

It's now the only thing we disagree about.

I laugh as I watch Camden try to wave to Hunter, who is handing the trophy to the game's MVP, which of course was Bryce. It's funny that all those years ago we wondered if he was going to be a bust. Five years later, under the guidance of Hunter and Davis, he's the best quarterback in the league.

I look back at my son, who is still trying to get his father's attention. He is one hundred percent McAvoy in every way. He was literally born with a football in his hand, Francine made sure of that. She also made sure to buy him his first Alabama onesie.

He only wore it when she came over. I'm still a Vol for Life, after all.

Camden is also very excited to be a big brother and tries to talk to his baby sister every day through my belly.

That makes me cry because it's damn adorable.

I wipe a tear away as I see Hunter and Davis walking toward our crew. They shake hands and give each other one of those back-slapping hugs before parting ways, Davis to go see his family, and Hunter to see his.

The pride and happiness on Hunter's face are unmistakable. He deserves to bask in every inch of joy he is feeling right now. The last five years haven't been easy.

Nothing worth fighting for ever is.

As soon as he can reach me, he scoops me in his arms and swings me around. Yes, I might be six-months' pregnant, but that doesn't stop Hunter from lifting, or carrying me, whenever he sees fit.

I don't mind it one bit.

"Holy!" *Kiss.* "Hell." *Kiss.* "We." *Kiss.* "Won!"

"Yes, you did. I'm so proud of you."

He sets me down and reaches over to his dad to take Camden, who immediately latches his little arms around Hunter's neck. But before he can step away, Bo extends his hand, which Hunter returns. The look the two share has so many unspoken words in it. Only now they are all of happiness and love.

And there I go, crying again.

"Won!" Camden shouts. "Daddy won!"

"Yeah, I did, buddy!" Hunter says, giving him a kiss on the cheek.

My heart melts every time I see them together. Which is a lot. I still work for *US Daily*, but I have transitioned my role to editor. I still get to work from home, only with a little more stable hours.

And I do it under the name Sadie Benson-McAvoy.

It was perfect when we found out I was having Camden. It will be even better when Carli joins us in a few months.

Hunter reaches for me with his free hand and kisses the top of my head.

"How does it feel?" I ask, looking up at him with all the love I can muster. "How does it feel to be the champ?"

He kisses Camden before leaning down and kissing me one more time.

"It now feels like I have everything I have ever wanted."

OFF TRACK

NASHVILLE FURY: BOOK 2

PROLOGUE
BETHANY

"ARE you sure this dress looks okay?"

I had asked Sadie this question when I tried the dress on at the boutique connected to the salon I work at. I asked her again when I was checking out.

And now, as I ask my stepsister the same question while we wait for our Lyft to pick us up, I'm pretty sure she is regretting the fact she agreed to set me up on a double date.

"For the hundredth time, yes, it looks fine. You look great. Sexy. Davis won't be able to take his eyes off you. Now the car is here, let's go."

Bless my stepsister's heart for saying that, even though I bet if I held a gun to her head, she couldn't tell me the color of the dress.

It's cream. Modest on top, but so short I'll need to watch how I sit.

In other words: It's perfect.

I've been eyeing this dress for months, and I finally had an excuse to buy it. Tonight's double date with Davis could be my last first date. So, obviously, it deserves a special dress.

Don't think like that, Bethany. You always think those kinds of thoughts before a date and it always ends up in disaster. Don't set yourself up for failure. He could be like every other guy out there and be a complete jerk. Quit putting pressure on this.

I let out a heavy sigh I don't think Sadie hears as we ride to a downtown Nashville bar for our double date. I hate thinking like this. I know it's not healthy to put expectations on a date, especially with a man you've never met. Yet, this is where my mind goes every time I go on a first date—that this one will finally be *the one.*

I love love. I want to love and to be loved in return. I want the kind of love that is written about in songs, the kind of love you don't think is real. I want the happily ever after. I want the husband and the house and the three kids running around with the golden retriever chasing them at our home in the suburbs.

Every date I go on, I hope it's with Mr. Forever. I build up every guy in my head because I'm so tired of waiting for my forever to begin. Yet the only guys I can find these days are the ones who say they want the forever at first but are just saying what they know you want to hear. In reality, they only want one night. Which, of course, I don't find out about until the next morning. You know, after the one-night stand.

And I fall for it.

Every.

Single.

Time.

Because you are so desperate to find your happily ever after you ignore the glaring red flags.

I shake away the voice inside my head as the car turns onto the street where we are meeting her boyfriend, Hunter, and Davis, my date and a fellow coach with Hunter of the Nashville Fury, the city's professional football team.

I don't know a thing about football, but from the picture she showed me of my hopefully, last first date, I'd be willing to learn. I know there is something about a tight end, and I liked the sound of that.

I'm also a fan of the pants the players wear.

"So, tell me more about Davis," I say as I take the compact from my purse to make sure my makeup is still in place. "You barely told me a thing about him."

When Sadie and Hunter first started dating, I asked if Hunter had any single brothers or friends. Sadie thought I was joking. You would think since we've been stepsisters for more than ten years, she'd know by now I never play around when it comes to trying to find my future husband.

It's like she doesn't even know me sometimes.

Then again, Sadie and I are complete opposites. Today's impromptu shopping trip for this dress reminded me of that. When we went prom dress shopping in high school, I wanted to try on everything at the store while she looked like she was ready to make a run for it.

Today, I was in my glory, wanting to make sure I had the perfect dress for tonight. Sadie, on the other hand, barely paid attention to me and was glued to her phone, likely working on a story. As a reporter for the local newspaper covering the Fury, Sadie is always on her phone. I could have come out of the dressing room wearing a burlap sack and she would have told me I looked good. Her usefulness past connecting me with Hunter's friend is the extent of her involvement, so it seems.

"He's nice."

"Nice?" I ask, looking over at Sadie who is still typing furiously on her phone. "That's all you got? I mean, nice is good. Nice is a requirement. But I'd like a little more intel than that! What if he has a weird feet thing?"

Sadie must pick up on my desperate tone as she puts her phone away. "First off, I'd like to remind you this setup is solely because you refused to leave Hunter alone, constantly asking him if he had any single friends. Considering Davis is pretty much the only guy Hunter hangs out with, this is who you get. Secondly, how would I know if he has a weird feet thing? It's not something I'd ask him during an interview."

"Does Hunter know? Text him really quick. I can't go on a date with a guy who wants to suck on my toes."

"Why on Earth would Hunter and I ever talk about if Davis has a weird feet thing?"

"I don't know," I say in frustration, sliding down a little farther in the back seat. "I just want this to go well. What if we hit it off and one day we get married and we live next door to each other? Our kids can play together and we can take back-to-school photos every year! How amazing would that be?"

Sadie shakes her head, letting out a small laugh as she places her hand on top of mine. "While yes, that would be great to one day have, remember what we talked about. Please don't go into this date with your hopes super high that Davis is the one. In all honesty, I don't know much about him except his football background and that he and Hunter have become pretty tight in the past few months. Hell, I don't even know his first name except that he goes by the initial *R*. But what I do know is he strikes me as a guy who doesn't take much seriously. The players call him the fun uncle of the coaching staff. So while I want you to have fun, don't get your hopes up too high, okay? Let's just go and have fun and see where the night takes us."

"You're right. Thanks for talking me off the ledge."

I let Sadie's words settle as our car approaches the bar. This is just a fun night with friends getting drinks. Meeting someone new.

No pressure.

No expectations.

No planning our wedding an hour into the night.

The car slows down, and I see two men standing in front of the bar, casually leaning against the fenced-in patio. I can tell one is Hunter. But it's the guy next to him I can't take my eyes off of.

Davis. The picture Sadie showed me did him no justice.

The first thing I notice is his arms. His biceps are barely contained in his light blue button-down shirt, which is a beautiful contrast to his tanned, olive skin. He has chestnut brown hair that is just long enough to imagine slipping my fingers through. If I had to guess, his beard is supposed to look like a five o'clock shadow but is styled like that on purpose.

This man, by far, is the sexiest man I've ever met in person.

I'm now really glad I bought this new dress.

Our ride comes to a stop, and I take a deep breath before getting out of the car, closing my eyes to give myself one more mental pep talk.

This is just a date.

Don't go into this thinking he could be Mr. Forever.

Even though you know you'd make beautiful babies.

Just enjoy the night.

Be in the moment.

After all, there'll be time to plan the wedding starting tomorrow.

I feel the air hit my legs before I open my eyes. When I do, I see Davis standing next to the car, extending his hand for me to take.

And they say chivalry is dead.

"Thank you," I say, accepting his hand, though my words don't come out as confident as I would like. Half of that is to do with how sexy this man is. The other half is because the second my hand touched his, shivers raced through my body, despite it being an unseasonably warm November night in Nashville.

"I would like to say it's because I'm a gentleman," he says, not hiding that he is openly checking me out. And I'm guessing he's a leg man for as much time as he spends not looking me in the eye.

"You're not a gentleman?" I ask as we walk to the bar, his hand now resting on the small of my back.

He lets out a low chuckle as I carefully sit on a barstool. He leans in close, and I can feel his breath on my neck, his hand still on my back. "The things I'm thinking about right now are the opposite of a gentleman."

Another shiver goes down my spine. Between the feel of his hand and the words coming from his mouth, my body is quickly overheating. Thankfully, I get a reprieve as he releases his touch, pulling up a seat next to mine. I look around for Hunter and Sadie as Davis flags down a bartender and see they found a table outside.

I guess we're on our own.

"What is the opposite of a gentleman?" I ask.

Davis doesn't answer as the bartender takes that opportunity to take our order. Vodka soda for me. Beer for him. As he's trying to convince the bartender to put the drinks on Hunter's tab, I take the opportunity to give him a better look.

His dress shirt is rolled at the sleeves in the way that makes most women, including me, go ga-ga over. His eyes are a fascinating shade of blue that almost looks gray. Then there is his cologne. It's a combination of a woodsy and manly scent that makes me glad I have to cross my legs in this dress.

"The opposite of a gentleman," he says, suddenly pulling me away from my unladylike thoughts. "is a man who just meets a woman and can't stop looking at her legs, or wondering what they would feel like wrapped around him. The opposite of a gentleman is knowing we are here with our friends, but not being able to wait for the time we can leave. The opposite of a gentleman is wondering how I could know you from just a photo and a few words of conversation, but I already know I'm about to kick my friend's ass for not introducing us sooner."

I reach for my drink that was just put down in front of me, needing the liquid to cool me down.

What man talks like that? Definitely none I have ever been with. In my quest to find Mr. Right, I have dated douchebags and fuck boys. They tried to talk like Davis just did, but failed epically. Just sending a text saying, "U up?" isn't the way to lure a woman to bed. Then there were the responsible guys. The ones with 401ks, savings accounts, and square footage with their name on the deed. They *definitely* never talked like that.

But Davis? Davis knows what he wants. And apparently, right now, he wants me. Sadie might have said he doesn't take things too seriously, but I'm guessing that doesn't mean inside the bedroom. Unless he's a big talker. But judging by the way he's looking at me right now—with nothing but fire in his eyes—I would bet all the money I have in my bank account that this man can not only talk the talk, but can also walk the walk.

This guy isn't Mr. Forever. This guy has Mr. One Night written all over him. My dreams of this being my last first date are once again crushed.

"Cat got your tongue, princess?"

I ignore the pet name, not having any clue where he came up with it, and take another healthy sip of my drink as I gather courage for what I'm about to say.

Because I've never said it before.

One night.

Maybe one night wouldn't be so bad? At least this time I know what I'm getting into. There wouldn't be any surprise when I wake up tomorrow morning and he's already gone, quicker than the afterglow of what I expect would be a phenomenal orgasm—or three.

And let's be real, it has been a *really* long time since anyone has been anywhere near my bed. And definitely not a guy as attractive as Davis. Or with a man who can make my toes curl just with his words.

Yes! This is perfect.

I can't get hurt if I know what I'm getting myself into. This time, I'm in control. Right?

Well, at least going into it. If the way he's looking at me right now says anything, I have a feeling he's going to be in control for most of the night.

And I don't hate that. Not one bit.

"Not at all," I say as I lean a little closer to him. "I was just thinking I like the fact you're not a gentleman. Being a gentleman doesn't sound nearly as fun."

He lets out a small laugh. "I'm all about fun."

"I like the sound of that."

One night.

No one gets hurt knowing the expectations. What could be the harm in that?

1

───────

BETHANY

THREE MONTHS LATER

THE AUDACITY.

The absolute and sheer audacity of Hunter McAvoy asking me what he just did sitting in the position he is in. Apparently, no one told professional football's golden boy you don't ask that kind of question to the woman cutting your hair.

"Did you really just ask me what I think you just asked me? Because I know you are smarter than that."

"What?" he says, feigning innocence as our eyes connect in the mirror at my station. "All I asked was if you could come to Memphis and take pictures when I propose to Sadie this weekend. That's it. I don't know what you're getting so worked up about."

"You know that was not all you said," I say, pointing my scissors at him for extra emphasis.

"But that's the only part you need to focus on. Forget I said the other thing."

If it were only that easy.

What my likely—because he may not make it out of this haircut alive—future brother-in-law would like me to erase from my memory is that not only did he ask me to come to Memphis to take photos when he proposes to my stepsister, but he also invited his best friend to come as well to get the video.

And therein lies the problem.

His best friend is Davis.

The man I can't say no to.

Believe me, I've tried.

So many times.

I've never succeeded.

I'm so incredibly weak.

"You know I can't do that," I say, going back to cutting Hunter's hair. "You said it and now it's in my brain."

"Maybe if he's in your head so much, then you two, you know, should become more than two people who pretend they aren't sleeping together?"

Yup. This man is about to get a chunk of hair removed from the back of his head.

I give Hunter my meanest glare in the mirror as I go back to cutting his hair. The right way. I may want to "accidentally" cut an outline of a penis into the back of his head, but I'm way too nice.

Because he's about to ask my stepsister to marry him. If he had a horrible haircut for the biggest night of his life, I'd never forgive myself.

"We aren't sleeping together," I say as matter-of-factly as I can muster. "I don't know where you got that idea from."

Hunter looks at me through the mirror, trying to decide if he's going to call me out on my crap or not. Apparently, he chooses the former.

"So, you're telling me you two didn't leave my house after the championship game to go back to one of your places to hook up? And you two haven't been secretly hooking up for months, even though both Sadie and I know it's going on, yet neither of you will admit it to us?"

I turn my focus to his hair. If I make eye contact, he'll know I'm about to lie through my teeth. Again.

"Nope. I have no idea what you are talking about. Can you look down so I can clean up the back of your neck?"

I'm going to hell. Liars go to hell, right? They do. And I've booked myself a one-way ticket to meet Lucifer himself. Is it wrong I'm hoping Davis is seated beside me?

Because everything Hunter just said is precisely right. What was meant to be one night with Davis has turned into a months-long, not-so-secret hookup fest we can't seem to stop.

We aren't dating.

We have sex.

Correction: we have amazing sex.

That's it.

The first night we hooked up, Davis confirmed what I thought the moment I laid eyes on him—he doesn't do long term. He doesn't do commitment. What he does do is me… over and over and over again.

Just like he did that first night…

We stumble into his apartment, shoes and clothes already coming off, and we aren't even two steps inside.

How we didn't get kicked out of the Lyft back to his place is a mystery.

My fingers are frantically trying to undo the buttons of his shirt while his hands are cupping my ass, his mouth sucking on a spot on my neck that I didn't know could give me such pleasure. Just as I get the last button open, he stops.

"You don't have to stop," I say, pushing the shirt over his shoulders.

"I need to be upfront with you before this goes any further."

The tone of his voice makes me pause. "Unless you're about to tell me you have a wife and this is your sex apartment, we don't need to talk anymore."

I try to let my fingers go down to undo his belt when he stops me.

"No wife," he says, tilting my chin up so I'm looking at him. "There will never be a wife. This is only tonight. Do you understand that?"

It takes all I have not to laugh. I knew I had this guy pegged.

"I had no intentions of it being anything more than that."

I want to go back to undoing his pants, but he refuses to let my hands go.

"You don't strike me as a hookup girl."

I let out a defeated sigh. "I'm not. I want the husband and the kids and the whole nine yards. But not tonight. Tonight is just about that... tonight. No strings."

He quirks his eyebrow at me. "You sure, princess?"

"Yes," I say, dropping to my knees. "Now, where were we?"

It was just supposed to be one night. Yet here we are, three months later.

I knew he'd be good. What I wasn't prepared for was the man to be a sex god and to make me wonder if any of the previous men I had been with have any idea what they were doing.

He's attentive.

He's primal.

He makes me speak in tongues.

He has the most beautiful dick in the history of dicks.

Yes, dicks can be pretty. He proved that to me.

His is glorious. Long and thick and… it's just perfect.

And it makes me weak when it comes to him. That and the dirty words he whispers when he's making me see stars.

Which he has done. Many times. In many ways. In many places.

I'm addicted to him. And his dick.

It's bad. I'm bad. So, so bad.

God, let him be sitting next to me on that one-way trip to hell.

"Bethany?"

Hunter's words snap me from my Davis-induced daze. "Yeah?"

"You know because you reacted like I asked you to help me bury a body is very telling that you two are more than you let on. But if you insist on not admitting it out loud, Sadie and I will continue pretending we don't know what's going on."

I let his words hang in the air because I have nothing to say. He's right. When he asked me to come to Memphis and tried to slip in that Davis would be there, I reacted like a guilty person. Like someone who had something to hide.

Because I do.

I'm not this girl. I'm not the girl who has a month's-long relationship based solely on sex. We've never gone on a date besides the first night we met. We don't share meals. We don't talk about our feelings.

We have sex. It's what we do. What we do very well.

Well, it's what we did.

A week after the setup date that resulted in three mind-blowing orgasms, I was out with a few of my coworkers when I ran into him at a bar not far from our salon in the West End of Nashville. Before I knew it, we were calling a car and going back to my place.

Then there was New Year's Eve when we celebrated by him drinking champagne off of my chest.

And when we left Hunter's place at halftime of the championship game. And that was after we had round one in Hunter's garage. We were both winners that night.

And last Thursday.

And a bunch more times in between.

It's wrong on so many levels. But I give him credit, he never lied to me that this was anything more than two adults enjoying each other's company. I agreed to those terms because Davis might be fun, but he's not the guy to bring home to meet your family. And for the time being, I'm okay with that.

Until last Thursday.

God, I hate last Thursday.

What changed? I did what I promised myself I wouldn't do that first night—I envisioned our future. A future with Davis.

And I loved what I saw.

I don't even know where the thoughts came from. One minute I'm watching his spectacular, naked ass walk out of his bedroom to get us some water, then the next, I was seeing our future in vivid detail.

I pictured myself walking toward him on our wedding day.

I pictured him walking out of that bedroom to get me a snack in the middle of the night because the pregnancy cravings kicked in.

I pictured us with Sadie and Hunter, watching our kids play in the backyard of our neighboring houses.

When he came back and asked me if I was all right, I couldn't leave fast enough. This wasn't supposed to happen. I wasn't supposed to catch feelings. I don't even know how it happened. It's not like we have in-depth conversations about anything. Those thoughts weren't supposed to creep up.

Yet there they were. As clear as if they were happening in real time.

The next morning I texted him we were done. No more. How can I find what I'm looking for if I'm hooking up with him on a regular basis without the promise of a future? He said he understood and wished me luck.

I ignored the part where his well-wishes stung more than I anticipated.

But I want more, and I know Davis isn't the guy who that can happen with. He has told me he doesn't do relationships. Plus, we are total and complete opposites. I'm born and raised in Nashville with no intentions of leaving. He's a coach for a professional football team, and his life could be uprooted at any moment. He's the guy who doesn't take life seriously and goes with the flow. I'm the girl who can't operate without her day planner and schedule book.

Hell, he won't even tell me his first name. I only know it starts with the letter *R* because of Sadie.

That's not what I want from the man I'm going to spend the rest of my life with. I mean, only knowing part of his name doesn't make for a solid marriage foundation.

I have been Davis-free now for six days. And just when I thought I was kicking the habit, here comes Hunter McAvoy strolling into my styling chair, asking me to spend an evening with the man I'm trying to quit cold turkey.

As I said, the *audacity*.

"So, can I count on you? To be there Saturday?" I look at Hunter, who is giving me his best puppy dog face. "I want this night to be perfect for Sadie. She deserves perfect. I want us to be able to remember it for years to come. And that only happens with photos and video. That is where you and Davis come in. Can you do it for me? For Sadie?"

I let out a sigh of defeat. Hunter knows I'll do anything for the woman who is not only my stepsister, but my best friend.

Even if that includes spending one more night in the presence of the man who is all sorts of wrong for me.

"Fine. But you owe me. Big-time."

2

———

DAVIS

THE THINGS we do for friends.

That is one of the many thoughts going through my head as I sit at a hotel bar in Memphis, sipping on a glass of chilled, top-shelf tequila, waiting on the princess to arrive so we can play the part of paparazzi for Hunter and Sadie tonight.

Usually, I'm a beer guy. But I knew tonight called for something stronger.

Tonight, I have to be around Bethany and not touch her. I have to respect her wishes. I have to know and be okay with the night not ending with her in my bed.

As much as I'd like her to be.

"Yup, tonight calls for the hard stuff."

I must say that a little too loud because the bartender turns to see if I need a refill. I shake him off and take another sip of the cold liquor.

When Hunter asked me to come video the proposal and also happened to mention he was asking Bethany to participate, too, I played it cool. I believe I went so far as to pretend I didn't hear what he said, despite the moment he mentioned her name, my pants started to get tight.

That's the effect she has on me. Just the sound of her name gets me going.

No one knows that, of course. Not Hunter, who is not only my coworker and technically my boss but has also become my best friend. I have a feeling he suspects Bethany and I are more than acquaintances who were set up on one date, but he's never called me out on it.

If he only knew what we did in his garage at halftime of the championship game...

Or that she drives me crazy in ways I don't like to admit...

But he doesn't know that, either. Neither do my sisters. Definitely not my mother. My personal life is just that. Personal.

I glance down at my phone to see that it's seven forty-five. We are supposed to be at our spots on Beale Street at eight fifteen. I told Bethany to meet me down here now, and it's surprising she's not here, ready to go. I mean, never have I had such a punctual friend with benefits.

> Davis: You almost ready?

> Princess: I'll be down in five minutes.

> Davis: Is the princess actually going to be late for once?

> Princess: Just for calling me that I'm making you wait another five.

> Davis: You know you love it when I call you that.

> Princess: See you in fifteen.

I smile as I set my phone down and signal for the bartender to close my tab. I know she hates it when I call her that, which is why I continue to do it.

I love getting her fired up. Early in our... whatever you want to call it, I discovered when Bethany was riled up, it translated to off-the-charts sex. And nothing got her more worked up than when I called her princess. I don't know why, but it did.

So I kept doing it.

Yes, I know she hates the name. And I know she has called off our arrangement. That doesn't change the fact that pushing her buttons is one of my favorite things to do.

That and making her toes curl.

There is something about Bethany that is addicting. It's definitely not her constant need to look perfect for every occasion. I still don't understand why a woman needs to have perfect hair and makeup for a booty call when I'm going to mess up both.

It for sure isn't her deep-seated want to get married and have a family. That's good for some people, but I'm not one of them.

Yet since that first night, there has been something that has drawn me to her. Something about her I've never been able to say no to. Something that kept me coming back for more.

It's how she became the only woman I've slept with on more than one occasion.

Not that she, or anyone else, knows that.

I'm not a relationship guy. I'm the guy you have fun with. I'm the guy who doesn't take life seriously and is the life of the party. I'm not the guy you bring home to your parents. I'm the one your parents tell you to stay away from.

The dumb jock. The class clown. You name it, I've been called it my entire life.

At least that's who everyone thinks I am. I know I'm much more than that, I just don't correct them when they make the assumption. It's how I've flown under the radar and taken care of the business I have needed to.

I have everything I need and everything I can handle. Personally and professionally. I don't have room in my life for anything else.

"That is why it was best she left when she did."

Apparently, the combination of tequila and thinking about Bethany makes me talk to myself. In public. It shouldn't surprise me. The woman keeps finding ways to mess with my head.

Take our last night together. When I left my bed with her lying naked and sated, nothing seemed off or different. It was like any other night we chose to spend in each other's company. It wasn't until I got back to my bedroom, holding two bottles of water, that it hit me.

Looking at her lying in my bed hit me in the heart like it had never done before. I thought she was gorgeous from the first time I laid eyes on her, but at that moment, she was truly a vision. Her makeup and hair were a mess and all I could think about was what she would look like in the mornings. We had never spent a full night together, so I didn't know what she looked like in the morning light, before she had a chance to do her hair and makeup. I rarely got to see her like that, and frankly, I loved it more than when she was all done up.

And in that moment, I wanted to. I wanted to see her without the makeup. I wanted her to wake up in my arms before we went down to the kitchen to make breakfast; her wearing nothing but my shirt as we made our coffee. I wanted us to get so distracted by each other we forgot we had started making pancakes. I envisioned lazy days on the couch and date nights with Hunter and Sadie.

In that moment, I envisioned our future. And that scared the ever-loving shit out of me.

Those were the pictures in my head when the flash of Bethany sprinting out of my bedroom knocked the thoughts away. I was too stunned to stop her, though I know it was best I didn't. It's also why I didn't fight her the next day when she called our arrangement off.

She wants the whole shebang. She wants the husband and the house and the kids. How can she find that when she and I have become very good friends with benefits who don't have conversations past the ones where we are whispering filthy things into each other's ears?

It was a good move on her part to call things off. Though the thought of her with another man pains me in ways I'm not ready to admit; I know I'm not the guy for her. She wants forever. I'm not in a position to give that to her. Now or in the immediate future.

That's what I need to remember tonight.

My phone buzzes and I pick it up, thinking it's Bethany needing another five minutes. Instead, I'm greeted by a message from my sister who likes to sometimes think she's my mother.

> Abby: Please tell me you are not sitting at home alone on a Saturday night. Or worse, at the bar you always go to. Never mind. Maybe I'd rather you be at home than at that meat market.

I laugh, because when I tell her what I'm doing, she will never believe me.

> Davis: Actually, I am sitting in a hotel bar in Memphis waiting to go take video of my friends getting engaged.

> Abby: I don't know if you're being serious or not. Pics or it's not happening.

I laugh and do something I rarely do, snap a selfie and send it to her, making sure I get the sign that clearly says I'm in Memphis in the background. She'll get a kick out of that.

"You're wondering where I am, and you're sitting here drinking and taking selfies?"

Bethany's voice startles me, and I quickly put away my phone. My reaction gets a laugh out of her as she takes a seat next to me.

She's so close I could touch her, but I keep my hands to myself. The smell of her perfume gets me just like it does every time. It's something floral and sweet and screams Bethany.

And it's just now fading from my pillows.

"I had to do something while I was waiting for you," I say, taking another drink of my tequila in an attempt to recover. "I'm not used to you making me wait."

The look she shoots me lets me know she has picked up on my double meaning. The Bethany of old? She would have come back with a witty, and just as suggestive, comment.

I'm going to miss that Bethany. Hell, I already miss that Bethany.

But this Bethany? She just lets the comment hang in the air. When I take another look, her sapphire eyes look almost pained. Like she doesn't know what to do or say, and it's like every second in my presence is making her uncomfortable.

Out of habit, I let my hand graze down the side of her arm, wanting to put her at ease. I don't even mean to do it. But when she's this close to me, looking like this, I can't not touch her. She shivers under my touch before stepping back.

Shit, I didn't mean to scare her off.

"I'm sorry," I say, truly meaning the words. "I know what you said and I need to respect that."

"No apologies needed," she says, quickly standing from the barstool. "Old habits die hard. We should go, shouldn't we? We don't want to be late."

"Have you ever been late before? Or am I getting to witness a moment in history?" I say jokingly, hoping I can put a smile on her face.

"Ha ha. You are such the comedian," she says, a hint of a smile showing as we turn to walk out of the bar. "Just because I love being punctual doesn't mean I don't slip up from time to time."

"I doubt that, princess."

She turns and shoots me a look. "Do not call me that."

"You love it when I call you that."

She gives me a huff as she turns to exit the hotel. Having her in front of me gives me the chance to look at her uninterrupted. She's wearing a sweater dress that hits mid-thigh and heeled boots that come up past her knees. The sweater hugs her in all the right places and hangs off of one shoulder. It leaves plenty of room for my lips to find skin. Especially with her blond hair over the opposite shoulder. Hair that I'd love to wrap my fist around as those killer legs are wrapped around my waist.

Stop it. It's done. No more.

I know we can't get together. She was adamant in what she said, and I'd be an asshole to not respect her decision. I have two sisters. If I knew any guy they were seeing didn't respect their wishes, I'd beat their asses without question.

But looking at her now? Remembering the way her body felt in my arms? Or how she felt when she came undone on top of me that last night?

Fuck, I think I need another drink.

"Are you coming?"

Oh princess, those are three words that could get you in a lot of trouble—especially with tequila flowing through my veins.

I know I'm a bastard for what I'm about to do. Maybe the tequila wasn't in fact my best decision because those words have now sparked something inside of me.

I might not be able to have one more night with her, but that doesn't mean I can't drive her wild.

I smile as I take a few steps toward her, putting my hand on the small of her back to bring her into me. Just like always, whenever we touch, an invisible spark passes through us. I thought it was a fluke the first time it happened, but every time it's the same feeling. God, I miss that feeling.

And it's another fact I choose not to overthink. So instead, I taunt her with the possibilities and the what ifs.

"Oh, princess," I whisper into her ear. "That will have to wait until later."

I press a small kiss on her neck right below her ear, and I can feel the shiver through her body.

"I told you we were done Davis… never again," she says quietly, though she isn't trying to remove herself from my hold.

"Never say never." I place one more kiss on her neck before letting go. "Now, let's go take some pictures."

3

———

BETHANY

I ask the question even though I know Davis doesn't know the answer. I check my phone for the hundredth time, reviewing the directions I now know by heart. We are right where we are supposed to be—outside a jazz club on Beale Street at 8:15 p.m. Yet, there is no sign of Hunter or Sadie.

"I'm sure they just got held up at the restaurant. Keep your panties on, princess. Or don't."

I shoot Davis a glare, even though he doesn't catch it because he's staring at his phone.

"Can you quit watching sports highlights for five seconds and concentrate," I say, tugging his arm so he can help me look for Hunter and Sadie over the crowd of people who have gathered at our meeting spot.

"I'm not watching sports," he says, reluctantly following me.

"Oh really? What could possibly be more important right now than making sure we don't miss Hunter's proposal?"

"I was checking to see how the stock I bought this week is performing."

"Funny," I say, not even giving him the time of day with that response. "Put your phone away and keep on the lookout for them."

I have no idea what Davis was really doing, but he doesn't argue with me. He slides his phone into his pocket as we pace around the area Hunter told us to be at.

"Can you believe they are about to get engaged?" I say, doing my best to not make the silence between us awkward. We've never been together this much with our clothes on. "And at the spot where it all started for them. Is there anything more romantic?"

"I mean, he could have done it the first place they had sex. Or while they were having sex, but I guess then he wouldn't want us for an audience."

"Of course, you would say that."

"What? I'm sure that moment and location holds a special meaning for them."

I hate that I immediately think if that were the case for Davis and me, he would be proposing to me in his living room. Because that first night we couldn't even make it to the bedroom.

"It's not just the spot," I say, trying to divert myself from the thought of a naked Davis. "It's the whole city. Recreating the night. It's romantic."

Davis doesn't reply. We just keep looking for Hunter and Sadie, our phones at the ready so we can start capturing the moment as soon as we see them. I'm in charge of the photos. Davis is in charge of the video. I assume it's because Hunter knows I will be meticulous in making sure I get every angle. Davis just has to point in the right direction. Surely he can't screw that up.

"Is this what you would want?"

Davis's question catches me off guard. "Is this what I want for what? My engagement?"

"Yeah," he says with a shrug. "I mean, you're the one always talking about the marriage thing. I imagine you have had dreams of how your proposal would be."

I give him a look out of the corner of my eye, trying to assess the seriousness of his question. Is he messing with me or is he truly interested?

"You really want to know?"

"Yeah," he says, though he doesn't make eye contact. "Tell me all about it. What will it be like when your future husband proposes to you?"

"Well, first, I would want it to be a surprise. I would hate to know if it was coming."

"You said first. How long is this list?"

I give Davis a playful shove. "If you keep interrupting me, I won't give you the abbreviated version."

"Fine," he says, dragging it out like he's a toddler. "Keep going, princess."

"*Second* of all," I say a bit more exaggerated, skating over the fact he used that pet name. "I would want him to put a lot of thought into it. And I'm not just talking about a hundred candles and a trail of rose petals. I have always wanted my engagement to be special between the two of us. While I don't know the what or the how, I do know I want it to be something I tell our children and grandchildren about because it was so amazing. I want it to be completely unique, because it will only be meaningful to us. Something we will remember every day for the rest of our lives."

I brace myself for some sort of snarky remark from Davis. Maybe something about the candles burning down the house during my hypothetical engagement, or that I wouldn't let my future husband propose because my nails weren't done.

That remark doesn't come, though. Instead, he stops and turns to face me. And when he does, I see something in his blue eyes I wasn't expecting. It's not the normal look of lust like I'm used to. The look where everyone in the vicinity of us knows he has seen me naked.

I don't know what this look is. And the only word to describe it is… more.

More of what, I don't know.

"What?" I ask, needing to know what he is thinking.

"Nothing," he says, though the look in his eyes hasn't changed. If anything, it is getting more intense. Like he's trying to see through my soul.

Or kiss me.

Both are very bad ideas.

"Then why are you looking at me like that?"

"Like what?"

He takes a few steps closer to me and my breath hitches. He doesn't take his eyes off of me as he slowly places a loose strand of hair behind my ear. A tremble goes down my spine, just like always. I figured that reaction would eventually go away. It never did. If anything, knowing we aren't sex buddies any longer only amplifies the feeling. It's part of why I had to walk away. I knew it would only get stronger as time went on.

"Like you... miss me."

Before he can respond, I'm pushed into Davis with a force I didn't see coming. My hands immediately grip onto his chest as his arms protectively go around me.

"Watch it, asshole!" he yells to the seemingly drunk guy who just ran into me. The man yells back something inaudible to Davis as he haphazardly stumbles away.

"Are you okay?" Davis asks, rubbing his hands up and down my arms.

I nod, but I don't try to push away. I know I should, but I can't make myself, which makes it all the more disappointing when Davis quickly takes a step back.

"What?" The word slips out of my mouth, even though I should be glad he broke the contact. Being in Davis's arms like that leads to things I don't want to happen anymore. Things that can't happen anymore.

"I see Hunter and Sadie," Davis says, pointing over my shoulder. "It's time."

I turn to look in the direction he's pointing, and there they are, a seemingly confused Sadie being tugged down Beale Street by Hunter, who looks slightly frantic and very nervous.

It's go time.

I hurry and bring my phone to life, firing up the camera app to take pictures. But before I can start making my way toward them, not wanting to miss a second, Davis grabs my hand, pulling me back into him.

"You were right."

I tilt my head, slightly confused by his words. "About what?"

He gives my hand a squeeze before leaning in, his cheek brushing against mine.

"I do miss you."

4

DAVIS

"YOU'RE TELLING ME, that you, Mr. Hunter McAvoy, the man who went viral for a fake press conference where he professed his love… that all day you were an ass to the lovely Sadie. Then you spilled water on her, and this was all before walking up and down Beale Street for the equivalent of two miles before proposing? Sadie, sweetheart, maybe this guy isn't the one for you? You know I'm still available. It's not too late to change your mind."

Everyone laughs at my recap of the events leading up to Hunter's proposal as Sadie reaches for her now fiancé's hand, giving it a kiss before he puts it around her shoulders. Usually, I'd give them shit about being all over each other, but not tonight. Tonight is for celebration.

My best friend is getting married to the love of his life. And I couldn't be more excited for the two of them.

"He was. He did. And yes, I did," Sadie says, looking at Hunter with nothing but love in her eyes. "Thanks for the offer, Davis, but I'll have to pass."

The conversation flows as the four of us make ourselves comfortable around a table at the hotel restaurant. As a thank you to Bethany and me, Hunter reserved both of us rooms at the same place he and Sadie were staying. He also felt the need to emphasize that Bethany and I would be staying in separate rooms.

After we took some pretty epic footage of Sadie saying yes, we made our way back to the hotel. I figured they would want to spend the night alone—I know I would if I had just proposed. Hypothetically speaking, of course. But Hunter insisted the four of us celebrate together.

"Why would you pass on me?" I ask, taking a sip of tequila. Yup, I went back to the hard stuff. Still probably not a good idea. "I'm quite the catch."

Bethany and Sadie both let out simultaneous laughs as soon as the words leave my mouth.

"What?" I gasp, putting my hand over my heart like I'm offended. "Tell me one thing that makes me not husband-material."

"Oh, where do I begin?" Bethany chimes in.

I shoot a look to Bethany, who is giving me a devilish smile, like she's ready to expose all of my secrets.

"Name one thing, princess."

She sets down her empty champagne glass and sits up straight, like she's about to give a presentation to the class. "For starters, you won't even allow yourself to have a girlfriend, let alone get married. Kind of hard to get married without dating first."

"Nope. Doesn't count," I say, grabbing the bottle out of the ice bucket to give her glass a refill. "That's by choice. Doesn't mean I don't have the goods to be one if I wanted. Try again."

"Fine," Bethany continues, this time giving it a little more thought. "Oh! Your name. Kind of hard to get a woman to agree to marry you when you won't even tell your closest friends that vital piece of information."

"Strike two, my dear. That is also by choice. When the right woman comes along, she will be worthy of knowing my deepest secrets."

"What about me?" Hunter asks. "I'm your best friend. And your boss. I can't believe you haven't told me. Though, you know I could figure it out if I wanted to. I could just go look it up."

"Good luck," Sadie says, a sound of defeat to her tone. "I work for one of the biggest media companies in the country. We have access to records not many do, and I *still* can't figure it out. Who did you pay off to keep it a secret? And more importantly, why is it a secret?"

I hold up my glass, giving Sadie a cheers for her failed reporting efforts. "Don't you wish you knew. Maybe one day I'll give you the scoop. But only after you tell me if Hunter hadn't snagged you up, you would have gone out with me."

"Whatever you need to tell yourself to sleep at night. Randy."

The look I give Sadie is of utter confusion, while Bethany can't seem to hold in her laugh. "Randy? Who the fuck is Randy?"

Sadie shrugs while taking a sip of her glass of champagne, snuggling farther into Hunter's side. "If you're not going to tell us, then I'm going to assume it's something awful or something you despise. I know in the media guide your name is listed as R. Davis. Therefore, I'm going to keep guessing random names that start with *R* until I get it right. Or until I drive you crazy."

"Ooh, I want to play!" Bethany says excitedly, nearly bouncing on her seat.

"How much have you had to drink?" I ask her.

"Don't try and change the subject," she says, pointing her finger into my chest. God, I wish I could take it and bite it.

"Fine," I say, pretending to be exasperated, though I think their game is kind of funny. "If either of you guess it within the next year, Sadie can write an exclusive story on me centering around my name. If I win, I get lunch every day for a month."

I reach my hand across to Sadie. "Deal."

"Wait! What do I get, Romeo?" Bethany asks, a slight flirtation in her voice.

"Romeo, yeah, that's cute. So, what does the princess get?" I repeat, tapping my fingers to my lips, pretending I'm thinking of something really good.

What I want to say is I'll give her as many orgasms as she wants. That I will set up shop between her legs for as long as she will let me.

That I will forever ruin her for that future husband she's so desperate to find.

Instead, I say the next best thing. I push her buttons in a way I know only I can.

"Why, the princess will get a tiara. Only the best, of course."

This earns me a playful slap across the chest, which I gladly take—anything to get her hands on me.

"You're going down, Davis," she says, leaning a little closer into me, not taking her hand off my chest. She's so close to me that all I can smell is her perfume. It drives me fucking crazy. Between that and the three glasses of tequila I've had tonight, my head is spinning.

Only thing is, I just don't know if I'm drunk off of the alcohol or her.

Probably both.

After a few more minutes and one more shot of tequila for celebration, Hunter and Sadie tell us good night, leaving just the two of us at our table. I order us each another drink, though we probably don't need it. But I'm not ready for my night with her to be over yet. And by the look she keeps giving me—filled with want and need—neither is she.

I'm going to blame that look on what comes out of my mouth next. That and the tequila.

"Want to make another bet?"

She gives me a flirtatious look, and if I had to guess, she knows where my brain is going.

"What do you have in mind?"

"You need to answer a question first."

She cocks her head to the side. "And what is that?"

"How drunk are you?"

She finishes off her glass of champagne, sets it down on the table, and inches even closer to me. Fuck, does she realize what she's doing? Any closer and she'd be straddling me. Not that I care, but she has to know she's playing with fire right now. Sitting beside her all night, I'm like a literal tinderbox waiting for a spark.

She's definitely the spark.

And by the look in her eyes, she absolutely knows what she is doing.

The little minx.

"Drunk enough to not care about what I said last week. Sober enough to remember this tomorrow."

Fuck. This woman is going to be the death of me.

"Then the bet is that I can have you naked in less than an hour."

I whisper the words in her ear, and as soon as they leave my mouth, I feel her shiver against me.

Good to know I have the same effect on her that she has on me. Not that I doubted it though. Together we've always been combustible.

"What happens if you win?"

I put my arm around her back, bringing her flush to me so I can whisper my next words. "Then I'm going to make you come with just my tongue."

"And what happens if I win?"

I lean back in, placing a small kiss just under her ear. Right at the spot I know drives her wild.

"Then you get my tongue and my cock."

5

____

BETHANY

THIS IS SUCH A BAD IDEA.

This is a very, very, very bad idea.

The worst idea ever.

I know that. My brain knows that. My heart knows that.

But my body? The body that is currently melting into Davis because he is doing something wicked with his tongue that is making me tingle in places I didn't know could tingle.

My body thinks this is the best idea ever.

One more night. What could be the problem?

You could fall for him... even more than you already have.

Drunk me is going to ignore that little voice. Because all I want right now is the man who is kissing my neck.

"I almost forgot how good you taste."

Davis's words bring me back to the present as we step out of the elevator and stumble down the hall to my room. I reach into my purse, fumbling around, trying to find the keycard. It would probably be easier if Davis wasn't sucking on my earlobe, but I love it too much to tell him to stop.

"Hurry up, princess," he says slowly into the ear he just finished nibbling on. "Or do you not want my tongue between your legs? You don't have to delay to win the bet. I'm going to eat that pussy, win or lose."

My legs nearly give out as I continue to dig through my purse for the keycard. If he only knew how badly I wanted him there. That every night since I told him we were done that I've dreamed about his mouth and the dirty, yet delicious, things he can do with it.

"Oh, thank God," I say as I finally locate the keycard and quickly insert it to unlock the room. Before I can take a step inside, Davis picks me up and swings me through the doorway, slamming the door shut behind him, pressing me against the hard surface. I don't even have a second to get my bearings before his lips find my skin again, this time concentrating on the exposed skin on my shoulder.

"God, I love your tongue." I know love probably isn't the best word to use with a man who is nothing more than a hookup. But it's true. His mouth can do things I never imagined. Can make me feel things that no other man has.

The first night we were together, I remember being surprised by how much he seemed to enjoy foreplay. I figured he would be one of those lick it once, flick it twice, three pumps and done kind of guys.

But not this man. This man loves using his mouth more than anything. His tongue should be deemed a wonder of the world.

And I have missed it every day.

"If you love that, then I think you'll love this even more."

He lowers me from his hold against the door. I start to make my way to the bed, but he kneels down in front of me.

"Not so fast. Let's see if you still taste the same."

Before I know it, my leg is over his shoulder, and I hear the sound of my lace thong ripping as Davis's tongue finds my center. My back is against the door again and I don't know how I'm going to keep my balance standing on one foot in heeled boots. All I know is that I'll do everything in my power to stay upright as long as he continues that thing he is doing with his mouth.

"Holy shit…"

The best part of Davis giving oral is that it's never the same twice. This man doesn't just have one move. He has every move.

Tonight? He has decided to devour me.

I'm not going to object.

He isn't just using his tongue; his entire mouth is in on the action. It's as if I am his last meal and he doesn't want to miss a single taste.

As many times as he has done this to me, he's never done it while I'm standing above him. The view from up here is… erotic. Powerful. Like even though he is the one pleasuring me, I'm the one in total control.

I might think I have the power, but as I glance down at Davis, I realize I am nothing but putty in his hands. Hands that are reaching around and grabbing my ass, bringing my core as close to his face as possible.

"Davis. Ah!" I moan as he sucks on my clit. The sensation drives me wild, and I start to move my hips, all but riding his face. All of this… it's too much. There are so many sensations and I'm not going to be able to last for long.

"Almost," I pant. "I'm almost there."

Yet he doesn't stop. If anything, he speeds back up. That's it. I'm done for.

"Davis!" I scream his name as I explode on his face. The man has made me orgasm many times from oral sex, but never this hard. Never this intense.

I don't have a chance to catch my breath before he scoops me up, takes five steps, and we both go crashing onto the bed.

The next few minutes are a flurry of limbs, torn clothing, and desperation. Each of us grabbing on to each other for dear life. Our mouths colliding in passionate kisses that could make me come again from the intensity of it all. Our clothes being ripped off—figuratively and literally—as we fall into the sheets.

"I need inside you," he says right before taking my breast into his mouth, sucking on it like his life depends on it.

"Condom…" I don't know how my drunken brain remembers to say that, but I have a feeling if I didn't, we wouldn't have used one. We've never been irresponsible before. But we've also never been so much in the moment.

Right now, we're in a bubble. It's just us. No thoughts of the future. No thoughts of how different we are. No thoughts of we ended this thing not that long ago, yet here we are.

It's just us.

Davis releases my nipple with one last pop as he quickly jumps off the bed, somehow immediately finding his pants. He quickly grabs a condom from his wallet and sheaths himself before he's back on the bed, kneeling between my legs.

"What is it you want tonight?"

He might be asking me, but I have been in this situation before to know that no matter what I say, I'm going to get what he wants to give me.

And somehow, it's always what my body craves.

"You."

He strokes himself once before positioning himself on top of me.

"Then that's what you are going to get."

With one thrust, he pushes himself inside me, his perfect length and girth filling me completely. I expected after what he did to me against the door, and the subsequent tearing of our clothes on the way to the bed, that this would be hard. Rough. That he'd have me on all fours and be taking what he wants from behind.

That's not what he is doing at all. Right now, he's slowly moving in and out of me, making sure that I feel every inch of his cock as he thrusts. Our hips are circling in perfect unison, meeting each other at every right moment.

He sits back up, bringing my legs so they are fully wrapped around his waist. "I can't hold on, Bethany. Come with me."

"Yes." It's all I'm able to say as he begins pumping faster. I grip on to his biceps as he hits the spot that only he can find. Before I know it, I feel another orgasm rising in me, readying to let go at any minute.

"Now, Bethany. Come with me now."

And I do. With one more push, Davis and I come together, long and hard and perfect. It's the kind of orgasm I used to only read about when I snuck a read of my mom's romance novels. I have had friends who said that they had experiences like this, but now I don't believe them. There is no way to describe what just happened between us. And if I tried, people would think I'm a straight-up liar.

Davis collapses on me, and while I welcome his weight, this act takes me by surprise. Yes, he has collapsed on me before, but normally after a few breaths, he's up and disposing of the condom.

Now? Now it's almost like he's… cuddling me?

No, it can't be.

I then really question if I'm dreaming as he presses a kiss to my cheek before rolling out of bed to dispose of the condom.

Okay. Now we're back on track.

This is the part of our arrangement I know by the book. He gets rid of the condom, cleans up, gets dressed, plants another kiss on my cheek before saying some witty banter, and shows himself out.

Except, this time, that's not what happens. Instead, I feel the bed move. Though I know it's him, I almost want to turn and look.

But I don't. I just let the moment happen.

Davis in my bed. Wrapping me in his arms as we fall asleep together for the first time.

This might be a bigger mistake than the sex.

Holy crap on a cracker. Who is this man?

6

———

DAVIS

THE MORNING LIGHT creeping in from behind the curtain startles me awake. When I'm at my apartment, I'm never woken by the light. Blackout curtains are the best invention since smartphones, instant replay, and mobile banking.

That's not the only thing telling me that I'm not in my own bed, though.

I feel the mattress move as Bethany rolls to her side so she's now facing me, and by the looks of it, she's still asleep. Good. I'm going to need a few minutes to process the events of last night.

Hunter's engagement.

Tequila. Champagne.

Bets.

Going down on her against the door.

Sex so good I don't even know how to describe it.

Two drunk and sated people falling asleep together in a blissful bubble.

It doesn't shock me that Bethany is the first woman I've ever woken up next to—and that it doesn't surprise or scare me. Tack this up to another first that she doesn't realize she is for me. It's not that I don't want a relationship. I just know I can't put any more on my plate.

Sometimes I wish I were in a different situation. But wishing doesn't get you anywhere. I have my priorities. I have my duties for my family. I have a job that could change at any moment if the team I'm coaching doesn't perform well. Plus, during the season, I'm on the road for most of the year, and that doesn't count the travel scouting and off-season duties. None of that is good for a relationship.

So, unfortunately, there is no room for any woman. But if I were to make room for anyone, it would be this woman right here.

I roll to my side so I can unabashedly look at her while she sleeps. This is what I thought of that night. This right here.

Her blond hair is a mess over the pillow. Her mouth is slightly open, and every few minutes, a soft snore comes out. I think there is a little drool on the pillow, which makes me silently laugh. She would die if she knew I noticed that. The covers are tightly wrapped around her, but I know underneath lies a naked body that I would worship every day if I could.

In other words? She's perfect. And if I'm being honest, this is the most beautiful I have ever seen her.

And this will be the first, and last, time I'll ever see her like this.

For real this time. No more slips. No more drunk nights.

I could fall for this woman. So easily. And that can't happen.

The scary thing is, I don't even know much about her. We don't exactly "talk" when we are together. But from the little bit I do know? She's the type of woman I would go for.

She loves her family. She is a loyal friend to Sadie. The times I've made her laugh, I never wanted to stop hearing the sound.

And when we touch? I know it can't be a fluke that after months together, I'm still feeling the same spark.

That is why this has to be over. There's no room for her, or any woman, in my life.

"Mmm."

Bethany's low mumble alerts me she's awake. I start making my way out of bed, not wanting her to know that I've been staring at her for the past ten minutes like some sort of creep.

"You don't have to get up just because I'm awake now," she says, her voice groggy and still heavy with sleep.

"It's probably for the best," I answer, standing up as I look for my discarded clothes that are all over her hotel room. I locate my boxer briefs and quickly slip them on.

"You know, if we wanted to do things that were for the best, we wouldn't be here right now."

Her words cut me, even though I know they are true. When I turn back to look at her, she's sitting up, the sheets pulled up over her chest. I don't know if it's to hide her body from me or it's serving as a proverbial shield from the conversation we both know we're about to have.

Maybe both.

"Yet here we are," I say, throwing on the rest of my clothes before sitting next to her on the bed.

We both take each other in for a minute, a heavy silence filling the air. I look at her face, and it's swimming with a bundle of emotions.

Sadness. Resignation. Acceptance.

"Why can't we stay away from each other?"

I don't acknowledge her question, because I don't have an answer. And the only possible answer I have is one I can't and won't think about.

"I don't know, but this can't happen again."

She looks down away from me and nods, and I'm pretty sure I see a tear falling from her eye.

"Because you don't want anything long term," she says, sadness thick in her voice.

I let out a sigh. "And you want something that will last forever."

Our eyes find each other again, and I can see the pool of tears welling in her eyes.

"Hey there," I say, gently taking my thumb and wiping away a stray tear. "There's nothing to cry over. Certainly not over me."

She nods, quickly trying to wipe away the few other tears that have leaked out. "I don't know why I am. It's not like we were ever a thing. We aren't breaking up or anything."

Bethany might have said the words, but we both know that we essentially are. I damn well know she's the closest thing to a girlfriend I've ever had.

"I wish I could give you what you want," I say, lacing our fingers together, hoping she can feel the weight of my words.

"And I wish I could be enough to make you change your mind."

If she only knew. If she only knew that she is likely the only woman who could make me change my mind.

But I can't. I have my career. And my responsibilities. There isn't enough of me to go around. It wouldn't be fair to her.

So, to give her the opportunity at what she wants—what a girl like her deserves—I have to do the last thing I want to do. I have to walk away.

For good this time.

With our linked hands, I bring her a little closer to me and I'm relieved when she doesn't fight me away. I need to kiss her one more time.

When our lips meet, I can tell this time is different. I don't know if I've ever kissed anyone like this. With meaning. With emotion. Like I'm trying to convey words through the act.

I hope she can feel my goodbye, because I can feel hers.

It takes all the power I have to break the kiss. I don't move right away, instead letting our foreheads rest against each other before I place one more kiss on her cheek before I get off the bed.

This is it.

Last night was our swan song. This morning is our goodbye.

"I'll see you around," I say, grabbing my phone and wallet.

"Yeah. I'll see you around."

I don't turn back to look at her. If I do, I'll crumble.

Instead, I walk out of the hotel room with the knowledge that I just gave up the only woman who could have made me want to change.

7
____

BETHANY

MAYBE IT'S because I'm southern, or maybe it's because I'm a blonde cosmetologist, but I've always had an affinity for the movie *Steel Magnolias*. Something about that movie just draws me in.

As an adult, I have truly come to appreciate the strong leading ladies, the story that will rip your heart out and show how people can be vulnerable yet strong at the same time.

Then there's the quote. The one line I feel so deep in my soul that I know I'll remember for the rest of my life... heck, maybe that's the whole reason why I went into cosmetology as my chosen profession. But the movie quote has resonated with me since the first time I saw it on the big screen.

I don't trust anybody who does their own hair. Dolly Parton is a true queen, and we should all bow down to her greatness. Of course, that could just be the southern girl in me talking too.

Ever since then, I have wanted to be a cosmetologist. When I was eight, all of my dolls had different hairstyles. When I was thirteen, I asked for wigs for my birthday to practice different cuts and styles. In high school, my friends came to me before prom to do their hair and makeup.

I must say, we had the best-looking senior prom dates this side of the Mississippi.

I first wanted to become a cosmetologist to make women, and men, feel their best. I remember whenever my mom came home from the hairdresser, she had a certain glow about her. She always looked different, and not because a few inches of hair were gone. She was confident. She had an extra sway to her step.

I wanted to make people feel like that. So, when my friends were agonizing over college finals and internships, I was graduating at the top of my class from cosmetology school, about ready to start at one of the most successful salons in Nashville.

Over the years, I've learned being a hairstylist is more than giving people a good cut and color. It's about giving people time to themselves. It's about giving people an ear if they need it. It's about helping people feel beautiful inside and out.

And I am darn good at my job.

"Can you believe it?"

Considering I have no idea what Ruthie, my eighty-six-year-old client, just asked me, I'll amend that last thought to say, "except today." Today I am failing miserably. Not at the hair part. I have done Ruthie's hair every week for five years now. I could do her hair in my sleep.

But the other part of my job? The chatting and the talking and the being interested in my clients' conversations? I am completely out of it. I've had five other clients in my chair today, and I don't think I said ten words total to them, much less could tell you about anything that they talked about.

"I really can't, Ruthie." Not looking at her, so hopefully, she can't tell I'm fibbing straight through my teeth. "But stranger things have happened."

"You think there is something stranger than a twenty-something hottie asking me to be his sugar mama? I mean, I am a catch, but even I know I can't snag a twenty-year-old anymore. Maybe a few years ago, but these days I'm focusing more on the sixty-and-over crowd."

"Wait. What did you say?"

"Oh my dear," Ruthie says, shaking her head in laughter as she looks at my confused face. "You were so out of it, I just started talking about random things to see if I could get your attention. You missed the one where I said Elvis was living in my basement, and that I think next time I'm here we should shave all my hair off."

"Oh wow," I say, trying to laugh off that I've likely been spacing out the entire time I've been styling her hair. "I'm sorry. I'm just a bit out of it today."

"That's not just any kind of out of it. That look on your face is because of a man."

I raise my eyebrow, wondering if I'm really that transparent. "And how would you know that? Weren't you the one saying last week men weren't good for anything anymore?"

She gives me a shrug. "Just because they are good for nothin' doesn't mean we don't want them. I don't want to want Lester at the senior center, but the man does something to my lady bits that I didn't think worked anymore. Even if he cheats at cards. Moral of the story, we might not want men, but that doesn't mean we don't need them in some ways. Now, talk to me, dear. Lord knows, I've told you enough of my problems over the years. What has my favorite hair girl looking lost?"

I let out a large sigh and a small smile as I look at Ruthie's reflection in the mirror. Not only is she my oldest client, but she's also my favorite. And that isn't because she makes the world's best chocolate chip cookies, or because she gives me a bottle of moonshine each year at Christmas (that I'm pretty sure she distills herself). She's a spitfire. She tells it like it is. She keeps me on my toes. She's the definition of age is only a number.

And right now, she is the only person I want to talk to.

"You're right," I begin. "It is a guy."

"I knew it. I'm going to guess he's got you in knots. And not the good kind."

I give a small shrug, not sure how I want to say this. "We had an… agreement."

"Y'all were naked bed buddies."

"Is that what you used to call it?" I say, trying to hold in my laugh.

"We didn't call it anything because it wasn't polite to talk about back then. But we aren't talking about me. Why did you two call it quits?"

"We want different things," I say matter-of-factly. "And neither of us are willing to budge. So we called it quits. I just didn't realize it would be this hard."

That is the truth. It's been nearly two weeks since Memphis. I was a wreck driving back to Nashville after that night, which was expected. But I didn't expect it to last this long.

It's ridiculous that I am feeling this way. We were never anything serious. We were friends with benefits. Plain and simple.

Friends who had one last unforgettable night that is making me wish for things I can't have with him. And it wasn't just the sex. Hanging out with Sadie and Hunter made me wish that we were a normal couple on a double date. It was easy. Effortless. And it made me want more.

"Giving up someone you care about is never easy," Ruthie says as I give her one last spray. "That's why you need to get back on the horse."

I wasn't expecting her to say that. "I need to what?"

"Sweetie, I'm the one who wears the hearing aids. Not you. You heard what I said, my dear. Get back out there. Find yourself a new man. The only way to get over someone is to get under someone new, isn't that what the younger crowd says these days?"

"What?" Did she just say what I think she just said? "I don't think that's how it works, Ruthie."

"Actually, my dear, I think that's exactly how it works."

"I'm not just going to go out there and sleep with the first man I meet to get over someone I shouldn't even be hung up on. I'll be fine. By next week I'll be good as new."

I can't believe I'm having this conversation with an eighty-six-year-old woman.

"You might be. But maybe you need a little help. Now I'm not saying you have to sleep with Gavin right away. I'm just saying he might help you get over the man who is haunting your thoughts."

Now she is really confusing me. "Gavin? Who is Gavin?"

"The man I'm going to set you up with."

I'm pretty sure at this point, my eyes are bugging out of my head. "You are what? Huh? Who? I am so confused."

I take the gown off of Ruthie and she slowly stands from my chair. "Gavin is the grandson of a very nice man I've met at the senior center. He's new to Nashville. Just got transferred for his job at a bank, if I remember correctly. So, he needs to meet new people his own age. And he's going to be your date this Friday."

"Oh, is he now?"

Ruthie nods before grabbing her cane so we can walk to the front of the salon. "Bethany, my dear, I love you like you were my own grandchild. And the look I saw on your face today was of someone who is in pain. And I don't want to see that. I only ever want to see your beautiful smile. Now, I'm not saying that you need to sleep with Gavin, or even marry him, but I'm saying that you need to do something to take that frown off your face. And Gavin is the way to go about doing just that very thing."

She's right. Because since Davis and I have been sleeping together, I quit dating. I didn't mean to; it just kind of happened.

And maybe someone like Gavin is who I need, even if I only know his name and his job. If he works at a bank, that means he has a stable job. I know the guys I've dated in the past who have jobs like his haven't been the most exciting, but maybe a little on the boring side is what I need now.

Yes. I need stable. Guys in the banking industry who are looking out for their future—both personally and financially. Not football coaches who refuse to think past the next game.

Maybe Gavin won't be so bad?

"Fine," I say, walking to the computer to ring her up. "I'll go out with Gavin."

"That's right, you will," Ruthie says as I help her put on her jacket. "And make sure you wear something nice. Something that shows off the girls. Even at my age, the guys like the girls to be on display."

"Goodbye, Ruthie," I say, waving and laughing as she leaves the salon.

Maybe this won't be so bad? If anything, it rips the Band-Aid off and gets me back into the dating world. And maybe it will help me get over a man I should never have had to get over in the first place.

8

———

DAVIS

I LOVE THE DRAFT. It's my favorite part about coaching professional football.

Don't get me wrong, I love helping players develop. A win on Sunday is a feeling you can't replicate. Calling a play that leads to a big score? It's a pure adrenaline rush.

But the draft? The draft is months of planning, strategizing, and scouting, concluding with a three-day chess match against thirty-one other teams to see who can put the best moves together.

It's like the stock market of professional sports.

And I fucking love it.

Except not right now. Right now, I'm ready to pull my hair out.

"What happens if Phoenix takes a running back at number eight? Then Orlando takes a defensive back at fourteen, and Sacramento takes a linebacker at twenty. Who let me remind you, is the guy we love. And where does that leave us? We need defense this draft."

This is about the tenth hypothetical question Hunter has asked me in the past half hour. And the only reason he is asking me is because I'm the only coach left at the Fury facility. The defensive coordinator and the other position coaches said goodbye a long time ago. They got the hell out of Dodge as soon as they could.

I told them to save themselves. I'd throw myself on the sword for them because I could see the spiral Hunter was about to go down. He gets this way around draft time. He tries to predict every team's every move. It's an impossible task.

And it stresses everyone the fuck out.

"Up shit creek without a paddle."

This gets his attention. "Huh? What did you say?"

"You heard me," I say, kicking my legs up on the table in our conference room that has turned into draft central. "We're up shit creek. Obviously, you have it all figured out, and it's not going to go well for us because of hypothetical picks that are likely to not happen, so we should just pack up and go home. Don't even bother drafting. Maybe I can cash in some of my stocks and take a vacation to Aruba. I hear it's nice there in April."

The look he's giving me screams he doesn't appreciate my sarcasm. I, however, think I'm hilarious.

"We have to plan for everything. We can't just draft by the seat of our pants."

I let out an exasperated sigh and pick up a football that was left on the conference table. "And like I've said for the hundredth time, there is no way we can plan what is going to happen before our pick is on the board. There are twenty-one other teams picking before us. Killing yourself to try and see the future is not healthy. All we can do is put together our board of best players and go from there. So sit the fuck down and take a breath."

Hunter lets out a defeated sigh before slinking into a chair, beating his head with the football I just tossed him.

"We can't fuck this up."

"I know," I answer honestly. "And we aren't going to. But you seriously need to get your panties out of a bunch and relax. You're stressing everyone out."

I believe in my words, but I get where Hunter is coming from. This draft is easier said than done. A big reason we made the playoffs this past season was because we had the number-one pick last year and drafted our franchise quarterback, Bryce Donald. We knew

Bryce was our guy from the moment we set eyes on him. He was the total package. Great athlete, hell of an arm, and he's the All-American boy that moms across the country want their daughters to bring home. He was a home run pick. From there, we just had to decide who our best players were and let the cards fall where they may.

We knocked the draft out of the park. It was a feeling like no other. It was the first draft I was a part of where I was in the room where the decisions were happening. I still get a rush thinking about that day.

It reminded me that I've come a long way since my lowly days as a glorified towel boy in Denver. That was my first professional coaching job, if you could call it that. After a few seasons there, I somehow was able to get hired with the Fury as a low-level offensive assistant. I didn't care though. I was moving up.

Now, three years later, I've gone from no-name assistant who was partying with the players, to wide receivers coach, to offensive coordinator. I'm Hunter's right-hand man to run his innovative offense.

So I get his stress. We need to nail this draft, even though we are picking at number twenty-two. We are a team on the rise and after last year's playoff season we don't want to lose momentum.

"How many players are we scouting this week?" I ask, trying to get his mind off of the actual draft.

"I forget the total number, but every coach is somewhere," Hunter says, looking at our scouting lineup. "You are going to be heading to Michigan and Ohio Friday."

"Sounds good to me. Both have a killer craft brew selection."

Hunter all but rolls his eyes at my response. "Between flights of beer, can you remember to scout players? I'm going to head down to Alabama for Pro Day. Always good for me to make an appearance at the alma mater."

"You just need your ego stroked since Sadie is out of town."

Hunter launches the football back at me, which I catch with ease. "Says the man who isn't getting anything stroked right now."

"Maybe I am. You don't know what I do when I leave here."

"I know you aren't sleeping with my future sister-in-law anymore. I also know that you're a dumbass for not even trying with her."

The look I shoot Hunter is meant to kill. I'm not an idiot to think he didn't have an idea what was going on with Bethany and me, but this is the first time he has brought it up to me.

"You don't know shit, McAvoy."

I throw the ball back to Hunter a little harder than I should as I stand from my seat and head to one of the many whiteboards around the conference room. I grab an eraser and find an insignificant portion to erase. Anything so I don't have to look Hunter in the eye right now.

If he knows we aren't… whatever we were, then why did he bring it up? Dick move, in my opinion.

Since I left her hotel in Memphis two weeks ago, I've been doing everything I can to keep busy and keep my mind off of her. I've put in twelve-hour days at the Fury facility. I'm at the gym twice a day. I'm in constant motion to keep my mind from going to that dark place where all I do is think about Bethany.

Because if I don't stop, I don't have time to play the what-if game. If there is one thing I'm good at doing, it's what-ifing a situation to death. I know I made the right decision, but that doesn't mean it doesn't suck any less.

I made my bed. Now it's time to lie in it.

"You know you can talk to me," Hunter says, his tone now not as harsh. "You helped me when shit almost blew up with Sadie. The least I can do is return the favor. However you need it."

I know he means well, but talking to people about my personal life isn't my favorite thing to do. Nor is asking for help.

When you ask people for help, they take it as an invitation to know everything about your life. The easiest way to get around that? Don't ask for help. Never show weakness. Paste a smile on your face and deflect with a joke. It works every time.

I found out at an early age that if you're joking around and always happy on the outside, no one asks how you are doing. How could you *not* be happy? You're the life of the party! You might be struggling more than you ever have in your life, but if you're laughing and joking, no one is the wiser to what's going on behind the scenes.

No one will know that your piece-of-shit father up and left one day and never came back, leaving you, your mom, and two younger sisters to fend for themselves.

No one will know that you had to become the man of the house at thirteen.

No one will know that those responsibilities still follow you to this very day.

"No favor to return," I say, though I still don't make eye contact.

"She's going on a date this weekend."

His words catch me off guard. I freeze at the board, not knowing what to do next.

She's going on a date? Already?

No, this is what I wanted. What she wanted. This is what I knew was going to happen when we called things off. She wants to settle down. Start a family. It just can't be with me.

But I just didn't think it would happen so soon.

"Good for her," I say, not looking back at Hunter. "I hope she has a good time."

"You're a fucking liar, Davis."

I let out an irritated breath. "How am I a liar?" I ask, finally turning to look at him. "She's a good girl. She deserves to be happy. If dating some random dude makes her happy, then great. I'm happy for her."

Hunter just shakes his head at me, notably frustrated at my reaction. "Fine, if that's how you want to play it, I'm not going to press you. But answer me one thing. Not as your boss, but as your friend. Why? Why won't you give her a chance?"

Fuck. I liked Hunter much better when he was spewing out random draft scenarios.

I really don't want to answer his question. That answer could open a Pandora's box of information that I have worked my ass off to keep stored away under lock and key.

If I was going to tell anyone, though, it would be Hunter. I didn't have a lot of close friends growing up; I kept everyone at arm's length to make sure that no one knew what me and my family were going through. Hunter isn't a shithead teenager who would run his mouth, though. He knows what it's like to want to keep family things a secret.

Yet, I can't bring myself to tell him the full truth.

"I have a lot on my plate. Family stuff," I begin, though I know I'm still being pretty vague. "My mom and my sisters come first. Always. There's no room in my life for anyone else."

Hunter nods, though I can tell he knows there is more that I'm leaving out.

"Does Bethany know this?"

I shake my head. "No. And I'd appreciate it if she didn't. I have my reasons. That's all anyone needs to know."

Hunter stands and walks over to me at the whiteboard. "You know she'd understand."

"I don't want to have to make her understand."

"I get it," Hunter says as he gives me a hard pat on the shoulder. "But I don't get it at the same time. Thanks for telling me. I promise that I won't tell Bethany, or Sadie."

"Thanks. I appreciate it."

"Actually, no, that's not it," he says, slightly frustrated. "I get that you have your reasons, and in your head, you've made sense of them. But the right girl? The one who is made for you and only you? She would understand that you have other people in your world besides her. She wouldn't make you pick. She'd be your teammate. Your partner. Your best friend. She'd be right there beside you, supporting everything that is important to you. And that feeling? The feeling of having someone like that in your life? It's better than any win on a Sunday will ever make you feel."

I let Hunter's words roll around in my head as we pack up our things and make our way to our cars in the parking lot of the Fury facility.

I get what he's saying. In theory. I know he's found his person in Sadie, but from what I can tell from other relationships I have seen, they are unicorns.

Do I wish things were different? Yes. I also know that dreams are for fools. The real world doesn't allow for dreams. Just responsibilities. Heavy responsibilities.

As for Bethany? She deserves more than just to be someone else I'm responsible for. She deserves a man who can put her number one at all times.

"Hey, Hunter," I say as I open my car door.

"Yeah?"

"Just make sure he's not a douchebag."

Hunter nods. "I'll kick his ass if he is."

9

____

BETHANY

I AM CONFIDENT.

I am beautiful.

I am not going to go into this date thinking I just met my future husband.

I have said these words to myself at least ten times in the fifteen minutes I've been sitting in my car outside of the Mexican restaurant where Gavin and I agreed to meet. I've been trying to psych myself up to go inside the restaurant, but I can't seem to move from the car.

I don't know why I'm so nervous. It's not like this is my first, first date. Heck, it's not even my first setup or blind date.

Liar, you know why you're nervous. It's because this is your first date since you met Davis.

Ugh, sometimes the voice inside my head is a real twat waffle.

I didn't mean to go on a dating hiatus when I met Davis. It just kind of... happened. I know we weren't a couple. We didn't go out to eat or get drinks or even see each other in the light of day. Yet somehow, it feels wrong for me to be dating other men. I've obviously taken the friends with benefits scenario with Davis to the next level.

I should have known then that I was in deeper than I should have been.

But that's no more. Tonight starts a new chapter. A Davis-free one.

"Just have fun. Don't put pressure on yourself or Gavin. Just have a nice dinner and see what happens."

Maybe since I'm saying those words out loud and not just in my head, I'll listen to them a little better.

I check the time, five minutes until seven.

Check the hair and lipstick.

Deep breath.

Here goes nothing.

Gavin and I exchanged a few texts before tonight—compliments of Ruthie and his grandfather playing matchmaker—and we figured out this place was a good central location for the both of us. Plus, Mexican is always a safe first date spot, in my opinion. There are drinks, chips and queso, and it's a laid-back atmosphere.

And if you don't like tacos, then we don't have a future together, and it's best I learn that early.

From the little I talked with him, he seems like a nice enough guy. He was polite. He didn't ask for a picture of my boobs before he learned my last name, and when I asked him for a picture so I would know what he looked like tonight, he didn't send me one of him holding a fish or his junk. He's already better than almost every guy I've met on the dating app I just rejoined this week.

"Bethany?"

I turn to my right to see the man who looks just like the picture Gavin sent me standing in the lobby, looking adorably nervous.

"Hi. Gavin?"

"Hi," he says, letting out a relieved breath. "I was so worried I wasn't going to recognize you and say hi to the wrong person."

"Well, put those worries aside. Here I am. It's nice to meet you."

I reach out my hand to shake his as he simultaneously takes a step toward me, arms open for a hug. What comes next is the most awkward thirty seconds in my entire dating history of fumbling hands and repeated apologies.

"I'm so sorry," he says nervously, taking a step back and rubbing his hands down the front of his pants.

I touch his shoulder, trying to ease his discomfort. I ignore that I don't feel one bit of a spark when my hand makes contact with his. "No worries. I never know if people are huggers, so I always err on the side of caution. Come on, let's go grab a table."

We follow the hostess back to our booth as we both get settled in before saying another word.

The silence lets me take him in a little more. He has light brown hair that I would bet my cosmetology license on gets more blond in the summer months. He has kind eyes hidden behind a set of stylish glasses. His shy smile is highlighted by the slight dimple in his right cheek.

He's very attractive. Some might even say that he's hot in a Clark Kent before he becomes Superman kind of way.

Unfortunately, since he doesn't look like a tanned, brown hair, blue-eyed football coach, I am feeling absolutely nothing.

Don't. Don't compare him to Davis. Davis isn't an option. Get him out of your head.

"So, since I'm new in town, what's good?"

"Do you want an appetizer?"

We laugh at our second awkward moment of the night. Luckily, the waitress saves us from ourselves to take our drink order while also placing two glasses of water down in front of us.

"Do you do this often?" he asks.

"You mean talk at the same time as my date and shake their hand when they try to hug me? Can't say I do."

His shoulders visibly relax as my attempt at humor does the job. "At least you'll be able to say this date is memorable."

I hold my water glass in the air. "To a memorable first date."

He returns my gesture, and just like that, the blundering part of our date seems to be over.

We get served our drinks, place our food orders, and begin what I like to call standard interview date questions. We are both twenty-nine, yet neither of us is dreading our next birthdays. He's originally from North Carolina, went to college at N.C. State and recently moved to Nashville when his bank transferred him here. He used to spend each summer here with his grandparents, and when the opportunity presented itself to move here, he jumped at the chance. He likes cats over dogs, though doesn't want either, isn't a big sports fan, and has no opinion on whether pineapple belongs on pizza.

When it's my turn for the inquisition, I tell him how I was born and raised here, and how these days, not being a Nashville transplant is a badge of honor. I tell him the CliffsNotes version of my family history—that it was just my mom and me until she met Sadie's dad, Mike.

Guys don't get the full version of my sad childhood until at least date five. No first date wants to hear that sob story, especially the part that I've never met my father.

"I want to apologize again for earlier."

I give him a questioning look. "What for?"

He lets out a breath like he's trying to give himself courage. "I was so nervous for tonight. It's been a long time since I went out on a first date. And then my grandfather showed me your picture and you are gorgeous and… yeah. Needless to say, I might have psyched myself up a little too much for tonight."

This guy really is too sweet.

I reach out and touch his hand, hoping to calm his nerves. I again ignore that there is zero zing when our skin makes contact. I hate that I look for that now. The spark never even crossed my mind until… him.

"There is nothing to be sorry for," I say, trying to reassure him. "I haven't been on a first date in a while either. So, I'm a bit out of practice myself. Normally, I'm better judging whether someone is a handshaker or a hugger."

He laughs, though there isn't much humor in it. "I doubt you're as out of practice as me."

"How about this, since we seem to be great at doing things at the same time, on the count of three we'll say how long it has been since we've been on a first date."

"Promise to not make fun of me?"

I shake my head. "Cross my heart. This is a judgment-free zone. Ready? One… two… three."

"Four months."

"Four years."

I don't mean for it to happen, but I choke on my water. "I'm sorry. I didn't mean to respond like that. Wow, four years?"

He laughs, handing me a napkin. "I'd probably react like that too. But that's the answer. I was in a long-term relationship before I moved here."

"Is that why you moved?"

He shakes his head and immediately reaches for the second round of drinks the waitress just delivered. "No, but I'm not going to lie and say that the opportunity didn't come at the right time."

"Can I ask what happened?"

"We wanted different things," he said, a somberness now to his voice. "I guess we should have figured that out earlier. I wanted marriage and kids and a family. She wasn't opposed to the marriage part, but she didn't want children. I thought after a while she might change her mind, but she didn't. We realized, way too late, that it was best if we went our separate ways."

His words hit me straight in the gut. Is this what Davis was trying to save me from? He knew upfront that he would never change. Was it better to cut ties early like he did? Or was it better to be Gavin? To have four years of love with someone before you decided to move on with your lives?

Honestly? Both sound pretty crappy to me.

"Why do I have a feeling that you understand everything I just said?"

I shake my head as I smile. "Am I that transparent?"

"Nah, I just recognize that look."

I take a drink of my margarita. "Why can't two people who have deep feelings for each other want the same things? Finding love shouldn't be this hard."

This earns me a laugh. "If I knew the answer to that, we wouldn't be here tonight."

We both let the comment settle and take each other in.

This man is going to make some woman very happy someday. He's nice and sweet and good-looking. He has a good job, he's family oriented, and wants the exact same things I want in life. On paper, he checks every single box.

That is, except one. He's not the man that I can't get out of my head and the one I want in my bed.

"Gavin."

"Bethany."

Again, all we can do is laugh.

"We are really good at that," he says.

"That we are."

"Though I think that might be the only thing we're good at."

Thank the heavens he said it first.

I reach for both of his hands and give them a squeeze. "It's not fair to you that my mind is still with someone else."

"And though I know I need to at some point, I'm not ready yet to get back out there."

We let our words hang in the air, though the silence isn't uncomfortable. In fact, it feels right. All in all, it's a very pleasant date. We finish our meals with great conversation because the elephant in the room has been let free. If I felt one ounce of attraction to this man, I know I'd already have our wedding planned out.

Instead, I'm going to go home and dream of the man and the life I can't have. I know I'm going to need to get over him and the idea of us, eventually. But that's not going to be tonight.

Or likely tomorrow.

Maybe someday.

"Bethany?" Gavin says as we approach my car. "I know this is going to sound weird, but I want to say thank you."

This I wasn't expecting. "For what?"

He brings my hand to his lips and gives it the gentlest kiss. "For making me realize that I can do this. Maybe not now, but eventually."

It's like this man can read my mind.

"Then I should say thank you as well."

He quirks an eyebrow at me. "For what? Talking over you three times?"

"No," I say, giving him a kiss on the cheek. "For showing me that I'm not ready either."

10

———

DAVIS

I'M TIRED.

I'm hungry.

I'm horny.

Put those all together and I am one grumpy-ass motherfucker.

I've been scouting for the past four days, making my tour through colleges in Michigan and Ohio. At the last minute, Hunter requested I swing over to Indiana to watch a few kids, and that was all before my flight was delayed twice due to a late-winter snowstorm.

I might be originally from Pennsylvania, but I have become quite acclimated to the mild winter Nashville offers. I have no love lost for Midwestern snowstorms.

Normally, after a trip like this, I'd go home, shower the day away, hop into the sports bar not far from my apartment and grab food and a drink. If the stars aligned in my favor, I'd meet a willing woman to help me scratch the itch that's been festering since Bethany and I ended our arrangement.

Unfortunately, that's not in the cards for me tonight. Instead of having a relaxing night, I'm heading into the Fury offices to have a debrief meeting with Hunter.

I told him it could wait until tomorrow. He then went on a

twenty-minute rant about draft strategizing and having to get this draft perfect, and the hidden gem of the draft could have been in the players I watched this week, but I might forget if we wait until Monday morning.

I know when to pick my battles. This wasn't one of them.

Just as I'm trying to think of ten different ways I can get Hunter back for making me come in on a Sunday night, including what I'm going to make him buy me for dinner, my phone rings. And since it's eight p.m. on Sunday, there is no question as to who it is.

"Hello, favorite sister."

"How do I know you don't say that to Sara too?"

"Have you no faith in me? I'm a man of my word."

I'm pretty sure she snorts before answering. "Whatever you need to tell yourself to sleep at night."

"I sleep just fine, thank you very much."

"I take that as code for I'm still not sharing my bed with anyone for more than a few hours at a time so no one is stealing the covers?"

Leave it to my sister to get to the real reason for tonight's weekly check-in. Some weeks she calls to give me an update on our youngest sister. Sometimes she calls to talk about Mom. Most weeks, she gives me hell about not settling down yet.

"Is this going to be the topic of tonight's phone call? To try and meddle in my life?"

"What are little sisters for?"

"I thought once we became adults you'd quit annoying me."

This earns me another laugh. "Again, what are sisters for?"

We might give each other shit, but besides Hunter, Abby is my best friend in the entire world. I know that might sound weird to some, but if you grew up how we did, it would make sense.

Abby and I are Irish twins, though that's the only thing Irish that flows through our veins. I was born in January, and by December, my mom was taking care of two kids under the age of one. Considering we both share our mother's dark hair and features, people just assumed we were twins for most of grade school. We got tired of correcting people and just rolled with it.

Being basically the same age helped later in life when our dad took off. We went from being seemingly normal preteens to adults overnight.

When my parents were together, we weren't rolling in the cash, but we weren't starving either. Mom worked in the school cafeteria, and Mitch—I try not to think of him as Dad even though I look nearly identical to him—had a steady job with a construction company. I never had a pair of new Jordans or the latest gaming system, but I knew even at a young age we were better off than most.

Then one day, everything changed.

Mitch left without warning. It was a Saturday, and he said that they were getting overtime on a job. We didn't think anything of it.

That was until it was dark out and there was no word from him. We didn't have enough money for a cell phone back then, so all we could do was wait.

Sometimes I think my mom is still waiting. She used to sit outside in our backyard on an old tire swing for hours, just staring off into the distance. She said she was doing it to clear her mind, but I think she was waiting to see if he'd come home.

He never did. We never saw him again.

Next thing we knew, our lives were turned upside down. Mom picked up a second job waitressing. Abby became a second mother to our younger sister, Sara, who was a toddler when he took off.

As for me? I hated seeing my mother working herself to the bone. So along with school and football, I picked up every odd job I could. Every penny was either saved or spent on necessities.

Abby and my mom hated me working. They both wanted me to concentrate on school and football. They promised me that helping around the house was enough. But I couldn't sit back and watch them suffer. I had to do what I had to do. That was the man-of-the-house mentality that was almost ingrained in me—not by my father, of course.

So, from the age of thirteen until the time I graduated, I never went to a party. I never had girlfriends or went to the prom. It was school, football, and work. That's all that mattered because at the end of the day, I needed to help my family.

And to this day, I'm still living that lifestyle. Now just for different reasons. But still for my family.

Anything for my mom and sisters. They come first. Always.

"Did you really call just to nag me about my personal life, or was there a real reason?"

"I'd be lying if I said it wasn't partly for that. I hate that you are alone, Davis. You know you don't—"

"Stop right there," I warn, knowing where my sister is going with this conversation. It's a speech she likes to give at least twice a month. "Why else did you call, Abby?"

I hear the defeat in her sigh before she goes on. "I stopped and saw Mom the other day."

"How was she?"

"It was a good day. She remembered my name."

I hate that this is now what's considered a good day for my mom. But that's the reality with early-onset Alzheimer's.

"That's good."

"I was also told to tell you to expect a call soon from the billing department at the facility. Something about terms in her insurance changing."

As if this night couldn't get any worse. "Can't wait for that one."

"As if getting older and sick wasn't hard enough."

"Don't worry about it, Abbs. I'll take care of it."

I hear her take a deep breath. It's the kind of breath these days she reserves for scolding my two nieces or me. "You know you don't have to carry the load anymore. We aren't kids, Davis. I'm a grown woman. And despite what you think, so is Sara. We are in this together."

"I said I'll handle it, Abby." My voice growing frustrated, but I don't know how many times I can have this conversation with my sister. "You have a family of your own, and that's where your energy should be. I want Sara to worry about college, not this. I said I'll handle it and I will."

Silence weighs heavy on the line, even though we've gone round-

and-round on this ever since my mother was diagnosed. The early signs started becoming apparent when I was in college, though I have always wondered if they were there earlier and I just didn't realize it. Abby stayed at home and went to community college because she felt guilty about leaving Sara, who was still in elementary school at the time. That turned out to be a blessing in disguise because when we realized something was wrong with Mom, things happened at warp speed.

From what started as forgetting a few things turned into her going missing, which led to the early-onset Alzheimer's diagnosis. We were able to find a facility for Mom within an hour of Abby, and she has been the point person physically since I can't be there. That and basically raising Sara.

As for me? I'm the one footing the bill. I don't mind. Take my money. Take it all. As long as my mother is getting the care she needs and my sisters are provided for. That's all that matters, and if I have to give up aspects of my life for that to happen, then so be it.

"I hate what all of this has done to you," Abby says, her voice now softer.

"What do you mean?" I ask as I turn into the Fury facility.

"Since the moment Dad left, you put your life on hold. Then Mom got sick and you went into overdrive about helping us. I know we had to back then. But now? Davis, this shouldn't be how it is. Sara and I shouldn't get to live our lives while you suffer."

"I don't suffer, Abby," I say, exiting my car and making my way inside the building. "I've made my choices. Mom is safe and cared for. You and Sara are happy. I don't regret a thing."

"One of these days, big brother, you will. And when that day comes, you're going to realize that a promise you made to yourself when you were thirteen wasn't worth it."

I let the comment go and say goodbye to my sister as I head down the hallway to our coaching offices. Every Sunday call is like that with her. She makes sure I'm alive, updates me on Mom, and makes some sort of comment about my personal life. If I didn't love her so much, I'd quit answering.

She acts like I'm suffering because I've chosen to prioritize my family's needs over my own. When Mitch left, I became the man of the house. It's a responsibility I have never taken lightly. A man doesn't turn his back on his family. A man doesn't let his family suffer when he has the means to make sure they don't.

The day he left, I vowed to myself that my mother and sisters would never want for or have to worry about anything. Not for food, for clothes, for anything.

It's a vow I still hold true to this day.

It's why I won't get into a relationship. If I did, I don't know if I could balance it all. How can I be there for someone else, as well as my mom and sisters? How could I provide for two families? How would I prioritize?

I never wanted to know that answer, which is why I've kept women at arm's length my entire life.

Except her...

As if my mind is playing tricks on me, I hear her laughter coming from one of the offices as I walk down the hallway.

No. It can't be. What is she doing here?

I take a few more steps toward the voices and realize my mind isn't messing with me. Sadie and Bethany are sitting in Hunter's office. The door is open so I'm able to hear what they are saying without them realizing I'm here.

"So how did it go?" Sadie asks. "You can't tell me about a first date, then give me no follow-up details."

Bethany doesn't answer for a minute. Then she does something I rarely hear her do.

She giggles.

"He was like no one I've been out with before," Bethany answers, a happiness to her tone that simultaneously makes me happy for her and want to punch a wall.

I forgot Bethany had a date this weekend. I was able to block that out of my mind while I was freezing my ass off scouting players we might draft.

"In a good way?"

"In the best way. Sadie, it was the best first date I had been on in a while."

"Tell me everything. Consider this payback for all the times you made me gush about Hunter."

"Well, he was nice, and sweet. Once we got past the first-date jitters, he was easy to talk to."

"And…" Sadie probes.

"And yes, he was very good-looking."

"You're holding out on me. What else?"

"He was just about perfect. He wants the same things I want. He wants a family and to settle down. He has family in Nashville and wouldn't mind staying here. I honestly didn't think a guy like him existed."

I don't hear whatever else Bethany says because every ounce of blood in my body starts boiling.

I knew she had a date, but I figured it would be with some tool. From the little bit of her dating history I know, that seems to be her luck. Selfishly, I hoped it didn't change.

From the sounds of it, that's not the case.

You knew this could happen. You didn't try to prevent it. You made your bed. Now lie in it.

"You're here."

I nearly jump out of my skin at Hunter's words. "Dude, give a guy a warning."

"Not my fault you were eavesdropping."

"I wasn't eavesdropping."

The look Hunter flashes me lets me know clear as day he doesn't buy it. "Whatever. And before you ask, Sadie and I were on our way to dinner when Bethany called her. Since we had to make a pit stop here to meet you, she told her to come here and catch up."

"I didn't ask."

"You didn't have to. Come on, let's get this over with so we can get out of here."

Hunter signals for me to follow him down to our draft conference room. In doing so, we have to walk past his office. I know I shouldn't, but I take a peek as I walk past.

Bad idea.

I almost forgot how beautiful she is. Especially now, talking and laughing with Sadie. She looks happy. Lighter. Like she doesn't have a care in the world.

And that's all I want for her is to be happy. Even if it's with some douche canoe who is "sweet."

Fuck a bunch of sweet.

As if she could hear my internal dialogue, she takes that moment to look up. The second our glances connect, I see the light leave her eyes.

I put that look there. Because I was a selfish bastard who couldn't stay away from her, I put that look in her eyes.

No more. If the douche canoe makes her happy, then I need to stay as far away as possible.

Because I can't give her what she wants. And apparently, he can.

"You coming?" Hunter asks, standing at the doorway to the conference room.

And I do the only thing I can. I walk away from her without saying a word.

11

BETHANY

"HELLO? WHERE Y'ALL HIDING?"

Normally, when I show up at my mom and stepdad's house for Monday night dinner, I'm greeted with the sights of my mother flying around the kitchen and Mike reminding her she's only cooking for five of us, not an entire army.

Today? Today I've walked into an empty house, though I see both my mom and Mike's cars in the garage. The oven isn't on; nothing is in the crockpot; there aren't any signs that my mom plans on cooking tonight.

"AHHHHH!!! MIKE!!!!!"

No.

No.

No. No. No.

Did I just hear what I think I just heard?

No. It can't be.

"YES!!!!"

Oh my God.

It is.

My mom is having sex.

And she's a screamer.

When you grow up with a single mom who never brought men home, this wasn't something that happened. I don't have the childhood memory of accidentally walking in on my parents and them giving me a flimsy excuse about why they were naked in bed that I only buy because I'm a kid. Even when she and Mike started dating, I don't believe they even spent the night together when I was home until they were married and we all moved in together. Then again, he was my English teacher, so I'm going to assume that also had something to do with it.

And now, hearing what I'm hearing, I'm glad that I don't have to sit in his class every day knowing these are the sounds that the two of them make together.

I will never be without the knowledge that when my mother orgasms, she screams for all the neighborhood to hear.

I don't know how long I stand in the entryway. It has to be more than a few minutes because before I know it, my mom is coming downstairs, fixing her hair like she just freshened up in the powder room, not getting a mid-afternoon quickie from my stepdad.

"Bethany! Oh dear! When did you…?"

Her question trails off because at this moment, I'm guessing she can read the horror on my face.

"Long enough," I say as I look away, trying not to make eye contact with her.

"Well, you're an adult. I'm sure you can appreciate the act of two—"

"Mom, please," I say as I follow her into the kitchen. "I beg of you. I never want to talk about this again."

"Oh, come on, Bethany," she says, pulling chicken out of the refrigerator. "We used to talk about this stuff all the time."

It's true. To an extent. My mother and I have always been extremely close. I never knew my father. They were engaged when she got pregnant with me but decided to postpone the wedding until after I was born. She says every day that was a blessing in disguise because after two months of fatherhood, he couldn't handle it and split. Signed away his parental rights, never to be heard from again.

Apparently, fatherhood is easier to dispose of than a used condom.

Since it was just me and her, we became this weird combination of mother-daughter and best friends. She never pulled punches with me. I had the birds and the bees talk long before my friends did. I wasn't embarrassed when I first got my period. I even ran home and told her all the details about my first kiss.

There has never been a part of my life when I didn't think I could talk to her.

That is, until now. Hearing your mom cry out her husband's name during an orgasm is crossing the line.

A big one. One that can never be uncrossed.

"Please, Mom, let's forget about it," I say, trying to busy myself by starting to make the salad.

"You know sex is a natural thing," she says, and I swear on my best flat iron that if she goes into the lecture she gave me when I was in sixth grade, I'm going to lose it.

"Yes, Mom. I do. Now please—"

"And it's natural as you get older your sex drive…"

Oh God, she's really never going to stop.

"Mom!"

"And you know you arrived a half hour early."

Just as I'm about to protest again, my stomach makes a sound that I've never heard it make before. Not even on my twenty-first birthday after ten lemon drop shots and a trip to Taco Bell. Who knew that my mom talking about sex could make me physically sick?

"Bethany?"

I hear my mom, but I don't answer as I sprint to the bathroom that is just off the kitchen.

There is no such thing as vomiting gracefully. And for the next ten minutes, I try to figure out what in the heck I ate to make this my current reality.

After I left the Fury facility last night, I was craving hot chicken, which I rarely do, and picked some up on the way home.

Maybe it was the potato salad? Yes. That had to be it.

"Bethany? Are you all right?"

Sadie's voice travels through the door, but I don't answer right away. First, I make sure I'm confident that whatever just happened is over before I stand and start rinsing my mouth out.

Gosh, that was a weird turn of events. And hopefully, a one-time thing.

"Give me a second."

Convinced I look like I didn't spend the past ten minutes unloading my guts, I open the door to see Sadie standing in front of me, a concerned look on her face.

"Are you okay?"

I laugh it off the best I can. "Yeah. I don't know what happened. I have it narrowed down to bad potato salad or hearing our parents having sex."

This makes Sadie's eyes go wide.

"Did you just say...?"

I give her a devilish smile. Because if I have to know this, so does she.

"Oh yes. And fun fact. My mom's a screamer."

THE REST of the night is Monday dinner business as usual. My stomach stopped revolting, my mom quit trying to talk to me about sex, Sadie retreated to the study to conduct a phone interview, and Hunter and Mike had their now-weekly debates over the best college football players of all time.

Just a normal Monday night at the Benson-Hall household.

"You sure you're okay?"

Ever since my episode earlier, my mom has asked me this question every five minutes or so. I thought me loading the dishwasher would give me a reprieve. Not so much.

"For the hundredth time, I'm fine, Mom. I think I just had some bad food last night. Please stop worrying."

"You're my baby, I'll never stop worrying."

She wraps her arms around my waist as I lean back into her

embrace. I know everyone says that their mom is the best, but I'm pretty sure mine would win every time.

"That's our job as parents. We will worry until the day we die," Mike says, entering the kitchen with Hunter and Sadie right behind him. "Even though you two are adults, and soon starting families of your own, you're still our little girls."

I know the second part of that comment was directed toward Sadie, but I'm not going to lie that it doesn't sting a bit that it's *only* directed to her.

I never really thought about having the stereotypical family growing up. I had my mom. We were happy. That was all I needed.

Then she met Mike.

I remember when she first told me about him. I remember thinking to myself that this was the happiest she ever looked. She couldn't stop smiling. She would just stare out the window in a daydream, and I never wanted to disturb her.

That was when I decided that I wanted to find a love like theirs. And I didn't want to wait until I was in my forties.

I want it now.

Maybe because I'm so desperate to find it is why I haven't. I know there's a saying about you find love when you're least expecting it, but I think that's a bunch of bull crap.

Although, my mom didn't expect to meet Mike during a PTA meeting.

And Sadie didn't expect to meet Hunter when she did. Heck, they never really should have ever even gotten together. A coach and a reporter dating is super taboo in their world.

Yet here they are. Happy and engaged.

And here I am. Puking alone because of bad potato salad.

"Bethany, are you okay?"

Just when I think my mom is asking me if I'm about to get sick again, I realize it's because I've started crying.

"Yeah," I quickly say, wiping away the stray tear. "I should get going. I have early clients tomorrow."

Considering how this night has gone for me, my mom doesn't

press about me leaving early. I quickly tell everyone good night and make my way back into the Nashville city limits toward my apartment.

Normally, when I'm in my car, I find my Top 40 country station and blare the radio. Tonight, I choose to drive back to my apartment in silence, only my thoughts keeping me company.

I've always been happy for Sadie and Hunter. I don't know why tonight, all of a sudden, I feel a pang of jealousy toward them. There's nothing to be jealous of. They found their love story. Mine is coming soon.

Hopefully. Maybe.

Crap... there go the tears again.

What is with me tonight? As much as I want to blame it on hearing things no child ever wants to hear, I know that's not it. One minute, I'm my normal happy self. One minute, I'm crying over nothing. One minute, I'm throwing up.

This isn't like me.

Maybe it's my time of the month? Yes, that has to be it. Good ol' Aunt Flo is on her way to town and it's throwing me all off.

At least, that's what I'm going to blame it on. Because being the depressed single girl who realized today her mom has a better sex life than she does is not an option.

12

BETHANY

I'm not even three steps inside Hunter and Sadie's condo when my stepsister says that statement and drags me into the half bathroom just off the entryway.

"Why am I hating you? Did you forget the wine? Sadie, I said I'd order the pizza. You had one job for girls' night, and that was to get the finest bottle of ten-dollar wine Target has to offer."

"No, I didn't forget the wine," she says in a loud whisper. "But I want you to know that when I invited you over tonight, I really thought it was just going to be the two of us."

That makes my eyes go wide. "What are you talking about?"

She looks toward the door, even though it's closed, before looking back to me. A look of guilt is written all over her face. "Between the time I told you to come over and now, Hunter might have moved the draft strategy session to here."

"Sadie…"

"And he might not be alone."

When Sadie asked me to come over tonight because Hunter was working, I jumped at the chance. For some reason, I was feeling extra emotional and really didn't want to be alone. What better way to fight the depression, pre-period blues than with pizza, cheap wine, and a binge-watch of the new historical romance series on Netflix?

Guess I'll never find out.

"It's fine," I lie.

Sadie raises her eyebrow at me. "Really? You aren't mad that Davis, whose name is not Ricardo, is here, and you had no prior warning?"

I mean, I am mad. Not mad, just… mentally unprepared. But I can't tell her that. Sadie knows the bare minimum of what went on with Davis and me. She definitely doesn't know what happened in Memphis. She doesn't know that the real reason my date with Gavin is going to be a one-and-done is that the entire night I spent comparing the two men.

I should have told her about us when we first started. It would have made everything so much easier. I don't even know why I didn't. Maybe because I felt ashamed? I'm not one to have a month's-long hookup. But what's done is done. I've made my bed, and now I have to awkwardly lie in it.

"I'm not mad. They can do their thing and we will do ours," I say, trying to play it off. Though I take the time in the bathroom to make sure that the little makeup I wore today still looks good.

"Are you ever going to tell me what happened with you two? I thought maybe after Memphis things would change. You seemed to be getting along so well at the bar."

I make eye contact with Sadie through her mirror, a sad look gracing her face. It matches the look on mine.

"Everything is how it is meant to be," I say, my tone resigned. "Now, where is this wine, and you better have bought more than one bottle."

She lets out a sigh. "As long as you are happy, that's all that matters. I love you, sis."

Sadie gives me a side hug before we exit the bathroom. I let her leave before I give myself one last glance-over, fighting back the unexpected wave of tears that almost hit me from Sadie's words.

Deep breath. Check.

Makeup? Good.

Hair? Messy, but in a cute and styled way.

Heart? Locked up. Tight.

I take one last resolving breath and leave the bathroom. I kind of hoped that I'd at least get past the kitchen before I saw him, but of course, that's not my luck.

Standing at the counter, in all his muscled, sexy glory, is Davis.

And he's wearing gray sweatpants.

Dear Lord Jesus and Queen Dolly, give me the strength to resist.

His back is turned to me, which gives me two choices right now. I can quickly walk past him and not say a word, hoping he gets the idea and doesn't talk to me. I do need a wineglass, but I'll just drink from the bottle if it affords me the chance of avoiding him.

Or I could suck it up, say hello, and attack the elephant in the room head-on. Be an adult. Let him know that I'm the bigger person here and that his presence means nothing to me.

"Why don't you take a picture? It might last longer."

Or Option 3: Get caught staring at him when I didn't even know he knew I was there.

"I have no idea what you mean," I say, even though I totally was just staring at his butt. "I'm just about to get myself a wineglass."

He turns to look at me, a devious grin on his face. "Wineglass, huh?"

"Yes, a wineglass," I say with more confidence than I'm feeling as I walk toward the cupboard.

I might have given myself the option of talking to him and being an adult, but I didn't take into account what it would feel like to be in his orbit again. Every step I take closer to him, the more my body reacts to his mere presence.

"I didn't expect to see you here tonight," he says, now leaning against the counter, his arms crossed in a way that should be casual yet is ridiculously sexy when he does it. God, that smirk on his ridiculously handsome face is more potent than I remember.

"I can say the same for you," I say as nonchalant as possible. "I didn't picture you as one who worked past five o'clock."

Yes! Fight off his vibe with sarcasm and snark. Good plan!

He quickly puts his hand over his heart. "You wound me, princess. What makes you think that I'm a clock watcher?"

"Excuse me for thinking that the fun uncle of the Fury works overtime," I say, now standing directly in front of him. "I didn't think those two things went together."

We might be playing a game of verbal cat and mouse right now, but I can't deny the pull I feel toward this man.

And I hate that I do. He is the worst possible man to feel like this toward. Is it ever going to not happen when we are near each other?

Even though I know what I'm feeling is all kinds of wrong, it doesn't mean I don't want to pull him into Hunter's garage and have a repeat of the championship game night where he made me see stars against Hunter's truck.

"Fun uncle, huh?" he says, taking a step toward me. "I've heard that I've been called that. I also get dumb jock a lot. But I don't know if I agree with that one."

I quirk my eyebrow at him, doing my best to ignore the overwhelming effect his cologne is having on my body right now. "Then how would you describe your work habits? I mean, you are the man who once told me that if it isn't fun, it isn't worth doing."

Just as I'm about to pat myself on the back for how I'm handling this interaction, Davis leans a little closer.

Oh God... No! Stay strong! He's just a man!

But I don't know if I have enough strength to fight back all of the feelings my body is processing right now. His lips are inches away from my ear and his breath on my neck right now has a direct path to my core.

I feel myself getting weaker by the second.

"I'm a much bigger proponent of the phrase 'work hard, play harder.' You remember that, right? You remember how hard I like to play, don't you?"

Dear seven-pound, eight-ounce baby Jesus, give me the strength right now because I don't think I can resist.

Before I can answer, Davis continues. "But the question is, does your new boyfriend play like I did? Does he play hard, Bethany?"

The noise inside my head right now sounds like a ten-car crash on Interstate 40 during rush hour.

"What did you just say?"

I'm genuinely confused. Who is he talking about? Gavin? How does he even know? Did Hunter tell him something?

Then it hits me.

Sadie... Sunday night... the Fury facility... making eye contact with him before he walked away without even an acknowledgment.

That must be it. He must have overheard me talking to Sadie about my date with Gavin. Though by how he is talking, he must not have heard the part where I told Sadie that there was no chemistry and we are going to just be friends.

Davis takes a step back, a satisfied look on his face. "You heard me. I was just asking if your new boyfriend likes to play hard, too? Or is he one of those guys who plays it safe? You didn't strike me as a girl who would be attracted to that kind of guy, but what do I know? I'm just the dumb jock who doesn't know the meaning of the word serious."

"Don't put words in my mouth," I say, my blood now simmering. "And who I do or don't see is none of your business."

"It's not," he says, trying to play nonchalant. "I just think it's funny that you go from me to what I'm now guessing is some nice guy who is all about giving you your two-point-five kids. But hey, whatever floats your boat."

Is this man serious right now? The sheer audacity of him!

I don't even justify his outburst with a response. I don't correct him about Gavin. I can't. I don't trust my words right now. Instead, I shove my way past him, open up the cupboard and get a wineglass. A big one. I'm going to need the whole bottle after this interaction.

"Nothing to say, princess?"

I take a breath, trying to even my tone as much as possible despite Davis being ridiculously infuriating right now.

"Who I am seeing is none of your business."

A shit-eating grin forms on his stupid handsome face. "Ah, then that's all the answer I need. I hope that Mr. Nice Guy gives you everything you want."

"You!" I scream, slamming my wineglass on the counter. It might have shattered, maybe just cracked. I'm not sure. "You have no right to ask about who I am or am not seeing. What Gavin and I do or don't do is not your concern."

"Ah-ha!" he says, a smug look on his face. "So you are seeing someone. Gavin's his name, huh? That didn't take long."

"This is all because of you! How dare you try and throw stones at the type of man he is. You've never met him. Remember, you did this. You're the one who didn't want more. You're the one who couldn't bear to have his perfect little fun life be complicated by such hassles like a girlfriend or responsibilities. Or God forbid, a family and a future."

"Don't you talk to me about family or responsibilities," he answers, his voice now going down an octave. "You have no idea what is on my plate."

I am livid right now. "How can I? How can you? You won't even tell me your name! You won't tell anyone. I don't know if you're an only child or you have eight siblings. I know nothing about you. And that's your doing. I wanted more. You didn't. That was that. So before you come around here giving me hell for moving on with my life, remember each and every reason that I'm doing it."

My breathing is heavy, and I can't believe all of that just came out of my mouth. This isn't me. I'm not the one to yell at anyone. I hate confrontation. I used to try and break up fights at recess because they made me sad.

Then I look over Davis's shoulder and see Hunter and Sadie standing outside the kitchen, looking at us in shock. Davis turns when he sees my eyes fixed on them, his shoulders dropping when he realizes that we just had a full-fledged screaming match in their kitchen.

"I'm sorry," I say, running to grab my purse, embarrassment and a million other emotions raging through my body. "I need to go."

"No," Davis says, gently putting his hand on my shoulder. "You stay. Hunter, I'll see you tomorrow."

All I can do is watch him as he grabs his keys and makes his way to the door. What happens next is something I never expected.

"You're right," he says, though he doesn't turn around. "This is all my fault."

And then he walks out.

Why does it feel like this time him walking away means forever?

13

DAVIS

I TURN the treadmill up to eleven, hoping that the punishing pace will do the damage I'm seeking. My normal run is somewhere around a nine, so hopefully, this does the trick.

It won't. Nothing will. Nothing will make up for how I treated Bethany tonight.

Could I be any more of an asshole?

The moment I left Hunter and Sadie's place, I wanted to turn around and apologize. I know I should have. Maybe it was my pride that didn't allow me to do it.

More like my shame.

When I drove away, I considered heading to the bar, and finding some faceless and nameless woman to get lost in for the night. But the more I thought about it, the more I couldn't stomach that thought.

Instead, I drove home and found myself in the gym of my apartment complex. When I was in high school and was mad at the world for the hand my family and I were dealt, I'd take my frustrations out on weights or a heavy bag.

And when that wasn't enough, I went on a run. A long, punishing run.

But tonight, even that isn't working. That's how much I fucked everything up.

Where did I think I had the right to question who she was seeing? Or to act the way I did? If I knew a man was treating Abby or Sara like that, I'd pummel him to within an inch of his life.

Bethany was right. Every word she said. I'm the reason nothing is happening between us. I'm the one who refuses to budge. Granted, my reasons are valid, but still, it's because of me. How can I be upset that she is seeing someone new?

I can't be. Yet I am. And I'm not sure how to process all of that.

"I don't regret a thing."

"One of these days, big brother, you will. And when that day comes, you're going to realize that a promise you made to yourself when you were thirteen wasn't worth it."

Abby's words from a few weeks ago come to the forefront of my memory. Is this what tonight was? Regret? No. While I might regret how I treated Bethany, I don't regret why we aren't together. I made a choice back then, and that was to put Mom, Abby, and Sara first. Always. Just because my balls had barely dropped at the time doesn't mean anything. I meant what I said, and I'm going to stick with it until my dying day. I won't be like my father and dismiss the family responsibilities that I have. Real men don't do that.

As long as they are taken care of, I will regret nothing.

Except living with the knowledge that I put the look of anger and sadness on Bethany's face tonight.

That sobering thought sends a jolt through me and I jump to the sides of the treadmill, letting the belt keep running as that image goes through my head.

What kind of man talks to a woman like that? I pride myself on being a man for my family, but what kind of man am I to make a woman feel bad about herself? To chastise her about her dating life?

Fuck, I really am an asshole.

I don't think this was the type of regret my sister was talking about. Neither is what I'm about to do.

"Hello? Davis?" Abby says when she answers, confused as to why

I'm calling. "Is everything all right? What happened? What did you do?"

I sit in a nearby chair, thankful that no one is in the gym right now. "What makes you think I did something?"

"Because you are calling me, unprompted, on a Wednesday night at nearly midnight. Spill it. What did you do?"

I run my hand over my face, wondering where to even start. "There's this girl."

I've never begun a sentence like that to my sister. Therefore, I didn't expect the high-pitched noise that came from the other end of the phone that I'm pretty sure only dogs can hear.

"Abby, settle down. It's not like that."

The line immediately goes quiet. "What do you mean, *it's not like that*? Oh God, did you fuck it up already? You are such a fucking man sometimes."

I let out a sigh I'm sure she can hear. "It wasn't supposed to be serious between us. But…"

"But then it got serious?"

I let out a sigh. How do I explain this? "Yes. No. I don't know. She wants more than I can give her. She wants what you have. The husband and the kids and the happily ever after. I can't give that to her, so I told her to move on. And she did."

"You did what?" Abby yells, and I'm pretty sure the only people who have ever heard her voice reach this volume are her children and husband. "Why on God's green Earth would you tell her to do that?"

"You know why."

"Are you meaning to tell me," she begins, then has to take a deep breath before continuing. I haven't been yelled at like this since I was ten. "That you met a woman you liked enough to actually keep around for more than a night. And I'm going to assume she felt the same way about you. And because you decided when you were thirteen that you were going to provide for us that you turned her away? Wow, big brother, you are a special kind of dumbass."

"You know I had to," I say, trying to defend myself.

"You did not. We are all adults, with our own families now, not children. Don't use us as an excuse to run from commitment."

This gives me pause. Is that what I'm doing?

No. She's wrong.

"Abby."

"Ri—"

"Don't. Do not use my full name."

"If a situation called for it, it would be this one."

"I didn't call you for a lecture."

"Then why did you? Why did you call me to tell me about a girl I'm never going to meet because you're an idiot who pushed her away because of a decision you felt you had to make when we were kids?"

I don't answer right away because I honestly don't have any idea how to. She's right. I made that declaration when I felt our backs were against the wall. We were struggling, and I hated seeing my family suffer. Mitch leaving put us in an impossible situation that no family should ever have to endure.

I never thought about the future when I decided to put the family on my shoulders. I never thought there might be a day when I'd want more. And now, to have more in my own personal life, I'll have to let down the family I'd die for.

That is not an option.

"I called because… I don't know. She and I, we have mutual friends. We saw each other tonight. It didn't go well. I said some stupid shit and… I don't know, Abby. I feel horrible."

"Do you feel horrible because of what you said or because you're in this situation to begin with?"

I take a moment to think about that. The real answer is both, but I wouldn't have to be sorry if we never started sleeping together.

But then I would have never known her. And I hate that most of all.

"Do you think I can do it all?" I ask, ignoring Abby's question.

"Brother, there has never been a time in your life that I didn't think you could do anything you put your mind to. You got good grades while working thirty hours a week, while also playing football well enough to earn a scholarship. You have put this family on your back—carrying a heavy burden that no one person should have to carry—while also moving up the professional coaching ladder. Don't sell yourself short. If you think she's the one, do not let us hold you back. You know that's not what Mom would want."

Abby's last words are a straight knife to the gut. "Low blow, Abby."

"I know when to play the ace. And now is the time. If you want to see where this goes with this girl, then go for it. Quit using us as a shield. You have to live your own life. If anyone deserves happiness, Davis, it's you."

Is she right? Can I do it all? I never thought I could. The mere thought of it made me panic. But not as much as just the mere thought of Bethany being with another man.

"I don't know if I can fix this, Abbs," I say, knowing how badly I fucked up tonight.

"Well, you better try. I want to meet the woman who made you finally get your head out of your ass and tell her thank you."

14
____

BETHANY

BEING BORN and raised in Tennessee, I pride myself on being a southern woman.

I always say please and thank you. I refer to my elders as sir and ma'am. I love anything with my initials monogrammed on it. I still say my prayers every night, and I believe that white shoes have no place on your feet after Labor Day.

I might be a lady, but that doesn't mean I don't cuss a little.

Not often. Only in certain situations.

Like when someone tells me they only have Pepsi products. Because Diet Coke is *not* the same as Diet Pepsi.

Or when a certain football coach is making me forget how to string together sentences.

Or when I'm two weeks late on my period.

That last one requires all the swear words. And it's all I've been saying all morning.

How in the fuck did I not realize I had missed my period?

I didn't even realize I was late until this morning when I looked inside my medicine cabinet and saw the box of tampons. The box that hadn't been opened this month. That unopened box caused a slew of cuss words to be formed in my head.

Then I did the math. I should have started two weeks ago. I've never been regular, but I've never been *this* late. I'm not on the pill, but I am always careful. Always. No condom, no entry.

We were careful, right?

The thought sends me into a whole new level of panic. Because if this is true, then it means...

Davis... what will he think?

Oh God. Davis. The last time we spoke at Hunter and Sadie's was... well, it wasn't pretty. The things we said to each other, neither of us can ever take back.

Besides that, the man fears commitment like I fear snakes. As in, don't put it within fifty miles of me unless you want me to full-on freak-out. If what is happening now is what I think is happening right now, he is going to flip the entire fuck out. There's no use in sugarcoating that reality.

Breathe, Bethany... deep breaths.

Maybe this is nothing. Yeah. Maybe this is just my body being weird and I'm panicking for no reason. We were safe. Every time. Yeah. No reason to freak-out.

Except I have been an emotional basket case recently. And there were those few times that I felt pretty nauseous. And the time I threw up at Monday night dinner for no apparent reason.

And now that I think about it, my boobs are super tender.

Shit. Shit. Shit.

Fuckity-fuck-fuck.

The next few hours are a blur. I vaguely remember canceling my appointments for the day. I know I had to be a walking zombie when I left my apartment because I did so without putting on makeup or doing my hair. That never happens. After all, southern cosmetologists never allow that to happen. Somehow, I managed to drive myself to a drugstore, where I proceeded to buy ten different pregnancy tests.

Now I'm standing on my mother's doorstep, frozen in place, holding a bag full of sticks I'm supposed to pee on that will tell me if my life is about to change forever.

How did I get here? I mean, I know that I drove myself, even though I don't remember much of it. But theoretically speaking? How did I get here?

We were careful. I think back to that night in Memphis, which is where this had to have happened. We used a condom. We always did.

Except they aren't always reliable. I don't know what's wrong with me, but for some reason, right now, I'm reminded of the scene in *Friends* when Ross and Joey find out that condoms aren't one hundred percent effective.

And I just start laughing.

Hysterically.

On my mother's porch.

It's official. I'm certifiably insane.

And this is how my mother finds me when she opens the door—no makeup, wearing clothes I don't think are clean, laughing my ass off as I hold a bag full of pregnancy tests.

"Bethany? What's the matter?"

I don't know why, but those three words snap me out of my hysteria. And I do what any woman in my situation would do.

I fall into my mother's arms and cry.

"SWEETHEART? CAN I COME IN?"

I stir when I hear my mom's voice. Why is Mom waking me up?

When I slowly open my eyes, I realize that I'm in my bed in my teenage bedroom and everything comes rushing back to me.

Missing my period.

Buying the tests.

Making my way here and proceeding to cry myself to sleep.

"How long was I out?" I ask, slowly sitting up in bed as my mom comes and sits next to me.

"A few hours."

She hands me a glass of water, and bless her heart, she doesn't start asking me questions. That's just her way. Helen Benson, formerly

Hall, does not prod. She waits. She makes you feel calm. Next thing you know, you're telling her your entire life story.

"I'm guessing you know why I'm here?" I ask, wanting to know where to start.

"I have an idea, but why don't you tell me everything from the beginning."

I look up at the ceiling, wondering where the beginning even is.

When Davis and I first met?

When we refused to stay apart, even though we knew it was for the best?

The night Hunter and Sadie got engaged?

"I'm late."

"By the bag full of pregnancy tests, I gathered as much."

"The fath... his name is Davis."

"The one who coaches with Hunter?"

All I can do is nod. "I swear, we were careful."

She puts her hand on my ankle and gives me a reassuring squeeze. "I have no doubt you were."

I don't know what to say next, so I say the only thing I know to be true right now. "I'm scared, Mom."

And I am. I'm scared for the result. I'm scared of the unknown. I'm scared of what Davis will say. I'm scared of everything.

"I reckon you are, but let's not completely freak-out until you take a test... or ten," she says, grabbing the bag and holding it up for me. "You have a variety to choose from."

I laugh, her bad attempt at a joke just what I need. I rummage through the bag and grab one and make my way to the bathroom to find out my future.

"Here goes nothing," I say to no one as I lay the test next to the sink and sit on the toilet, setting my phone timer for three minutes.

The longest three minutes of my entire life.

Do I want children? Yes. One day. But I never thought it would be like this. It wasn't supposed to happen like this. I was supposed to meet the love of my life, date, get married, have some years that we got to spend together, then babies. It's always ended with babies in my scenario.

In that order.

At that moment, I think back to growing up with just my mom. I love my mother and I treasure the bond we have together. Growing up, I never thought about what my life would have been like if we had a traditional family. Then she met and married Mike.

What would it have been like to have a father? Someone to take me to the father-daughter dance and teach me sports? What would it have been like to have a sibling? Yes, I consider Sadie my sister, but we didn't grow up together. And we are the same age. What would it have been like to have a little sibling?

Once I knew what I missed out on, I vowed that I was going to do things differently than my mom. I was going to date and find a man I couldn't live without, and in turn, he couldn't live without me. We would get married and eventually start a family.

If this test shows what I think it's going to, that is likely never going to happen.

Davis doesn't want a family. Hell, he doesn't want a girlfriend. Am I going to be alone like my mom? My dad couldn't handle the responsibility and left before I knew him.

Will that be Davis? Will he want nothing to do with me or the baby before it even arrives? Will he think he wants a part of it, then realize he can't handle it?

I don't even let myself think about him accepting us and becoming a family. No sense in dreaming of an outcome that will never happen.

Beep. Beep. Beep.

The timer on my cell phone goes off, and though I stop it, I don't move. I don't reach for the test. I just sit there, allowing myself a little more time before knowing whether or not my life changes forever.

You can do this.

You're a strong woman.

No matter what this says, you'll do what you need to do.

One… two… three.

I stand up and turn toward the counter. With one last breath, I look down at the test, and staring right back at me are two distinct pink lines.

"Bethany?"

My mom's voice comes through the closed door, but I don't answer.

I'm pregnant.

"Bethany, are you okay?"

The tears start slowly coming down my cheeks as I turn and open the door. As soon as I make eye contact with her, she can read it on my face.

And for the second time today, I fall into my mother's arms and cry.

15

———

DAVIS

TO SAY the Fury front offices are a dumpster fire right now would be the understatement of the year.

The draft begins tomorrow. Hunter has gone through so many scenarios and driven himself to the brink of insanity. He was doing no one any good, so the other coaches and I kicked him out. I'm guessing he made it home by the last texts Sadie sent me.

> Sadie: You're an asshole.

> Davis: I mean, I am. But why this time?

> Sadie: Because you sent my fiancé home the night before his first draft as head coach, and instead of driving you crazy, he's driving me crazy.

> Davis: This is what you signed up for when he put a ring on it.

> Sadie: You're a fucking asshole, Randall.

> Davis: Still wrong. Keep trying. You still have 11 months.

I laugh as I prop my feet on the desk and take a look around my office.

My office.

Who would have thought a mid-level college football player from bumble fuck Pennsylvania would one day be the offensive coordinator on a team that every football pundit is saying is the future of football?

Surely not me. And probably not any teacher or coach I had back in school. The only one who saw me for my potential was my mom.

Football was the only thing I did growing up that was for me. I had to keep a part-time job to help out around the house when Mitch left, which my mom reluctantly agreed to. However, she gave me one condition when she signed my work permit, I had to still play football.

I didn't know at the time why. In middle school, I was good but not great. It's not like a lot of middle school football teams are making big plays with their wide receivers. If you ask my coaches from back then, they'd probably remember me more for my wisecracks in the huddle than my playing ability.

Then came high school.

My body developed, I gained some speed, and I was playing with a quarterback who could throw the ball. Next thing you know, I'm getting scholarship offers. I knew that was going to be the only way college was going to be an option for me, so I went to Pitt. It wasn't the highest ranked school that offered me a scholarship, but it was close to Mom, Abby, and Sara if they needed me.

I learned a lot in college.

I learned it was easy to transition from the class clown in high school to the life of the party.

I learned that I was never going to have a career as a professional wide receiver in the league. I was good, but not great. Plus, players are always one injury away from having their careers eliminated. My focus was on how best to provide for my family after college. It didn't take me long to realize that you could have a longer career coaching than playing. And if I wanted to provide for Mom, Abby, and Sara for the long run, that was my better move.

I also learned I was really good at finance—a skill that has served me well over the years. Turns out having a side hustle as a stock trader earns you and your family a pretty penny. So, while being a graduate assistant on the Pitt football team, I also received my MBA. I figured it was a good Plan B in case coaching football didn't work out.

I know using the MBA would be more responsible, but it didn't sound nearly as fun as coaching. And trading stocks on the side means I can have my cake and eat it too.

And that's a lot of fun.

"Coach? You wanted to see me?"

I look to my doorway and see our quarterback, Bryce Donald, leaning against the frame. I almost forgot I asked him to come in tonight.

"Yeah, Bryce, have a seat."

At this time last year, Bryce was about to be our number-one pick in the draft. When we were scouting him, he had all of the makings of a franchise quarterback. At Clemson, he guided his team to a national championship. He is a good-looking kid who comes from a good family. He's well-spoken and has a cannon for an arm.

Last year, he was named Rookie of the Year. He's exactly who you want to build your team around.

And all of that is going to his head.

And I need to put a stop to it. Now.

"I'm guessing you know why I asked you to come in?" I ask, taking my feet off my desk.

"Not really," he answers, almost sounding bored with my question. "I kind of figured you needed a wingman for tonight."

The fact that I used to party with players is not serving me well right now. "I heard that you've been having some fun this offseason."

He laughs, a cocky tone to it. "So you *are* asking if you can tag along. Coach McAvoy too boring now that he's wifed up? I mean, I could always use another wingman. I hate to send home too many ladies disappointed."

Who is this kid? This isn't the guy we drafted last year. That guy was polite. Said please and thank you.

After the season ended, it was like a switch flipped. It started with an article from one of the blogs showing Bryce and a few other players partying on Broadway. It was the end of the season and we had a good run. We didn't think anything of it. It was twenty-somethings letting off a little steam.

The problem is, for Bryce, it didn't stop. His name has been popping up on blogs, both local and national, nearly every night showing him at a different bar. Usually with a different woman on his arm.

This kid could break every record in professional football if he does things the right way. But if this train continues? His career is going to be over before it starts, and he doesn't even realize it.

"Are you listening to yourself? You sound like any other fuck boy running around this town."

"Except I'm not. My face is on twenty billboards in the city limits alone. Those country music guys got nothing on me. So what if I'm blowing off some steam before the season begins? Is it now a crime to go out and have some fun? That's rich coming from you."

"It's not," I say, trying my best to keep my temper even. "But it is going to be a problem if your antics carry through into camp. And you do have a behavior clause in your contract. I'm just trying to talk to you before things get out of hand."

I pause to try and get a read on him. All he looks is annoyed.

"You're my quarterback, Bryce," I continue, hoping I'm not talking to a wall right now. "This team depends on you. You do your teammates no good if you're drunk every night. You do us no good if you knock up some girl whose name you don't know and have your face plastered across the tabloids every day. Or if you wreck a car and get arrested for DUI. You're better than this."

The look he is giving me screams of privilege and the it-will-never-happen-to-me mindset.

"I thought you were the cool coach. What the fuck gives? Why you riding my ass?"

That's it. I'm about done with this kid.

"I'm riding your ass because someone has to. I'm not saying you have to live like a priest, but for God's sake, Bryce, you have to see that this behavior is only going in one direction."

"I can do whatever I want and spend my free time however I want. I'm a grown man."

"Then act like one!"

He stands up, fire now in his eyes. "You sound just like Cole. Neither of you know what it's like to be me."

Cole Campbell is his best friend and a lineman on the Fury. The two have played together since they strapped on their first shoulder pads. At least someone is trying to talk some sense into him.

"No, I don't," I say, trying to calm my voice. "All I know is that I see a talent like this league has never seen, and he is one bad move away from ruining it all."

He doesn't reply. Instead, he just stares at me like I'm wasting his precious time.

"Are we done?"

I let out a defeated breath. "With this conversation? Yes. And I'd rather not have more like this in the future."

He turns and storms out of the office, and if I'm not mistaken, I hear a wall being hit on his way down the hallway.

I had hoped to talk some sense into him. I've always had a good relationship with the players, and I was hoping I could get through to him before Hunter had to sit him down for a come to Jesus meeting.

Sometimes being the fun coach isn't always so fun.

16

———

BETHANY

I HAVE NEVER BEEN a football fan.

Growing up, it was just the sport I cheered for in the fall on Friday nights. I knew that when we ran the ball to the end of the field, it was good, and when the other team did, it was bad.

When Sadie and Mike came into our lives, they lived and breathed it. Whenever they talked football at the dinner table, it sounded like a foreign language to me. My mom wanted to learn a little because she knew it would make Mike happy. Me? I was fine not knowing anything.

Therefore, it's safe to say that I have never in my twenty-nine years on this Earth sat at home and watched the draft. I had no idea what to expect. Sadie made it sound like it was as exciting as the Grammys.

Newsflash: It's not.

"Are we really just going to sit around all night and watch guys talk, then announce a name, some clapping, and then more talking?"

"Yes," she says, acting like I just asked the dumbest question in the world. "I told you to bring your wine because we were in it for the long haul tonight. We have another hour before the Fury pick."

I let out a groan as I slink back into her couch, bracing myself for what this night has in store for me. I told Sadie I would watch the draft with her because, well, she's a little out of sorts tonight. It's the first time in her career she hasn't worked on draft night because of her promotion to the investigative team at *US Daily*. She doesn't know what to do with herself. Add on that this is Hunter's first draft as head coach, and she is pacing around their condo like a southern mama at a beauty pageant before they name the ultimate grand supreme winner.

Or like me trying to figure out how to tell my baby daddy that he is a baby daddy.

Oh God, I have a baby daddy.

I always hated that phrase. It sounds so juvenile. But at the end of the day, that's who he is.

Who am I? I am a confirmed, seven-weeks pregnant, confused, scared, expectant mother who vomits every morning at eight thirty like clockwork and is currently craving apples.

Oh, and I'm the person who still isn't sure how to tell the man who wants nothing to do with her that he's about to become a father.

"What? They took Jarrett! You've got to be kidding me! This fucks everything up!"

Sadie's outburst nearly makes me jump off the couch that I have become quite comfortable in. "What are you yelling about?"

"That!" Sadie says, pointing to the TV like I'm supposed to know what *that* means.

"What? It says that Milwaukee took a linebacker."

"Exactly!" Sadie is back to pacing. Between watching her walk around and the nausea that likes to creep up sometimes at night, I'm about to be sprinting to the bathroom soon. "Milwaukee was supposed to take an offensive player. *Everyone* thought that. And that was the guy Hunter wanted. And their second choice was also already drafted. This screws everything up!"

Sadie turns on a dime and heads to the kitchen. "Did you bring wine? I'm out and I need more if this is how the night is going to go."

Oh shit.

"I forgot it."

This makes her stop in her tracks. She hasn't stopped moving since I got here. "You forgot wine? Who are you and what have you done with my sister?"

I shrug and try to look anywhere but at Sadie. "I had it on the counter and then just forgot."

She just shakes her head at me, though she must have bought it because a few minutes later, I hear her giving a "woo!" from the kitchen.

"I have vodka!" she yells, her voice much more excited than it was a few minutes ago. "Want me to make you a drink?"

I'm not an alcoholic by any means, but if it's me and Sadie and a girls' night—even if we are watching football stuff rather than our normal Netflix or reality shows—I always have a cocktail. She was so nervous tonight she hasn't noticed that I haven't been drinking.

"I'm good," I say as nonchalantly as possible.

"You're good?" she asks, making her way back to the living room. "Everything okay? Is watching the draft stressing you out where you don't drink? What gives?"

No, Sadie. Everything is not okay.

"Yeah, just had a headache today. Figured I should play it safe with water."

Sadie seems to buy my flimsy excuse and turns her attention back to the talking guys on TV.

No, I have not told Sadie yet. It's killing me not to. Especially now, when it's just the two of us.

Luckily, the day that I showed up at my mom's house crying with a bag full of tests, she was the only one home. I left before Mike got home from work, and I begged her not to tell him yet. Or rather, not to tell anyone.

I don't want anyone else to know before I have the chance to tell Davis.

It only feels right. I have no idea how he's going to take it. But I couldn't stand the thought that he would be the fifth person to know.

If Sadie knew, that would mean Hunter would know. I didn't want to put him in an awkward situation.

So, for right now, only my mom and I know the secret. Even though I have to tell Davis soon. And that thought has scared the crap out of me.

I have tried to think of a million ways to do it. And like the universe is mocking me, I swear every video I see on Facebook right now is cutesy ways women are telling their husbands they are pregnant. Just today, it was a man going on a scavenger hunt leading to the positive pregnancy test. Of course, he was over-the-moon excited, scooped his wife into his arms, and kissed the heck out of her. You know, because she'd just made them one big happy family and all with that little gem of an announcement.

And here I am, just hoping that when I finally get the courage to do it, he doesn't tell me to get out of his life and slam the door in my face.

I need to do it soon. I'm driving myself mad with the "what will he do or not do" scenarios. I wanted to do it this weekend, but Sadie kept saying how the draft is super important and stressful, so I told myself I'd wait until it's over.

She informed me the draft ends Saturday night.

Sunday it is then.

"Woo-hoo! Great pick guys! Great fucking pick!"

I turn my head to the TV where I see the cameras first following a guy who is no more than twenty years old up to the stage.

"That's Dexter Smith," Sadie says, even though I didn't ask her. "He's the best wide receiver in the draft. They wanted defense, but you can't pass a player like him up. He is going to be a game changer for Hunter and Davis. They have to be ecstatic!"

I can't share in Sadie's excitement because the cameras have now shifted to the Fury draft room. I recognize it from when I was there a few weeks ago. The cameras are zooming in on Hunter and Davis giving each other that one-arm hug thing that guys always do. They break away and Davis is pumping his fist and clapping his hands.

I've never seen this side of him before. He looks so excited. Light. Happy.

And I'm going to be the one to ruin that for him. Literally crush that carefree vibe right out of him.

"Bethany! Why are you still sitting down? It's time to celebrate!"

But I can't. Instead, all I can do is run to the bathroom and cry. And pray that I don't puke.

17

———

DAVIS

Somehow, someway, we came away with a better draft than we did last year.

In every scenario that Hunter dreamed up over the past few months, none of them had Dexter Smith dropping down to us. In the rest of the rounds we were smart, took players we personally scouted and drafted needs for our team.

The talking heads on sports radio are already calling us the favorite to win it all this year.

And this is why I love the draft.

"Thank God, it's over," Hunter says, falling unceremoniously into his desk chair. "I'm wiped out."

"Oh, come on," I poke, taking a seat on the couch in his office. "It's not like the last four days were busy or anything."

The draft is a three-day affair, and Sunday is the day we invite all non-drafted players to rookie camp. It's a four-day whirlwind when you are not only putting together your team puzzle but also watching what thirty-one other teams are doing as well.

Screw Christmas and New Year's, these are my favorite days of the year.

"What now?" I ask, genuinely curious as to what Hunter is going to want to tackle next.

"Right now, we are going to leave this building—that I feel like we've lived in since Thursday—knowing that we've earned a few days off. I don't know what you're going to do, but I'm going to go home to my fiancée and do many things that I'd rather not talk to you about."

"Yeah, yeah," I say as I stand up from the couch. "You go home to your woman. I'm going to go out with the boys. Celebrate our draft haul."

Hunter lifts an eyebrow. "Boys? Who the hell are your boys?"

I gesture down the hall to the other assistant's offices. "Gumont and Martinez. I think I still saw them around earlier. They can wingman me."

"I'm pretty sure they have already taken off," Hunter says as he gathers his things. "Because they also missed their wives or girlfriends since they've barely seen them in four days. Face it, Davis, you're the lone bachelor on this staff."

I am? When did that happen? And why is that realization not sitting well with me?

Being a bachelor has never bothered me in the past. I was happy for my friends who were coupled up or getting married. Hell, I'm your go-to guy when you want a bachelor party thrown. I'm the guy who will lead everyone to the dance floor at your wedding.

Now the thought of everyone in my circle going home to someone is hitting a little harder than I care to admit, even though it's my choice that I'm going home to an empty apartment.

"Whatever," I say, trying to play it off. "Tell Sadie I said hi. And that my name isn't Robert."

Hunter lets out a small laugh as he gets up to leave his office. "Will do. See you in a few days."

And then there was one.

"Fine," I say to no one, gathering the rest of my things and making my way to my truck. "I've been going to bars by myself for years. Who cares if I'm celebrating alone?"

That's at least what I tell myself as I pull out of the Fury facility and make my way to the sports bar by my apartment that has never let me down.

Though the more I think about it, the more I wish I was going home to someone.

And not just anyone.

Bethany. The blonde beauty who knocked me on my ass the first time I saw her.

After my talk with Abby, when she basically called me a dumbass for how I treated Bethany after our last encounter, I really sat down and thought about it. Could I do it? Could I be a boyfriend? A husband? Could I give a woman forever?

I had honestly never thought it before. I was the guy women came to for a good time. My family always came first, and that stretched me thin enough on top of my job responsibilities. It was easy if I kept women at arm's length. Better safe than sorry.

Then I thought of the morning I woke up next to Bethany in Memphis. How content and happy I felt. It was a damn good feeling. One I wouldn't mind having more of.

But then I fucking blew it.

For a second, I had convinced myself I could do it. That I could be there financially and emotionally for Mom, Abby, and Sara while still being able to be a good partner for Bethany. I grew up with a father who was barely there before he was completely gone. I don't want to be that man. I refuse to be that man.

Then I think about the other side of the coin. She's moved on. I'm assuming she's still dating the douche canoe. But even if she isn't, would she even give me a chance?

I know for damn sure I wouldn't after the things I said to her.

So I never called. I never texted.

And now, here I am. Alone after the biggest weekend of my coaching career and no one to share it with.

I pull into the parking lot of the sports bar, and as soon as I turn off the ignition, I hear a text ping from my cell phone.

I do a double take as I read the message again.

Bethany? Wants to talk? Important?

This has to be some sort of sign. Half of me is excited and the other half is confused as fuck, though.

Why does she need to talk? Is it because of our blowup at Hunter and Sadie's? I can't think of another reason why.

Then there is the excited part of me that can't help but think this is a sign of some sorts. I usually don't believe in that cosmic bullshit, but I can't deny that I've been thinking about her nonstop for the past twenty minutes—okay, weeks—and here she is. Asking me to come over.

To talk.

This is it. This is my opening. I can do this. If there's a woman worth taking the leap for, it's her.

And this is my chance to make that jump.

Now I'm even more confused.

18

BETHANY

Even though I had all weekend—and the better part of a few weeks —to figure out how to tell him, now that he is here and knocking on my door, I have no clue what I'm going to say.

How do you tell someone their life is about to change forever?

I know you said you didn't want a family...

So, remember how we used a condom? Funny story about that...

Surprise! You're going to be a daddy!

Honestly, when I texted him, I had no idea how I was going to tell him. I just knew if I didn't do it tonight, then I didn't know when I'd work up the courage again to do so.

Be strong.

Be brave.

No matter what, everything is going to be okay.

I take one last deep breath and open the door. My legs almost give out at the sight of him. He's dressed very casually in a Nashville Fury hoodie and joggers, his beard is a little longer than usual and his hair looks like he's been running his hands through it all day.

"Hey, princess."

Oh God. The tone in his voice is so gentle. Tender even. Likely because he has no idea why I've asked him over here, and the last time we saw each other it was a toss-up of whether we were going to fight or fuck.

"Hey. Come on in."

My words are lame, but I'm just happy I'm able to find some. Between the sight of him, the smell of his cologne that is slowly taking over my body, and the insane amount of hormones swimming through me right now, I'm a jumbled mess inside.

I take a seat on the couch and instinctively grab a pillow to put over my stomach. I know I'm not showing yet, but the defense mechanism makes me feel a little more protected. Davis takes a seat next to me, but somehow I feel like we are miles apart, not just one cushion.

"Thanks for coming over."

"Actually, you beat me to the punch."

I quirk an eyebrow. "I did?"

"Yeah," he says, turning slightly so we are now facing each other. "I've thought about messaging you a dozen times since the last time I saw you."

This is a surprise. "You have?"

"Yeah," he says, taking a deep breath before he goes on. "Bethany, I was an ass that night at Hunter's. I could spew twenty different reasons about why, but they are all bullshit. You did nothing wrong, and I acted like a jackass. I'm sorry."

Wow, I wasn't expecting this. I know his admission is delaying the reason he's here, but I can't say I hate his words.

Maybe this won't go so bad after all?

"Thank you. I appreciate the apology. But I need—"

"Wait, let me finish," he says, inching a little closer to me. "I know you're seeing someone else right now, and this is the absolute wrong time to say this, but I can't stop thinking about the possibility of an us."

Wait, what?

"I'm… You…. What? I'm confused."

He laughs quietly while reaching for my hand. "Bethany, when I found out you started seeing someone, it drove me insane. I know I told you to. I know I told you to move on because I couldn't give you what you wanted. That I'm not the guy you need. Hell, I still don't know if I am. But I do know that I'd never forgive myself if I didn't take this chance now."

Is he?

Did he just?

What in the name of Dolly Parton is happening right now?

Out of all the things I thought might happen tonight, this is the *last* thing I considered. And if this were three weeks ago, I'd be shouting from the rooftop. I'd be calling Sadie and screaming in her ear. I'd be kissing the ever-loving daylights out of him before he uttered his next words.

Now? Now, I don't know what to do because everything that I wasn't expecting to ever happen with us, he's now telling me is a possibility. Giving us the green light. My emotions are all over the freaking place right now.

So I do the only thing that I've become good at over the past few weeks.

I cry.

"Bethany?" Davis asks, concern laced in his voice, as he puts his arms around me. "Shh. What's wrong? What did I say?"

"Nothing," I'm able to say in between sobs. "You said everything I've dreamed of hearing."

My tears last for another few minutes, and in that time, he just holds me. I'd be lying if I didn't say I took a few extra seconds to relish what it feels like to be in his arms. To have his protectiveness surrounding me.

Because this might be the last time I'm ever here.

"Talk to me," he finally says, brushing a loose strand of hair off my face. "I can't handle tears. Tell me what I can do to make them go away."

Oh, if it were only that simple. There's not a thing he can do to make this baby growing inside of my stomach go away. And as happy as what he told me makes me, I'm still so unsure of how he will react when I break the news to him.

I sit up, wiping away the stray tears running down my cheek. "I just wasn't expecting that. You took me by surprise, that's all."

Not half as surprised as I'm about to make him.

"I know. And I'm sorry. You're dating someone and it took me so long to get my head out of my ass and—"

"No," I say, cutting him off. It's my turn to talk. "I'm not seeing anyone."

"But I thought?"

I shake my head, wishing that this was the biggest hurdle we were going to have to overcome tonight. "I went out on one date with someone. I'll admit, I let you think it was more because I was mad at you, but it was never anything serious. He was nice. We wanted the same things in life. But…"

"But what?"

I take a deep breath, ready to admit a truth I've been trying to deny. "He wasn't you."

Before I know it, Davis's lips are on mine, and I'd be a liar if I didn't say this was the single best feeling in the world right now.

We've kissed before. Usually in the heat of the moment as we are in the process of ripping each other's clothes off. Those kisses have been sloppy and desperate. A means to an end.

This kiss? This is different. This has warmth. Feeling. Emotion. Commitment.

Dare I say something deeper?

His hands are cupping my face, holding me with a tenderness I've never felt before. Our tongues are meeting in perfect harmony. I feel this kiss in every cell of my body. I wish I could just stay here for eternity, letting this man consume every part of me.

But I can't. I know I need to stop this. This can't go on without him knowing everything.

With every ounce of strength I possess, I gently push him away. My body goes cold the second our lips part, but I can't let this go on anymore.

"Davis…"

It's now or never.

"I don't know why you stopped that, but I'm going to need you to change your mind," he says, trying to scoop me onto his lap.

"Davis. Wait," I say, holding my hands up. "Before anything else happens, I need to tell you the reason I wanted you to come over tonight."

He lets out a defeated breath but doesn't retreat back to his end of the couch. Instead, he takes my hands in his, placing soft kisses on the tops of each of them.

Okay, so I haven't scared him away completely, that's a good sign.

"Then tell me. Because I almost forgot how much I have missed your lips and plan on doing a lot more of that tonight."

The smile on his face right now is boyish with a touch of mischief in it. I hate that with my next words, that smile is likely going to fall from his face. That with what I have to tell him, I'll either go from being a hero to a zero in a few minutes. I'll go from that perfect familial unit to a single mom, like my own, as soon as the words leave my lips.

Damn… I can't do this.

Maybe I should wait.

Ease him into being in a couple before I drop this bombshell. Let him get used to an us before we become a family.

What's going to happen next, though?

"Hey, it's okay," he says gently, seeing the level of panic on my face. "Whatever you need to tell me, it's okay. It's you and me now. If you're willing to give me a chance, then we are in this together."

I can't stop myself from laughing. "You say that now."

He shakes his head. "I'm confused. And you're killing me, princess. Just tell me whatever it is."

I take a deep breath and resolve myself to say the two hardest words I've ever said in my life.

"I'm pregnant."

19

DAVIS

"YOU'RE WHAT?"

I couldn't have heard her right. No. No way she just said that.

Though the more I look at her, the more I know that she said just that.

And at this second, I feel the ground falling out from under me.

"I'm pregnant, Davis. It's… It's yours."

Instinctively, I stand up and start pacing around her living room. I know I heard her correctly. She has said it twice now, yet I still don't believe her.

I'm pregnant, Davis. It's yours.

"You're pregnant?"

"Yes."

"And you are telling me it's mine."

Fuck. I shouldn't have said that. And by the look she is giving me right now, she's thinking the exact same thing.

"Yes, like I said, it's yours. Contrary to what you might have thought about my dating life before, I don't sleep with every man I meet."

"I'm sorry," I say, knowing how it came out. "I'm just… This is a lot."

She nods. "I know. Trust me. It's been a lot for me. But it's true. We're going to have a baby."

We're going to have a baby.

I pick up the pace of my steps, my mind going in circles because right now, nothing makes sense.

How did I get here in the blink of an eye?

Just a few minutes ago, her lips were on mine and everything was right in the world. I was just a guy who was praying this amazing woman would give me a chance to date her properly. And I didn't even know what I was getting into then. But I knew I wanted to try. For her.

Now… now everything has changed.

"But we… we always used condoms," I say, still trying to wrap my mind around this. "Didn't we? I don't know how this happened? We were always safe."

"I know," she says, her voice weak and distant. "I guess they mean what they say that they aren't foolproof."

I mean, I knew that. But… that doesn't happen in real life. Does it?

"When?"

"Memphis. I'm seven weeks."

"That means you're due…"

"The doctor said she'd give me a firmer date next appointment, but it's looking like end of November."

I don't reply, because I have nothing more to add.

Instead, I just keep pacing.

It's the only thing keeping me upright at this moment.

My universe is slowly toppling over right before my eyes and I can't make it stop. I've only ever felt like this once in my life, and that was the day we realized Mitch was gone for good. Then I knew my world was never going to be the same, but that was different.

This? This is so much more.

I'm going to be a father.

It's my job to make sure that Bethany has everything she needs. I'm the one who is going to be responsible for this child's well-being. I'm responsible for making sure it is clothed and fed and provided for.

I've assumed this role before with my own family, so it won't be a problem, right? Only this time, I also need to be a partner for Bethany. To make sure I never make her or this child ever want for anything and to always have her back.

It's my job to make sure I do everything Mitch didn't do for us growing up.

Which means there is only one thing left to do.

"Marry me."

My words shock her. At least, that's what I think by the look on her face. Her jaw is open, her eyes are big, and she is looking at me like I have three heads.

"What did you just say to me?"

Shit. I'm doing this all wrong. But this is uncharted territory for me. I really have no idea what I'm doing, just what will be expected of me, and I'm already screwing up.

So I get down on one knee and take her hand in mine.

"Marry me."

"Is that a question or a command? I'm kind of confused here."

"Does it need to be a question?" Now I'm the one confused. "We are having a baby. We should get married. You've always wanted a husband and a family. So, let's do it. Let's be a family."

She doesn't answer. Instead, she stands from the couch, throws her hands in the air, and storms into the kitchen.

So, is that a yes?

"Where are you going?"

The sound of cupboard doors being slammed shut is the only answer I get until Bethany comes charging out of the kitchen, carrying three bags of different-flavored potato chips.

"What are you doing?" I ask because I genuinely have no clue what is going on.

"Well, I wanted vodka. I thought if I got drunk, I could understand your level of crazy," she says, throwing the chips on her coffee table before sitting back down on the couch. "But I can't have vodka because of your super sperm breaking through the condom. So, then I thought that maybe eating my frustrations and emotions would serve two purposes since I'm hungry all the freaking time. But my cravings change every three seconds, and right now it's potato chips, but I didn't know what kind I wanted. So, I brought all the chips. Get it now?"

I don't think I've blinked since she started talking.

"I... I don't—"

"Exactly. What I'm doing is nuts to you. Well, guess what, bucko, what you just said? Marrying you because you think that's what is expected—and not because it's something that you wanted? That's equally insane."

I sit down next to her because I need to steer this conversation back around.

"I thought you wanted to get married? That was the whole reason we ended things before. And now that there's a baby in the mix, marriage is the obvious solution."

She lets out a deep breath, almost trying to calm herself as she tears into the bag of Funyuns and shoves a few in her mouth, taking a moment to chew and swallow before speaking. "I did. I do. I don't know. But I don't want a husband just because of the situation. I want to get married for love. Not out of pity. What you are asking of me right now is clearly out of pity and obligation."

"Pity? This isn't because of pity or obligation." I take her hand in mine, hoping I can get through to her. "Bethany. You? This child? You're my responsibility now. It's now my job—"

"Your what?"

"My responsibility."

"Oh! Your responsibility," she says as she shoots back up and starts walking in circles, now tearing into the bag of Flaming Hot Cheetos as I silently wonder if that's the best choice of food to eat while pregnant. I don't dare ask that, though. She's starting to scare me. "Well, that makes the proposal *all* that much better! Where do I sign up for that?"

"Yes," I say matter-of-factly, ignoring her sarcastic remarks. "You're my responsibility. You are carrying my child. You both are my responsibility now."

She turns to face me. The look on her face, I admit, scares me a little.

Bethany. Is. Pissed.

"Why are you mad? I thought this is what you wanted?"

And now she's crying.

Holy shit. I heard about pregnancy hormones; I knew they were a thing, but I've never seen them in action.

"Not like this," she says, trying, but failing to hold back her tears. "Not like this."

I walk to her and bring her next to me on the couch. "What do you want then? Tell me, because I can't take the tears. But please know, you tell me what you want, and I'll make it happen."

She takes a few breaths, letting the tears subside.

"Do I want you to be a part of this child's life? Absolutely. And if you want to be with me because you care about me and you meant the things you said earlier tonight? Great. Let's give us a try. And yes, someday I want the husband and the house and the family and the golden retriever. I didn't lie to you when I said that. But not like this. I don't want a proposal or a husband out of some sort of misplaced feeling of guilt and responsibility. I don't want you to regret me in ten or twenty years. I don't want you to see our baby and realize you can't do it, but you feel tied to me. I want a husband who wants me because he can't imagine spending the rest of his life without me. Not one who only proposed because he got some life-changing news and feels that it's the right thing to do. So, no, Davis, I won't marry you. Not now. But if you meant what you said earlier, I do want to give us a try. I want you in my life."

Fuck. She's right.

I did all of that. I asked her the most important question of her life because I was panicking.

"I'm so sorry," I say, bringing her on to my lap. "You're right. But yes, I did mean it. I do mean it. The baby changes nothing."

She snuggles in a little closer. "I like the sound of that."

"Which part?"

"The one where you say I'm right."

I tickle her sides, and the sound of her just-been-crying laughter is music to my ears.

For the next few minutes, we just sit with each other, letting the night's events replay. At least, I am. Bethany's breathing has slowed down and her eyelids are starting to flutter.

Holy fuck, I'm going to be a father.

Why does that not scare me more than it should? Yesterday, I didn't think I could even handle a girlfriend, let alone a family of my own. Yet somehow, while this news is the most shocking of my life, I'm not as rattled by the enormity of it as I would have thought.

I have a feeling I know why.

Because of the woman in my arms right now.

"We're going to have a baby," she whispers, her eyes still closed.

"Yeah, we are. From this point forward, it's you and me, princess. Team Davis."

She lets out a laugh. "You know what this means, right?"

"What's that?"

"I'm eventually going to have to know your first name."

20

____

BETHANY

I'M STIRRED awake by the feel of Davis's arms wrapping around me, bringing me closer to his naked chest.

If this is what it's like waking up with him every morning, then sign me up.

I don't open my eyes yet for fear that the second I do this bubble will burst. That last night didn't happen. That if I open my eyes, he won't actually be here. Instead, I take in the feel of his warm body against mine, his muscular arms holding me tight as I replay the events of last night.

Will you give me a chance?

I'm pregnant.

One of those announcements would have been enough for one night. But the two put together? That's a lot for anyone, especially for a man who just weeks ago wanted nothing to do with a committed relationship, let alone a family.

How could he change his mind so fast? What happened that made him want to give us a try? And then throwing a child on top of it and he didn't run for the hills?

No. Not only did he not run, he threw out two words I never thought I'd say no to.

Marry me.

What was he thinking?

How did I have the sense to say no?

I mean, I've been denying my true feelings for this man for months. And here he is, saying that he wants to give us a chance and that he wants to be a family.

Yet, I know he wasn't saying it for the right reasons.

I believe you should get married for love, not out of responsibility or obligation. I meant what I said, I don't want him to regret anything. I don't want him to leave because he made a rash decision and he didn't know what he was getting into.

I don't want to feel like my mother did. I don't want our child growing up like I did, even though I had a wonderful childhood, never knowing my real father still bites.

"Good morning, princess."

Jesus, take the wheel; his morning grumbly voice is enough to make my panties melt off.

I don't respond, instead snuggling closer to him while cracking open an eye to see what time it is.

8:28 a.m.

Oh no.

No. No. No.

Please, let this be the one morning I'm not sick. Please, just let me stay here for a little longer. Don't burst the bubble with…

The sound my stomach makes screams that it does not care that I'm in bed with a sexy as hell man. And from the sound and feel of it, I have approximately ten seconds to get to the bathroom or else Davis is going to see something that might completely change his mind.

I furiously break away from his hold, throw the covers off of me, and sprint across the hall to my bathroom.

"Bethany? You okay? Princess? What's happening?"

I don't answer him. If I answer, I'm not going to make it. Instead, I slam the door shut and lift up the toilet seat for what has become my new morning ritual.

Morning sickness, like my inner voice, is a real twat waffle.

No. Scratch that. Whoever named it morning sickness is the twat waffle.

Because it's not just morning sickness. At least for me, it isn't. I find myself kneeling before my toilet like clockwork at eight thirty each day. It also hits me somewhere around mid-afternoon. And any time I smell freshly cut grass. Which in the spring in Nashville is a lot. What in the name of all that's good and holy causes puking from that?

Like I said. Twat waffle.

I don't know how I don't hear Davis come into the bathroom. Yet I feel his presence without even looking up. My forehead is resting on my forearms across the toilet as I feel his hands bring my hair away from my face. Next, I hear the water running before I feel a cold washcloth on the back of my neck.

Since I found out I was expecting, I mentally prepared myself that I could be doing this on my own. That I'd be okay being my own wingman during these next seven months and beyond. I mean, how many times did he tell me he was never going to have anything serious, let alone a family? I believe his words were, "I wish I could give you what you want." I figured, if anything, he'd send a few checks and be on his way.

But for at least for right now, he's here. And this cold washcloth means more to me than he could ever know.

"You're probably going to want to rethink sleeping arrangements," I say, slowly backing away from the toilet until my back makes contact with the bathtub.

"Not a chance," he says, taking the washcloth and wiping away the sweat on my forehead. "I told you last night, we're in this together. The question now is, what can I get you? Water? Food?"

The sincerity in his voice is enough to send me into an emotional spiral. And the look in his eyes? There is so much caring and warmth in them that I don't know how I keep back the tears.

"Nothing," I say, giving his hand a squeeze. "Just you being here is more than enough."

"WHAT IS ALL THIS?"

Davis looks up at me, a big smile across his face. "It's breakfast. Now, sit."

My oh my, he's bossy today.

I forgot how much I love bossy Davis.

It's likely the very reason we are in this situation. Except last time it was Bossy Davis in the bedroom, not Bossy Davis in the kitchen. But with this baby growing inside of me, I'm really, really liking Bossy Davis in the kitchen.

After my morning episode, Davis insisted that I take a bath, relax, and that he'd take care of breakfast.

Who was I to argue with that? I figured I'd be greeted with a bowl of cereal. Maybe a bagel from the coffee shop down the street.

I was not expecting a breakfast buffet.

"Here," he says, placing a glass of orange juice in front of me as I take a seat at my small dining room table. "Is orange juice okay?"

"Yeah, it's great," I say, still a little confused and shocked by the feast laid out before me. "Did you order everything DoorDash had to offer?"

"Pretty much," he says, putting a plate down in front of me filled with bacon, eggs, pancakes, and waffles. "I didn't know what you liked. Or how much you were eating now. So, I played it safe."

I know I'm pregnant when a man hitting a few buttons on a food app is cause enough to make me cry.

I'm able to hold back the tears and dig into the best breakfast I've had in a very long time. Eventually, Davis makes himself a plate and joins me at the table.

It strikes me at this point that this is the first time we've shared a meal together. Well, by ourselves, where Hunter and Sadie weren't with us.

"God, we've done this completely backward."

I meant to say that to myself, but apparently, I said it a little louder than I intended.

"Not completely," he says, taking a sip of coffee before continuing. "We did at least go on one date first."

I laugh. "You're right. Though, I wouldn't say we dated."

"No, we didn't, princess. No, we didn't."

We sit in silence for a few minutes, and at least for me, my brain is going in twenty directions right now.

But the biggest question is, what now?

I didn't think past telling him because I couldn't predict the outcome. That was the major roadblock, and until I knew how he felt about everything, I didn't want to think about anything past that. There wasn't any point until I knew where he stood.

Now it's here. And now I don't have a flipping clue what to do next.

"We need to figure some things out," he says as if he's reading my mind.

"We do. I feel like there is so much to do and no time to do it and it's overwhelming."

Davis puts his fork and coffee down and takes my hands into his. Before, every time we touched, I felt a spark go through us. Now? The spark is still there, though this time there is something more. Now the spark is followed by a sense of warmth that makes me feel like everything is going to be okay.

"I agree. I suggest that first we figure out our living arrangement."

I offer him a confused look. "Well, I have a place to live and so do you. I don't see why that is the top priority?"

"Bethany, look around," he says, scanning my small one-bedroom apartment. "There is not enough room here for a baby. My apartment is bigger, but I'm too close to downtown. That's not a place we want to raise a baby."

He's not wrong. My apartment is very small. I didn't have to think of anyone else when I leased it. I can barely fit my clothes in here, let alone things for a baby. His place is nice, but he's right. I don't want to be listening to crowds when I'm trying to get the baby down for a nap.

"Okay, I see where you're coming from, but there is one important thing you're missing."

"And what is that?"

"I said I wasn't marrying you."

He picks up on my teasing tone as the look on his face goes from serious to mischievous in a heartbeat. How does this man have so many sides to him? He's serious and practical. He's also playful and boyish.

I don't know which one I love more.

I'm also going to ignore that my brain went to the word love rather than like.

"That's right, you did say that," he says, now a glint in his eye that screams he's up to something.

"What is going through that head of yours?" I say, taking another bite of bacon because we might be having a huge, life-altering conversation, but it's still bacon. And I'm still pregnant.

"You might have said no last night, but I do intend on marrying you one day. And it's going to be the proposal of your dreams."

"Oh, do you now?" I'm trying to play it off, but inside? Inside, I'm screaming like a teenage girl. Does he remember what I told him in Memphis? About what I wanted my proposal to be? Something special for just the two of us? I wonder what he would do?

I shake my head from those thoughts. That is a long time from now. Right now? I'm just going to focus on that he is here and he wants to give us a shot.

For now, that's more than I could have ever hoped for.

He brings my hand to his lips before continuing. "I thought about my life without you in it. Or you spending the rest of your life with the douche canoe—"

"His name was Gavin."

"Whatever. He's irrelevant," Davis says, scooting my chair closer to his. "What I'm saying is, that if I'm going to marry you one day, then one big thing needs to happen first."

"And what is that?"

He stands up, takes my plate, and places a kiss on my forehead. "I need to take you on a proper first date."

21

———

DAVIS

I MUST SAY, for knowing that I'm going to be a dad for less than twenty-four hours, I'm pretty much already killing it.

After I left Bethany's today—she kicked me out after her second wave of nausea hit because she wanted to nap before our date—I decided to do what I do best.

And that is to come up with a plan.

Not many know this side of me. My former teammates saw the guy who would play pranks on the freshmen. My players see the fun coach who makes jokes in between drills. My fellow coaches expect me to make the inappropriate comment during staff meetings.

That might be part of my personality, but the other part is on the complete opposite end of that spectrum.

I plan until the very last detail is in place.

It started when Mitch left. There were budgets to create in order to make sure we had enough for food and anything extra we needed that month. There were calendars to keep so Mom, Abby, Sara, and I knew when any of us had anything going on. The refrigerator in our house always had notes and reminders on it written in Mom's handwriting. Was this the first sign of Mom's eventual diagnosis? I always wonder that.

No matter what the reason they were there, it's how we survived. And it's how I've been surviving ever since.

The second I get home, I pull out my laptop and start googling everything from "how much does it cost to have a baby" to "best daycares in Nashville."

Both of those answers have price tags that slightly terrify me.

I order four parenting books off of Amazon, quickly skim a blog about what Bethany is feeling right now and tips to help with morning sickness, and even look at pictures of what a seven-week-old fetus looks like.

Just as I'm closing my laptop, and before I get lost in the rabbit hole that is birthing videos—those look positively terrifying, by the way—my phone vibrates on the table with an incoming call.

"Hello, favorite sister. To what do I owe this pleasure?"

"Because, dipshit, you didn't answer your phone last night, and you didn't call me back," Abby says, her voice scarily creeping up to her mom tone. "God forbid me wanting to check in on my brother to make sure everything is okay."

I laugh as I make my way into my bedroom to start getting ready for tonight. "Everything is fine, Abbs. Actually, more than fine."

"Why do you sound so cheerful, and what have you done with my brother?"

If there is one person on this Earth who knows that my class clown persona is more of a diversion than anything, it's Abby. And she's not afraid to remind me of it.

"I'm no more cheerful than normal," I say, entering my closet to look for something to wear.

"The only thing that makes a man sound like this is that he's getting sex, about to have sex, or is having sex right now. Which, when it comes to you, I'd rather not know about."

I laugh. "No sex for me. Sorry to disappoint you."

"Then what has you sounding like you just won the lottery?"

I could drag this out a little more, but I'm expecting a solid half hour freak-out from her, and I don't want to be late picking Bethany up.

"Remember the girl?"

"The one who I told you to get your head out of your ass about? Vaguely."

I'm glad my sister can't see me roll my eyes. "Yeah. Her. Well… I have some news."

"Are you about to tell me you're in a relationship? Holy hell, I never thought I'd see the day! Oh my gosh, you're actually not going to die alone! Wait. Let me record this so I can play it for Sara. And Mom. They will never believe me."

The next few minutes are filled with Abby shouting exclamations, asking questions so fast I'm not sure what she said, and ramblings about how I better bring her home soon for the rest of the family to meet.

"Are you done yet?" I ask, loving that I still have one more big bomb to drop on her tonight.

"I… I think I am," she says, catching her breath. "What can you tell me about her? What's her name? Is this serious? Or are you getting my hopes up only to break up with her in a week?"

"Well," I say, finding a black button-down and dark jeans. "It's serious enough that you're going to be an aunt."

My news has its desired effect on Abby. Complete and blissful silence. Never once in my entire thirty years of existence have I ever been able to shock my sister silent.

I'm going to need to write this down somewhere in a journal or some shit to revisit time and time again.

"Abby? You okay?"

"Did you just say… You're going to? I'm going to be?"

I chuckle, setting the phone down and putting it on speaker so I can put on the shirt. "Yes, Abby. You heard me correctly. And before you ask, no, it wasn't planned. Yes, it's a surprise. But Bethany is pregnant. She told me last night."

If I thought my sister was screaming gibberish earlier, then I don't know how to explain what happens next. All I know is that by the time she starts speaking coherently again, I've finished getting dressed, brushed my teeth, and styled my hair.

"I have so many questions I don't even know where to begin," she says, wrapping up her incoherent conversation with herself.

"Well, the answer to one of those questions is no, you can't post all over social media about this. Not yet. I haven't asked her when she wants to tell everyone, so please wait until I give you the okay?"

"Fine," she says, though I know her grumble is only half serious.

"Are we done here? I'm taking Bethany on a proper date tonight and you're holding me up."

"Look at you. My big brother is finally leaving Neverland."

"You're such a comedian."

"I'm quite serious. You have gone from eternal bachelor to ready to buy a minivan in the blink of an eye. Then again, you are the one who doesn't back away from a challenge. Nope, my older brother meets the bull head on."

She's not wrong. When Mitch left, I didn't flinch. We came up with a plan and it was full steam ahead. That plan never included me having a family of my own. My sisters have always hated that I made that choice. Abby and Sara have been on me for years to try and settle down. They said just because I insisted on helping the family on the financial end years ago, that didn't mean I had to put my life on hold now. I'm sure if Mom was mentally capable of knowing what was going on each day, she'd have my ass as well.

Turns out, all I needed was the right woman to give me the push I needed.

"Any other questions, sister?"

"Yes. When do I get to meet her?"

I smile because there is nothing more that I want right now than to introduce Bethany to my family. Next month being May will be tough with rookie camp. But by June, we will have some downtime before training camp opens. Sara will be out of school and living with Abby for the summer. And Mom... it's been a while. Even if she doesn't know who I am.

It's time to go back to Pennsylvania.

"How does June sound?"

22

BETHANY

"I AM SO SORRY."

I reach for Davis's hand and give it a squeeze. "For the twentieth time, you don't need to apologize. You didn't know."

"But I should know. I should have known all of this!"

If this is truly going to be my last first date, it's going to be memorable for sure.

And not in a good way.

Things started off great. Davis picked me up, and I was able to keep my hormones in check from the sight of him in a black button-down with the sleeves rolled up and dark-washed jeans. He wore the cologne that makes me go weak. I deserve a medal for not pulling him into my house and skipping dinner altogether.

From there, it went downhill fast.

We drove into downtown Nashville and as soon as he parked the car, I knew where he planned on taking me.

A sushi bar.

Being pregnant, I can't eat raw fish.

If that was the only oopsie moment of the night, we still could have chalked this up to a win. However, that might have been the highlight.

In an attempt to make it up to me, he tried to surprise me again, and drove a few streets over to an Italian restaurant.

If this were a normal date, I would have been all for it. I love lasagna. Except right now, the smell of garlic and I are not friends. At all. As soon as we pulled up to the restaurant, the scent overtook my senses, and I had to make a mad dash from his truck.

Throwing up in a Nashville parking lot at seven on a Monday night, completely sober, is not one of the highlights of my life.

His last attempt at trying to surprise me came in the form of Indian food. The only problem is that I'm allergic to peanuts and peanut oil. With so many dishes using those ingredients, I play it safe and don't eat there.

"How could you have known?" I ask, trying my best to soothe him as he drives back to his apartment.

"I should have known about the sushi," he says, his voice still edged with frustration.

"Okay, maybe. But the garlic thing just started this week. And the Indian? It's not like our restaurant preferences ever came up in conversation."

He pulls the truck into a spot, puts it in park, and lets out a defeated breath. "I know. I just hate that I don't know any of these things. I'm your... I should know."

I lean over the center console and bring his lips to mine. Not a deep kiss, but one I hope tells him that he's doing nothing wrong.

"How about this," I say, placing one more kiss on the corner of his lips. "We go upstairs. Order our weight in hot chicken because that is the only thing I am craving right now, and we get to know each other in all the ways we skipped over before."

He smiles and leans over, taking my face in his hands for one more kiss. When he releases me, the smile on his face is one that makes the rest of this disastrous date worth it.

"Let's do it, princess."

"WHAT DO YOU MEAN, you've never seen *Die Hard*!"

The look on Davis's face right now is a combination of horrified and hilarious. Well, he's horrified. I find it hilarious how horrified he is.

"So? What's the big deal?"

"What's the big deal? What is the big deal!" he shouts as he paces around his living room. I think he's pacing harder now than when I told him I was pregnant. "How are we supposed to raise our child with the knowledge that *Die Hard* is, in fact, a Christmas movie if you've never seen it in the first place!"

I want to laugh. It is so cute how serious he is about this. But if I laugh, I'm afraid I'll open up another can of worms about the merits of *Die Hard* as a Christmas movie, and I'm not ready for that.

Plus, the man has never seen *Steel Magnolias,* so I think we're even. How can he lecture me about the greatness of *Die Hard* when he doesn't know the amazingness of a cast featuring Dolly Parton, Julia Roberts, Shirley MacLaine, and Sally Field?

The answer: he can't.

The beginning part of our date might have been disastrous, but the last few hours have been amazing. After our food arrived, we began learning all of the things about each other that we should have already known for two people who have seen each other naked as many times as we have. Take, for example, I had no idea he was from Pennsylvania. He was equally surprised to discover that I have never traveled west of the Mississippi.

Things we agree on: Pineapple doesn't belong on pizza; dogs over cats; and neither of us see what the big deal is about *Star Wars.*

Things we don't agree on: I think Christmas is the best holiday while he is Team Thanksgiving; I'm a morning person, while he is a night owl, which will be great when it comes time for late-night feedings; and of course, the atrocity that I've never seen *Die Hard.*

"Come, sit down," I say, patting the spot next to me on the couch. "You're making me dizzy."

He makes his way over, and not only does he sit down next to me, but he also brings my feet across his lap, rubbing small circles into my arches.

Oh, I could get used to that.

"What else do you want to know?" he asks, continuing to work my arches. If he keeps doing that, the only thing I'm going to want to know is how quickly he can get me naked.

"Tell me something no one else knows about you."

The circles on my feet stop almost instantly and the temperature in the room drops a few degrees. I didn't realize that question was so loaded. But now I'm wondering what his answer will be… or if he'll even respond.

"Remember when we were in Memphis and you were giving me shit for being on my phone and I told you I was checking a stock?"

I laugh. "Yes. I remember thinking that was a pretty well thought-out fib. You could have just said you were checking Instagram. Or sending another selfie."

He laughs. "Well, it was the truth."

"It was?" I say, the curiosity heavy in my voice. Though by the look on his face, he is one hundred percent serious. "You… are you a stock trader?"

"Kind of," he says, readjusting my feet on his lap. "When I was in college, we weren't allowed to have jobs. NCAA rules and because of our scholarship, but I helped support my mom and sisters, and needed to figure out a way to still be able to do that. I had taken a few business and finance classes and started reading up on the stock market. Apparently, I'm good at it. I made smart buys, sold when the time was right, and I made a pretty penny from my investments. Ever since then I've been buying and selling on the market to help support my mom and sisters, without having to dip into my coaching salary."

When I asked this question, I expected the answer to be something like, "I have a sixth toe" or "I can tap dance." No way did I expect all of that.

"Can I ask why you had to support your family while you were in college?"

He takes a deep breath before answering. "It's two-fold. My dad took off when I was thirteen. One day he was there, the next day he was gone. We never saw him again. On that day, I made a promise to my mom and sisters that I would help in any way I could. So I picked up part-time jobs while I was in school and continued playing football. I hated seeing my family suffer because my asshole father left us in the dust."

I reach for his hand, wanting to offer some comfort. "What's the second part?"

He slowly rubs his thumb over the top of my knuckles. "When I was in college, my mom was diagnosed with early onset Alzheimer's. It… we didn't see it coming. She needed medical help that neither my sisters nor I could provide. We found a facility for her, but it isn't cheap, and insurance only covers a fraction of what she needs. I take care of the rest."

Wow. Out of all the answers he could have given, this wasn't what I expected to hear.

Though, now I feel like I have a few more pieces to the puzzle that is Davis. I can't imagine what it's like feeling like the provider of a family, especially when you live hundreds of miles away from them. And he's been doing this since he was a teenager? Now his words about "I can't give you what you want" make more sense.

He was already trying to juggle life. He was trying not to add more to his already-overloaded plate.

Then here I come, baby on board. Adding more to his responsibilities.

"Is that why you pushed me away? Why you didn't want a relationship?" I ask, wanting confirmation.

He nods. "I've always felt like if I tried to settle down, I'd let down someone. Either them or my hypothetical girlfriend or wife. It wasn't fair, so I decided a long time ago to never have someone else in the equation, and then I didn't have to worry about letting someone down."

"Then I came along. With baggage."

He smiles, kissing my hand. "Then you came along. And with baggage I'm excited about."

I know he didn't ask me, but after his confession, I feel like I owe him one as well. One that's been weighing heavily on my mind since we decided to give this a shot.

"I didn't have a dad either," I say, my voice soft. "That is something else we have in common."

Concern covers his face in an instant. "Do you want to talk about him?"

I shake my head. "There's really nothing to talk about. He and my mom got pregnant with me when they were engaged. They decided to not get married until after I was born. That was a blessing in disguise, because not long after I arrived, he realized he couldn't do it and took off. I've never met him."

Davis gathers me in his arms and places me on his lap, his lips softly kissing my cheek. "I'm so sorry."

"I'm not," I say, meeting his tender gaze. There's not a trace of the alpha man I know he can be. Or the jokester.

This… this is the true Davis.

And now I know, right here and now, that I could fall head over heels in love with this man. That if he were to leave me down the line, I don't know if I could recover.

"Davis?" I ask, my voice quiet.

"Yeah, princess?"

"Make me a promise."

I hope he can hear the sincerity in my voice right now. "Anything."

"If you can't do this. If you sit back and realize fatherhood isn't for you, please let me know. There will be no hard feelings. I think I turned out okay because I never had a dad, so I honestly didn't know what I was missing. I think it would have been worse if I had memories of him. So please… I know we are giving this a shot and we've made no promises, but promise me this. If you don't think you can handle it, leave now. I'll be all right. But I'd rather this child not know you at all than miss you every day of its life."

He doesn't answer. Instead, he takes my face in his hands and kisses me like I've never been kissed before—with so much passion that I can feel his answer without him saying a word.

This kiss is more than the one we shared in Memphis when we thought it was goodbye. This is more than the kiss the other night when we decided that we would give this a chance.

When our lips release and I look into his eyes, I can see everything he is thinking and what this kiss means.

This kiss screams of forever.

"I'm in this. I'm all in. You'll never have to worry about that. Our child will never not know me. I give you my word."

And then he kisses me again, and I know that we might have done things completely backward, but we are right where we are supposed to be.

23

DAVIS

OVER THE LAST week or so, Bethany and I have gotten on the same page about a lot of things.

We have agreed that we are going to find out the gender of the baby when the time comes.

We have agreed to at least start looking for a bigger place to live. Even if something happens where we don't work out, I want to make sure she has the room she will need for our child. Surprisingly, she didn't put up a fight on that one.

Probably because I convinced her of that while I was rubbing her feet and kissing her senseless.

We have also agreed that we don't want to announce this to the world until the twelve-week mark. Her mom knows. Abby knows. However, there are two important people who don't know. Yet.

Hunter and Sadie.

As in, they still don't know.

And it's more than time that they know—about everything.

"Do you think they are going to be mad?" Bethany asks as she straightens the pillows on my couch for the twentieth time.

"No. I don't think they are going to be mad," I say, bringing out the appetizer tray that Bethany insisted we make for them. I didn't tell her I know she only pushed for it because she's craving mozzarella sticks. "I think they are going to be excited for us. And relieved everything is in the open."

When we decided to come clean with them, I thought the best way to do it was to invite them over under the ruse of watching the hockey game—our fellow hometown Music City Rockers are in the playoffs. Little do they know Bethany will also be here and we will finally tell them everything.

I'm not worried a bit. Bethany has been freaking the fuck out all morning. Case in point? She's now reorganizing the appetizer tray.

"Hey," I say, taking her hand and pulling her into my chest. Her arms immediately go around my neck as I place a reassuring kiss on her forehead. "Relax, princess. Are they going to be surprised? Yes. Are they going to be happy for us? Also, yes. Imagine how good this is going to feel when we don't have to pretend in front of them anymore."

She nods, but I don't think my words reassure her as much as I'd like. "I just don't want them to think we are trying to steal their thunder."

"We aren't stealing their thunder. This little one will be here long before they walk down the aisle."

After two months of being engaged, and two months of listening to Hunter's mom nag them on a daily basis, they finally set a wedding date. They are getting married in June of next year.

Gotta love planning a wedding around the calendar year of professional football.

I realize then that not only did my words not cheer Bethany up, they actually make her start crying.

I should have known better. She cried at a dog food commercial yesterday. And again at a drug commercial that promises to clear up warts.

These hormones are no joke.

"What's wrong?" I ask, wishing I could say something to help her. I have figured out how to soothe her when she's sick in the mornings. I've figured out how to help her wind down after a long day at the salon. But the crying? The crying I haven't figured out a remedy for yet.

"Our baby," she says between sobs. "Is going to be six months old when they get married. She'll almost be a year!"

While yes, she is correct, unfortunately, I don't have time to help her work through this one because as soon as the words leave her mouth, a knock on the door signals Sadie and Hunter are here.

"I'll get that," I say, wiping away some stray tears with my thumb. "Go to the bathroom and do what you need to do. Come out when you're ready. We got this."

She nods and gives me a small kiss before making her way down the hall.

Here goes nothing.

I barely have the door open when Sadie comes barging in. "Where is she?"

"Good luck, man," Hunter whispers, patting my shoulder as he enters my apartment.

"What are you talking about?" I try to play dumb, but it's no use. Sadie is currently looking in every corner of my living room and kitchen as if Bethany is hiding in plain sight.

There go the fluffed pillows.

She shoots me a look that very clearly says that she isn't buying my act. "Bethany. I saw her car outside. I'm tired of y'all sneaking around. At first, I was fine with y'all doing your thing on the down low. If anyone can appreciate a secret relationship, it's us. But come on, it has gone on long enough, Rudolph. Just admit you two are sleeping together so we can quit pretending we don't know when we obviously do know!"

All I can do is laugh at Sadie's tirade, which only earns me an even meaner look.

Damn, she can be scary when she wants to.

"Oh, Sadie. You have it mixed up on so many levels," I say, really wanting to laugh at her outburst. "And my name is not Rudolph."

"I figured it wasn't, but I'm running out of *R* names. And don't try to distract me. Just tell me what I have wrong. We'd love to finally know the whole story."

"I don't know personally if I'd go so far as to say love," Hunter chimes in. "But I am interested."

Just as I'm trying to figure out a way to stall, Bethany returns from the bathroom. She doesn't even stop to say hi to Sadie and Hunter. She just immediately comes to me and slides her hand into mine.

"Where would you like for us to start?" Bethany asks, her voice much stronger than it was just a few minutes ago. "Because you're right, we need to come clean about a lot."

Sadie stares down at our joined hands, then back up to us, confusion now covering her face. "I don't know? I guess we'll start with why all of a sudden you asked us to come over today after months of us begging for you two to tell us what the hell was going on. And don't say that you really invited us over to watch hockey because that's a bunch of crap."

"You sure that's where you want to start?" Bethany asks.

"Yes, Bethany!" Sadie exclaims, becoming more frustrated. "Just spit it out. You're killing me here."

"You sure you don't want to sit down?" I ask, because I know the effect of the bomb about to be dropped. And I wish I had been sitting down.

Sadie lets out a groan. "For the love of all things holy, spit it out. I can't—"

"I'm pregnant."

"... keep waiting for you to tell me. Wait, what did you say?"

Sadie's eyes grow large as she realizes what Bethany said.

"What did you say?"

Bethany softly laughs as I decide I'll clean this one up. "How does the name Aunt Sadie sound?"

BETHANY

"Oh my God. When? Where? How? I mean, I know how, but… how? I need every detail. Well, not every detail, but a lot of them."

Once we tell Hunter and Sadie the news of the day—followed by five minutes of shock and bewilderment—the two rush toward us in a flurry of hugs and congratulations.

I must say, it's a huge relief.

Things have settled down, and now it's time to face the firing squad. Though now I'm not as nervous for their line of questioning as before.

"Memphis," I say, loving that I'm finally able to talk about this in the open.

Hunter's jaw drops as he stares wide-eyed at Davis. "This is because of me! You are welcome, dude!"

Davis laughs. "Sure, McAvoy. Take all the credit for something you had a minimal part in."

"I'm serious," Hunter says, taking a jalapeño popper from the appetizer tray. "If I wouldn't have pushed so hard for you two to come to Memphis for the engagement, I doubt we would be here now. And if I wouldn't have invited you back to the hotel that night to celebrate with us, then I'm guessing you wouldn't have ended up in the same room together. Therefore, this is all because of me, and I will accept you giving your child Hunter as a middle name and yes, I will become his godfather."

We all laugh. And it feels so good to laugh about this. Today is really the first time since I found out I've felt good about this whole unexpected pregnancy. I'd been so worried about what Davis would think, then what Hunter and Sadie would think, that laughter hasn't been present much. Combine that with general worry about how everything is going to change, well, I really haven't sat back and enjoyed this change of life plans.

Until now. Right now? I feel like everything is going to be okay.

"What if it's a girl?" Sadie asks. "You do know that's a possibility."

Hunter waves her off. "Nope. My money is on a boy."

"Well, I'm going with a girl," Sadie says, setting down her glass of iced tea. "I have to keep things interesting. Plus, I love you, Bethany, but you raising a boy is slightly terrifying."

"Hey! I could raise a boy. He could play football and stuff."

"That's right, princess," Davis says, bringing me in for a quick kiss. "You can do whatever you set your mind to."

"This is just weird," Sadie says.

"What?" I ask, wishing that Hunter and Sadie weren't here so that kiss could go a little deeper.

"You and him kissing. In the open. Not hiding. I'm not used to it yet."

Davis and I look at each other and all we can do is smile. She's right. That's the first time we've kissed in front of people. Out in the open. Free to be… whatever we are. I feel the weight of months of hiding, questioning, and frustration lift off my shoulders.

"Well, get used to it, Benson. It's going to be happening a lot more," Davis says, scooping me onto his lap. "Did we sneak around for months? Yes. Why did we hide it? I guess because it wasn't a real relationship, and we didn't want you two, or anyone else, judging us for the arrangement that at the time, we were both okay with. At that time, that reasoning seemed logical. Now we know it was a bunch of bullshit. All that matters now is that we're in this, and we're going to have a baby together."

I really need Hunter and Sadie to leave now. Between that speech and my hormones? I need this man naked and me on top of him.

Which would be the first time I've seen him naked since we decided to give us a real shot. Don't ask me why now, all of a sudden, he's taking things slow. It's driving me bonkers, and if he doesn't have sex with me soon, I'm going to combust.

"So, from the time we set you two up, until Memphis, you were sleeping together?" Hunter reiterates.

We both laugh. "For the most part. Yes."

Sadie slaps Hunter on the shoulder. "I told you they hooked up after the championship game!"

Davis and I both look at each other before busting up laughing again.

"What?" Hunter asks. "What is so damn funny?"

By the time we get our laughter under control, Sadie and Hunter are looking at us like we are from another planet.

"Let's just say," Davis begins. "Your truck is quite durable."

24

BETHANY

"WHY IS everyone looking at me funny?"

I have to look up from my phone to see what the heck Davis is talking about. We are sitting in the waiting room of my ob-gyn for my ten-week appointment. I told him there was nothing super exciting that was going to happen today, but he was insistent on coming with me.

It's pretty adorable.

As I take a look around the waiting room, I can only guess as to why every woman here—and even a few men—are looking at Davis.

Frankly, he's the best-looking man in here. And he's covered in Fury gear from head to toe since he came straight from the facility to the appointment. Rookie camp starts soon, and apparently, that's a big deal to prepare for. Or so I've been told.

He's also built like a brick house and looks almost cartoon-like sitting in these small waiting room chairs.

"They probably think you're a player," I whisper, giving him a look up and down, signaling to his clothing. "Also, if you didn't know, you're pretty good-looking. I bet they are checking you out."

This earns me the smirk I love so much. "I did know, but it's always nice to hear it from the mother of my child, princess."

"Are you ever going to stop calling me that?" I ask. I used to loathe that name, but I must admit, it's growing on me. Though, I refuse to tell him that.

"Not a chance."

"Why do you even call me that?"

He leans in like he's going to kiss me on the cheek, but instead whispers in my ear. "That's my secret to keep."

I'm half-tempted to roll my eyes, but I'm stopped as a nurse calls us back.

"You ready?" I ask.

He stands up and holds his hand out for me. "I'm ready. Let's go meet our baby."

I don't know if he knew the double-meaning I packed into my question, but either way, I'm glad for his answer.

Every day I wake up wondering if this is going to be the day he realizes this isn't what he signed up for. He has given me no indication that he has one foot out the door, but my insecurities—packed with my own childhood ordeal—keep letting my mind travel down that road.

"Right in here," the nurse says. "Let's get all your vital signs checked out."

"Is she okay?" Davis asks, his voice concerned as the nurse takes my blood pressure.

The nurse smiles at him. "First time?"

Davis looks slightly embarrassed. "Yes, ma'am."

The nurse takes off the blood pressure cuff and enters it on my chart. "Everything is fine. We just need to do this each time she comes in. Everything is normal. Just wait here a few minutes, then the doctor will be in."

The nurse leaves and all I can do is laugh.

"What?" Davis asks. "I'm just making sure you're okay!"

"It's just my blood pressure. What are you going to do when they start strapping heart rate monitors to me?"

"Why would they do that?"

On cue, Dr. Janet Stewart walks into the exam room. "Because we like to make sure that the baby's and the mom's heart are working. You know, that's kind of my job."

"Hi, Dr. Stewart," I say, trying to hold back my laughter at her response to Davis. "Let me introduce you to the baby's father."

"Hi, ma'am. I'm Davis." He extends his hand, and if I'm not imagining things, I think he's shaking.

Is he nervous? The Davis I know is the definition of calm, cool, and collected. The man who is the center of attention and thrives when the spotlight is on him.

I knew there were going to be many layers of Davis. And every day since I told him about the pregnancy, I get to see a new one.

"None of this ma'am stuff. That is one thing I've never gotten used to living in the south. You can call me Dr. Stewart. Now, what million questions do you have for me, Mr. Davis?"

Bless Dr. Stewart's heart, because Davis came in today with no less than fifty questions, and she answered each and every one of them. I knew he's been reading parenting articles, but I had no idea how deep he had gotten. As in, he asked her if I was allowed to talk on my cell phone because of possible radiation transfer.

He also asked her about sex.

So many questions about sex.

If she was shocked, she didn't show it. Instead, she took the opportunity to ask him about the Fury's upcoming season. Apparently, she's a huge fan.

And she reassured him that sex is just fine.

"Now, if we're done with that, let's get to the good stuff," Dr. Stewart says, putting on a set of gloves. "Bethany, lie back and lift your shirt up. It's time to look at this baby."

I do as she instructs as Davis positions himself next to me. I'm now glad that I didn't have an ultrasound at my first appointment. All we did then was confirm once and for all that I was pregnant. It feels right that the first time we are seeing proof of our baby is together.

As Dr. Stewart gets her equipment ready, I sneak a peek at Davis. Were his eight-million questions a bit over the top? Yes. Were they also extremely thoughtful and gave me butterflies? Also, yes.

"How you doing?" he asks, taking my hand in both of his.

"I'm nervous. Excited. Anxious. Before, it was just talk, but now…"

"But now this becomes real life."

I nod, loving that he knows how I feel. "Exactly."

He brings my hand to his lips as Dr. Stewart begins the exam.

"Everything is looking good," she says, moving her wand around on top of my stomach. "The baby is right on track size-wise at ten weeks' along."

Was Memphis just ten weeks ago? It feels like it has been a lifetime.

I hear Dr. Stewart talking about size and a few other things, but right now, all I can look at is Davis.

His eyes are transfixed on the monitor. I can tell he is taking in every word Dr. Stewart is saying. His hand is gripping mine tighter each time she says something about where the baby is at in terms of development.

I want to look at the monitor, but I can't take my eyes off of him. Watching his face register the joy and love simply from seeing our child for the first time is a memory I'll never have the chance to have again.

Plus, I tried to look at the monitor. I didn't see anything when she pointed to the place I should have seen something and I don't want to admit that.

"By the looks of everything, clear your calendars for the end of November," Dr. Stewart says, as she begins what I assume is printing out pictures of what we just looked at. "And let's hope you don't go into labor on a Sunday."

My eyes go wide. "Oh my gosh! I never thought of that!" I say, sitting straight up. "What if you're on the road for an away game? What if I go into labor early? What if I go into labor during a game and we can't get ahold of you? What if there's a freak snowstorm? What if—"

Davis chuckles and brings my face to his, doing his best to kiss away my worry. "Don't worry, princess. No matter what, I will be there for you. I promise. Nothing is going to keep me away from the birth of our baby."

"We have plenty of time to come up with a plan," Dr. Stewart says, handing us pictures of the sonogram. "Until then, do everything you've been doing, and we'll see you in a month."

I want to worry. I want to panic. But I can't. Because all I can look at right now is Davis, who is looking at the picture of our baby in pure awe. It's like he's staring at the best gift he could have received on Christmas morning.

I'll panic later. Right now, I'm just going to watch this and let my heart melt a little more for this man.

25

DAVIS

I'VE ALWAYS BEEN ATTRACTED to Bethany. That was never the problem for us.

And as the days go on and we spend more time together, my attraction and feelings for her are only getting stronger.

I remember the first time I saw her. The sun was setting when she exited the car in front of the bar where we were meeting. As she walked toward me, her long legs on display in that cream dress, I could have sworn the sunlight radiated from her and it almost made it look like she was wearing a crown.

Like a princess.

As I look at her now, standing in the kitchen doing something as mundane as loading the dishwasher, she's just as beautiful as she was that first night. No. That's wrong. She's more. I never knew what people talked about when they said women have a pregnancy glow. But looking at her now? I can see it. Or maybe it's the knowledge that she's carrying my child.

Combine that with the fact we got to see our baby today? There are a lot of emotions flowing through me right now. And they are all for this woman.

I can't believe I was going to deny myself this. I'll never tell Abby, but she was right. For years, I let myself use my family as a shield. As an excuse because I was scared of what kind of partner I would be. Would I be like Mitch? Only half present and then gone when things got too hard? Or would I be the person I had to become when he left? The dependable person who would provide no matter the odds stacked against him?

I was hoping I'd be the latter, but Mitch's blood does run through me. I'm reminded of that every day when I look in the mirror.

But looking at Bethany right now? Knowing that in a matter of months we are going to be bringing a child into this world together? I know that I am the furthest thing from my so-called father. I am going to be the best father and provider I can for Bethany and our baby. And I'm still going to make sure my mom and sisters have everything they need. Just because I'm adding more into my life doesn't mean I have to subtract others.

I know that now. And that knowledge is freeing.

"What are you looking at?" she says, noticing me staring at her as I lean against her kitchen counter.

"You," I say, walking behind her and wrapping my arms around her stomach. Her stomach that is growing our child.

Why does that thought turn me on so much?

"Me loading the dishwasher, does it for you?" she teases as she rinses another dish.

"You doing anything turns me on. I thought you knew that by now."

I begin kissing her neck, which has its desired effect as her body begins to go limp in my hold. "I... I didn't know if you were still attracted to me."

My lips freeze on her neck. How could she think something so outrageous?

I spin her around, lift her up and place her on the kitchen counter, her legs opening and giving me the perfect spot to stand between. "What did you say?"

She doesn't look me directly in the eye. Not liking that at all, I take her chin and lift it so our eyes meet. "There has never been a day since we met that I haven't been attracted to you. Since the day we met, you have driven me so crazy I couldn't say no. You have made me realize that I want so much more out of this life. So why... why on God's green Earth do you think right now that I'm not dying to be inside you?"

I keep hold of her chin, not roughly, but just enough so she can't look away. "Because since we... got back... got together... whatever we are... you haven't tried to have sex with me. And I, well, I puke every morning, and I'm putting on weight and I'm tired all the time, so I figured—"

I don't let her finish. I crash our mouths together and show her just how much she turns me on. She immediately opens her mouth for me, and our tongues find each other, taking everything we want. The counter is the perfect height for me to rub my rock-hard cock against her center, showing her just how much she, in fact, turns me on.

"Feel that?" I ask, taking her hand and bringing it down to my dick. "That is you. That is all you. My beautiful princess. And as to what we are? You're mine. And I'm yours."

Her hand begins exploring, and I almost forgot how good her touch feels. If I was a selfish bastard, I'd let her explore.

But not tonight. Tonight, I need to show her that not only is she the most beautiful woman I've ever seen but that she's desired in a way I didn't know I could desire another.

"Lift up," I command, which she does the second the words leave my mouth. I push up her skirt and take off her panties before spreading her legs even more.

"Oh!"

It's the only sound she makes as I bend down and dive into her sweet pussy. Going down on a woman in the past was always more of a means to an end for me. But with Bethany? I could live here if she would let me. Between the sounds she makes when my tongue hits her clit just right and the feeling of her legs clenching around me when I make her come?

It's fucking heaven.

"Davis!" she says, and I can't believe that she's almost there, but I feel her contracting.

"What, baby?" I ask, replacing my tongue with two fingers. "What do you want from me?"

"You. I only want you."

How can I argue with that? Especially since the doctor has given the green light for sexual activities.

I give her pussy one more lick before I come up and begin taking my pants off. Out of habit, I reach for my wallet when something hits me.

Do we need a condom?

I look back up at Bethany, who is biting her lip while also giving me the sexiest smile I've ever received.

"I'm clean," I say immediately, needing her to know that.

"I trust you, and it isn't like I'll get pregnant or anything," she answers with a smirk, bringing me back in close to her.

While I'd love nothing more than to dive into her right here on the kitchen counter, I can't. This isn't just another roll in the hay between two people sneaking around and denying their feelings for each other.

This is the first time as an us. The first time without anything between us.

The first of many more.

She shrieks as I scoop her off the counter and quickly make my way back to her bedroom. As soon as we find the bed, we frantically strip each other. We are nothing but lips and hands and clothes flying off.

"I've missed you," I say, lying her back and reaching down for one suck on her taut nipple.

"I missed you too," she moans. "Now, please…"

"Please what?" I ask, lining up my cock with her center.

"Make me feel everything you said earlier."

And I do. I drive into her, with nothing between us, and the feel of her hot pussy against my dick is almost too much to handle.

"Fuck, you feel so good," I say, trying to control myself when all I want to do is fuck her hard and fast.

"More," she says, as if she's reading my mind. "Don't hold back. I want to feel all of you."

"All of me." I groan, bringing her legs onto my shoulders. "Give me everything, princess."

And she does. Our hips meet in perfect rhythm as the angle drives her insane. Her hands are reaching for the sheets, the pillows, whatever she can get her hands on. And before I know it, her center is clenching around me in a feeling I've never experienced with a woman.

"Now, princess. Give it to me now."

She does, and I follow right behind her. We come undone with nothing between us, a perfect harmony of pent-up lust, emotion... and, dare I say, something more.

I knew that first night this woman is something special.

Little did I know that she is it for me.

26

———

BETHANY

"WHAT DO YOU MEAN, you've never met someone's parents?"

I know my voice got a little loud there, but I'm seriously confused about how he never went through this rite of passage in his life. Then I look over at Davis, who is just laughing at my reaction as we drive to my mom and Mike's house for Monday night dinner.

"I mean, I've never met a girl's parents before. I've never had a dad greet me with a bat or give me mildly veiled threats of treating his daughter right. I've never had to kiss up to a mom."

"How does that happen?" I ask, still confused how this is actually a thing that he hasn't experienced before.

"What?" he asks.

"I'm just baffled how you've never had to meet parents."

"I didn't date in high school," he says matter-of-factly. "When you don't date, you don't have to meet the parents."

"How did you not date?" I turn and face him because I'm genuinely intrigued by how this is a thing. "Did you not go to prom? Or homecoming? Or even out to the movies?"

He shakes his head. "Nope. I was working. My family came first. When my dad left, I made a vow to my mom and sisters that I would help provide. I was the man of the house and I took that job seriously.

It's the reason I was a hard-headed asshole to you for months. That meant every second I wasn't in school or playing football, I worked."

"That's kind of sad," I say, reaching for his hand that's not on the steering wheel. "I mean, I think it's admirable that at a young age you took on that responsibility. I don't know many teenagers who would do that. But I also wish that you could have had a normal childhood."

He shrugs. "It is what it is. So now I ask, how many of your boyfriends did you bring home?"

"Only a couple," I admit. "In high school I had a few boyfriends, and they met Mom and Mike because of circumstance. Proms and what not. Though, I wouldn't consider that the firing squad. Mom was pretty laid-back about things, and Mike had just married my mom, so I don't think he felt right playing the role of my father. Plus, he was my English teacher. Things would have gotten really weird. As of late? None have lasted long enough for me to make it worth my time."

"And I'm worth your time," he says with a cocky tone to his voice.

I lean over and give him a peck on the cheek. "Without a doubt."

We sit in silence for a few minutes and my mind drifts back to a younger Davis. I picture the boy who had to become a man too early in life, working likely at some fast-food restaurant on a Saturday night instead of going to the movies. The boy who barely slept because of everything on his plate.

"Do you regret it?" I ask, curious now that he has hindsight.

He doesn't have to ask what I'm talking about as he turns into the driveway. "Not even a little bit. I'll never regret putting my family first."

He puts the truck in park and flashes me a smug grin. "Plus, if I had met parents back then, you wouldn't get another one of my firsts."

"Another one of your firsts?" I ask, a little confused. "I didn't realize I had any firsts. I'm going to guess I didn't have the *big* first."

This makes him laugh. "No, you didn't get that first. But the firsts you have, they mean more than any of the other ones."

"Can you tell me one?" I ask with a hint of flirtation in my voice, hoping this gets me my answer.

He leans in and gives me a quick kiss. "You're the first woman I ever spent the night with."

This leaves me speechless. I am? I was?

As I turn this new information over in my head, Davis gets out of the truck to come around to my side to open my door. I tried to open it myself the first night we went out, and I was told to never do it again.

Who knew this man had such a chivalrous side?

"Will you tell me more firsts later?" I ask.

"Of course," he says, taking my hand as we walk up the sidewalk. "But let's get this first out of the way, shall we?"

Now that we're nearing the second trimester and Davis and I have fallen into a consistent groove, we figure it's time to meet the families. We've booked flights to Pennsylvania in June when he has some downtime so I can meet his sisters and Mom. And with rookie camp starting next week, now is as good a time as ever to meet Mom and Mike.

"Are you nervous?" I ask as we approach the door.

"Nah," he says, giving my hand a squeeze. "If Hunter can survive this, then it will be a piece of cake."

The door opens before I have a chance to knock—I now knock whenever I come over—and standing there is a very stern Mike in the doorway.

"Hey, Mike," I say awkwardly, wondering why he's taking up the entirety of the doorframe.

"Hello there," he says, his voice stern and very un-Mike like. The last time he was like this was when he met Hunter.

Oh, Jesus, take the wheel.

"You must be Davis," he continues, stepping slightly to the side for us. "Why don't you come inside. Let's get to know each other a little better."

"WHAT DO you mean that the SEC is overrated! Helen, are you going to let this man be the father of our first grandchild with that kind of blasphemy coming from his mouth!"

"Now, now, Mike," Mom says, patting Mike's arm like he's a toddler throwing a temper tantrum. "Every person is allowed their opinion. And I don't think I can really have a say about him being the father. That's already sorted itself out."

"Hunter!" Mike yells, turning to look to his left at Hunter, who is trying, but failing, not to crack up. "How does this man work for you!"

Hunter just shrugs. "It's nice to have someone who keeps my ego in check."

"Mike, I'm sorry," Davis says, casually putting his arm on the back of my chair. "But if you take away Alabama, the conference is mediocre at best."

Mike takes his fork and points it across the table at Davis. "We aren't done with this conversation."

"But we are tonight," Mom says, standing up and clearing the plates. "Enough football talk for the night."

"I agree," I say as I start to stand.

"What are you doing?" Davis asks, taking my hand and pulling me back down to my chair.

"Helping clear the table?"

"You will not," Mom says, sweeping the dishes out from in front of me. "You need to stay off your feet."

"You do know I'm still on my feet for hours a day working."

"I do. That means you should be off your feet whenever you can. Davis, can you talk some sense into her?"

"I can try, Mrs. Benson. She doesn't listen to me very well."

"What did I tell you about Mrs. Benson? It's Helen," she says with a smile before she walks with Sadie into the kitchen.

It's safe to say that Mom and Mike are smitten with Davis. As soon as we walked through the door, Mike took him back into the office with Hunter. It was reminiscent of what he did with Hunter when Sadie first brought him home. That lasted for about thirty minutes before they came out laughing and talking football jargon that sounded like a foreign language to me.

Davis then helped my mom in the kitchen. He didn't flinch when she asked him not so casually how many cribs we needed to buy—also known as are you two going to be living together or staying apart.

He explained to her that we're going to start looking for a house, and he made her a promise that no matter what, baby and I will always be provided for.

I'm pretty sure Mom melted a bit at that declaration.

The conversation at dinner was easy and natural. I was worried it would be awkward considering the whole "first time you met this guy was after he got me pregnant thing," but everyone has been wonderful. We talked about our family, he told us a little about his, and we started spitballing ideas for nursery themes.

He wants football. Boy or girl.

I want teddy bears. Either pink or blue ones.

We'll see how this goes down.

"I think she likes you," I say as I reach for his free hand under the table. "Same with Mike."

He gives my hand an extra squeeze. "You could have warned me he and Hunter were going to gang up on me about college football."

"You know I don't know anything about that stuff," I say, leaning back into his shoulder. "For all I know, they were talking about TV shows. It sounds like reality TV."

"I still don't know how none of my football knowledge rubbed off on you over the years," Sadie says, taking back her seat next to Hunter.

"The same way you never listened to my hair or makeup tips," I say, pointing to the messy bun on top of her head that I'm pretty sure is there twenty-four seven. Just once, I'd love to see her with loose beach waves.

"Touché, sister. Touché."

"Enough football talk," Mom says, taking her seat next to Mike. "I want to talk about all things baby."

"Yes!" Sadie says. "First thing's first. Do we have a gender yet? And if you do one of those elaborate reveal parties, I will no longer call you my sister."

I shake my head, suddenly embarrassed that all eyes are on Davis and me right now. "We are going to find out. That's about eight weeks away. As for the reveal party, I am not doing one. I'm not taking the chance that I'm one of those gender reveals gone wrong and end up on the national news. We will stick to telling y'all at dinner one week, then posting on Facebook."

"I like the sound of that," Davis says, bringing my hand to his lips. When I look back at my Mom, I think she's actually going to cry from the act.

"Have you thought about names?" Mike asks. I'm guessing to save my mom from an emotional episode.

"Not really," I say with a shrug. "We still have a few weeks before we have to start worrying about that."

"Names, you say," Sadie says, leaning forward on her elbows as she locks eyes with Davis. "What do you think about names, Davis? Maybe as in, is there a family name that needs to be passed down if it's a boy?"

I laugh at Sadie's horrible attempt to get Davis's first name out of him. Do I want to know? Heck yes I do. But at this point, I'm kind of enjoying the game these two have going on.

"Yes, there is. But I'm not worried about it," Davis says, confidence oozing from his voice.

"Really?" I ask, looking up over my shoulder at him. "Why?"

"Because," he says, placing a slow kiss on my lips. "I think we're having a little girl. And she's going to be just as beautiful as her mother."

If my mother wasn't crying before, she most definitely is now.

It's okay, because so am I.

27

———

DAVIS

IT FEELS like forever since the Fury has been on the field.

And even though this isn't our full squad today—this week is just rookies and unsigned players looking for a shot at the big time—it's still good to be back on the field.

"Again!" I yell, signaling for my running back coach to run the agility drill again. Satisfied that he's doing what he needs to, I make my way over to the receivers. Also known as my former position group. The group that now has the best young receiver in the league with Dexter Smith.

"Oh, the offense we can run with you," I say to myself as I watch him make a forty-yard catch.

"You aren't wrong," Hunter says as he steps up next to me. I didn't even hear him approach. "Imagine the plays we can run with him."

"As long as he has someone to throw it to him," I say, trying to gauge Hunter's feelings on Bryce and his offseason antics.

"Let's just hope it's a young kid blowing off steam," he says, patting me on the shoulder. "I have to go pay attention to the defense. Apparently, that's my job now, too."

I laugh. "Better you than me, boss."

He holds up his middle finger as he runs across the field to watch the defense. Happy with what I'm seeing out of the receivers, I head over to watch the offensive linemen.

I'm not like Hunter. I never had big dreams and aspirations to be a head football coach. Whereas he wants to turn the professional football world on its head, I just want a job where I can have some fun while also providing for my family. I want to be a coach who is found reliable and can help a team win. I'm also the coach who gives every rookie an unflattering nickname when camp starts.

It's all about balance.

Coaching offers me financial stability as well as getting to do something I love. Yes, I could have used my MBA to work at a bank, but that didn't sound too fun. Though I would have loved the rush, a stock trader or hedge fund manager was a little too risky. I might not make the kind of money that head coaches do, but between that and my investments, it's more than enough to provide for myself, while making sure Mom's bills are paid, Sara doesn't have to work while in school and helping Abby whenever she needs it.

That's all I ever wanted; to give my family stability and to not have to go to bed each night worrying how they were going to put food on the table or pay the electric bill.

And now I have two more to take care of. But instead of that giving me anxiety like it used to, now I think about it and all I do is smile.

I'm about to have a family of my own.

"Is a shiny new receiver putting that smile on your face or is it someone else?"

The comment comes from Cole Campbell, our left guard on the offensive line and Bryce's best friend. They were in pee wees together before going to the same high school. They both won national championships at Clemson, and because of an injury, Cole fell to the second round last year so we were able to draft him along with Bryce.

He's also the most mature twenty-four-year-old I've ever met in my life. Hence, why his nickname is Dad.

"What are you doing out here, Dad? Miss me too much?"

"You know that's it. Figured I'd come out and see what we have to work with. Not like I'm doing anything else these days."

Cole is one of those players I don't know a lot about personally. I might be his coordinator now, but last year I was the receivers' coach, so I didn't have a lot of interaction with him. From what I know, he keeps his nose to the ground, doesn't party, and is the most responsible player in the locker room of any age, and that's including our veteran tight end who has three kids.

"No girl keeping you busy this offseason?" I ask, half curious and half hoping I can steer him into a chat about Bryce.

"Nah," he says as his gaze turns back toward the group of practicing rookies. "Maybe one day."

Judging from his tone, I would put money on there being more to that story. And that he's also not going to talk about it.

"So, what have you been up to this offseason?"

He just shrugs. "Working out. Went and visited my family for a few months. Just lying low, you know?"

"I hear that," I say, knowing that it's now or never if I want to talk to him about his childhood friend. "Have you talked to Bryce much?"

He lets out a big, frustrated sigh. "No. And don't bother asking me to. I've already tried. He won't listen."

That is the last thing I want to hear. This could be our season. With Hunter's offensive mindset, a defense that has reloaded, and the reigning Rookie of the Year as quarterback, we could be unstoppable this year.

That is, as long as Bryce gets his head out of his ass and shapes up.

Quick.

The talk I had with him did no good. In fact, it might have made him worse. *The Nashville Banner,* the local newspaper and where Sadie used to work, rarely prints gossip. But Bryce has been so out of control lately that even they are writing about it. The other night a video went viral of him dancing on a bar with two women before making out with each of them within seconds of each other.

I don't know what has gotten into him. But if he doesn't clean up his act, he's going to be out of the league before he really even made his mark.

"I tried to talk to him," I say, wanting Cole to know that it's not all on him. "He pretty much blew me off."

"Yeah, he's good at that," Cole says, still looking out at the players. "He's done this from time to time. Rebelled. He did it our freshman year of college, but it never made the news. And it wasn't nearly this bad. Before, I knew what to do. But now? Now I don't even think that will work."

This gets my attention. "What is it? You tell me and we'll make it happen. He's the future of the franchise. You both are. Whatever needs to be done, you tell me and I'll do it."

Cole finally turns to look at me, a sad look in his eye. "That look in your eye. The one from earlier. Is she special?"

Confused by his question, but wanting more information, I go along with it. "Yeah. Yeah, she is. We're actually having a baby together."

"Then you know. What would happen if she left you? That you thought, albeit selfishly, she'd always be in your life, but then for whatever circumstances, one day she up and leaves. What would you do?"

My blood temperature spikes from just the thought of it. "I'd go nuts. Probably off the deep end."

Cole nods and looks back to the position group. "That's Bryce right now. He's off the deep end. He never thought she'd be gone. I've tried to talk to him. His sister has. We don't know what to do."

Fuck. This is all because of a girl? I remember last year when he started off rough, Hunter said it was a personal matter, but he worked through it so it was completely forgotten.

Is this the same thing? And if Cole is right, can it be fixed? If this is a personal matter, we can only help Bryce so much before he has to do something about it himself.

I can fix his throwing motion. I can fix a play that's not working.

But this? I don't know if I can help him fix this.

"What can I do?" I ask Cole.

"I wish I knew, Coach. I wish I knew." Cole sighs and gives my back a slap before walking away. "Oh, and congratulations on the baby."

28

____

BETHANY

"WHAT DO you mean you won't tell me his name!" I cry out, though I'm only half mad that my efforts have again been derailed. "I thought I could bring you to my side! What happened to our girls' day this afternoon! I thought we bonded."

Abby and Sara both fall back into Abby's couch in a fit of laughter. All Davis can do is plaster on a smug smile as he puts his arm around me.

"We did. Never did I ever think I'd be able to go makeup shopping with Davis's girlfriend. Hell, I never thought Davis would have a girlfriend. And I really wish I could tell you," Abby says, straightening herself back up. "But that man has sworn me to secrecy. Plus, he has all the dirt on us. If it was just me, I'd dish away, but I'd rather he not one day tell my daughters what I was like in high school."

"You're damn right I would," Davis says, a smug smile on his face. "I told you, princess. They have sworn a vow of silence."

"If it makes you feel better, Bethany, I also hate our last name," Sara says as she stands up from the couch. "I would have changed it too, except I'm holding on to the hope I'll get married and not have to go through the paperwork. I don't tell anyone unless I know they are going to be around for a very long time."

I snap my head to Davis and turn on my best overly dramatic southern accent. "You had your last name changed? I thought we were just trying to figure out your first name! This is brand new information! Who are you even? I'm having a baby with a complete stranger!"

"That's it. You're dead," he says, jumping up from the couch and running after Sara.

"I didn't know about that part being a secret! I'm sorry!"

Sara's voice trails off and all Abby and I can do is laugh.

"There wasn't enough of that in our house growing up," Abby says out loud, though I don't know if she really means to voice it.

"What was he like?" I've been dying to ask this question and now seems like the perfect chance.

Abby sits back into her couch and doesn't answer right away. Instead, she's looking in the direction that Davis and Sara ran off, like she's trying to see through the walls.

"It's like I grew up with two different brothers."

"What do you mean?"

She lets out a sigh and turns back to face me. "I like to call our childhood pre-Mitch and post-Mitch. He did tell you about our so-called father, right?"

I nod. "Yeah, but not a lot. I get the feeling he doesn't like talking about him."

Abby lets out a humorless laugh. "That's the statement of the year. The Davis before Mitch left was so full of life. Not that he's not now, but before he was the definition of a carefree kid. There wasn't a room he couldn't charm or a crowd he couldn't make laugh. He didn't get into big trouble, but he was mischievous. Then, the day we realized that Da—Mitch—wasn't coming back, it's like a light switched off for him. He made it his mission to take care of us. I don't even know where he got that idea in his head from. Mom surely didn't ask it of him. But once he made up his mind that he was going to help financially provide for the family, we couldn't talk him out of it. Lord knows, Mom and I tried. We hated seeing that light in his eyes go out. I know he still kept up the act around people at school and his teachers. They had no idea what was going on at home. But to those who knew him, who really knew him, we never saw that same spark again."

My heart hurts as Abby tells me this, and I subconsciously put my hands over my stomach. I can only hope that our child will have that same playful side.

For some reason, at that moment, I let myself imagine a little boy. But it's not Davis. Abby showed me pictures earlier. This little boy I'm imagining does have Davis's brown hair, but it's lighter. The lightest brown hair can be. And his eyes aren't the same blueish-gray color as Davis's. No, they are lighter, almost as if they are a combination of the two of ours.

For the first time since I found out I was pregnant, I let myself envision a little boy. A boy with Davis's smirk who is a tad bit ornery in the best way. A little boy who might be tough on the football field, but deep down is a mama's boy. One who gets to have the spark in his eye forever because I'll make sure I do everything in my power to make sure it never fades away.

"That is, until I met you."

Abby's words bring me back from my daydream. "I'm sorry. What did you say?"

Abby stands up and comes to sit next to me, taking my hand in hers. "I never, ever, thought that Davis would find his spark of happiness again. I don't know if you've realized this about my brother, but he's quite hard-headed."

"I've noticed."

We both laugh before Abby continues. "I might bug him every week about settling down, but I really thought I was talking to an empty room. Then one day he talked about you. You were the first one he's ever told me about. Then I met you and… now I see it. The spark is back in his eyes. The way he looks at you? It might not be the same trouble making look he used to have, but for the first time in years, there is life in his soul. And I have you to thank for that."

I laugh because that's the only thing that's keeping the tears away.

"I'm pretty sure a faulty condom also had a little something to do with it."

"While that might be true, don't for one minute discourage how crazy he is about you." She looks up and Davis and Sara are on their way back to her living room. She quickly leans in, close enough to whisper now. "I knew you were someone special before I knew you were going to make me an aunt."

I look at her confused, and all she does is nod as Davis and Sara retake their seats.

He talked to Abby about me before I told him about the baby?

If I needed another piece of reassurance about how he feels about me, then this is it. I've always believed him, but that twat waffle inner voice of mine always perked up with thoughts of "this is working out too well" and "don't you think this happened a bit too fast?"

But knowing that he talked to Abby about me before I told him I was pregnant? That's everything.

"Uncle Davis!"

My head snaps to the doorway to see a little girl no more than four years old running as fast as her little legs can carry her toward Davis and me. Before she crashes into us, Davis quickly kneels to the ground and scoops the little one up.

"How's my Livvie doing?" he says, scattering kisses on her face. "What did you do today?"

"Went to park!" she says between giggles.

"We were quite fond of the swings today," Abby's husband, Joe, says as he comes in the house with a sleeping Sophia in his arms. "One fell asleep on the way home. One picked up her fourth wind."

"Uncle Davis! I want to show you my toys!" Olivia yells, dragging Davis up the stairs. "Come on!"

I laugh as I watch Davis being manhandled by a four-year-old. Though it is nice to see him with his nieces, today was our adult day. Joe volunteered to take both girls to the park to give us girls time to get to know each other. Davis had some things he needed to take care of at his mom's facility, so we decided to go shopping. This mama was in need of some maternity clothes.

And of course, no girls' day shopping trip is complete without a trip to Sephora.

I have a feeling that by the look Abby is giving him right now, his efforts today earned him some husband points.

"Thank you for taking them," she says as she starts to stand up. "Want me to go lay her down?"

"Nah," he says, waving her off. "I got it. I'll see you guys in a bit."

As soon as Joe goes up the stairs, I see movement coming down it.

And it's a sight that I will never forget for the rest of my life.

Davis, my two-hundred-pound, muscled, former football player, is walking down the stairs in a blond wig.

With a tiara.

It is freaking adorable. And weirdly sexy.

"We're having a tea party!" Olivia says. "Come on, Uncle Davis! Bethy! Come play too!"

We've now been in Pennsylvania for two days. The first day we laid low and recovered from a day of travel. Yesterday, we made our way over to Abby's house, where I officially met everyone. From the second I met this little girl, my heart melted. She's everything I could want in a daughter. Spunky and sassy, while also sweet and kind.

And she loves her uncle Davis.

She's not the only one.

Since we've been here and seeing him with his family, I've seen a side of Davis I could only hope existed. I know there are a lot of layers to this man, but seeing him with his nieces? With his sisters? It confirms what I hope for deep in my soul.

This is a man who knows the worth of family.

This is the man I want to have a family with.

This is the man I want to spend the rest of my life with.

"What are you looking at, princess?" he whispers as Olivia "makes" more tea.

I almost crack a joke about how right now, technically, he's the princess. I also almost say those three words that are on the very tip of my tongue.

I don't say either of those things. Instead, I say what's in my heart.
"I'm looking at our future."
He smiles, taking my hand in his. "Do you like what you see?"
I nod and say three different words instead. "It's simply perfect."

29

DAVIS

EVERY TIME I go to enter my mom's memory care facility, it takes me a second to gather my resolve.

I wasn't there when the memory lapses started. I was away at college and had to get my updates from Abby and Sara. At first, we thought it was just the byproduct of getting older.

Then one day Sara got home from school and she wasn't there. She wasn't working either of her jobs that day. Her car was in the garage, and the front door was unlocked. Sara panicked, called Abby, and the search began. They ended up finding her a few blocks away at a park where she was sitting on a bench, none the wiser about what she had done or how she had gotten there.

We knew then it was time to get her help.

I've only made it here a few times since then. But every time I stand on this sidewalk, staring at the doors that take me inside, I'm reminded that Mom—the woman who kept us together when everything could have fallen apart—is in there. And this is her life now.

No more singing Motown in the kitchen. No more of her knitting while we watch TV. No more pushing us on the tire swing in our backyard.

That woman is still there, but she's not. She's never going to get better. And this walkway reminds me of that every time I'm here.

Even more so today. I have no idea how she is going to be when Bethany and I walk into her room? Will she recognize me? If I tell her Bethany's name, will it register for more than a few seconds? Will we be robbed of the moment when we tell her we're having a baby?

Will she ever be able to meet our baby and know who it is? Will my child ever get to know the woman who did everything in her power to keep our family together when it could have crumbled?

I hate this disease. Today, more than ever.

"You okay?" Bethany asks, giving my hand a squeeze. "We don't have to do this if you don't want."

I take a breath and bring Bethany around to my front, wrapping my arms around her waist. Her arms instinctively go around my neck.

"It's always hard walking in," I say, allowing her touch to give me resolve. "Yesterday she was napping when I was here, so I didn't want to disturb her. But now? Now I know I'm going to see her and I'm always… I just never know how she'll be."

"It's okay," Bethany says, her soothing voice having its desired effect. "No matter what kind of day she is having, we will make the best of it. And we'll do it together."

"You're right," I say, placing a kiss on her forehead. "Let's go tell my mom she's going to be a grandma again."

I walk through the front door and go to push the button for entry. One of the best features of this facility is its security and round-the-clock, in-person monitoring they have of the residents. However, when I push the button, nothing happens. Normally, it signals a worker to buzz me in. Right now? Nothing.

"That's weird," I say, pushing the button again. "It worked just fine yesterday."

"Maybe it's broke?" Bethany says as she tries to pull the door open. Just when I'm about to tell her it won't work, it opens right up.

"That's not supposed to happen," I say, my anger growing slightly. "The security here is supposed to be state of the art."

"Oh my goodness, I am so sorry!" A woman in her mid-forties says as she comes rushing toward us. "Mr. Davis, I'm so sorry about that. I don't know what happened with our alarm, but it went offline for five minutes. Security is double-checking all of the residents now, which is why there was no one to let you in. Trust me when I say that this has never happened before."

"Thank you for the explanation," Bethany says, taking my hand in both of hers before I can snap at this woman. "Technology has its quirks sometimes. We appreciate the explanation."

I let out a breath, glad that Bethany stopped me from making a scene. "Yes. Thank you, Ms. Hathaway. Can we see my mother now?"

"Of course. Right this way."

I don't need directions to Mom's room, but I have a feeling that Jennifer Hathaway, the director of the facility I met with yesterday to talk about my mom's care, needs this more than I do.

"Here you go," she says, ushering us into a room that looks more like a studio apartment than a nursing home room. "She's having a good day today."

"Thank you," I say, as I gently knock on the door. "Mom? It's me. Can I come in?"

Bethany and I slowly walk into my mother's room, not wanting to startle her. Though, I doubt she can hear me with the sound of *The Price is Right* playing at full blast.

"Mom!" I say a little louder, hoping to get her attention. I'll have to ask Jennifer about her hearing.

"What do you want, Richard!" she says, muting the television as we walk in. "I heard you the first time."

Well, at least she remembers my name.

My birth name, that is.

"Richard!" Bethany whisper-yells. "Is that a part of the Alzheimer's, or did your mother just out your name?"

"I should have known she would do it," I say in defeat.

"Oh, you have so much explaining to do, mister."

"Are you two just going to stand there and have a conversation, or are you going to tell me who this is, Richard?"

My mom is sitting on her reclining chair, looking slightly

annoyed that I interrupted her television time and confused as to why I'm not alone. But the best part of how she looks? Her eyes look clear. Not confused. She knows who I am from the second I walk in.

Jennifer is right; today is a good day.

"Hey, Mom," I say, walking over to her and giving her a kiss on the cheek. "How are you feeling?"

"Today is good," she says, turning off the television. "Now, enough stalling. Who is this beautiful woman?"

I smile. "Mom. This is Bethany Hall. Bethany, this is my mom, Marie."

"It's so nice to meet you," Bethany says, holding her hand out.

"Nonsense," Mom says, holding out her arms. "Come over here and give me a hug."

Bethany smiles and walks into my mother's embrace. The sight hits me in the heart in a way I wasn't expecting.

"I've been waiting fifty-five years to do that," Mom says as Bethany comes and takes a seat next to me on her small couch. "About time."

I laugh, loving how much she sounds like herself right now. "I was making sure she was perfect."

Mom turns her gaze to Bethany. "Do you fall for his smooth words? You know half the time it's a bunch of crap, right?"

Bethany laughs. "I can't resist them, ma'am. It's probably why I'm here today."

This makes Mom laugh. "I like you. But don't ever call me ma'am again. I might be getting old. I have trouble remembering some things. The least you can do is just call me Marie."

Bethany smiles. "I can do that."

The three of us fall into conversation. We tell her about how we met through Hunter and Sadie—though we leave out the part where we spent four months of that time as friends with benefits. She tells us about a recent field trip they took to a botanical garden that she enjoyed, though the way she's telling it, I don't know if it was last week or last year. She struggles a few times with remembering certain things like Olivia and Sophia's names, the name of a recipe she used to love making, and a few times stumbles over Bethany's name. But for the most part, it has been smooth sailing.

Which will make telling her the big news so much easier.

"Mom, there is something we want to tell you," I say, bringing Bethany a little closer to me.

"If it's that this lovely woman here is pregnant with my grandchild, then you should have told me that a lot sooner."

My jaw drops in shock. I look over to Bethany, whose eyes look like they are about to jump out of her head.

"How did you know?" I ask, and if the answer is Abby told her, I'm going to beat my sister's ass.

"Oh, Richard," Mom says, and I hear Bethany snicker a little bit at the use of my real name. "I've been pregnant four times. Some were on purpose, some were gifts from God. I might not remember a lot of things most days. But I'll never forget the look of someone who is expecting. The subtle ways she's been holding her stomach? The glow on her face? My dear, pregnancy looks wonderful on you and I am so glad you are going to give me another grandchild."

Bethany stands and rushes over to my mom, giving her a big hug. But I replay those words over in my head.

Pregnant four times? That's not right. There are only three of us. I'm not going to correct her though. I don't want it to trigger anything if that was just a lapse in words.

Instead, I take the moment to look at two of the women most important to me in this world. I can usually keep my emotions together, but seeing this before me? It's a struggle to keep the tears at bay.

With my schedule, I don't get here too often. Hell, probably the next time I see her will be after the baby is born.

Will she remember then what we told her today? Will she know me? Or Bethany?

I wish I knew. But at least today, we all get this. We get to enjoy this moment together.

I'll take that as a win.

30

―――――――

BETHANY

"ARE we just not going to talk about the truth bomb your mom dropped today… Richard?"

I waited until we were back in our hotel room before I asked Davis… I mean, Richard, to talk to me about the little tidbit of information his mother disclosed.

Now that we are here, he has nowhere to run.

After months of dancing around the topic, I'm finally going to know the true story behind his name.

Oh, I wish Sadie could be here for this one.

"You think you have jokes," he says, coming up behind me and putting his arms around my waist as I take my earrings out at the bathroom vanity. "And here I thought you were a nice girl. A southern lady. Who knew you would manipulate my sweet mother into telling you my secrets?"

"I did no such thing." I gasp, turning around so I'm now leaning against the bathroom counter and touching his hard chest. His chest that feels darn good against me. "She offered that information freely. I can't help that I'm such an easy and appealing person to talk to."

"Easy and appealing, huh?" he says, his mouth attacking my neck in a swarm of sucks and kisses that make my body go weak. "Actually, this dress makes things very easy. And I find you very appealing."

"You can't get out of this conversation through sex," I say, though not with as much resolve as I would have liked. I mean, his tongue is tracing circles on my neck that is sending a straight shot to my core.

"Fine," he grumbles, picking me up and sitting me on the counter. "What do you want to know?"

The giddiness in my voice can't be hidden. "You're seriously going to let me ask?"

"You can ask three questions about it. And you can't tell Sadie because I want free food from her. Then I'm getting you naked. Choose wisely. And hurry."

He still tries to distract me by bringing his finger up the side of my leg and traveling underneath my dress. I have found that sundresses are a savior for a pregnant woman in the summer. They are flowy, comfortable, and don't make me feel like I'm roasting all the time.

It's also easy access for Davis—I mean, Richard, or Dick… oh, I like the sound of Dick. Pregnancy brain is off the charts real. Regardless, the easy access is an added benefit for both of us.

"Quit trying to distract me," I say, doing my best to ignore his traveling hand. "Why don't you go by Richard?"

He lets out a sigh and his fingers stop searching. I'd be more upset if I wasn't about to get the answers I've been wondering since the day we met.

"My grandfather's name was Richard. My mother named me after him. And she hated it when I tried to go by Ricky or Rick. I even tried Richie. That made it for a few months before my teacher called me that when she sent a note home and I got grounded for a month. Mom said she gave me that name to honor her father, and that I was to respect it. So, much to my dismay, I was Richard. She is also the only person on this Earth who calls me that."

"Okay," I say, still a little confused by the secrecy of this all. "So you have an old-fashioned name. Is that a reason to not go by it?"

"You try being an eight-year-old kid whose jackass classmate figured out that Richard is a form of the name Dick."

I laugh, because hello, was just thinking about Dick, but there is more. I can tell. "What are you not telling me? Is your name unfortunate? Yes. Is it easy access for bullies? Also, yes. But this seems all a bit extreme. What's the scoop, sir?"

Davis looks up at the ceiling and lets out a breath before meeting my eyes again. "I just want you to know. You are the only one besides my mother and sisters who are about to know this."

I take my finger and make a cross over my heart. "Your secret is safe with me."

"The first name would have been bad, but I could have gotten through it," he says, taking another breath before continuing. "But then there was also our last name. That... that was the dagger, the literal sword that I could not fall on."

I beg him with my eyes to go on. "What is it? You can't just leave me hanging like that."

He smiles. "You've already asked three questions."

"I'll make it worth your while later if I get a few extra," I say seductively, letting my hand fall down and grazing his dick.

He lets out a moan. "You play dirty."

"I learned from the best. Now, spill it."

"Fine," he says begrudgingly. "My legal last name now is Davis. It was my middle name. When we fill out the birth certificate, our baby, if we agree to it, will have the last name of Davis. It was legally changed to that the day I turned eighteen."

"Should I ask from what or why first?"

"Because," he says, pulling me a little closer, "for one, it is the worst last name to have in the history of last names. I was teased mercilessly for it. And it was Mitch's name. His actions might have turned me into the man I am today, but he doesn't deserve to have his name carried on. So the day I could, I stopped it. I would have changed my first name, too, but I couldn't do that to my mother, so I opted to just go by my initial and given middle name, which is now my last name. Hence, Davis."

I stare at him, not believing he is keeping me in suspense. "Are you not going to tell me? I'm dying over here."

He laughs. "You promise you will not tell anyone? Not even Sadie."

I cross my heart again. "Scout's honor. Now tell me."

I don't know what I'm expecting. But what comes out of his mouth next? I could have had a hundred years to mentally prep for this, and I still wouldn't have been ready.

"Semen."

I shake my head a little.

Did he just say?

"Excuse me?"

"Yup. My name growing up was Richard, aka Dick Semen."

I try not to. I summon all the power I have, and even some from the baby, to not laugh.

But it's no use. I laugh. I laugh so hard I almost pee my pants.

I'm having a baby with Dick Semen.

"Oh, you think that's funny?" he asks, scooping me off the counter. "I'll show you funny."

Before I know it, we are landing in the center of the king-size bed and his mouth is on mine. If he wanted to get me to quit laughing, this is definitely the way to do it.

"You want funny, huh?" he says, sliding down the strap of my sundress. "Is it funny when I do this?"

His mouth moves down my neck, over the tops of my breasts, before he pushes my bra down, freeing my breasts that are larger than they have ever been in my life.

"Not funny." I moan as he takes one nipple in his mouth and twists the other with his fingers. In my first trimester, they were so swollen I couldn't bear him touching them. But now? I'm craving his mouth on them. I need him there. He switches it up and puts his mouth on the other, and I've all but forgotten the admission of his name and even what my own name is.

He releases my nipple and leaves me panting on the bed, half-dressed and turned on as well. "If that's not funny, then how about this?"

He sits me up, bringing me on his lap as he unsnaps my bra and lifts my dress over my head. I think once I'm undressed he's going to continue whatever magical thing he was doing to me with his mouth, but instead, he just lays me down, stripping me of my panties, and runs his hand across my stomach before he gets off the bed.

"You think this is funny?" he asks, taking his shirt off over his head with one motion.

"No," I say breathlessly.

"How about this?" Next to go are his shorts, showing his hard cock that is begging to be released from his black boxer briefs.

I shake my head. It's hard to find words right now as I watch this magnificent man strip for me.

"Maybe this?" he asks, stripping off his briefs, freeing his perfect cock.

"No," I barely say as my hand begins traveling to my center that's begging for any kind of release.

"Well, then maybe this?"

He slowly crawls into bed, taking my hand that was just rubbing my clit and sucking on my two fingers.

Holy hell, that's hot.

"Davis," I moan, shocked I can find words at this point I'm so turned on.

"Shh," he says, covering his mouth with mine in a kiss that is pure fire and lust. "No more talking."

I couldn't talk anymore if I tried. All I do is feel as he enters me, his cock filling me in a way only he can. His thrusts are fast and hard and perfect. I don't know how every time he knows what I need, but he does. The man can read my body better than I can, which is evident by the orgasm he gives me in a matter of minutes.

"Davis!" I yell, hoping that the walls in this hotel are a little soundproof.

He doesn't let me recover from the orgasm. Instead, he scoops me up under my back and brings me to where I'm sitting on his lap. Our eyes are locked on each other as I ride him, taking from him everything I want and everything he will give me.

"You're mine," he says, holding me still as he drives into me. "Forever."

"Forever," I repeat as I fall apart again, only this time he's right with me. I grab on to his shoulders, burying my face in his neck as my orgasm rolls through me. Unable to hold us up anymore, Davis collapses on the bed with me lying on top of him.

We don't say anything for a few minutes. I revel in feeling his heartbeat beneath me and get lost in the feel of his fingers tracing my skin.

This man. I've learned so much about him on this trip. And not just the reveal of his name. I see him as a son. As a brother. As an uncle. As the provider he has become. I see the love he has to give and the love he has for his family.

I realize that I'm one thousand percent, head over heels, crazy in love with this man.

"I love you," I say, not able to hold the words in any longer. "I love you so much."

His fingers stop, and for a second, I'm nervous that I should have kept my mouth shut. Is this like the other times? When I would think there is more to a relationship than there is? Does he not feel the same about me?

But before my brain can go down too many dark alleys, he lifts my chin so I'm looking in his eyes. And all I see is nothing short of love.

"I love you so much," he says, leaning forward and kissing me deeply. "You're it for me, Bethany Hall."

I don't know how we got here. Lord knows, we didn't take the conventional route, but at this moment, I don't want to be anywhere else.

31

———

DAVIS

WHEN I STARTED GETTING interested in finances and stocks, real estate never really captivated my interest. The thrill of watching stocks go up and down? That's exciting. Betting on the housing market? Not so much.

Now, I can tell you everything there is to know about the Nashville real estate market. I'm also an accomplished bluffer.

It's driving Ken the skeezy real estate agent insane.

"It's going to go fast. It will likely sell for seven-fifty K," Ken says in his best used car salesman voice. "If you want it, you better make a quick offer."

"I don't know," I say, pretending to check out a nonexistent fault in the open-concept first floor. "We looked at a similar one two streets over that's just sold for six seventy-five. And that had more square footage."

"Well," the agent stutters, trying to think of a reason, "this one has newer appliances. State of the art."

I don't get to make a comeback to him because at that moment, Bethany comes rushing into my arms. "Did you see the kitchen? And the deck? Imagine how many parties we can throw!"

I laugh and pull her aside to the office that sits just to the right of the entryway. I don't want Ken, the realtor who is hosting the open house today, to know that by far, this is the best house we've seen. And by the look in Bethany's eye, this is her favorite as well.

Once we decided on where to look, it was full steam ahead. This neighborhood will add a commute for both of us to work, but it's going to be worth it. This house is move-in ready, never lived in, and ten minutes from Mike and Helen.

We've looked at our fair share so far. One was too small. The other was way overpriced. Another we liked, but it needed too much work, and with being halfway along with the pregnancy and training camp opening soon, we don't have time to fix up a house.

But this house? This house has the layout she wants, the number of rooms I want, and comes at a price tag we are more than comfortable with.

And it has a pool. With a fence. I would pay all the money in the world to have access to Bethany wearing a bikini every day in the summer, pregnant or not.

"What do you think?" she asks, looking around the room that I envision to be an office. "It's perfect, right?"

I pull her into my arms before giving her a quick kiss. She's so damn adorable when she's this excited. "I do. It has everything we need."

I don't know why at this moment it hits me that this comment would have scared the absolute piss out of me just a few months ago. Buying a house? Putting down roots? Those were things for some other guy. Some guy who didn't have another family who relied on him.

Now? Especially after visiting Mom, Abby, and Sara? I realize what an idiot I was. I can have it all. I can help them and still have love and happiness of my own.

All it took was the right woman to show me that.

"Want to see where I think the nursery should go?" she says, grabbing my hand and leading me out of the office.

"I have a feeling you're going to show me no matter what," I say, though I notice as we climb the stairs that Ken is talking to another couple in the living room. "If we want to put an offer in, I'd like to do it before we leave. I don't want to lose this place."

I send a text message to my realtor, letting him know that I'll be in touch with him soon, as Bethany yanks my arm and pulls me into a bedroom.

One that looks awfully big to be a nursery.

"This is where you want the nursery to go?" I say in confusion as I look around the room that is obviously the master suite.

"No," she says before she literally jumps into my arms and starts kissing me. "This is going to be our bedroom."

"Princess," I say when I can catch my breath. "What are you doing?"

She doesn't answer me. Instead, she takes the opportunity to start rubbing her pussy against my growing cock as she continues to kiss the life out of me.

I love second-trimester Bethany.

I mean, I love all Bethanys. I meant what I told her in Pennsylvania and every day since. But second-trimester Bethany? The one who loves sex almost as much as Flaming Hot Cheetos, is horny all the time and is happy about everything? I'd like to keep her.

"Bethany," I say, already hating myself for what I'm about to say next. "This house is going to be ours. Trust me on that. We will have plenty of time to break it in. There are other people here. We should get going."

She gives me a pouty lip before unwrapping her legs from around me. But just as I think we're going to leave the room, she takes my hand and yanks me toward a closet, shutting the door behind us.

"What are you…"

I can't even finish the sentence because I realize Bethany is on her knees in front of me, undoing the zipper to my jeans.

"This is going to be our house," she says, stroking my cock. "And I love that you are doing this for me. For us. And I want to show my gratitude."

I can't answer before she takes me fully in her mouth. Usually, she is gentle when she and I have done this. Hesitant, even. But now? This woman is determined to give me the best blow job of my life.

And she's succeeding. Her hand and mouth are working in tandem, and that is already making my balls tight. And when she goes to lick the underside of my cock, I almost lose it right there and then.

"Fuck," I groan, hoping my voice isn't too loud. Then again, maybe if they hear us, then they will leave, and the house will be ours.

"Don't hold back on me," she says, still working me with her hand. "I want you to come in my mouth."

Jesus tap dancing Christ.

I have never come in her mouth. Then again, most of the time, when she goes down on me, it's before we have sex, and I know I'm going to finish inside her. Now just the thought of her swallowing me does me in.

"Bethany… shit!"

I don't know how loud I yell that as I release into her mouth. And I honestly don't care. I just got the best blow job of my life from the mother of my unborn child in a house we haven't bought yet while there are people in the other room.

There is nothing hotter than that.

She slowly releases me from her mouth, and I hurry and help her off her knees before I take care of my… situation.

"Where did that come from?"

She giggles, and even in the dark, I can tell she's doing her best to fix her hair. "I wanted to break in this house correctly."

I kiss her nose as I finish tucking my semi-hard cock back into my pants. "You know I'm never going to be able to look at this closet without thinking about this."

"Good," she says, opening the door. "Maybe that will be our sneak away spot once the baby is born."

We both laugh as we leave the closet but stop in our tracks as soon as we see the scene in front of us.

Ken, the realtor, and the couple I noticed downstairs, both staring at us with horrified looks on their faces.

"What are you doing?" Ken says, though if he really looked at us, he would absolutely know what we are doing. I look at Bethany, whose hair gives away that something was going on in the closet. That and she hasn't stopped giggling since we exited the closet. I'm guessing my face has the smile that every man who has ever gotten a phenomenal blow job knows.

Judging by the look on Ken's face, he's never received a blow job from a woman in a closet. Or maybe ever.

"Excuse me!" Ken yells, now annoyed with us. "I asked you what you were doing."

I laugh and pull Bethany to me. "I'd like to put in an offer on this house. How does cash sound?"

32

BETHANY

I THINK I've handled pregnancy quite well now that I'm through my first twenty weeks.

I battled and conquered the morning sickness. I've adjusted my diet and made sure that I'm taking all my vitamins. I even gave up Diet Coke.

And I really love Diet Coke. I love it more than my current pregnancy craving, peanut butter and pickle sandwiches.

Don't knock it till you've tried it.

That being said…

Shit! Shit! Shit!

Fuck! Fuck! Fuck!

Fuck! Shit! Dammit all to hell!

There, I feel better.

Except I don't.

It's why I'm standing on Sadie's doorstep banging on her door to let me in. I need to figure out what to do, and she drew the short straw to help me fix this.

"What in the—?" Sadie asks as she opens the door. "Bethany? What are you—"

I don't give her a chance to finish the sentence as I barge into the condo and unceremoniously flop onto the couch and scream into the pillows.

"I'm going to go get you some water. Though I wish I could get you something stronger."

Same, sis. Same.

I make myself sit up and take a breath. I'm freaking out over nothing. The baby is healthy. The baby is strong. Everything on the ultrasound was perfect.

Except now I know a secret I'm not supposed to know, and I don't know how to handle that.

Hence, the freak-out.

"Okay, what the hell is going on?" Sadie asks, handing me a glass of water before taking a seat next to me on her sectional. "Is everything okay with the baby?"

I nod. "Yes. I just came from my twenty-week check. Everything is great."

"Then, what's the problem? And where is Davis?"

Oh, Davis. If Davis was with me at this appointment, none of this would be an issue.

Yes! This is all his fault. He doesn't get sex for a week!

Oh, who am I kidding. I feel so guilty right now, I'll probably give him a blow job before and after dinner. Hell, maybe even while he's eating dinner.

"We had a scheduling mix-up between the appointment and the coaches' meetings he had today," I say, starting to calm down a bit. "So, I went to the appointment alone."

"Wasn't today the day you were going to find out the sex?"

I nod, taking a big gulp of water. "Yes. But I told him… I promised him I wouldn't find out. That we would do it together. So, I was all prepared to tell Dr. Stewart to put the results in a little envelope and we would open it up together tonight."

"I'm guessing that didn't happen."

I shake my head. "Dr. Stewart got called in for an emergency c-section, so the nurse practitioner saw me."

Sadie's eyes grow large. "Oh, no…"

"Oh, yes."

"You know?"

"I know."

I don't know why I didn't tell the nurse from the moment she stepped into the room that the father wasn't here, and I didn't want to know the gender without him. I could have said that. I should have said that. But we got to talking—turns out she gets her hair done at the salon by one of my best stylist friends—and next thing I know, she's squirting the gel onto my stomach.

Looking back, I also could have told her right then, too. But at that point, we began talking about hair styles that need to go away. If you ever want to distract me, bring up this topic. I could go on for hours.

Next thing I know, she's saying the words I'll never forget.

"Bethany, she looks great!"

And that's how I found out Davis and I are having a little girl.

"No!" Sadie gasps as I deliver the not-so-funny punch line.

"Yup," I say in defeat. "We're having a girl. You were right."

"Screw me being right. I can't believe she slipped like that! And Davis… oh hell, how are you going to tell him!"

I collapse back into the sectional in defeat. "That, my dear sister, is the million-dollar question."

I hate it. I hate this. He didn't get to be there for the first appointment when I found out I was pregnant. I have wondered from time to time what his reaction would have been. I thought that I could make that up to him by being there when we found out the gender.

I pictured it a dozen times. Him sitting next to me, holding my hand as we watch our baby on the screen. Then, the doctor would do her thing and ask us if we wanted to know. We say yes, but not now. We have her put it in an envelope so we could find out later at home.

Then, later, we would open it together and celebrate whether or not we were having a baby girl or boy. We'd profess our love for each other and this child and have a perfect night celebrating.

But no. None of that can happen now.

Because Nurse Nancy ruined it.

"What if you pretend you don't know," Sadie says. "Make another appointment, and then when the doctor reveals the gender, you act super surprised. Boom, it's like today never happened!"

"I thought of that," I say defeatedly. "Except I'm a horrible liar around him. I can't even lie about eating the last cookie. He'd know immediately."

"Hmm," Sadie mutters. "And we agreed to not have a gender reveal party. Though we are in a different situation, I don't think we've resorted to that yet."

"No we have not," I say. "I'm not letting the next people to know the gender of my baby be a bakery or a balloon company."

We both sit in silence for a few minutes. I know I'm being dramatic about this. I know I could just wait for him to come home tonight, sit him on the couch and tell him what happened. I'm sure he would understand. He'd be a little upset, but at the end of the day, he is just going to be happy that we have a healthy baby girl who's planning on making her way into this world at the end of November.

But then my heart hurts that he doesn't get a moment. I want to give him that moment.

"I got it!"

Sadie's exclamation makes me jump a little. "Good Lord, woman, you scared the pee out of me. Which isn't hard to do these days."

"I'm sorry, but I have an idea. Though it is a little dramatic and over the top."

I raise an eyebrow to her. "I thought I was the over-the-top, dramatic sister."

"You are. I guess you're rubbing off on me."

I laugh, grateful that I can laugh about something right now.

"What's this plan?"

Sadie gets a devilish smile on her face. "You want to give Davis a moment? I can make it happen. But you need to give me a few days."

My eyes go wide. "A few days!"

She grabs my hand and gives me a squeeze. "Yes. Put on your best lying face and be willing to distract that man with sex for forty-eight hours. But I promise you, it will be worth it."

33

———

DAVIS

I don't know how many times I've yelled that today since practice started. I know it's about ten times too many for a quarterback who should already know the playbook, yet he's the one fucking up every time.

This is our second day of camp. We don't have pads on yet, but I'm liking what I'm seeing for the most part.

The offensive line looks great. Cole is stepping up as a leader, and if you don't have a good line, you don't have a good offense. The running backs are doing everything I have asked of them. The receivers are running good routes.

They just can't catch. And that's not their fault. Can't catch a ball that is five yards off the mark.

"What the fuck is his problem?" I mutter as Hunter and I watch another drill break down because Bryce goes the wrong way.

"I can't believe he looks this bad," Hunter says. "The press is going to eat him alive."

I look over to the media gallery that gets to watch the morning session of practice and can hear the cameras click with every movement—correction, every wrong movement—Bryce makes.

Fan-fucking-tastic.

"Cole said it had something to do with a girl. Know anything about that?"

Hunter shakes his head. "Last year, when he and I talked, he wasn't specific, though I had a feeling. But this? This is nothing like last year. Last year he looked lost. This year he looks like he doesn't give a fuck. He has another few days like today and we need to be looking at other options for quarterback. I benched him last year, and I'll do it again. I can't wait around for him to get his head out of his ass."

I let out a defeated breath as Hunter signals for the players to huddle up and head to the locker room for their lunch break.

"Bryce!" I yell, wanting to catch him before he heads inside. He lazily jogs to me, which pisses me off more than any missed throw he just made.

"Care to tell me what all that was?" I ask as discreetly as possible as there are still some players and media outside.

"Not my fault they weren't where I put the ball," he says in a cocky tone. "New guys need to figure me out."

It takes every ounce of strength I have not to ring this kid's fucking neck. "You didn't run one drill right. Now that I'm up close to you, I can tell you're hungover. What the fuck is wrong with you? And if you tell me nothing, I swear to God…"

"It's not your problem, and quit trying to figure me out," he says in a defensive tone as he turns away from me.

I grab his shirt before he can walk away. "Not a fucking chance. You're benched for the rest of the day. You come to my camp again hungover and lazy, you can find yourself a new team."

He just stares at me before he starts laughing. "You think you can do that? My contract is worth more than yours and half the team's combined. You can't do anything to me."

"Try me," I say, getting in his face. "Now get the fuck out of here. I don't want to see your face for the rest of the day."

Bryce rolls his eyes but stomps toward the locker room. I follow him to make sure he doesn't cause a scene in the locker room as he packs up his stuff. Luckily, he doesn't. He quickly changes, grabs his bags, and storms out of the locker room. As I watch it unfold, I catch Cole's eye as he watches his best friend leave without a word. He looks to where Bryce had been standing, then back to me before giving me a slow nod.

He gets it. He doesn't like it, but he gets it.

Once I know Bryce is gone, I make my way back to my office, thankful for a few hours of quiet time. If I could get everything figured out with Bryce, my life would be just about perfect. The coaching staff with Hunter at the helm is clicking better than any staff I've worked with. Every player, save for Bryce, came to camp in shape, focused, and hungry. We have a favorable schedule this year, so it's playoffs or bust.

Then there is my personal life. Bethany and I closed on the house quickly. I have a feeling real estate Ken wanted to be rid of us as fast as possible. We have everything moved, unpacked, and we are settling into our new life together.

And soon we will find out if we are having a boy or a girl. I hate that I couldn't be at her appointment the other day, but I know the wait will be worth it.

It also doesn't hurt that second-trimester Bethany is still here, which means that she is always ready. Whenever. Wherever.

I never thought I'd say that my dick is tired, but it is. It's a good problem to have.

I don't even realize that I've nodded off at my desk until I hear a banging on my office door. I shoot up to see Hunter standing there, laughing his ass off.

"Bethany wearing you out?" he teases, tossing me a pre-wrapped sandwich that we have catered for lunch each day of camp.

"In the best way possible," I say, digging into the turkey and cheese before we have to go back onto the field.

"I must say, this looks good on you," Hunter says, taking a seat across from me.

"What's that?"

"Happiness."

I let that sink in. While he's one hundred percent right, I can't let him know that.

"Who says I wasn't happy last year? You've known me going on two years and you think you know everything that is the book of Davis?"

Hunter laughs. "No, you asshole. But I can tell when someone is putting on a show. I did it for most of my life, so people didn't know about the real relationship between me and my dad. That always happy-go-lucky guy front you put on? The one who pretended he didn't have a care in the world? I knew at least half of it was bullshit. But now? Seeing you with Bethany? The way you talk about her and the baby? That, my friend, is true happiness. And I'm glad you've found it."

Well, damn, maybe he really does know me.

Close friends aren't something I had growing up. Sure, I had buddies I ate lunch with or played ball with, but no one who really knew me. Honestly, the closest friend I had was Abby. In college, I still kept people at arm's length. It was all I knew how to do at that point.

Now? Now I have family on multiple levels. I have friends who I can call on when I need it.

He's right. I am happy.

"All right, enough of this mushy shit," I say, crumbling the sandwich wrapper and tossing it in the trash. "Don't we have football to coach?"

Hunter laughs and gives my back a slap as we walk out of the offices and toward the practice field.

Everything seems normal until we step outside, though. Normally, there is rap and heavy rock music blaring from the practice field speakers. Instead, I hear a ballad, and I'm pretty sure it's one of the Motown songs my mom used to listen to. The one about having sunshine on a cloudy day.

I take another few steps onto the field, confused as ever. When I get a full view, I see the team doing their normal warm-up routine. Only it's what they are wearing that is throwing me off. They each have on their normal practice jerseys and shorts. However, each of them has a pink mesh vest over top.

What in the actual fuck?

The strength and conditioning coach who runs warm-ups blows his whistle and every player drops to the ground. I have to blink my eyes to make sure that I'm seeing what I think I'm seeing.

Standing in the middle of my professional football team is Bethany, wearing a pink dress and holding something in her hands.

I run over to her, paying no attention to anyone around me. "What are you doing here?"

She laughs nervously. "I wanted to give you your moment."

"My moment?" I say confused. "What do you mean?"

"The other day, at my appointment..." Bethany trails off, fighting back tears, though I still don't know why she's crying. "The nurse accidentally told me what we were having. And you weren't there, and I feel terrible about it. I should have told her. I should have stopped her."

She takes a breath, and I take the opportunity to wipe away a tear from her cheek. "It's okay. But why didn't you tell me that night?"

Another tear gets loose. "Because I felt horrible. And I know we said no big gender reveals, but you deserve to have a moment you'll never forget. I want to give you another first."

Now it's my turn to get choked up. I look around again. All of the players wearing pink have stopped stretching and are now looking at us. I listen a little close to the song that is still playing. I catch Hunter's eye, who is standing next to Sadie, who looks like she is crying.

"Are you saying?"

My question trails off and she nods. "I am."

"We're having a girl?"

She nods again. "Congratulations, Daddy. We're having a girl."

Applause roars from the players and coaches as I pick Bethany up and twirl her around, kissing the life out of her.

A girl. I'm having a little girl.

The next several minutes are a mixture of back slaps, congratulations, and sneaking a few moments with Bethany when I can. When the scene calms down, I pull her to the sideline where Hunter and Sadie are standing, both with conspiratorial looks in their eyes.

"You," I say, pointing to both of them. "This has the two of you written all over it."

Sadie just shrugs. "My sister needed my help, Reginald. And I figured this would be the best way for you to find out and not be mad at the nurse who spilled the beans."

I laugh. "You're right. And my name is not Reginald. Isn't that right, Bethany?"

Sadie's eyes go wide as she shoots a look to Bethany. "You know! And you haven't told me! I helped you coordinate this whole thing, and you've been keeping this from me! How dare you!"

The girls walk off with Sadie still going on about sisterhood bonds trumping baby daddies. All Hunter and I can do is laugh.

"You're right," I say.

"About what?"

"Happiness. I am. I've never been happier in my entire life."

34

———

BETHANY

I READ THE TEXT AGAIN, a little bounce to my step as I climb the
stairs to our bedroom.

Our bedroom.

I still can't believe everything that has happened in such a short
amount of time. At this point last year, I didn't even know who this
man was. Heck, Sadie and Hunter hadn't even come out publicly as a
couple. I was still going out on bad date after bad date, and Davis…
well, I really don't want to think about what he was doing.

Now? We have a baby due in about four months. We have a house
that I can see myself and Davis growing old and raising a family under
its roof. I've found a man who loves me the way I've always wanted to
be loved and whom I love equally in return.

In no way did I do this in the order I thought it needed to be done.
First comes love, then comes marriage and all of that. But who's to say
what is the right order? At the end of the day, isn't the result all that
matters? I have the man of my dreams, a baby girl on the way, a career
I love, and a house we plan on making a home. If I had to go through

every bad date, every guy who ghosted me and do this all over again in the wrong order to get here? I'd do it again in a heartbeat.

I now understand the line from *Steel Magnolias* about wanting thirty minutes of wonderful rather than a lifetime of nothing special. I never truly understood that until now. But this. This is what Shelby meant. This is the wonderful. And I'll take as many minutes as I can get.

> Davis: I will be home in ten minutes. This is your warning.

After today's grand announcement of the gender of our baby, Davis unfortunately couldn't come home with me right away to celebrate. Something about limited practice time and the league rules. All of that confuses me.

However, he did promise that he would make it up to me the second he got home. And by the tone of these text messages, I'm not going to be disappointed.

I hurry and strip the sundress over my head, quickly disposing of my bra and panties as well. As I make my way to our bed, I catch my reflection in the full-length mirror by our closet.

Just in the past week or so, my baby bump has gone from "is she pregnant or gaining weight?" to "Yup, she's preggo." I've always been slender—being five foot seven helps narrow me out—so this ball that's sitting in my belly right now is pretty obvious.

What's it going to look like in a few weeks? A month? Am I going to have one of those bellies that just looks like a beach ball took residence in my body?

"You are fucking stunning."

I look up and see Davis standing in the doorway, looking at me with pure desire in his eyes.

"I didn't hear you come in," I say, making my way toward the bed.

"No," he says as he begins to walk to me. "Stay right there."

I can't take my eyes off of him as he slowly walks toward me. Though his eyes are on nothing but my stomach.

He obviously knows that my bump has started to show. But that's over clothes or under covers when the lights are off. This? In the daylight with not a scrap of clothes on my body? This is the most naked I've ever felt in front of a man before.

"Do you know how sexy you are right now?" he says, standing behind me and wrapping his arms so his hands are sitting on my bump.

I meet his eyes in the mirror and almost melt from the intensity of his gaze. "I don't."

I don't get an answer right away. I don't complain though. He's currently kissing the top of my shoulder, traveling up to my neck, and slowly moving his fingers up and down the sides of my body. I can feel myself getting wetter by the second.

"You have always been sexy to me," he says, his fingers still exploring my naked body, one hand tracing my bump as he takes hold of one of my breasts. "I remember that first night I saw you, the physical attraction I felt for you was instant. But here? Now? Seeing you carrying our child? You are, without a doubt, the sexiest woman I have ever laid eyes on. And you are all mine."

He spins me around and our mouths meet in perfect unison. As my fingers slide through his hair and his hands pull me into him, I can only hope that this part of us never wavers. That even after a child, and whatever else the future has in store for us, that we always have this.

The passion. The desire.

The love.

"Now, princess, I believe I told you to be naked in bed waiting for me. And while this isn't a bad view to come home to, there are things I plan to do that will be much better for you if they are done lying down."

I giggle as Davis scoops me up and carries me the few steps to our bed.

"Why do you call me that? And no more of this 'it's my secret' crap."

He lets out a small laugh as his fingers travel down my body, headed straight to my center.

"The first night we met. When you stepped out of the car, the way the sunlight radiated from you, it looked like you were wearing a crown. That, and you were the most beautiful woman I had ever laid eyes on."

My eyes go wide at his admission. I was *not* expecting that.

"I thought you were making fun of me," I say a bit shyly. "I thought it was because I always had my hair done, or because I wear so many skirts. That's why I didn't like it."

"Never," he says, his eyes locked onto mine. "From the moment I met you, I knew you were someone different. Someone special. It might have taken me a while to realize it, but you're not just my princess. You're my queen. My love. The woman who is about to give me a baby girl. You're my forever, Bethany."

His lips are on mine before I have a chance to respond, which is fine by me because he has left me thoroughly and utterly speechless. And a tad bit emotional.

Our tongues are tangled in a perfect symphony, and his fingers have found their way to my opening, slowly entering me and beginning to explore. I slowly reach down and slide off his pants, taking his cock into my hand, slowly stroking it, loving the feel of his hardness against my skin.

"I want you inside me," I say, not being able to stand any more of his fingers teasing me.

"Your wish is my command."

He strips off the rest of his clothes and before he can position me in the way he wants to, I push his shoulders down and swing my leg over his body, seating myself on top of him. By the look in his eye, this was a good decision on my part.

I lean forward to align myself, my heavy breasts dangling in front of his face. He takes full advantage of the position, taking one in his hand and bringing it to his mouth. The sensation of his lips around my nipple feels so good, I can't help but slowly rub my pussy on his cock.

"Quit teasing," he groans, taking my ass in both hands and lifting me up. "Ride me."

He takes his cock and lines us up, allowing me to sit back and feel every inch of him enter me. My hands go to his chest as I slowly find my rhythm, loving not only the way he fills me but the look in his eyes.

"So goddamn beautiful," he says, taking my hips and slowly beginning to move me faster. "I could watch you all day."

His words only spur me on. Before I know it, my pace is quickening. His thrusts are meeting mine, and by the look on his face, he is as close as I am to finding release.

"Yes," I say, loving how even though I am on top, right now, he's in complete control. "So close."

He doesn't say another word. Instead, he flips me over, somehow never leaving me, and begins rapidly pumping into me. His finger comes to my clit, and with just one flick, I'm done for.

"Davis!"

Thank goodness we don't have any close neighbors, because I'm sure they would have heard me clear as day. If they didn't, they surely would have heard him seconds later.

"Fuck. Bethany. Fuck!"

Neither of us moves for a long time after we come down from another set of earth-shattering orgasms. I actually might have fallen asleep when I feel Davis's fingers start to trace my sides.

"You know," he says quietly, his fingers still exploring, "I pictured something like this once."

"Hm?" I ask, my voice heavy with sleep.

"Right before you called it off. I pictured you in my bed. I wondered what it would be like to wake up with you. For us to have lazy days on the couch, and nights where we couldn't keep our hands off of each other."

I turn toward him. "When was this?"

He kisses me gently before answering. "The night you told me we were done."

"Oh, really?"

"Yeah," he says, now a bit confused. "Why is that so funny?"

I lean in for a deeper kiss, one which he obliges. "Because that night, I had the same thoughts. That was the night I knew my feelings had grown. And I had to leave you before you could hurt me."

"Are you serious?"

I nod. "Funny how things work, huh?"

I'm greeted with another kiss. This one more intense. "I'd leave you all over again if it's how I end up here."

35

DAVIS

I REALLY THOUGHT I was doing fine.

I have not panicked once since Bethany said those few little words that changed my life forever. She might say I lost my mind when I asked her to marry me. That's still up for debate.

I didn't even freak-out the first time I heard the baby's heartbeat. That was a whole different feeling. I remember feeling shocked. Almost paralyzed when I heard that thumping. I knew Bethany was pregnant, but at the moment, it felt real. Yet, I didn't panic. I cried like a baby. But I didn't panic.

How do I know I didn't panic then? Because if that was panic, then what I'm doing right now is full-on hysteria. The racing of my heart? The shortness of breath? The feeling I have that the room is spinning and there's nothing I can do to stop it. This is panic.

The worst part is it came out of nowhere. One minute I'm fine, the next, I'm talking to Wes, our veteran tight end and father of three.

"Getting everything ready?" Wes asks as we leave the practice field.

"For sure. We're ready. Baby could come tomorrow and everything would be great."

Wes laughs. "I wish I was as confident as you are before my first. Hell, I was so nervous putting together the crib it took me a week. I was so scared I was going to screw something into the wrong hole and that it would break the second we put the baby in it."

Oh shit. The crib. "Well, we still have to get that."

"Did you two decide on a stroller? Personally, I like the travel ones. Easier for transporting."

"Oh... We... We haven't settled on one yet."

"Oh," he says, a bit surprised. "Well, if you need any help, let me know. I also know a guy who started this line of baby carriers for men..."

I have no idea what the fuck else Wes said. All I knew was at that moment, I might have set up my insurance to cover the baby and started her college fund, but I forgot to buy a fucking stroller and a crib for her to sleep in.

"McAvoy!" I yell, charging toward Hunter's office. What kind of fucking father am I? How do I forget to buy a damn stroller and crib?

"What?" he asks, looking up from his pile of paperwork. "What the hell are you yelling about?"

"Are you doing anything important?"

"Just going over the scouting report. I know it's just preseason, but I like to be prepared. Why are you breathing heavy? Are you okay?"

"I'm fine. I'm not fine. Fuck. Just get your keys and let's go. We have shit to take care of."

"WHEN YOU SAID, 'we have shit to take care of' this is not what I had in mind."

Hunter's remark comes as I stare at no less than thirty options of cribs at a store that is called Everything Baby. Felt like a good place to come to buy all the things that I forgot to get.

Some provider I am. If the baby comes tomorrow, she'll be sleeping on the floor.

That's a lie. I would be. Because I'm pretty sure Bethany would have kicked me out of bed and Baby Girl Davis would be on my side of the bed.

How have we not done any of this yet? We talked about it a few times. But first, we wanted to wait to find out the gender of the baby. Then training camp hit, and next thing we knew, any free time we had was spent unpacking boxes and getting the house settled. Now preseason is here, and pretty soon, games are going to start, and holy hell, I am not ready.

Well, that all ends today. My baby *will* have a place to sleep by the time the sun sets.

"Don't you think Bethany is going to want to pick some of this stuff out with you?" Hunter asks as I eye the seemingly endless amount of cribs in front of me. "I might not be a dad yet, but I at least know that Sadie would kill me if I did these things on my own."

"I'm sure she will like what I pick," I say, eyeing a white one with a better headboard than we have on our bed. "Plus, I know how she wants the nursery. I can get the changing table and the dressers and the nursing chair all today. How hard can this be?"

"How does she want the nursery?"

"Girly. Pink. Bows. I got this."

Hunter grabs me by the shoulder so I'm now looking at him. "Are you listening to yourself? Are you really telling me that Bethany, the woman who has three pairs of shoes for every occasion, is going to be okay with you picking out your baby's entire nursery without her input?"

I hear what he's saying. He's right. But I can't leave here without something.

"I'm not ready," I admit, plopping down on a rocking chair that is the most uncomfortable thing I've ever sat on. I'm definitely *not* buying this.

"Talk to me," Hunter says, taking a seat next to me. "What happened today? I thought everything was okay?"

I let out a heavy sigh. "It was. Or so I thought. I thought I had everything ready. Then I talked to Wes."

"The man who just looks at his wife and gets her pregnant?"

I laugh. "Yeah. He was asking me pretty basic questions of things we were getting ready for, and we didn't have any of them done. It made me panic. It made me... I don't like to be unprepared."

Hunter slaps me on the back. "Dude. Cut yourself some slack. You still have more than two months before the baby gets here. You just moved into a house. You don't have to get it all done today."

"Except I do," I say, urgency coming in my voice. "You never know what's coming tomorrow."

Hunter raises an eyebrow at me. "What are you not telling me? Is everything okay with you two?"

I let out a breath. "Yeah. It's just… when I was growing up, one day my dad was there. The next day he was gone. Haven't heard from him since. I was thirteen."

"Fuck, man," Hunter says. "How come you never told me this?"

I shrug. "Not really one of my favorite subjects, you know?"

"Yeah," he says as he leans his elbows on his legs. "But what does that have to do with this? I know you. You aren't just going to one day leave. You would never leave Bethany hanging like that."

"I know," I say, standing up, pulling at my hair in frustration. "But I also know what it's like to be unprepared. The day before my dad left, we didn't have to worry about if we had enough money to cover groceries and utilities that month. We didn't have to worry about rationing food. Then, the next, we did. I had no idea what to do. I was unprepared. I vowed to myself that day I'd never be unprepared again. That I would make sure we were ready for anything, so my family didn't have to suffer. And here I am, a baby on the way and nothing ready for her. I just… I need to do this, Hunter. I need to feel like I did something to help prepare for this. For her. For Bethany."

Those words have been living in my brain for months now, I just wouldn't admit it. Now that I've said them out loud? I feel the weight lifted off my shoulders.

"All right then," Hunter says, standing up. "Let's get my niece a crib."

36

———

BETHANY

"OH, yeah. Right there. That's the stuff. Yes. Yes!"

"Mom!" I yell, scaring the very nice woman who is currently buffing my feet. "Can you please not make sex noises when you're getting a pedicure?"

"But it feels good," she defends, turning her attention back to the magazine she's reading. "I can't help it if I vocalize when I'm feeling good."

"Don't remind me," I say under my breath as Sadie tries not to crack up in the seat next to mine.

Pedicure day sounded like a great idea two hours ago. Now that I'm having flashbacks to the day I heard Mom and Mike having sex? Not so much.

Mom, Sadie, and I used to do this all the time. Not at first, though. Sadie and I are the same age and were even in the same class in school, but I wouldn't have considered us close. We had nothing in common and no mutual friends. We didn't hate each other, we really just didn't know each other.

I remember the first time the four of us got together when Mike and Mom were dating. We just sat there staring at each other with nothing to talk about. Mom and I were the definitions of girly girls, and Sadie was a tomboy who was raised by Mike the sports fan.

Then one day Mom took Sadie and me to get our nails done. For the two of us, this was a semi-regular outing. For Sadie? It was a first. And that was when we found out that there was a little bit of "girl" in that tomboy.

Since then, we try to go every few months. And since my feet are starting to swell in ways I didn't know feet could swell, and it's getting harder each day to reach my toes, Mom thought lunch and pedicures were what the doctor ordered.

I'll never turn down lunch and pedis.

"So, enough about Helen's sex noises. Let's talk names," Sadie says.

"I told you, I'm not telling you Davis's name. You have to find it out on your own."

"Whatever," she says, waving me off. "I'm talking about baby names. What are you thinking?"

"Oh! I really love Gretchen," my mom says. "You know you were almost a Gretchen."

Sadie and I look at each other and give each other a gagging look.

"What was that for?" Mom asks.

"Gretchen was the queen bitch of our high school," Sadie explains. "Bethany and I might not have been in the same circles back then, but that didn't mean we both didn't hate Gretchen."

"Fine," Mom says, a little defeat in her voice. "What is your suggestion then, Sadie?"

"You mean, what is about to be the name of my future niece because Bethany is going to love it so much and it's absolutely perfect?"

"Oh, really?" I ask, wondering when she had planned to tell me this amazing name. "Well, don't hold back, sis."

"Ready?" she asks, doing a little drumroll on her legs. "Magnolia."

I slouch a bit in disappointment. "That's your great name?"

"What?" Sadie yells a bit too loudly for a packed salon. "You love *Steel Magnolias*. It's a perfect name! You could call her Maggie. Or Nola. What is the matter with it? I thought I did so good!"

"I take it you haven't watched *Hart of Dixie* yet?" I ask. She shakes her head in confusion. "Watch two episodes. You'll know why. That character ruined that name for me."

"Fine," Sadie says defeated. "So, what have you and Davis talked about?"

"Honestly, we've vetoed more than we've put in the good column," I say, staring at my toes that are currently having a bright pink being painted on them. "We aren't fans of anything that starts with the same letter of our names. We don't want people to think we did that on purpose. I suggested Emma, but he wasn't a fan. He suggested Memphis, but then I asked him if he was going to be the one to eventually tell our daughter that her name is where she was conceived. He quickly put that idea into the no column."

Everyone gets a laugh out of that. "Hey, that could be your thing! Maybe all your children could have 'where they were conceived' names. If you have a boy and you're here, his name could be Nash. Or take a road trip to watch a Tennessee football game and he could be Knox. The possibilities are endless!"

"No, thank you," I say, slipping my flip-flops back on. "We'll find the perfect name. It will just take time."

We gather our things and tell Mom goodbye before Sadie takes me back to my house. Even though I told her I was more than capable of driving, she insisted on picking me up today. Though I think it was just an excuse for her to come to the house and try to snoop to see if she could find anything that signaled Davis's name.

She's never going to guess it.

I've been thinking so much recently about how much things have changed between Davis and me in such a short amount of time, but the same could be said for Sadie and me. After Mom and Mike got married, we got closer, but I still wouldn't have called us besties. Then, last year, Sadie needed an ear when she caught feelings for Hunter. I was there with an open ear and a bottle of wine. During that process, she became my best friend.

What if Hunter hadn't been hired as Fury's offensive coordinator? If he didn't get the job, he would have never met Sadie. They would have never fallen in love. Maybe she and I wouldn't have gotten as close as we are now? They wouldn't have set Davis and me up on a date.

I wouldn't be pregnant.

Crazy how one event can trigger so many things.

I'm pulled from my nostalgia as Sadie turns onto my street and something catches my eye from my driveway.

"What is Hunter's truck doing here?" Sadie asks as she pulls into the driveway. "I thought he and Davis were going to be at the facility all day?"

"I did too." I open up the garage door to see Davis's truck there as well. Now I'm really confused.

"Maybe they decided to work here?" I say, opening the door that goes from the garage and leads into our mudroom. "Change of scenery?"

Sadie and I aren't even two steps inside the house when we hear a loud crash come from upstairs, followed by the loudest yelling of the word *fuck* I've ever heard in my life.

"What the hell?" she says as we both take off toward the noise. Well, she takes off, I quickly do a half-walk half-waddle.

When we get upstairs, the scene before us is one that I never thought I'd see. In the room that is going to become the nursery are Davis and Hunter. They are surrounded by what looks like a million pieces of wood and screws, and they have no idea we are here.

And Davis is wearing a tool belt. I didn't even know he owned one of those.

"I told you that piece *A* needed to connect to piece *D* with the *E* screw. Not the *F*."

"How the fuck am I supposed to be able to tell!" Hunter says. "They all look the fucking same!"

"I told you to read the directions! Do you want your niece's crib to fall apart!"

"I don't need any goddamn directions!"

"Just hand me the fucking *E* screw!"

"Oh, I'll hand you something!"

What in the name of Jolene is going on in here?

Sadie and I bust out laughing at the scene in front of us, which catches their attention.

"Bethany! You're home early!" Davis says frantically, trying to recover from something. I just don't know what.

Hunter chimes in, trying to right himself as well. "Sadie! You're here too!"

"Oh, this ought to be good," Sadie says, chuckling next to me. "Hunter. Why don't we leave and you can tell me all about how you got roped into this?"

Hunter all but runs out of the room as Sadie and I continue to laugh at the scene before us.

I can't walk more than two steps into the nursery without stepping on a piece of wood or a screw. When I finally make it in, I see the box leaning against the wall. Pictured on it is the most gorgeous crib I have ever seen.

"Did you buy a crib?" I ask, my hand going to my stomach like I do a lot these days.

"I wanted it to be a surprise," he says hesitantly as he walks toward me. "Do you like it?"

I look at the mess on the floor, then to the box again. There could have been two hundred cribs to pick from, and I doubt I would have picked any other one. "I love it."

"Oh, thank God," he says, relieved at my reaction. "Hunter had me worried you'd be mad that you didn't get to pick it out. I wanted to put it together for you before you got home, then we didn't realize how many pieces were involved—"

I cut his ramble off with a kiss. "You're just lucky you have good taste," I say, looping my arms around his neck. "Now, I'm going to need you to help me with something else since you are all about trying to make me happy today."

He wraps his hands around my back. "Anything, princess."

"Apparently, I have a thing for guys in tool belts. And I think we need something fixed in the bedroom."

In a second, Davis throws down the directions he's holding and scoops me into his arms.

"Just call me Mr. Fix It!"

I don't know when he's going to finish building the crib, but it's not going to be tonight.

37

———

DAVIS

WHEN I ACCEPTED Hunter's offer last year to become his offensive coordinator, I did it because I knew I was attaching myself to something special. Hunter, even though I won't tell him this to save his ego, is one of the brightest football minds in the business. He's not the youngest head coach in history by accident.

Becoming his offensive coordinator means I get to help run an innovative offense with a man I respect who is also becoming my best friend. I couldn't ask for more in a job.

What I didn't foresee happening is being the offensive coordinator of a team who is led by the Rookie of the Year in one season to that same player not being able to throw ten yards the next.

"Are you sure this is what you want to do?" I ask Hunter, standing next to him in his office as we wait for Bryce to come in. We are not even two hours removed from our latest loss—by a team we beat by double digits last year—and Bryce looked like he had never thrown a football before.

"When I benched him last year, it helped get his head out of his ass. I hate that I have to do it again, but we can't function as a team with him right now. He's a liability."

Last season when we started off bad—as in couldn't score a

touchdown and lost our first four games—we didn't know what was going on. Nothing was working. I remember spending hours with Hunter trying to figure out why the offense couldn't click.

This year it's the same start, only this time there is one specific culprit. Not only is his play suffering, but his antics have become regular national news. Bryce has gone from football's golden boy to football's bad boy in the span of months. Sports radio's new favorite topic is "where was Bryce last night" and usually, the answer is drunk with a flock of women around him.

"I've got your back," I say to Hunter as I see Bryce slowly walking into Hunter's office. He doesn't knock. Instead, he just slouches in, drops into one of the chairs like a high school kid who got called into the principal's office, and doesn't care that he's about to get detention.

"Bryce," Hunter begins, but before he can say anything else, Bryce interrupts.

"I know. We sucked today. Your new shiny wide receiver can't catch any of my passes. He needs work."

"Dexter has nothing to do with this," I say, feeling defensive of my former position group. "It's not his fault that he ran the correct route and his quarterback underthrew him by ten yards."

"Like I said," Bryce continues, cockiness oozing from his voice. "The receivers need to be where I put it. Not the other way around."

"Who the hell are you?" Hunter asks as Bryce rolls his eyes. It takes all the power I have not to smack that look off his face. "I'm being serious, Bryce. You aren't the kid we drafted. You aren't the player who led us to the playoffs last year. You aren't the leader of this franchise like you're supposed to be. This guy… I don't know this guy. And I don't want to."

"No one says you have to," Bryce says, beginning to stand up. "Just leave me alone and let me play football."

"We aren't done," I say, pushing him back down into his chair. "You want to play football? Then start fucking playing football. What you showed us today was pathetic. If you want to start playing football, quit the partying, get your priorities straight, and get your head back in the game."

"Here we go again with the partying," he says, the annoyance in his voice clear as day. "What I do outside of this facility is none of your damn business."

"It is when it affects your play," Hunter says, his voice growing sterner. "And it is. Bryce, you're a liability right now. Today's loss? That is all on you. Until you can prove to us that you are the leader and player we drafted, you're benched."

His eyes go wide. "I'm what? You can't bench me. I haven't violated anything in my contract. I'm your star."

Hunter laughs. "Damn right, I can. And I am. I never thought I'd have to do this again after last year, but here we are. Maybe this time it will work. As for your contract? Consider this me helping you to make sure you didn't break it."

Bryce shoots up from his chair and slams his hands against Hunter's desk. "Fuck this! This is all his fault!" he yells, pointing to me. "This fucker has been on my ass since the summer. He tell you to do this?"

"While I take stock of all recommendations from my coaching staff, this decision I came to on my own," Hunter says with a calmness I don't know if I could pull off right now. "If you can't clean up your act on your own, we will demand you go to a rehabilitation center to get treatment."

"Treatment!" Bryce yells so loud that teammates are now starting to gather outside Hunter's office. "I don't need fucking rehab. I'm fine. Why can't you just get off my ass?"

"We are on your ass because despite what you think, we care about you and we don't want you to run your life into the ground," I say, trying to keep my tone even. "This is for your own good."

Bryce looks at me, a humorless laugh coming from him. "You know, it's funny that you've been telling me to clean up my act all summer. Like you have the right to fucking talk."

My blood is now officially boiling. "What is that supposed to mean?"

"I remember last year you were partying with us. The fun uncle coach. Isn't that what they called you? Now I hear you knocked up

McAvoy's sister-in-law? Real responsible, Coach. Great role model. Maybe take your own advice and get your shit right before you come after me."

Oh, fuck no, he didn't.

In that moment, I don't even think. I just charge. I'm two steps from clocking my own player before I feel Hunter's arms wrapping around me, picking me up and holding me back. Bryce's eyes are inviting me to try something, but before he can get any further, Cole comes into the office, stepping between us.

"You need to go," he tells Bryce. "Get the fuck out of here and get your head straight."

"Shut the fuck up," Bryce yells, shoving his best friend in the chest. "How many times have I told you to mind your own fucking business, too? You aren't my father."

"And how many times have I told you I'm not fucking going anywhere," Cole says. "I promised you when we were kids that I'd protect you. And that's what I'm doing. Do what coach says. Get out of here. Go home. Get help. Do something. But I'm not protecting your ass anymore until you're the Bryce I know. This guy? This isn't him."

Hunter lets go of me as we watch the scene unfold in front of us. Cole's eyes are challenging Bryce to try something, or to defy him. I've always thought of Cole as a gentle giant. But right now? This man would rip off the limb of his best friend if he made a wrong move.

"Go," Cole says again, putting his hand on Bryce's shoulder.

Bryce doesn't say anything before he turns to leave. Cole doesn't either, but turns to us, nods his head, and exits the office.

"Did we do the right thing?" Hunter asks. "I feel like we just made it worse."

"Only time will tell," I say. "Only time will tell."

38

———————

BETHANY

I don't know how many times I have said those words today. By the looks of the unopened presents on the table, I'm going to be saying them at least twenty more.

But I don't care. Today is the baby shower, and my heart is overflowing with love.

And it's not about the presents. Though they are wonderful, needed, and thoughtful. But it's about the people who are here with me.

Mom and Sadie did an amazing job planning this. They invited my friends, coworkers, and my favorite hair clients, including Ruthie, who swears she's not mad at me that my date with Gavin didn't go as planned. They were even able to coordinate with Abby and Sara to make sure they were here. It hurts my heart Marie wasn't able to travel, but it hasn't been a good few weeks for her, according to Abby, so the doctors didn't want to take any risks.

The shower isn't even the best part of the weekend. Tomorrow is a Fury home game and the whole family is going to watch from one of the boxes. It's not only my first professional football game, but it's the first time Abby and Sara have been able to see Davis in action as a coach.

I'm ready. I have my Fury gear that is now decked out in rhinestones. He has been quizzing me all week to make sure I at least have an idea of what is going on so I don't have to keep bugging Sadie, who will be attending as the fiancée of the head coach, and not as a reporter.

Turns out, I know more than we both thought I did. I know the quarterback throws it. I know if the other team scores it's bad. I know somebody did something wrong when the yellow flag is thrown. And I know if I don't know the answer when he quizzes me on football knowledge, I just distract him with sex.

Football is officially my favorite sport.

"Now that is just precious!" Mom says as I hold up a onesie that says "Daddy's Little Cheerleader" in Fury colors.

"You better hope he never loses his job!" Ruthie belts out. "That kid will need a whole new wardrobe!"

I try to hide the worried look on my face as I glance at the gifts we've received. Ruthie isn't far off. Besides the bigger items that people bought for us—the girls at the salon chipped in for our stroller that is nicer than my car, and Mom and Sadie bought us the rest of the furniture for the nursery—every piece of clothing is either baby girl pink or Fury orange.

At least our daughter is very on brand with her parents.

"Don't worry about what she said," Sadie whispers, handing me another gift. "He's under contract for four years. Unless things go horribly bad, he and Hunter are safe."

I might be just learning about football, but even I know this season isn't off to the best start. They just won their first game last week, and Bryce is MIA. The company line in the media is he's rehabbing an injury. The truth is, no one has heard from him since he was benched and stormed out of the locker room. The whole thing ate at Davis for days after it happened. He feels horrible that he couldn't do more to help him. I tried to console him as best I could, but I don't know if it helped. The team has done its best to move forward, but it hasn't been easy.

If Sadie is right, they aren't going to lose their jobs this year. But what happens if next year it's more of the same? Or worse? What happens if the whole coaching staff is fired? Could they do that?

"Oh my gosh, that is the most adorable thing I have ever seen!"

At this point, I'm unwrapping the presents on autopilot as the thousands of scenarios play through my head.

What if he's fired? We have a house here. I have family here. We said this was where we were going to raise our family.

Would we split our time between Nashville and wherever he ends up? Would we live here while he lives wherever he found a job? I can't imagine being anywhere without him for that long of a time, but if his job takes him to a different city, he'd have to be there. Can I just pack up and leave?

Would things be different if we were married?

We've talked about a lot of things in the past few months. Yet somehow, the topic of marriage hasn't come up since that first night when he asked me out of shock and panic.

I know he loves me. And I love him more than I thought possible. If he were to ask me today, without a doubt, I would say yes. But he hasn't.

When I told him no, it was because I wanted him to be sure. It's not that I'd *never* marry him. I just didn't want him to propose because he felt he had to.

I shouldn't be worried though. It will happen. Is he waiting for the baby? Yeah. I bet that's it. We have enough going on. We're committed to each other. We bought a darn house together.

It's fine. Everything is fine. Right as rain.

A collective gasp breaks me from my thoughts. Since I'm not opening a gift, I look around to find Davis walking in, looking as handsome as ever. He's wearing black slacks, a light pink button-down with his sleeves rolled up, and that smile I can't get enough of.

"Hello, ladies," he says, oozing charm, as he walks over to me, placing a kiss on my lips while gently rubbing a hand over my now very large bump. "How are my girls doing today?"

"We're great," I say, clearing my head from the thoughts earlier. "What are you doing here?"

"Well, I can't let you have all the fun," he says, which gets a good laugh from the ladies in the room. "Plus, I heard one of these presents is for me."

"Of course, you would think something is for you," Abby says.

"Am I wrong?"

"Sometimes I hate you, big brother," she jokes, giving him a kiss on the cheek and handing him a package. "This is for both of you. From Mom."

I'm not telling a lie when I say it takes all of my willpower not to cry as soon as Abby says that. As for Davis? He doesn't even pretend to hide himself wiping away a few stray tears.

"Go ahead," I say gently, giving his arm a squeeze.

He clears his throat and begins gently unwrapping the paper. His hands are shaking a bit, so I lean over to help him take the top off the box. Inside the box is the most beautiful, softest, pale pink, baby blanket I have ever seen.

"She still knits on her good days," Abby says as we look at it. "She wanted to give you guys something she'd made all by herself while she still could."

There is now not a dry eye in the house.

Davis, blanket in hand, stands and goes straight to where his sisters are sitting. The three of them embrace in a hug that is the most touching thing I have ever seen.

As I go to put the box down, something inside catches my eye. It's a note, and it's addressed to me. My fingers can't open it fast enough.

Bethany,

Every baby girl should have a pink blanket, and my granddaughter should be no different.

I'm about to tell you something none of my children know. I was pregnant a fourth time. After Sara. No one knew besides Mitch, but I miscarried early.

As you know, Davis was named after my father. Abby and Sara were named after women on my ex-husband's side of the family. I always wanted to name a child after my grandmother, and don't ask me how I knew, but I knew that baby was a girl. The kids never knew Grandma, but she was the strongest woman I had ever met. Survived the Depression and raised a family with my grandfather fighting in the war. When Mitch left, I asked myself, "What would Grandma Charlotte do?" And the answer was survive. And that's what we did.

I tell you this because I want you to know that I saw the strength in you the second I met you. I saw the strength that my grandma had. That I tried to have. That my kids had when they were too young to ought to need it. You are the absolute perfect woman to love my son. Thank you for loving him. And I'm glad I got to meet you before it was too late.

Love,
Marie

39

DAVIS

"YOU KNOW we don't have to put everything away tonight?" I say as I bring in the last two boxes of baby items from the truck.

"I just want to get a jump on it," Bethany says from her spot on the floor as she folds another onesie that is so small, I have no clue how it will fit a baby. "I plan on doing most of it next week when you guys are on the road."

The nursery currently looks like the baby store exploded in here. There are clothes everywhere. Tons of boxes of diapers to put away. Everything a baby could want is here.

Our child is already so blessed.

We are so blessed.

The sight of a pink blanket laying at the bottom of the crib catches my eye. I don't know how I didn't completely lose it when I opened that today. Knowing my mom made that? That even though her good days are dwindling, she was still able to create something so beautiful for my daughter? It's too much to think about.

At that moment, the small box that has been sitting in my pocket all day taps my leg, reminding me it's there. Before my sister dropped that surprise gift on me, I was planning on proposing to Bethany at the shower. But after opening that beautiful gift, I couldn't.

No worries. It just wasn't the right time. I'll know it when it comes.

"Today was amazing," she says, holding out a stack of onesies for me to put away. I do before taking a seat next to her on the floor. She immediately leans back into me, my hand instinctively going to her stomach, where I feel our little one kick.

"That feeling will never get old," I say, placing a kiss on her temple.

"I'd love it if she kicked more during the day. Currently, her favorite time is at three a.m. She's already exhausting me."

I laugh. "She's a night owl like her dad."

"Well, then does Dad want to try and eliminate a few more names for his mini me?"

This has become our nightly ritual. Neither of us has come up with names we like, so instead, we have continued to throw out names we don't like. Last night we eliminated Heather, Jessica, and Kathryn for no reason except they didn't feel right to us.

"I heard the name Layla today. I gave it a test run. Doesn't fit."

"I agree. No to Layla."

"What about you? What's your veto of the night."

She doesn't say anything for a minute, and I feel the air in the room shift.

"Actually. I might have a name to keep this time."

This surprises me as I turn her toward me. "Really?"

"Yeah," she begins nervously. "What do you think about the name Charlotte?"

Charlotte.

"I love it," I say, playing it around in my head again. I don't know why, but it just... fits.

"I do too," she says, a smile growing on her beautiful face. "And if you don't mind, I'd like her middle name to honor my mom. I was thinking her middle name could be Elizabeth. It's my mom's middle name."

Charlotte Elizabeth Davis.

"It's perfect," I say.

"You think?" she asks.

"It is the most perfect name for the most perfect baby girl in the world."

Like a magnet, our lips come together, sealing this moment in the only way we know how. I never knew I could have this much love in my heart. How did I survive for so long thinking that my heart had a limit on how much love it could hold? That I couldn't have more people get close to me because it would take away from others?

There is no limit when it comes to love. There is no cap on how much you can love. You don't have to ration it out to people who are worthy.

My love for Bethany grows every day. From what started as simply physical attraction has grown into a love I can't imagine my life without. I already love Charlotte and I haven't even met her yet. I love the children I want to have with this woman in the future.

When our kiss breaks, neither of us moves. Instead, we just look at each other, our foreheads touching, and nothing but love in our eyes.

This. This is the moment.

Not when she told me she was pregnant. Not today, in front of a bunch of people. Not something elaborate like Hunter did for Sadie.

Just the two of us. Right here. Right now. This is where I ask her to marry me.

"Do you remember what you told me after you said that you wouldn't marry me?"

She laughs slightly. "I said that the next time you ask me to marry you, it needs to be because you can't imagine spending the rest of your life without me, not because you were panicking."

I position her so I'm now fully facing her, taking both of her hands in mine. "You also once said that you wanted a proposal that was just for you and your partner. It didn't have to be fancy, just something special that only the two of you would know."

I see the tears begin to well in her eyes. "I did say that. I can't believe you remembered."

I lift myself up, now facing her on one knee. "Bethany, as I sit here tonight and think back on our story, it's nuts to think that we are here today. I know this wasn't the order it was supposed to happen, but I don't regret one minute of our journey. I don't regret you ending things all those months ago. It made me realize you were more to me than I was ready to admit to myself. I don't regret having this baby before we even knew if we'd last, because I already know she's going to be the greatest gift either of us has ever received. I don't regret you telling me no the first time I asked you to marry me, because then we wouldn't have had this moment."

I pause, allowing myself a minute to breathe, and take the ring from my pocket. Bethany's tears are now full-on sobs, but I need to keep going.

"I love you, Bethany Hall. I didn't know I could love someone like this. You showed me I could be the man you needed, even when I didn't think I could be. You helped me see that one day I can be the father neither of us had. And not just to Charlotte. I want to have a whole bunch of babies with you."

This makes her laugh. "We'll talk about that later."

I wipe away a tear with my free hand. "What do you say, princess? Spend the rest of your life with me?"

She frantically nods her head as tears come streaming down her cheek. "Yes. Yes. A million times yes."

With shaky hands, I put the ring on her finger, thankful that Sadie was smart enough to tell me to go up a ring size just in case. As soon as the ring is on, our lips collide, kissing with a passion I've never felt before.

This woman. She bewitched me from the first moment I laid eyes on her. I remember feeling a jolt of energy the first time we touched. I thought it was strange, but I never thought anything of it.

Now, I know what it was. It was the universe telling me that I was done for.

40

———

DAVIS

EVERY FOOTBALL TEAM hits a point of the season when it goes into cruise control. Yes, you want to win. Yes, you want to keep preparing for the next opponent because every win counts in some way.

But it also comes to the point where if they don't know it by now, it's never going to happen.

This is where we are at the beginning of November. Somehow, despite Bryce not playing since the beginning of the season, we have just as many wins as we do losses. By some miracle, we aren't the laughingstock of the league, considering our franchise quarterback hasn't been heard of since that fateful day when we told him he needed to get his act together.

We thought he might come back in time for the bye week. That's always the week for teams to hit the reset button. That was three weeks ago, and the week came and went without a word from Bryce. Well, we got a message from his agent that he was alive but that it was best for everyone that he sits out the rest of this season. We placed him on injured reserve, gave a bullshit line to the media about an old injury that flared up, and kept going about our season.

One where we are probably not going to make the playoffs.

The fact that we are still mathematically in contention is actually a miracle, though it's a long shot. Once Bryce left the locker room, the mood drastically shifted. The offense didn't seem as tense. The veteran quarterback we picked up to hold us over is doing a well-enough job. The defense is keeping us in games, and we've managed to win a few. It could have gone a hell of a lot worse.

I might sound like a horrible coach, but the thought of playoffs right now is the last thing on my mind. Bethany is in the final weeks of the pregnancy, and things are becoming very real. We've hit the thirty-seven-week mark, and Dr. Stewart said everything looks great. I'm freaking out daily because I think she should be at home resting. She's fighting me every step of the way. Not only is she still working, when she isn't at the salon, she is in what I've read to be the "nesting" stage.

She also insisted on coming down here to meet me for a lunch date. I've learned to pick my battles. I knew I wasn't winning that one.

"Hey there," Hunter says as he lightly knocks on my open door. "Got a minute?"

"For the boss? Anytime."

He laughs as he takes a seat in the chair across from me. "It's still weird when you call me boss."

"Would you like me to call you something else? I gotta admit, that's a little weird, but if that's what you're into, we don't need to let Sadie know."

He grabs a loose football from the corner of my desk and chucks it at me. I catch it with ease.

"You forget sometimes that I was quite the receiver back in the day."

"Why didn't you try to go to a bigger college?" he asks, his voice back to being serious. "I've watched your tape. You were good, man."

I shrug, tossing the football back to him. "I didn't want to be too far from Mom and Abby. Mom was starting to show symptoms then. Though at the time we didn't know what it was. Abby was around, but Sara was just a kid. Pitt was the closest college who offered me a full ride, so I took it."

"I get it, man. I just wonder..."

I shake my head. "I don't. If I've learned anything over this past year, it's that everything happens for a reason. If I hadn't gone to Pitt, I might not have had the chance at the graduate assistant position. That introduced me to the coaches in Denver and put me on track to come here. I wouldn't mess with a day. Who knows how else it would have turned out?"

"You might not be sitting at my old desk," he says, tossing the ball back to me. "And you might not be on the way to becoming my brother-in-law."

"Like I said, I wouldn't change a thing," I say, a smile growing on my face as I watch Bethany slowly walk down the hall toward my office. Hunter catches my gaze and just shakes his head.

"God, you're whipped," he says, standing up.

"I learned from the best."

He kisses Bethany on the cheek before turning back to me. "See me before you leave. I have scouting reports for this week."

"Am I interrupting?" she asks as I guide her to a chair. "I know I'm a little early, but I didn't know how long it would take me to walk from the parking lot."

"I don't know why you walked at all. I hate that you're even out. You should be at home resting."

She just waves my comment off. "I'm pregnant, not dying. I'm fine. Plus, I'm craving a wrap from that place across the street. And you wouldn't deny your pregnant fiancée food now would you?"

It's her ace card and she's been playing it a lot these days. But she's right. If the woman asked me right now to find Dolly Parton to preside over our wedding and baptize our child, I'd make it happen.

"Of course not, princess. How are you feeling today?" I ask as I straighten up the folders on my desk and grab my cell phone. "Any discomfort?"

She gives me a look that would make a weaker man crumble to the ground. "I'm thirty-seven-weeks' pregnant with a future soccer player who has taken up residence on my bladder and Braxton Hicks contractions are hitting me. What do you think?"

I've learned this is a trick question.

"I think you look beautiful," I say, walking back to her and placing a kiss on her cheek. "Are you sure they are just Braxton Hicks?"

"Yes, and good answer," she says, taking my offered hand to stand up. "Speaking of your daughter, she is signaling to me that it's time to go to the bathroom. I'm going to do that before we go."

Before I can respond, my phone vibrates from my pocket.

"It's Abby," I say, though I'm confused as to why my sister is calling me on a Monday afternoon. We had our weekly talk last night.

"Well, answer it," Bethany says. "I'll go do my thing, then we'll go."

"You remember where it is?"

She nods and walks out of the office as I answer the call.

"Abby? What's up?"

"Davis..."

Abby's voice is panicked and mixed with what sounds like traffic noises.

"Abby? What's wrong. Talk to me."

"It's Mom. She's missing."

Four words. That's all it takes for my blood to go cold.

"What do you mean, she's missing? She lives in a secure facility! What the fuck do you mean she's missing!"

"I don't know," she says, evident she's trying to hold back tears. "I just got the call. I don't know anything yet. I'd never ask this of you but—"

"I'm on my way. I'll be there as soon as I can."

I hang up the phone before she has a chance to respond.

Mom.

Missing.

I know she hasn't been having many good days, but this... this hasn't happened since right before we found her the treatment facility. The last time she got out, she was so disoriented we didn't know what to do.

Where could she be? Where would she go?

I have to go. I have to find her. My family needs me.

I sprint down the hall to Hunter's office. "Hunter! The plane. Is it available?"

He looks up at me, confused about my sudden request. "It is. Why do you need it?"

"It's my mom. She... she's lost. She wandered away from the treatment facility. My sister just called me—"

"Go," he says as he picks up his office phone. "Don't worry about anything here. Take the plane. We're home this week, and we don't need it. Take all the time you need. I'll make the arrangements."

I turn to leave his office when I see Bethany walking toward me.

Shit.

I can't leave her. She's three weeks away from having our baby. What kind of father would I be if I leave her right now?

"Davis?" she asks, clearly seeing the worry written on my face. "What's the matter?"

"It's," I swallow, now finding it hard to say these words, "it's Mom. She... she's lost."

"Lost?"

"Apparently she wandered off. I don't know. Abby didn't know much. All we know is she's missing."

"Well, then, what are you doing here?" she says, marching back toward my office. "You need to go!"

I look at her, confused and torn on what to do. "I can't leave you."

"The hell you can't," she says, finding my keys on my desk and tossing them to me. "Your mom and sisters need you. Get your butt to Pennsylvania."

I stand there stunned, not even sure what to say.

Bethany lets out an exasperated breath as she walks to me with my coat in hand. "Richard Davis, you listen to me and you listen to me good. I am fine. I have Mom and Mike and Sadie and Hunter. We still have three weeks before Charlotte graces us with her presence. You need to get on a plane this instant and find your mama, do you hear me?"

At this moment, I realize two things. One, that when Charlotte is ever in trouble, Bethany will instantly turn into a stereotypical southern mother.

Two, I love this woman more than I even realized.

"Thank you," I say, leaning in and kissing the ever-loving hell out of her. "I'll be back as soon as I can."

She takes both of my hands, placing one over her heart and one over her stomach. "Find her. Then come back to us. We'll be here waiting. I love you."

"I love you more," I say before I give her one more kiss, then run as fast as I can to my truck.

41

BETHANY

"HAVE YOU HEARD ANY UPDATE YET?"

Mom's question pulls me from my daydream. One where I'm holding Charlotte in the blanket Marie made for her, smiling up at Davis after she's born.

"No," I say, grabbing a potato to start peeling. Anything to keep me busy as I sit and wait. "Nothing new."

Davis texted me when the plane landed in Pennsylvania to say that he made it, but I haven't heard from him since. I didn't expect I would hear from him. He has much more important things to do than text me every ten minutes.

When there is an update, he will let me know. And until then, I sit and wait.

"They are going to find her," Mom says, bringing me a glass of water as she comes to sit next to me. "We have to keep the faith."

I'm trying to, but the longer she is missing, the more I worry. After Davis left to take the team plane to Pennsylvania, I decided to come to Mom and Mike's for the day. It's Monday, so I was going over tonight for weekly dinner anyway. Something didn't feel right about going home to an empty house. But now, sitting here, it doesn't feel right doing nothing, either. Though every time one of these fake contractions hits me, it's a reminder of why I'm here and not there.

For being fake, they are quite uncomfortable.

"I hate that I can't be there helping," I say, putting down the potato. "I could be another set of eyes."

"I know, sweetie," Mom says, wrapping her arms around me in a side hug. "All we can do is send them good thoughts and hope that everything works out."

I try to think back to the day we went to visit her. The facility is large, so she could be somewhere on the grounds that they haven't checked. Though I doubt that. It's also in the middle of a residential neighborhood with a lot of side roads. She could have gone down any number of them.

I hate this. I hate this for Davis. I hate this for Abby and Sara. I hate this for Marie.

God, she must be scared. Or is she? Does she know what's going on? Does she have any idea how many people are trying to find her right now?

"I can't believe my baby is having a baby," Mom says so softly I almost don't hear her.

"That was random," I say, though I'm glad for the change of conversation.

She just shrugs. "I mean, I've obviously thought about it. But seeing you here, all belly, it just hit me today."

"What do you want to be called?" I ask, adjusting in my seat after another cramp hits me. This one wasn't too bad.

"I guess I haven't thought about that yet," she says, taking a sip of her Diet Coke. God, how I miss Diet Coke. I think the minute this baby is out of me, I'm going to request an IV drip of Diet Coke into my veins. "I don't want to be Grammy. That just sounds…"

"Old?" I say, finishing her sentence with a laugh.

"Yes. I don't like that. Grandma would be fine. Maybe Gigi? Do I look like a Gigi?"

I shake my head. "I'm pretty sure Sadie told me that Hunter's mom already requested Gigi on the day that they told her they were engaged."

Mom laughs. "Both of my girls are growing up. I remember the day we first moved into this house. It feels like so long ago now. But I still remember how nervous I was."

This takes me by surprise. "You were? But you and Mike were so in love. What was there to be nervous about?"

"Oh, sweetie," she says, taking a seat next to me, her hand resting on top of mine. "I was nervous about everything. It had been you and me for so long. Honestly, I had forgotten what it was like to live with a man. And even when your da… even when he was there, he really wasn't. I was nervous that you and Sadie wouldn't like each other. I was nervous that I'd screw something up just when I finally thought I found happiness. I was nervous that once we got here, Mike would change his mind. I still wonder sometimes how I got so lucky, but I thank the heavens every day I'm here now."

"Do you ever wish he would have stayed?" I ask. That question has been on my mind for as long as I can remember, but I've never asked.

"Oh God, no," Mom says, shaking her head. "Your sperm donor, because let's be honest, that's all he is, gave me the greatest gift of my life. I can't imagine my life without you. You have given me so much joy and I'm so proud to be your mama. But if he would have stayed? He would have only brought us down. He wasn't ready to be a dad. He left because he knew that. I don't hold any ill will toward him. I did for many years, but I don't anymore. He tried and he just couldn't do it. Him leaving made us who we are today. And I quite like how we turned out."

"I love you, Mama," I say, wrapping my arms around her the best I can with a beach ball in my stomach. "The only way I know that I'm going to be able to do this is because of you."

"I love you too, baby girl," she says, giving me a kiss on the cheek. "But you have something different than I did. You have Davis. That man, I know you were worried at first, but he is going to be the most amazing father."

"How do you know?"

She laughs, standing up from her seat. "Because I see the way he looks at you. That man would rather die than let you down. Your daddy never looked at me that way. But Davis? That man would move Heaven and Earth and walk through hell for you. That is the man you want by your side forever. That is the man to start a family with."

Mom gets up to check on dinner. I reach for my phone, instinctively checking to see if there is any word from Davis, even though I know there won't be. It's six thirty in Nashville, which means seven thirty in Pennsylvania. It's November. It has to be completely dark by now. And cold. God, she must be so cold.

If they don't find her tonight...

No. I won't let myself go down that road. He will find her. She will be okay.

She has to be.

Another pain hits me, this one a little bit longer than the others. When it subsides, I decide to get up and stretch my legs. But before I can even take a step, the oddest feeling happens between my legs.

No.

It can't be.

It's too early.

I haven't had a symptom all day except... well, shit. Were those contractions? Like real ones?

I take a deep breath and look down at the floor.

Oh shit.

"Um, Mom?"

"Yeah, sweetie?"

"How do I know if my water broke?"

She turns to look at me, her eyes growing wide. "It will feel like you peed yourself. Why?"

I look down at the puddle on the floor and back up to her. "Well, then someone better go home and get my bag. I think I'm fixin' to have a baby."

42

———

DAVIS

I FEEL like I have walked down this street a dozen times.

I haven't, it just feels like I have since every fucking street in this goddamn neighborhood looks the same.

Where in the hell could she be?

As soon as I got the call, I raced to the airport. Two hours later, I was in Pennsylvania.

Turns out the security system shorted out again. Mom was outside when it happened, as it's an unusually warm November day for Pennsylvania. Somehow, when they were doing a check on all the patients to make sure that they were safe and secure, Mom wandered off.

It could have happened to anyone, they said.

Well, it didn't. It happened to my mother. And now she's been gone for going on eight hours. When the sun went down, so did the temperature. She has to be freezing. If I don't find her soon…

I turn down yet another side street, looking every direction I can to see if anything catches my eye. Abby and her husband are out looking, as well as the local police and a group of staff from the center.

How far could she have gone? The staff and police seem to think she has to be somewhere in this neighborhood, but I'm starting to doubt them.

I check the time on my watch again. It's almost eight o'clock. The sun is now completely set, but I can't make myself stop looking. She's out there somewhere.

I should call Bethany. It's not like I'm doing anything except looking back and forth right now. But just as I go to pull my cell phone out of my pocket, something catches my eye. A shadow moving in a backyard.

I check the front of the house and there is a for sale sign posted, which makes me pick up my pace. As soon as I get to the backyard, I see her clear as day. Mom, sitting in a tire swing, slowly swinging back and forth.

I hurry up and grab my phone, ignoring the twenty texts and missed calls, and message my sister that I found her and send her my location. I slip my phone back into my pocket and gently start making my way toward her.

"Mom?" I say, hoping to not startle her. "Are you okay?"

"Dinner isn't ready yet," she answers without looking at me, a sadness to her voice.

The way she says that makes me pause. Dinner isn't ready?

Then it hits me. She's not here right now. She might be physically here, but in her head, she's not. If the answer she just gave tells me anything, she thinks I'm a kid.

"Mom, it's dark out. Why don't you come with me?" I say, taking a few more steps toward her.

When she turns to look at me, the sadness in her eyes nearly breaks my heart. "I'm not coming inside, Mitch. You can heat up leftovers."

Mitch? Does she think I'm…?

"Mom, it's me, Dav… It's Richard, Mom. How about we go inside?"

She smacks down the hand I just offered to her. "Shut up, Mitch. I know you aren't Richard. He's at school. And I'm not coming in with you."

Fuck. I should have known better. I remember when she was first diagnosed, one of the therapists told us that if she was ever having an episode to not scare her. To go along with it. It's the best thing to do so as to not to agitate her.

That means, right now, I have to pretend to be the man I hate more than anyone else on this planet.

"Okay, Marie," I say, her name feeling foreign on my tongue. "What do you want me to do?"

"I want you to leave me be. You left us. You walked away. Don't you dare think about coming back."

I don't know what to say to this. Is Mom reliving a real event? Did Mitch try and come back? She had always told us that once he left, she never saw him again.

"I just want to make sure you're okay," I say, hoping she thinks Mitch is still talking.

"Okay? I'm not okay. I lose my Charlotte and the next day you leave. Of course, I'm not okay!"

What did she just say?

"Who is Charlotte?" I ask, wondering if this is just a coincidence. It has to be, right?

"You know who Charlotte is. She was our baby, Mitch. But I lost her. I lost our Charlotte. And then the next day you go and leave. And now you're back. You need to leave. Let me be in peace. I don't want the kids to see me like this or know you were here."

I stand there in front of my mother, who thinks I'm my father, stunned silent.

Is all of this real? Did this really happen? It sure as hell feels like it did, even though I have no idea what is going through her mind.

If all of this happened, then Mom was pregnant, but lost a baby right before Mitch left. And she was going to name her Charlotte? Does Bethany know this somehow?

And why did he come back? What did he have to gain from coming back? Was he trying to get her to forgive him? Did he forget something? I guess we'll never know since no one has spoken to him in more than fifteen years.

"Mitch, you need to leave," Mom says, wiping the tears from her eyes. "The kids will be home from school soon. You made your choice. You left us. You chose her. Now leave us be."

What did she just say?

Mitch had an affair? That's why he left?

I don't know why I'm shocked by this, but I am.

"Leave, please," she says as I hear the sound of cars pulling up to the house.

I know this next move is risky, but I can't just walk away from her right now. She might think I'm my piece of shit father, but I can't let this be how I leave her as I see Abby and the team from the hospital coming toward us.

"I'm so sorry. I'm sorry I couldn't do more." I lean in and kiss her forehead, meaning those words as both identities. As Mitch, I hope wherever the bastard is that he's sorry for hurting her and leaving us. As for me? I'm sorry that she felt she had to live with this pain, with these secrets, for all this time.

Her mind might be betraying her right now, but she is still the strongest woman I know.

"SHE'S RESTING COMFORTABLY," Jennifer says, greeting Abby and me in the small waiting area at the facility. "Again, I would like to profusely apologize for this. I… I just feel awful."

I want to rip her a new asshole. I want to scream that she better get that fucking door fixed. That I will pay for it personally, so this never happens again.

But I don't, because I know it will do no good. That, and Abby threatened me that I would never have another child if I cause a scene. It could have happened to anyone. All that matters is that Mom is back in her room and safe.

"Thank you, Jennifer," Abby says. "We'll be by to check on her in the morning."

"That will be no problem. Come whenever." She shakes our hands and walks away.

"Holy fuck, that was scary," I say, collapsing back into the chair, my body and mind exhausted from the day.

"You're telling me," she says, taking the seat next to me. "What happened with you and Mom?"

I sit up and rest my elbows on my knees, not knowing where to start. "Do you know if Mitch ever tried to come back?"

"Not that I was ever told. Did he?"

"Apparently. At least, that's what Mom was remembering tonight. If it was real. She… she thought I was him."

"Can you blame her? When she's in a state like that? You're the spitting image of him."

"Don't remind me."

"What else did she say?"

I take a deep breath, preparing myself because this is news that I still haven't come to grips with. "Mom thought Mitch was back. In her mind, by my guess from what she was saying, it wasn't long after he left. She told him to go back to the woman he left us for."

"I always knew that bastard was cheating on Mom," Abby says, the anger clear in her voice.

"Yeah, well, are you ready for the rest?"

This surprises her. "There's more?"

"When I got there… She was crying on a tire swing. Just like the one we used to have as kids. She… she was crying over a lost child."

"A lost child?"

I nod. "She said she was pregnant but lost the baby. She was calling her Charlotte. She said she lost the baby and the next day Mitch left."

"Oh my God. I had no clue."

"I don't think anyone did."

"Poor Mom."

"Want to hear the most fucked-up part?"

Abby's eyes grow wide. "That *isn't* the most fucked up?"

"The night after Bethany's baby shower, we were doing our nightly elimination of baby names and she said that she had a name that she liked and wanted to see what I thought about it. Abby, she said Charlotte."

If Abby's eyes were wide before, they are all but popping out of her head at this point. "You have got to be shitting me."

"We both love it. That's our baby's name. We're... I'm... we're naming our child after the sibling we never knew."

Abby gets up from her chair to sit on the arm of mine, wrapping her arms around my shoulders. "Mom is going to love it. Hopefully, she still has a few good days so we can tell her."

I pat Abby's arm when I feel a vibration go off in my pocket.

"Oh shit," I say, scrambling for my phone. "I never called Bethany to tell her we found her. She has to be worried sick."

"Good move, Richard," she says, moving back to her seat. "Why are you staring at your phone like you've seen a ghost?"

I didn't realize the color in my face drained that fast. When I check my phone for the first time tonight, there are dozens of missed texts and calls from Sadie, Hunter, and Helen.

I ignore all of them and immediately call Sadie, who answers on the first ring.

"What's going on, Sadie?"

She takes a deep breath. "First, tell me if you found your mom."

"Yes," I say, already standing and walking out of the facility, Abby not too far behind. "Now, what's the matter? Bethany? The baby? Is everyone all right?"

"They are fine," Sadie says, though her voice has an urgency to it. "But you need to get here sooner rather than later."

"Spit it out, Sadie," I say, now sprinting to my rental car.

"She's in labor, Davis. And if I were a betting woman, this baby is going to be here before the sun is up."

43

____

BETHANY

ONE OF MY guilty pleasures during pregnancy has been to watch videos of women doing ridiculous things to speed up or induce labor. Some of the dances they did were pretty entertaining. It was also pretty interesting to see what food combinations they were willing to try, all in the name of an old wives' tale that said it would jump start labor.

Who would have known that I needed to be watching videos of how to keep a kid inside me, because that would have been a lot more educational at this point.

This kid is ready to come out. But she needs to hold her damn horses until her daddy gets here.

"Ahhhh!" I yell, another contraction tearing through me. It's three in the morning, I've been having consistent contractions for nine hours now and this kid is one accidental push away from crowning.

Davis and I talked about the possibility of him missing the birth. The weeks surrounding my due date were away games. There was a very good chance he would be on the road when I went into labor. But knowing that he's on his way back, I need to do everything I can within reason to wait for him to get here.

I don't want him to miss this first.

"You're doing great," Sadie says, placing a cold washcloth over my forehead. "What do you need?"

"What's his status?" I ask, trying to even my breathing as I feel another contraction coming on.

"I haven't felt my phone vibrate, so likely nothing."

I shoot her a death glare. "I'm sorry. I didn't know we were going to assume things tonight. *What. Is. His. Status!*"

"Okay, hold on," she says, pulling her phone out of her pocket with hesitancy because I'm even scaring myself right now. "The last text was a half hour ago, and he just landed. Hunter is waiting with a car for him so they could go as fast as they could. He's on his way."

I had Sadie look up for me earlier how long it would take to get from the airport to the hospital. According to the map app on her phone, fifteen minutes.

If Hunter knows what's good for him, he better make it here in ten.

"I don't want him to miss this," I say, trying to hold back tears. He missed when I found out I was pregnant. He missed the accidental gender reveal. I don't want him to miss this as well.

I don't want him having to regret making an impossible choice. He made the right one. He did what he had to do for his mom and sisters. But if I can do anything to make sure he doesn't have to miss this, then I'm going to do it.

Maybe if I just cross my legs she won't come out? Seems reasonable.

"I know, sis," Sadie says, taking hold of my hand again. "You know he's doing everything he can to get here. You just need to keep breathing."

We always had a backup plan if Davis was out of town when I went into labor. Though at the time, I thought I'd be using it because of a football game. First, Sadie wasn't to contact him until we were one hundred percent sure I was in active labor. Tonight, we just amended that to make sure she did not tell him until she had confirmation Marie was safe. I didn't want to have him make that decision, and making sure she was safe was the top priority.

Sadie is also my backup birth coach if Davis isn't able to be here. Mom wanted to be in the room with me, but frankly, she's just too nice. I need the drill sergeant. I need Sadie.

But now that I'm here? I want Davis. I want his strong hands holding me. I want his soothing voice telling me everything is okay. I want him to be here with me the first time we lay eyes on our daughter.

"How are we doing?" Dr. Stewart asks, taking a seat at the bottom of my bed.

"I…" I don't get to finish that sentence because another contraction comes roaring through me. This one is the worst yet.

Holy hell, these things are no joke.

"Bethany, I know this isn't what you want to hear, but it's time to start pushing. We can't wait any longer."

I flash a panicked look down at Dr. Stewart. "What do you mean, it's time? He's not here yet. Just give him a few more minutes. He's on his way."

"Bethany, if we wait any longer the baby will be in danger," Dr. Stewart says, doing her best to be patient with me. "We tried, but we need to do what's best for the baby now. It's time."

I nod, tears now pouring down my cheeks as my birthing team gets into position.

How did this happen? I wasn't supposed to go into labor for another three weeks. Those contractions earlier today? Those were supposed to be Braxton Hicks.

Why can't one thing in this whole freaking pregnancy go according to plan? I had come to terms with not doing things in the right order when it comes to Davis and this baby. Why can't one little tiny thing like having the baby on time with my fiancé here be an option?

Though, honestly, it's fitting. This whole freaking thing has been off track since day one. Might as well keep on going. No sense trying to right our journey now.

"Are you ready, Bethany?" Dr. Stewart asks as I see a man sprinting past my labor and delivery room.

"Davis!" I scream, knowing that's who just ran past my room.

"What?" Sadie asks confused.

"Davis, he just ran by. Go get him! Now!"

Sadie looks at Dr. Stewart, who signals for a nurse to go chase down Davis. I've lost track of minutes and seconds, so I have no clue how long it takes for the nurse to find him. But when I see him through the window of my room, he isn't moving as fast as a man who's about to miss the birth of his daughter should be moving, in my opinion.

"Richard Davis Semen, you get your fucking ass in here right now!"

Everything stops in the room. Every doctor and nurse just stare at me. And Sadie? I'm pretty sure I just sent her into shock.

"What did you say?" Sadie asks, her voice laced with excitement. "Is that his name? Like his real name? Oh my God, this is the best day of my life."

I shoot her another glare. "Get my fucking fiancé in here NOW!"

Before she can move, Davis comes crashing into the room and sprints to the side where Sadie is no longer, taking my hand and kissing it.

"I'm so sorry, princess. I'm so fucking sorry."

"Apologize later! We have a baby coming!" I say, biting through a contraction. "It's... FUCK!!!"

44

DAVIS

ON NOVEMBER 9, three weeks early, Charlotte Elizabeth Davis was born at 3:58 a.m., coming in at seven pounds, eight ounces. She has a full head of brown hair like me and has blue eyes that are clear like her mom's.

She is the most beautiful thing I have ever seen, next to her mother, of course.

And I almost missed it.

If not for the grace of a good tailwind, Hunter driving one hundred miles an hour across Interstate 40 and a little luck, I would have missed the moment my daughter came into the world.

I almost let this beautiful little girl down before she even knew who I was.

I'm really nailing this fatherhood thing out of the gate.

"You look exhausted," Bethany says from her bed where she is nursing Charlotte.

"I'm fine," I say, shaking away the yawn that is fighting to come out of me. "You're the one who should get some sleep."

"I'll sleep when I'm done here," she says, smiling down at our baby girl.

I sit next to Bethany on the bed and just watch her nurse for a few minutes. I don't know which of these two I'm more in awe of right now.

That's a lie. It's Bethany. This woman… this woman who just gave me a child… she is so fucking strong. She was prepared to have this baby on her own if I would have said no to her all those months ago. She was ready to have it without me if the curveballs of life kept me away. She fought with everything she had to make sure she gave me the best chance of being able to see the birth of our daughter.

And what did I do? Ignored text messages and calls all night while I was hundreds of miles away.

"What's the matter?" she asks, looking at me out of the corner of her eye. "I know that look. Where's your head at?"

That's the question of the year. I have no idea where my head is. The last forty-eight hours are such a blur. Did all of it really happen in that short of a time span?

"How did you come up with the name Charlotte?"

Though that's not the first question on my mind, it has been one that has been nagging me since the episode with my mother. It can't be a coincidence, can it?

Bethany takes a breath and situates Charlotte to burp her. "In the box with the baby blanket, there was a note for me. In it… she told me about a miscarriage she had. And that she was going to name the baby Charlotte, after her grandmother, but didn't have the chance to. She didn't ask us to name her that, but… it just felt like we should."

I lean in, needing to feel her lips against mine right now. I don't know what I did in this life to deserve this woman, but I know I don't.

"When I found Mom… she was sitting on a tire swing. It was like one we used to have in our backyard. She was talking about a baby named Charlotte. It freaked me out. On top of that, she thought I was my dad. It was like I was living in two worlds at once."

"Oh, Davis," she says, giving me another kiss, the one of reassurance. "I can't imagine what you had to have been going through."

I shake my head. "I didn't know what to do. I hated being away from you, and I wanted to get back to you as soon as I could. And I didn't even know then you had gone into labor. I wanted to help my mom, but having to do it while she thought I was my asshole father was not my first choice. Then everything happened so quick to get her back and safe. Then I forgot to check my phone. If something would have happened to you or the baby…"

I trail off, the emotions and feelings of the past few days finally catching up to me. Bethany puts Charlotte down in her bassinet and brings me into her arms.

"You did everything you could," she says as she runs her fingers through my hair. "You had no idea I was in labor. I had no idea I was in labor. The system breakdown at the center was an accident. It was a perfect storm. But at the end of the day your mom is safe, Charlotte is healthy, we are fine, and we have a perfect little girl we get to take home with us in a few days. That's what counts."

I nod, hearing her words but not really fully letting them digest. Even two hours later, as I'm holding Charlotte while Bethany sleeps, I let her words wrestle in my head.

I still can't find peace with them.

All I can think about are the what ifs.

What if I wouldn't have made it back in time? I know we had a plan in case, but I never would have forgiven myself if I missed the birth of my daughter because I forgot to check my phone.

What if something were to have happened to her during delivery and I wouldn't have been here? What if there would have been a complication with Charlotte? Or, God forbid, something happened to Bethany?

If any of those would have happened, I don't know if I could have lived with myself.

Then there are the what ifs with my mom's situation. What if I wouldn't have been able to find her and I would have learned my daughter was born while I was wandering the streets of suburban Pennsylvania? What if she didn't respond to me and I couldn't have brought her back? What happens the next time? Because she might not get lost again, but there will be more episodes that I'm going to need to be there for my family.

But then there is my family here. The one I created with the woman who has shown me I could love.

This is why I said I never wanted this. I'm only one man. In the first hours of my daughter's life, I've already been pulled in more directions than I know how to bend. Now I'm worried that I will continue getting pulled and will finally break.

I rub Charlotte's back as I take a glance down to my chest to look at my sleeping daughter. Feeling her little body against my chest is the most surreal feeling in the entire world. Right now, she's counting on me for warmth. For love. And I'll do everything in my power to give her anything she needs.

But does that mean letting down others? When something like this happens again, which family am I going to let down the most? The one who raised me or the one who is now my future? I'd rather cut off my own arm than disappoint either of them.

The worst part is the little voice in the back of my head. I've pushed him away for months, making myself think I could be enough for everyone in my life. But right now, as I hold my sleeping daughter, he comes back to the forefront of my brain, louder than ever, and says the words I've been denying for months, though right now I'm realizing are absolutely true.

I don't know if I can do this.

45

____

BETHANY

WE HAVE BEEN HOME for four days.

I think Davis and I have argued for the better part of three of them.

Take last night, for example. We made a deal a long time ago that he would take at least one late-night feeding. If my memory serves me correctly, he volunteered to do it on his own. I believe his exact words then were, "I'm a night owl, it's the least I can do." So each night before I go to bed, I make sure I have at least one bottle pumped and ready to go for Davis' shift.

When Charlotte woke up for her three a.m. feeding, I rolled over and nudged him. I'm still trying to figure out if what happened next actually happened or is a product of my postpartum imagination.

"She's up. There's a bottle downstairs."

Davis grunts and rolls back over. "I'm tired. Can you do this one?"

"I did the last one. You promised me one a night. Please, I'm exhausted."

"Join the club."

That was his response. A "join the club" and a snore a few minutes later.

Frustrated as all get out, I got up, went to my daughter's room, and whipped out the boob. After I was done, I decided it was best for all involved if I didn't go back to bed, so I slept in the rocking chair in Charlotte's room. It might not have been the most comfortable, but it saved me from accidentally smothering my fiancé with a pillow.

I don't know where his sudden mood shift has come from, but I'm not a fan. I thought everything was fine in the hospital. Since that first day, he's been distant. Quick to the trigger. If it's not a fight, it's a dismissal.

I don't know who this man is, and I pray to the heavens that this isn't some sort of new Davis. Because if this is Davis as a dad, we are going to have big problems.

I'm not expecting him to give everything up to help me, but a little bit here and there can go a long way. Since we've been home, he hasn't changed one diaper. He has fed her twice. Yesterday, I asked him to get me a Diet Coke because I can have Diet Coke again, and his response was, "what do I look like?" and he walked away.

During all of this, he was in the kitchen. Two steps from the refrigerator.

I'm hoping today is better. It's Sunday, but Hunter told Davis that he was not to show his face in the stadium today, even though they have a home game. I'm hoping for a nice easy day with minimal arguments, a chance for both of us to catch up on some sleep, and maybe, if I'm lucky, a shower.

Because I don't remember the last time I took one of those.

Needless to say, it takes me by surprise when I see Davis coming down the stairs, bookbag in hand, and decked out in his normal Fury coaching attire.

"What are you doing?" I ask, checking the time to see that it's just after eight a.m.

"Going to the game," he says, like it's the dumbest question I've ever asked. "Did you make coffee?"

"No," I say, following him into the kitchen. "I didn't think you'd be taking it to go."

"Fine, I'll do it myself," he says, annoyed as he heads into the kitchen and pops in a K-cup.

"Why are you dressed like you're going to the game?" I ask, trying to keep my voice down so as not to wake up Charlotte, but I'm having a hard time. "I thought you weren't coaching today. Hunter told you to stay home."

"Hunter isn't the boss of me."

"Actually, he is."

The sound he lets out is somewhere between annoyance and dismissal. And it's pissing me off. "Don't get literal on me, Bethany. It's my job to coach. We have games on Sundays. I'm going to coach my team."

"I thought you would want to take this time to be here with me and Charlotte? We've had a long week. Take the day and relax. We both could use some down time."

He's standing facing away from me, almost like he's willing the coffee machine to brew faster. I step up behind him and put my hand on his shoulder, hoping to ease some of the tension for him.

Then he does something that throws me more off guard than any way he's been acting the past few days.

He shrugs off my touch.

Never, not once since the day we met, has he ever done that.

I take a step back, wondering what is going on. "Who are you right now?"

He turns to face me, and the look on his face is confused. Like I just asked him what color the sky is.

"What do you mean who am I? I'm the one who has to pay for this house and buy our kid diapers. I'm the man of this house, and I'm trying to go to my job so I can provide for my family like I'm supposed to."

Whoa. That came out of left field.

"Why are you being like this? And when has money ever been a concern for us that you can't take one day off? You're acting like I forced you to buy this house. You wanted it as much as I did, and now you're throwing it in my face?"

His eyes grow cold as he puts on the lid of his coffee cup. "Hard to say no to someone in the position I was in."

Did he really just make a reference to the closet blow job? By the look he is giving me right now, he sure as shit did.

The *audacity.*

I have never wanted to punch a person as much as I do right now. But I don't. Because I'm a fucking southern lady.

"That was completely uncalled for."

He lets out a heavy sigh but doesn't apologize. "I'm only one man, Bethany. And today I have to go to work. Maybe tomorrow I can be a dad. I'm leaving."

I stare at him as he puts on his shoes and grabs his coat.

That's it? That's how we are going to leave it? Somehow, in the months of dating and preparing for Charlotte, we never fought. This is completely foreign territory for me.

I just know that I hate him leaving today with us angry at each other.

"When will you be home?" I ask, desperation clear in my voice.

"When it's done."

That's all I get as he walks out of the door.

"WHAT YOU'RE TELLING me is that Richard is acting like a real dick?"

I shoot a look over at Sadie. "Please don't talk like that while you are holding your niece."

She rolls her eyes. "You know she is going to hear a lot worse from my mouth over the years, might as well get her accustomed to it from the start."

I fall back into the couch, flipping on the television to turn on the Fury game. "I know. I'd just rather her not hear it this young. Plus, this isn't a laughing matter. Something is seriously wrong with Davis and I have no idea what it is."

I don't know how long I stood in the kitchen stunned this morning after Davis walked out. I do know the only thing that got me moving was the sound of Charlotte crying. Feeling confused and not really wanting to be alone today, I called Sadie and asked her to come over. Since she doesn't cover the Fury anymore, her Sundays are more open.

"Okay, let's think back," she says, switching arms as she holds Charlotte. "He started acting funky when you came home from the hospital?"

I nod. "Yeah, but even when I was there, he was starting to act a little aloof. But I didn't think anything of it. We were so tired, and everything was a whirlwind. I just chalked it up to that."

"Makes sense. I probably would have done the same thing."

"I thought we were good, Sadie," I say, unable to hold back the tears anymore. "Everything was going great. I hate to say that it changed the second the baby was born, but unfortunately, that's the case."

We sit in silence, well, except for the sound of my tears that I can't control, neither of us really sure what to say. What can we say? It's not like either of us has a pathway into Davis's head. For a while, I thought I did. I guess I didn't.

"Oh, turn it up," Sadie says, signaling me to grab the remote. "I always love to hear what the announcers say when they talk about Hunter. I think this guy is going to lean into his age."

Sadie is right. The announcer goes on and on about Hunter being the youngest coach in pro football history and that just last year he was the offensive coordinator.

"But today, McAvoy's offensive coordinator isn't with us as he is home with his fiancé, welcoming their new daughter into the world." The television flashes to a picture of a newborn Charlotte. "We want to wish Coach Davis and his fiancée, Bethany, congratulations. Now, calling plays today for the Fury is running backs coach..."

I snap my head to Sadie, who does the same to me.

"What did he tell you he was doing today?" she asks.

"He said they had a game, and he didn't care that Hunter told him to stay home."

Sadie looks back to the television and back to me again. "If he's not at the game, and he's not here, then where is he?"

I stand up and begin to nervously pace around the living room.

If there was an accident, we'd know by now. He left the house more than five hours ago. The television is making it sound like he's here. He told me he was there.

I collapse back onto the couch and I can feel my face drain of color. Sadie hurries and puts Charlotte in her carrier and rushes over to me.

I'm pretty sure she starts talking to me. I have no idea what she is saying. All I know is that my worst fear is happening.

He wasn't ready.

He wasn't ready and he left.

He left me. He left our daughter.

Just like my own father.

46

DAVIS

"YOU ARE some kind of fucking asshole."

Hunter's voice should startle me as he takes a seat at the bar next to me, but it doesn't.

Part of me knew he'd show up sooner or later.

The other part of me is just drunk, so I don't give a flying fuck about anything.

"This is where you spent your day? Back to the bar where you used to pick up nameless women to get your dick wet?"

I look around the sports bar by my old apartment. "Yup. Right here. Though, no women today. Just booze. My man Patrick here kept my glass full!"

I raise my glass to the bartender, who is now ignoring me. That's kind of rude.

Also, Patrick looks like a woman now.

I meant to go to the stadium this morning. I had every intention to. Being in the house with Bethany and Charlotte was becoming too much. Over the past week I drummed up every what if and hypothetical scenario. I was starting to feel suffocated. I needed out. So I was ready to defy Hunter and coach in today's game.

Then, on my way to the stadium, all I could hear was the sound of disappointment in Bethany's voice. I replayed the fight that I started for no other reason than I'm an asshole over and over in my head.

The part where I told her I bought our house because I was getting a blow job. How I dismissed her touch when she was trying to soothe me despite me being a grade A asshole.

I don't deserve her sympathy.

I don't deserve her.

I don't deserve to be a father.

So, instead of driving to the stadium, I somehow ended here. Where I've been for the past... fuck, I don't know. I've been here all day.

"What are you doing, Davis?" Hunter asks, his voice full of disappointment. Seems like I'm good at getting that reaction from people lately.

"I'm getting drunk," I say, finishing off my glass, hoping he will drop this conversation and leave me be.

"I mean, what are you doing here? Why are you not at home with your fiancée and newborn daughter? When I said take the day off, this isn't what I meant."

I shoot a look at Hunter, who has the gall to look at me like he's upset. At least I think he does. There's two of him right now.

Both look pretty pissed off.

"It's too much," I admit. Damn, drunk me for being honest.

"What is too much? How much you've had to drink? Because that I will agree with you on."

I set down my glass and turn to face Hunter. "Everything."

"You're going to have to be a little more specific than that."

I try and gather my thoughts before responding. Which is hard because I'm pretty sure I killed a good amount of brain cells today. "I almost missed it, Hunter. I almost missed her being born."

"But you didn't," he says. "You did everything you could to make it there for her. And you did. You got to hold that little girl of yours in the first moments of her life. You were there for both of them."

"But I wasn't," I admit, hating having to say this, knowing I'll live with it for the rest of my life. "Bethany had to go through labor alone.

Yeah, I know she had Sadie, but I should have been there. I promised her I was going to be there and I wasn't."

"Davis, no one could have predicted what happened to your mom happening at the *exact* same time that Bethany would go into labor three weeks early."

"But it did happen," I say, my anger starting to creep back up. "I had to choose between my two families. There was no right or wrong answer. Do I say no to helping find my mom who doesn't know what day it is half the time, or do I stay with the mother of my child? This is why I never wanted a family of my own. Having to make these choices. This is why I stayed single. This is why I denied Bethany for so long. I don't want to have to make these choices. My mom and sisters count on me. Bethany and Charlotte now count on me. I can't be in two places at once. And before my child was even born, I had to make that choice."

"We all have to make choices sometimes," Hunter says, looking at me confused. "You know that Bethany wasn't going to be upset if you missed the birth, right? She understood. Did she want you there? More than anything. But do you know what her instructions were to Sadie when she was in labor?"

I shake my head because I obviously don't.

"She said specifically, 'until he says that Marie is found and safe, you do not tell him I'm in labor.' She knew where you needed to be. There was a backup plan for her. There wasn't a backup plan to finding your mom. Bethany was prepared to sacrifice her want to have you next to her during the birth of your child so you didn't have to make an impossible decision."

She did that? I know Sadie asked me if Mom was safe before she told me she was in labor, but I didn't realize it was because it was on Bethany's demand.

"That doesn't change anything," I say, though I'm finding it harder to believe my own words. "This isn't going to be the last time I have to pick between my two families. I'm always going to disappoint someone. It was the first, but it won't be the last time. I can't do this, Hunter. I can't fucking do this."

"Can't do what?" Hunter asks, his voice now pissed off. "Can't be a father? Can't be a son? Can't be a brother? Can't be a partner to your fiancée? What are you going to give up? Who are you going to disappoint, your words, not mine, when you tell someone that because you are one thing you can't be another?"

I don't answer, but only because he's right. I hate when he's right.

"I'd love to hear this conversation," Hunter continues, clearing his throat. "'Hey, Bethany. Engagement is off because on the chance something happens with my mom or sisters again when something big in our life is happening, I don't want to disappoint you guys. So I'm just going to end things here. Disappoint you from the fucking get go. Tell Charlotte I'll see her at her graduation.'"

"I wouldn't ever—"

Hunter cuts me off. "Or maybe it will go like this. 'Hey, Abby. I know I'm your brother and power of attorney for our mom, but I'm going to have to dump all of that onto you and Sara because you might need me sometime down the line when I have to be there for my future wife and child. Sorry. See you at some point.'"

"That's not what I mean—"

"Oh. Maybe this one will be the best. 'Hey, Mom. Hope you're having a good day today. I'm just going to let you know that I can't help your daughters anymore because I'm a dad now.'"

"Shut the fuck up!" I yell. I can see eyes across the bar flashing toward me. "That isn't what I meant."

"Then what did you fucking mean?" Hunter asks, his voice more even. "Because I just laid out your three choices if it's really too much for you. You have to pick."

He's right. I hate to say it, but he's right.

Until the day I die, I will do everything in my power to be there for Mom, Abby, and Sara. But Bethany and Charlotte? I would rather take a bullet to the chest than not be there for them in every way I can.

"How do I do this?" I ask, my voice now barely above a whisper. "How do I be enough for all of them?"

Hunter laughs. "You don't be."

"What?" That isn't the answer I was expecting.

"What you want to be for everyone? It's an impossible feat. But you know what you do have that not every man can have?"

I think I know where he's going with this, but I let him finish because I'm a glutton for punishment.

"You have women around you who are stronger than most men I know. Bethany? She might seem all sweet and southern, but that woman had every hospital worker at her will that night to give her just another minute to try and get your pathetic ass there. Your sisters? I might have only met them once, but I'm pretty sure they can shoulder a little more than you let them."

"I don't want them to have to worry about things I can handle," I say, all of a sudden feeling like the thirteen-year-old boy who had to become a man in a day. "I can handle it."

"But you obviously can't," Hunter says. "No man can. It's admirable you want to do everything. But you're right. You are only one man. But the women in your life around you? They are damn good ones, and you are going to piss all of them off if you keep this shit up."

I laugh. "I hate it when you're right."

He smiles and begins to stand up. "Last question."

I let out a breath. "What's that?"

"How are we going to sober you up so Bethany takes you back? I really don't want you sleeping on my couch tonight... or in the future."

47

———————

BETHANY

I REMEMBER the day I realized I wasn't like other kids—that most kids had a mom and dad.

I was in first grade. We were making Christmas cards, and our teacher told us to make ones for all of the relatives in our family.

My mom was an only child, and her parents passed away before I was born, so I only had the one card to make. I remember Gretchen, the girl who grew up to be the queen bitch of my high school, teasing me because I only had one card to make.

"You don't have a daddy? What is wrong with you?"

When I got home from school that day, I was crushed. I remember crying to Mom, wondering why other kids had a mommy and daddy and I didn't. She explained to me that some families have a mommy and daddy, some just have mommies, some just have daddies, and some have two mommies or two daddies. But the important thing was that no matter how many parents you have, as long as they love you with all their might, that's all that counts.

As I sit here and hold Charlotte, looking down at the beautiful little girl I am blessed with that is the perfect mix of Davis and me, I wonder if I'm going to have that conversation with her? Am I going to have to one day tell her that it's okay that you don't have a daddy, because I have loved her enough for the both of us?

I hope I don't have to, but the longer Davis stays away, the more I can't shake the feeling that this isn't going to end well.

I tried to call his cell as soon as I realized he wasn't at the game. It went straight to voice mail. The second the game was over, Sadie called Hunter, and I know he left to go look for him as soon as he could.

Sadie messaged me a while ago saying that he found him. And while I'm glad he's safe, it doesn't help knowing that now hours have passed and he's still not home.

"If it's going to be you and me little girl, then it's going to be you and me," I whisper to Charlotte, who is currently fighting to keep her eyes open. "You and me against the world."

I pull her to me a little tighter, not wanting to put her down in her crib. It's funny, the parenting books say that your children need to feel your skin and feel close to you in the days right after their birth. Little did I know I'd need her just as much as she's needing me.

We must both drift off because I'm startled awake by the sound of a door opening. When I open my eyes, I see Davis standing against the door of the nursery, looking a bit worse for wear. He doesn't say anything, instead just nods his head, silently asking me to follow him.

I don't want to, but if he's leaving, I can't let him go without saying my piece. And I can't let him just leave. If he's going to do this, he's going to look me in the eye and tell me he's leaving.

I stand up, put Charlotte down in her crib, and make my way to our bedroom where I find him already sitting on the bed.

"Are you coming back just to leave again?" I ask, needing to not beat around the bush with this one.

He looks up at me, his eyes bloodshot and confused. "I don't want to. But if you want me too, I will."

I laugh, though it probably sounds like an evil one. "I don't want you to leave. What I do want is the man you have been the last few days to kick rocks and never come back."

Davis smiles, and I hate that he has that effect on me. Will that ever go away? How can one smile melt me so instantly? It worked on me that first night we met. I have a feeling it will work on me until we are old and gray. "He was a pretty big asshole."

"The biggest," I say, walking to sit on the bed, though there is significant space between us. "What happened? What's going on? I'm… I'm so confused right now."

He takes a deep breath and reaches out his hand for mine. I don't move closer but place my hand in his.

"My entire life, all I've wanted to do is not let the people in my life down," he begins. "It started with Mom and Sara and Abby. It was my teammates when I played football. It's my players. But now, more than ever, it's you and Charlotte. I'd rather cut off my arm than disappoint you."

"Then why have you been acting like you have?" I ask, still confused. "Because the last few days? Even though you've been here, that man, that man is not who I fell in love with. That man doesn't have a place in this house."

"I know. And I will never be able to say I'm sorry enough. It's just…" he pauses, slightly turning toward me. "Knowing that I almost missed the birth because of having to choose others, it started getting to me. I've been playing what-if scenarios in my head for days now. What if it happens again? What if I can't get to Mom because you need me? Or what if I disappoint you because Abby needs me and I need to go to Pennsylvania? It was just too much and I…"

"You started acting like an asshole?"

"Yeah," he says, a little laughter in his voice. "I started acting like the biggest asshole of all."

I take in a deep breath, letting that all settle in. It makes sense. While him leaving Charlotte and me is my worst nightmare, not being able to be enough for the ones he loves is Davis's.

"You know I wouldn't have been mad at you if you missed it," I say, hoping he knows that. "I wanted you to be there, yes. But finding Marie was the most important thing you could have done that night."

"I know," he says, inching himself a little more toward me. "All I could think about was that our daughter wasn't even born yet and I almost let her down."

Now it's my turn to face him. "Richard Davis, you listen to me and you listen to me good."

He takes my other hand in his. "I love it when you go all southern mama on me."

This gets a smile out of me. "Hush and listen while I say what I need to say. Your daughter would not have known if you were there or not. And if she ever did? I would have told her that her daddy was being brave and making sure that her grandma was safe and sound. And that if anything were to ever happen to you, he'd make sure he does the same thing for you. Because you... you're the only man I want to keep us safe. You're the only man I want to raise this child with. But if you're going to retreat into yourself and be an asshole when you start feeling overwhelmed? That I won't accept. We're teammates. We're partners. If we're going to do this, we have to do it together."

He doesn't answer. With words at least. Instead, his hands travel to my face, bringing our lips together.

And just like that first night, I feel the zing from my head to my toes.

"I love you," he says, pressing our foreheads together. "I love you so much. Can you forgive me?"

Little does he know I forgave him the second I sat down on this bed. "Possibly."

He quirks his eyebrow at me. "What do I need to do to make it up to you?"

"Two things," I say, my voice growing more playful.

"Name them."

"One. Never, ever, and I mean ever, act the way you did this morning."

"Done," he says, taking my hand and bringing it to his lips. "I will never be able to say I'm sorry enough for that. What else can I do?"

I smile. "You owe me a few middle-of-the-night feedings. Oh, and some more foot massages."

He laughs. "Consider it done, princess. Consider it done."

48

DAVIS

LAST YEAR during the championship game, I was sneaking out during halftime with Bethany for a quickie in Hunter's garage.

Oh, how much has changed in a year.

"What are you doing?" Bethany asks as I pull her into the bathroom, already kissing every part of her neck I can. "Davis, we can't do this."

Well, not that much. So what if I'm still trying to sneak moments with my girl? I think it's a good thing.

Especially since Aunt Sadie and Uncle Hunter are here to watch the game with us. And watch Charlotte while I sneak away with her mama for a few minutes.

"I'm kissing my fiancée because it's been an hour since I've done so last and that's unacceptable," I say, finding her mouth and willing her to open for me with my tongue.

I don't know if I'll ever get tired of kissing this woman. Or making love to her. Or watching her with Charlotte. It baffles me that I was stupid enough to think at one point I could live without her. Without them both.

"We can't do this," Bethany says, though her roaming hands say otherwise. "Hunter and Sadie are in the next room!"

"I don't care," I say, sneaking my hands up the front of her shirt to get a feel of her full breasts. "Let's make it our tradition. Every year during halftime we sneak away for a quickie."

She laughs, her hand searching for my growing erection. "What happens when you are in the game? I don't think we can do it then."

"We'll cross that bridge when we get there," I say, hoisting her on the counter, our lips crashing together in a frenzy.

Despite being in playoff contention until the final week of the season, the Fury did not make the postseason. However, the year could have gone a hell of a lot worse considering our franchise quarterback sat out for pretty much the entire season and is still off the grid.

To be honest, I'm kind of glad we didn't make the playoffs. Charlotte is almost three months old, and she changes every day. Being able to be here for her and see all her little milestones is something I'll never take for granted. Bethany is back to work part time at the salon, and I'd be a liar if I didn't say I love the days that all I do is the job of daddy.

I even considered giving up coaching and being a stay-at-home dad. Maybe trade some stocks in between changing diapers? Then Bethany reminded me that additional cooking responsibilities go along with that job, so I figure I'll stick with the football thing.

Plus, Hunter is bound and determined that he and I are going to be the youngest head coach and offensive coordinator duo to ever win a championship. And the man is nothing if not determined.

I've had to make a few trips to Pennsylvania for Mom and Abby— we decided to move her to a facility closer to Abby to make it easier on her. Mom is getting great care and the miles are easier on Abby.

Bethany and Charlotte came with me once, and seeing my mom hold her grandchild was easily one of the best moments of my life. It wasn't a great day for her, so I'm not completely sure Mom registered what was going on. But when we told her the baby's name was Charlotte, her face lit up in a way I hadn't seen for years. Then she snuggled her granddaughter tight as she was wrapped in the pink baby blanket.

It's a memory I'll cherish always.

And then there is Bethany. I don't know how I can love her any more than I already do. I knew she would be an amazing mother, but seeing her with Charlotte makes me want to put another baby in her immediately. I have been told that's not happening until we are married.

So I booked a venue for July. I would have done a courthouse ceremony, but I know how much a wedding means to Bethany. We've done everything else out of order; the least I can do is give her the wedding of her dreams.

"If we're going to do this, let's do this now," she says, hurrying and sliding down my joggers and boxer briefs.

"I love it when you talk dirty," I say, quickly removing her leggings and panties. It only takes me a second before I'm lined up and entering her with ease.

She might say she doesn't want another baby just yet, but she hasn't made me wear a condom since we got the okay from Dr. Stewart to "resume intercourse." Yes, that's what she called it when I asked the question. And as far as I know, she's not taking birth control.

I smile to myself as I think that Charlotte could be getting a brother or sister sooner than we think.

The thought of Bethany being pregnant again spurs me on, making my thrusts faster than normal. I'm not even thinking about how she's only balancing on a small piece of counter.

"Davis," she whispers in my ear, wrapping her legs around me tighter. "You feel so good."

"Fuck, I love you," I say. "I love you so fucking much."

Our pace is now furious and I feel her tighten around me. "Come for me, princess. Now."

I move my hand to the top of her clit, and with two strokes, Bethany comes completely undone.

"Davis!"

It takes all I have not to yell her name as I empty myself inside her.

Holy fuck, that was intense.

Neither of us moves for minutes, both finding ways to catch our breath.

"That was…" I say, but am unable to finish the thought.

"My new favorite tradition," she says, leaning in for one more kiss.

But before it can go too far, we are stopped by the sound of banging on the door.

"Richard! Bethany!" Sadie yells, still banging her fist against the wood. "We know what you're doing!"

"We don't care!" I yell, sneaking one more kiss as we finish putting our clothes back on. "And just because you know my name now doesn't mean you have to use it."

"I can and I will," Sadie says. She has been calling me Richard every chance she gets since she found out my real name. Though the bet was technically a draw since Sadie didn't guess, neither of us won. Being the nice guy I am, I still gave her the interview—after she bought me lunch, of course. "And when you two are done in there, your daughter has decided to invent a new definition for 'blowing through a diaper.' I did not sign up for that today."

We look at each other, each of us smiling from ear to ear.

"I'll take the diaper if you take the feeding tonight?"

I lean in and kiss her one more time. "You've got a deal, princess."

EPILOGUE
BETHANY

FOUR YEARS LATER

SOME TRADITIONS ARE MEANT to be broken.

For the first time on championship Sunday since I met Davis, we haven't snuck away at halftime for a mid-game quickie.

And I couldn't be more excited about it.

The Nashville Fury has won the league championship for the first time in franchise history. It has been years of hard work, frustration, and determination, but Hunter and Davis did what they set out to do all those years ago.

They are the youngest coach and coordinator duo ever to win a title.

And I couldn't be prouder of them.

"They did it, sis. They really did it."

The words come from a very emotional and very pregnant Sadie as we watch Hunter receive the championship trophy. I bring her into a side hug as Hunter hoists the trophy above his head, his team cheering behind him as they all hold up their phones to capture the moment.

"Look at him up there," Hunter's mom, Francine, says. "I'm just… I'm just so proud of him."

Sadie gives my hand a squeeze as she goes to stand next to Hunter's parents as I take in the scene in front of me. Standing off to the side of the makeshift stage in the middle of a huge stadium are Mom and Mike, along with Hunter's parents, who are basking in the moment of their son winning the championship. Bo, Hunter's dad, keeps pointing to the jumbotron to show Camden, my nephew, his daddy on the screen.

Unfortunately, Abby and Sara couldn't make it. It's the middle of the school year and Abby didn't feel right about having the girls miss, and Sara just started a new job with a tech company in Seattle. Then there is Marie. Hopefully, she's watching and understands what her son just did. Though these days, it's unlikely. She's still with us physically, but mentally each day it gets a little worse.

Then there is Charlotte and me. I'm watching her dad in awe of the accomplishment he just made. She's more interested in the balloons and confetti that are still raining from the rafters. As much as Davis tries to get her to take an interest in football, she wants nothing to do with it. She is my daughter through and through.

And he loves every minute of it. What no one knows is that last night Charlotte wanted to have a spa night at the hotel, and my husband's toes are painted pink because he can't say no to his daughter.

Maybe things will be different with our next one. The one that Davis doesn't know about yet.

We didn't mean to wait this long between kids. In fact, we tried for a few years with no luck. But in classic Davis and Bethany fashion, nothing happens the way we plan. We had all but given up and resided ourselves to Charlotte being it for us.

I took the test this morning. And I can't wait to tell him.

I look up on stage, where Hunter is still giving his television interview with the championship trophy in hand. I would guess most everyone here and those watching on television are watching Hunter speak. But me? I'm taking in the moment behind him.

The moment where Bryce and Davis are hugging, basking in the glory of what the two of them accomplished tonight. At that moment, I look to my right and see Bryce's wife crying, holding her very pregnant stomach. We share a look, and somehow without speaking, we have a full conversation with our eyes.

My look is meant to say thank you. I don't know if we'd be standing here if she hadn't come back into his life.

Her look is soft and welcoming. Though she hates taking credit for what she did for Bryce, everyone knows she's the one who pulled him from the gutter.

It's almost unreal to think that just a few years ago we wondered if Bryce was ever going to play again. Now? Now he's taking the championship trophy from Hunter, holding it above his head as the MVP of the game.

Yes, I know what that stands for. And yes, I know that because Davis quizzed me last night.

As the television announcer turns his attention to Bryce, Hunter and Davis start exiting the stage. As soon as they step off, they turn to each other and embrace in one of their manly back-patting hugs.

Sadie and I like to tease them about how much they man hug, but today they get a pass. It wasn't easy for the two of them to get here. But they never gave up on each other or the team. And now they can call themselves champions.

They part ways, and Davis makes a beeline for Charlotte and me, scooping her up with ease and planting a kiss on me that I feel in every inch of my body.

"Daddy!" Charlotte shrieks. "You won!"

Thank God she at least knew they won. Her favorite part of the day was the halftime show and the fact I allowed her to drink the complimentary Diet Coke that I wasn't drinking.

She really is my daughter.

"I did!" he says, placing her on his hip. "Did you have fun?"

"Can I take some of these balloons home?" she asks, her voice so sincere.

He laughs, putting her down. "Of course. Go get some right there by Gram and PopPop."

Charlotte goes running to Mom and Mike as Davis brings his hands around my waist.

"We did it," he says, his voice more emotional.

"You did it," I say, wrapping my hands around his neck. "I love you."

He leans in and kisses me. Nothing too X-rated, but enough to make me know that tonight is going to be a fun night.

Thank God Gram and PopPop are keeping the kids tonight for both Sadie and me.

"I can't believe this happened," he says, still holding on to me. "I didn't think this would ever happen. And now that it has? I don't know how you can top this feeling?"

I smile and bite my lip. "I bet I can make it better."

He wags his eyebrows. "You ready for that quickie? I bet we can sneak into the locker room."

I laugh, shaking my head. "No, but I still think you'll be just as excited."

"Well, I'm now officially intrigued."

I raise up on my tiptoes and lean in. "I'm pregnant."

He immediately pulls back to look at me. "You are? We are?"

I laugh, nodding my head. "I took a test today. We're having another baby."

He picks me up and twirls me around, shouting for everyone to hear that we're pregnant again.

All I can do is laugh and enjoy this moment.

Who would have thought that two people who were so different and wanted such different things could be so happy? I know things didn't go the way I had planned, but if that's what needed to happen for me to be here right now, I'd do them all over again.

And I'd do it with him every single time.

OFF SEASON

NASHVILLE FURY: BOOK 3

PROLOGUE
BRYCE

ONE WEEK AGO

"GOODBYE, BRYCE. GO BE AMAZING."

I jolt up from the bed, a cold sweat covering me as I try to catch my breath, as I try to figure out why she continues to haunt my dreams every night. I look to my left to see Cole still asleep in the second bed in the hotel room as I roll off my bed and stumble to my duffle bag where I pull out a half-finished bottle of whiskey and my cell phone. Yes, it's the night before a game. No, I'm not supposed to be drinking while staying in the hotel, which the team mandates we do the night before games.

Frankly, I don't care. If they want me to be any sort of a functioning quarterback tomorrow, then they want me to finish this bottle. It's the only way I'm going to fall back asleep and make sure I don't dream of her again.

I quietly slide open the door to the small patio and fall into the chair as I down a healthy swig of the burning liquid. I look at my cell phone, hoping I can find something on here to take my mind off the dream I just had. Instead, I see a text message from my father. Fucking wonderful.

Dad: Don't fuck tomorrow up. I have a lot
riding on this game. Ten grand to be exact.

I squeeze my phone until it nearly breaks because it's better than throwing it over the balcony. Instead, I take another drink from the bottle.

"Why?" I say to no one. "Why can't I stop dreaming about her?"

I've been having some sort of version of that dream for what feels like every night for the past nine months.

Sometimes I'm watching Lucy get married, and I can't do anything about it. I'm just sitting in the back of the church, wondering why it wasn't me she was pledging to spend the rest of her life with.

Sometimes I'm kissing her before she's pulled away from me.

Tonight I dreamed of the last time we were together. It was during my rookie season a year ago, and I was a wreck. The transition from college to pro football was more than I could handle, and my play was paying the price.

And, just like always, Lucy made it better. She silenced the doubt in my brain and got me back on the right track. I really thought that the next time I saw her, we'd finally be starting our life together, that it was finally our time.

Until it wasn't. Until I found out she moved on. That she got engaged.

When she told me goodbye and to go be amazing I never thought they were going to be the last words she said to me.

She's gone. My rock. My first love—the only person in this world who knows how to fix me when things get bad—is out of my life for good.

She's someone else's now. I was too late.

So, I'll just sit here on this balcony, drink the rest of this whiskey, and do my best to forget her.

Too bad there isn't enough whiskey in the world to ever make me forget her.

But that won't stop me from trying.

"DONALD. COACH WANTS YOU."

Fucking fantastic.

Not only am I still nursing a hangover from hell after last night's whiskey-on-the-balcony bender but also now I'm going to have to get chewed out by my head coach. If only that last jackass reporter wouldn't have asked me the stupidest question in the history of press conference questions I'd already be out of here. But no, because of that dip shit, I'll have to listen to Coach McAvoy drone on about how we need to fix the offense and how it's my job to do it.

No. It's his job. I'm doing mine. Not my fault his offense can't hang with me.

I toss my bag into my locker, and if I didn't know better, I'd swear that every one of my teammates was watching my progress across the locker room toward Coach McAvoy's offices. It's like I'm getting called into the principal's office or something.

"Hey"—Cole's hand on my shoulder stops me mid step—"whatever happens, I'm here for you. You know that, right?"

It takes all I have not to roll my eyes at my teammate and lifelong best friend. Because what he just said? That is the most Cole shit I've ever heard.

"How many times do I need to tell you I'm fine?"

"And how many times do I need to tell you that I don't believe you?"

"Whatever, man," I say, shrugging away his hand and making my way to Coach McAvoy's office. I don't have time today to listen to Cole's latest spiel about how I need help and should talk to someone. I don't. I'm fine. And the quicker I get this meeting over the quicker I can get to the bar tonight. If I have my way, I'll be forgetting about today's loss with a blonde or two.

Coach McAvoy is standing next to Coach Davis when I walk in, which is fucking wonderful. He's been on my ass more than McAvoy has. I swear, the man feels like it's his personal mission to be my counselor.

Or worse. My friend.

I don't need either. I need to be left the fuck alone.

"Bryce."

"I know. We sucked today," I say before either of them can say anything else. "Your shiny new wide receiver can't catch any of my passes. He needs work."

"Dexter has nothing to do with this," Davis says. "It's not his fault that he ran the correct route and his quarterback underthrew him by ten yards."

Of course, he'd say that. In his eyes, everything that goes wrong with the offense is my fault.

"Like I said, the receivers need to be where I put it. Not the other way around."

Why is it so hard for these two to get that? Hell, McAvoy was a quarterback. He should know. I don't understand why they aren't comprehending this.

"Who the hell are you?" Coach McAvoy asks.

Here it comes. The attempt at the intervention.

I'm Bryce fucking Donald. I'm the former number-one draft pick and best up-and-coming quarterback in professional football. My contract was the largest for a rookie in the history of the league. My face is on billboards all around Nashville. The city might be known for its country music, but since I arrived and led the Fury to the playoffs last season, it's my town now. I can get into any bar, club, or restaurant. I see a woman I want? She's mine. I'm living the life every twenty-four-year-old dreams about.

Though, by the looks that McAvoy and Davis are giving me, they don't care about that.

"I'm being serious, Bryce," McAvoy continues, his tone conciliatory and calm. "You aren't the guy we drafted. You aren't the player who led us to the playoffs last year. You aren't the leader of this franchise like you're supposed to be. This guy . . . I don't know this guy, and I don't want to."

"No one says you have to." I stand and turn to leave. I'm over this conversation. "Just leave me alone and let me play football."

"We aren't done," Davis says, pushing me back into my chair. "You want to play football? Then start fucking playing football. What you showed us today was pathetic, so quit the partying, get your priorities straight, and get your head back in the game."

"Here we go again with the partying," I say, sounding as bored as I feel. I don't have a fucking problem, yet he's acting like I'm drunk twenty-four hours a day. "What I do outside of this facility is none of your damn business."

"It is when it affects your play," Coach McAvoy says, his voice growing sterner. Uh oh. Good cop is getting mad. "And it is. Bryce, you're a liability right now. Today's loss? That is all on you. Until you can prove to us that you are the leader and player we drafted, you're benched."

I have to shake my head a few times because I clearly didn't hear him correctly.

I'm the starting quarterback. The future of this team. The face of the franchise.

I don't get benched.

"I'm what?" I demand, still not believing what I've heard. "You can't bench me. I haven't violated anything in my contract."

Coach McAvoy laughs. He fucking laughs. The asshole.

"Damn right, I can. And I am. I never thought I'd have to do this again after last year, but here we are. Maybe this time it will work. As for your contract? Consider this me helping you to make sure you don't break it."

I start pacing in circles. My hands grab pieces of my hair and if I'm not careful I might pull some out. They can't do this to me. I won't let him.

Then I catch Coach Davis out of the corner of my eye.

Him. He's the reason McAvoy is doing this.

Well, this isn't going to fucking happen. Not if I can help it.

"Fuck this! This is all his fault!" I yell, pointing at the fucking traitor who calls himself my offensive coordinator. "This fucker has been on my ass since the summer. He tell you to do this?"

"While I take all recommendations from my coaching staff into consideration, this decision is mine," Coach McAvoy says. "If you can't clean up your act on your own, we will demand you go to a rehabilitation center to get treatment."

"Treatment?" My teammates are starting to gather outside the office, but I don't give a shit. Let them hear what our coaches are doing to me. "I don't need fucking rehab. I'm fine. Why can't you just get off my ass?"

"We're on your ass because despite what you think, we care about you and we don't want you to run your career into the ground," Davis says. "This is for your own good."

I laugh, though there is no humor in my tone. "You know, it's funny that you've been telling me to clean up my act all summer. Like you have the right to fucking talk."

Davis's face gets red. Apparently, I touched a nerve. Good. I have him right where I want him.

"What is that supposed to mean?"

"Last year, you were partying with us. The fun uncle coach, isn't that what they called you? Now I hear you knocked up McAvoy's sister-in-law?" Yeah, I know I'm throwing Davis's own drama in his face, but ask me if I care. He's over here acting as if he's a fucking saint when, this time last year, he was asking us what bar we were hitting up. "Real responsible, Coach. Great role model. Maybe take your own advice and get your shit right before you come after me."

My eyes are locked on Davis, and I see the minute he snaps. Good. Serves the asshole right for getting me benched.

I don't flinch as he charges toward me, and he probably would have landed the punch I know he's dying to throw, but Coach McAvoy got to him before he got it in.

Too bad. I would have loved to have told the owners that a coach hit a player.

"You need to go. Get the fuck out of here and get your head straight."

Cole's voice takes me by surprise. When did he get in here? And when did he place himself like the brick wall he is between me and the coaches? I swear, this man is fucking everywhere. He's almost as bad as Davis.

"Shut the fuck up," I yell, shoving my apparent former best friend in the chest. If he's telling me to go, that means he's on their side and he's no friend of mine. "How many times have I told you to mind your own fucking business? You aren't my father."

"And how many times have I told you I'm not fucking going anywhere," Cole says. "When we were kids, I promised you that I'd protect you. And that's what I'm doing. Do what coach says. Get out of here. Go home. Get help. Do something."

I look up at Cole, and for the first time since we met when we were six years old, I'm staring into the eyes of a stranger. My best friend wouldn't side with coaches over me. He would have my back. He's always had my back.

He turned on me. Lucy turned on me. Everyone has fucking turned on me.

"Go," Cole says again, putting his hand on my shoulder, which I promptly shove off.

I look at the three sets of eyes in the office, ones that are all trying to show sympathy.

Fuck their sympathy. They have no clue what it's like to be me.

Fuck Cole. Fuck the coaches. Fuck all of this.

They want me gone? Fine. I'll leave.

I don't need them.

I don't need Cole.

I don't need her.

I don't need anyone.

1

BRYCE

"THE NASHVILLE FURY win their first game of the season, and they do it without franchise quarterback Bryce Donald, who will be out for the remainder of the season."

Wait, what?

I blink a few times. I was just about to take my daily afternoon nap so I'm not sure I heard the announcer correctly. Did he just say that I'm out for the season?

If so, my agent has a hell of a lot of explaining to do.

I grab the remote from the coffee table and turn up the television as I grab my phone. And here I thought it was a good idea to turn it off for the game so I didn't have the temptation to see what was being said about me on social media.

Instead, I watched my team play the best they had all season. My backup looked like a starter. Dexter caught every pass, and the defense played out of their minds.

All I could think about during the entire game was that I should be with them. We should be celebrating our first win of the season together. I shouldn't be watching it from my mother's couch in my small hometown in Southwest Ohio because I've been benched for the season.

"According to Donald's agent, Dean Braxton, who released a statement in conjunction with the Fury at the end of today's game, the second-year quarterback out of Clemson has been placed on injured reserve to focus on his mental health, which is the first time we've seen this happen in league history."

I mute the television and shake my phone, begging it to turn on faster. When it finally comes to life, there are seven voice mails from my agent. There are thousands of social media notifications, and a handful of texts. Three from Cole, two from my sister, and one from my father, which I'm sure is telling me that I'm no son of his now because he can't make money off me.

I don't have a chance to search for Dean's number before I see his name flash across my screen.

"I'm done for the season? This how you normally deliver news to your clients?"

"Only ones who make it their goal to be a pain in the ass."

"I'm your highest-paying client." I stand, needing to pace because all of this is too much to deal with sitting down. "You should have told me before the rest of the world found out. And mental health? I don't have a mental health problem. Where the hell do you and the team get off saying that without my permission?"

"I tried. Seven times. But it couldn't wait," he says, a long and frustrated breath following. "So we released the statement, and your tweet about taking the season off just posted."

"My what?" I shout, putting the conversation on speaker as I navigate to Twitter. And just like he said, a picture of a statement that I didn't write is there for the world to see.

"Fans, thank you for your support. I haven't been in a good state of mind for many months. My off-field actions have carried over on to the field, and that isn't the player I want to be. I owe it to the Fury, the fans, and my family to make sure I am the best version of myself. Mental health is an important topic today, and I hope that you will respect my privacy as I work

on becoming the best version of myself. I'll see everyone next season. Go Fury!"

I re-read the tweet. When Dean told me that, from time to time, he or someone on my PR team would be tweeting for me, I didn't think anything of it. But this? Admitting to my fans—and to the professional football world—that I've been having mental health problems? How fucking dare they.

I'm fine. I'm definitely not crazy. I'm fine. How many times do I have to tell people that before they start to believe me?

I swallow my anger. "I don't have mental health problems. I'm not crazy."

"No one said you were," Dean says, his voice trying to soothe the anger that is pouring from mine.

"Apparently, I did. And you did. And the team did. Without my consent, may I add."

"We did what we thought was best. It's important that you get help, which you need, so that you avoid a potential suspension after the shit you pulled with Davis last week. It's the smartest solution for everyone involved."

The last week has been kind of a blur to me—I was so mad I was being benched I couldn't see clearly. I remember throwing words at Davis. I know that Cole and McAvoy had to keep us apart. Next thing I knew, I was walking out of the facilities to find Dean waiting for me in a non-descript car with tinted windows. Roughly four hours later, we were pulling into the driveway of my childhood home.

Dean told me to lay low and keep out of trouble until he and the Fury could work something out. Apparently, that answer was to tell everyone I was nuts.

I feel my face getting redder the more and more it seeps in what my team and my agent did. "So, instead of suspending me, this is what they are doing? Putting a stamp on my forehead that I'll wear for the rest of my life?"

"You can't look at it like that," Dean says. "Just because you are working through mental health issues doesn't mean you're crazy.

Mental health is just as important as physical. Only for mental health, we can't send you to the trainer at halftime and have you ready to play in the second half. You need to talk to someone to help you through this. And that's what you're going to do because, whether or not you're ready to admit it, there is something going on with you that no trainer or coach can fix."

I try to listen to Dean, but I'm too angry. How dare they? How dare he? Especially when I'm fine. I've told everyone this for months but no one will listen to me. I don't need to talk to some shrink.

Everyone just needs to leave me alone and let me be.

"So what? Am I stuck here in Ohio?"

"You aren't stuck."

"My apologies. I should have asked if I'm being held hostage here."

I hear the exasperated breath from Dean. At least we're both over this conversation. "No one is holding you hostage. The Fury and I just don't think Nashville is the best place for you right now. That is, unless you can promise us you won't end up shitfaced drunk in the nearest bar."

I'd be lying if I said I hadn't thought about doing exactly that. Shit, that was the first thing I thought of when I got to Laurel Heights last week. The bars here might not have the same ambiance as Nashville, but I'm sure they still pour a stiff drink.

And maybe I could have found a girl from high school who wanted to live out a fantasy from the past.

I was told under no circumstance was I to drink or even leave the house. And not only was I told it but also my mother was told as well.

There's no security guard quite like Pamela Donald.

"So, that's it? I'm done for the year?"

"Yeah. Yeah, you are," Dean says. "Listen, it was either this or they were going to start looking into legal avenues. So, keep your head down, stay out of trouble, and go talk to someone like they asked you to. I have three sports psychologists lined up when you're ready. Two of them offer online appointments or you can drive out to Cincinnati for a face-to-face; I don't care which you choose, but you have to pick one. If you don't, then you might not have a team to go back to next year."

He hangs up the phone, and I fall back into the couch.

The phrases *mental health* and *out for the season* roll through my head as I process everything Dean just told me. When I arrived in Laurel Heights last week, I really thought it was only going to be for a few days, but now it looks like I'll be stuck here for God knows how long.

During which time, I will no doubt end up seeing her.

I let out a laugh that has absolutely no humor in it. The Fury think they have everything figured out. They really think sending me to Laurel Heights will be the key to fixing me, when the person who broke me is right around the corner.

2

BRYCE

"I DIDN'T KNOW there was a new landscaping company in town. Do you have a card or should I just find you on Facebook?"

Each day in Laurel Heights, I get another reminder of how I was whisked away like a thief in the night. Right now? I realize I don't have any headphones to drown out the sound of my twin sister's voice.

Note to self: Order some online and pay for overnight shipping.

"What brings you by Brenna?" I ask, raking the last of the leaves into a pile.

"Can't a girl come by and visit her mom and brother? A brother she hasn't seen in months?"

I don't even need to use my twin telepathy to know this girl is lying out of her ass. "She could, but that's a bunch of bullshit. And don't lie and say it's for pizza night either."

It's been two hours since it was announced to the world that I was done for the season to focus on my mental health. When I got off the phone with Dean, I was so pissed I almost punched a hole in my mom's living room wall.

I wanted a drink, but then remembered that Mom cleared the house of any alcohol when I got here.

Then I looked outside and realized that her yard could use tending to. Figured I might as well burn off some of this energy in a more productive way than stewing on the couch, or trying to resist putting holes in walls.

"Fine. I watched the game today and heard the announcement. Sue me if I wanted to come and check in on you."

"I'm fine," I say through clenched teeth. "It's what the team needed to say."

"Who's spewing bullshit now?"

"What's that supposed to mean?"

I throw down the rake and stare at my sister, who is returning my glare right back. Brenna Donald has never stepped down from a fight or challenge. Apparently, she's not going to step down now.

"It means maybe, just maybe, they know what you need more than you do right now."

"So, you're on their side?"

"No. I'm on your side," she says, taking a seat on the steps leading to our front door. "No matter how bad you fuck up, or how many times I want to smack you on the back of the head, I will always be here for you. I might not agree with everything you do, but I'm always on Team Bryce. However, if this is what needed to happen to get my brother back, then I'm going to side with them."

"So, you are on their side. You think I'm crazy?"

Brenna lets out an inaudible grumble as she rubs her temples. "I don't know who said you were crazy, but it sure as shit wasn't me. I do think you need professional help to figure out a better way of dealing with life without Lucy's help. Oh, and Mr. Jack Daniels is not an acceptable replacement."

"You have no clue what you're talking about." I turn my back from my sister in the act of looking for trash bags to shove the leaves into. What I'm really doing is hiding the fact that she hit the nail on the head.

Though I'm not ready to admit that to anyone.

"I think I do," Brenna says. "The quicker you realize that none of us are out to get you, the quicker the old Bryce can come back."

I want to laugh at the thought of "the old Bryce." The old Bryce thought he had the world in front of him. The old Bryce thought that once things got settled in his life, he'd have it all—the career, the fame, and the girl.

Obviously, that's not going to happen.

"Maybe the old Bryce is gone. Or maybe this Bryce was the real Bryce all along."

"Nah," Brenna says, walking up next to me and taking the trash bag from me and holding it open. "He's there. He's just lost. The real Bryce isn't the guy who parties every night and leaves with a different woman each night. The real Bryce doesn't blame his teammates for losses. That's not my brother. You're not that guy. That guy is a stranger to me. And frankly, from what I can tell, he's a fucking douchebag."

I let her words hang in the air and drop my gloves to the ground. I'm not replying because she's right. Though, I'm not ready to admit it yet. Frankly, I'm over this conversation. Actually, I'm over this whole fucking day.

I try to walk past Brenna, but she grabs my arm to stop me.

"I know she hurt you," Brenna says, her voice soft as if trying to comfort me. "But she did nothing wrong. Neither did you. You guys just grew up and your lives took you separate ways. Don't ruin your life—don't ruin your career—because it didn't turn out the way you wanted it."

My blood turns cold as I shrug away from my sister's hold.

"You think you know a lot more than you do Brenna. Just stay the fuck out of it."

"I know a lot more than you're willing to admit. Remember who was here for her all those years. It wasn't you, Bryce. It was me."

Brenna is now toe-to-toe with me, well, as much as she can be for someone who tops out at five-foot-four.

"You might have been here for her. But you don't know what it's like for me out there. A spotlight always on you. Every decision, every play, every waking moment under a fucking microscope. Your own father texting you about how you cost him money because of one pass or play call."

"Fuck Dad. You should just block his number."

"That's not the point Brenna. The point is you have no idea what's it's like to walk in my shoes. So, until you do, don't try to pretend you know what it's like. Because you don't. No one does."

I turn and storm past Brenna, really needing this conversation to be over. Actually, I need this whole fucking day to be over.

"So that's it? You're just going to hole up here?"

I turn back and look at my sister, who looks as over this conversation as I'm sure I do. "That's the plan. Got a problem with it?"

She shakes her head and gives a shoulder shrug. "Nope. It's your life. You've made that abundantly clear."

"Hey. Do me a favor?"

She raises an eyebrow, which I don't blame her for. It's not like I'm in the best position to be asking for favors right now. "What?"

"Don't tell her I'm back in town. Don't tell anyone."

"Bryce, people are going—"

"I know they're going to find out. Just . . . let's try to keep it hush for a minute."

Brenna lets out a defeated breath. "Fine. I promise. But you have to promise me something."

I should have known my words would come back and bite me in the ass. "And what is that?"

She gives my arm a playful punch. "Find the old Bryce. I miss him."

3

———

LUCY

"IT WAS GOOD SEEING YOU, Lucy. You tell your mom and dad hi for me."

"Will do. Have a nice day, Mrs. Latimer. Congrats on the new car!"

"Thank you, dear. Oh, and you make sure that wedding invitation of mine doesn't get lost in the mail. I bought a new dress for the occasion and everything!"

"Mm-hm." That is the only sound I manage to get out before a coughing fit like no other overtakes my body.

"Oh my goodness, dear!" Mrs. Latimer says, running to grab the bottle of water from my desk and handing it to me. "Are you okay? This is so adorable. Just the thought of your wedding gets you all choked up!"

I take a big gulp of the water and nod my head, praying that the worst of it is over. "Something like that."

When she's convinced that I'm not going to die, and at this point, I'm considering it as an option, Mrs. Latimer exits my office at the bank and I fall back into my seat.

I really thought these coughing fits were over. It had been almost two weeks since my last episode. That was when I went for my dress fitting and the seamstress told me that, the next time I was in, I'd be taking the dress home with me. Then there was the time before that when the florist reminded me that I needed to make a decision because my wedding was just a few months away.

Now, here I am, six weeks before the big day, still getting fits every time someone brings up my wedding. And yes, as a former mathlete, I realize that the common denominator to all of my coughing fits is my wedding.

The wedding that my family has been planning since my birth.

The wedding I have yet to send the invitations out for.

The wedding the entire town is talking about.

"It's about time they realized they were meant to be together!"

"I heard their mothers started planning this wedding when they were in the hospital right after they gave birth. How adorable is that?"

"It was meant to be. Luciano and Lucy? They have their own celebrity name! They are LuLu!"

I take another sip of water before my thoughts send me into another coughing fit.

This is normal, right? Doesn't every soon-to-be bride have near panic attacks every time her wedding is mentioned?

God, I hope they are normal.

Though I've never been called normal in my entire life, so there really isn't any point in aiming for it now. I'm the smart girl. The girl who is just slightly on the weird side of things. The super-analytical, loves-math-and-anything-with-numbers girl.

I'm also now the coughing-when-thinking-about-her-wedding girl.

I slouch back into my seat in my office at the bank, thankful it's in the corner. No one can see me unless they look but I can still hear and see everything. It makes days like today great because, after that episode, I need a few minutes to myself.

Maybe the coughing bouts are because I'm ready to get it over with and just be Mrs. Luciano Tripoli. I mean, I *know* I'm not coughing out of excitement, but lying to myself and saying that is better than admitting the alternative.

Don't get me wrong, I'm excited for the day, but I was never that little girl who had her whole wedding planned out with a color-coded binder. I couldn't tell you the difference between a gardenia and an orchid. All I know is that they cost a lot of money for something that is just decorative.

Honestly, it all seems very impractical when one could buy a brand-new car for what it cost to throw a wedding.

Maybe that is the source of the coughing fits?

Yeah, keep telling yourself that. Maybe one day you'll believe it.

"Heard this one almost took you out. You know if I have to do CPR, you might not get back up."

"Ha, ha," I say as Megan, my assistant manager, sits in the chair across from me. "Your humor is too much for me to handle. Really, you should go on the road with that act."

"You're being sarcastic. Something must be wrong. Tell me all about it."

I consider lying and telling her that I'm fine and it is no big deal, but I know better than that. The woman can sniff out a lie a mile away.

"I'm fine. Just hit me out of the blue."

"Are you ready to talk about why you start coughing every time someone mentions the wedding? Or are we still ignoring that? Just tell me which one we're doing, and I'll make sure I follow suit."

"Don't all brides get jitters?" I ask, hoping to play this off.

"They do," she says as she stares into me, likely trying to assess my level of bullshit. "I was nervous as all hell before Joe and I got married. Then again, I was pregnant with the first one, and I was hoping that no one could tell. But you? This isn't just normal jitters."

"I didn't know there was a difference in pre-wedding jitters?"

"There is when the bride doesn't want to go through with it."

Did she just . . .

"What? Of course, I want to go through with it!"

She tilts her head, and all of a sudden, I feel like I'm a criminal being interrogated. All she is missing is the lamp. "Between you and me, are you sure you want to do this? It's okay if you don't."

"Yes!" I say, probably a little too loudly. "Yes, I want to marry

Luciano. He makes me happy. He's a good man who loves me. One day, he'll be a good father. He's the man I'm going to marry."

The most important thing is that he puts me first. It doesn't matter how busy he is with the restaurant or with his obligations around town, at the end of the day I'm what matters most to him. It's a crazy concept for the man I'm with to want me more than anything else in life. For a while, I thought that was only a myth. It's not, and I'll never have to worry about being second when it comes to Luciano.

So, what if he doesn't make me feel butterflies? Who cares that the few times he's kissed me I didn't feel a spark in every part of my body?

Butterflies and sparks are overrated.

Stability. Stability and commitment. That's what matters the most.

Just when I think I've convinced Megan that what she said was preposterous, the silence that she lets sit between us allows for the chatter in the bank lobby to filter into my office.

"I heard he's back in town."

"Heard the same thing, but no one has seen him."

"I heard he got kicked off the Fury for partying too much."

"I heard he's been cooped up at his mama's house. Won't even step foot outside."

"Too bad. That boy had such potential."

No. It can't be. They can't be talking about . . .

"Bryce was something special to watch on the field. No one ever played like him."

He's special off the field, too; though, no one chooses to see it.

"Remember when he led that ninety-nine-yard drive in the state championship game?"

I do. I was wearing his jacket and was so proud of how he played. After the game, he kissed me like we had a forever full of kisses to look forward to.

"That was a good season. No other Laurel Heights football team is ever going to be that good again."

And no other man is ever going to make me feel the way he did.

"There!" Megan yells. "That look. That's the look you need to have when you're about to marry someone. The look that tells anyone who sees it that nothing else matters besides you and that person. How have I never seen that look on you before? Hell, I was at your engagement party."

All I can do is shrug. She's right. She has never seen this look on my face. Megan is five years older than me and only knows me as an adult. She never knew the girl who fell in love with the hometown hero.

"I looked like that because I was thinking about the date Luciano has planned for us tonight," I lie, straightening papers on my desk that don't need to be straightened. "You're reading too much into things."

"If you say so," Megan says as she stands. "Otherwise, you have a lot to think about."

I shoo Megan away from my office, praying my face doesn't give anything else away.

Shoot. That was close.

As soon as Megan is gone, I hurry and grab my cell phone from my purse. If what I heard in the lobby is true, someone has a lot of explaining to do.

> Lucy: Is there something you want to tell me?

> Brenna: Whatever do you mean?

> Lucy: Cut the crap. Is he here?

> Brenna: Before you get mad at me . . . I wasn't allowed to tell anyone.

> Lucy: BRENNA! How could you not tell me?

> Brenna: He's not leaving the house so I was kind of hoping you wouldn't see him. Or hear that he was home. In my defense it was a great plan and would have totally worked if the gossip mill in this town wasn't on paparazzi level.

> Lucy: It's Laurel Heights. You think that Bryce Donald being home was going to stay a secret?

I toss my phone back into my purse and resist the urge to scream in frustration at the top of my lungs. When I look back up, the picture of Luciano and me at our engagement party on my desk is suddenly all I see.

I pick it up and look at it, maybe really looking at it for the first time. We're smiling at each other, but I can't remember if it's because it's natural or if the photographer told us to smile. While his arm is around my waist, I wouldn't say I'm pressing into him, dying to be closer.

No, that isn't our relationship. Yes, I love him, but I learned a long time ago that love with sparks only burns you. The love Luciano and I have? The love that's built on friendship and respect? That's the one that will last forever.

That's the one who will always choose me first.

And that's the one I'm choosing to spend the rest of my life with.

Butterflies be damned.

4

———————

BRYCE

BRENNA WAS RIGHT.

I hate saying that, but she was right about so many things. Yet, there are only a few right now that I'm ready to admit.

The biggest one is that she said I couldn't hide in Mom's house forever. There's only so much television you can watch without going stir crazy. It's why, when Coach Roberts texted me, I jumped at the chance to come down to visit my old high school.

It isn't just getting out of the house that brought me to my old stomping grounds, it's also that Nick Roberts will always give it to me straight. The man isn't a teddy bear, but he's not a dick. Once I tell him my side of what's going on in Nashville, I'm sure he'll agree with why this mental health bullshit is just that, bullshit.

When I enter the doors that lead toward Coach Roberts's office and the weight room, a flood of memories come rushing back to me. It doesn't help that as soon as I walk into the facility, there is a huge trophy case with the championship trophy we won my senior year prominently displayed. Next to the trophy is a framed photo of Cole and me celebrating our win. Shortly after that picture was taken, Lucy came running toward me, wearing my jacket, with tears falling from her eyes as she leaped into my arms. That photo might not be hanging, but it's one I'll never forget. I can still feel her arms squeezing my neck.

"Seems like just yesterday."

I give my head a little shake as I hear Coach Roberts walking up next to me. "Can't believe it was seven years ago."

"A lot can change in seven years. For example, the best player I ever coached could go from rookie of the year to water boy in a matter of months. Oh wait, that didn't take that long at all."

I whip my head to my coach, who is far too focused on the trophy case. "Not you too?"

"Not me what?" he asks, signaling for me to follow him into his office. "Did I misspeak? Did my former star player go from top of the league to sitting at home on Sundays watching his team on television? Or do I have you confused with another player?"

I take a seat across from him at his desk. A lot might have changed in seven years, but not this space. Coach Roberts's office is exactly the way I remember it. Yes, it might have a few extra trophies, but that's it.

"I really thought our days of having to have a come-to-Jesus talk were behind us," he says as he takes a seat.

I let out a small laugh. "What can I say? I missed your words of wisdom."

Coach Roberts takes in a deep breath, his gruff demeanor seemingly melting just a bit. "I talked to Cole."

"Of course, you did," I say, annoyed that yet again Cole has taken it upon himself to try to fix things in my life. "What did my locker-room Dad have to tell you? Does he think I'm crazy too?"

"He never used the word crazy, so we're going to come back to that. He did say that you're partying until all hours, fucking anything that walks, and coming to practice and playing hungover."

My blood starts to boil just like it does every time someone tries to tell me that I'm fucking up my life. Why is everyone so concerned about what I'm doing off the field? "What I do with my life is nobody's business but my own."

"That may be true, but when it spills over onto the field, then you lose that privacy."

"It's not affecting—"

He slams his hands on his desk. In all my years of knowing this man, I've never seen him this angry. "Bullshit it's not. I watch you every week, and I can't believe the young man I knew has turned into this. I love you like a son, but damn it, boy, you are fucking up everything you've worked for. Now, I want you to watch this and tell me everything is fine with the way you're playing."

He fires up his old DVD player that he still uses to watch game film. The man does not care that everything is available online. Nope. He refuses to get rid of his trusty DVD/television combo that he's had since 1999.

"Are we really going to break down my film? Coach, while I appreci—"

"I said watch."

Feeling like I'm back in high school, I sit back and do what he says. If this were anyone else, I probably would have gotten up and left. But Coach Roberts is more of a father to me than my own ever really was. This is the man who made sure I kept my grades up to get into Clemson. He has always had my best interest at heart and never texted me to see if I'm going to cover the spread.

He was who introduced me to Lucy.

Don't. Don't think of her. Thinking of her does no good.

I shake my head and sit back, knowing what play is about to happen. Another pass to my would-be star receiver, Dexter Smith. I do my part right, I drop back, roll right, and I launch it to Dexter.

Only, he is ten yards short, and I overthrow him. Luckily for the defense, they have a safety there who catches my pass and runs it back for a touchdown.

"What happened here?" Coach Roberts asks.

"Smith stopped short. Pass got intercepted."

"Did he?"

Confused as to what he's asking, I watch the next play. Only this isn't from the last game I played. This is a game from last season because Coach McAvoy is calling the plays, something he doesn't do now that he's head coach.

I watch the play develop, and it's the exact one that Smith fucked up last week. I drop back, my receiver rolls out, and . . . stops exactly where Smith did.

I found him with a perfect pass.

What the hell?

"What are you showing me?" I ask, confused even though I know what I just saw.

Coach Roberts fast forwards the DVD to the next play. "Just watch, Bryce."

If the person who edited this video together wanted me to feel like a piece of shit, they succeeded.

Holy hell, is this how bad I've been playing all year?

It's like a bad 80s montage of the worst playing of my career. Bad passes, not looking for all my options, rolling right when I should have gone left. I overthrew targets I haven't missed since I was in middle school. I've seen all of these plays before. I've watched them ad nauseum with Coach McAvoy and Coach Davis, but it's like I'm seeing it with a new set of glasses.

Probably helps that I'm sober.

Just when I think the video is over, the video zooms in on me as I break the huddle in last week's game. It's worse than any bad play I've been shown.

All I can see are my eyes under my helmet. My bloodshot, tired eyes that are barely open. When I don't think it can get any worse, a video flashes on the screen of me dancing on a bar with three girls. I lick salt off one girl's chest and then another one pours tequila into my open mouth.

That wasn't all I licked that night.

"Fuck . . ."

It's all I can say as I slump down into the chair as the video goes black. Ten minutes of concise footage perfectly outlining the train wreck that is now my career and my life.

"I'm sorry I had to put it out there like that, but someone had to."

I sit back up, lean forward and drop my head into my open palms. "I didn't think it was this bad."

"What's going on with you, Bryce? I know I'm not there to see this, but from what Cole told me, and from what this shitty video showed me, this isn't the player . . . this isn't the man you are. You are better than this."

"There is nothing going on." I have to force the words out of my mouth. I've been asked what was wrong with me more times in the past nine months than I ever have in my entire life. My answer is always, "Nothing," or, "I'm fine."

I'm not fine. Nothing is fine.

She broke me, and she's the only one who can put me back together.

"Bullshit," Coach Roberts says, his voice louder than it's been all day. "You know it, and I know it."

"You don't know shit," I say, growing angry—at him or myself, I'm not sure. All I know is that the walls are starting to close in on me and I need to get the fuck out of here.

"I know the team said you were dealing with mental health problems, and I don't think they're wrong. Never use the word *crazy* because that's not it, but that doesn't mean you shouldn't talk to someone," Coach says, standing and rounding his desk. "Have you talked to Lu—"

"I said I'm fine! Thanks for the intervention, Coach. Don't quit your day job."

I stand and stride out of his office. I need air. I need to feel like the walls aren't closing in around me.

I mean to run to my truck. Away from this school and one of the few people who can see through my bullshit. Away from the memories threatening to puncture my brain.

But because karma is a devious bitch, I don't end up in my truck. Or even outside.

No, somehow, I run right to the place it all started.

5

BRYCE

SEPTEMBER, SENIOR YEAR, HIGH SCHOOL

"ARE YOU BRYCE DONALD?"

I bite back my grimace and ignore the girl's voice as I delete yet another message from someone I've never met. He isn't the first guy to reach out and tell me all about how great their old college's football program is, and he won't be the last.

It doesn't help that he caught me on a really shitty morning. Coach Roberts told me that, until further notice, instead of lifting each morning with the team, I'm to come to the library to work with a math tutor. He said her name was Lucy and that I was to listen to her or else. I didn't know what "or else" actually meant, but I could read the look in his eyes that said he wasn't messing around.

When I look up at this girl, who I'm guessing is around my age, she looks thoroughly annoyed. "I'm not happy being up this early so please just answer my question."

"I am. Can I ask who you are?"

My question isn't to play the role of dumb jock. I honestly don't know her, which is odd considering my graduating class is going to be seventy kids. It's not hard keeping everyone straight when you've known them since kindergarten.

From the way she is looking at me, she doesn't know me either.

"Yes, of course. I'm Lucy. Your math tutor."

My eyes grow wide at her introduction. "You're the math tutor?"

I never expected a girl who is . . . well, she's gorgeous. She's not one of those model types who guys my age go ga-ga over. But she's beautiful in her own right. Her long brown hair and black-rimmed glasses make her stand out from the crowd. She's not wearing anything flashy like some girls here who try to show off with expensive clothes, but that doesn't make her any less beautiful.

And I can't stop staring at her.

She takes a seat across from me, clearly unfazed by my confusion. "Yes. I am. Ready to start?"

I blink a few times, trying to decipher if this is real life or if I'm still sleeping and this is some really fucked-up dream.

I wish it were a dream, but the longer I sit here watching Lucy take out books and notebooks, the more I realize that no, this is real life. I'm also definitely feeling things below the belt as my apparent tutor pulls her hair up on the top of her head in that messy way girls do.

Why is that so hot?

"I'm sorry . . ."

"Lucy."

"Yeah. Lucy. Listen, I'm sorry you woke up early for this, and I'm not sure what Coach Roberts told you, but I don't need a tutor."

"Why would he tell me you did if you didn't?"

Damn, she's right. I can't think clearly. I want to blame it on being up and at school before six thirty in the morning, but it's really her big brown eyes. They are making me stupid.

"I know what I'm doing in trig," I begin, trying to figure out how to word this without sounding like a complete dumbass. "I just . . . haven't done it."

What I'm not going to say is that I'm barely passing because I've been too busy to study or do homework. In my defense, I've had a lot going on. Like football and trying to decide where I'm going to play football in college and working out for football. Oh, and there is also the constantly deleting of emails and messages from crazy fans.

Though if I don't pass trigonometry, I don't play. If I don't play, there's no chance for a state title and my scholarship offers will be out the window. But I'll pass. The teachers always make sure I do.

Lucy stops fiddling with her textbook and looks up at me. "So, you know what you're doing, but you just aren't doing it? Does Uncle Nick know this?"

"Yes. No—wait, who is Uncle Nick? And while we're at it, who are you again?"

She smirks and then tries to stifle a laugh.

"Yes, let's start over. My name is Lucy. I moved back at the beginning of this year, and Uncle Nick to me is Coach Roberts to you. He's my mom's brother."

"Coach Roberts has a niece?"

"He does."

"And you just moved here?"

"Technically, I just moved back," Lucy says matter-of-factly. "I was born here, but then my family moved to Indianapolis. Now we're back. So, here I am."

"Here you are."

I don't mean for it to come out sounding creepy, but I can't stop staring at this girl. She has a blush creeping up on her cheeks that stands out against her ivory skin, and I can't help but hope that blush is there because of me. I internally slap myself for letting my head— both of them—think like that. I don't date during football season because I need to stay focused. I barely talk to girls during school just to resist temptation. Little did I know, the biggest temptation of all would come in the form of a five-foot-nothing math tutor.

"Why haven't I seen you around school?"

She shrugs, her messy ponytail bouncing around on the top of her head. "I'm going to guess we don't exactly have the same friends."

I lean forward on my elbows. "You didn't answer my question."

She gives me a look that suggests I'm dense—or, at least, that's what I assume it is. Brenna gives me that look all the time.

"You're Bryce Donald."

"We've established that."

"Do I really have to say it?"

"Considering you haven't answered my question yet, I'm going to say yes."

She lets out a frustrated breath. "Fine. I'll say it. You're the captain of the football team, you broke Ohio's high-school record for yards passed in a season, you have your pick of which college to play for, and you are on the trajectory to be a top draft pick when you go pro. Based on high-school stereotypes and assumptions, I'm going to guess you date the head cheerleader and you're most likely to be voted homecoming king. Then there is me—captain of the mathletes and newest member of the debate team. I don't care if this is a small school, the captain of the football team doesn't hang out with the mathletes."

While everything she just said may actually be true, I like to think I'm an approachable guy. Still, high school is what it is. The jocks pal around with other jocks. The band kids stick together. If she's smart enough to be tutoring math, I'm going to guess she's in the honors classes. I'm in the classes where kids go just to pass.

"You're right."

Her eyes go a bit wide with shock. "I am? I mean, I know I am. I just didn't expect you to admit it."

I shrug, leaning back in my chair. "Can't argue with facts. Just takes one look at our cafeteria to know that. Though, I must point out that you weren't completely right. You did get a few things wrong."

"And what may I ask was that?"

I lean back forward and get the slightest whiff of her perfume. Something floral. Hmm . . . Miss Math Wiz didn't strike me as a perfume wearer. Good to know.

"I don't date the head cheerleader," I say. "First of all, she's my twin sister. And second of all, I don't date during football season."

She tilts her head, almost as if she's studying me. Usually, when I say that I'm single, I can tell the moment a girl decides it's her mission to try to lock me down.

But Lucy? That look never comes. She just studies me as if I'm an equation she can't figure out.

"Interesting. Not what I thought I would have got wrong. Based on the size of the population of the school and town, it would have been a more than forty-six percent chance that—"

"Is everything a math problem to you?"

My interruption takes her off guard. "Math is everywhere. A football player should know that."

"Touché, Lucy. Touché. Now, let's dive into this math stuff. Teach me your ways."

Ten minutes ago, I wanted nothing to do with a tutor. I still don't think I need one. But thinking about spending a few mornings a week with her? I think I can handle it.

Plus, I don't date during football season. No one, not even this girl, who is throwing me for all sorts of loops, is going to change that.

6

LUCY

COUGH DROPS. That's what I need, cough drops.

Honey lemon. Cherry. Menthol-lyptus. Give me all of them.

I put two of each flavor into my basket, scanning the rest of the aisle to see if I need anything else. Right now, talk of my wedding only makes me cough, but who knows? The closer it gets, the worse the reaction might get. I might start breaking into hives.

I pick up a box of Benadryl, some Midol for good measure, and then head to the checkout counter, only to pull to a sudden stop.

No, no, no . . . Please, God, let that not be him.

I could ask every holy being in existence not to let that be Bryce Donald, but unfortunately, they'd all let me down. It might have been more than a year since I've seen him, but I could go fifty without laying eyes on him and I'd know that profile from a mile away.

Stupid chiseled jawline and perfect features.

Bryce has always been good looking. In high school, he was your stereotypical teen heartthrob. Light brown hair that was never purposefully styled but always looked good. A muscled frame that made every girl lose their mind. Blue eyes that sucked you in from the moment they made contact with you. And don't get me started on his smile that, when he aimed it at you, made you feel like you were the only girl in the world.

But the Bryce who is standing thirty feet from me isn't the boy from high school. No, he is all man. His hair is just as messy but a little longer that he used to wear it. The muscles he had back then are nothing compared to the ones he's sporting now. I believe the term Brenna uses is "arm porn." Though she wasn't talking about her brother because that would be weird.

The longer I stand and stare at him, the more I feel like I'm being stabbed with a thousand knives that are slicing open old hurts.

I miss him so much.

I want to hit myself for thinking that because it's ninety levels of wrong. I'm engaged. I made my choice, and that was to spend the rest of my life with Luciano. I decided to quit waiting for it to be the right time in Bryce's world for him to finally be with me.

I'd be a liar if I didn't say I missed him, though. I miss our talks. I miss the way he made me feel. I miss the way he'd look at me, like he's looking at me right now.

"Shit!" I yell, realizing that in fact he is looking at me and I was caught staring. So, I do the only logical thing a grown woman can do —I turn around, run to the back of the store, and hide behind a display of potato chips.

With any luck, he'll finish checking out and then leave. There is no reason for him to come looking for me, and if he does, my hiding spot is fantastic. He'll walk right by—

"Hiding from me now, Lulu? I knew you weren't talking to me, but I didn't know hiding was also a part of it. Should have figured though."

I jump at the sound of Bryce's voice, knocking down six bags of potato chips in the process. I don't want to look at him not only because I'll have to have a conversation I've been putting off for months but also because I can hear the pain behind the arrogant tone he's trying to project.

He has every right to be mad at me.

"I wasn't hiding from you," I say as I begin to pick up the mess.

"Sure, you weren't."

The last time I looked Bryce in the eyes was the last day we were *us*. Whatever that means. I lied to him that day. Well, I didn't lie. I just didn't tell him the whole truth. I didn't tell him I was engaged. I didn't tell him that I was done waiting for him. I let him believe there was a future for us.

It was the most selfish thing I have ever done. I knew it was the last time we'd be like that, and I wanted as much time as possible. Had I told him, things would have ended far worse than they did.

And now that act of selfishness is about to bite me in the ass.

"Oh, for God's sake, Lulu, stand and look at me."

"Don't call me that," I say, reluctantly standing. "And I'm not avoiding you."

Wow, I haven't gotten any better at lying to him.

When I finally manage to look at him, I want to flinch and turn away. He's looking at me in a way I don't deserve—full of longing and hope—and I wish he would stop. I deserve his ire and mistrust.

"Oh really? You aren't avoiding me? Then what is this? Or did you mean when you wouldn't answer my phone calls after I found out from my mom you were engaged? Which time are we talking about? Cause I'm starting to lose track."

His voice is angry, and honestly, I don't blame him. But I had to dodge his calls and cut ties with him. It was the only way I'd survive. I had to make a clean break or the cycle I've come to coin as the Bryce and Lucy Saga would have just continued.

It was the same thing every time. Bryce would tell me that the season was almost over and then we could finally be together. I would wait for Bryce. The season would end and then something would happen in Bryce's life that would make this not the right time for us. Bryce would ask me to wait again, and I would. Then the cycle would start over again.

That had been my life since senior year. I had to break it. My heart couldn't handle it anymore.

I square my shoulders, doing my best to try to seem the confident woman I've become. "I'm sorry, but it was for the best."

"The best for who? And don't say it was for me because, in case you haven't heard, I'm pretty much a train wreck these days," he says bitingly.

He might as well have punched me in the heart, but his inability to handle his own life isn't really my problem. It used to be, sure, but he's an adult. It isn't fair that he would blame me for his own terrible choices. I want to be so indignant that he would do that, but I'm too full of my own guilt for doing what I did in the way I did it. He may have hurt me on a fundamental level, but that doesn't mean he doesn't deserve an explanation.

Only . . . I can't. I can't hurt him even more than I already have. I can't say the words. So, I make the second most adult decision I've made today.

I drop my basket and run.

Before the cough drops and Benadryl even hit the floor, I'm making a beeline for the exit. I know Bryce is behind me, but I have to get out of here. I may never be able to have this talk with him, but if that moment comes, it won't be at five o'clock inside the town convenience store with ten or so people watching us. It's not the place to air out our dirty laundry.

"Lulu, Stop!"

I stop and turn to find Bryce inches from me. "Don't call me that. Not anymore."

"Why? Why can't I call you that?" His face is so close to mine as he silently begs for answers. He might be trying to come off as intimidating, but my heart says otherwise having him this close.

"Because I hate it."

"Liar."

"I didn't lie to you!" I yell, knowing we're causing a scene. I feel the eyes of Laurel Heights on us.

"Yes, you did. You did then and you are now."

"I did what I thought was best."

"So you've said." His voice drips with disdain.

"I can't do this. Not now, and not here."

"Then when? When are you going to give me the explanation I

deserve? Coincidentally, it all started right after you decided I wasn't worth having in your life anymore."

Tears are burning in my eyes, but I push them back. I know I owe him an explanation, but I'm not ready.

Every time he's low, he needs me to pull him back up. Every time there is a hard decision or his dad decides to pop back into his life, I'm there to talk him through it. And, as much as it kills me not to help him, I can't. He has to learn how to navigate his problems without my help.

"Yes, you can. You've always been able to."

"Is that a joke? In case you haven't seen—"

"Oh, I've seen," I say, taking a fortifying breath. "I've seen it all. The headlines. The pictures. The games. But Bryce, you've always been able to. I've been your crutch for years, and I can't be that anymore. I'm sorry. I can't be the girl who you go to when things get hard and then leave behind with empty promises of a future that is never going to come. It's not fair to me, Bryce. It hurts me too much."

"But it was finally time!" he yells, his hands gripping my shoulders. "It was time for us."

I laugh, but there's no humor to it. "What made that time different?"

My question silences him. If he's honest with himself, he knows that's just another promise he wouldn't have kept.

I use the silence to shrug away from his hold and race to my car down the street. Thankful that I left it unlocked, I hurry and get in, immediately locking it and firing up the engine.

When I look back toward the front of the store with tears streaming down my face, I don't see the man who has been on the front page of every tabloid in America.

I see the lost boy I first fell in love with.

7

———

LUCY

OCTOBER, SENIOR YEAR, HIGH SCHOOL

"BRYCE! EARTH TO BRYCE! HELLOOOOO!!!"

I know I shouldn't be yelling in a library, but I don't feel bad considering he and I are the only ones here.

And he is currently asleep.

"Bryce!" I yell again, giving his arm a nudge.

"What?" he says, jumping a bit, which would be funny if I weren't so annoyed that he fell asleep.

"I know morning tutoring sessions aren't ideal, but the least you could do is try to stay awake."

"I can't help it," he says mid yawn. "This is boring, and I was up late last night."

"I don't care if you think it's boring. You have a test tomorrow, and you aren't ready for it. What were you doing up anyway? Don't tell me studying because I know that's a lie."

"You wound me." He puts his hand over his heart. "If you must know, I was going over college brochures."

I have to blink a few times because that was not the answer I was expecting. I was waiting to hear something football related. In the month I've known Bryce, I have come to learn that the man eats, sleeps, and breathes football. I suppose it's why he's so good. Though, I can't imagine one thing taking up so much time of my life. I mean, I love math and all, but I'm not up at two in the morning simplifying equations.

"Really? You don't know where you are going yet?"

He just shrugs, pulling the textbook back in front of him. "I have a bunch of offers, but I haven't been able to figure out which school is going to be best for me. So, I figured maybe if I looked at the colleges a little more it could help my decision."

I'm pretty sure my mouth is open a bit.

"What?" he asks

"I'm just surprised."

"Why?"

"Because I didn't think of you as the guy to go through college brochures to help make your decision on where to play football."

"And why is that? Because I'm the dumb jock who needs trig tutoring?"

"No. I didn't say that," I say, closing the textbook. "I never said you were dumb. In fact, I don't think you need me at all. It's just that, in the time I've known you, every decision you have made has had football as the deciding factor. I figured you would have already made a decision on school."

He seems to calm down a little and slouches down in his chair. "Thanks. Too bad it was a waste of time. I can't figure anything out, and I need to make a decision soon."

"Says who?"

"Everyone."

"Who is everyone? Because by the definition of everyone, I would be included, and I can guarantee you I am not waiting on pins and needles for you to tell me where you're going to college."

That makes him smile, which makes me feel . . . well, I don't know how to describe this feeling. Maybe it's as if a family of butterflies have taken up residence in my stomach.

"Fine. Everyone is Coach, my parents, and Cole, who is insisting we honor a blood oath we made when we were ten and swore we would play football on the same team for the rest of our lives. Fans, recruiters, and even other quarterbacks around the country who are waiting to see what I do so they don't commit to the same team I do. It's . . . it's just a lot. How do you make a decision that pleases everyone when it can make or break your entire future?"

I take a second to look at him and don't see the football player who walks the fine line between confident and cocky.

I see a teenage boy who is just as confused about life as the rest of us.

"Is there anyone you can talk to? Maybe someone can help you make a pros and cons list? Uncle Nick? A guidance counselor?"

He just laughs and shakes his head. "Every person thinks I should do something different. Mom wants me at Ohio State because she wants me close to home. Coach thinks I should go to Auburn because of their track record of putting quarterbacks in the league. Dad wants me to go to Alabama, but I'm pretty sure a booster is padding his pockets so he'll talk me into going there."

"What?" No way I just heard him right. "Fans are paying off your family to get you to go to their school?"

"I think. I'm not sure," he says, the defeat clear in his voice. "I can't figure out another reason why my so-called father, who barely cared to come watch my high school games, is so intent on me going to a school I haven't even visited."

"Wow," I say. "College football is a whole other world."

"Tell me about it," he says, starting to doodle in a notebook. "I just I wish I knew the right answer. I never thought I'd say this, but I wish it were like trig. Only one right answer."

I pause and wonder if I should point out that he never once said what he wanted to do. He only outlined what everyone else wanted him to do. He is trying so hard to please other people that he is putting the most important person's wishes on the back burner.

His own.

"You want this to have a right answer? Then let's figure it out," I say as I grab the notebook from under his hand.

"Lucy, I appreciate it, but there is no—"

"Shh. Who is the tutor here?"

This earns me another smile. "You are."

"Then let me help you figure out this problem. First, where do you not want to go. Don't think about anyone else. Just you."

"But, Lu—"

"Nope," I say in my best no-nonsense voice. "This is your decision. No one else's. While you respect their opinions, you have to figure this out on your own. This is your career. Your future. So, let's start with the places you cannot imagine playing a day of football."

"But they are all good—"

"Are you listening to me, Donald? Shut off the brain for five seconds, and then, on the count of three, I want you to tell me the one school you'd rather quit playing football than to play for."

"You'd be a great football coach," he teases.

"You aren't doing it."

"It's not going to work."

"Humor me."

"Fine," he says reluctantly.

"Ready? One . . . two . . . three."

"Ohio State."

His eyes grow wide, and his hand immediately covers his mouth.

"See? It worked."

"My mom is going to be so mad, and it's my in-state school. Fans are going to go ape shit."

"Who the heck cares what the fans say, and your mom will be fine so long as you're happy," I say, ripping off a piece of notebook paper. "She might like you to be close, but at the end of the day, she wants you to be happy. And those fans? They only want you for how far you can throw a football. They don't matter. Now, let's keep going."

For the next half hour, Bryce and I write a pro-and-con list for every school that has made him an offer. We quickly eliminate the state schools. Any schools with snow are a no. I don't blame him. A chance to get away from snow sounds amazing. We also cross off Alabama just in case his dad is getting paid off.

Five pieces of paper later, he writes down one word: Clemson.

"Is that it?" I ask, hoping I didn't rush him. "Is that where you want to go?"

He looks at the paper and back up to me with confidence back in his eyes. "Yeah. Yeah, it is. I love the atmosphere. They have a great rate of turning players pro. I can win a championship there. They want Cole just as much as they want me. It's . . . that's it. That's where I'm going to go."

I grin and clean up the papers I've strewn over the table. "See? That wasn't so hard, was it?"

He laughs, also gathering his stuff as the first bell of the day rings. "Who knew a good pro-con list was what I needed?"

"I find most life decisions can be made with a solid pro-con list."

I start to walk out of the library when I feel his hand on my arm. When I turn back around, I see a look on Bryce's face that I've never seen before.

It's . . . happy. Relaxed. Free.

Before I know it, Bryce's arms are wrapped around me. I'm too stunned at first to return the embrace. It's not like I've never been hugged before. I've even shared hugs with guy friends. It's just that, as I wrap my arms around his waist, I realize that being in this position with Bryce is like nothing I've ever experienced before.

"Thanks, Lulu. For everything."

His words are a whisper against my ear and send a shiver down my body. It's probably why I don't realize for a few seconds that he called me . . . Lulu?

"What did you call me?"

"Lulu," he says, and even though I can't see him, I know there is a smile forming on his lips. "Is that okay?"

"I guess so?"

"Well, get used to it. From now on, to me, you're Lulu."

"What if I don't like it?"

"Too bad."

I've never had a nickname. Well, my real name is Lucia, but no one calls me that except my mom and the Tripolis. It's always just been Lucy.

For some reason, the thought of having a name that only Bryce calls me . . . well, it makes me feel the same way it does when I make him laugh or smile.

Like a million butterflies are fluttering in my stomach.

Though, I'd never tell him that.

"Come on," he says, taking my books from me. "I'll walk you to your next class."

8

———————

BRYCE

FOR THE SECOND week in a row, I watch my team win without me, and it feels just as bad as it did the first time.

Though, it's not just because I've been told I'm done for the season.

Last week, I hadn't seen Lucy. Last week, I hadn't been reacquainted with her big brown eyes or her floral perfume. I had almost forgotten what it smelled like.

Almost.

It took all I had not to try to wrap myself in her orbit, where everything is always okay.

She's my safe space. My calm when things get too loud.

At least, she used to be.

The diamond on her hand reminded me that she's no longer my Lulu. She's someone else's. I don't even know who she's marrying. When I found out, I didn't ask because the only thing that mattered was that it wasn't me.

"Well don't you look like a ray of sunshine."

I glare at Brenna, who is walking into the house with my mom, grocery bags in tow. "Have you ever thought of giving up teaching for comedy?"

"Nah. People aren't ready for my brand of humor," she says as she begins to unpack the bags. "What did you do today? Wait. Let me guess. You watched your team play football without you then moped instead of working on getting reinstated."

"Brenna, be nice to your brother," Mom says, her tone the same one she used when my sister and I fought when we were kids. "He's working through things, and that doesn't happen in a few days."

"Thank you, Mom, and I'm not moping," I say, doing my best not to sound like I am. "I'm lying low, which is what my agent and the coaches told me to do."

Brenna puts the last of the groceries away and takes a seat on the other side of the couch. "I'm pretty sure they didn't mean for you to come here and do nothing. If I were to guess, I would say they meant for you to work out your shit so you can go back and play the game they are paying you millions to play. Have you set up an appointment with any of the therapists your agent recommended?"

I haven't, which I don't admit. I'm not ready to talk to anyone about what's been going on in my head or admit I have issues I need to work on. After this past week, though, it's getting harder for me to deny it.

It's hard opening up to someone, especially when I used to have a person to talk to about that stuff and that person is gone.

"You know you can stay here as long as you'd like," Mom says, taking a seat on the other side of the room. "I like having you back."

"You like having a lump on a couch?" Brenna jabs.

"He's not a lump," Mom says. "I've always liked having my children home. In fact, it makes me wish he played closer or that my only daughter didn't move out the second she could afford her own place."

"Don't start, Mom," I say because I already know where this conversation is going. "You know there was never a chance I was going to play pro ball in Cincinnati."

"A mother can dream," she says as she stands and grabs her phone. "I'm going to call for the pizza. Brenna, are you staying for dinner?"

"Do I have a choice?"

"No you don't."

"Then get one with pineapple and one without."

"Anything for my babies. Oh, I just love having you both here."

Mom leaves the living room, and I swear I see her skipping. That woman is way too excited for me to be home. It doesn't matter that I'm here against my will and for reasons no mother should be proud of.

"You think she's going to kidnap me and make me move back in?" Brenna asks.

I laugh, but only because it's an actual possibility. "I'm surprised she let you move out in the first place."

She turns off the television. "I didn't tell her. Signed the lease and was moved in before she realized my stuff was gone. It was the only way."

"You broke free. I'm proud of you, sis."

That makes it sound like Brenna was serving a jail sentence, but it was nothing of the sort. Everyone thinks their mother is the best, but ours truly is. She never missed a game when I was growing up or an event that Brenna and the cheer squad were performing at.

Then there is our Sunday pizza tradition. It started when she had to tell us that she and Dad were splitting up. She thought that if she had our favorite meal—pizza from Tripoli's—that it would lessen the blow.

Somehow, it did. It also helped that she talked to us like adults, even though we were still three months away from our eighth birthdays. Our mom just has a way of knowing what we need even when we don't.

Ever since then, Sunday has been pizza night. What started as a way to heal our hearts became a tradition. On the weekends we spent with our dad, she always had the pizza ready for us when we came home. During high school, it was the one meal each week we made sure to eat together.

"Speaking of breaking free," Brenna says, turning to face me. "How long *are* you going to stay here? Don't get me wrong, I love that the town gossip has switched from the installation of solar panels to you and Lucy fighting in the street, but I don't think that's why the coaches sent you back here."

I groan. "Heard about that, did you?"

"Who hasn't? You should be happy I didn't call you a second after it happened. What were you thinking?"

"Clearly, I wasn't thinking at all. It was the first time I'd seen Lucy since everything happened, and I wanted answers. She owes me answers."

Brenna raises an eyebrow. "What if someone had recorded it and posted it online? I'm sure that video would have gone great right next to the one of you getting a lap dance from the cleat chaser."

Shit, I hadn't even thought of that. When I saw her hiding behind the aisle, thinking a bag of Doritos was going to mask her from me, all I could think about was that I needed to talk to her. The last time I saw her, we were supposed to have forever in front of us, and then she was gone, and I needed to know why.

"It might not have been the best move, but what should I have done? Ignore her? Pretend like she didn't exist? Not confront her with questions I've been saving for nine months?"

When I found out Lucy was engaged, I bypassed the whole five stages of grief and went right to drinking myself stupid every night and fucking any woman who wanted a piece of me. Her absence broke me in a way I couldn't deal with, and I acted like an ass. I've been a shitty teammate. I've turned into a PR nightmare. And I've pushed away everyone and anyone who tried to reason with me simply because they weren't her.

Lucy is the only one who can. That's what she does. She fixes me. She takes the broken pieces of me and puts them back together.

Or, at least, she used to.

"You never answered my question."

I look over at Brenna, feeling completely defeated. "Which one?"

"The one about when you're going back to Nashville?"

"Not sure," I admit, my voice filled with defeat.

A silence falls over the two of us as Mom makes her way back to the living room.

"I'm going to go get the pizza," she says, grabbing her keys and purse.

"No," I say as I push to my feet. "I can get it."

Mom shoots Brenna a panicked look before looking back at me. "You sure? You said you didn't want to go out a lot. It might not be a good—"

I take her hand in mine, lowering her keys. "It's just pizza, Mom. I think I can handle a pickup. Consider this me not being a lump on the couch. Plus, I haven't driven my truck since I've been home. It will do me some good to get out."

"Bryce!" Brenna shouts. "Mom is right. I don't think this is a good idea."

"Oh, for the love of God, Brenna. It's pizza. I'm not in high school anymore. I'm not going to cause a scene at Tripoli's. There is nothing to worry about."

9

______

LUCY

BENEFIT OF HAVING a fiancé who owns the town pizza place? Access to my favorite food whenever I want it.

Downside of having a fiancé who owns the town pizza place? Access to my favorite food whenever I want it when I also need to fit into a wedding dress in a few weeks.

It's been three days since I saw Bryce, and I swear I have eaten four large pies with extra cheese, three orders of cheese bread, and a whole dessert pizza. Apparently, I cough when I think about my wedding and stress eat when I think about my . . . whatever the hell Bryce is.

Ex-boyfriend? I mean, technically yes. Though, we were actually together for such short a time that I doubt it even counts.

Friend? Friend doesn't really scratch the surface of what our relationship was.

What Bryce and I shared was something that can't be explained. Our friendship was a force so deep I thought it could never be broken. I was his calming voice when things got too loud. He was the one who taught me that it's okay if not everything had an exact answer or neat formula. We understood each other like no one ever has or likely ever will. I could feel him in a room before he even entered. It's like my heart knew when he was near.

He was my best friend. Until he wasn't. And yes, I may be the one to blame for that, but no one told me that the worst thing I could have done was fall in love with my best friend.

"Amore! What do I owe the pleasure on a Sunday?"

Luciano's voice pulls me from the unhealthy rabbit hole my mind was about to go down. I hurry to plaster a smile onto my lips as he comes around the corner from the kitchen.

"Can't a girl want to see her fiancé and maybe grab some dinner?"

He wipes his hands on the front of his apron before bringing me in a little closer and placing a gentle kiss on my forehead.

Oh, Luciano . . . if there is one thing I can count on about this man it's his predictability. Whenever we see each other—it could be him coming over to my house for a date night or in the middle of a crowded restaurant—I'm greeted with a quick kiss on the forehead.

Never anything more. Never anything less.

It's one of the many things that makes him, well, him. Even when we were kids, Luciano was an adult in a child's body. He was a rule follower. He was the student teachers always made line leader. It's why his parents made him a manager here when we were seventeen. It's why he's about to take the family business and grow it by leaps and bounds, leading up to a franchising endeavor that would put Tripoli's all over the state of Ohio.

He's a good, upstanding man. I may not ever get surprised with flowers just because, but I also never have to worry about what's around the corner.

"A girl can, and I know you love my pizza, but this is the third night in a row. Everything okay?"

Luciano guides me to an open booth and we sit across from each other. I would reach for his hands, but I know he doesn't like PDA, so I keep them to myself.

"Everything is fine. I'm just stressed with the wedding and cooking is the last thing I want to do. Besides, why would I go anywhere else when I can come here and get my favorite food and see my favorite guy?"

He gives me a soft smile. "I hate that you are stressed about the wedding. I wish I could do more to help."

"You are doing more than enough. You organized and planned all the food at a discount. Do you know how happy that made me? You're already the best husband ever."

He laughs softly and reaches for my hands, twining his fingers through mine.

I barely manage to stop myself from raising my eyebrows in shock.

"I want to be."

His words are so soft I'm not sure I hear them. That and I can't stop staring at our joined fingers.

"Want to be what?"

He lets out a sigh before saying, "The best husband. You deserve that. You deserve the world. And I'm not sure if I'm the man to give that to you."

"Luciano, I don't know why you're worrying. You make me happy. I can only hope I make you as happy as—"

The sound of the bell over the door has me glancing toward it. Blood rushes to my brain so fast that I might pass out as I watch the door of Tripoli's swing open.

That's the effect Bryce Donald has on me. Always has.

It happened the first day I met him when I was his trigonometry tutor. Back then, it took me almost ten minutes to work up the courage to go over and introduce myself.

It's happening now as I feel his presence as he charges toward our table.

"Bryce . . ."

He doesn't say anything, which is making me more nervous than if he were yelling. He just looks down at us completely expressionless.

That's when it hits me. What he's looking at. Why he's not saying anything.

I follow his eyes down to the table where my hands are linked with Luciano's. My engagement ring glinting in the fluorescent lights of the restaurant.

"Him! Out of all the men in this town and you pick him?"

The neutral-to-anger shift is so sudden it makes me jump in my booth. Though, I should have expected this reaction.

"Bryce, you need to calm down."

"Why, Lucy?" His voice grows louder with each word. I'm pretty sure the cooks in the back can hear him. "You don't want me to cause a scene? Maybe that's our thing now. Hell, I've caused plenty here over the years, why not another one for old time's sake?"

Luciano lets go of my hands and quickly stands, going toe-to-toe with Bryce. "How dare you come into my restaurant and talk to my fiancée that way."

Oh God . . . it's high school all over again.

I stand, quickly putting myself between them.

"Luciano, how about you go back and finish making our dinner. We'll take it to go."

"But, Lucia—"

I put my hands on his chest, hoping to calm him down. "It's okay. I'll handle it."

Luciano takes my hand and gives it a quick kiss, never dropping his stare from Bryce. I wish I had two seconds to be shocked that my fiancé kissed my hand for the first time in our relationship, but no, I have to deal with Bryce before he explodes.

"You. Outside. Now."

"Oh, come on, Lulu, we were just getting reacquainted."

I narrow my eyes at Bryce. "Get. Outside. Now."

Bryce laughs, which fuels my anger, but he does as I said and heads to the door, pushing it open more forcefully than need be.

"What the hell was that?" I ask the second I'm outside.

He stops and turns to me, but his face is no longer angry. It's blank. Emotionless. I think I preferred anger. I know how to handle angry Bryce. Indifferent Bryce? It leaves me floundering.

"Like a brother to you, huh?"

"Listen, I can—"

"In high school," he says coolly. "I always thought he had a thing for you, but you always said you only saw him like a brother.

Something about your families being friends? Funny how that worked out, huh?"

Now, it's my turn to be angry. "That was the truth. Back then, there was nothing romantic between us."

"And now?"

I open my mouth to say something, anything, but nothing comes out.

Maybe because if I said there was something romantic between us it would be a lie. I love Luciano, just not in the romantic way. This is a marriage of convenience—at least, for me it is. I've denied that for long enough, and it feels good to admit that to myself.

Luciano was the right man at the right time when I finally realized I was done waiting for Bryce. I wanted to begin the next part of my life. I wanted to be with someone who would put me first and never make me wonder if I'd make the cut of things he'd care about that day. Yes, I could have dated and tried to find someone I loved and who was ready for a committed relationship. But I didn't. I said yes to the first man who asked me to marry him. I said yes to the first man who asked because all I wanted to do was break the vicious Bryce Donald cycle and let me move on with my life, even if I don't feel "that" kind of love toward him.

"Why didn't you tell me you were engaged? And to him? Why Lucy? Just tell me why."

I look down, unable to meet his eyes. They are too full of hurt and anger. It's too much.

"I didn't know how to tell you. When I saw you last season, you were already dealing with so much, and I didn't know how to tell you I was engaged. So, I didn't. I took my ring off and didn't tell you."

Bryce just stares at me, his face emotionless. "When did you start seeing him?"

Tears threaten at the corners of my eyes because this might be harder to tell him than anything else.

"Right after the draft."

I look up and see the moment the realization hits him. His body goes from still and stoic to looking like a volcano about to erupt. Let him be mad all he wants at the timing, but at the end of the day, he's the one who broke another promise.

He's the reason I went out with Luciano in the first place.

"How could you?"

"How could I?" I scoff. "I was *tired*, Bryce. I was tired of hearing the same lines over and over. I was tired of waiting. So, I stopped waiting."

"You could have told me. You could have told me our time ran out. Have a little respect for me."

"I do respect you."

"No you don't. If you did, you would have told me about him. You would have told me you were engaged. You would have told me that we didn't have a chance."

"I tried!" I scream, my voice just as loud as his because, how dare he make this out to be all my fault. "I tried, Bryce, but someone—that would be you—would never take no for an answer. Every time I tried to give us a clean break, you came back with talk of next year, asking me to wait just a little longer. You were the one who refused to listen, but I was the one who fell for it. Every time you let me down, my heart broke a little more. After the draft? What we shared that day? That just sealed the deal."

"You still didn't tell me you were engaged. That we can both agree on. Why, Lucy? When were you going to tell me about that? When I got an invitation to the wedding?"

"I don't know, okay? I don't know!" I begin pacing because it's all I can do to keep from ripping my hair out. "When I saw you in Cincinnati, you were a mess. Your rookie year wasn't going as planned, and I didn't think hearing about my engagement was what was going to pull you out of your slump. So, did I withhold the truth? Yes, but I did it for you. I didn't want you to spiral."

"Well, that worked out exactly to plan," he says sarcastically. "Look at me, Lucy. You did this. If you would have just told me—"

"Oh no you don't!" I stop pacing to glare at him. "You don't get to put your spiral on me. I didn't put a bottle in your hand. I didn't tell you to become a playboy. I didn't tell you to quit caring about your career. You did that, Bryce. Do you really think that if I had told you that day, or even when it happened, you would have acted differently? No, I don't think you would have. So, vilify me all you want, but don't try to tell me your garbage choices are my fault. I was just smart enough to finally realize that there's never an offseason with you, which meant there would never be a time for us."

He doesn't say anything or try to dispute my final claim, and I'm not waiting for him to.

He knows I'm right.

I take a few steps toward him, gently placing my hand on his heart. "I'm sorry. I truly am."

His hand covers mine, and for a second, I let myself get lost in the feel of his touch. Of the feel of his calloused fingers against my skin and the warmth that soaks into me every time we touch.

Then I remember where I am and the choices I've made and quickly walk back into the restaurant.

10

———

LUCY

NOVEMBER, SENIOR YEAR, HIGH SCHOOL

"WHY DO I give a shit about how tall a tree is? When in the hell am I ever going to have to know something like that?"

I let out a frustrated sigh and redraw the equation. "Probably never, but you need to understand the equation to pass this test and play this week, so focus."

I begin to cross out what he did wrong, and Bryce reaches across the table to try to grab a slice of pizza.

"No," I say, slapping his hand. "No pizza until you correct this."

"Ouch!" He shakes his hand as if I actually hurt him, which is unlikely. I saw how hard he gets hit during a game. I highly doubt my little slap did more than annoy him. "Why would you invite me to study at a pizza joint if I can't eat pizza while I do this crap? That's pretty mean of you Lulu."

"Listen, I'm still not sure if I'm a fan of that name," I say as I push the notebook back in front of him. "And I have to work at six and you have to take a pizza home to your mom and sister. We're being practical."

"That's my Lulu. Always the practical one." He flashes me that cocky smile before bending to begin reworking the problem, and I fight away my own.

It might be the nickname, or the fact that we now spend every day together, but I can't seem to stop smiling when it comes to Bryce. There's something special about him, and I'm not just talking about on the football field.

After he begged me to come watch him play, I caved and went to his game last week. The whole time I sat in those stands, I was in awe of what he could do on the field.

The Bryce I'm talking about, though, is one not many people get to see. I'm talking about the guy who follows me home every time we study late to make sure I get home safely. I'm talking about the guy who got me my favorite donut last week because I said on one of our now nightly FaceTimes that I liked them. He's the guy who walks me to every class even if it means he's going to be late to his own.

I'm talking about the guy who I think I'm falling for but who doesn't see me as anything more than his math tutor.

I shake my head, refocusing on Bryce working through this math problem. This is what I'm here for. Uncle Nick told me to make sure he passes trigonometry. I'm not supposed to be swooning over him like every other teenage girl in Laurel Heights.

But Bryce wasn't lying when he said he doesn't date during the football season. When he first said it, I didn't believe him. Then I watched him turn down Moriah Marks, who was very up front with him about what she would let him do to her while she was in her cheerleading uniform.

The man is focused on the game and nothing else.

"Am I right? Do I get pizza?"

"Sure. Yeah. Go for it."

"I knew you'd cave," he says, passing the notebook to me as he grabs a slice of Tripoli's famous supreme pizza.

"I was just tired of hearing you complain," I say as I check over each step of the equation. "But you would have gotten one anyways. You got it right."

"Hell yeah!" he says, pumping his fist like he just threw a touchdown. "That means another slice."

"How about another problem," I say before I start to draw a triangle. His hand covering mine stops me, and I blink at it dumbly for a second before slowly forcing my attention to his face.

"How about we take a break from math and you enjoy a slice of pizza with me?"

Honestly, no one has ever looked at me like the way Bryce is looking at me right now. It's as if there is no one else in the restaurant but us. Like life outside of this booth doesn't exist.

It's just him, me, and this moment.

"Lucia, it's time to clock in, and I believe this is for you, Donald."

Luciano drops the pizza box onto the table, and I quickly pull my hand out from under Bryce's. Just when I'm about to tell Luciano that I'll be right back there, Bryce takes back my hand.

"She'll be there in a second," Bryce says, cockiness oozing from his words. "I don't think I *really* understand this math problem yet, so we're going to be a few more minutes. But thanks for bringing me my pizza. The service here is impeccable."

Luciano stares at our joined hands with narrowed eyes before he turns his gaze back to Bryce. "You are not her job or her boyfriend. You should not be holding her hand in public. Tripoli's is her job. She needs to get to work. Lucia, let's go."

"You can't tell her what to do," Bryce says, letting go of my hand to stand as if he's about to go toe-to-toe with Luciano.

"I'm her boss," Luciano says, not backing down. "And if I understand correctly, you are nothing more than the boy who she is helping pass math class."

I quickly stand from my side of the booth and slide between them.

"Luciano. I'll be right there," I say, pleading with my old family friend and boss to cut me a little slack. "Please let me finish then I'll clock in."

I don't move as Luciano and Bryce send each other one more round of dirty looks before he goes back into the kitchen.

"What was that?" I ask as I take my seat again.

"You know he likes you, right?"

I give Bryce a confused look. Maybe he got hit in the head last week and I didn't know about it. "No, he doesn't. It's . . . he's Luciano. He's like a brother to me and I've known him as long as I've been alive."

"Yes, he does, Lulu. His thoughts? Not very brotherly."

I feel the blush creep onto my face as Bryce reaches for my hand again.

The first time I wasn't sure what was happening. But now?

Oh my God, Bryce Donald is holding my hand.

On purpose.

Cue freak out.

"Well, he shouldn't feel that way," I say with as much confidence as I can muster. "Because we're just friends even if our moms like to joke that we are going to get married one day."

Bryce laughs. "Believe me, Lulu, he wants what your mothers want. And now he hates me because I'm the one holding your hand and he's not."

I shake my head. "Whatever. I need to go to work before he comes back out here."

I hurry and stand from the booth, but before I can leave, Bryce grabs my elbow.

"Was it okay that I held your hand?" Bryce asks softly, the cockiness and anger now long gone.

I nod. I want to tell him it was more than okay and that he can do it whenever he wants, but the words won't come.

Without letting go of me, Bryce stands. "He said something that I'm not sure I like."

"Yeah? And what was that?" He actually said more than one thing that I didn't like, but I'm curious as to what set Bryce off.

He takes my other hand in his. "He said that I'm not your boyfriend, and I don't like the sound of that very much."

I'm pretty sure if I saw myself in a mirror, my eyes would be as big as basketballs.

"But . . . I . . . I'm sorry?"

Talk about throwing a girl for a loop. Of all the things he could have said, that was the one thing I hadn't expected.

"What I mean is, when he said I wasn't your boyfriend, it felt like I was punched in the gut. Sure, it may be true, but if I were your boyfriend, I'd get to hold your hand all the time. Give you a hug and a kiss like I want to every day but I can't."

"But it's football season . . ."

I know that probably isn't the best thing to point out, but I'm in a bit of shock. Yes, I'm going to blame it on the pure shock over what he just admitted.

"I know, and while I might not be the best boyfriend over the next few weeks because of the playoffs, I can't go another day just being your friend."

Be Bryce Donald's girlfriend? I can't lie, I've thought about it. Many times. Many nights when we were on the phone, talking way too late into the night about stupid things like television shows or our favorite toys when we were kids.

"I don't want to get in the way. I know how important football is to you. I don't want to rock your boat."

He grins. "I know. That's also how I know you're it for me. You know what football means to me. So, I think I've come up with a solution."

"Is that right?"

"Yup. So, I'm going to ask you to give me six weeks."

"Six weeks?"

"Yup. That's when the state championship game is and also when the season ends."

Could I wait six, short weeks to be his girlfriend? I'm pretty sure that's the dumbest question I've ever asked myself.

When I don't answer right away, Bryce laughs softly and shifts closer to me. "In six weeks, I'm going to ask you on a date. A real one. Our real first date. Not one where you bring math books and bribe me with pizza. One where I put on a shirt with buttons and you wear something that will make me crazy and we spend the entire night together. Just you and me."

"I like the sound of that."

He smiles at me, and it's as if he just got the perfect present from Santa.

"You just agreed to a date, we're in the playoffs, and Clemson is processing my scholarship information. All my dreams are about to come true."

"That's amazing, Bryce."

He brings our joined hands to his heart. I'm thankful that his is beating as fast as mine is.

"I'm so close to finishing out my high school career exactly how I wanted. But I can't go another day without being able to sneak a kiss from you when I drop you off for English class. I want to drive you to school and hold your hand the whole way. I want you in the stands at every one of my games with my number painted on your face. Hell, I want to go to your math tournaments and make signs and cheer you on when you get the answer to a problem I don't understand."

This makes me laugh because, somehow, I'm imagining him and Cole at a math tournament with painted chests.

"I can't get you out of my head, Lucy. You and football, it's all I think about. So, right now, if you'll have me, I'd love for you to be my girlfriend. And in six weeks, when things settle down, I'm going to take you on a night you'll never forget."

"Yes."

The word comes out of my mouth before I can stop it—not that I'd have said anything different.

The smile he gives me is the biggest one I've ever seen. Then he presses his lips to the back of my hand, and yup, there they are . . . the butterflies are back.

Or maybe they are here because I just officially became Bryce Donald's girlfriend.

11

BRYCE

WHEN I FIRST FOUND OUT THAT Lucy was engaged, I got drunk. Feels fitting that I do the same thing on the night I find out who she's marrying.

Correction, I am drunk and getting drunker. With any luck, it will only take a few more beers and another shot of Jack for me to erase the image of Lucy holding hands with that pizza fuck face.

Yes, I've known for months that she was engaged, but seeing her tonight with him hit me in a whole new way.

It's real. She's engaged. She's his.

It's no longer a hypothetical thing I try to drink away every night.

"Fuck 'em all!" I yell, tossing another empty beer can from the bed of my truck toward Lake Laurel in the distance. It's called a lake when, really, it's an overgrown pond. But what do I know? I'm just the guy who can't seem to get anything right.

"That's the best throw you've made all year."

I turn and squint at the hallucination of Cole Campbell standing behind me. He's in Nashville.

Without me.

With the winning team.

"Get out of here, imaginary Cole," I say as I crack open another beer. "I betchu are here to judge me just like real Cole. Well, I don't need it from either of you! Unless imaginary Cole has more beer. Then he can stay."

Imaginary Cole laughs as his shadow—well, shadows because I think there are three of them—walks toward my truck.

"You have always been a shit drunk," imaginary Cole says, hopping up to sit next to me on my tailgate.

Damn, imaginary Cole weighs a lot. I didn't know imaginary people weighed anything, but the tailgate bounced around like real Cole sat on it.

Or maybe I'm that drunk. Probably that.

"Not a shit drunk. Imma good drunk. Except I usually don't talk to imaginary people when I'm drunk, so maybe I am a bad drunk. Imma bad quarterback. Imma bad drunk. Imma bad boyfriend. I fucking suck."

It takes me a solid five seconds to register the fact that the smack I just felt on the back of my head was in fact real. Only then do I look to my right.

Holy shit, imaginary Cole is real, and he looks pissed. All three of him.

"What are you doing here?"

He cracks open a beer and takes a drink before answering. "Early game. Bye week next week. Was planning on coming back anyway to check on you and see my folks. Then I got a text that said I should probably get here sooner rather than later. Honestly, I'm just glad I'm not bailing you out of jail."

"I'm really not a fan of you and Brenna talking as much as you do." Though I don't blame my sister for calling him. After I left Tripoli's, I texted Brenna that she needed to go get the pizza. When she asked me what happened, I hung up, turned off my phone, and drove to the liquor store before coming here.

"It wasn't your sister."

I don't have to be sober to know he means Lucy. Why she would call Cole when she wants nothing to do with me, though, is a mystery.

"So, you drove all this way to do, what? Lecture me again? To pass along how disappointed McAvoy is in me? Fine then. Let me at least get another beer before you tell me for the millionth time that I'm a train wreck. Good news. I have figured out that I'm a train wreck. To being a train wreck!"

I sway back and forth as I wind my arm back to throw my newly empty beer can toward the lake. I try to reach for a new one, but Cole rips it from my hand and throws it toward the shoreline.

I liked him better when he was imaginary.

"No more."

I try to focus my eyes but the damn world won't hold still long enough for me to do it. "You always were the fun killer."

"Someone has to be the responsible one, and God knows it's not you."

I shoot him a look. At least I think I do. I really can't feel my face. "No one ever told you that you were responsible for me. You aren't my father."

"Thank God for that."

I mostly fall to my ass in the bed of the truck, too pissed that Cole chucked my last beer to say anything else.

"Do you remember what I told you before our first game?" Cole's voice is back to even, which means he's about to go into lecture mode, and I groan.

"Which first game?"

"The very first."

I fall backward and look up at the sky as I think back to all those years ago. We were six. It was Laurel Heights Little Tigers football. I was the quarterback and Cole was my center. Later in his career he was moved to left tackle to protect my blindside. Back then, he was the only one who could figure out how to snap the ball.

"You told me not to drop the ball."

He barks out a laugh. "The other thing, asshole."

I let out a sigh. "That you'd always protect me. That no one would get to me if you had anything to do with it."

I remember thinking that he was nuts because he was talking like an adult, but that's always been Cole—the guy was six going on thirty.

We were also in Pop Warner football. It wasn't like I was about to be tackled by a three-hundred-pound linebacker.

In true Cole fashion, he kept his word. I don't think I got sacked until high school, and that was because he was out with mono and couldn't play that game.

Who knew the words of a six-year-old would hold so much truth? This man has lined up with me in every level of football, which is unheard of in this day and age of recruiting and professional ball. From what started with the Little Tigers that led to high school, which led to college at Clemson, and then to Nashville with the Fury.

The man has had my back, and my front, for my entire life. He's kept me alive—literally and figuratively.

"Whether you care to admit it or not, you need me," Cole says. "Only this time, I'm not blocking guys who want to rip your head off."

"Then who are you protecting me from?"

"Yourself, you asshole. I'm protecting you from yourself. The fact that you can't see that means you haven't figured out shit since you've been here."

He's right, of course. He's been right all along. I was just too stubborn or prideful or stupid to admit it.

Probably all of the above.

I'm spiraling. I'm out of control. I'm my own, and everyone else's, worst enemy. And it's all because, for the first time in my life, I lost. I lost her, and I didn't know how to handle it. Correction, I *don't* know how to handle it. Throw that on top of the other things in my life that I'm barely holding on to with a string, and that leads to the absolute shit show that has become my life.

"Is this the right time to tell you I'm sorry?" While I didn't expect Cole to give me a big hug and tell me everything is okay, I definitely didn't expect him to laugh. "What's so funny?"

"That you need permission to apologize. I find it amusing. Has the great Bryce Donald never done this before?"

I can probably count on both hands how many times I've had to admit I'm wrong, and most of them have been to my mom.

"What I was going to say is that I'm sorry. I was a dick to you. Not just the day I left Nashville but also over the past nine months. Ever since I . . . well, you know. You tried to help me, but I didn't want it."

"And now? Are you ready for help now?"

Isn't that the million-dollar question.

"I have no idea how to do this without her," I admit, the words tasting vile as they pass through my lips for the first time. "She was my calm. My center. You've always been there for me, but with her? It was different. I love her. I love her so fucking much I can't see straight. I waited too long, and now she's gone and there is all of this . . . this . . . shit that I've let build up. Endorsement deals are ready to drop me. The team probably hates me. My dad won't leave me alone. For the last seven years, when something like this happened, I would go to her. And now I can't. She's not mine anymore. Maybe she never was to begin with."

"You're right."

I have to blink a few times because did I hear him right or is that me making things up because I'm still pretty drunk. "Did you just say I was right?"

"Focus here, Donald. But yes, you're right. You have shit. Some of it you built on yourself, some of it comes with the price of being a professional football player. And yes, you have to learn to do this without her. It has been nine months. She's moved on. Now it's time for you to. I guess the question is, how do you plan to do that? Because it's not just moving on from her. It's also getting your career back as well."

I sit up and start to answer, except I'm at a loss for words. All that's going through my head right now are the last nine months of my life.

All the booze. All the women. All the times I treated my teammates like trash. How I treated my coaches.

"God, I've fucked up so bad," I say, my hands catching my head in defeat. "How can I even come back from all of that?"

"Do you want me to tell you or let you figure it out? If I'm the new Lucy, I need to know the protocol."

He may have known when it was time to call her, but he never understood how she was able to get through to me when he couldn't.

No one can fill the space her absence has created, but that doesn't mean her method won't still work.

"Apologies. I owe so many apologies."

"That's definitely on the list. What else?"

I think about it before saying, "I should probably start working out again. Can't come back to the league if I can't throw a football."

"Also a good idea. Anything else?"

I let out a breath because I know what I need to say, but saying the words are harder than I thought.

"I need to talk to the therapist," I admit. "I need . . . I need help."

Cole gives my back a slap. "It will be hard, all of it, but I'm proud of you. You need to move on. These are the first steps."

I jump off the tailgate, which might not have been the best idea as I stumble before I catch my balance. "Do you realize that I never went home with a brunette? Always a blonde."

"I just figured you had a new type."

I shake my head, which is also a bad decision. "She's my only type. She was it. She was my end game. And it was almost time. I was almost ready. Last offseason. After the playoffs. That was going to be it. That was going to be our time. I was finally going to be able to show her how much she really meant to me."

I hear Cole's footsteps coming from behind. "I know, man, but maybe this just wasn't in the cards for you two. Hell, maybe it was and the opportunity has come and gone, but you need to take the steps to move on. You need to get back to being the Bryce I know. Only this Bryce is without Lucy. I need the Bryce who was going to take the league by storm. The Bryce I am going to win a league championship with."

A Bryce without Lucy. I don't even know what that guy would look like.

Cole is right, though. I need to take the steps and figure this out.

Starting now.

12

———

LUCY

Well, not really dying unless I could die from too many consecutive minutes of coughing, then I probably would have keeled over seven minutes ago.

"Lucy! Are you okay? I'm coming!"

The coughing fit continues as Brenna runs up the stairs to my bedroom where she finds me sitting on the edge of my bed with my wedding dress on my lap as I gasp for breath.

"Here. Take a drink of water."

Why Brenna has a bottle of water at the ready I'm not sure, but I'm not about to look a gift horse in the mouth. This woman literally just saved my life.

I take a few sips before finally calming down enough to take a deep breath. That was by far the worst coughing fit I've had since they started.

If I'm like this just from looking at my dress, I can only imagine what it's going to be like when I'm wearing it on my wedding day, which is in five weeks.

Not that any of my guests would know that since I still have not sent the invitations.

"I came by to drop these off," Brenna says, tossing a few bags of cough drops onto my bed. "I know I'm a few days late, but I heard you went to buy them but left before you could check out. From how you sounded when I walked in, it's a good thing I grabbed them, too."

"Something like that," I say as I finally catch my breath.

"Are we going to talk about it?"

"Talk about what?" I ask, trying to play dumb as I hang the dress up on the back of my bedroom door. "Oh! Luciano held my hand in public last night! At the restaurant. In front of customers. How exciting is that?"

Brenna plops down on my bed. "Are you listening to yourself? This should not be big news."

"I am listening, but this is a big deal. I think we should talk about that and only that and nothing else that has happened over the last week."

"Nice try," Brenna says. "While I'd love to dive into the fact that it should not be major news that your fiancé held your hand, I'm more interested in what happened between you and Bryce when he walked in on such an exciting milestone in your relationship. Or would you rather talk about how, if I hadn't shown up today, you might be dead from coughing as you held your wedding dress? You can pick."

"What if I don't want to?"

"Then I'll pick, of course. It's like you've learned nothing in the six years we've been friends."

I sometimes wonder why we're even friends. What started as just someone I knew who ended up in my freshman English class in college has turned into a friendship of a lifetime. She has been my shoulder to cry on more times than I can count. In return, I'm her shoulder when she is ghosted by another shitty online date. She's my person.

"I was at Tripoli's last night."

Brenna falls back onto the bed. "Ugh. I thought that would happen. We tried to get him not to go in case you were, but he was insistent."

"It's not your fault," I say, falling back next to her. "He had to see us together at some point. Might as well rip the Band-Aid off."

"Was it as bad as I heard?"

"What did you hear?"

"That he and Luciano almost fought in the middle of the restaurant and that he broke the door when he left. Oh, and that he took out someone's mirror when he sped away"

I roll my eyes. The Laurel Heights Facebook gossip page will never cease to amaze me. "Partially. They did argue, but the door is still intact, as far as I know. As for the mirror, I'm not sure. I walked back inside before he drove off."

While I hate how last night went down, in a strange way, I'm glad it happened. I owed Bryce an explanation. Yes, I wish I didn't give it to him while we were screaming at each other in a parking lot, but I'm glad I got it out.

He needed to know how I felt and why I made the choices I did.

Even if I question them every day.

"Well, that explains why Cole showed up at my place at three in the morning carrying in a very drunk and very passed out Bryce."

I sit up, putting my hands to my head. "I hate that he's drinking as much as he is. I know he's responsible for his own choices, but I can't help but feel guilty—"

"No. Do not put that on yourself," Brenna says as she sits up next to me. "You did what you had to do and made a decision for your life and your future. My idiot brother's inability to figure out how to cope with adult things without a bottle of booze is not on you."

"I know," I say. "But what if I made the wrong decision?"

I don't make eye contact with Brenna as my words linger in the air. Instead, I move my hands from my head to a suddenly very interesting piece of thread that is coming undone from the bottom of my T-shirt.

"Excuse me? What did you just say?"

I stay focused on the thread, wondering how I'm going to play this.

Reverse. Reversal seems good.

"Nothing. Absolutely nothing. I said no words. Want to go get tacos?"

Brenna moves closer to me, forcing me to look at her. "Bullshit and don't you dare try to distract me with the deliciousness that is the best food in the world. You just said you're wondering if you made the right decision. Need I remind you of the pro-con list that took us five hours to make? Do I need to go find it so you can reacquaint yourself with it?"

"No," I say, though it would be nice just to look at it one more time. It was the biggest list I'd made to date—fifteen pages. Front and back.

On it listed every reason I should continue to wait for Bryce.

Pros: He was my first love and my best friend.

Cons: It will never be the offseason. Football will always come first.

Then it had the reasons Luciano would be a good life partner for me.

Pros: My family loves him. He makes time for me and our relationship.

Cons: Not overly affectionate.

There were many more reasons than those—and Brenna made an entire section of cons when she found out that Luciano and I hadn't slept together yet—but that's what it all boiled down to.

Luciano wants what I want. He's ready to start the next chapter in his life that involves marriage and, eventually, kids. I don't need to be pregnant tomorrow, but I want to get the journey started. Most importantly, I never have to wonder if he'll break promises he makes to me. I know he won't.

As for Bryce? Yes, the last time we spoke he said that he was ready to settle down and start our future. He said the same thing when we—well, before the draft. He's been saying that in some way, shape, or form since our senior year of high school. Yet, his actions have always spoken louder than his words. Actions that always leave me waiting and wondering. That was what happened the night I decided I was done waiting. So, I moved on. Even though it hurt like hell.

"List aside, why did you say it? Because if you ask me, which you kind of did, it's that you're finally willing to admit that you're marrying Luciano because you were so desperate to get over my brother that you said yes to the first man who asked."

I stand and take my wedding dress off the hook, holding it in front of me. I feel a cough, but I swallow it.

"Furthermore," Brenna yells, making sure I can hear her from where I stand in the back of my closet. "I may never have been in a relationship like you're in, but I do know that if you're going to marry someone, then you should have zero doubts. You should be counting down the days until you become husband and wife, not counting the days since your last coughing fit. If you're having any hesitations—any at all—you need to figure them out soon."

She isn't telling me anything I don't already know. The longer I let this go on, the more people this is going to hurt, and Luciano deserves better than that.

"This shouldn't be so hard," I say, hanging my dress back where it was.

"Right? Decisions like this need to come with signs from the universe. They are too big to make on our own. Even though I think you already know what to do."

I already know I can't marry Luciano. I'm not in love with him. It isn't fair to him. It isn't fair to me.

Though it would be nice to have a sign from the universe confirming that is the right choice.

Maybe lightning could strike.

Or maybe something in your closet can catch my attention after years of being ignored.

Something like Bryce's high school letterman jacket.

13

———

LUCY

DECEMBER, SENIOR YEAR, HIGH SCHOOL

I AM GOING to kill Bryce Donald.

That is, after I find him.

I thought it was strange when he didn't show up for tutoring before my Sunday shift at Tripoli's. It is state championship week, so I thought maybe he had extra practice that he forgot to tell me about.

Then he didn't come in to pick up the pizza his mom ordered. I tried to call and text him, but both went unanswered. I messaged Cole, but he thought Bryce was with me. Same with Brenna.

So, now we're searching. Cole is checking the high school while Brenna is searching around their house. As for me? I'm going out on a limb and heading to check Lake Laurel.

It's not like Bryce not to message me back. Or Cole or Brenna. No one has heard from him since this morning, and it is already well past dusk.

I pull on to the main road that leads back to Lake Laurel, and at first, I don't see anything. Just trees and the remnants of last week's first snow. Then I turn on my bright lights and, in the distance, right in the middle of a picnic area, I think I see an outline of a gray truck.

I put my phone away and exit my car. It's not until I take a few steps toward the truck that I see Bryce sitting on the end of this tailgate. If he hears me, he's not reacting.

"Hey," I say as I walk toward him. "Are you okay?"

The only reason I know he is alive and not a mannequin is because I can see his breath in the cold Ohio air.

"Bryce? What's the matter?"

I look at his hand, and narrow my eyes.

"What is this?" I ask, walking in front of him and grabbing his hand. "Whiskey? Where do you even get a bottle of whiskey? You're not even eighteen yet!"

He jerks his hand away from me, causing liquid to spill on both of us. "I have my ways." At least if it's full enough to spill like that, then he hasn't drunk that much of it. "Besides, I've only had a sip of it. Turns out I'm not that big of a fan of it."

Well, that's good.

"Why do you even have it in the first place? And what are you doing here?"

I wait for him to answer even though I'm freezing and am already having to clench my teeth to keep them from chattering.

"Do you know that if we win this Friday, we'll be the first state champions in school history?"

"I do." Friday's game is all anyone in town is talking about. It's in Columbus, and the town is shutting down and renting buses to take the two-hour drive to watch the game.

"What happens if we lose?"

The question takes me by surprise. In all the months I've known Bryce, I've never heard anything but confidence in his voice when it comes to his football abilities. It's why he works as hard as he does. He talks the talk and walks the walk.

"Why would you ask that?" I ask, doing my best to ignore the cold. "You guys are undefeated this year. No one has even come close to beating you. This is your year. You've said so yourself."

"I don't know. It's just . . ." He sighs, and just when I think he's about to take another sip of the whiskey, he tosses it to the side of the truck. "We've worked our entire lives for this game. When we were ten, we had a coach tell us that if we couldn't win a state title one day, then no one in Laurel Heights could. Now it's here, and . . . and I . . . I don't feel ready."

"Why wouldn't you be? You do nothing but think about football, despite my best attempts to make you focus on math."

Usually, this kind of joke got a laugh out of him, but not tonight.

"Do you want to make another pro-con list?"

When he turns to me, the look in his eye breaks my heart. He looks . . . lost. Defeated. Tired.

"I told Mom this week about Clemson."

Oh no. I know he had been putting it off because he was scared of her reaction. "I'm taking that it didn't go over well?"

He shrugs. "She freaked out and cried. Brenna couldn't even get her to calm down. I tried to tell her all the good things about it. I even showed her the list we made, you know, to show her I put thought into it. All she could say was how far away it was and how she'd never get to see me."

I lift his hand and give it a kiss, which feels natural to do even though I'm still navigating this girlfriend thing.

"I'm so sorry about your mom. But I have a feeling that she'll come around. That she was just taken by surprise."

"I hope so. I really need at least one parent on my side."

And there it is. I had a feeling this was big, and if his dad has anything to do with it, then it's huge. Bryce hasn't told me much about his dad, except that he comes in and out of his life, usually at the worst possible times. And that when he comes in, it's because he wants or needs something.

Which, I'm sorry, is just shitty.

"Did you talk to him?"

He nods. "He called me when I was on my way in to study with you. I shouldn't have even answered it, but he's my dad, you know? How can I ignore him?"

"What did he say?"

"That he arranged a visit for me next weekend at Alabama. I told him that I didn't want to visit and that I was planning to commit to Clemson."

"I take it he didn't react well?"

"He told me I was worthless and that if I knew what was good for me I'd visit. I asked him why he cared so much about Alabama, and he gave some bullshit reason. Then I asked him if he was coming to the game this weekend, and he said, and I quote, 'why bother when I'm not going to do what he wants.'"

I'm not a violent person. I believe in trying to find peaceful resolutions to problems. But if I saw Bryce's dad right now, I would punch him straight in the throat.

"Oh, Bryce." I let go of his hand so I can wrap him in my arms. If there were ever a person who needed a hug, it would be Bryce.

His arms tighten around me, and he leans his head on my shoulder. If I listen closely, I'm pretty sure I could hear his sniffle.

All he wants to do is make everyone happy. He wants to make his parents and his coaches proud. He wants to win a state title for the town and his teammates more than he wants it for himself. He is worrying about everyone else at a time when most teenagers—heck, most humans, would only be worrying about themselves.

"I'm sorry all of that happened, and I'm sorry it's happening now," I say as we let go of each other.

"It's not your fault, and I'm sorry I scared you. I actually came to Tripoli's to talk to you tonight, but when I pulled in, I saw pizza boy with his hand on your back. Between that and the call with my dad, I didn't trust myself in there."

Luciano did put his hand on my back briefly, but it was to guide me around a spill on the floor. I hadn't thought anything of it.

"There is nothing going on with him. I'm with you. Please know that," I say, trying again to ease his mind when it comes to Luciano.

"But, Bryce, whiskey? You know that isn't going to make anything better. In fact, it will just make things worse."

"I know," he said, his voice resigned. "I was . . . I'm just all over the place. I can't focus. I can't figure out what's right and wrong. I'm . . . I'm lost, Lulu."

"Well, then let's get you unlost," I say, patting my thigh. "Come on. Lie down."

He quirks an eyebrow. "What are you doing?"

"Just trust me," I say. "Now put your head down and close your eyes."

He gives a groan but complies, laying his head on my lap. I begin gently massaging his scalp, hoping that it helps alleviate some of the tension I know he's carrying.

"That feels good," he says as he slowly relaxes.

"Shhh. Don't talk." I give him a soft smile as I continue to rub small circles around his temples. "All I want you to focus on is the game this week. That's what you've worked for. That's what you want more than anything else right now. You've worked too hard to let everyone else get in the way. So just lay here and focus on that. Let all of the other noise go away."

I'm not sure how long we sat like that. At some point I think he might have fallen asleep. I know for a fact that my butt is frozen to his truck. But it's all worth it because soon I hear the best words I could hear.

"One week."

I can't help but smile at his words. "One week."

He slowly sits up, and the picture in front of me makes my heart swell. Gone is the lost boy from an hour ago who felt like the world was crashing down on him. Now here is the person I'm falling for more and more every day.

"Thank you."

"You don't need to thank me."

"Yes, I do," he says as I visibly shiver.

"Lulu, why didn't you say how cold you were?" He's quick to tug his jacket off, but I hold my hand up.

"No," I say, trying to refuse it. "It's cold for you too. I'm fine."

"Don't care," he says, reaching behind me so he can put it over my shoulders. "Wear it."

"Thanks," I say shyly because I secretly love how it's huge on me and how it smells of him. I have to do all I can not to bring it to my nose and sniff it.

"And I do need to thank you. Not just for tonight but also for . . . well, everything."

"I didn't do much." I shrug.

"You did everything," he says, reaching for my hand. "You get me. You know when I need to vent or when I need quiet. You know how to talk me off the ledge or how to encourage me. You're amazing."

I open my mouth to thank him or tell him that I am just trying to be a good friend.

But neither of those things happen because before I can, Bryce Donald is kissing me.

And it is warming me in every cell of my body.

This isn't our first kiss, but every time our lips touch, I notice something new. His lips are soft, which is maybe the only part of his body that is. I taste the faint hint of whiskey, and I think for the rest of my life I will associate that taste with Bryce. He opens his mouth, and I follow suit, our tongues meeting in a way that is both weird and thrilling at the same time. Bryce is the first guy I've kissed, so I find myself wondering how I'm doing, which I probably shouldn't do.

Oh God, what if I'm bad at this? What if he has kissed dozens of girls, and I'm on the low percentile of kissability?

"I can hear your brain," Bryce says, slowly pulling away from me. "What is going on in that beautiful head of yours?"

Our foreheads touch as he links our hands together.

"Promise not to laugh?"

"You can tell me anything, Lulu."

I take a deep breath, hating that I'm about to say this. "You're the only guy I've kissed."

He backs away, and his eyes grow wide. Oh geez, I've scared him off.

"I was your first kiss?"

I nod. "Embarrassing, isn't it?"

I try to back away, but he pulls me back to him. "Not embarrassing at all. In fact, I kind of like that you had never been kissed."

I give him a sideways glance. "And why is that?"

"Because now I know I don't have to beat up any other guys who have kissed you before."

I shake my head. "That's a little much, don't you think?"

He shrugs, pulling me on his lap. "Don't care. Want to know what else I like?"

"What is that?"

"You in my jacket."

I pull it a little tighter around me. "Good, because I like it too."

"Will you do me a favor?" he asks while giving me one more small kiss on the cheek before pulling me tighter.

"Anything."

"Wear this to next week's game? I feel like I could use a good luck charm in the stands."

"You don't need luck," I say, wrapping my arms around his neck. "You're Bryce Donald. You got this. You're going to be amazing."

He leans in to kiss me again, only this time I don't overanalyze it. I just revel in the feel of his kiss and his arms around me as I mentally count down the days until next week when it will just be us.

14

______

BRYCE

I'VE BEEN hungover a lot over the past nine months.

Some of those nights I was able to completely forget what happened the night before. Other nights, I wasn't so lucky. This is one of those mornings. My head hurts, my mouth feels like it's stuffed with cotton balls, and my stomach is revolting.

I remember everything from Tripoli's and fighting with Lucy to getting shitfaced at the lake to Cole appearing out of nowhere. The only thing I can't seem to remember is how this bruise got on my knee. Though, I do have a vague memory of trying to jump off the tailgate of my truck and not actually landing. That might have something to do with it.

I deserve it all. And frankly this hangover is making up for the times that I thought nothing was wrong.

Everything was wrong. I knew it, but I just didn't want to believe it.

But Cole is right. Hell, everyone is right. I can't keep doing this. I can't keep going down this path. I can't jeopardize my career all because things didn't go my way.

And as much as I never thought I'd admit it, the team isn't wrong. I am going through something. And it is definitely a mental problem.

I'm not making the right decisions for myself or my team. I'm allowing myself to self-destruct. As much as I hated them for doing it at the time, the Fury did exactly what they had to do for me.

Step one was admittance. But what's next? I've fucked up so many things over the past nine months that I don't even know where to begin.

"Numbnuts! Are you going to wake up today or should I just plan on you being on my couch for the foreseeable future?"

I blink a few times, hating every ounce of light in Brenna's living room. "What time is it?"

"Time to drink this," she says, throwing a full bottle of Gatorade at me.

I sit up slowly, though that doesn't stop the room from spinning. "Why aren't you in school today?"

"Because it's four o'clock," she says. "And it's Columbus Day so I had the whole day off."

I fall back onto the couch. "Thanks for letting me crash here."

"I didn't have much of a choice. One minute Cole is messaging me to open my door and the next he is dropping you—literally—on my couch."

Okay so maybe I don't remember everything from last night. Now that I think about it, everything is kind of blurry after leaving the lake.

"Well, I appreciate it," I say, trying my best to sit up again. "Fuck, I drank a lot."

"So I heard," she says, taking a seat on the chair next to me. "If this was how you were when you lived in Nashville, I have no idea how you functioned."

"Denial is a powerful thing," I say, taking as big of a swig of the drink as my stomach can handle. "It makes you think nothing is wrong when, in reality, the world is crashing down around you."

"Do my ears deceive me or is my brother admitting that he does in fact have a problem?"

"What is your brother admitting?"

I look over to see Cole standing at Brenna's door. I'm starting to seriously question on whether or not he has magical powers that just make him show up at places.

"That he's a jackass," Brenna says.

"We knew that," Cole says as he sits next to me on the couch.

I take another sip of my Gatorade, watching Cole and my sister stare at each other.

Then again, the room is still spinning when I try to move so I can't trust anything I'm seeing right now.

"What are you doing here?" I ask.

"Giving you this," he says, tossing my cell phone to me. "It fell out in my truck last night. Figured you'd want it when you came back to the land of the living."

I pick it up, almost scared to see what is waiting for me. Numerous texts asking where I was last night. Most of them from Cole. Twelve missed calls from Brenna and Mom. A shit load of emails that I'll deal with later.

Nothing from Lucy.

I drop my phone on my lap, disappointed when I have no right to be.

Though I can't shake the feeling that we're not done yet. That our story isn't over. Maybe because we're in the same town? Maybe because I felt the same spark I always do when I touched her the other day?

I know she did too. I know that's why she ran.

Spark or not, she made her choice. She's marrying pizza boy. And now I have to learn how to navigate life knowing that Lucy isn't my end game anymore.

"So, what now?" Cole asks in his serious "dad" voice as he takes a seat next to me.

"I'm not sure," I say defeatedly.

"Well, are you staying here?" Brenna asks. "I mean, not here with me because I love you, but I'd kill you. I mean as in Laurel Heights."

This gets a smile out of me. "No, Brenna, I will not cramp your style. But I . . . I don't think I'm ready to go back to Nashville."

Cole pats me on the back. "If you're not ready, then you're not ready."

If I go back to Nashville now, still this raw and vulnerable, I know it would be easy to pick up the first bottle I see, or call any of the faceless women in my cell phone for a night of meaningless sex to make me try to forget. I know Cole would keep an eye on me if I asked him to—hell, he'd move in with me if he thought it would keep me above water—but I can't ask him to do that.

I need to do this myself. For the first time in my life, I need to figure out life on my own.

"How are you going to stay here—"

"Without fighting with Lucy every time I see her?"

Brenna nods. "Well, yeah, that. Or you need to figure out a way to just steer clear of her. Can't fight with her if you don't see her."

The Jack Daniels threatens to come up from my stomach because I know Brenna is right.

Hell, maybe that is why I should stay here. I can work on getting back in football shape—both physically and mentally—while also learning how to live in a world where Lucy is there, but just not in the way I'm used to. And if I stay away from her, I'll get used to her not being in my life.

"Can you do that?" Cole asks. "And don't just say that you can because that's what we want to hear. You have to mean it or I'm dragging your ass back to Nashville and you're moving in with me."

I lay my head back against the couch and close my eyes, knowing that going back to Nashville isn't an option. I need to stay here.

Here I can't ignore that Lucy has moved on. I can't ignore that I'm not with my team. I have to work to get back to Nashville. I have to earn it.

And that's what I'm going to do.

"Yeah . . . I can do it. And I will."

15
———

BRYCE

"COME ON, Donald. That all you got? Give me five more!"

I had forgotten what kind of drill sergeant Cole was in the weight room.

My arms feel like they are going to fall off, I think I'm sweating out the last nine months of whiskey while I plot my best friend's murder.

But the pain is good. It's a reminder of what I did to myself.

It's a good reminder never to do it again.

"Three . . . two . . . one. Done!"

Cole takes the weight bar from my hands as I lie still on the bench press. "Remind me never to half ass off-season lifting again."

"Not a problem," he says as he adds more weight to the bar for himself. "How about you go fill up our waters while I knock out this set."

"You don't need me to spot you?" I ask jokingly.

"I think I got this," he says, putting up his first rep. "Maybe next time, I'll just bench you."

"I'd like to see you try."

I talk a big game, but Cole could easily bench me. He could probably do it without breaking a sweat. It's not that I'm small, but compared to Cole, who is six-foot-four and two-hundred and ninety pounds, I'm nothing.

I make my way over to the water station as I hear Cole grunting through his set. It's the only sound in high school weight room at six in the morning.

One of the first phone calls I made during the hangover from hell was to Coach Roberts. I owed the man an apology. He tried to help me the other day, and I stormed out of his office because I couldn't handle the truth when it was right in front of my face.

I also needed a favor.

If I'm going to eventually earn my way back onto the Fury, I need to get myself back into shape. I half-assed training camp and was too busy drinking and fucking during the off-season that I don't think I went to a gym once. Looking back, I can't figure out how I survived the few days of training camp I participated in, which didn't sit well with me. But I'm not about to go to the town gym where the equipment is subpar and the people will start gossiping up a storm.

Nope. I'm not about to put myself through that. So, I asked coach if I could come in before school to get in my workout. Yes, the league frowns upon players working out at non-team facilities, but I can't sit around and get even more out of shape. Plus, the equipment at my old high school is state of the art—Cole and I made sure of that the second after our first checks cleared.

Plus, I like working out in peace. Well, I will when Cole goes back to Nashville at the end of the week. It will give me time to think. To figure out the rest of my new plan.

I know what I need to do on the football field. I know what I need to do in the weight room. And Coach Roberts will help me get there if I need additional support.

Personally? That's a whole other story. The person I always had to help me with that I can't have anymore.

And I get why.

I kept Lucy on the hook for years—unintentionally, of course. I never wanted to hurt her. Hell, I would have cut off my own arm before hurting her on purpose.

Yet, that's what I did.

I just always felt like I couldn't give her what she deserved until the time was right, not even considering that my promises wouldn't be enough for her.

When my clock ran out, I only had myself to blame for not starting the play earlier.

"You done?" Cole says, setting the bar back on the rack. "Or you want to do another set?"

"No, I'm good," I say, tossing him his water bottle. "Baby steps are probably best for me at this point."

"What is that I hear? Bryce Donald making a good decision?"

I give him the finger and walk to where I dropped my gym bag. "Isn't it time for you to go back to Nashville? Don't you have other friends to annoy?"

"Nope. Just you, and you're stuck with me for another three days. Don't hate me, but I'm going to ask one more time, are you sure you don't want to come back with me?"

I take a seat on a bench across from him. "Thanks, but I'm good. I did think about it for longer than five seconds. I know you'll be there for me and you'd do whatever needs to be done to make sure I don't slip back into old habits, but you have to be with the team. Plus, there are still six away games on the schedule. I promise you, the second I am ready, you'll be the first to know."

He nods. "I'm proud of you, you know that, right?"

I laugh. "What do you have to be proud of me for? For almost fucking up my career, being two steps away from a thirty-day program, or treating you like a piece of shit?"

"While you might have done all of those things, I'm proud because you're owning up to them. Not many people could do that. They would just keep going down the path until they hit rock bottom."

"Rock bottom isn't getting kicked off a team that thought you were worth ten-million dollars a year?"

"You weren't kicked off. You were put on personal leave for the season. There is a huge difference."

"Sometimes you can polish a turd in ways no one else can."

"It's my specialty," Cole says, standing from his bench. "Rock bottom would have been you in a hospital after a night of black-out drinking. Rock bottom would have been one of your many nameless, faceless blondes telling you that you were going to be a daddy. Rock bottom would have been getting fired by the league for breach of contract. That would have been rock bottom."

Cole is right, all of those things would be far, far worse than what I'm dealing with, but even that bit of perspective doesn't make me feel any better. It just makes me feel like more of an asshole.

As angry as I was with Coach McAvoy and Coach Davis for sending me away, I now know that they needed to. As much as I hated seeing the tape Coach Roberts showed me, I'm not sure if I would have realized how bad things were had he not done it. And I don't know if I hadn't seen Lucy with Luciano—God I hate even thinking his name—that I would have realized that she is not mine anymore.

I needed all of that. Sometimes, the truth hurts and you need it to smack you in the face so you can feel the pain.

"Well, thanks for making sure I didn't get there," I say as we begin to walk out of the weight room. "I know I wasn't the easiest person to get along with for a while."

"Understatement of the year," he says as we walk past Coach Roberts's office just as the door opens.

"See you soon, Uncle Nick. Keep me updated on Brandon's test scores."

Lucy's voice freezes me mid-step. I knew I was going to see her around town. I knew I couldn't avoid her entirely, but I thought I would be safe at the school.

Apparently not.

"Oh!" she yelps, taking a few steps back as she almost runs into me and Cole. "Bryce . . . Cole . . . I didn't . . . I didn't know you would be here."

"No problem, Luce," Cole says as he pulls her into a hug. "Come here. It's been too long."

She lets out a breath and slowly accepts Cole's hug. I want to look away, not because my best friend is holding the only woman I have ever loved but because I know a hug for me isn't coming next. Hell, I'll be lucky if she says two words to me. She hasn't even looked at me.

"What are you guys doing here?" she asks nervously, still avoiding eye contact with me.

"Coach is letting Bryce work out in the mornings. I'm just tagging along until I go back to Nashville. What are you doing here?"

"I . . ." She releases an uneven breath that betrays her nervousness. Why? My Lucy isn't nervous. My Lucy doesn't care what the world thinks, and she says it like it is. Maybe that's another thing that has changed? "Apparently, I'm the only one Uncle Nick can find when he needs a math tutor. So, I come down a few days a week to help out a few of the players."

Of course she would because she's the type of girl who would wake up early and tutor kids before she goes to work. It brings me right back to all those mornings we spent together when I acted like I didn't know trig. All the conversations we had that changed my life. All the secret looks we gave each other as feelings we both didn't know how to handle started developing. All the times I would sneak a kiss because I couldn't help myself.

As if she's thinking about the same things, when she finally looks at me, her eyes are bright with remembrance.

"He's lucky to have you," I say as I contemplate what I'd give to have Coach Roberts bust out of his office and launch into one of his tirades about technology in football just to break the tension between Lucy and me.

"Well, I need to get going," Cole says as he backs away. "Call me later, Bryce? Good to see you, Lucy."

Cole makes a quick exit, and if I thought the silence was awkward a second ago, it has nothing on what it is like right now.

"Hey, can I—"

"We should—"

We both awkwardly laugh as we talk over each other.

"You first," I say.

She glances at her phone. "I have to be at the bank in twenty minutes."

"This won't take long," I say, guiding her to the empty locker room. I know this is my one shot at an apology, which also means I need to bury all thoughts about bringing her in my arms, kissing the hell out of her, or trying to convince her to call off the wedding.

"Cole said he was going back to Nashville," Lucy says as she takes a seat on one of the benches. "Does that mean you're going back with him?"

"Actually, I'm not," I say, taking my own seat. "I need to figure out a few things before I head back, so I'm going to stay here for the rest of the season."

Her eyes grow wide. "You're staying here? In Laurel Heights? But what about the Fury? Your contract?"

"My agent worked it out. I'm technically on the injured reserve list. So, I'm taking the rest of the season to work through my . . . issues."

"Oh," she says, the nervous tone back in her voice. "Well, I'm glad you're doing what you need to do."

She starts to stand, but I reach for her arm. "Lucy, wait. I need to apologize."

She looks down at my hand, but she doesn't move to pull free. It's almost as if she's just as desperate for the connection as I am.

Then, slowly, she slides her arm free, and my heart sinks. "You don't need to apologize," Lucy says. "We both said what needed to be said, and that's that."

"But it's not," I say standing. "You said what you needed to say, and I deserved every word of it. I didn't do right by you for many years, and I know that now. I'm so sorry, Lucy. I never wanted to hurt you. I loved you. I still love you."

"Bryce—"

"No. Let me finish. I will *always* love you, but I know you've moved on, so I have to accept that. If Luciano is who makes you happy, then I'll support you because, before you were my first love, you were my best friend."

I wasn't expecting laughter mixed with fits of coughing that's more of a wheezing gasp, but it's what I get.

"What's so funny?"

"I think that's the first time in all these years you called him by his first name."

"I'm growing," I say as a smile forms on my lips.

"Apparently." Her smile is so brilliant that, when her phone beeps, I want to break it and snatch the moment back.

"It's the bank," she says looking at it then tossing it into her purse. "I need to go."

"Yeah. Sure," I say, walking to the door and holding it open for her as she walks out. "And, Lucy?"

She turns to look at me. "Yeah?"

"I meant what I said. If you're happy, then I'm happy."

"Thanks," she says, quickly turning and walking away. All I hear as she walks down the hallway is echoes of her coughing.

16

———

LUCY

"THIS ONE IS from your Aunt Linda, and I snuck another cough drop under the bow. This is the last gift. You got this."

I couldn't have asked for better bridesmaids than Megan and Brenna. Megan made it her mission to get this shower over with in record time, all while sneaking me cough drops like a boss so I didn't start coughing. Brenna is steering the conversation away from specific wedding talk to avoid the chance of coughing fits, which is really hard at a bridal shower, but Brenna is pulling it off.

In fact, I haven't had a spell all day. The only downside is that my mouth and throat are numb and all I can taste is honey lemon.

That's fine. It's a small sacrifice to pay.

"Aunt Linda, they are lovely!" I say, as I hold up the embroidered towels I picked out. Though, Aunt Linda went a step further and had them personalized with our town nickname instead of our initials. How . . . thoughtful.

"Those are precious, Linda!" my mom says, which is what she's said about every gift I've opened, including the vase shaped like a penis that was not on my registry.

I thought Brenna was going to lose it on that one.

"I'm so happy," Mom continues as she takes the towels from me. "Guiliana, can you believe this is finally happening? Who would have thought that our babies would actually get married, just like we planned!"

Damn. We almost made it through the whole shower without this conversation. Though, someone would have been a fool not to bet on it. The math nerd in me set the odds at a hundred-to-one.

"Do you remember lying next to each other after we gave birth to them? All we could talk about was their eventual wedding. We just knew that this day was in our future," Guiliana says standing, very clearly wanting this conversation to be about her and my mom and not me and Luciano. Again, that is fine. I've never been comfortable being the center of attention anyway. "I'd like to propose a toast. To Luciano and Lucy, may your days be filled with love and ours be full of lots of grandbabies."

"You'd have to have sex with him for that to happen," Brenna whispers as she walks past, and just like that, my throat closes faster than a door being slammed. It's more from trying not to laugh than from the thought of sleeping with Luciano.

"Oh, I remember crying tears of joy when Lucy told me she and Luciano were going on a date. Lucy, why don't you tell everyone how you two reconnected?"

I look to my mom, who is looking at me like she's a child wanting to hear her favorite bedtime story.

"Well," I begin before taking a sip of water, "he had just gotten back from his internship in Italy, and I was in the mood for mint chocolate chip. We ran into each other in the freezer aisle, and *boom*, he asked me out, and I said yes."

The oohs and aahs I'm getting from the room make it sound like I just told the greatest love story ever written. I might prefer mystery novels to romance, but even I know that our love story isn't one they make movies about. Or pornos. Or anything that's not rated PG.

What I don't tell the forty people here, who are all friends of my mom's and Guiliana, is that the only reason I said yes to Luciano was because it was days removed from Bryce breaking his last promise to me. I figured one date couldn't be a bad thing. It would be a good way for me to start putting myself out there, and Luciano was someone I knew and trusted. Heck, when I was in high school and didn't have a date for the prom because Bryce couldn't make it back, Luciano agreed to take me. That night was nothing to write home about, so I figured a date with him wouldn't blow me away but it would be good enough to make me feel like I was moving on.

I was right. We had a pleasant time and had a lovely meal. We talked about our families, his time in Italy, and what my plans were now that school was done. It was bland and boring and exactly what I hoped for.

It was only supposed to be one date. Next thing, I knew it was seven months later and he was proposing at our surprise engagement party.

"I heard there was a beautiful bride who could use some help taking these gifts to the car?"

Everyone's head turns toward the door of the coffee shop, where Luciano stands holding a bouquet of red roses.

"Luciano!" Guiliana squeals, walking to greet her son. "This is for ladies only!"

He leans down and presses a kiss to his mother's cheek. "I know, but I thought my future wife could use some help after you lovely women spoiled her. Plus, I heard there was cake."

This makes everyone laugh. I even hear a few *awwws* and someone whispers, "What a lucky girl Lucy is."

"Well, this works perfectly," Guiliana says, grabbing my mom as they make their way toward us at the front of the coffee shop. "Anne Marie and I had this game prepared for the wedding, but it will be more fun here with a more intimate crowd."

I do everything I can to hold in my sigh. "I said no games, Mom."

"Oh, you can play one," she whispers as she pulls me from my seat and rearranges it so I'm now more front and center. Guiliana does the same to Luciano, and then, somehow, they both produce notebooks and pens for us. Do they carry those around in their purses?

"Now, Guiliana and I are going to ask the engaged couple a few questions. They are going to write down their answers, and we will see for sure how perfect you are for each other!"

I can feel the color drain from my face as I frantically look for Megan or Brenna, begging them with my eyes for another cough drop, but neither of them seems to be here any longer.

"I'll start with the first question," Mom says, her voice oozing with pride. "What is Lucy's favorite color?"

I don't start writing down my answer right away, trying to look out of the corner of my eye to see what he's writing, though I can't make anything of it. Shit, I honestly don't know if my fiancé knows my favorite color, which is navy-blue.

"On the count of three, turn your notebooks around. One . . . two . . . three!"

We do as they say as a group of my mom and Guiliana's friends laugh. Clearly, the answers are not the same.

"What did you put?" I ask.

He shrugs, turning to show me his notebook. "I went with pink. It felt safe since those were the wedding colors."

"Colors my mother picked," I remind him. "It's okay. It was a safe guess."

"Next question!" Guiliana yells. "What is Luciano's favorite movie?"

Shit. I know this one. I remember because it's one of my favorites, and it was one of the first ones we watched together. I mean, a historically accurate tail of a female mathematician? Sign me up.

Until we both turn around our notebooks. Mine says *Hidden Figures*. His says *The Greatest Showman*."

"What?" I ask, really thinking I nailed it. "I remember you saying the night we watched it together you couldn't believe I liked it too."

A blush creeps over his face. "I just said that because I wanted to impress you."

"Oh," I say, a little taken aback. "Okay, let's try again."

We are asked five more questions, and five more times, we get our answers wrong. Even I can't do the math of how long it would take until one of us gets an answer correct. I really thought we were going to find out, but Brenna saved the day with an announcement that everyone needed to leave because coffee shop had to close due to an emergency.

I could have kissed her.

"It's okay, Lucia. We have the rest of our lives to learn this stuff about each other," he says before leaning down and giving my forehead a kiss. This, again, drives the women in the room crazy. All it does is remind me of how little chemistry there is between him and I.

That had never bothered me before. I chalked it up to the fact that Luciano and I have a love based on friendship and respect.

Only, I want more. I want the spark. I want it all.

Who knows when it will happen or who it will be with, but I deserve a once-in-a-lifetime love. Everyone does.

I watch Luciano walk away, heading to take the first round of presents to the car. He's a good man, and he deserves that kind of love too. That person would know what his favorite movie is and look at him like he hung the moon.

Like how my parents still look at each other after thirty years of marriage or how Megan and her husband look at each other when they don't think anyone is watching.

Like how Bryce is looking at me right now.

Wait, what?

I shake my head, wondering if I'm seeing what I think I am.

Outside the glass window of the coffee shop, is Bryce. When I first got a glance of him, he was looking at me like I was the most beautiful woman in the world.

Now? Now, all I see on his face is conflict and hurt.

There is only one other time he's looked at me like that, and it was the day before the draft.

I can't stop looking at him. I want to run outside, bring him into my arms, and tell him everything is going to be okay. I want to scream at him because he did this before whispering that I've never stopped loving him and that I'm about to call off my wedding.

Oh my God, I'm going to call off my wedding.

I look back at Luciano and then back at Bryce, and for the first time in months, I don't feel like I'm going to cough.

17

BRYCE

DECEMBER, SENIOR YEAR, HIGH SCHOOL

I SHOULD BE on cloud nine right now.

We won the state championship game last Saturday. I played the best game of my life. Cole and the rest of the offensive line were on another level. Our defense was unstoppable.

The best part? Seeing Lucy run toward me wearing my jacket, her eyes shining with pride as our fans stormed the field. The kiss I gave her after she jumped into my arms was icing on the cake.

I'll never forget that moment for as long as I live.

And I have a feeling I'll never forget this night either.

"Bryce?" Lucy says as she walks out of Tripoli's. "What are you doing here?"

It's a fair question. It's Friday night and she had to work all night. In fact, between her work schedule and my unexpectedly busy week, we haven't gotten to see each other at all.

I missed her, but after tonight, missing her is going to be something I better get used to.

I hold open my arms, and she immediately comes into them, wrapping herself around me.

"You smell like pizza," I joke, placing a kiss on the top of her head.

"Comes with the territory."

I take her hand and guide her to my truck. "Do you mind if we go for a ride?"

She shakes her head. "No. My parents are with the Tripolis. They won't be home for another few hours."

I let out a sigh of relief as I get into my truck and rev the engine. As soon as it's in drive, I reach for her hand, needing to feel her touch.

How am I going to tell her my news, especially after I promised her that once football was over, things would be different? That I would be able to focus more on her, on us.

I really do want to be her boyfriend and walk her to class so I can steal kisses in the halls. I want to treat her the way she deserves because Lucy Valenti is the best girl in the world. She deserves everything.

Now I have to break that promise, and it's killing me even thinking about it.

"Do you mind if I turn on the radio?" she asks, already reaching for the dial.

I shake my head. "Nope. Just please no Taylor Swift."

"Hey now." She laughs. "Don't you dare speak ill of Taylor."

"I would never." I really just love to tease her about her crappy taste in music. Though, I must admit, the song that's now playing is catchy. And fitting.

It's a song about goodbyes. About tears. About heartache and heartbreak.

It's like the world is fucking with me as we make our way to the lake.

"What are we doing here?" she says as I put the truck in park.

I don't say anything as I round the truck to help her out of her seat. I take her hand in mine and walk her back to the tailgate, which is already set up with blankets.

"For some reason, when life gets tough, I always end up here," I say, helping her onto the tailgate before I join her and tug her back to my front. "Then, one day, I went missing. Neither my sister nor Cole could find me. Yet, you knew I was here."

"I took a guess," she says, snuggling closer to me. "All I could think about was that stupid conversation we had on the differences between a lake and a pond."

I laugh. "Well, no matter what, you found me, and I like to think it's because we have a connection. One that not many people have."

I know this probably sounds cheesy, and if the guys on the team heard me right now, they'd give me hell for weeks, but it's Lucy. I can always tell her the truth, no matter what.

"I think so too," she says, laying her head back on my shoulder. "But why are we here? I feel like you have something you want to say, and it's killing me not to know what it is."

How is one person able to see through me like that? It doesn't make sense.

Then again, Lucy and I don't make sense. I'm the jock whose whole life is going to be determined by how far I can throw a football. She's a smart-as-hell girl who could run the world one day if she wanted.

That's just one of the reasons I'm in love with her.

It's also why I have to break both of our hearts tonight.

"The guidance counselor called me into her office on Monday, and to my surprise, Coach Roberts and Coach Carvill were in there waiting for me."

"From Clemson? Your recruiting coach?"

I nod. "One in the same. Apparently, if I take an online course this month, I'll have enough credits to graduate high school early."

She gives me a confused look, and I don't blame her because it took me awhile to wrap my head around this. "What does that mean?"

"It means that if I graduate high school early, I can enroll at Clemson for spring semester, which is what the coaches want me to do. They think it will help me start as a freshman if I'm there for spring practice."

I let the silence settle over us as I wait for some kind of reaction from Lucy. It's better than when I talked about this with Mom. She cried for two days before realizing what this could do for my football career. That, even though it's sudden, it's the best decision for my future.

"When would you leave?"

I let out a sigh. "The day after Christmas."

"That's in two weeks."

"Yeah," I say as we fall silent again. I know I need to be a man and bring up the topic of she and I, but how do I do it? I don't want to do it. If I had my way, I'd be taking her with me. I can barely navigate the waters of high school and Laurel Heights before it becomes too much for me to process. I need her with me, even though I know I can't have her.

"I'm guessing our date tomorrow night is off?"

"I'm so sorry." The words barely scratch the surface of their meaning. "I wanted this so bad. I wanted us. I just . . . wonder how it will work with me being in South Carolina and you being here."

She sits up and pulls out of my hold and turns around to face me. I wish she would have stayed where she was. Then I wouldn't have to look at her as she fights back tears.

"It wouldn't," she says, reaching for my hands, which I willingly give her. "Maybe if we had been together longer, maybe we could make it work. But long distance is hard. And especially when you're going to college and starting football right away. You'll be busy with football and classes and just being in college. You don't need me here holding you back."

"Holding me back?" I shake my head in denial. "Lucy, you will never hold me back. From the moment I met you when I thought you were a dream, you have made me a better person. This might be the end of us now, but it's not the end forever."

"What's that supposed to mean?"

I shrug, bringing her back into my arms. "I don't know. All I know is that our story isn't done yet. It can't be. There are too many things we still have to do."

"You want things for us?" she asks.

"Hell yes. For one, I want to take you to prom."

"Prom is in April. You'll still be in classes."

Shit, I didn't think of that. "Nope. I'll make it home. I promise. Plus, there's more. Like, I want to meet your parents. I want Uncle Nick to give me the sit down about being respectful while dating his niece."

This makes her smile. "Those all sound great, Bryce, but—"

"No buts," I say before giving her a quick kiss. "I know we can't do long distance, but I also know that I'm not ready to say goodbye to you. I know that sounds selfish, but it's the truth."

She looks up at me, tears filling in her eyes. "I'm not either."

Who knew three words, well, *those* three words could fill me with such hope for the future?

"Listen," I say, turning her so I'm looking directly into the brown eyes I'm going to miss every day I'm away from her. "You're my Lulu, and I know that this might seem insane, but I love you. The thought of leaving you kills me. When I was asked to come to Clemson early, you were the first one I thought of because I didn't want to hurt you."

"You're doing what you have to do, and I'm proud of you for doing this."

She settles back into my arms, and we sit in silence for who knows how long. I know I still have two weeks before I go, but it's going to be so busy that I doubt I'll have time to come up for air. This is it. This is our last night, and I'm determined to take every second of it I can.

"I'm going to miss you," I say before placing a kiss on top of her head. "I'm going to miss you so fucking much."

"I'm going to miss you too," she admits. "But you know you can still call me. We might not be together, but that doesn't mean I'm not your friend. I'll always be there for you, Bryce."

I take her face in my hands and crash my mouth to hers. If I don't, I will start crying. That is how much I hate this, and the only thing that will make me hate it less is her lips against mine.

I'm not sure why I never thought to do this before, but I memorize her taste. The feel of her lips. The way her tongue feels as it dances with mine. I memorize a lifetime of moments in a handful of minutes.

God I'm going to miss her.

I'm going to miss her. So damn much.

"I'll be here. Always," she says after breaking the kiss. "There's no one else. Only you. I love you, Bryce. Now, go be amazing."

18
____

BRYCE

THERE ARE things I always miss about Laurel Heights, and one of them is Heights Park. The running trail here is perfect. Just enough shade to block the sun. It's paved so I can let my mind go and not worry about things like twisting an ankle on debris.

I have enough to worry about.

Granted, it's better than it was a few weeks ago when I arrived back in town, and it's a hell of a lot better than it was during the months leading up to my return.

I'm still not back where I want to be, but I know that's going to take time.

Dean has me on weekly calls with a sports therapist, and though I was against it at the beginning, I will admit that some things he's said have made sense.

Today's discussion was about pressure. I'm a professional quarterback. My job is literally done in one of the most pressure-packed situations there can be. Then he talked to me about a different kind of pressure—the kind I face off the field.

In the past, it was about trying to win a state title for an entire town and making my college decision. Today's pressure is more about the expectation to live up to being the most talked about rookie in pro football history and not letting down my teammates, my fans, or my sponsors.

Admittedly, I've never been good at that kind of pressure because I always wanted to please everyone. Malcom tells me that likely stems from wanting my father's approval, which is simultaneously something I need to work through as well as never want to talk about, ever. Nevertheless, the pressure of pleasing everyone became overwhelming, and somewhere along the line, I decided that Lucy was the only one who could help me navigate it. With one little pro-con list, she became my fixer. My go-to when anything in my life felt out of balance.

Then I found out she was engaged, and it was as if someone snapped the supports to my safety net and I was in a freefall. Of course, I was going to crash and burn because I hadn't ever learned to handle that stress myself.

Malcolm asked me today what I did when I felt overwhelmed, and I didn't have an answer for him because I couldn't say, "I call Lucy." He asked if I had hobbies to take my mind off the game. When I said no, he asked if I went to the movies or even took a drive out of the city to decompress.

The answer to all of it was no. I'm a football player who has only ever focused on football. I don't have a life outside of the game.

That was when he suggested I take up running because the physical exertion would help clear my mind so I could focus on the important things. So, here I am, letting the trail take me wherever it may and trying not to stare at the woman in front of me.

That part wasn't suggested by him, but if he were here, he'd understand why I can't take my eyes off her. She's wearing shorts that are glued to her ass. Her petite frame has curves in all the right places, and the brown hair on top of her head gives me all sorts of ideas.

If I hadn't known better, I would have thought it was Lucy. That's probably my mind playing tricks on me. I might not be as familiar with her ass as I'd like to be, but I know my girl, and Lucy hates running. Or walking. Or really any form of physical activity.

I know those things about her, but the longer I look at her like a creeper, the more convinced I become that it's Lulu. There is no one else in this town whose body makes me react like mine is right now.

"Lucy?" I call out as I lengthen my strides, hoping to meet hers. It doesn't take me long to get within a step of her, but she must still not hear me.

"Lucy!" I yell a little louder, putting my hand on her shoulder.

That apparently is the wrong move because, before I know it, her arms are flailing, she's yelling "Danger!" at the top of her lungs as she tries to locate something to subdue me with.

"Lucy! It's me!" I say, grabbing her shoulders. "I'm sorry. I didn't mean to scare you."

"Well, you did!" she yells, shoving away my touch before taking out her earbuds. "You can't just come up on someone in a park and touch them, Bryce."

"I'm sorry, I wasn't thinking. I just saw you, and . . . well, I was surprised to see you."

"What do you mean you were surprised to see me?" she says as she tries to catch her breath. "It's Laurel Heights. Based on the population of the town, and the activities that you and I both like to do, the probability stands high that we are going to run into each other at least four times a week, maybe more depending on the weekly circumstances and event schedule."

"Are you mad at me? I mean, I know I'm probably not your favorite person right now, but I thought after our talk in the locker room last week that we were getting to a better space."

"No, I'm not mad at you—actually, I am. You scared me, and I was just getting into my run."

I send her a questioning look. "You hate running. In fact, I was surprised to see you walking."

"I've changed," she says, starting to speed up. "A lot has changed, Bryce. Like now I'm a runner. See, I'm running."

She takes off, and it takes all I have not to start laughing on the spot. Her version of "running" is more of a fast walk, almost hobble, with a strange arm swing. I don't really know how to describe it, but

I'm pretty sure if her gym teacher/football coach uncle saw this, he'd disown her on the spot.

The faster she goes, the more awkward she looks. Somehow her legs are coming out from the sides instead of going back and forth, and her arms have taken on more of a windmill motion.

It's adorable.

Fuck, I still have it bad. I probably always will.

I follow her, picking up my pace to catch up with her. Though, that doesn't take long considering her strides have her running almost in circles. I'm nearly next to her when she turns her head to look at me, which is a horrible decision on her part. It's like her brain doesn't tell her feet to stop, and before she knows it, she's about to tumble to the ground. I quickly reach for her, breaking her fall.

"A runner, huh?" I ask, a hint of teasing in my voice as I help her up.

"Fine, I don't run," she says, smoothing out her shorts. "I do walk, though. Slowly. Sometimes. Usually alone. What are you doing here?"

"It's a public park, is it not?" I ask, doing my best not to stare at the sweat dripping down her face. "I needed a run, and I hate running on the treadmill. Figured I could get in a few miles and enjoy the weather before the temperatures drop."

"That's understandable I guess," she says. "The days of running outside are numbered where you will be able to run outside . . . especially . . . without..."

I crack a smile because I just realize that Lucy is staring at my chest.

My naked, covered-in-sweat-from-this-abnormally-hot-day chest.

Interesting.

"Without what, Lulu?"

"Without your . . ."

"Come on now, use your words."

She shakes her head. "Without your shirt. See. Shirt. Easy word."

I smile, happy to know that I still have an effect on her because she sure as hell still has an effect on me.

How can she not? She's perfect. From her big brown eyes that always pull me in, to the curve of her hips, to her smile that makes me feel like I'm worthy of whatever she's willing to give, she's absolutely perfect.

"Do you have time to sit and talk, or do you have more walking to do?"

She looks toward the end of the trail, then to her watch, and then back to me. "I can stay for a few minutes. I have . . . I have somewhere I need to be tonight."

We walk a few more steps until we find a bench.

"Hot date?"

I might say the words with nonchalance, but they taste like poison on my tongue. Still, I give myself a point for effort just because I am being nice and asking about Pizza Boy.

Malcolm will be so proud.

"No—I mean, yes."

"Having a hard time putting words together today? Do you need me to put on a shirt so you can concentrate?"

She playfully smacks my shoulder. "No. And I wasn't staring at your chest."

"Sure, you weren't."

"Whatever. For your information, I am meeting Luciano tonight."

Okay. This is it. This is when I show that I'm supportive. That I'm a friend and not a jealous ex who wants to ring Pizza Boy's neck for being able to touch and kiss and hold the only woman who has ever meant anything to me.

"That's nice. Going over wedding stuff? When is the big day, by the way?"

Instead of answering, Lucy starts coughing.

Like, I-think-she-might-break-a-lung coughing.

"Are you okay?" I ask, patting her back, wishing I had some water to give her. "Why are you coughing so much recently? You did this the other day too. What's wrong? Are you sick? Do you need a doctor?"

I'm mentally going through the doctors in Laurel Heights I can call when I feel her hand on top of my palm. Her coughing is dying down, but she still looks worn out, as if that coughing fit just sucked the energy right out of her.

"I don't need a doctor," she says, taking one last breath in and out. "I just get these coughing fits from time to time. It's nothing to worry about. I haven't had one in a while, and I didn't bring any cough drops with me."

Cough drops . . .

Those are what she was buying that day I ran into her at the convenience store. At least, I think that was what she dropped on the floor. I was too busy staring at her to really take notice of anything else.

"If you're not okay, you can tell me. I know things have been weird between us, and I say this as a friend, you kind of look like you haven't slept in a week."

"That's a really nice way of telling me I look like shit."

I scramble to backpedal, but then she smiles. God, I've missed her smiles.

"I didn't mean it like that, but as someone who has been through the ringer lately, I kind of know what it looks like when something is weighing heavy on you. And you, Lulu, look like you're carrying the weight of the world on your shoulders."

She lets out a sigh before turning to me. Her eyes are . . . sad. Torn. Heavy.

"Talk to me, Lulu. I might have messed things up with us more times than I can count, but that doesn't erase our history. We can talk to each other about anything. So, talk to me. What can I do to help?"

She lets out a humorless laugh. "Isn't this backward? Aren't you the one who's supposed to be coming to me for advice?"

"Consider this my first repayment on years of old debt."

"You're lucky I didn't charge interest."

"I've always been lucky when it comes to you," I say, reaching for her hand. "Now, talk to me, and if you tell me nothing is wrong, I'll call bullshit. In case no one has told you, I'm kind of the king of bullshit and am in recovery."

I almost pull my hand back, thinking it was too much, but she hasn't moved yet, so I'm not going to disturb the waters.

"How do you know when you're happy?"

I look at her, utterly unable to answer that question.

"What?"

"How do you know if you're happy? Like, what if you think you are but you aren't but you really have never been happy so you aren't sure what it actually should be like?" Her voice cracks at the end, and it almost destroys me.

I still don't have a clue how to answer her, but for years, this woman did all she could to take the pressure off me, so I have to try. It's my turn to give back.

"I think you're happy when the littlest stuff doesn't get you down. When you sit down at the end of the day, and you can smile. That when you look at everything and everyone you have around you, you realize you have everything you need and are wholly content."

She pulls her bottom lip between her teeth and watches a squirrel run across the running track.

"Do you remember the other day when you said that if I was happy, then you were happy for me?" she asks.

I nod. How could I ever forget that day?

"I don't know if I am."

This takes me by surprise. God, there are so many things I could ask her, but I have a feeling it will be best if I just play it simple.

"You aren't?"

She shakes her head. "I don't think so."

"Maybe a pro-con list will help."

She laughs and rewards me with her smile. "A pro-con list is what got me in this situation in the first place."

"Maybe it's time for another?"

She looks at me, then down at our adjoined hands, then back to me again. "Yeah, maybe it is."

19

———

LUCY

PRO: Parents love him.

Con: You don't love him and you know it's the easy way out.

Pro: You can get pizza whenever you want.

Con: You haven't had sex with him.

Pro: He puts you first.

Con: He's not Bryce.

I throw my notebook into the air and scream into my pillow. This is the fourth time I've tried to come up with a new pro-con list, and when one of the higher pros is pizza, then something isn't adding up.

It's clear. My heart, my lists, and my lungs have been telling me the same thing for weeks—I need to call off the wedding.

How do you tell someone who you do love as a friend but not a lover that you can't marry them? Am I going to crush him? Does he know I've been having doubts? I honestly have no idea which way this is going to go. Some people wear their hearts on their sleeve. Luciano wears his under four layers of wool sweaters.

All I know is that I can't go another day feeling like this any more than I can leave him to stand outside my front door any longer.

"You can do this. This is the right decision. This will be the best for both of you in the end. Be confident. Be strong."

I take a few deep breaths to try to center myself, grab the doorknob, and twist it before I chicken out.

"*Amore*," he says as I open the door. "How are you tonight?" He leans down and kisses me on the forehead. This is normal, any day of the week Luciano. Me, on the other hand? My palms are sweating, my heart is racing, and I kind of want to vomit.

"I'm fine." My voice comes out about three octaves above what it normally is. So much for being strong and confident. "Can we talk for a minute?"

"Of course." If Luciano is thrown by why my voice is switching between octaves or why I'm visibly jittery, he doesn't show it. Instead, he takes a seat on my couch like this is just a normal night.

It's now or never.

I can do this.

I'll never have to buy cough drops again.

"Thanks for coming over tonight," I say, taking a seat next to him as I wipe my sweaty hands on my jeans.

"When your future wife says come over, you come over. Look at us, just a few weeks away, and I already have the concept of happy wife, happy life down."

God, I wish I could read this man. He doesn't seem curious or stumped about why he's here. The lame joke he just made is the same one he'd make any other day of the week. He seems so normal when I'm so twisted in knots.

"Actually, that's what I wanted to talk to you about."

That's good, Lucy. Rip the Band-Aid off.

"The wedding?"

"Yeah, the wedding. I don't really know how to say this, but . . . okay, here it goes. I love you, Luciano. However, I . . . I'm not *in* love with you—not like that. So, I don't think we should get married."

Silence falls over the room, and I actually have to think back over what I said to make sure I spoke aloud and not just in my own tangled mess of a mind.

He hasn't blinked.

He hasn't taken a breath.

He's frozen. Oh God, is he devastated? Paralyzed from shock? I'm going to need him to say something soon because I have no idea what to do right now.

"Luciano, I'm so sorry," I say as I default to panic mode. "I know this probably seems sudden, and I know how much this is going to screw up, but I—"

His thunderous laughter stops my words.

I didn't even know he could laugh like that. Normally, his laughter is pleasant and almost choreographed. This one? It's like he just heard the world's funniest joke for the first time.

"Are you okay?"

It takes him a second to catch his breath, and he has to wipe tears away from his eyes before he responds.

"Do you know how long I've wanted to call this off but couldn't figure out how to do it? And then, here you are, just *BOOM*! Oh my God, this is such a relief."

Wait, what?

I'm so confused.

"Okay, back it up," I say, still trying to figure out what the hell is going on. "Not that I'm trying to win the award for who called the wedding off, but . . . I had no idea you felt that way."

"Well, then I'm a better actor than I thought I was," he says. "Why do you think I've never kissed you or tried to have sex with you? I was dreading our wedding night, but now we don't need to worry about it! We're not going to get married!"

He sounds almost giddy about that, and I feel like I should be offended . . . or offended that I'm not offended?

"Dreading? Am I that revolting?" I mean, I'm not mad he's happy, but I'm starting to feel a little self-conscious over here.

"No, no!" he says, inching closer to me and taking my hand. The last time he touched my hand was a few weeks ago at the restaurant, which I thought was monumental. This time feels more natural and sentimental then that one could have ever hoped to be. "You are beautiful. I have always thought that about you. Quarterback boy wasn't wrong to be jealous of me back in the day."

"Then why were you dreading the wedding night?"

"Because—" His voice cracks for the first time since we began this conversation and he has to clear his throat. "Because I'm in love with someone else."

My eyes grow wide. Damn, I thought it was going to be big, but I wasn't expecting that. "Who? I mean, not that it's any of my business. I'm just . . . I calculated fifty different ways this conversation was going to go, and I did not see it happening like this."

He chuckles and stands to head into my kitchen. "Would you like some wine, Lucia? I feel like we could both use a glass."

"Oh God, yes please," I say, hoping he brings back the whole bottle I can't help but notice when he comes back into the room, he seems more relaxed. More natural. It's like the stick he's had up his butt for months has been removed.

"So, let's recap," I suggest as I accept one of the two glasses and he sets the bottle on the coffee table. "I don't want to get married. Neither do you. Neither of us love each other in that way, and you are in love with someone else."

He smiles before he takes a sip of his wine. "Something like that."

"Okay, I'm going to need the whole story because I feel like your story is so much better than mine."

He takes another sip of his wine and puts his glass down. "Her name is Celine. I met her during my internship in Italy."

"Wow. Okay. How long after you got there did you meet her?"

He nods. "We met on the first day and were inseparable for the entire year. I fell in love with her from the start. She's beautiful and smart and an amazing cook and . . ."

"And what? You can't leave me on a cliffhanger!"

"And she's French."

My jaw drops. Luciano's parents might have been born in America, but just like their ancestors, they view anyone from France as an enemy.

It has something to do with the wine.

"So, what happened? Did you two break up in Italy?"

He shrugs. "I wanted to bring her back with me. She had never been to America and was so excited. When I told my parents, they flipped out. I believe my father's words were, 'You can leave Frenchie where you found her or you can kiss the expansion location goodbye.'"

"Are you kidding me? That expansion was your idea. You were transforming the menu! And they threatened to cut you out of it because they didn't like a girl based on an age-old stereotype?"

"I know. It sounds ridiculous, which I told them. In no way did I think they were serious. So, I came back from Italy and brought Celine with me. Only they were serious, and Dad signed over the franchise rights to some corporate schmuck from Chicago. I was devastated. I've worked for years on that. That was . . . Celine and I had dreams. We were going to take Tripoli's and make it ours."

"Oh my gosh, Luciano, I'm so sorry. I can't believe your parents would do that."

"Neither could I. It was infuriating. I had my bags packed and was ready to tell them goodbye for the last time, but then Celine left. She wrote me a note, saying how much she loved me but that she wouldn't be the reason my dreams couldn't come true. She went back to France so I could get the franchise back."

Holy shit. I've never met this woman, but I love her already. I'm also now very invested in this story.

"So, why did you ask me out if you were still in love with Celine?"

He laughs. "Would you believe it was because you were there?"

Now it's my turn to laugh. "Yes, because that's actually why I said yes."

"When Celine left, I didn't want to tell them it was so I could get the restaurants back. They would have thought it was some sort of grand plan, which it would have been. I figured that, to prove we were truly broken up, I needed to start dating. What better person than the girl they've wanted me to be with since birth?"

"I get it. I needed to get over Bryce. We . . . well, it had been a whirlwind few days with us that did not end well. When you asked me, it felt like the universe telling me that I made the right decision to move on from him, so I said yes. I must admit, going out with you got my mom off my back about why I didn't date. When she found out it was you, I think I made her year."

We just stare at each other for a second, and for the first time in a year and a half, I don't feel awkward or that I have to force something that's not there.

I definitely don't feel like I'm going to cough.

"I didn't mean for all of this to happen," he says. "I thought that, if I asked you out a few times, it would get them off my back."

"And I thought if I went out with you, then I'd slowly start moving on with my life. Then you proposed, and I didn't know what to do. So, I said yes."

"I really need to apologize for that," he says, shaking his head like he can't believe what's going on. "I never meant to propose to you. Dating was one thing. But marriage? It was never supposed to go that far. Then one day, I came home and my parents were waiting for me, ring in hand. They told me that they reserved the restaurant that night and invited all of our family and friends so everyone could be there when I proposed to you."

This is news to me. "They did what?"

"Yes. That is the true story of our engagement. News flash: my parents are nuts," he says, finishing off his wine. "I really think they were worried I wasn't serious about you. It was like we were both playing this epic game of chicken."

I can't wait to tell Brenna and Megan everything.

"So, let's add all of this up," I say, needing to get my analytical mind around all of this craziness. "You not loving me and being in love with Celine, plus me not loving you and only dating you in a futile attempt to get over Bryce, plus our crazy parents putting unwanted pressure on us equals an engagement neither of us wanted and a marriage we were both dreading?"

"Ding, ding. We have a winner."

I can't help but laugh, and soon Luciano joins me. I mean, what else can we do? This has to be, by far, the most messed-up situation in the world.

Luciano pours us each another glass as our laughter dies down. "What do we do now?"

"We start canceling stuff?" I ask.

"I'll cancel the food."

I nod. "I'll take care of the cake and the flowers. What about the honeymoon?"

"You take it," he says. "The next time I go away, it will be to bring back the woman I am supposed to marry."

This makes me smile. "I can't wait to meet her."

He squeezes my hand. "And I hope that football boy treats you the way you deserve."

This takes me by surprise. "Who says I'm going to be with Bryce?"

"Oh, Lucia. It was only a matter of time before he came back for you. I see the way he looks at you. That man is insanely in love with you, and you might not want to admit it, but your feelings for him have not gone away."

I can't make eye contact with him because if I do I have to admit he's right. Love has never been a problem for me and Bryce.

It's everything else.

"We do have one small problem," Luciano says.

I raise an eyebrow. "Besides figuring out how to get deposits refunded?"

"Worse. We have to tell our parents."

20

BRYCE

The sound of Lucy's voice makes me jump a little from the seat on the back of my tailgate. So much so that I almost drop the iPad I'm holding.

"Lucy? What are you doing here?"

I came to Lake Laurel to get some peace and quiet—I love my mother but she will talk my ear off if I let her—and I had homework to do for Malcolm.

I slide over to make space for her, and like she's been doing it every day for her entire life, she settles in next to me. "When I need to get away from things or if I'm having a bad day, I come out here. What about you? What brings you out here?"

I put the iPad down and angle myself so I can look at her. "My therapist gave me a quiz to take. I thought maybe if I came out here, it would help me focus a bit instead of being at my mom's."

"Oh," she says, her eyes going wide. "I don't want to interrupt. I'll let you go then."

She begins to get off my truck, but I quickly put a hand on her forearm. "No. Don't go. Stay."

"Are you sure?"

"Of course, I am." I grab a blanket from the pile I have sitting behind me, glad I thought to bring them, and offer it to her.

"Thanks," she says, taking the blanket from me and wrapping it around her shoulders. "So, what is this quiz on. I hope it's not math because I'm going to guess your trigonometry skills have not improved in seven years."

"I didn't know you took up comedy in your spare time." I give her shoulder a little shove with mine, loving the easiness of this conversation. "No, it's about different situations that could cause stress. I'm supposed choose how I would react. We're working on . . . well, we're just working on stuff."

The smile she gives me resembles one she gave after the state title game. It was a smile of pride.

"I'm glad you're talking to someone. I really hope it helps you."

"Thanks," I say as I start rocking back and forth, all of a sudden uncomfortable having this conversation be all about me and my problems. "What part of wanting to get away from life brought you out here?"

She looks away for a few seconds, and it gives me a chance to really look at her. Have I ever really studied her profile and the beautiful lines of her face? Her hair is up on top of her head, which gives me a perfect view of her long neck. If this were seven years ago, my mouth would be on it in a heartbeat.

When she turns back to look at me, the look of pride she had just a minute ago is gone. She doesn't look tired or stressed like she did the other day. She also doesn't look sad like she did when I watched her through the window at her wedding shower. No, right now she looks like everything is finally okay, almost peaceful even.

"Luciano and I called off the wedding."

I'm doing my best not to crack a smile, but it is damn hard. Is it appropriate to stand and start cheering? I wonder if she'd be mad if I did a backflip. I've never tried, but it doesn't look that hard. Or maybe I can hire the high school marching band to do an impromptu parade tomorrow? That's probably too big.

"You can wipe the smile off your face," she says.

"What smile?" I say, giving up and letting it stretch wide.

"That one," she says around her laughter. "How do you know that I'm not crying on the inside?"

"Because I know you, Lulu," I say, leaning back on my hands with my legs stretched over the tailgate. "If you were really upset, you'd be at home, eating your weight in mint chocolate chip ice cream and watching those movies I hate."

"I did that *once*," she says. "And don't you dare speak ill of *Twilight*."

"She should have ended up with the wolf guy."

This makes her laugh. "I'm not sad. I meant what I said the other day, I wasn't happy, and the closer the wedding got, the worse the anxiety got. He wasn't what I wanted."

"Yeah? And what is?"

I know the question is a risky one, but I have to know because every muscle in my body is aching to touch her. I know I'm supposed to be working on myself and learning to live my life without her, but if she opens that door, there is no way I won't step through it.

"I want to say you . . ."

"I feel there is a *but* coming."

She nods, reaching for my hand, which I gladly give her. "I've never stopped loving you. As much as I've tried, as much as I thought that moving on would be the way to somehow erase my feelings for you, I never stopped."

"Neither did I. I know I fucked up, broke promises, and let you down more than I deserve to be forgiven for, but you have to know that everything I did, every decision I made, you were always on my mind."

"There's a difference between being on your mind and being in your life, Bryce. For years, I lived on empty promises and pipe dreams. I'm not going to deny that I love you, and I believe when you say that you love me, but . . . there is a reason there was never an us. If you tell me, right now, that it's our time, and something ends up becoming more important than us, I won't survive. Not again."

"It is our time," I say too quickly.

She grabs my hand, putting it between both of hers. "I know you think it is, but stop and think. How would this work? And not just right now but also in the long-run. How do you have someone in your life during the season? How do you have someone as a part of your daily life?"

I do as she asks, and really think about it. The problem is that, every time I pictured us together, it was effortless. We were just together and happy and nothing else mattered. Logistics never came into consideration. I just wanted to love her and for her to love me back. For us to be together. To be the team I always thought of us as.

"I know that's not a question you can answer quickly, and you do too," she says, taking a breath. "So, I want you to think about it until I get back in two weeks."

"What? You're leaving?" I say, probably a little too loudly.

"Luciano is friends with a chef at a resort in St. Thomas. It is where we were going to honeymoon, and since that isn't happening anymore, he made a call and got me a room there instead. I had some extra money laying around now that I don't have to pay for flowers or caterers, so I booked myself a ticket. I need to get out of town and think some things through. I want you to do the same."

"But, Lu—"

"No," she says, pressing a finger to my lips. "We love each other. That's not the hard part. That has *never* been our struggle. What we need to figure out is what we want, and you need to figure out where and how I fit into your life."

I let her words settle in. I believe her when she says that if I screw up again, that's it. I'll have squandered my final chance with her, which is the absolute last thing I want to do.

I refuse to do that, so I'll take the time she's telling me to take, and really think about how this would work.

"You know, sometimes I hate how smart you are," I say, pulling her a little closer.

"You're lucky I didn't give you a breakdown of the statistics of long-distance relationships."

"I love it when you get all math geek on me."

"I'll remember that for when I get back from my non-honeymoon at Indigo Royal Resort."

"Or I could go with you and you can give me all the statistics you want? I'm a very good learner, and I haven't had someone give me a breakdown of probabilities and statistics in a very long time. I think it would be good for me to go so you can teach me all of that while you're wearing a bikini."

She smacks my chest playfully before cuddling against me. "As much as I would love to do that, you know we need to do this by ourselves."

"I hate it when you're right," I say. "Though, I would like you to send me daily updates. If pictures are included, I won't be upset, but I require one math fact from you a day."

"Deal."

We fall into a comfortable silence as the water gently ripples in front of us. Soon, her head falls on my shoulder, and instead of moving it, she moves in closer to me.

This. This is what I want. I want her next to me, in my life, and if she wants me to figure out how it's going to happen, then damn it I'll do it.

"So, what do you plan to do on this non-honeymoon?"

She shrugs, but her head doesn't move from my shoulder. "What any girl on the cusp of a breakup and possibly getting back together with her high-school sweetheart would do. Drink a copious number of daiquiris and make pro-con lists about the future."

"That's my girl," I say, kissing her temple. "Nothing gets me going quite like a pro-con list."

"Don't mock the lists."

"I would never."

She turns to face me. "Two weeks. We take that time to figure this out because I might not be marrying Luciano, but I'm not going to settle. I don't care how in love with you I am, I'm not going to be—"

I don't know what she was about to say, but I refuse to hear it.

This is the present, and in the present, I'm going to kiss this girl and make sure she knows how crazy I am about her. That I'm going to move mountains to make sure this works.

I'm definitely not going to let her go away for two weeks without the taste of me on her lips.

Our mouths connect, and for the first time in God knows how long, I feel like I'm home. Her lips are soft and warm and fall into a perfect rhythm with mine.

I feel like I'm more alive than I have ever been. That's what she does to me. Always has, always will.

I also know this. I don't care what I need to do or what needs to happen: Lucy is going to be in my life.

I know what life is like without her, and it almost killed me. If I let this chance go without doing everything I could to be with her, then I deserve to be miserable.

No more waiting. No more excuses. It's our time.

21

LUCY

"LUCIA MARIE VALENTI, you get your ass out here right now and tell me to my face that the rumor making its way around town isn't true!"

Brenna's voice makes me physically jump out of bed. I put my hand over my heart, making sure it's still there and not somewhere beating outside of my body.

Did I not lock the door? I really thought I did. Then did she pick the lock? I mean, I wouldn't put it past Brenna to do something like that.

"Good morning to you too, Brenna," I say, sitting back down on my bed as my best friend comes into my room.

"Don't good morning me," she says as she aggressively takes a seat at the bottom of my bed. "How can you call off your engagement and not tell me *immediately?*"

"I meant to. I promise. Things just didn't go as planned."

"How do they not go as planned? Oh no. Did Luciano cry? I like the guy and all, but I can see him being a crier."

I shake my head. "No. He laughed."

Breanna's jaw drops open. "I'm confused. Start from the beginning. Leave nothing out."

"Fine, but at least let me get up and make coffee. You might not drink it, but some of us need it to function."

"Can you imagine me on caffeine? The world can't handle that."

I laugh as we make our way to my kitchen where I begin to brew a cup and fill her in on everything from last night.

I tell her about his trip to Italy, why he asked me out in the first place, and how all of this snowballed into something neither of us could stop.

"That doesn't seem so bad," she says as we take a seat at my kitchen counter. "Seems like you two did what was right for both of you."

"We did. Then we told our parents that the wedding was off."

That was our biggest mistake, but at least we did it together.

Pro: We only had to say it once.

Con: Double the Italian outrage.

Dishes were thrown. Voices were raised. There was swearing in both Italian and English. More than once, I heard the phrase "French hussie."

When it was over, I felt like I got ran over by a truck. I needed calm, so I went to the lake. Bryce being there felt like kismet.

I have no idea when I got home. All I know is that I slept better last night than I had in months. Whether it was because the stress of the wedding was gone or because I could still feel Bryce's arms around me and his lips on mine, I'm not sure.

"Damn," Brenna says, her mouth hanging open as I wrap up the events of the night. "That's a lot to unpack. Also, I feel oddly invested in the Celine-Luciano romance."

"Right?" I say, getting up to pour myself another cup. "Is it bad that I'm glad he is in love with someone else?"

"Absolutely not. You guys love each other like family, not like husband and wife. Him loving her helps you know that the decision you made was the right one. Now he can be happy with her, and you and my brother can *finally* be together. Oh my God, we're going to be sisters!"

"Calm down," I say, taking a seat back at the table. "We're a long way from another wedding."

"Semantics. But at least you two are back together now, right?"

"Not exactly."

"What do you mean not exactly? You talked last night. You kissed, which is gross but I'm willing to pretend he's not my brother for you and the sake of our friendship. You both are clearly in love with each other. What else do you need?"

When she says it like that, it all seems so simple when it's anything but.

"We have a lot to figure out," I say. "He might be seeing a therapist now, but he still has a lot of issues to work through. That doesn't happen overnight. Also, I need to make sure what we have isn't something I've built up in my head for seven years. I need to make sure this is the real deal before I uproot my life to Nashville. There's a lot to figure out."

"You're right," Brenna says. "So, what are you going to do?"

She follows me as I stand and head back to my bedroom. "First, I'm going to call all of the vendors and see what kind of refund I can get back on my deposits."

"I wonder if I can get money back on my bridesmaid dress."

"Sorry about that."

"No worries. I'll add it to my growing collection. What about after that??"

"After, I'm going to go on my honeymoon. Alone."

"Why would you do that? And why wouldn't you take me?"

"Can you get two weeks off work in the first two months into the school year with zero notice?"

"No," she grumbles, plopping onto my bed. "But why go alone?"

"Why not? I won't be able to do anything for a while around here without someone asking me what happened. Maybe if I go away for a few weeks, some other scandal will pop up and take over as the biggest news in Laurel Heights."

"If it doesn't, I'll start a rumor about Moriah Marks. Chances are it will be true."

"You're a good friend."

"Damn right I am. Why don't you take Bryce? It would give you two time to reconnect without our nosy, prying eyes looking at you."

"Did he tell you to ask me that?"

"What? No. Why would you ask me that?"

"Because he was trying to convince me last night that I shouldn't go alone."

Saying no to that was harder than I thought because two weeks alone with Bryce at a romantic resort sounds like a dream come true. Beaches. Candlelit dinners. Couples' massages.

Bryce shirtless for most of that time.

Sometimes I really hate being responsible.

"No, we need this time to figure things out. Alone," I say, walking to my closet to get my suitcase. "If we're together, we won't do our due diligence of making sure this is what we want. For so many years, we've been living off teenage dreams and promises. We need to be adults about this. We need time to really figure out if we can do this."

"You're making him make a pro-con list, aren't you?"

I fling the suitcase onto my bed. "Damn right I am. Now hand me my cell phone. I have overpriced flowers to cancel and a plane ticket to change."

22

BRYCE

Today is the day that the rest of my life begins.

Sure, there's a chance that, at some point over the past two weeks, Lucy has decided that it's too much of a risk and we shouldn't be together. Maybe one of the ten lists she made said this wasn't a good idea.

I might love the woman, but if that fucking list exists, I'm setting it on fire.

I know they are part of her process, and to love her is to love her lists, but I don't need a piece of paper to know that I want to be with her. To know that I love her with all my heart.

The clock on my dashboard reads nine in the morning, which I'm hoping isn't too early to ask the woman you've been in love with for seven years to give this a shot. Hell, she's lucky I wasn't waiting on her doorstep when she got back from St. Thomas last night and that I waited until now instead of knocking on her door at five AM when I woke up.

I reach over to the passenger seat to grab the donut and cup of coffee I bought for her this morning, and with one last deep breath, I make my way to her doorstep.

Here goes nothing.

More like, here goes everything.

I knock on her door and look around at the outside of her house as I wait for her to answer. It's white with light-blue shutters and yellow flowers blooming in the garden. Her flowers are perfectly trimmed and planted. The paint is perfect without a chip to be found.

It's the most Lucy house I've ever seen.

I hate that I'm only just now seeing it. I also hate that I had to ask Brenna for her address.

After I left for college, things didn't go the way I thought they would. I thought I'd have the chance to come home more. I thought I'd have the chance to call or text her more often.

Instead, I went silent for months until I needed something, until I needed my Lulu to help me calm the chaos in my head.

Like the angel she is, she always answered.

Like the bastard I am, I took it and ran.

Well, no more. That shit ends right now.

"Bryce?"

Lucy opens her door a few inches, and I almost drop my coffee.

If this is Lucy first thing in the morning, I never want to go another morning without seeing her.

Her hair is in a messy nest on the top of her head. She's wearing pajamas that should not be sexy but are making my mouth water, her face is free of makeup, and if I didn't know any better, I would think the glasses she has on are the same ones she wore in high school.

"Hey, Lulu," I say, holding out the donuts and coffee. "Welcome back."

"What is this?" Her voice is that perfect mix of sleepy and sexy.

"I figured you'd need breakfast."

"So, you came over to my house at nine in the morning, the day after I get back from my vacation, with coffee and donuts because you were worried about my need for nutrients?"

"Um . . . yes?" Though, I'm not sure if that's the right answer. This is what happens because I went my entire life without seriously dating. I've never had to think about this stuff before.

Just when I'm about to apologize for overstepping, a smile forms on Lucy's lips. "You're my hero. I didn't remember that I had no groceries until I woke up this morning and realized I was out of coffee. Come in, but fair warning, I'm not sharing any donuts."

I follow her back to her kitchen, and I can't help but smile—and not just because the sleep shorts she's wearing give me just a tease of her amazing ass.

I'm smiling because I'm here. It's finally time. The off-season is finally here. I can feel it.

She sets the coffee and donuts on the table, and I grab her hand and spin her around, bringing her flush to me as my lips find hers.

"Bryce," she says, inching herself away. "I told you we needed to talk about everything once I got back."

"I know," I say without letting go of her. "And I thought. I love you. I'm ready. Now, can we kiss some more?"

She raises an eyebrow. "Anything else? What did you put on your pro-con list? We need to compare."

"I didn't make one."

Her eyes grow wide. "You didn't make one?"

I'd be scared right now if her exasperation didn't make me laugh. "Nope. I don't need a list. Pro, I love you and have always loved you. Cons, None. There."

She pushes away from me. "We need to be serious about this. I gave you one job over the past two weeks, and you didn't even do it."

I laugh because I can't wait for this to be the argument for the rest of our lives. "I didn't need one."

"Yes, you do."

"No, I don't. I guarantee that, anything you wrote down on the con side, I have an answer or a solution for."

"You have never been that decisive about anything in your life."

She has me there.

"I am about this," I say, reasserting myself. "Try me."

She raises an eyebrow. "Fine. One of my cons is that I would eventually need to move to Nashville."

"Are you willing to do that?"

She shrugs. "It would be scary. I'd hate not knowing anyone but you and Cole, especially if you're on the road for long periods of time."

She's right. During the season I'll be on the road a ton, and where does that leave her? Alone in a new city?

"All right, how about this," I say, looping my arms around her waist to bring her closer to me. "You don't move right away. I won't be going back to Nashville until the spring. That gives us four months here to figure out what you're comfortable with. It will also give you a chance to meet some people out there before you make your decision."

"That's smart, though we do need to come back to it eventually," she says. "When did you become good at making decisions? You're the king of indecision. That therapist must be really good."

"That was then. This is now," I say, kissing her temple. "Apparently I just needed to make the easiest decision of my life."

This makes her smile. "Fine, but there are more cons."

"And what would those be, Lulu?"

She fights an eyeroll. "What if we sleep on the same side of the bed? What if you're a horrible slob and I can't handle it? What if the other football girlfriends or wives don't like me? Will my relationship change with Brenna?"

"Do you have this list?" I ask, realizing exactly what I need to do.

"I do," she says, walking over to her purse and pulling out multiple sheets of paper.

"Can I see it?"

She hesitates for a second before handing it over. "Sure, but I'm not done with the cons—"

I rip it in half.

"What did you do!" she screams, trying to grab the two halves from me but I am holding them well out of her reach.

"I'm getting you out of your head," I say, throwing them in the air so they scatter across her kitchen.

"Bryce!"

I grab her hands and pull her back into me. "What were your pros?"

"What?"

"I asked, what were your pros? You had valid concerns, and I'm sure very spot-on cons, but what were your pros?"

For a second or two, she lets her fingers play with the fabric of my shirt, her eyes focused on the task.

"That I love you."

I take two fingers and lift her chin up. "What was that?"

"That I love you."

"That's a pretty big pro."

"But is it enough?" she asks, her voice unsure and hesitant. "What if, after all these years, we aren't a good fit? What if love isn't enough?"

I sit down and bring her with me so she's on my lap, which she doesn't fight. "Want to know why I ripped up your list?"

"Because you like driving me crazy?"

I laugh. "Besides that."

"Because you hate making lists?"

"While that might be true, that's not why." I bring her in a little tighter and hope that she hears everything I'm about to say. "I ripped it up because there are some things you can't pro-con. There are things in this world that don't have a predetermined answer and can't be solved by a formula. Sometimes, you just have to see where things go. I don't know how this is going to work. We might drive each other insane or never fight. All I know is that, if we go another day without trying this, then we'll never know, and that seems like the worst con of all."

She looks at me, and for a second, I'm not sure what to think because her eyes aren't giving anything away.

In fact, I'm getting the vibe that she thinks I'm an idiot.

"You really think we're never going to fight?"

I laugh. "That's what you took from that?"

"Well, that . . . and you're right."

"I'm sorry, what? I didn't quite hear you."

Now I get an eyeroll. "You're right. We'll never know until we try. I'm just scared."

"Oh, Lulu," I say, holding her a little tighter. "You don't think I'm scared? I'm terrified. I'm scared I'm not good enough for you. I'm scared that I'll fuck all of this up. I'm scared of what Coach Roberts and your parents and Brenna will do if I fuck this up. Hell, I'm scared of Cole because I know he likes you better than me. Do you want to know what scares me more than all of those combined?"

"What's that?"

"I'm scared of going my entire life and not knowing what it was like to be with you, not to know what it feels like to be yours and for you to be mine. So, what do you say? Want to be scared with me?"

Her answer is to wrap her arms around my neck and tug me closer. The second our lips touch, I feel all of the doubts she has, and all the fears I have, melt away.

And just like that, I know that this is going to be worth it.

It's finally our time.

And I'm not going to fuck it up.

23

LUCY

If my first date with Bryce Donald would have been seven years ago, I might not have been able to handle it. In fact, I *know* I couldn't have handled it because I'm twenty-four years old and can barely handle it.

The touches. The looks. The electricity. It's almost too much to handle.

And to think I was going to marry someone who I didn't feel any of this with.

It started when he picked me up. When I opened the door to find him standing there holding a bouquet of fall wildflowers, wearing tailored black pants and a white button-up shirt with the sleeves rolled to his elbows, my legs almost gave out.

Then there was the hour drive to Cincinnati in which he insisted on holding my hand the whole way. Every so often his thumb would brush back and forth over my knuckles and I know that's not supposed to be anything more than a simple touch, but I felt it in every cell of my body.

Now I'm sitting across from him at a candlelit table at one of the most exclusive restaurants in Cincinnati. The wine is perfect, the meal is mouthwatering, and the view of the river is exquisite.

None of that compares to him.

"You snuck into a bar?" he says in between laughter. "Let me guess, my sister had something to do with it."

"She's the yin to my yang," I say with a little shrug. "We were twenty. Brenna knew one of the bouncers, so she got me in. I was so nervous the whole night I didn't drink and spent the whole time trying to calculate how many ounces of liquor the bar would go through in an entire night. I sat at the bar with my phone calculator open, writing equations on cocktail napkins."

"Now that's the mathlete I know," Bryce says, a warm smile coming over his face as he reaches for my hand. "Who would have thought that you lived the crazier college life than I did?"

Now this takes me by surprise. "No way. You were at Clemson. I've seen pictures of the parties and the sorority girls. No way you didn't have a little fun."

He lets out a breath and takes a sip of his water. "I went to a few parties my freshman year. They were fun, but football was a lot more than I expected. So was school."

"I remember," I say, hoping that talk of college doesn't lead us down a touchy road of past memories.

"I realized that if I wanted to go pro, then I had to stay focused. I think I maybe went to five parties the whole time I was in college, and that was because my teammates dragged me to them. No, I saved my partying for adulthood when I thought I was untouchable."

The silence becomes thick as his words hang in the air.

"I'm so sorry," I say. "I just didn't know how—"

"It's in the past," he says, bringing my hand to his lips. "The past is what it is. It happened. We learn from it. But now? Now I'm only focused on the future."

I smile because that's exactly what I needed to hear.

"Speaking of the future," he says as he stands. "This night is not over yet."

"Really?" I ask, standing as he pulls my chair out. "And what does that have to do with the future?"

"Because," he says, wrapping his arm around my waist to bring me in for a quick kiss. "Tonight is the first night of our future. Come on, I have somewhere I've always wanted to take you."

———

"HEIGHTS PARK? This is where you couldn't wait to take me?"

He laughs as he puts the truck in park. "What do you mean? You don't like it?"

"I mean . . ."

It's not that I don't like it. Being anywhere with Bryce is better than being most places, but I guess I just thought that maybe we'd take a romantic walk on the riverfront or catch a show.

Not go to the high-school make-out spot back in our hometown.

"I know I was talking about the future," he says as he opens my door a few seconds later and helps me out of the truck. "But before we move on to the future, there are some things in the past I need to make up for. This date is one of the biggest."

He takes my hand and walks me to a spot under a big tree, and I have to blink a few times to make sure my eyes aren't deceiving me.

Laid out is a blanket surrounded by candles. I'm pretty sure if I look close enough, I see a box of cannoli from Tripoli's and two bottles of what look like root beer chilling in a bucket.

In the middle of the blanket is Bryce's old jacket.

"How did you do all of this?" I ask, stunned as I take a few steps closer.

"Turns out my sister isn't that big of a pain in the ass after all." He picks up his jacket and holds it up for me to put on. "And when I told her what I had always planned for our first date, well, let's just say there was no stopping her."

I take another look around, and everything screams seventeen-year-old Bryce and Lucy.

"This is perfect," I say, taking a seat on the blanket. "I can't believe you did all of this. I'm also trying to decide how I feel that you wanted to bring me to the Laurel Heights make out spot on our first date."

Bryce couldn't wipe the wicked smile off his face if he tried.

Though, I bet he doesn't want to. "Let's just say that teenage Bryce was very ready to make out with you."

I laugh as Bryce takes a seat behind me, immediately bringing me in between his legs so my back is to this front.

"Lucy, I know I've said it before, and I'm pretty sure I'll be saying it for the rest of our lives, but I'm sorry. I'm so sorry. We've wasted so much time because I was an idiot—"

"Don't apologize." I smile and trap his face between my palms.

"Yeah, but—"

"No buts. We can't change the past. We can only learn from it and move on and work for the things we want."

He lets out a sigh as he weaves his fingers through mine. "How do you do it?"

"Do what?"

"Always know the thing to say to get me out of my head?"

I shrug. "I guess that's my superpower."

"One of many," he says, bringing me the few inches onto his lap where I immediately wrap my arms around his neck.

"I have others?"

"You do." Then he places the softest kiss on my neck.

Sweet baby Jesus.

I hadn't known I could feel a kiss on my neck all the way in my pinkie toe.

"You, my Lulu, have the power to drive me crazy. Do you know how hard it was to keep my hands to myself tonight? That dress just about killed me."

"It did?"

"It did," he says, placing another kiss on my neck, this time just a bit lower. "I'm powerless when it comes to you. Don't you know that by now?"

It could be the moonlight, the candles, his words, or all of the above, but I have never felt a need like this before in my entire life. If I don't kiss him in the next two seconds, I might explode.

I bring his lips to mine and as soon as we connect, a fire rages through my entire body. A fire I never want to put out.

His lips are perfect—soft but demanding. I turn so I can straddle him, and I'm pretty sure I hear the faint sound of my dress ripping. I don't care. I need to be closer to him. I need to be as close as possible.

Kissing him is all-consuming in every part of my body, and I'm pretty sure we are both close to combusting.

My hands slide up the back of his head, my nails grazing his scalp as I urge him closer to me. He must read my mind because his hands trail down my sides and then cup my ass, lifting me slightly so I'm as flush against him as possible. Where he has placed me makes it impossible to ignore his hardness beneath me.

"Lucy," he says, his lips trailing to my neck. "We need to slow down."

"We do?" I ask as I shift away slightly. "Why? Did I—"

"Absolutely not," he says, bringing me in for another kiss. "You are perfect. God, you are perfect in every way. I would kiss you all night if you let me."

"Then what?" I ask, hating how insecure I sound.

"I have waited years for you. For *this*," he says as he brushes a lock of my hair back and tucks it behind my ear. "I don't want it to be rushed in a park. I don't want it to be in the heat of the moment. I want it to be perfect."

God, this man. Every time I saw him cast as the newest bad boy of football or saw a picture of him with his arms draped around multiple women, I couldn't bear to look at it. I knew that wasn't him.

I refused to entertain the idea that I was wrong and the Bryce I fell in love with was the imposter.

I'm glad I dug my heels in because this is the real Bryce. The caring man. The man who remembers inconsequential conversations from years ago and what my favorite dessert is. He's the man who gives me butterflies just from a look across the room and a touch of the hand.

The man I'm in love with.

24

BRYCE

DECEMBER, COLLEGE, FRESHMAN YEAR

I MIGHT HAVE BEEN GONE for a year, but Laurel Heights hasn't changed a bit and neither has this view at the lake.

There is still construction downtown, which has been going on since I started high school. The same old men were talking in the coffee shop when I walked past the other day—no doubt talking about football after their weekly trip to the bank. The only difference was not seeing Lucy's big brown eyes and smile when my mom, Brenna, and I walked into Tripoli's on Christmas Eve. The whole night, I had to see fucking Pizza Boy with a smug grin.

I still hate him, so at least that's the same.

Even hours after dinner was over, I couldn't stop thinking about how much I missed Lucy. I tried my best to stay in touch with her when I was gone, but I really never realized how much football and classes would take over my life. I've never been great at school, so when I wasn't at practice or in classes, I was studying to make sure I was keeping my grades up. It was truly a whirlwind. One minute it was spring semester, which rolled into summer classes, and next thing

I knew, it was time for training camp and I'd missed my chance to come home and visit.

"Bryce?"

Lucy's voice pulls me from my thoughts, and I hurry and jump off the bed of my truck.

The second my eyes land on her, it's as if my whole world slams to a stop. I can't believe how much she's changed in subtle ways and my eyes race to note every difference.

She's impossibly more beautiful than I remember, and she isn't wearing glasses, which I strangely miss even if it means I can see her doe eyes all that much better. The curve of her hips are more pronounced, and I have to fight the urge to hold on to them. And her curves up top? When did that happen?

Snap out of it, man. I need to stop acting like a horny teenager.

Except, I still am, I guess. Sometimes college makes me forget that because I may still be a teenager but I have all adult consequences and responsibilities.

"Hey," I say quickly, realizing I've been standing and staring at her. "How are you?"

I hold open my arms for a hug and then immediately put them down.

What's the protocol for how I greet my technical ex-girlfriend who I'm only exes with because I couldn't pack her in a bag and take her to college with me is fuzzy. Oh, and I shouldn't forget that she should hate me for breaking all sorts of promises I made her.

"If you're trying to figure out if you're allowed to hug me, the answer is yes," Lucy says, reading my mind. "You were making the face you used to make when you couldn't figure out an equation."

I let out an uncomfortable laugh as I take the final few steps to her and pull her into my arms. As soon as her head rests against my chest, the stress of the last year lifts into the crisp December air.

"God, I've missed you," I say, squeezing her a little tighter. "Thank you for meeting me."

"Of course," she says, lifting her head to look at me. "I figured it was important considering—"

Considering I haven't talked to her in months. That is what she leaves unsaid. In fact, the last time we spoke was when I texted her to let her know that I couldn't make it home for prom. That was eight months ago.

"I'm sorry," I say, leading her back to my truck and helping her up on the tailgate. "I've been so bad at calling or texting. I just . . . well, the last year has been . . . hard."

Hard doesn't even begin to scratch the surface. Overwhelming. Intense. Those are much better.

"I'm actually surprised you're home. Aren't you going to a bowl game?"

"We leave the day after Christmas. Coaches made everyone go home for the holidays before reporting back."

"Well, that's nice," she says. "I'm sure your mom liked that."

She was thrilled I was home and cried when she found out it was only for two days, but that isn't what I want to talk to her about.

"Lucy—"

"How is—"

We laugh, but it sounds weird. Forced. Not us.

God, I hate this. When did this become how Lucy and I are around each other? Oh, right. When I went off to college and dropped off the planet.

"You're probably wondering why I texted you tonight," I say, rubbing my hands together. Why I thought coming to the lake in December was a good idea is beyond me.

"Honestly? I did," she says. "After six months of silence, I figured I no longer warranted texts or calls."

"I'm sorry. I'm so sorry. It's just . . . college is nothing like I expected."

She lifts an eyebrow. "What do you mean? I thought you were ready for nonstop football."

"I thought I was," I say, leaning back on my hands. "It's so much more than that, though. It's film, then practice, then classes, then more practice, then study tables. It's nonstop. All day, every day, and for what? For me to barely pass classes and ride the bench while a guy I know I'm better than takes the starting position? It's just—it's too much. I'm barely holding on. That was why I never called or texted you. I was embarrassed that nothing was going the way I wanted it to, and . . . and I didn't know how to hide the fact that I'm barely staying above water. So, I just disappeared."

I don't mean to admit all of that, but at the same time, it feels good to finally say everything aloud.

"Bryce, that's nothing to be ashamed of. College is hard for a lot of people, when you add in a demanding sport, it's probably impossible. Your first year is done, so now you have a better handle on everything for next year."

"If there is a next year."

The lake is already eerily quiet. But now? I could hear a pin drop.

"What are you saying, Bryce?"

I take a deep breath because if I say this aloud, then it's out there in the universe. I haven't told anyone these thoughts, not even to Cole, who is the only person who has an inkling of how unhappy I am.

"I'm thinking about transferring." The admission tastes bitter on my tongue and I swallow hard.

"Transferring?" she repeats, clearly stunned. "Bryce, are you sure?"

I shrug. "Maybe? All I know is that I can't sit the bench again next year. And my classes? I know I've never been a great student, but I struggled this year. Bad. I passed, but it wasn't easy. Maybe I should have stayed home and gone somewhere in-state. Maybe a smaller college? I don't know, but if this semester is a preview of my next three years, I'm not going to make it."

I'm scared to look at Lucy because I know how that must have sounded. Pathetic. Embarrassing. Like a failure. That's why I'm startled when I feel her hand rest on top of mine. When I look to her, I don't see someone who is ashamed of me.

I see someone who believes in me.

"Bryce, if it wasn't hard, everyone would do it," she says, bringing our hands together on her lap. "But now I know why you called me."

"You do?"

"I do. It's because you needed to make a pro-con list and you know I'm the best at them."

She smiles, and I can't help but do the same.

"That must have been it," I say, turning to face her. "Too bad we don't have any paper."

"You think this is my first rodeo? We don't need paper. Now, let's talk this out."

For the next hour, that's what we do. Only we move the conversation to the inside of my truck because it's Christmas Eve and cold as fuck outside.

After our hands unthawed, a list has been made and it's clear I'll stay at Clemson.

"You know that's not actually why I texted you," I say.

"It wasn't for my masterful list making?"

I laugh. "Shockingly no. It was just a bonus."

"Then, why? I mean, I'm glad you did, but I figured you needed my help."

I reach over and move a stray hair back behind her ear. I can't stop staring at her. This new Lucy with no glasses and full lips is . . . it's too much.

"I messaged you," I say, placing a kiss on her cheek. One she doesn't pull away from, "because I miss you. Because you get me. Because you're the only one I can talk about what's going on in my head without judgment. You're my best friend, Lulu—no, you're more than that. You're everything to me, and I'm so sorry I didn't call, or text. I'm so sorry."

I feel her hand on my cheek, and I know I'm going to regret being this selfish, but I don't care.

I need to kiss her. I need it more than I need to take my next breath.

"Bryce," she whispers, and that snaps the last of my resolve.

I take my hands and cup her cheeks, bringing her to me. The second our lips touch, I know I'm not wrong. The warmth and electricity I feel every time I'm with Lucy courses through my body.

She wraps her arms around my neck, and I pull her over the console so she's straddling me in the driver's seat. I sure as hell didn't mean for this to happen when I called her earlier, but I can't lie and say I'm mad about it.

It's Lucy. In my arms. On my lap. Kissing me like her life depends on it.

I let go of her hands and trail my palms down her body. I feel the curve of her breasts, and it takes all the willpower I have left not to cup them. I wonder what they would be like in my hands.

Or in my mouth.

"Bryce." She moans my name, and fuck, I am as hard as I've ever been. I'm not a virgin—that ship sailed sophomore year of high school—but I feel like I am.

Wait, what am I doing? As much as I enjoy kissing Lucy—I really need to figure out how I can smuggle her back to college with me— this isn't right. We're in my beat-up old truck at the lake. We haven't seen each other in months.

I'm being a selfish bastard, that's what I am doing.

"Lucy," I say, pulling away from her lips, which I immediately regret. "Wait."

"What?" she asks. "Is everything okay?"

"No—I mean yes. I mean . . . shit." I'm clearly fucking this up. "I don't want it to be like this."

"What do you mean?"

I adjust her so she's looking right at me, even though that makes me want to kiss her all over again.

"If we keep going, I know where it's going to go, and you deserve more than a quicky in my truck. I want to give you so much more. Romance and candles and the whole nine yards."

"Bryce, I don't need—"

"Yes, you do, and I'm going to give it to you. Some day."

"Bryce. Don't say things you don't mean."

"Don't mean? Lucy Valenti, I'm crazy about you. I know I have a weird way of showing it, but I love you, and I promise I'm going to do better. I'm going to call you every week, text you every chance I get, ask you how your days were. You're going to tell me about school and life, and I'm going to complain about classes. And then, guess what?"

"What?" she says, a hint of a smile coming through.

"Next off-season? It's ours."

25

LUCY

I roll my eyes as I wipe my hands on the dish towel in the kitchen.

"Are you ever going to get tired of that?" I ask as Bryce comes into the kitchen, dropping the bag of groceries I asked him to pick up on his way over.

He wraps his arms around my waist and places a kiss on my cheek, one that might seem tame but warms me from head to toe. "Nope. Never."

I might joke with him about the lame throwback to *I Love Lucy*, but it's the favorite part of my day because it always leads to this. Just a few minutes of quiet time for us as our individual days melt into our nights together.

He trains during the day while I'm at work, and he has his appointments with Malcolm twice a week. Sometimes, we cook together, and other times, we get takeout. It's so . . . normal.

I love it.

"How was your day?" he asks. "Anything . . . interesting happen?"

The man might be the best quarterback in pro football, but he's a horrible actor.

"Nope. Pretty normal" I say, going back to chopping the peppers.

"People wanted money. I gave them money. Megan complained about being pregnant. Same old, same old."

I'm glad I'm facing away from him because I'm having trouble keeping the smile off my face. I know he's trying to egg me on about the ginormous flower arrangement he had sent to the bank today. It was so big that when Megan brought it into my office, I couldn't see her face. The bouquet is a beautiful red and white rose arrangement that screams Christmas. It also makes my budget-loving heart pound a little harder wondering what it had to cost him.

While the arrangement was gorgeous, it was the card that came with it that sent my emotions into overdrive.

I'm sorry it took me this long to send you flowers.
Love you most, Bryce.

I wanted to text him and thank him right away, but as soon as I picked up my phone, we got busy and stayed that way until I locked the doors at five.

"So, you didn't get anything special at work?" he asks, spinning me around so I can't hide behind the peppers anymore. "Nothing at all?"

I shrug as I loop my hands around his neck. "Not that I can think of. Oh wait! I did get something! It was this little bouquet of flowers. I think one of my clients sent it to me."

"I'll show you little . . ."

Bryce scoops me up and sits me on the counter, bringing our lips together as our laughter fades. I knew what it was like to kiss Bryce when we were teenagers, but kissing him now is a whole new experience. Maybe it's because we're adults and we aren't afraid to hold back. Or maybe because it means something more. I'm not sure, but every time I kiss the man, every time I feel his lips on mine, it makes me feel like I am the most loved and cherished woman in the entire world.

"If we don't stop, we aren't going to eat dinner," I say, though I don't make an attempt to stop him from kissing my neck.

"I don't need to eat," he says before his lips suck on my neck as his hands begin searching underneath my sweater. "Well, food that is."

"Yes, you do," I say. Despite the fact that he has spent every night here since we decided to give this a go, we haven't slept together yet. We're trying to wait and not rush into it. That's becoming easier said than done.

It sounded like a good idea at the time. I guess I didn't factor in that Bryce could make me see stars with just his mouth.

"Fine," he grumbles, placing one more kiss on my lips. "In all seriousness, did you like the flowers?"

I return the kiss and jump off the counter. "I loved them, but they were too much."

"Nonsense," he says as he begins to put away the groceries. "When you told me you had never gotten flowers from anyone, it was basically a challenge."

"You could have just got me a regular bouquet."

He laughs into the refrigerator. "Again, nonsense. You will learn, Lulu, I don't do things halfway. It's all or nothing, baby."

I scoop the carrots into the salad bowl and place it onto the kitchen table as Bryce follows behind, setting out our preferred dressings.

"So, where did we leave off last night?" Bryce asks as he pours us both waters as I put down the lasagna.

"Fears and phobias," I say, sounding more like a category on *Jeopardy* than dinner conversation. "You were telling me about your very real, and very paralyzing fear of spiders."

"Yeah, let's move on from that one," he says, taking a huge bite of my lasagna. "Oh! I know. Guilty pleasures. We all have them. What is the one that gets my girl going?"

I laugh at the way he says it, his eyebrows wagging up and down like he's about to pull a juicy secret from me.

"Well, you know at night when you see me playing with my phone and I say I'm playing solitaire? I'm really browsing real estate apps and looking up extravagant houses that I'll never be able to afford."

"Really? That's your thing?"

"Definitely. You should see some of these houses. I'm talking about ones that sell for millions and millions of dollars. They are fascinating to look at, but who needs a house with six bathrooms? Then there are the ones that listed for like, two million, and then you look inside and it's like the worst version of a freaky, real-life dollhouse."

"Have you looked at any in Tennessee?" Bryce asks, trying to sound nonchalant. "I've heard there are some pretty nice ones down there."

"I haven't, but maybe I will," I say, feeling the blush creep across my cheeks. I don't know why the thought of looking up extravagant homes in Tennessee makes me nervous, but it does. Maybe because that means I'm thinking about a future with Bryce, which still makes me feel all sorts of ways. "Now, what about you. What's the one guilty pleasure the gossip sites would love to know about Bryce Donald."

He lets out a breath and puts his fork down. "I'm not sure if you're ready for this."

Oh, now I'm intrigued. "Lay it on me, Donald. Tell me that secret love you have."

"I need to preface this by saying it's not just me. It's most of my team, even Cole. It started as something to do together, and it has . . . well, it has grown legs none of us could have predicted."

"Are you going to make me guess, or are you building anticipation? Because if it's the latter, it's working."

"I'm trying to figure out how to tell you so you don't look at me differently."

"That is now out the door. Spill it."

"Fine," he says, picking up his glass and taking a healthy sip of water. "Most of the guys and I on the team are a part of Bachelor and Bachelorette nation. We are in fantasy leagues for them. We never miss an episode. Our Tuesday meetings can't begin until we've done episode recaps, and we send each other articles updating each other on past contestants. I'm actually glad we brought this up because the new season starts next week, so guess what your Monday nights now include."

My jaw drops a little more with each word that comes out of his mouth. Of all the things he could have told me, that was the absolute last thing I thought would be said.

"Come on. Give me shit. I know you want to," he says, digging back into his lasagna.

I don't. Instead, I stand and walk to the other side of the table, where I situate myself on his lap.

"I think that is both hilarious and amazing. I can't wait to watch with you."

This earns me a quick kiss. "Remember that when I go crazy on the hometown dates."

"I'll try to remember that. Now, if I'm going to be watching the show with you, I need you to do something for me."

"Anything, Lulu."

"You say that now . . ."

"Oh, come on. What could it be? Want me to buy you a ridiculous house in Tennessee? You got it. Want a bigger flower arrangement each day of the week? No problem. Hell, I'll even let you tutor me for old time's sakes. There is nothing you can ask me that I would say no to."

I glance down before letting out a breath. "I'd like you to come to Christmas Eve dinner with me at my parents' house."

His eyes go wide, realization setting in about what I'm asking him to do. This isn't a normal meet the parents. This will be the first family get together since I called off the wedding.

My parents and I have spoken, but it hasn't exactly been warm or loving conversations. They didn't come out and say it, but I know they think I called off the wedding for Bryce. When I remind them that neither Luciano nor I loved each other, they ignore it.

But it's Christmas, and Christmas is meant to be spent with those you love.

"My answer does not change. I will absolutely be there," he says right before placing a kiss on my nose. "Though, I might need a bit of encouragement beforehand. You know, something to pump me up."

I wrap my arms around his neck and pull his lips into mine a little more forcefully than I usually do. I'd say this takes him by surprise by the sudden bulge I feel underneath me. Though I wouldn't say he's complaining about it considering his hands are now digging into my hips in the best way.

"Like that?" I say, placing one more kiss on his upper lip.

He swallows hard, readjusting me on his lap. "Something like that."

"So will you come with me?"

He plants one more kiss into my neck as he quickly sweeps me up into his arms. "I'm still not sure," he says, carrying me away from the dining room. "I think I need more convincing."

26

BRYCE

"BREATHE," Lucy says as we walk up to her parents' door, and I slightly adjust the bag full of gifts we brought. "They are going to love you. Plus, Uncle Nick is here as a buffer."

I relax a little as Lucy kisses my cheek.

I wanted this, right? When we were younger, this was one of the things I couldn't wait to do. Except then I was a dumb teenager hoping her parents would like me enough that they would let me take her out to a movie. Now I'm the guy she started dating days after calling off her wedding to the man they might have loved more than Lucy.

Her words, not mine.

It doesn't help that it's Christmas Eve because, why not meet your girlfriend's parents on a major holiday?

"Are you sure this is a good idea?" I ask, unable to hide the nervousness from my voice. "I don't want to ruin Christmas. I can meet them on December twenty-seventh. That sounds like a great day."

"Stop," Lucy says as she puts her hands on my cheeks. "Get out of your head. It's game time, Donald. You ready?"

Her attempt to sound like one of my coaches makes me smile. "You hyping me up?"

"Hell yeah I am," she says, putting our foreheads together. "Let's do this."

I lean down and give her a quick kiss. "You're really cute when you do this."

She smiles. "I'll remember that for the future."

I kiss her again, but as soon as our lips touch, I hear the sound of her front door opening.

"Are you going to stand there and make out with my daughter or are you going to come in so we can get this night started?"

I jump away from Lucy and clear my throat. "Hello, sir. Nice to meet you. I'm Bryce Don—"

"I know who you are. You cost me money in the season opener last year. Now get in here so I can start eating the appetizers."

He walks away, and I'm left stunned as I follow Lucy into the house.

"See, that went well," Lucy says, taking off her coat. After a second, I set the bag on the floor and pull my own jacket off.

"How in the world did that go well?"

"He let you in, didn't he?"

I blink a few times. "Was there another option?"

Lucy just shrugs. "Honestly, I have no idea. This is all new to me, and I'm just hoping we make it out of here tonight with minimal tears and bloodshed."

I pick up the bag and as soon as I do, I feel a cold blast of air hit my back.

"Lucia?"

You have got to be fucking kidding me.

Pizza Boy is standing in the open doorway, wearing a fucking Christmas sweater. Why does that not surprise me?

"Luciano," Lucy says, clearly as confused to see him as I am. "What are you doing here? And is this . . ."

My gaze shifts to the blonde to his left.

"Lucia, meet Celine," Pizza Boy says, his eyes never leaving Celine, who is wearing a matching sweater.

I don't care how much I love Lucy, I will never, ever, wear matching sweaters.

Oh, who am I kidding? If she asked me to dress up as a reindeer I would.

"It is nice to meet you, Lucia," Celine says, her French accent thick as she and Lucy shake hands.

"You too." She turns to Luciano. "I thought this year our parents were doing Christmas Eve apart?"

"I thought so too," Luciano says, taking off his coat before helping Celine out of hers. "But yesterday Mama messaged me to come here instead."

"Oh God," Lucy says, her face turning whiter by the second. "Our parents are unbelievable. They knew I was bringing Bryce, and your parents knew Celine would be here. Whatever they're up to, it's nothing good."

"Sounds about right," Luciano says. I guess I can refer to him as that now that I know the French girl exists. "What's the plan?"

Lucy looks to me, to Luciano, and then back to me. "We stick to our guns. No matter what emotional blackmail they try to use, we are with the people we want to be with and we are happy."

"Sounds good to me," Luciano says as he extends his hand for me. "And, Bryce, I know we've never seen eye to eye, but for tonight, can we leave the past in the past?"

I don't offer mine back right away because years of jealousy is hard to drop in a second or two. Yes, I can admit I was jealous that he got to be around Lucy and that he knew her longer than I did. In my mind, it meant that he knew her *better*, even if that wasn't the case. When I found out they were engaged? I'd never had murderous thoughts before, but I was certain I wanted to kill him.

Now I know where Lucy and I stand and can appreciate that they needed each other for different reasons over the course of their dating and engagement. It probably doesn't hurt that he looks at Celine the way I look at Lucy. I might not want to go golfing with the guy, but I can at least make it through the next few hours with him.

"Sounds good to me," I say, extending my hand. "Now, let's go see what we are in for."

I WASN'T READY.

Though in my defense, even if I'd had years to prepare and a cheat sheet, I wouldn't have been prepared.

This dinner, is by far, the most uncomfortable thing I've ever been a part of, and I once had to take pictures with a very handsy female senior citizen group who were lifelong Fury fans.

There have been subtle digs at Celine and me. Apparently, I'm a dumb, manwhore jock, and she's unable to understand their inside jokes because she's French. I don't know how Luciano kept his cool with that. I almost punched a wall, and she's not even my girlfriend. It's one thing for them to say shit about me—I deserve it, but making fun of this woman because of her nationality? There are names for that.

Then there was the not-so-sly remark about how this was supposed to be their first Christmas as a united family.

Now we're seated around the table, and the passive-aggressive comments are through the roof.

"How have workouts been going?" Coach Roberts asks, doing his best to try to break up the awkwardness. "Thanks for letting a few of my players come in and lift with you. It's good for them to see what it's going to be like at the next level."

"Anytime. They're cool kids," I say. "But I should be thanking you for letting me use the facilities. It's really been a help."

"I mean, you paid for it. It's the least I could do."

"What did you pay for?" Mrs. Valenti interrupts.

"Mom, he and Cole upgraded the high school football team's weight facility," Lucy says, reaching for my hand under the table, which I gladly give to her. "You knew that. Uncle Nick couldn't stop talking about it for months."

"Oh, I must have forgotten," she says nonchalantly as she sips her wine. "But do you remember when Luciano donated new jerseys to the little league team and gave them a pizza party after their season? How nice was that?"

"Mrs. Valenti, our family has done that every year since I was a kid. That's nothing special."

"Oh, shush now," Mrs. Valenti says. "Don't downplay your efforts in the community. And when did you start calling me Mrs. Valenti? It's Anne Marie. Or Mom. You know that."

I clench my jaw as I listen to her talk to Luciano, and for once, the rage isn't toward him. I've never met Lucy's parents before, but it doesn't take a rocket scientist to see that it doesn't matter who I am or what I mean to Lucy. I'm not Luciano. That's all that matters. Her dad, on the other hand? He hasn't said a word since he opened the door for us. Maybe if I pay him back what he lost on our game last year it will get me into his good graces.

"Celine, how are you liking Laurel Heights?" Lucy completely ignores her mom's comment as she turns to Celine with a smile. "Have you made it down to Cincinnati yet? The restaurants down there are amazing."

"I love it here," she says. "Actually, we stayed in Cincinnati a few days when—"

"Lucy, how is the bank?" Mrs. Tripoli asks. "You must be really busy with it being the holidays."

Lucy's eyes show nothing but shock as she stares at Mrs. Tripoli. "They are, but I was asking Celine a question—"

"So, Bryce, when are you going back to Nashville?" Mrs. Valenti asks.

Apparently, we're not going to let Celine talk tonight.

"Sometime in April. I have some things to take care of before optional camp starts. Celine, what were you saying about Cincinnati?"

"That's too bad," Mrs. Valenti says, not giving Celine a chance to talk. "I'm sorry you and Lucy will only have a few months together."

Excuse me?

"Mom, just because Bryce has to go back to Nashville, it doesn't mean we are going to quit seeing each other."

She starts laughing under her breath. "What are you going to do? Move with him? Be a football player's girlfriend? Ha! Quit acting foolish, dear."

"He's a good kid, Anne Marie," Coach Roberts says in my defense. "You don't need to treat him like a drug dealer."

Mrs. Valenti waves off her brother. "He's a manwhore and not good enough for my daughter. I saw the tabloids last year. Despicable."

If that is the only objections about me, then it would be easy enough to clear the air. Only, it isn't. It's just a convenient excuse.

"Ma'am, I know what you saw last year, and I'm not proud of what I did," I say, my words as apologetic as I can make them. "But please know that I would never cheat on Lucy. I love her, and I'd never want to hurt her."

Mrs. Valenti looks directly at Lucy. "You know, if you and Luciano would just get back together, you wouldn't have to consider moving or worry about what he's doing on the road. You'd be here. Where you want to be."

"Mrs. Valenti, we are not going to be getting married," Luciano chimes in. "We don't love each other like that."

"Oh, stop, Luciano," Mrs. Tripoli says. "You and Lucy belong together, and the quicker you both get over"—she waves dismissively —"whatever these are, then you two can get back together and the wedding will go on as planned."

Lucy stands and screams, "There. Is. No. Wedding!"

I didn't even know her voice could get that loud. "There is no wedding, and I refuse to sit here and listen to you bad mouth the man I love and a woman who is perfectly wonderful and is clearly in love with Luciano."

"You don't love him. You love Luciano. He loves you. You can't fake what you two had."

"Oh my God! Were you that blind?" Lucy yells. "The man could barely stand to touch me in public. The kiss at the engagement party? That was the first time we kissed. Ever. For God's sake, we never even slept together!"

Did she just say what I think she just said?

"Wipe that smile off your face," Coach Roberts whispers to me. "Though, thanks for providing the most entertaining meal in family history."

"Well, I think that waiting is romantic," Mrs. Tripoli says. "You both were waiting for the wedding day."

"No, Mama," Luciano says, reaching for Celine's hand. "I was in love with Celine, and I couldn't bring myself to do it. Plus, Lucy is like my sister. It was . . . well, the thought of it was kind of gross. I was dreading the wedding night as much as I was dreading the marriage."

"Speaking of the wedding day," Lucy chimes back in. "Did no one notice that every time it was brought up, I went into coughing fits? No way you missed that, Mom. I went through two bags of cough drops at the shower."

"You were just caught up in the excitement of the wedding," Mrs. Valenti says as she chugs the rest of her wine. "Once Bryce goes back to Nashville and Celine goes back to France, we can all sit down and get this all back on track."

"Are you not listening to anything we are saying? We aren't in love. We aren't getting married. I love Bryce, and I'm eventually moving to Nashville."

"Shush. You have no clue what you're talking about."

"No, you two are the ones who don't know what you're talking about. You know the only reason Luciano and I didn't call the wedding off sooner? Because of you all. We each felt this immense pressure not to let all of you down. Then, when we both come to you, asking you to let the people we truly love into your lives, all you can do is bad mouth them because they don't fit in to the story you started writing when we were kids. Well, I'm not going to sit here a minute more and listen to this. Merry Christmas."

Lucy moves her chair back to exit the dining room, and I am two steps behind her. As I pass him, I make eye contact with Coach Roberts, who gives me a subtle head nod.

At least one person in her family likes me.

I catch up to Lucy at the door, where she is frantically trying to get our coats out of the closet. I put my hands on her shoulders, hoping to calm her down.

"Hey," I say, my words finally breaking her trance, "breathe for me."

She does, but I can still feel the tension and anger radiating from her as I turn her toward me.

"What you said in there was amazing. You are amazing. I didn't know I could love you any more than I already did." I press a kiss to her forehead.

"For once, I agree with Bryce," Luciano says as he comes into the foyer, hand-in-hand with Celine. "You said everything I wanted to but couldn't. Just like always, you're the brave one. Thank you, Lucia. I owe you."

Lucy seems to relax a bit, despite the background noise of yelling in the dining room. "You don't owe me anything. I meant what I said. I'm just sorry the night went like it did."

"Is this not traditional American Christmas?"

We all look at Celine and immediately start laughing. We're so loud we actually drown out the yelling coming from the other room.

"Well, we really didn't eat," Luciano says, checking his watch.

Lucy furrows her brow. "What are you thinking?"

Luciano reaches for Celine's coat and holds it open for her. "I can't believe I'm saying this, but would the two of you like to come back to the restaurant? Maybe a double date of sorts?"

I look at Lucy, who is giving me a pleading look.

My first Christmas with Lucy is going to be spent with the man I've hated most of my life, who is also her ex-fiancé.

It's a damn Christmas miracle.

"Fine, but only if we can get a supreme," I say. "And don't hold back on the breadsticks."

Luciano laughs. "I would never. Though, this will be the first time I've made you a pizza without spitting in it."

My eyes grow wide. "What did you say?"

"I'm kidding. I swear, but your face was priceless. That was the only Christmas gift I needed."

27

____

LUCY

"Depends. Did I really volunteer to help move Celine in with Luciano?"

I laugh as I take off my coat. "You did, and then I offered to help them decorate."

I have no clue what to call tonight. A disaster? A breakthrough? A fight twenty-five years in the making? Honestly, I'll go with all of the above.

About an hour after the epic fight at my parents' house, Uncle Nick messaged Bryce to tell him he was leaving because he couldn't take it anymore and they were out of wine.

Then there was dinner at the restaurant with Luciano and Celine, which was actually pretty great. We all got along, laughed, and told stories. Luciano and Bryce tried to decide who won every fight they had ever been in. The night ended with hugs and handshakes. Bryce even invited Luciano to be a part of next year's Bachelor fantasy league.

I feel like I'm living in a jacked-up version of some Christmas movie where you're in an alternate reality but you don't realize it until you wake up.

"Please tell me tomorrow isn't going to be as eventful," I say as I ungracefully plop onto my couch.

"Unless the Grinch steals the presents and tree from my mom's or Brenna doesn't get her yearly wine subscription, tomorrow will be much less eventful," Bryce says as he sits next to me and then tucks me against his side. "And I bought Brenna her wine."

"I still can't believe my parents treated you like that," I say, laying my head on his shoulder.

"Your dad wasn't so bad."

I sigh. "He and Mr. Tripoli learned long ago not to get involved with any scheme involving my mother and Guiliana. This one, though? This might have taken the cake."

Bryce kisses the top of my head as the weight of the night comes down on me.

"I'm so sorry." I've probably said it a hundred times tonight, but it doesn't seem like enough.

"Don't be," he says, running his fingers up and down my arm. "Plus, the night wasn't a total wash. I learned some interesting tidbits tonight."

"Like what?"

"I seem to remember you telling everyone at your parents' house that you and Luciano never slept together."

I freeze for a second. Crap. I completely forgot that I admitted that.

"Did I say that?"

"You kind of yelled it, but yes," he says, picking me up so I'm now straddling his lap. "Was it true? Or was that just something you said to get your mom off your back?"

I look down, not really wanting to have this conversation, but his finger under my chin tilts my face back up.

"You can tell me anything, you know that right?" he asks. "If you aren't comfortable talking about it, then that's fine too."

"It's fine." I clear my throat before saying, "No, Luciano and I never slept together. In fact, I can count on one hand how many times he kissed me. The wedding night would have been interesting, to say the least. The man could barely hold my hand."

When he laughs, I wish I hadn't admitted any of that to him.

"Don't laugh." I try to shift off his lap, but his hands clamp on to my hips and hold me in place.

"I'm sorry, I can't help it," he says. "I'm just thinking back to all those times that I was jealous as hell of him. And all he was doing was playing pretend."

"That's actually kind of what we were both doing. It was a relief when I found out we were in it for the wrong reasons."

Bryce's laughter dies down, and he gives me a quick kiss. "How could you want to marry someone you've barely kissed, Lulu?"

"We should go to bed," I say before trying to slid off his lap again. "We have a long day tomorrow and it's late."

"Whoa, wait there." All signs of levity have melted away, and his brow pinches with concern as he catches my eyes. "Did I say something wrong?"

I tip my head to the ceiling and try to find the words I want to say —no, that I *need* to say.

"You really want to know how I could marry someone I didn't love?"

"I do."

I let out a breath. "Because I didn't think I could marry the man I actually loved. I said yes to the first man who asked me because I thought the man I wanted was never going to."

I can see the moment my admission hits him where it hurts, and I hate it, but I couldn't lie to him.

"Lucy, I'm so sorry. I know it's not enough, but—"

I shake my head. "It's in the past, Bryce. We're here now. No use dwelling on it."

I try to stand, but once again, Bryce keeps his hold on me. "You got to talk, now it's my turn."

"You don't need to say anything."

"But I do. I did you wrong for so many years. I made stupid promises that I wanted to keep, I just didn't know how. Since I've been home, I really see that. I've also come to realize that it doesn't have to be one or the other, that I should be able to have both. It was stupid of me to think I had to wait for one to be ready before I could invite in the other."

"Life doesn't work like that."

"I know that now. I don't know why you have given me another chance because we both know that I don't deserve it or you. I never have. But please know that I am never, ever going to let you down again. This? You and me? It's forever, Lulu. Now, that I have you, I'm never letting you go."

For years, I have heard versions of this speech. For years, I've heard words like "forever" and "love" and have latched on to them like a lifeline.

In this moment, there is something different. It could be what we've been through or that the emotions and adrenaline of the day have caught up to me, but this time? This time, I believe him.

This is it. This is happening.

Our off-season is finally here.

"Bryce . . ." I say seconds before my lips press into his. He claims me as fiercely as I claim him, and the second our tongues meet, I feel a surge of heat that I've only ever felt one other time in my life.

His hands travel up my back and quickly make their way to the sides of my breasts. Before I know it, he's cupping each, and if my mouth weren't so busy memorizing the feel of his, I'd be crying out for more.

His fingers find my nipples through my shirt, and with a gentle tug of each, my core clenches and begins throbbing for more.

My hands find the hem of my shirt, but before I can pull it up, Bryce's hands are there, doing it for me. I barely have time to notice the chill of the air on my skin before he's unclasping my bra and tossing that to wherever my shirt landed. Then his mouth is trailing down my neck and chest before it closes over one of my peaked nipples.

Oh sweet baby Jesus . . .

His tongue circles my nipple before he closes his lips around it. I can't help but stare at the act as my hips begin to writhe in his lap.

"Bryce." I moan as he changes his focus to the other side. "More. Please. I need more."

"More of this?" he asks before his tongue starts doing something I hadn't known tongues could do. "Or maybe this?"

"Ah!" I scream when he gently bites my nipple and his hand cups my center through my pants. He might not be making direct contact, but the pressure is enough to set my body on fire.

"Take me to bed, Bryce. Now."

Our eyes lock, and I see nothing but fire in his as I'm sure mine are burning for him.

"Are you sure?" he asks. "Because this is it, Lulu. Once I have you, I'm never going to let you go."

"Promise?"

His smile turns devious as he stands, and I hook my ankles around his back. Then he's kissing me again while he ascends the stairs and strides into my bedroom.

"I love you," he says, laying me on my bed. "I love you so fucking much."

I want to say the words back to him. They are on the tip of my tongue. However, I'm currently rendered speechless as I watch Bryce strip in front of me.

I've seen him shirtless. That is enough to stop traffic. But as my eyes travel down as his pants slide down his muscular legs, I can't help but stare at his very hard, very well-endowed, penis.

I hurry up and do about fifteen calculations in my head. In none of those does the math work out that his dick is going to fit inside me.

And I don't mess up math.

"Hey," he says, climbing onto the bed with me. "I don't want to see your thinking face right now."

"My thinking face? I don't have a thinking face."

He laughs and places a kiss on my nose. "You do. And it's adorable. Now, whatever has you doing math in that head of yours, I want it to go away. Just lay back and relax. All I want you to do tonight is feel."

I try to do as Bryce says as he kneels in front of me, slowly sliding my leggings down.

"You are so beautiful," he whispers, kissing his way up my leg before placing a gentle kiss on my center. "Are you relaxed yet?"

I close my eyes, doing my best to melt into the feeling of being touched by Bryce. His lips are softly kissing my stomach as he slides off my panties. When they are off, his fingertips slowly trace back up my legs, his feather-light touch leaving goose bumps in its wake. When he lands at my pussy, his fingers begin to circle in my wetness.

"Fuck, Lulu. You're ready for me, aren't you?"

"Please, Bryce," I beg, but I can't help it. Between his touch, his lips, and his words, I'm a mess of emotions.

"Shhh. No more talking," he says. "Close your eyes and feel."

I do as he says, not knowing what to expect next. I want to peek because the anticipation is killing me. Then I feel his mouth on my breast, his tongue circling my hardened nipple again, and it takes all I have not to moan and embarrass myself. Then his warm palm blazes a path down my side, over my hip, and then to my center before he slides a finger into my core.

"Mmmm." I hum, my back arching and my hips raising as I silently beg for more. His free hand cups my breast, giving him more to suck on as his finger works in and out of me. I don't know which one to concentrate on. His mouth is warm, and each time he nips my skin, it sends a throb of heat straight to my clit. The finger he's sinking into me is making my toes curl, and when he adds a second one, it steals the breath from my lungs.

"Oh!" I whimper as Bryce hits the spot inside me that sends sparks dancing along every nerve in my body.

"That's it, Lulu. You're so close. I can feel how close you are." Bryce's finger continues to work inside me, but his lips have made their way to my mouth. I grab his face and pull his lips against mine, needing to drink in the taste of him as much as I need something to hold on to. God, I feel like I'm about to explode all over this room.

I want to beg him to stop in one breath and demand he keep going with the next because he's making me feel too much all at once. I'm not sure I can handle it. Then his lips swallow all the needy noises that fall from me as his thumb presses against my clit.

My entire body starts to vibrate, and the only thing I can focus on is the press of his fingers inside me and the slow circles of his thumb on me before I'm exploding for him.

He brings me down slowly from my orgasm, and when he releases his fingers, I immediately miss the feeling of him inside me. I want to scream for him to get back here and to keep doing whatever it is that he was doing.

Because that was really freaking good.

I open my eyes, feeling slightly drunk, and before I know it, Bryce is back on the bed, sheathing his thick cock.

Please math be wrong. Please math be wrong.

"I love you, Lucy," he says, slowly kissing me as he lines himself with my center. "I have loved you for so long."

"I love you," I say back, wrapping my arms around his neck as he slowly pushes into me.

I tense, expecting it to hurt, and he pauses, tucking his face against the crook of my neck. There is a slight tremor in his shoulders, as if it's taking everything inside him to hold still so he doesn't hurt me.

"I got you, Lulu. I got you," he says as he presses open-mouthed kisses up the column of my neck. "I've got you."

Slowly, I relax around him, but it isn't until I rock my hips a fraction, inviting him to push deeper, that he relents. His arms snake under my body so his hands can hold on to my shoulders and tuck me against him. The man is everywhere around me and inside me, and it's so much more perfect than I thought it would be.

That is, until he starts to move. The way he withdraws from me is close to torture, and when he sinks back in, I'm so full it's almost as if I can't breathe. His lips are relentless as they taste my skin. His words are sweet nothings that become a litany of praise as his hips move.

"God, Lucy." He moans into my neck. "You feel so good. Too good."

"You feel—" Whatever I was going to say is stolen from my thoughts when he seats himself deep inside me and rolls his hips.

I thought it felt good when his fingers were doing the work. But now? Feeling his cock inside me? It's better than anything I can think of.

"Bryce!" I rock my hips up to meet his. My eyes close so I have no choice but to only feel everything he's doing to me. "Bryce, don't stop."

He's going to make me come again, and I chase the high like an addict. I didn't know before tonight that orgasms like that even existed, and now, I get two of them? My mind wants to figure out that probability, but then he leans back, flips me, over, and pushes back into me so I couldn't do basic math if I tried.

When he pulls my hips back against his thrusts, it's almost too much, and my arms collapse, dropping my chest against the mattress. His pace falters, and he lets out a low groan of appreciation.

"Do you know how hot you look right now?" he asks as one of his palms burns a line along the length of my spin, coaxing me to arch my hips higher before reclaiming its grasp on my hip. "So beautiful, LuLu."

Holy fuck, I want to hold out longer, but the feeling of this position is too good to ignore. So, when my body clamps around him and my vision narrows down to the flood of pleasure rioting through my blood, I let myself fall into it.

"So perfect," is the last thing I register before he stills, his release pulsing into me as his grip on my hips turns bruising. I'm too blissed out to care, though.

The math was wrong. Thank God the math was wrong.

Soon we collapse on the bed, Bryce just to the side of me as we try to catch our breath. I almost think we fall asleep until I feel the bed move as Bryce gets up to dispose of the condom.

For years, I wondered what this would be like. I've had fantasy after fantasy, each and every one a little different from the one before it.

Never once did I imagine it would be like that simply because I had no idea sex like that even existed.

28

BRYCE

"YOU OKAY?" Lucy asks, squeezing my hand. "You know you don't have to do this today?"

"No, I do," I say as I try to force my feet to move forward. "It's been too long."

I'm standing staring at the Nashville Fury facility, paralyzed by the fear of what I'm about to do.

Apologize.

I haven't been here since I was put on the injured list three months ago. The last time I was here, I told off my coaches and said a bunch of stuff I'll never be able to take back.

The fact that Coach McAvoy and Coach Davis are even willing to talk to me today is some sort of New Year's miracle in and of itself. I wouldn't talk to me if the situations were reversed.

"I'm right here," Lucy says. "I'll be right beside you for as long as you want me in the room. You've worked hard, Bryce. They have to know that or else they wouldn't have agreed to meet you."

They did agree to meet with me. However, to make sure we didn't stir up a story that didn't need to be reported yet, they are meeting me at six in the morning on New Year's Eve. Also known as the butt crack of dawn on a day the reporters all have better things to be talking about.

"All right, let's go." I say, taking one last deep breath as I walk into the facility hand-in-hand with Lucy.

I didn't expect anything to change in three months, yet, it feels almost foreign to me. The murals of Fury teams of the past are still on the walls. Pictures of great plays and memories are still in the same places, and at the end of the hall, there's the newest addition to the mural—Cole lifting me up in celebration after we made it to the playoffs our rookie year.

We could have done it again this year had my head not been so far up my own ass.

I fucked it all up because I acted like a spoiled brat who didn't get his way.

"Bryce," Coach McAvoy says as we turn the corner to the locker rooms and his office.

"Coach." I extend a hand, which he accepts. Just that act alone relaxes me slightly.

"Good to see you," he says. "And this must be her?"

Lucy's cheeks turn red as I bring her a little closer to me. I almost forgot how much I loved that blush. "Yes, sir. Lucy Valenti, Coach Hunter McAvoy."

"It's nice to meet you, Lucy," he says. "Come on back. We are all waiting for you."

All? Who else is here besides him and Davis?

Turns out that the answer is everyone. It's a full house when we enter Coach McAvoy's office. Sitting on the corner of his desk is his fiancée Sadie, a sports reporter who used to cover the Fury. That is until her and Coach McAvoy started dating. Now she's a national reporter with *US Daily,* who is kicking ass and taking names.

Coach Davis is sitting on a chair, but he hasn't made eye contact with me yet. He's too busy holding who I'm guessing is his daughter, as his fiancée, Bethany, looks on.

Leaning against the wall, wearing a shit-eating grin, is Cole.

"What are you doing here?" I ask as I give him a hug.

"Coach told me you reached out and asked me if I could come in. I debated, then he said Lucy was coming and she's really who I wanted to see."

"It's good to see you too, Cole" she says, stepping to him so he can give her a kiss on the cheek.

"Well let's get started," Coach McAvoy says, sitting down. "How you doing, Bryce?"

I begin to answer, but the sound of a wail cuts me off.

Damn Davis's kid has a pair of lungs.

"She's hungry," Bethany says. "I'll take her so you guys can talk."

"Lucy and I will come!" Sadie says as she jumps off the desk.

"You don't have to," Bethany says, giving Sadie a questioning look.

"Apparently, you missed the part of the plan where the only reason we came at this ungodly hour was so we could meet the woman who made this man act like a fool. No offense, Bryce. You boys have fun. Come on, Lucy. I want to know how you pulled his head out of his ass."

Lucy looks slightly horrified and confused as Sadie leads her out of the office.

I just give her my best reassuring smile because she's in good hands. Sadie might be a little over the top, but she's good people. She and Bethany are exactly the kind of women I can see Lucy becoming friends with.

"Does she have a filter?" Davis asks Hunter as Sadie shuts the door.

"Never has, and I hope she never will," Hunter says with a smile. "Now, where were we?"

All eyes in the office shift back to me. The only thing that is missing is one of those old-time interrogation lamps. My throat goes dry, and everything I'd planned to say somehow disappeared the second Lucy walked out of the office.

"I swear I knew what I was going to say when I woke up this morning," I say, trying to figure out the best place to start.

"How about we help," Hunter says, sitting back in his chair. "How are you doing? And if the word *fine* comes out of your mouth, this meeting is done."

I crack a smile. "I'm . . . better. Well, getting there. As Malcolm likes to tell me, I'm a work in progress. He's done a lot to help me identify my triggers and is helping me find healthy ways to deal with my issues. We're starting to focus on my return to football, and how I need to take on little bits at a time so I'm not overwhelmed and shut down."

"And the drinking?" Davis asks. Just like him to cut to the chase.

"Besides one lapse in judgement three months ago, I haven't had a drop. It's just easier to stay away from it."

"So, you're sober?" Davis reiterates.

"I guess I am," I say, though I've never thought about it like that. The transition to being sober wasn't one I made consciously. I just knew that, when I was drunk, I made bad choices. I almost ruined my career as well as the two best relationships in my life.

I needed those back, and to make sure that happened, I needed to stop making bad decisions.

"Well, you look good," Hunter says. "Working out? Doing drills?"

I nod. "Every day. Doing as much as I can without a receiver. It will be nice to get back into the routine with the guys."

A silence falls in the room.

Shit . . . did I overstep? I assumed the injured tag meant I was free to come back when next season started. Did I assume wrong? Am I not going to be back in Nashville next year?

"You know it's not going to be as easy as you walking back into the locker room and saying you're back, right?" Hunter says. "You alienated a lot of your teammates before you left."

I look at Cole, who raises an eyebrow as if to say I should have expected this. I never thought coming back was going to be easy, but I guess I underestimated how hard it was going to be.

I was an asshole to everyone. Cole tried his best to defend me and defuse situations, but I know that only went so far. When I think about how I treated Dexter, I want to throw up. I was horrible to him, and the kid did nothing wrong. He's also not a kid. He's a year younger than I am, and I treated him like shit on my shoe.

"Seems like I'm going to have a lot of steak dinners to buy," I say, trying to make a joke.

"The words 'I'm sorry' will also go a long way."

I meet Davis's eyes. Out of all the people I treated horribly over the past year, he's the one I need to be apologizing to the most. He was the one who noticed before anyone that I was falling down the slope. He tried on more than one occasion to pick me up, but I wasn't having it.

"They will," I say as I move to stand in front of him. "And you need to be the first one in this room that I say that to. I'm sorry, Coach. I'm sorry I acted like an idiot. I'm sorry I didn't take your help when you offered. And . . . I am so sorry for the things I said on that last day here. That was one of the worst things I've ever done in my life, and I'm ashamed thinking about it. Please know that's not who I am, and if you and Coach McAvoy will allow me, I promise you I'll be the best damn quarterback you ever coach."

I have no idea what's about to happen. Is it too little, too late?

"I don't want that. We don't want that," he says, motioning to Hunter as my stomach drops to my feet.

"No," Hunter says, standing and walking around his desk. "We know you're a good quarterback. We wouldn't have drafted you if we weren't. What we want is for you to be the best man you can be for your teammates, your family, yourself, and that girl out there who clearly loves you."

I look over my shoulder and see Lucy holding Davis's baby. She looks up and meets my gaze, gifting me a smile that could melt an iceberg.

"It's not going to be easy," Hunter says, bringing my attention back to him. "There are going to be questions. You're going to have to do a media tour. You're going to have to mend a lot of bridges with your teammates. Are you ready for all of that?"

I look at Cole, who gives me a nod. It's one that screams that he's had my back since we were little and that isn't going to change anytime soon.

"I am," I say. "Let's get to work."

29

———

LUCY

"IT'S SO LOUD!" I yell as Bryce and I try to move through the groups of people packing the sidewalks on Broadway.

"It's Nashville, Lulu!" Bryce says as we break free so we can cross the street. "Come on, we're almost there."

I grip Bryce's hand a little tighter as we walk another block to the restaurant where we're meeting Cole. Bryce told me that Nashville on New Year's got a little crazy, but I had no idea this is what he meant.

I also didn't realize how many people I would see not-so-discreetly taking pictures of us. Then there were the two girls who didn't know the meaning of the word discreet as they pushed me out of the way to take a selfie with him.

Is this going to be my life if I move here?

We enter the dimly lit restaurant, and Cole's voice stops me from going down that rabbit hole. "Bryce! Lucy!"

"Hey, man," Bryce says, dropping my hand so he can man-hug Cole. The two slap each other's back a few times, and I can't help but get a little choked up at the sight.

These two have been best friends for so long, and I'm really glad that Cole has been there for Bryce when he needed someone.

"Hey, Lucy," Cole says, leaning in to give me a kiss on the cheek.

"Even though I know you've been here for a few days, let me officially welcome you to Nashville."

"Thanks," I say as the hostess takes us to our table at the back of the restaurant. I don't know if it is on purpose, but I'm thankful for the semblance of privacy.

"Has the news broke that Bryce Donald is back in town? Or did the meeting stay quiet?" Cole asks as we take our seats.

"Not that I've seen," Bryce says. "Though, judging by the pictures I know were taken tonight on our way down here, I'm sure the news will get out soon enough."

"Better you than me," Cole says as the waitress places waters on our table and takes our drink orders. "So, how is Laurel Heights?"

"Same as usual," Bryce says. "Except now I've replaced you as my best friend."

"With who?"

"Luciano."

Cole nearly spits out his water. "I'm sorry, are we talking about the man Lucy almost married?"

"One and the same. Oh, and he wants in on our fantasy league next year. The man knows his stuff."

I look over the menu as Bryce and Cole catch up on the events of the last week. Normally, Cole would have been home for Christmas, but his family decided to spend the holiday in Florida this year with his sister and her family.

If my family had done that, maybe we would still be speaking.

I figured we would need a few days to calm down after what I'm dubbing as The Laurel Heights Christmas Massacre. Then they somehow found out I was coming to Nashville, and my mom lost it. I'm not going to let that stop me from having a good time, checking out the city, and maybe taking a drive through Franklin to see the houses I bookmarked on Zillow.

"What do you think of Nashville, Lucy?" Cole asks after the waitress drops off our drinks and takes our orders.

"It's something," I say, not wanting to lie, but not knowing the exact words I want to use. "It's busier than I thought it would be."

"Maybe New Year's wasn't the best time to bring you down here," Bryce says, reaching for my hand under the table. "It usually isn't this packed."

"The country music festival would have been worse. Oh, and most weekends, which are bachelorette party central."

"If the Rockers make the playoffs. Then the city becomes hockey crazy."

"I can't wait until we make the championship game," Cole says. "This place is going to be nuts."

My eyes bug out a little more with each event they name. While I'd love nothing more than to be here for a championship parade for the Fury, I could do without the other random, loud weekends.

I didn't realize until I got here that I'm a small-town girl at heart. The people and the crowds are okay in small doses—like, maybe once a year.

"I'm glad we could do this," Bryce says. "I hope I didn't take you away from a hot date."

Cole laughs under his breath. "Why in the world would you think I had a date?"

"Oh, come on. It's New Year's. You're a good-looking, single guy. Why wouldn't you have a date?"

"Aw, you think I'm good-looking."

"Of course, I do," Bryce says. All I can do is shake my head. These two are like an old married couple. "Plus, when Lucy moves here, I'm sure she'll want a friend to hang out with when we're on the road or in training camp hell."

"Oh no," I say, shaking my head in disagreement. "Do not bring me into this. I'm sure Cole is very capable of finding a date whenever he wants one."

"Thank you, Lucy," Cole says. "Plus, I'd never take a girl out on a first date on New Year's Eve. That's way too much pressure."

"Brenna is on a first date as we speak."

"What? With who?" Bryce asks.

"Not sure. She met him online." I shrug. "I asked if she wanted to come so I had someone to hang out with when you were meeting with the coaches, but she already had plans made. Plus, I think it's romantic. If it goes well, she can say she started her year by finding love."

"Excuse me," Cole says, standing so quickly that he almost runs into the waiter bringing our food.

"What's that about?" More specifically, why did Cole's face drain of color when I said Brenna was on a date.

Interesting.

"No clue," Bryce says, leaning over and silently asking for a kiss, which of course I give to him.

"Oh my gosh, Bryce Donald!"

Our kiss is interrupted, and the second our lips release, Bryce goes from my Bryce to football player Bryce.

I haven't seen this version of him in person since high school, and I don't miss it. Correction, I didn't miss the women throwing themselves at him.

"Hi," he says to two blondes, who apparently aren't fans of skirts that cover more than a bare minimum of skin. "Nice to meet you."

"Oh, we met last summer at Tootsies," the girl on the left says, inching her way closer to him. "Don't you remember?"

Bryce's face goes white for a second, and I know exactly what he's thinking.

He's trying to remember if he slept with them or not, and considering it isn't going back to its natural color, I'm going to guess the answer is yes.

Breathe, Lucy. You knew this was a possibility. It's just happening sooner than you thought.

"Can't say I do," he says, bringing me closer to him. "Now, if you ladies can excuse me, I'd like to get back to dinner with my girlfriend."

Their gazes immediately snap to me, and I think they honestly didn't realize I was here.

Bitches.

"Oh, we didn't think this was . . . a thing," the one on the right says.

"Ladies, I don't want to be rude, but I'd really like to go back to having dinner with my girlfriend."

"Oh, come on, Brycie, just one picture for old time's sake?"

"He said no," I say. Or did I yell? I'm not sure but I probably yelled it. There are far too many people staring over at us for me to have just said it.

"Excuse me? What did you say?"

I square my shoulders because, apparently, this girl woke up today and chose violence. "I said, he said no. So, move it along and take her with you. Find another jock to chase."

I don't know where this sudden burst of confidence is coming from. It's like Brenna is sending me her don't-fuck-with-me vibes all the way from Ohio.

"You heard her, ladies," Bryce says, and the smile on his face stretches from ear to ear. "Have a good night."

With a huff, an eyeroll, and a turned heel, the two cleat chasers stomp off. Before they are even five steps away, Bryce's mouth is on mine in a kiss that is not appropriate for public.

"We need to go," he says as he breaks away, grabbing his wallet and throwing a few hundred-dollar bills onto the table.

"What?" I ask, still dazed from the kiss that almost knocked me off my chair.

"That was the hottest thing I have ever seen, and if we're not back at my place in ten minutes, I'm going to fuck you in the street and I don't care who is watching."

Well then.

30

BRYCE

"NOW THIS IS part of Nashville I can handle."

I chuckle as Lucy situates herself between my legs and rests her head against my bare chest. We're relaxed on one of the chase loungers on the patio of my penthouse apartment, watching the sky light up with New Year's Eve fireworks.

There are a few perks of signing the biggest rookie contract in league history. One of them is being able to afford this penthouse with a spectacular view that overlooks the whole city.

It also has enough privacy that Lucy and I can be out here naked under a blanket after having the most intense sex of my life.

Watching her tell off those groupies was a shot of pure adrenaline straight to my dick. We weren't even inside five seconds before I had her stripped and was eating her pussy against the door of my penthouse. I really meant to take her to bed because I needed to be inside her more than I needed to breathe, but we only made it to the living room.

"I can't believe you have this view," Lucy says.

"I know," I say, lifting the blanket to get another look at her spectacular tits.

"I meant of the city," she says before playfully slapping my hand.

"How do you live here? Maybe I've been in a small town too long, but there were . . . just so many people."

"I know," I say, kissing the top of her head. "This may be about as crazy as it gets, but it's still a pretty busy city."

"I guess I'll have to get used to it." There is a lilt of sadness in her tone that I can't ignore.

"You know we don't have to live in the city," I say. "Those big ol' houses that we drove by earlier? We can get one of those. Or we can build you one."

She turns her head to look up at me. "But won't it be hard for you to get to the facility during the season?"

"There are things called cars. And, you might not realize this, but I make a lot of money and can afford one," I say, situating her so she's now sitting across my lap, which is probably how I avoided an eyeroll for my smartass comment. "I know the city isn't for you. All night, I could tell how uncomfortable you were. I want you to be happy here. Though, I'll admit, living downtown was fun for me these last couple of years."

"Sure, it was," she says with an exaggerated eye roll. That one I couldn't hide from.

"It *was*. That's not who I am anymore. There are plenty of really nice areas that aren't a bad drive in and out of the city. You never know, we could move in next door to some famous country stars. If that doesn't work, then I bet I could talk Cole into moving in next to us. Then whenever he meets his future wife, you two can become best friends and we can raise our kids together. Despite what he said earlier."

By the time I'm done, I'm sitting up straight and I'm pretty sure my voice hit an octave I'm not used to hitting. I can't help it. The thought of planning my future with Lucy gets me all sorts of excited. It's like I'm a kid seeing Santa a week before Christmas and I'm rushing to tell him everything on my list.

"You have it all planned out, don't you?"

"I do. It doesn't hurt that Cole and I have had this plan since our freshman year to either marry sisters or best friends and live next door to each other so we could grow old together."

"Speaking of Cole, have you heard from him since he took off?"

"Yeah, he's fine," I say. "He said something came up."

"On New Year's Eve? He seemed pretty upset when I brought up Brenna. Is that why he left?"

"To go to Ohio and chase her down? Absolutely not," I say. "She's a little sister to him. That's Bro Code 101. Thou shalt not think another bro's sister is hot."

"Still, something seemed off," she says, but I really have no interest in talking about Cole. I'd much rather be kissing her, so that's what I do. I lower my mouth to hers and kiss her as if there is nothing else in the world but us and this moment.

"What was that for?" she asks as I slowly pull away.

"Because I wanted to."

She giggles as I lean forward to claim her lips again, and quickly, that laughter turns into moans. Moans that go straight to my cock.

I could kiss this woman forever. What am I going to do when I'm on the road and I can't wake up next to her? Or steal a kiss just because I can? It's going to be miserable, which is why I need to make sure I don't waste a second that we are together.

In such a short amount of time, I've become addicted to her. Yes, I've wanted her for years, but I never let myself have her. Now I know what she tastes and feels like. I crave her when she's not around. Her kisses, her body, her laugh, her everything.

As I kiss her under the open sky, fireworks glowing above us, I know for a fact it's only her. It's only ever been her. It will only ever be her. She's it for me.

I'm going to marry this girl.

Our mouths separate, and she slowly starts placing kisses along my jawline before she's trailing them down my neck. Then to my chest as her body slides down the front of mine.

"What are you doing, Lulu?"

She moves a little farther down, placing one last kiss on the tip of my cock. "You had your fun earlier. Now it's my turn."

Then Lucy's mouth is taking me all in, which is not an easy feat. Her hand is working me in conjunction, and holy hell, this is the best thing I have ever felt in my life. And not just because my girl knows what she's doing but because she's the one doing it. It's my Lulu, and watching her take me in and out of her hot mouth? Hearing her little moans as I slowly thrust up and down? It might be the best thing I have ever seen in my life.

"Jesus, Lucy." I moan as I fist my hands at my sides so I don't sink them into her hair. "Baby that feels so good."

When I bump the back of her throat, my restraint almost snaps, but when she hums her pleasure and I feel the vibration in my balls, I can't take it anymore.

"Come here." I pick her up and shift her so she's straddling me.

"I didn't want to stop."

"Tough," I say before dipping my head and closing my lips around her nipple. I've learned if there is one thing that gets my girl going, it's this.

And I make sure to do it every damn time.

She arches her back, giving me all the access I want. I switch to the other one, flicking my tongue across her nipple.

"Bryce," she moans as she slides herself over my hard cock. "I need you."

"I got you, Lulu."

Just as I'm about to line myself up with her, I stop and groan in frustration.

"Hold on," I say, lifting her off my lap. "Do not move a muscle."

"Wait," she says grabbing my arm and pulling me back down. "Are you . . . are we safe?" I pause and raise an eyebrow, silently asking her for clarification. "I'm on the pill, and I know you've—" She presses her lips together to stop whatever she was going to say.

I sit back down and press a kiss to her lips, hopefully chasing those thoughts right out of her head.

"I've always been safe," I say. Even in my drunkest hook ups, I always remembered to wrap up. "And I got tested at the start of camp because the team required it. I'm safe. I'm clean. But are you sure?"

She nods and kisses me again. "I trust you."

I didn't know those three words could have such an effect on me, but they do. It's like she just gave me a gift I didn't know I wanted.

Without breaking the kiss, Lucy pushes me back and then shifts to straddle my lap again. The second she lowers her hot, wet center onto me, I swear to God I see stars.

Being with Lucy is a dream. This? With nothing between us? This is something that there are no words to describe.

"Fuck." I hiss the word through gritted teeth as I sit up and smash her chest against mine. "Fuck you feel so good."

My tone is deep as I take her hips in my hands, guiding her up and down as she rides my cock. I lay back, wanting to see every moment of this. I need to capture the beauty that is Lucy as she braces herself on my chest as she rides me. She is so uninhibited, so free. She rarely lets herself go like this, but when she does, it's a beautiful sight to watch.

"Yes," she cries as she grips my shoulders for balance. "More, Bryce. I need more."

That is a request I can fulfill. With her tight against me, I shift us so her back is pressed to the lounger. She's gasping for breath, and her whole body arches in pleasure as I force her thighs wide before moving her legs to rest against my shoulders.

Almost desperately, she reaches for me, for something to hold on to, and I groan in encouragement as her nails bite into my hips.

"More," she begs, and I kiss away her plea as I give her everything.

"Ahhh!"

Her orgasm is too much for me to handle, and I thrust so deeply into her that I hope I stamp myself onto her soul as I explode. Never in my life have I climaxed so hard that it made me dizzy, but I'm pretty sure I black out for a second. Holy shit . . . I want that again.

I don't have the words.

My brain is broken.

As I scoop her into my arms, kissing every part of her I can, all I know is that I'm never letting her go.

Yup. I'm marrying this girl.

31

____

BRYCE

"BRYCE."

I hear Lucy's sleepy, sexy voice as she gently tries to wake me up, but I don't open my eyes. Instead, I just reach for her, bringing her warm body closer to me.

"Bryce, you need to wake up. Your alarm is going off."

I blink my eyes open, wondering why it didn't wake me up.

Actually, I do know why I didn't hear my phone: It's all the way across the room in the pocket of my jeans. Last night Lucy yanked them off me and tossed them after we got back from our double date with Celine and Luciano, and I had better things to think about other than my cell phone.

Have I said before how much I love this woman?

Unwillingly, I let Lucy go and roll out of her bed, stumble across the room, find my phone, and then silence the alarm. Instead of staying up and getting dressed, I climb back into bed with her, quickly bringing her back into my arms. It's March in Ohio, which means the mornings are still cold. What better place to be than in bed with a naked, soft, and usually horny in the mornings Lucy?

"What are you doing?" She might be asking me the question, but that doesn't stop her from burrowing her head into my shoulder and hiking her leg over my hip.

"I'm going to take the day off," I say, kissing the top of her head.

"Can you do that?"

"I've been working out or running drills or watching film every day for five months. I think I can take a little break and have a lazy Sunday morning with my girl."

I don't tell her that today's lazy Sunday is brought to us courtesy of Malcolm. While he said that he's proud of me and the strides I've made, he doesn't want me to burn out before I'm even back.

I'm not going to argue with him about getting to spend more time in bed with Lucy.

"So, what do you want to do today?" I ask. "Options are to stay naked all day, go grocery shopping, or start to pack your things for Nashville. I, for one, am a big fan of options one and three."

My hands move across her soft skin before she shifts off me and rests her hand under her head.

"Actually, we need to talk about Nashville."

"That wasn't an option," I say, leaning in for a kiss, which I'm denied.

"Bryce, we need to figure some things out, and we don't really have a whole lot of time left to do it."

She's right. I know she is.

"Fine," I say, sitting up against her headboard, "but we're talking naked."

She rolls her eyes and pulls the sheet up to cover herself. Guess that means no morning sex. "Fine. But you can't look, you won't concentrate."

She knows me so well.

"First things first," she begins, and even though she doesn't have a list in front of her, she might as well. "Time frame."

"I have to go back at the end of April," I say. "Everyone thinks it's best that I get in early and meet with the public relations department about how we're going to handle my coming back. Then there is rookie camp in May, which I'd like to be there for, then training camp at the end of July."

"Megan's baby is due in the second week of May," she says. "And she'll be on maternity leave through July. I promised the bank that I would get them through that before I left."

"I can come home in early July," I offer. "That will at least break it up a little before I report back for training camp."

"You can?"

"I don't see why not," I say, reaching for her hands and linking our fingers together. "July is everyone's last chance at freedom. All of the coaches and players are with their families. Plus, after the media tour, I'll be ready for a few days with you."

I thought that would make her happy. Hell, just the thought of coming back and getting to see her makes me happy. Only, she doesn't look as happy about it as I am.

"Lucy? Talk to me. What's the matter?"

She looks away, quickly catching a rogue tear that has fallen from her eye. "I want to believe you. I want exactly what you just said. This is balance. This is us talking and planning together to make sure you do what you need on the field while making sure I'm still part of your life. It just . . . it seems too good to be true. All I can think—"

Nope. I know what she's about to say. She's going to bring up the last seven years, but I need her to know this time is different.

"I know I can't erase the past no matter how much I want to. But I promise you, Lucy Valenti, I will do everything I can to come back in July. I want this more than I want my next breath. Now that I know what it's like to wake up every day with you in my arms, there is no way I'll give it up. I can't do this life without you. I love you, Lucy. So, trust me—trust us to make this work, okay?"

That stray tear that escaped a second ago is nothing compared to the tears falling from her beautiful eyes right now. I'd be worried if she weren't also smiling and biting her bottom lip like she does when she gets overwhelmed.

"That's all I ask is that you come back to me."

"And I will. I'll be back in July for a few weeks before I go to camp."

"I know you'll be busy with training camp that you won't even know what day it is, which I'm prepared for. I'll take that time to move down there so we're settled before the season starts. How does that sound?"

How does it sound? It sounds too good to be true. It sounds like everything I've ever wanted.

I lean in and kiss the corner of her mouth. "Nashville by September?"

She smiles, giving me a little nod. "Nashville by September. We can do this."

We can do this. For the first time in my life, I feel like I have everything I could ever want or need. I have Lucy, I have Mom and Brenna, and my football career is back on track.

This is it. Now, not to screw it up.

"Well, if this conversation is over, then I suggest we get back to what I want to do today," I say, reaching for Lucy and bringing her to my chest.

"Maybe I'm not done," she says.

"Yes, you are," I say before kissing her, and it isn't just any kiss, either. It's one that screams we aren't going anywhere today. "We only have one more month before I leave. I'm not wasting a second."

32

———

LUCY

I FEEL as if I've been holding my breath for two days, waiting to see if the other shoe is going to drop.

I don't think anyone would blame me considering my history with Bryce.

Yes, he says all the right things. Yes, his actions match his words, but it's easy to keep his promises when I'm his only focus. It's when he has to split his focus that I worry about. He's always drawn that line between football and the rest of his life, and my gut tells me that changing that habit isn't going to be quite as easy as he seems to think.

We hadn't spent a night apart in four months until two nights ago. The first night made sense since he was exhausted after helping his mom relandscape the yard for spring and crashed at her house.

Last night, though, I didn't so much as get a call telling me that he wasn't coming over. No good-night text or quick message to let me know he'd talk to me in the morning.

Nothing.

When I finally got ahold of him today, he blamed it on the fact that I had to tutor this morning and he didn't want to wake up that early. It's never stopped him before, but I didn't press.

I've been trying not to let these thoughts stir in my brain, but when I'm not busy, it's all I can think about. More specifically that it's two weeks until he leaves for Nashville, and something happened in the last few days that made him realize this.

And now he's starting to pull away.

"Have you had a chance to sign the loan approval papers yet?" Megan asks, which causes me to jump out of my seat.

"Shit! You scared me!"

"Sorry," she says, waddling her way over to my desk. The woman is thirty weeks pregnant and looks like she could pop at any time. "I knocked so I thought you heard me."

"You're fine. I'm just . . . let me grab those for you." I scramble to find the papers that are stacked somewhere on my desk.

"Everything okay?" Megan asks, taking a seat in one of the chairs in front of my desk. "I'm getting vibes of pre-Bryce Lucy, and I don't see rainbows coming out of your butt. What's going on? Oh shit, do you need cough drops?"

Ugh, it's really annoying that Megan's bullshit meter has only grown during her pregnancy and she's even less cautious about calling me on my own shit.

"It's Bryce," I say. "He's been acting strange the past few days, and I don't really think it's a coincidence that it's getting closer to when he has to go back to Nashville. I'm . . . I'm just worried he's starting to pull away."

I tell her about the past few days, hoping that she'll pull me out of this spiral of paranoid thoughts and tell me I'm overreacting.

"That is weird," she says. "I don't blame you for freaking out."

"Really? No, 'Don't worry, Lucy, everything is going to be fine?'"

"Do you want me to lie to you? I mean I can if you want."

"No," I say, sliding down farther into my chair. "I know I need to talk to him, but he won't answer my texts."

"Have you tried to call him? Or Brenna? Maybe she knows."

"I did," I say. "She was acting weird too, which doesn't make any sense. Unless she knows something that I don't. Oh God! What if he's going to break up with me, and she knows but doesn't want to be the one who lets it slip?"

Now I'm panicking for a whole other reason. Is that what's about to happen? Has he realized that push is coming to shove, and he can't balance football with what it takes to make a relationship work? Is he going to end it before he leaves for Nashville?

"Okay, you need to calm down," Megan says. "Do my breathing exercises with me. I feel like they could help."

"I don't need to do Lamaze," I snap. "I need to talk to him. I need to nip this in the bud before I have a panic attack."

"We don't need that," Megan says, slowly pushing herself up from the chair. "How about you take an early lunch. Try to find him and hash this out so you can quit having your mind go in all sorts of directions. Take all the time you need."

"Really?" I ask, a little confused as to why she'd volunteer that option. "It's your lunchbreak, and the last time you missed lunch, you almost attacked a customer because you were hangry."

"I'll be fine," she says, waving me off. "Plus, I have a feeling you won't have to go far."

I have no idea what she's talking about, but I grab my purse out of my desk drawer and I all but sprint out of my office. I'm not even two steps out when I'm stopped in my tracks.

There are balloons everywhere, and there are bouquets of flowers on almost every surface.

"What in the world . . ."

My eyes don't know where to look, but as I scan the room, I realize I missed the five people standing in front of me, each holding a piece of posterboard with a letter on it.

Brenna is holding a P.

Luciano is holding an R.

Celine is holding an O.

Cole is holding the M.

Then there is Bryce, who is holding a question mark and wearing the biggest grin I have ever seen.

"What is this?" I ask as I fight back tears.

Bryce lowers his sign and comes to me, taking each of my hands in his. "Apparently, this is how guys these days ask girls to prom. It's called a Promposal—or, at least, that's what my workout buddies tell me. The balloons were their idea."

"The flowers were mine," Luciano chimes in proudly.

I can't help but laugh. Also, somewhere deep inside me, seventeen-year-old Lucy is freaking out.

"Seven years ago, I had to break my first promise to you. I promised you that I would take you to prom. I wanted nothing more than to see you in a beautiful dress, put on a tuxedo, and dance with you all night. Now, I know it won't be the same and we will be going as chaperones because apparently twenty-four is too old to go to prom, but Lucy Valenti, will you go to prom with me?"

"Yes," I say between laughter and tears. "Yes, I will go to prom with you."

Cheers erupt as Bryce scoops me in his arms, stealing a kiss in the middle of the bank lobby.

"Is this why you've been acting strange?" I ask.

"Yeah," he says as he puts me down. "I was scared I was going to slip. I figured it would be safer if I stayed away."

"I thought you were breaking up with me!" I yell, gently slapping his chest. "And you!" I yell, pointing at Megan, "Were you in on this?"

"Of course, I was," she says as she blows the imaginary dust off her nails. "I was the distraction so they could get this all ready. If you weren't in a talkative mood, I was going to force you to talk about baby names."

Everyone congratulates us before making their way out of the bank. Bryce is the only one who hangs back, and he moved to lean a shoulder against the threshold to my office.

I walk over to him and snake my hands around his waist.

"I love you," I say, going up on my toes for a kiss. "But next time you plan a big surprise, please don't pull away. I honestly thought you were going to break up with me."

"I'm sorry," he says before he flashes me his best pouty lip. "I promise I'll make it up to you."

"You better." I steal another kiss. "Now, I have another ten minutes for my lunch break. Want to—"

Bryce picks me up, cutting off my words, and slams the door to my office closed behind us.

33

―――――

BRYCE

PROM NIGHT seven years ago might have been one of the worst nights of my life. Maybe only second to the night I found out Lucy was getting married.

I found out that day she was at prom with Luciano—a fact I had to pry from Brenna. I laid in my bed all night, frustrated as all hell that he was the one who got to dance with her. That she was in his arms and not mine. All I could picture was his smug smile taunting me that he was with her and I wasn't.

Funny how life works out sometimes.

I laugh as I think about that as I hold Lucy close to me and we dance to some slow song I've never heard. I didn't think I was old until I heard what kids listened to these days.

"What's so funny," she asks without looking up. She keeps her cheek on my chest, exactly where it belongs.

"I was thinking back to prom night and how I wanted nothing more than to murder Luciano because he was here with you and I wasn't."

"That was funny?"

"Not back then. Though, it is funny now that Luciano is the one insisting on throwing my going away party."

"I always told you he was a good guy," she says as she looks up at me.

"Yeah, yeah," I say, leaning down to give her a kiss. Before I can make it too illicit, a hand on my shoulder is pulling me back.

"Hey! None of that!" Coach Roberts says "I didn't set this all up so you two could make out all night. You're supposed to be chaperones."

"Relax, Uncle Nick," Lucy says, "At least we're not as bad as those two over there. Would you like to break that up or have us do it?"

He glances to where Lucy is pointing, and sure enough, two kids are . . . holy hell, are they going at it.

"Son of a bitch," Coach Roberts says before stalking toward the teenage couple. "Stop that now! There will be no nookie on my watch!"

We both laugh and exit the dance floor when the song ends.

"Have I told you tonight that you look beautiful," I say as we head back to our table in the back of the gymnasium.

"Only about twenty times," Lucy says, wrapping her arms around my bicep. "And if I haven't told you, you look incredible."

"Have I told you tonight that I love you?"

"Not tonight."

I take her hand off my arm and spin her around so she stops in front of me. God, she's beautiful in her pale-pink dress that hugs every single curve on her body. It has one strap that goes over her shoulder, which leaves the other one completely bare. I've kissed that spot every chance I've gotten tonight. As soon as she stepped out of her house when I came to pick her up, all I could think about was taking that dress off her tonight.

Slowly. Methodically. Maybe with my teeth.

Then again, she looks good in an oversized T-shirt and a pair of my boxers. No, Lucy's true beauty comes from within. Her soul and her spirit make her the most beautiful woman in this world. It's in the way she sees the good in everyone, how she believes in people when they don't deserve that kind of faith.

She has seen that in me from the first time we met. To her, I was never the dumb jock or the kid who could only throw a football. I was always Bryce. I could live for a million years and not be able to return that kind of love.

But damn I'm going to try.

"Well then, I need to tell you for the first of many times tonight. I love you so damn much, Lucy Valenti."

She takes each of my lapels in her hands and pulls me to her. One more kiss won't hurt.

"I love you too, and thank you for all of this. This is . . . it's more than I ever dreamed of."

"Do you ever think about this night?" I ask, unsure of where the question came from, but I keep going with it. "If I had been able to come home. Do you ever wonder what would have happened?"

She fidgets with my lapels. "I'd be a liar if I said I didn't."

"And?"

Her big brown eyes fill with a twinge of sadness, and I cup her face between my palms.

"Hey, none of that," I say. "If it makes you sad, I don't want to talk about it. I don't even know where the question came from. Forget I said anything."

"No, it's fine," she says, taking a deep breath. "It's just . . . I had the stupid fantasy that every stereotypical girl has about prom night, and I figured that we would . . . that it would have been the first time for us. Silly, right?"

Her admission is a punch to my gut. Because it's the exact fantasy I had.

"Not silly at all. If it makes you feel better, I had the same one."

This gets me a smile. "You did?"

"I was so mad that I wasn't there. All I could think about was you and me dancing. The way you'd feel in my arms. I pictured us slow dancing and then sneaking off to the library and kissing you in the spot where we met. And then, if I was lucky enough . . ."

The way her body shivers in my hold tells me she knows exactly what would have happened that night.

"You know"—she runs her hands up and down my jacket lapels—"we could make one of those things happen tonight."

I look down at her, a little confused. "And what is that?"

She presses onto her toes and leans in close enough to whisper, "I have a key to the library. They gave it to me when I agreed to tut—"

I grab her hand, snag her purse from our table, and all but sprint with her out of the gym.

"Bryce!" Lucy laughs, trying to keep up with me in her heels.

Heels that I'm going to need her to leave on all night.

I take a look around to make sure no one followed us as Lucy frantically tries to open the door. Luckily, the coast looks clear.

We're really the worst chaperones ever.

"There," she says, turning the lock.

I guide her inside, turning back to immediately lock the door as well as the deadbolt.

Then I'm pulling her out of view of the door and kissing her like I've wanted to all night. Judging by the way she's kissing me back, she has wanted this as much as I have.

Our mouths are hurried and sloppy. Our hands are trying to be in every spot possible. She begins to undo my shirt, but a sliver of the light from the hallway distracts me.

"Not here," I say, breaking our lips as I pull her toward the back of the library. "Go to our table."

Somehow, even with no lights on, we find ourselves exactly where we met all those years ago. The place I first fell in love with her. I still remember that first day she walked up to me. Those big brown eyes penetrating my soul. Her no-nonsense demeanor throwing me for a loop, and her beauty taking my breath away.

"Come here," I say.

I bring her to me, and as soon as our lips connect, the rush from earlier fades away. This kiss isn't frantic like before. It's not messy or chaotic.

No, this one is tender. Loving. We both know the significance of where we are, both figuratively and literally. This is seven years of emotion pouring through our mouths.

"I love you," I whisper, my lips trailing down her neck and over her exposed shoulder. "I love you so damn much."

"I love you too," she says, arching her back as my lips trail to the top of her tits.

Her hand begins to slide down the front of my suit, stroking my aching cock from outside of my pants.

"You better watch it. I've been hard for you all night."

"Oh really?" she says, stroking it more. "Well then, we should probably take care of that."

Lucy undoes the button to my pants and quickly lowers the zipper, giving herself room to reach down through my boxers and take me in her hand.

"Who knew Lulu was such a bad girl," I tease, letting my fingers trail over her hips before I start to work her skirt up. Only then do I realize that my girl has been hiding something from me all night. "Are you not wearing panties?"

"Can't have lines, now can I?"

I didn't know my cock could get any harder, but it has. I lift her up and place her on the table before I kneel in front of her.

"I've wanted to do this all night," I say, lifting both of her legs over my shoulders and diving into her sweet and wet pussy.

She moans as soon as my tongue makes contact with her. Honestly, the sounds she makes when I do this are enough to make me lose it. I almost have a couple times. There is nothing quite like having the girl of my dreams sinking her fingers into my hair and forcing my mouth against her harder.

It's the hottest thing I've ever seen.

I slide two fingers into her center, working them around like I know she likes it.

"Yes," she moans as I begin flicking her clit with my tongue as my fingers hit the spot inside her that makes her crazy. Soon, she's squeezing around me and my fingers are coated with her juices.

"Oh my God," she says between breaths. "Bryce . . . that was . . ."

"Shhh," I say, bringing her lips to mine so she can taste herself. "We're not done yet."

I shove my slacks and boxer briefs down just enough to free myself and spread her legs as wide as they'll go. As I slide into her, I swallow her moan and smile against her mouth.

"Fuck, Lucy," I say, slowly beginning to work in and out of her. "You feel too good."

"Harder, Bryce," she says, reaching to grab on to each of my biceps. "I need to come again."

The thought of getting caught is real, and it's only making everything that much hotter. Not to mention her heels digging into my ass as I thrust into her.

"I love you," I say as I pull out, force her to her feet, and then bend her over the table. In her heels, she's just at the right height for me.

When I push back into her, the whole table shakes. I'd be worried that I'm being too rough, but she doesn't seem to care at all. If I listen close enough, I swear I can hear her begging me for more with each pant of breath she releases. Pleasure saturates her features as her body grips me and she loses herself to the orgasm.

I'm a goner. I spill into her as she also comes down from her own orgasm. How we both don't fall to the ground in a puddle I'm not sure.

"That was . . ." she says, her voice hoarse.

"Yeah," I say, placing a kiss on her back as I slowly pull out of her and tuck myself back into my pants. "If I would have known you had a key for here earlier, we would have done this a long time ago."

This earns me a laugh as she stands and begins fixing her dress.

Her hair is mussed. Her makeup is smeared. Her dress is wrinkled.

She has never looked more beautiful.

"Come here," I say, pulling her to me so I can kiss her long and deep.

"What was that for?" she asks when I finally release her lips.

"I'm trying to remember . . . I think I did, but I wanted to make sure . . . have I told you tonight I love you?"

Her laugh hits me in all the right spots. "Only a few times."

I lean back on the table, keeping her in my arms.

"You know"—I turn a little and pat the table—"this is the spot where I fell in love with you."

Her eyes grow wide at my statement. "You did? When?"

"The day you asked if I was Bryce Donald."

Her eyebrows go up so high it's comical. "The first time you met me? Bryce, you didn't even know me. I was the new girl in town who spouted off math stats to anyone who would listen."

"Yeah, you were." I can't help but smile at the memory. "I knew from the first moment I laid eyes on you that you were different. I didn't know it was love then. I was a teenager and stupid and thought the only thing that mattered was football. Yet, from the moment you walked into my life with your big brown eyes and your huge heart and random math facts, you've made me a better man. You've made me want to be a better man, even though I didn't always show that. You changed my life that day, and I've loved you ever since."

Her eyes soften as her hands travel up to cup my cheeks. Usually when she does this, she's bringing me in for a kiss. But this time all she does is let her thumb slowly stroke back and forth. Like she's memorizing my face. I should know. It's what my hands do every time they touch her body.

"Do you want to know the moment I knew I loved you?"

I lean forward so our foreheads are touching. "When was that?"

"The first time you called me Lulu."

I chuckle softly before kissing her forehead. I stay there a little longer than I intend to. It helps me push back the stray tear that's trying to come out.

"I knew you loved it."

"I only loved it because it came from you."

I tip her chin up and lean in, bringing our lips together for the hundredth time tonight.

"I'm going to miss you so fucking much."

My voice cracks, and she runs her hands through my hair, trying to soothe me. "I'm going to miss you too, but it's only a few months. We're different now then we were then. We love each other and have thought this through. We've got this. You and me. September will be here before we know it."

Her words are strong. Confident.
She believes in us. She believes in our love.
She believes in me.
I guess I only have one thing to do: make sure I'm worthy of it.

34
———

LUCY

APRIL, SENIOR YEAR, COLLEGE

"HEY, LULU."

This isn't the first time I've been to Lake Laurel since high school. In fact, I come here pretty regularly. It's been the place where I can get out of my head. Today, is a beautiful spring day so I decided to take advantage of the warm April weather and study for my finals where I can smell spring grass instead of the inside of a pizza parlor.

In all the times I've been here, I've spent my fair share of time thinking of Bryce since this is kind of our spot. I've replayed dozens of conversations we've had here, and even imagined dozens more we might have in this spot. However, not once in any of my daydreams did I hear his voice quite so clearly.

So, imagine my shock when I turn and find Bryce Donald standing there in all his future-pro football player glory.

"Bryce?" I blink a few times because I'm still not sure if my mind is playing tricks on me.

"Yup. It's me," he says, his smile piercing through my senses as he takes a few steps toward where I've laid out a blanket on the grass. "It's been a long time."

I want to tell him exactly how long it has been—three years, three months, and twenty-nine days. Not that I was counting. The last time I saw him was the Christmas Eve when he was thinking about transferring. We sat at this lake. We talked about his future and football and caught up on life.

He kissed me like I've never been kissed before.

"Yup. A long time," I mutter. "What are you doing here? Why aren't you in Cincinnati for the draft?"

The fact that the draft just happened to be in Cincinnati this year, which is just about an hour away from our town, has only added to the frenzy that has taken over Laurel Heights. Busses are shipping people down to watch Bryce and Cole get drafted. Others who can't make it have set up a watch party at the high school gym. This is a big deal for our town. Two guys from Laurel Heights about to make their dreams come true playing professional football? This is the stuff movies are made of.

Uncle Nick has been over the moon for the past few weeks because the media has been talking up Bryce as the eventual top draft pick. It looks like Nashville is going to draft him. Cole is projected to go in the second round, and that's only because he was injured last year. They even say there's a slight chance he could also be drafted by the Fury.

"I've given every interview I possibly can," Bryce says as he takes a seat next to me on my blanket. "I just . . . I needed to get away for a minute. It has been insane the past few months. So, I got in my truck and started driving. Somehow, I ended up here."

"It always has been a good spot to think."

"Yes, it has."

For long minutes, the only sounds around us are the gentle ripples of the lake and a few birds flying back and forth between the trees. I keep sneaking glances at him, though. In the one-thousand two-hundred and fifteen days since I saw him, he's changed so much. His muscles are more defined than I remember. I keep thinking his shirt is about to rip if it gets any tighter. His hair, which he's always kept short, is longer than I've ever seen it.

"What are you staring at, Lulu?" he asks, that smile that does me in every time forming on his mouth.

"You, I guess." No sense in hiding it. "I can't believe you're here."

He turns to look at me. At least his eyes haven't changed. I always thought they could see through my soul, which is what they seem to be doing right now.

"Honestly, neither can I," he says, letting out a breath. "Tomorrow, I'm going to be the number-one draft pick. Before I drove up here, I gave my agent the nod to finalize a contract that is worth more money than I'll ever spend in my life. Nashville promised me they were going to do what they could to also draft Cole. It's more than I ever could have asked for."

"But?"

"How did you know there's a but?"

I let out a chuckle. "I might not have talked to you in three years, but that doesn't mean I can't tell what's going through your mind."

It's his turn to laugh. "You always got me. When no one else understood, you did."

"Quit stalling. Tell me what's wrong."

He shifts his eyes away from me to the ground.

"What if I fail?"

Years ago, we sat in almost this exact spot and had the same conversation. It was the only time I heard Bryce Donald unsure of himself.

"What if you don't?"

He shrugs. "I'm about to set a new rookie contract record. I already have four endorsement deals. After I'm introduced to the media tomorrow, I'm scheduled to do a photo shoot with the PR department for the campaign they are going to run with my face plastered on it. I'm going to be across billboards all over the city."

"Sounds exciting." I don't know if I mean that, but it feels like the right thing to say.

"It's not exciting; it's terrifying. What if I don't produce? What if I can't hang? What if it's like freshman year of college when I didn't get the starting position? What if this team invests all this money and time into me, and I can't do it? What if I fail, Lucy?"

"Again . . . what if you don't?"

"I know you're trying to make me feel better, but there is a very good chance—"

I turn to face him more, cupping both of his cheeks to turn his head and make sure he hears this loud and clear.

"Bryce Donald, don't you dare start talking about chances because I will come back to you with statistics and probabilities that will make your head spin. I don't care if we don't talk for another ten years, you don't take that away from me."

He starts laughing, which is good to hear. He gets like this before every big decision and moment in his life, which is probably why I haven't heard from him in three years. He hasn't had a decision to make. When it comes to pressure on the field, the man is a pro. Off the field? When there are so many people riding on his success or failure? It paralyzes him.

"Now, as I was saying," I continue, "what if you get to Nashville and this is the best group of guys you've ever played with? What if your coaches are great? What if you don't fail? What if you take the league by storm and be the Bryce I know you can be?"

I really don't expect him to answer me, but I really don't expect him to say what he does next either.

"I miss you."

I'm pretty sure I stop breathing, unsure if I'm shocked, angry, or confused by that statement.

He misses me? While I love hearing those words, how dare he drop that now after all this time.

"Bryce, don't say things like that."

"But I mean them," he says, turning toward me and taking my hands in his. "I miss you. I have missed you. Not talking to you these past three years? I hated it. I felt like a part of me was missing."

"Then why didn't you call? And don't blame it on football."

"I don't know," he says. "Because I'm a guy, and I'm an idiot? What would I have said? 'Hey, Lulu. Sorry I haven't called and that I broke all my promises to you. Can we chat?'"

"That would have been a decent start."

"I never knew what to say, so I didn't say anything at all." He pauses to take a breath, and I'm glad he did. It's allowing my brain to catch up on what's happening here. "There were so many times I had your number ready to go, but I chickened out."

"Why now, Bryce? Why say all of this now?"

He lets go of my hands, pulling at his hair a bit. "Because I always thought . . . that when tomorrow happened, we'd be together. That you'd be sitting next to me, holding my hand when a team called my name. I'd turn to Mom and give her a hug and then turn to you and kiss the hell out of you before walking on stage to receive my jersey. That was the dream."

"Bryce—"

"I know. It's silly. We were high-school sweethearts what feels like a million years ago. Hell, we haven't talked in years. All I know is that, when I think of my future, or my perfect partner, or who I want to go on this life's journey with, you're the only face I ever see. So, yeah, I miss you. I miss what we could have had. I miss what we could have been. I just . . . miss you."

"I . . ." Even though my heart knows this is true, I'm scared to say the words. If I do, then they are out there in the universe and I won't be able to take them back. It has been three years, and I'd finally gotten over the fact that Bryce and I were never meant to be.

"What, Lulu? What is it?"

I take a deep breath, mustering all of the courage I can. "I miss you too."

I barely get the words out before Bryce's lips are on mine. At first, I'm too stunned to respond. Never in my wildest dreams did I think this is where today would lead, but here I am, my tongue tangling with his. All the while, my brain is stirring with crazy ideas like a future with the only man who has ever made me feel like I was more than just the smart girl.

Bryce lowers me back to the blanket, one hand on the back of my head while the other guides my lower back. Our lips release, and all I can do is stare up at this man. This man who somehow dug himself a place in my heart when I didn't even know he was doing it. A man who is so much more than people give him credit for. A man who I know I'll love until my dying day.

"Is this real?" he asks, his hands gently pushing back a piece of hair off my forehead. "Because if this is a dream, I don't want to wake up."

I bite my bottom lip because it's all I can do to stop the tears from coming. This. This right here is why I was never able to move on. I tried. Lord knows I did. I tried dating or going to parties and meeting people, but every time I thought a guy had a chance, I would always come back to Bryce. No other guy gives me the million butterflies like Bryce did.

"You need to quit doing that," he says, a wicked grin coming over his face.

"Doing what?"

"Biting that lip like that."

I loop my hands around his neck, gently letting my fingers play with the hair at his nape. "Why is that?"

"Because it makes me want to kiss you again."

"Maybe that's what I wanted you to do."

And he does. God does he kiss me. He kisses me like I'm his. Like this is our first kiss and the promise of a million kisses to come. I never want this to stop.

Unfortunately, his ringing cell phone has other plans.

"Are you going to get that?" I reluctantly ask. I know he should, but I'd rather him not stop doing whatever he is doing to my neck right now.

He lets out a groan before taking his phone out of his pocket. "Yes, Dean?"

I don't know who Dean is, but it must be someone important because he's quickly sitting up, leaving me strangely cold without his body weight on top of me.

"Fine. Yeah, yeah. I'll meet you at the hotel in a few hours."

He ends the call and lets out the most frustrated breath I've ever heard.

"You have to go back, don't you?"

He nods as he brings his knees up, letting his arms hang over them. "That was my agent. Apparently, there are a few things the Fury want to go over before tomorrow. I need to meet with them tonight."

"I understand," I say as I sit up. It doesn't mean the selfish part of me likes it, though.

"Lucy. Will you come with me to Cincinnati?"

How many times had I wished for him to ask me that? Hundreds? Thousands? Each time, I always figured my answer would be a resounding yes, and I hate that I can't have that.

"I can't. I have finals this week."

"Oh," he says, letting his head hang back down. "I just thought maybe . . ."

"What did you think?"

He finally looks back up to me, and the sadness in his eyes reminds me of when we said goodbye before he first went to Clemson. "I thought maybe this was it. That this could be our take two."

"Really?" Even though those were the words I wanted him to say, I honestly didn't think he would. "You'd be willing to have a relationship during the season? Because you're about to go pro, Bryce. This isn't high school anymore. This isn't even college. This is the big leagues. Are you sure, in your heart of hearts, that you're ready for this? For us?"

I wish I didn't have to say all of that. Every cell in my body is screaming at me for giving him this out, but I'd rather him tell me that maybe he isn't ready then promise that he is and get my hopes up again.

I start preparing myself for the speech. The one he gives me every time about things being different if I only give him a few months. That's usually what it is. So, I can't hide the shock on my face when he turns toward me and moves to one knee as he takes my hands in his.

"I know I've always said I can't date during the season. I know I've always felt that I needed to wait for the perfect time, but this is our perfect time. We're starting new chapters of our lives, and I want to do it together. So, even though it can't happen tonight, it's going to happen soon. You're going to nail your finals and graduate. I'm going to go to Nashville and find us a place to live. Then you're going to come down, and we're going to be together. For real this time."

"And what about during the season?"

"You'll be my biggest cheerleader. The one I come home to every day. My partner in crime. What do you say, Lulu? You in?"

Is he for real? I search his eyes, looking for any hesitation or hint of unsurety, but all I see is love. Love for me. For us. For our future.

"I'm in," I say, a smile so big you can see it a mile away.

Bryce scoops me into his arms, picking me up like I'm a feather and twirling me around. I'm sure if someone were watching us, they would probably think we were crazy, smiling and laughing like we are.

And maybe we are a little crazy. Bryce and I have never computed on paper, but in actuality, we are a perfect formula.

"I hate that I have to go back to Cincinnati," he says, putting me down.

"It's okay," I say. "I'll be watching tomorrow. They're having a huge thing at the gymnasium."

"I'll be thinking of you." He links our fingers together. "And the first second I have to call you, I will."

"I believe you," I say, bringing him into me for one more kiss. "Now, go be amazing."

THREE DAYS.

It has been three days of unanswered calls and unreturned texts. I thought about sending him a picture of my boobs just to see if that would get a reaction out of him, but I was worried that maybe he didn't have his phone on him. Then I saw a live report on television with a picture of him walking into the Fury facility, phone in hand.

I don't know who he was texting in the footage, but it sure as hell wasn't me.

When he told me he would call me on draft night, I actually didn't expect that. He was the number-one pick. I knew he'd be doing countless interviews, but by Sunday? I figured things would have died down. I figured wrong.

"How stupid am I?" I ask myself as I get in my car to go to the grocery store, slamming the door behind me.

I can't believe I let myself fall for his lies again. Maybe it was because I was seeing him for the first time in so long. Maybe because I was drunk from his kiss and I would have believed anything he said, but it doesn't really matter what the excuse is. I fell for the song and dance yet again.

If he can't do something as simple as return a call or a text, how can I uproot my life and move to Nashville? Graduation is next week, and I have a job lined up at the bank in town. Why would I leave stability behind for a man who can't be bothered to text back something as small as a thumbs-up emoji.

"Ice cream," I say as I pull into the grocery store. "Ice cream will fix it. Ice cream and a supreme pizza."

I call in my order at Tripoli's before making my way in to the grocery store. I sure as heck hope I don't see anyone. Between finals this week and crying each night because of Bryce, I can safely say I look like hell.

I keep my head down as I walk into the store, taking a basket just in case I see anything else along the way. I hurry down the first aisle and take a sharp left, making a beeline for the frozen foods, which is why I don't see the person making a right. The person I promptly run into.

"Ouch!" I say, losing my balance and falling backward onto my ass.

"Are you okay?" Luciano says, and my face blushes scarlet as I accept his hand and let him pull be back to my feet. Of course, he would be the one I run into because, why not?

"I'm fine." It's when I release his hand that I finally look up.

I haven't seen Luciano Tripoli since the day he left for his year-long internship in Italy. I've heard his parents talk about him coming back, but I guess I hadn't realized he was home already.

"Wow, it's good to see you." We both come in for a hug that's part awkward, part friendly. "I didn't know you were back in town."

"Just got in a few days ago."

The silence that settles between us is awkward. Do I say thanks for helping me up or ask how his trip was?

"Well, it was good seeing you," I say because, frankly, I just want to go home, put on my comfy sweats, eat a stupid amount of food, and watch a sappy movie. "Maybe I'll see you around the restaurant."

I start to walk away, but I only get a few steps before I feel Luciano's hand on my elbow.

"Lucia?"

"Yeah?"

"I was wondering . . . well, I was curious . . . I thought that maybe—"

"Luciano? What are you asking me?"

"Will you go to dinner with me?"

I'm taken aback a bit because, wow, that's not what I was expecting.

"Luciano . . ." I'm about to tell him thanks but no thanks. That we'll see each other soon enough at the next dinner party our mothers throw. I'm about to say all of this to him when my cell phone starts vibrating in my back pocket.

I hurry and grab it, knowing that it has to be Bryce finally texting me back.

Brenna: Finals are done! What are we doing tonight?

It takes all I have not to drop my phone and fall to the floor in tears. That's what I want to do. But I won't. I can't.

It's right there, in the middle of the town grocery story, that I decide that I've wasted enough time and tears on Bryce Donald.

I'm. Done. Waiting.

"You know what? Yes, I will go out with you. How does tomorrow sound?"

35

BRYCE

"TWENTY-NINE, toss . . . twenty-nine, toss . . . ready . . . set . . . hut!"

I take the snap from my center and roll to the right, all while faking a handoff to the running back. The defense can't touch me, the benefits of being a quarterback during camp, but I still feel the pressure as they come toward me. I look down the field, and exactly where he's supposed to be is Dexter. I reach back, wind up and give my wrist a flick as I throw the ball thirty yards down the field, right into the arms of my wide receiver in the end zone.

It might only be minicamp, but throwing a touchdown never gets old.

"That's how we do it, boys!" Davis yells from the sideline. "Offense, bring it in. Defense, gassers. Go!"

I can't help but smile as we jog over to Davis and Hunter, who are waiting on the sideline.

"Good practice today, guys. Good way to finish this session," Davis begins as we all take a knee around him. "Take the next weekend to rest up. I'll see you next week."

"Bring it in, guys," I say as we all stand and huddle up. "Team on three. One, two, three, team!"

We all start dispersing back to the locker room when I feel a hand slap me on the shoulder pad.

"Looking good out there. How are you feeling?"

"Feeling really good." For the first time in a while, it's not a lie. "It's like riding a bike."

"And the other stuff?" Davis asks, stopping in front of me. "You've had a busy few months. How are you handling it?"

I will give Davis credit. He's really had my back since my return. Apparently, it was his idea to put me on the injured reserve list. I'll never be able to pay him back for the way he's looked out for me. Even when I didn't want him to.

"I'm still getting there, but feeling good," I say as we start walking again. "I'm not going to lie. The press tour was rough. Interview after interview about mental health and what happened last season. How I handled coming back to the team. It was a lot."

"I can imagine. I watched a few of the interviews, though. You did a great job and handled yourself well."

"Thanks," I say even though, somewhere inside me, I don't think I deserve praise for coming back from self-destruction. That's a conversation to have with Malcolm and not Davis for a different day. "I'm not going to lie, admitting to the world that I let down my team, my family, and my fans was hard. But I'm better for it."

"You are. And you look like a decent quarterback too," Cole says as he comes to a stop next to me and Davis. "I forgot you knew how to throw like that."

"Me too. Nice to know I can put some throws in the playbook this year."

"Very funny," I say as Davis is called back over to the field. "I'll talk to you guys later."

Davis makes his way back to the practice field as Cole and I continue walking to the locker room. Cole's locker is right next to mine—it's been that way since high school—and I might be straight as the day is long, but I can't help but stare at Cole as he takes off his pads and shirt.

"How the hell did you get bigger? I didn't think that was physically possible."

Cole laughs as he tosses his pads and helmet into his locker. "I hit the weights a lot this year. Not like I had anything else to do."

"I hoped that, once you were done pulling my ass out of the gutter, you'd get yourself a girlfriend."

"I've told you, I'm not interested," he says.

"Why not?" I ask, taking off my jersey. "I meant what I said at New Year's. When Lucy gets down here, we're going to need double-date partners. Are you really going to make me ask Wes and his wife?"

"Hey now!" Wes, our veteran tight end, calls out. "Just because I've been married longer than you've been shaving doesn't mean the wifey and I aren't fun."

"So, you and your wife would be down for a night of doubles bowling?"

He shakes his head. "Me? Hell yeah. I'll even buy the first pitcher of beer. Cara, though? The day I see her in rented bowling shoes will be a cold day in hell."

"See!" I say, pointing at Wes. "That leaves you, buddy. Do I need to download an app for you? How about that Left for Love app? Hell, I hear that video app, what's it called? ForU? I hear that people are hooking up off that."

Cole mumbles something under his breath that sounds strangely like, "Fuck you." Man, I forgot how fun it was to mess with the big guy.

"What was that? I didn't hear you."

He flashes me a look that would make a normal person piss themselves. But to me? It's just Cole trying to look tough.

"Maybe you were better as a drunk. You didn't talk as much."

"Whatever man," I say, tossing my sweaty jersey at him. "You missed me."

He gives me an eyeroll before he heads to the showers. "I hate that I did."

"Love you too, buddy! See you tonight. It's *Bachelor in Paradise* premiere, so bring your notebooks because we're drafting right after."

I laugh as I hear him continue to grumble toward the shower and I take the moment of privacy to grab my phone out of my locker.

> Lulu: Hey you. Hope you have a great practice.
> I miss you. Counting down the days.

I can't hide the shit-eating grin that comes across my face when reading that. It has been a few days since we've talked, and I'm just glad to see her name on my screen. Sometimes, she'll send me a funny text, and other times, she sends me updates about her day. My favorite text of all time was the pro-con list of sexual positions. That was a fun conversation later that night.

Then there are days like today when I just get one that says "I miss you" and it takes all that's in me not to jump in my truck and drive the five hours back to Laurel Heights just to kiss her.

> Bryce: I miss you too.

I start to get ready to hit the shower when my phone buzzes. All someone would have to do is look at my face to know who it is.

> Lulu: How was practice today?

> Bryce: Great. We won. Again. Cole is being
> pissy because he hasn't been laid in a while.
> How was your day?

I don't get a response right away, and I know that means it was another rough day for her. She's been having a lot of those lately. Megan is officially on maternity leave. She and her parents still aren't talking, and as if that weren't enough, her car stopped working last week and it's going to take at least two weeks to fix.

I offered to get her a new car, but before I'd even finished suggesting it, she was spewing all the reasons why I shouldn't. I knew it was best not to argue.

I'll just get it for her when she moves here.

> Lulu: Mrs. Tripoli came into the bank today. That was awkward. I'm pretty sure she called me a bitch in Italian. But I don't want to talk about my day. I want to talk about good things. Tell me everything about practice today.

She deflects a lot. It's as if she doesn't want to bother me with her problems. But what she doesn't know is that I want her to. For years, she has carried the weight of my problems for me. She never asked for it. I just put it on her, and like the true angel she is, she bared it.

Well, now, I want to take some of that from her.

> Bryce: Don't deflect. You know you can tell me everything, right? Get your bad day off your chest. I'm here Lucy.

> Lulu: Can I call you later? It's just too much to text, and I need to finish closing things up.

> Bryce: Absolutely. I love you.

"How's Lucy?" Cole asks as he comes back to his locker.

"Busy," I say as I start stripping off my sweaty practice gear. "I wish she'd let me do more for her."

"All you can do is be there for her. Make sure she knows that."

I look back at my text messages, hoping she knows I meant every word of what I just wrote.

> Lulu: Love you more.

"She does," I say confidently. "She absolutely does."

36

———

LUCY

"I'M SO SORRY, Lucy, I really thought I had my checkbook."

"It's fine, Mr. Coffman. Take your time."

That might be what I said, but inside, it was more like: *you don't need your fucking check book to take out cash even though you insist you do.*

It's fine. Everything is fine.

I try to make myself take a few deep breaths as my ninety-year-old customer writes a check to cash. I should be happy that I have a few minutes just to breathe, but not going eighty miles per hour also gives me time to think.

And that is the last thing I want.

"Here you go," Mr. Coffman says, handing me a check written to cash for seventy-five dollars. "How is that boyfriend of yours? Hopefully he's going to play better than he did last year."

I try to laugh off the comment because I know he doesn't mean any harm by it. "He does too. Have a good day, Mr. Coffman. See you next Friday."

"Goodbye, dear," he says as he slowly walks out of the bank with the help of a cane. I know I need to make sure he gets to his car safely, but the feeling of my phone vibrating in my pocket makes me want to shove him out the door.

"Come on . . ." I say, bouncing on my heels as my phone continues to ring. Finally, Mr. Coffman is out of the door, and I sprint back to my office, simultaneously swiping right to answer the call.

"Hello," I say, sounding as if I just ran a marathon.

"Are you trying to run again? I didn't think that went well last time."

The tension immediately eases just hearing Bryce's voice. "I'll never make that mistake again."

We both laugh as a comfort washes over me and I sit in my desk chair. "How are you?"

"I was going to ask you the same thing. Been a few days since we've talked."

Four. Four days. "Yeah, I'm sorry about that. Things have just been nuts here."

"Still struggling with Megan on maternity leave?"

I slide a little farther down into my chair, the stress of the day, hell, the week, finally catching up to me. "Yeah, working open to close every day has been rough. But that's not the only bad news."

"Oh no. What happened?"

"Well, a teller quit on me last week. Said she wanted to chase her true passion or some crap like that."

"I know it leaves you in a bind, but I think it's cool that someone wants to chase their dream."

"Her dream is beekeeping, Bryce. Beekeeping."

"Well"—I can hear him taking a big swallow, not knowing how to navigate out of this conversation—"good for her."

"I hope she gets stung."

"No you don't. You're too good of a person for that. You're just stressed."

"I know," I say, which almost comes out like a sigh. "But that's not even the worst part."

"There's more?"

"Unfortunately, yes. I thought Megan would be back from maternity leave in August. Turns out, now it's going to be more like September."

He doesn't say anything, and he doesn't have to. I know what he's thinking. That means I won't get there until October. I haven't even begun to start thinking about packing or anything along those lines. If these were normal circumstances, I could ask my family for help. But they still aren't speaking to me because of the Christmas catastrophe. If I ask them to help me pack my house to move to Nashville, I'll likely get called a football floozie or get flooded with guilt about how I'm not following their wishes.

"Well, I guess this is the time for me to tell you my bad news."

This makes me sit up in my chair. "What? What happened?"

I try to steel myself for whatever bad news is about to come my way.

"I'm not going to be able to get home in July," he says dejectedly.

It takes every fiber of my being not to scream in frustration. Though, if I'm being honest, I should have known. This is how it always happens.

"Here we go again," I say softly I'm not sure I actually said it or just thought it.

"Excuse me? What did you say?"

Well, apparently, I did. No sense in taking it back now. Especially when it's the truth. "I said 'here we go again.' Because I should have known this was going to happen."

"How was I supposed to know the team would want me to do a second press tour? That wasn't part of the plan they gave me."

"It never is. It's always something that just pops up." I let out a breath because I'm trying to keep my cool, but it's really hard when the world feels like it's crashing down on me. "This is how it always starts, though. First, it's a few missed phone calls, which we've already managed to check that off the list."

"I can't be the only one blamed for the missed phone calls. You've missed your fair share as well."

Oh, he wants to go there? Let's go there. "I'm sorry I fell asleep at seven last night because I was exhausted from work and missed one phone call Bryce. I didn't see that you called until this morning, but I didn't want to wake you up."

"You know you can call me anytime," he says, his voice fighting back anger. "I don't care about getting woken up."

"Ha! Is that so?"

"What's that supposed to mean?"

"It means that when I called you last week at eight in the morning, I was told to call back in an hour. Then later that night when I asked why you were in a mood, you said it was because I woke you up."

"That was because I was out late and grumpy. You caught me on a bad morning."

"You were out?" This is news to me. "Who were you out with?"

"Some teammates. Dexter. A few of the defensive guys. They invited me to a bar, and we got home late. It wasn't a big deal. I was just more tired than usual."

"No big deal? Bryce, were you drinking? I thought you quit. You chose to quit! I thought that was part of your plan?"

"I can have a beer, Lucy," he says, his voice filled with annoyance. "I chose not to for a while, but I'm doing better. I feel that I can have one beer with the guys on occasion. Don't worry. I'm a grown man. I know what I'm doing."

"I know you're a grown man, and if you think you can have a beer here and there, then who am I to stop you?"

"Exactly."

"Then again, I can't even get you to keep a promise about coming home when you were the one insisting you would."

"That's low. You know I can't control what the team wants me to do."

"I know you can't. But that's not the point."

"Then what is? Because I have no idea which way is up in this phone call."

I suck in a frustrated breath. "I'm sorry. I apologize for what I said about not making it home. You can't control what the team wants you to do. Those were words of frustration and stress. I do take those back."

"I understand you're frustrated by it. So am I. But I have to go.

After the first press tour went so well, public relations and Dean think it will be good to do a full-scale Bryce-is-back campaign. Morning talk shows, guest spots on *SportsCenter*, the whole nine yards. They have me booked from now until the week before camp starts. They think that if I do this then I won't be hounded by reporters during the season. That we can officially put last year behind us."

I sink back into my chair. It makes sense. I might not like it, but I get it. And I know it's what he needs to do.

"I understand," I say, hoping not to sound as depressed as I feel. "But Bryce, drinking? Going out until all hours?"

"It was just one night Lucy."

"I don't care if it was one night or every night since you've been back. You worked hard and you even admitted that drinking was part of your problem so you cut it out. I just don't want to see you throw away months of hard work just to be with the boys."

"You have nothing to worry about," he says. "It was one night. I know the work I did. I was just tired of sitting at home. Let's not fight, okay?"

"Okay," I say, hoping that everything he is saying is on the level. "Also, I know you have to go back on the road. But that doesn't mean I have to like it."

"You can say you hate it," he says. "Because I do."

"You do?"

"Of course I do. I miss the fuck out of you. I was counting down the days until July. I also hate fighting with you, and I'd rather never do this again."

I smile. "Same. I miss you too. I'm sorry I flew off the handle, it's just . . . I'm scared, Bryce. I'm stressed, and I'm scared, and this is a hell of a lot harder than I thought it would be."

"I know," he says. "But we're almost there, right? Three more months. And your birthday is in August. I'll definitely be home to celebrate that. I can't do this without you. I need you here with me. I know it's hard, but we're almost there."

I look at the calendar, which I just turned to July the other day.

"Three more months."
"Three more months," he repeats. "I love you, Lulu."
"Love you more."

37

___

LUCY

"HI. You've reached the voice mail of Bryce Donald. Leave a mess—"

I toss the phone onto my couch and resist the urge to scream into a pillow. I could recite every word of Bryce's voice mail because I talk to it more than him these days.

"I know that look," Brenna says, walking into my living room with two glasses of wine. "What did my idiot brother do this time?"

Poor Brenna. She has had to take the brunt of my moods these past few months.

I sigh, taking the wine glass from her. "Just another day I get sent to voice mail. Happy birthday to me."

This isn't exactly how I thought I'd be spending my twenty-fifth birthday—fighting the urge to cry into my wine glass because my idiot boyfriend hasn't called. Brenna begged me to go do something, even if it was just to have dinner with her, Luciano, and Celine. Only, it didn't feel right without Bryce here, so I said I wanted a quiet night at home.

I should have taken her up on her offer.

"Maybe he doesn't have his phone on him?" she says, taking a seat next to me. "Or maybe he's in an interview and can't answer. I'm sure he's going to call. You never know, he could be on his way up here to surprise you?"

I just shrug because we could play the guessing game all night and still not know what the heck he is doing.

Most of July was filled with press tours and appearances. I was proud of him when he spoke of his struggles with anxiety and how mental health was just as important as physical health. He admitted to using alcohol to try to cope with it, which only created a bigger problem. Bryce was also doing his best to normalize seeking help in terms of therapy.

The one thing he hasn't done is return most of my calls or messages. After our fight in June, I made sure that I did my part. Even if I worked a ten-hour day, I made sure to call. I sent him a text every morning and every night.

Sometimes, I get to speak to him, but more often than not, my call goes to voice mail or the message goes unreturned for days. I know he's busy, and I know he's back and forth between traveling and Nashville, but he's managed to find time to go to dinner with his teammates and the opening of a new bar on Broadway. At least, according to some of his teammates' Instagram stories.

Ugh . . . I hate sounding this way. I don't want him to be a hermit. I want him to have a life. I want him to bond with his teammates and have a life outside of football. I just want him to miss me as much as I miss him.

I thought maybe today of all days he'd put his football responsibilities and his teammates to the side and be with me on my birthday. Even if he couldn't get here, it would have been nice of him to FaceTime me. Heck, I would have settled for a happy-birthday text.

Anything.

I already know what it's like not to be first on Bryce Donald's list. But this? This is the worst of all.

If I were to make an assumption based off the events of the last month, tonight, and—if I'm honest—the past seven years, I know exactly how this is going to go.

It's football season. Nothing else matters.

Not even me.

Especially not me. I know I should be upset about that. I should be in a full-on rage, but I don't have the energy. I'm just . . . I can't. I'm too deeply disappointed to be angry because on some level, I only have myself to blame.

"When was the last time you talked to him?" Brenna asks.

"Tuesday."

She gives me a small smile. "That's not so bad."

"Of last week. Tuesday of last week."

"What is wrong with him?" she asks, though I think it's rhetorical. "He messaged me last week to ask what color you preferred in jewelry. I just don't understand what is going on with him right now?"

"He's busy . . ."

"Bullshit!" Brenna's voice gets so loud it nearly makes me jump out of my skin. Apparently, the anger I can't feel has been transferred to her. "People can be busy and also make time for the ones they care about. There is always time, especially on their girlfriend's birthday. It's just about wanting to find it."

She's right. I've been making excuses for weeks now.

"Why doesn't he want to use his time on me?" I ask. "How could he say he loves me but then push me aside like this?"

The tears burst out of me like a breaking dam. I've been keeping them in for too long, so I was bound to burst at some point. Brenna hurries toward me and wraps me in her arms. I just cry. These are tears that I've been holding in for weeks now. Oh, who am I kidding? These are tears that have been building since the first time he made me a promise he didn't keep.

Why did I ever think that this time would be any different? Why did I think he'd change? I always thought I was a smart girl, but apparently love has made me stupid.

It's the only explanation.

"I wish I knew what to say," Brenna says. "Except that I hope you know that in no way, shape or form is this your fault. Frankly, I'm ashamed to call him my brother. What is he even doing right now? It's your fucking birthday, and he's making you cry because he's an idiot? Not on my watch. Fuck this shit."

I hear Brenna start clicking through her phone. If there is one thing I can say about Brenna Donald it's that the woman has zero fear. She also gives zero fucks. She's the borderline crazy girl who should be hired by the FBI because she can find something online in five seconds with just the first name of the person's cat. It's kind of impressive.

It's also kind of frightening that she teaches children.

"Oh hell no!" she yells.

"What?" I ask, though I don't look up.

"Who is Dexter?"

"One of his teammates," I say, inching closer to her to see what she's looking at.

"He's hot."

"Focus, Brenna."

"Oh shit. Sorry. Apparently, you and Dexter are birthday buddies. And judging by the pictures, the Fury guys are having *quite* the time at his birthday party."

I take the phone from her and have to blink a few times because, even in my worst thoughts about Bryce, I didn't think this was a possibility.

Bryce and the entire Fury team are at a VIP lounge at some bar. Cole is there, though, it seems as if he'd rather be anywhere else. As for Bryce? He looks quite content holding a glass of something in one hand as a girl takes up residence on his lap.

And not just any girl; it's the girl from New Year's Eve.

What the fuck?

"I . . . who . . . what the . . ." My brain can't form coherent sentences.

"I'm going to kill him. I don't care if he's my blood. I'm going to fucking kill him."

I hear Brenna, but I can't say anything. It's as if I'm stunned silent and the only thing tossing around in my brain is the events of the last few weeks.

Yes, we've had trouble reaching each other, but then there has been the drinking and the partying. Apparently, there has also been the other girls since I'm not in Nashville to keep them off his fucking lap.

"You need to call him. Now," Brenna says, taking the phone from my hand and handing me mine. "He needs to fucking explain himself."

She's right. I need to hear from him what the hell is going on.

It rings and rings. With every ring my imagination runs a little wilder.

Why haven't we talked in more than a week?

Is that woman more than just someone he hooked up with once?

Why isn't Cole stepping in? Isn't he on Team Lucy or is he helping Bryce with this?

"Hi. You've reached the voice mail of Bryce Donald. Leave a mess—"

I hit the red button and launch my phone across the room.

"What do you need?" Brenna asks as the tears start falling again. "Because right now, everything from a shoulder to cry on to committing a felony is on the table. Just let me change my shoes if we're burying a body."

I want to laugh, but I can't make myself.

"I just want to go to sleep. Hopefully, I wake up tomorrow this will all have been a bad dream."

Brenna brings me into a hug again. "I'm sorry you're hurting. I wish there was more I could do."

"Me too."

I'm not sure how long I sit crying on Brenna's shoulder before I pass out, but when I wake up in the middle of the night with a blanket draped around me, there still isn't a response from Bryce.

38

BRYCE

"She is going to be so surprised," I say to myself as I press on the gas a little harder. I've cut the five-hour drive from Nashville to Laurel Heights down by a half hour, but I don't care if I get a ticket. I'm making it home for my girl's birthday.

Today is going to be perfect. And that's what we need, a reminder of how perfect we are together. So, despite my still being slightly hungover from last night's festivities and that I'm going to have to explain why I haven't answered her calls the last few days, I know that after today we're going to be back to the old Bryce and Lucy.

These past months have been hell for both of us. We've missed calls, got in arguments, and went days without talking. Most of that is because of me and my insane schedule this summer, but that isn't something that I didn't warn her about. Yes, I've had some fun too. Not the fun I was having when I was trying to forget who Lucy Valenti was, but it was nice to be out and act like a normal twenty-five-year-old. Well, as normal as a bunch of professional football players can act when they have black cards to burn in a city they rule.

Then there was the past week where I was too scared that I'd give something away about her birthday surprise that I'd dodged her calls.

I pull off the freeway and expertly maneuver my way through the roads of Laurel Heights to Lucy's house. I'm pretty sure I run five stop signs, but again, I don't care.

I take a final breath as I make my way onto Lucy's front porch. If she heard me pull in, she hasn't showed it yet. In fact, I don't hear anything as I step up to knock on the door.

"Brenna?"

I know it's not crazy for Brenna to be over at Lucy's house, but what isn't making any sense is why my sister is looking at me with such hatred. It's like little knives are coming out of her eyes.

"You have a lot of fucking nerve," she says, stepping outside and closing the door behind her. "What the hell are you doing here, Bryce?"

"What do you mean? I'm here to surprise Lucy for her birthday."

I try to step around Brenna, but she moves to block me from the door. "You aren't going in there."

"Excuse me?" What gives her the right to say that I can't go into my girlfriend's house? "I don't know what's up your ass today, but let me in."

"I said no," she says. "Not until you fucking explain yourself."

"Explain what?" I ask, thoroughly confused by this situation. "I'm here to see my girlfriend on her birthday. Does that need an explanation?"

Brenna laughs, only it sounds like how a super villain would laugh. "Her birthday was *yesterday*."

I blink a few times as I let that process. Then I decide that I'm hungover and must have heard her wrong. "What?"

"I said that, her birthday was yesterday, you fucking dumbass."

I think I'm going to vomit.

Oh God, I missed Lucy's birthday.

"I have to see her," I say, trying to push past Brenna. "Lucy!"

"No," she says, blocking me again from going inside. "You don't get to barge in there. It's more than just the missed birthday. You really fucked—"

"Let him in, Brenna," Lucy says softly as she opens the door. As soon as I see her, my heart drops to my feet. Her eyes are puffy as if she's been crying all night. Her nose is red. Her hair is a scattered mess.

God I am such a fucking asshole.

"Lucy," I say, "I'm so sorry."

"We need to talk," she says as she steps to the side to let me in. "Thanks, Brenna. I'll call you later."

"Are you sure? The offer for me to go change my shoes is still on the table."

"I'm good," Lucy says as she gives my sister a hug. Brenna starts walking to her car, which I hadn't noticed when I pulled up.

"Lucy," I say as I step inside. "I'm so sorry. I—"

"No, Bryce. Sit down first. Let me go get dressed. I'll be down in a few."

I nod and do as she says. When I walk into her living room, all I see are pillows, blankets, and used tissues. There are also two empty wine glasses and a half-eaten pizza.

God, she spent her birthday crying and eating pizza on her couch while I was out celebrating with Dexter at a fucking club.

Fuck I am the worst.

Lucy comes back down the stairs in a pair of leggings and an oversized sweatshirt. "What are you doing here?" she asks as she sits about as far away from me as she can get.

"I was going to surprise you for your birthday, but I am the worst person in the world and got the dates wrong. I honestly thought your birthday was today. I don't know how I fucked it up. I would have been here yesterday had I known, and I am so fucking sorry, Lucy. God I am so sorry. How can I make it up to you?"

"You can start by explaining why another girl was sitting on your lap last night."

I shake my head in confusion. "What?"

"Dexter's party. The girl on your lap. The girl who tried to pick you up on New Year's? She looked comfortable on your lap last night."

I rack my brain, trying to remember back to last night. Dexter got us in to a club that just opened. It started out as just us, but eventually, a bunch of groupies talked their way in.

"Can't remember? Maybe I can jog your memory."

Lucy tosses me her phone, and as soon as I see it, my stomach falls.

There I am, sitting in the VIP area. I'm holding a glass of whiskey —one that just kept getting refilled without my having to ask—and looking at one of the guys with the groupie sitting on my lap.

"Yes, it was her. Yes, she got in to the VIP area. She somehow always does. That picture was taken at the exact moment she sat. It took me a split second to realize what was happening, and when I did, I told her to get off. Call Cole. He'll vouch. He'll tell you that after I told her to leave, she got so mad that she and her friends stormed off. Dex and the rest of the guys got pissed at me for chasing off the women. But I swear, Lucy, nothing happened."

She doesn't say anything right away, and I wish I could hold her, but it's clear that is the last thing she wants from me.

"Please say something," I plead. "You have to believe I didn't cheat on you. I never would."

"I know," she says softly.

"And you have to know that, if I were any good at keeping things straight, I wouldn't have been out with those guys last night. I would have been here. With you."

I start to move closer to her, but she holds her hands up to stop me.

"No, Bryce. You don't get to come in here and spew apologies when I spent the last twenty-four hours crying and wondering why my boyfriend doesn't love me."

"What?" I ask, leaning closer to her, but I stop as she holds her hands up again. "How can you not think I love you?"

"Gee, let me see," she says sarcastically. "We haven't talked in weeks. When we do, it's either a fight or so short it was barely worth it. You never have time for me, but you always seem to find time for your teammates and football. There will always be time for football."

"You know what I had to do this summer. We talked about it. You were okay with it."

She nods. "I was, and I'm proud of you. It took a lot of courage to talk about what you did."

"Then what's the matter? What do you want from me, Lucy?"

"What do I want?" she yells, all but jumping from her seat. "What I want is to have my boyfriend, the man who says he loves me, to put me first for a change. For him not to make me feel like I'm somewhere down the list of things in his life he needs to attend to or that he'll get to eventually. I deserve to be first too sometimes, and I never am with you. I never have been, and I don't think I ever will be. It's football or your teammates or your public relations responsibilities. Hell, I wasn't even important enough for you to write down the right day for my birthday. I'm never a priority, and damn it, I deserve to be."

"What do you mean you're never a priority?" I say, my voice getting louder as I also stand. "You're the *only* priority!"

"You have a funny way of showing it."

"You are!" I yell, beginning to pace as I pull at my hair. "Everything I do is for you. For us. For our future."

"Forgetting my birthday and getting drunk with your teammates is putting me first?"

"I said I was sorry!"

"What are you sorry for? Because I don't even know if you know." She takes a breath, which I think is to stop herself from crying, but the tears welling in her eyes are threatening to kill me. "We can't talk on the phone because you're either playing football, prepping for an interview, or sleeping because you had to do one of those things. You go out with your teammates at night because you think you need to bond with them, never mind that you said you were done drinking. That has been your life for the past four months. Do you want to know what mine has been? I work and then come home, hoping that maybe my boyfriend will take an hour from his day to see how I am doing. But he never did. I have waited so damn long for you, but I don't think I can do it anymore. It hurts too much. Last night? Last night was the final straw. I'm done. I can't wait anymore."

I blink a few times because she can't have said what she just said.

"Lucy, no." I scramble off the couch and literally fall on my knees in front of her begging. "Let's talk. I'm sorry. For everything. What do you want me to do? I'll do anything. I'll quit football. Right now. I'll call the team right now."

I move to grab my cell phone, and Lucy puts her hand on top of mine, lowering it back to my side. "You're not quitting football. I'm not about to be the Yoko Ono of professional football."

"Then what do you want? Because I can't lose you. I can't."

Tears well in her eyes again, only this time a few spill over. "Nothing. You can't do anything. You're football, Bryce. That's what you were meant to do. This? You and I? It just wasn't meant to be."

"Not meant to be!" I yell, as I push down tears of my own. "If there was anything in this world that was meant to be, Lucy, it's us. I have known I've loved you since the first day I met you. This is our time. We are so close."

"And then what happens when I move to Nashville? You go out with the guys after a game and forget to tell me? I have to see pictures of you out with the guys and the cleat chasers of whatever city you're in taking convenient pictures with you? I'll be alone while you're off being King of the Town. At least here I have friends, and maybe one day, I'll have a family again."

"It won't be like that," I say. "I prom—"

"Stop," she says. "Don't say that word. I hate when you say that word because you don't know what it means. You've broken every promise you've ever made me, and I refuse to let you do it again. No more empty promises. No more desperate pleas. I can't do it anymore. I won't do it anymore. This is over."

The finality in her voice is clear, but I refuse to acknowledge it.

"Lucy, please—"

"Don't. Don't make this any harder than it needs to be," she says, standing and walking past me toward the door. "This is for the best."

"For who?" I say as I follow behind her. "Cause it sure as hell isn't what's best for me."

"It will be," she says. Then she pulls the door open while refusing to look at me.

I grab her shoulders and sink down until she's forced to look me in the eyes. I need her to see that this isn't what I want, that I love her, and that I'm willing to put in the work if she's willing to let me. "You don't mean this."

She finally looks at me and shrugs out of my hold. "I do. I deserve to be on someone's priority list. I deserve good morning texts and calls at the end of the night. I deserve a boyfriend who writes down the right day for my birthday. I love you, but you will never be able to give me that. Now, please leave."

I stare at the tears streaming down her cheeks. Tears I caused.

"This isn't over," I say. "It can't be."

"It is," she says, opening the door wider for me. "Goodbye, Bryce."

I take a step out but turn around to take one more look at her. This can't be how it ends.

"I love you, Lucy. Please. Don't do this."

She blinks away her tears, and for a second, I think she might take back everything she just said. I slip my hands into my pockets to keep myself from trying to take her in my arms.

Instead, I wrap my right hand around the small velvet box in my pocket. The one that holds the ring that I was going to give to her today.

I almost blurt out the question that will prove to her that I'm all in. The four words that I've practiced saying to her a thousand different ways. They are on the tip of my tongue, but just when I'm about to let them slip free, she says the four words that make me know that we're done. That I've ruined the best thing to ever happen to me.

"Go be amazing, Bryce."

Then she shuts the door.

39

———

LUCY

SEPTEMBER, ROOKIE YEAR

"WHAT DO you think of a fall wedding?"

"Or maybe winter? Do you remember when we dressed our dolls up as brides and had a Winter Wonderland wedding, Anne Marie? It was just perfect. Lucia, what do you think?"

Out of nowhere, a coughing fit takes over my body, which is weird since I don't feel like I'm getting sick.

"Here, take a drink of water," Mom says, handing me a glass. "Now, what do you think. Fall or winter wedding?"

I drink the water, though it doesn't help the cough. Either way, I have to answer my mother and Mrs. Tripoli or they will just start making decisions on their own. They are having a little bit of a hard time understanding that it's not their wedding.

"Um, fall," I say. "Fall is fine."

"Fall it is then," Mom says as she makes a note in her book. "Fall flowers can be beautiful."

"Pumpkins!" Mrs. Tripoli offers.

My mom smiles. "And the leaves are stunning around here."

"Oh, it will just be wonderful."

"Our babies are getting married! All of our dreams are coming true!"

I get up from my childhood kitchen table and head outside. If I have to listen to them take another trip down memory lane, I might pull my hair out. This is the third wedding "meeting" they have called. It's also the third meeting that has ended with them talking about how they can't believe their babies are getting married.

Not like they haven't been planning this for the better part of twenty years. I'm honestly surprised they let me pick the season. Usually, they ask for my opinion but just go with what they want.

Which is fine. I've never been that girl who had every detail of her wedding planned out.

But if I did, it wouldn't be to who I'm marrying.

"No, don't go down that road," I say to myself. "Bryce isn't coming for you."

Every so often, I let the thought of Bryce go through my head. Then I remember every broken promise he has ever made and remind myself that it's for the best that I've moved on.

My cell phone vibrates in the back pocket of my jeans, and I laugh because Brenna is punctual as always. I told her to call me around this time to get me out of wedding planning. I wonder what crazy "emergency" she's going to come up with to get me out of here.

Last week, she needed help walking her pet octopus.

Except, when I look at the screen, it's not Brenna's name. In fact, it's a name I don't think has ever called my phone.

"Cole?"

"Hey, Lucy, sorry to call you out of the blue."

"It's fine. I'm just surprised. Is everything okay?"

I haven't the faintest idea as to why Cole is calling me, not that I've been paying any attention to what's happening in football. After the draft, it took Bryce nine days to send me a text message, and all it said was, "Hey, Lulu." I never responded to it. I haven't talked to him since that day at the lake.

"I'd be lying if I said yes. He's not good, Lucy. He's in his head. Ever since training camp started, he hasn't been able to throw the ball. He can't focus. I'm pretty sure his dad popped back up. He's just . . . I've never seen him like this."

I sit on the porch and let out a deep breath. "What does that have to do with me?"

He doesn't answer right away, and I hate the way anxiety is twisting inside me.

"I hate asking you this, and you can tell me no and to go to hell, but he needs you. I've tried to talk to him, and he keeps shutting me down, and I'm worried about him. His head is all over the place. It's like he's forgotten how to throw a football. He's been drinking more than usual. I'm worried about him, and I was hoping you'd be willing to talk to him. You're like the Bryce whisperer, so if he'll listen to anyone, it's going to be you."

I pinch the bridge of my nose, wanting to scream at the top of my lungs because no matter what I do, I can't yank myself out of Bryce's orbit. Something is always trying to drag me back in.

"I don't think that would be a good idea," I say.

"Why not? You don't have to come to Nashville. I'll bring him to Cincinnati. Could you meet us there?"

"It's not the distance, Cole. I'm . . . I'm engaged. I've moved on. Plus, I've been fixing him for way too long. He needs to learn to do this without me."

Nothing I said was a lie, and I owe Bryce nothing, but the guilt still wraps around my throat and squeezes.

"Wow, you're engaged," Cole says, though his voice doesn't sound very congratulatory. "Congratulations."

"Thanks. I'm sorry, Cole. I can't do it. The box is finally shut. It needs to stay that way, but I hope Bryce is able to work through whatever he's dealing with."

I'm just about ready to hang up when I hear words that I don't think I'll ever be able to resist.

"He still loves you, Lucy. He might not say it, but I know it. And I know it's really unfair of me to ask this of you, but . . . I hope you change your mind, if only for this last time. He really needs you."

"WHAT ARE WE DOING HERE?" Bryce says from the adjoining room. I can't hear what Cole is saying, but I'm guessing he's either lying about why they are in Cincinnati or bracing him for what's in the other room, which is me and Brenna.

Bringing her was my condition to talking to Bryce.

"Am I really doing this?" I ask Brenna as I pace the room. "Maybe this isn't a good idea."

"You're helping a friend. And your best friend's brother," she says. "Now quit pacing before you leave tracks on the carpet."

I sit and clasp my hands together as I try to prepare myself to see him. It's only then that I feel the metal on my hand.

"Shit! My engagement ring," I whisper-yell, not knowing if they can hear me. "What do I do with it?"

As far as I know, Bryce doesn't know I'm engaged. Cole promised he wouldn't say anything, and considering he's in an apparent fragile mental state, it's probably for the best he doesn't know.

"Take it off. Now," Brenna says, holding out her hand as I slip it off my finger. "I'll hold on to it. The last thing he needs to know is that you got engaged, let alone to Luciano."

She's right. He hates Luciano, and if Cole is to be believed and Bryce still loves me, the last thing I need to do is throw gas on the fire with news of my engagement.

I hear the sound of the adjoining door begin to open and I take one last breath.

This is it. This is the last time. Do it for your friendship. Do it for Brenna. Do it for the first boy you ever loved.

I fight back the tears as Bryce enters the room, confusion etched on his face as he sees Brenna and me sitting on the beds.

"Lulu? Brenna? What are you two doing here?"

I'm frozen, too caught up in the memory of that day at the lake. I still remember what his weight on me felt like. I can still taste his lips as he kissed me, and still feel his hands as they slid over my skin.

I know I'm engaged and that this man is my past, but Bryce Donald will always be the most beautiful man I've ever met.

Then I look at his eyes. I've always loved them. Except now they look . . . blank. I've never seen him look like this, and my heart breaks for him.

"I asked Lucy to come," Cole says, stepping into the room. "Brenna is just an added bonus."

"You know you missed me," she says as she pulls Bryce into a hug and then Cole, who seems to tense when she wraps her arms around him. "Now come on, Campbell. Let's get out of their hair. Know of any good parties around here?"

"Never again," Cole grumbles as they exit the room, leaving Bryce and me alone.

Wonder what that was about?

After a long moment, he's the one to break the silence.

"I'm sorry—"

"No," I say cutting him off. That's not why I'm here, and I can't go down that road. "We don't need to talk about that."

His shoulders slump as he hangs his head. "Did Cole call you here because I'm broken?"

"Something like that," I say as we take a seat on the bed. "I take it professional football isn't going well?"

He laughs, but there is no humor behind it. "I think Brenna could play better than I am."

"Bold statement."

He laughs again, and this time it sounds lighter. "Well, it's true. I have no idea what's wrong with me. It's like I got to the league, and my brain decided that it was going to forget every ounce of football I ever knew."

"Why is that?"

He just shrugs.

"Yes, you do," I say, my voice as gentle as can be. "It's me. You know you don't have to hold back. Talk to me. What's going on in that head of yours?"

A sad smile crosses his beautiful lips. "You don't have to do this, you know? I know how much I screwed up."

I inch a little closer to him, but not close enough where he can reach for me. "That's in the past, so let's focus on how I can help now. Come on. Let's figure this out."

I turn to grab the hotel notepad and pen off the end table.

"A list? We can't pro-con this, Lucy."

"Do you think that's the only kind of list I can make? It's like you don't know me at all."

"Fine." He sighs. "We'll do it your way."

And for the next three hours, Bryce tells me everything. The stress of his schedule. The complexity of the playbook. The pressure of living up to the hype as the top draft pick. The endorsement deals that are almost like a separate job. And yes, the infrequent-but-frequent-enough calls from his dad asking him for money or seeing if Bryce was willing to throw a game.

It's a lot for anyone, but when it comes to Bryce, who has let other people's demands and expectations rule his brain for his entire life, it's overwhelming. No wonder he can't throw a football.

So, we make a priority list. What he needs to focus on first, then second, and then last. Sometimes the lists change. Sometimes his focus shifts. But having a list gives him focus.

"There's one thing missing," he says as I hand him the papers.

"What's that?"

"You're not on here."

I freeze, not knowing how to react or what to say. I've been able to keep his attention off me for this whole conversation, and he seems to be a better Bryce than the one who walked into this room a few hours ago. Still, I know I should tell him about Luciano, but I can't. He'll find out eventually, but today isn't the day.

"That's okay," I say, cleaning up pieces of paper that weren't used. "You have a lot on your plate right now. Those need to be your focus."

"I meant what I said before the draft," he says. "I guess I just got a little ahead of myself. These lists? They're going to help me have the best rookie year ever. And then, I'm coming home and I'm picking you up, and I'm finally taking you on that date."

He leans in to kiss my cheek, and I don't move. It's the last time Bryce's lips are going to touch me, and selfishly, I want it for as long as possible. I know I'm never going to make a priority list for him or ever come before football or his career. I know that. It's why I'm marrying Luciano.

At the beginning, I truly believed Bryce and I would get a happily ever after, and it took me years to realize that was nothing but a daydream of a naïve little girl.

I never thought it would end like this though. With me being the one to say goodbye.

Only, it's what I have to do. It's what's best for the both of us.

"Goodbye, Bryce," I say, finally stepping away. "Go be amazing."

And with that I turn and walk out of the hotel room.

40

BRYCE

I saw his truck where he normally parks it, so I know he's home.

"Coming!" he yells before he opens the door. "Bryce? What are you doing here? Why aren't you with Lucy?"

His question is valid. He knew I was going home today to see Lucy. He also knew that I planned on popping the question. If everything were to have gone right, I should be in the middle of celebrating with her—hopefully naked—before we went out and screamed to the entire town that we were engaged.

But no, I fucked up. Royally. And I need to fix it.

I just don't know how.

"Because, and for the life of me I can't figure out how I did this, I wrote down the wrong day for her birthday."

His eyes grow wide as he falls into one of his oversized leather loungers. "Oh fuck. So, on her birthday . . ."

"Yup. I was drunk with you, Dexter, and a handful of groupies. As an added bonus, there are pictures all over the internet to show it."

"In my defense, I wasn't drunk and actually didn't want to go. You made me."

"Not the fucking point, man. The point is that, while we were at some fucking club, Lucy was crying herself to sleep and Brenna was figuring out how to kill me and bury my body."

"Fuck. What did she say?"

"She ended it. She said she couldn't do it anymore."

He shakes his head in utter disbelief. "She can't mean that. It's Lucy. How do you know she just doesn't need a few days to cool off?"

I fall into his other oversized chair, the defeat coursing through my body and finally taking over. "She told me to go be amazing. Those were the exact words she told me in Cincinnati. She's done, Cole."

For the next hour, I fill Cole in on everything. It really doesn't take an hour. For most of that time, we just sit in silence. I can't believe twelve hours ago I was on my way to Laurel Heights, thinking that today was going to be one of the best days of my life.

"Does she know about the ring?"

I shake my head. "Honestly, I forgot about it the second Brenna opened the door. I knew something was off. One second, I'm psyching myself up to ask the woman I love to spend the rest of her life with me, and the next, I was trying to figure out which way was up. It all happened so fast."

"What did you do after? Did you drive straight back here?"

I crack my neck, trying to figure out how I want to answer this. "Yeah. Straight back here."

His eyebrow goes straight up. "Really? You did nothing between leaving Lucy's and driving here."

"I stopped for gas and a Gatorade."

"Quit bullshitting me, Bryce. Did you go to the liquor store or a bar? And don't lie to me. We've come too far for you to try to talk your way out of this."

I fall back, letting my head hit the back of the chair. I could lie to him or I could be honest. After everything we've been through, and as much as I've bullshitted him in the past few years, the man deserves my honesty.

"When she first shut the door on me, I was stunned. I don't think I moved for ten minutes. When I finally made it back to my truck, my gut reaction was to drive to the liquor store then drive to the lake and drown myself in the bottle. When I pulled into the liquor store parking though, I cut the engine, and . . ."

"And?"

"I didn't go in."

Just saying those words feels . . . freeing. Like some sort of weight has been lifted. I don't know how else to describe it.

"You didn't go in?"

"No. I just sat there. Hell, I probably sat there longer than I stood on her porch. All I kept thinking about was how my drinking got me into this situation. Everything comes back to my using alcohol to cope with stress. Instead of manning up and figuring out a way to move on with life, I dove into the bottle. That isn't something I want to do again. So, I turned the car around, got back on the highway, and came straight here."

"Wow," Cole says, shaking his head in disbelief. "I'm proud of you. That was a really big moment for you."

"Yeah. A little too late, though."

"Says who?"

I give my head a shake, because clearly, he didn't hear me. "Says me. Lucy's done. You should have seen her. She was devastated, and I don't blame her. This wasn't just some other broken promise that I made to her. I forgot her birthday. I spent a day that I should have been worshiping the ground she walks on with you guys and some cleat chasers. This was the final straw. I could see it in her eyes. The play clock has run out. Game over."

Cole leans forward, putting his elbows on his knees. This is when I know I'm about to get a speech. This is Cole's version of the Dad-lecture pose.

"You say she's done, but do you really believe that?"

I think back to everything that has not only happened today but also over the past seven years. "Yeah. I think so. Who could blame her Cole? I broke every promise I ever made."

"You did. That's true."

"Gee thanks."

"Am I wrong? When was last time you kept a promise you made to her?"

I sit back and think. I think all the way back to that first time I met her in the library. I promised her a date after our championship game. That didn't happen. I promised to come back for her prom. That didn't happen. I promised her I'd come back this summer. I never did. Between all those are a hundred smaller unkept promises.

"I don't know if I ever have."

"Exactly," Cole says, inching a little closer to me. "Actions speak louder than words. She needs you to show her that you're the man she always knew you could be. The guy you could be if you could just get out of your own way. Want to know how I know that?"

Oh man, he's really in Dad mode. "Please, Father Cole, tell me in all your brilliance, why you know I can do it?"

"Because you didn't drink today. Not one soul on this planet would have blamed you for drinking a bottle of whiskey after the love of your life told you it was over, but you didn't. That's your first action. So now, the real question is, what's going to be your second?"

I let his words sink in, and the longer I sit here, the more I realize he's right.

I did something today that the old Bryce could have never done.

Maybe this isn't as over as I thought?

I push myself up from the chair, but in doing so I feel something between the cushion and the arm rest.

"What are these?" I ask, holding up a pair of lace panties, which I guarantee do not belong to my best friend.

Cole jumps up from the couch and rips them from my hand. "Not your concern."

I smirk, a little mad at myself that I didn't throw them in his face. Literally. "I have so many questions."

"None of them I'm going to answer," he says. "Focus. This is about you. What are you going to do to get Lucy back?"

"I'll make you a deal. I get Lucy back, and you tell me who those belong to."

He gives me a healthy eye roll. "Fine. Now, what's the plan?"

I'm not exactly sure yet, but I do know this. It's not going to be quick. It's not going to happen overnight. Cole is right; this isn't about my words. This isn't about empty promises. This is about actions.

"I need to call Sadie. I need a favor."

41

LUCY

Brenna shuts off her car and snaps her head at me. "Yes. I love you like a sister, but you have to come back to the world of the living. Plus, opening night of Luciano and Celine's restaurant is something you have to do. You'd never forgive yourself if you miss it. Now, buck up, buttercup. Put on your big girl panties, and let's go."

I scowl at her and contemplate refusing to get out of the car. I haven't worn jeans and a sweater in who knows how long. The only reason I have makeup on is because I had to go to work today, and even then, I only wore it to cover the bags under my eyes.

It's been a rough month since I shut the door on Bryce, and well, the chance of a future with Bryce. I get up, go to work, come home, and lay on the couch. I have eaten my weight in mint chocolate chip ice cream and can't remember the last time I ate a real meal.

Most nights I cry myself to sleep. I always wonder what could have been different. And every night I hurt. I thought by now it would have gone away. I've gone months—hell, even years, without Bryce in my life. It's not like this is foreign territory.

The difference is now I know what it's like to be with him. I know what it's like to fall asleep in his arms. I know what it's like to feel him inside me. I know what it's like to be surrounded by his love.

That's when I cry because I know I'm never going to feel like that ever again.

"You can do this," Brenna says, giving my arm a squeeze. "We'll get dinner. Say our hellos and get out of here. Okay?"

I give myself a mental shake. "Let's do this."

As soon as we open the door, the smells of sauces and herbs attack our senses. This is one way to wake someone up who has been a zombie for the past month.

"Lucia! You made it!" Luciano says before we're more than two steps into the restaurant, and then he's wrapping me in a hug. Funny to think that at this time last year we were still faking it and this hug would not have existed.

"Of course I did," I say, hoping that comes out more enthusiastic than I feel. "It looks great."

Luciano's father held strong that he wasn't going to give him what he needed to franchise. So, Luciano decided to strike out on his own. He realized he didn't need his family to be happy with his career or with who he chose to love. He had been saving money for years because that's the kind of responsible man he is, and between that and what Celine brought to the table, the two of them were able to open their own restaurant—Lucine. It's a romantic Italian restaurant that looks as if it should be in a big city, not little Laurel Heights. The tables are covered with beautiful crème-colored tablecloths and each has a small tea candle floating in a shallow bowl. The music is soft and beautiful. I can already tell it's going to be the perfect date night restaurant.

I push back the tears, not letting myself go down the depression hole as Celine comes up to us. "Lucia, I'm so happy you could make it! Brenna! Good to see you!"

I give her a hug and Brenna does the same as she takes us back to a table. The restaurant isn't full since it's the soft opening for family and friends, which I'm glad for. The last thing I need is someone walking up to me and asking why I'm here and Bryce is in Nashville. Though, I do wish we were in a private dining room. The few that are here I swear are staring at me. At least, I feel like they are.

"Let me get you some wine," Celine says as we take a seat in a comfortable booth. "And whatever you want from the menu just let us know. Tonight, it's our treat."

I start looking at the menu, which makes my stomach turn. Not because of the food itself—it all looks delicious—but because the thought of eating more than a few bites of soup sounds horrible.

"That boy has been playing out of his mind." I hear a man say from the booth behind me. I want to ignore them, but it's hard to when the music is soft and there are only a handful of tables seated around you.

Where is Celine with the wine?

"I know it's only the preseason, but he's looking damn sharp out there," another voice says. "If this is a preview for the season, the Fury will be in the playoffs for sure."

"I'm going to have the calamari!" Brenna yells loud enough to draw everyone's attention, and my eyes go wide with shock. She's at a volume thirteen while everyone else is at a six. "What do you think you're going to have, Lucy?"

"What are you doing?" I whisper-yell.

"I know your no-Bryce-talk rule, but others don't. Since I can't police the entire town to make sure they don't talk about him in your presence, I'll just talk loud enough to drown them out. Now, where was I, oh that's right!" Her voice is getting louder and louder with each word. "The chicken francaise sounds delicious!" By the end, she's full-on screaming, her face is red, and everyone seated around us is staring at her slack-jawed.

I just stare at Brenna, and before I know it, I feel something weird coming from my stomach. I try to hold it in, but I can't, letting the sip of water I just took come out of my nose.

Oh my God. I laughed. I'm laughing. I don't remember the last time I did that.

"There she is," Brenna says in a normal voice and with a sympathetic smile. "I've missed you."

"Is that a smile I'm seeing on our girl's face?" Luciano says as he brings out our wine and a dish of Italian greens with bread. "What did you have to do to coax that out of her?"

"Just be my usual, ridiculous self," Brenna says proudly.

"Well, whatever works. I know Celine said you can have whatever you want tonight, but that's a lie. I'm already making you two something special, so you will eat what I put in front of you."

"That's so nice of you," I say.

"Well, I'm doing it so you aren't mad at me."

I scoff. "Why would I be mad at you?" Only he and Brenna look far too serious for him to be joking. "What did you do?" I ask.

"Your parents are here."

I shoot up from my seat, nearly knocking over the table as I watch my parents walk in to the dining room. When I realize I likely look like a lunatic, I sit back down, but not before my mother sees me and begins walking toward my table.

"Sorry," Luciano says before disappearing back into the kitchen.

"How do you want to play this?" Brenna asks.

"I don't know," I say truthfully. We've been in a standoff since Christmas. From what Uncle Nick told me, she won't talk to me until I come to my senses. I won't budge because she's crazy.

"Lucia. Brenna. How are you tonight?"

I take a healthy sip of wine before making eye contact. "Good. Thanks."

An awkward silence falls over the table. One of those silences that only last for maybe five seconds but feels like five minutes.

"I'm going to go pee!" Brenna says, right back to her yell she was using before. "I mean, I'm going to use the restroom. Why don't you have a seat, Mrs. Valenti?"

"Thank you, Brenna."

Brenna slides out of the booth and doesn't make eye contact with me as she walks away, which is good. If she had, she would have seen me trying to kill her with my stare.

"I'd ask how you've been, but I think I know the answer."

"Really, Mom? This is how you're going to start a conversation after ten months?" I really don't want to cause a scene on Luciano and

Celine's big night, but if she keeps this up, I can't promise good behavior. "If you came over to gloat about how things didn't work out with Bryce, please leave. Enjoy your dinner. I don't want to hear it."

She doesn't say anything, nor does she get up. In fact, the only movement she makes is to hang her head.

"How did it get to be like this, Lucia?"

I let out a sigh and take another drink of my water. "You wouldn't accept anything other than me living the life you wanted me to. You made me feel guilty about not doing what you wanted, and when I put my foot down, you refused to return my calls or texts. Your best friend called a very nice woman, who I now consider a friend, a slut to her face and you did nothing to stop her. You refused to accept that I loved a man you didn't approve of. Any of this ringing any bells?"

She raises her head to look at me, and I'm pretty sure her eyes are welling with tears. "Why did she have to be French?"

I chuckle. "You can't help who you fall in love with, Mom."

"And you're sure you're not in love with Luciano? Look around. This here? This could be yours."

"No, it couldn't. Lucine would make no sense if it was the two of us."

"Don't joke," Mom says, though I can see a smile creeping onto her lips.

"In all seriousness, you have to know that the decision that Luciano and I made didn't come lightly. We were both unhappy, and we love each other enough to know that we would never have been happy. Plus, when a man is more affectionate with you after you call off your engagement, that's a pretty good indication that he's not in love with you."

She lets out a big sigh. "I just wanted you two together so badly."

I reach for her hand. "I know, and it would have been a great story. Two best friends have their children fall in love. It's the kind of story you read about in books. But that's not our story. He's with Celine, who is amazing and loves him the way he deserves to be loved. You guys would know that if you got to know her. And as for me . . ."

I trail off because I'm speechless. How do you admit to your mother that even though you followed your heart, it wasn't enough? That love wasn't enough?

"I'm sorry it didn't work out."

I just shrug. "It just wasn't meant to be."

"I don't believe that."

"What?" I ask, clearly confused. "What don't you believe?"

"That it wasn't meant to be." She wipes the stray tear from her eye and sits up a little taller. "I might have been pushing Luciano on you, but I would have had to be blind not to see how you two looked at each other. That's real love. You never looked at Luciano that way. Guiliana and I were just too blinded by our own selfishness to see that."

I feel the tears building in my eyes. "Well, that's in the past."

"It is? I read an article the other day, and I swear he was—"

"Please, Mom." I hold up my hands as I try to also hold in my tears. "I . . . I can't know about him. I can't read articles about him. I can't watch him. Nothing. This last month . . . it's been the hardest one of my life. This is the first time I've gone anywhere besides work, and Brenna had to drag me kicking and screaming. So, please, whatever you know or think you know about Bryce, please . . . just keep it to yourself."

"I understand," she says as Brenna comes back to the table. "Well, I'll let you two get back to dinner."

"Why don't you join us?" I say before I realize the words are coming out of my mouth. "Bring Dad over."

"Is that all right?" Mom asks, looking back and forth between Brenna and me.

"Of course," Brenna says as she slides in next to me. "The more the merrier."

For the next two hours, I sit with my best friend and my parents, eating and laughing and . . . just being normal. Yes, Bryce was accidentally brought up a few times, and while it hurt, it didn't kill me.

I might not be better yet, but I'm getting there. Slowly but surely, I'll get there.

42

———

BRYCE

BALL IS at the twenty-five-yard line, we have no more timeouts and we're down by four. I take a look up at the game clock and see there are ten seconds left.

Plenty of time.

"Fake seven power zero drag. Now, go win us a damn football game."

Davis slaps the top of my helmet before I run back onto the field, making sure my chin strap is adjusted as I head into the huddle.

"How about we win ourselves a football game today, boys?"

My words are met with a mixture of hell yeahs and other grunts of some sort.

"Fake seven power zero drag. Fake seven power zero drag on three. One, two, three, break!"

We turn and line up. I check to the right and then to the left. I always know my left is good. That's where Cole is. My right isn't so shabby either.

I look across the line to the defense. They are lined up exactly like the coaches thought they would be. All we need now is Dexter to do his job and for me to do mine.

"Red, twenty-two! Red, twenty-two! Set . . . hike!"

As soon as I feel the ball in my hands, the rest of my movements are on auto pilot. I block out everyone else and keep an eye on my receivers, trusting that my back is covered.

I roll out to my right, and waiting for me, exactly where I want him, is Dexter.

Pull back . . . launch . . . release . . .

Dexter plucks it out of the air as if the ball was drawn to his hands, and then he runs across the goal line for a touchdown. My haze goes away, and all I hear is the roar of the crowd as we celebrate our first win of the season. It wasn't as easy as we would have liked it to be, but a win is a win, and I'll take one of those any day of the week.

"Hell yeah!" Cole yells, picking me up like he has since high school. "Great game, man. Welcome back."

We give each other a few slaps on the back before I'm grabbed by the arm by one of the interns in the media department.

"Television wants to talk to you. You good?"

You good? Who knew that could be such a loaded question?

On the field? I'm great. I had a great preseason, have been having regular sessions with Malcolm and have been keeping my nose clean.

Off the field? Not so much. I miss her. I miss her every damn day. The only reason I'm not more of a mess is because she might think we're done, but I know we're not. And I'm doing everything in my power to show her that I'm worthy of her. Even if she doesn't know it yet.

"Bryce Donald. Three-hundred-and-six yards passing today and three touchdowns. What a return after last year. How did you feel out there today?"

I stare at the reporter who has a microphone two inches from my face and contemplate how to answer this. I could answer with my canned media responses. The ones I've learned and perfected since I was in high school. Or I could say how I really feel.

Actions speak louder than words.

And just like that, I know what I need to do.

"Physically, I felt great. My arm strength is where it needs to be, and I've been making sure to keep up with my conditioning after last year. I couldn't have asked for a better first game on the field."

"I thought after your first win back you'd be livelier. Why isn't Bryce Donald jumping through the roof about his first win back with the Fury?"

Here goes nothing . . .

43

———

LUCY

"WHY IS that on the television? You know the rule."

I don't mind that Brenna might as well live here with as much as she's over, but if she's going to be in my house, she's going to follow my rules.

And my rules are that we don't watch, talk, or read anything about Bryce Donald.

"In my defense, you were taking a nap and I wanted to watch his first game back."

"You know you could have watched him at your place. You remember? The one you couldn't wait to get so you could finally move out of your mom's house?"

"I don't have cable."

"Just turn it off please," I say as I walk through the living room to get a bottle of water from the kitchen.

I knew today was the first game of the season, that's why I've been hiding for the past three hours. I figured that, if I took a nap and ignored the world, I could wake up and pretend as if the game never happened.

Yes, one of these days I'll need to be able to hear his name without crying. I'm just not there yet.

"So, do you still want to go run errands today? Or are we putting that off again?"

Brenna doesn't answer, and when I walk back into my living room, I stop in my tracks. Not only is the game still on but also his stupidly handsome face is right there.

He's sweaty from the game, his hair all over the place from being in his helmet, and I can tell by the marks on his face that he got hit more than once. He's the most breathtaking man I've ever seen.

I allow myself to look at his eyes. Those have always been the gateway to his emotions. When he was at his lowest of lows last year, they were hollow. Now? They aren't as sparkling as I know they can be, but they aren't dead.

Good for him. At least one of us has been able to move on.

"I thought after your first win back you'd be ecstatic. Why isn't Bryce Donald jumping through the roof about his first win back with the Fury?"

"Turn it off, Brenna."

"You're going to hate me, but no."

I snap my head to her. "What do you mean no?"

"I mean that you have to hear him sometime. You can't ignore him forever. Consider this a test to see if you're any closer to doing that. The longer you ignore his existence, the harder it's going to be for you in the long run."

I start to argue back, but the sound of his voice silences me. God I've missed that. The way it was always so gravelly in the morning when he would whisper good morning to me. Or how excited it got when he would explain some football thing to me that I'd barely understand. Or when he told me he loved me.

I miss it all. I miss him.

"Don't get me wrong, I'm excited for this win today," Bryce starts, and as much as I want to walk away, I can't. "But it doesn't mean as much when you can't celebrate and be with the one you love. I let a lot of people down over the past year, but none more so than one woman in particular. She's the most amazing person I know, and I thought when I came back on the field, she'd be here with me. I thought after I did this interview, I'd run to the stands and find her waiting there for me. But that's not what happened, because . . . well, because I still have more work to do. Today might have looked like I was back, and maybe Bryce the quarterback is. But Bryce the man? He still has work to do. I only hope that I'm worthy of her sooner rather than later."

"Is this the same person you talked about in the *US Daily* article?"

He nods. "It is. I've learned that I can win all the football games I want, have all the money in the world or accolades I ever dreamed of, but if I don't have someone to share those experiences with, then what's the point? Football will only last for so long. But love? That one-of-a-kind love that only a select few ever know? That is what will last forever."

Bryce looks at the camera one last time, and I swear he is looking straight at me. I know that's not possible, but I swear that's what he's doing. His eyes are begging, no pleading, for another chance.

He said all the right things, but words have never been a problem for him. How do I know he's seriously changed?

"What article are they talking about?" I ask, vaguely remembering my mom also bringing up an article.

"Do you really want to know?" Brenna asks. Not because she doesn't want to show me but because she knows that if I read it, then there won't be any turning back. Everything I've done over the past month to ignore Bryce will be for nothing.

"Yes. I need to."

Brenna assesses me to make sure I mean it before bringing the article up on her phone. It was written by Sadie, his coach's fiancée and from what I've heard, a very well-respected national football writer.

Then I see the headline: "Bryce Donald ready to be a better man, on and off the field."

I think I read the article five times and then have to remind myself that Sadie wouldn't make things up for Bryce and everything in the article is true. They talk a lot about his mental health and how his problems began long before he stepped foot in Nashville. About how he didn't realize he had them because he had someone to confide in, but when that person wasn't in his life anymore, he didn't know how to process. He goes on to talk about how not many others have someone they can rely on in their life like he had, so his goal in the next year is to open an afterschool center for athletes. He wants it to be a safe place where high school athletes can get help with homework. Psychologists will be on hand to talk them through the trials and tribulations of their changing lives and help getting into college if they so wish.

"Oh, Bryce."

Then I get to the quote from Bryce that guts me. It's also likely that this is what my mother was talking about that night at dinner.

"I always thought I was just a football player. That I was put on this earth to throw around a football. And don't get me wrong, that's a large part of who I am. But someone . . . someone so special that there aren't words adequate enough to describe how amazing she is, never thought of me as just a football player. She always thought I was so much more than a player. She believed in me from the very start. And everybody should have someone like that in their life. Someone who believes in them and makes them want to be a better man."

That's it. I can't hold them in anymore.

I collapse onto the couch, holding the phone to my chest.

He's saying all the right things, which he always does. But something about the way he spoke today, and something about this interview . . . they feel different.

I need to know. I need to know now.

"Are you okay?" Brenna asks, reaching for my hand.

I look up at her, and I don't know if this is a good idea, but I know I won't be able to do anything else until I do this.

"Call Bryce. I need to see him."

44

———

LUCY

I KNOW I told Brenna I wanted to see him.

I know I *need* to see him regardless of if we work things out. Ignoring him was not helping me get over him. It was only making me more miserable by the day.

Now that I'm here, at Lake Laurel, because where else would he pick to meet me, I don't know if I can do it.

"You okay?" Brenna asks as we pull up to the lake. "You know you don't have to do this."

"No, I need to," I say, taking a few more deep breaths. "I don't like the way we ended things."

"Are you going to get back together with him?"

Well, that's the million-dollar question, isn't it?

"Honestly? I'm not sure. That's why I need to talk to him. I need to hear what he has to say and see if he's truly changed."

As soon as the words leave my mouth, Bryce walks from the back of his truck. And for a second, I stop breathing.

It's not because he's wearing a shirt that defines every muscle in his chest. It's not because his hair is crazy in that way I love so much.

It's because it's him. He's here. In Laurel Heights. During football season. To see me. Because I asked him to.

That, and I'm pretty sure the sight of Bryce Donald will always take my breath away.

"Listen to what he has to say," Brenna says. "If you still don't want anything to do with him, I'll be right around the corner ready with the getaway car."

Tears are already welling in my eyes as I slowly exit her car. As he walks closer, I can see he has his high school jacket over his arm, the one that I used to sleep in every night because I missed him so much. In the other hand, he's holding a piece of paper.

"Hey, Lulu," he says softly.

"Thanks for meeting me. I know you're busy—"

"No. I'm exactly where I need to be."

I'm speechless as he leads me back to the tailgate of his truck, which is down and covered in blankets. There's a bouquet of flowers sitting on top of a Tripoli's pizza box.

"Here, I believe this belongs to you," he says, holding open the jacket for me. Like I'm under some sort of hypnosis, I turn to let him put it on me before he lifts me up and sets me on the truck.

"What is all this?" I ask.

"This is the first of many things I do to make up for how bad I have messed up over the years. I figured I could start with your favorite pizza and flowers. The jacket is because, even after all these years, I still love it on you."

I bring it tighter around me, remembering everything this jacket once represented. It was his first promise to me. It was my memory of him. It was how I knew I wasn't supposed to marry Luciano.

"I remember when I first gave you that. I felt like the king of the world because the most amazing girl was wearing my jacket," he begins. "For years, I never thought of anything but football. It was my life, and my ticket out of this town. Then, one day, this girl walks up to me, wanting to teach me math. Her big brown eyes knocked me on my ass, and her smile took my breath away. It was the first time in my life that football left my brain and all I could think of was how to make her mine. I should have known then that you were going to be the only woman in my life I'd ever love."

I wipe the tears from my eyes but don't dare say anything.

"I worked hard to be the best at football, and that dream came true. Well, when I wasn't trying to destroy it. I haven't worked at all to be the man you deserve. In fact, I have epically failed at it. Yet, somehow, you gave me chance after chance. Chances I didn't deserve. Chances I didn't *earn*."

"Bryce—"

"No, Lucy. Let me finish," he says, unfolding the piece of paper he's been holding. "I've been thinking a lot about us. Not next offseason. Not when things settle down. Now because now is all we have. And this here is the list of things that I plan to do to be the best man for you."

I laugh. "You made a list?"

"Damn right I did." He smiles as he looks down at it. "Number one. We are going to talk every day. You will never not hear the words I love you every day from me."

"That's a good start."

"I thought so. Number two, every year on your birthday, I will take you wherever you want to go. You name it, it's done."

"Bryce, you don't need—"

"Shhh. I'm just getting started. Number three, I'm going keep my promises." His eyes lift and hold mine. "I know for years I have broken them, but not anymore. I promise that I will always put you first. I promise that, one day, when we have children, I'll never take the family you will have given me for granted. I promise that I will continue to work on myself because you deserve the best version of me."

A whole new batch of tears comes streaming at his words.

"And finally, I promise, that every day I will love you with my whole heart. Lucy Valenti, I am so sorry for taking this long to tell you all of this. I don't deserve you, but I want to. I want to deserve your love every day for the rest of my life."

I jump off the truck and take a deep breath. All I want to do is run and jump into his arms, but I can't.

Not yet.

"How do I know I can trust you this time?" I ask, crossing my arms as if to guard my heart. "I heard what you said after that game and I read the article. I heard about the things you wanted to do. How do I know it's not just to get me back? I have to know, Bryce. I know, deep down, even when we were miles apart, that you love me, and you know I love you, but how do I know this isn't the start of another cycle?"

Bryce walks toward me, reaching for both of my hands.

"Because now I know what it's truly like not to have you in my life, and it is absolute hell."

"You've not had me in your life before."

"This time was different. When we were young, we had the hope of us. It's what kept us afloat all those years. Then, these past few months, I had you. I knew what it was like to be with you. To kiss you. To hold you in my arms and know what it was like to have your love. It was better than anything I ever felt in my life. Then it was gone because of something I did. I've worked hard at football. I've never worked hard at being yours. Let me work my ass off to be the man you deserve."

One of the first things I ever noticed about Bryce was his eyes. I remember thinking that they could see through my soul.

Eight years later, as I look into his beautiful blues, it's as if he's begging me to look into his soul, to see how much he wants to change. He's laid bare, vulnerable, and telling me he wants to be a better version of himself.

That he wants to be better with me as well as for me.

All I've ever wanted was for Bryce to be the best version of himself. To be the man I always knew he could be.

"You know you'll have a lot of work to do," I say.

"I can't wait to get started," he says as he cracks a small smile before wrapping his arms around my waist, bringing his lips down to meet mine.

For the first time in what feels like months, everything is right in the world.

I know we have a lot to figure out, but we have love and a list. How can we go wrong?

45

BRYCE

FOR MY ENTIRE LIFE, when I had big decisions to be made, I didn't hesitate to call Lucy. When I was feeling nervous or overwhelmed, she was the only one who could clear my head.

That doesn't do me any good when I'm minutes away from asking her to marry me. I need my Lucy. I need her calm presence. I need her wisdom. I need her to make me a list.

Instead, I get Cole.

He might be good at keeping big ass defensive lineman from sacking me, but he's shit at love advice. I really need to find this guy a girlfriend, or at least finally force him to fess up about the owner of those panties I found in his couch.

"You sure you want to propose to her like this?" Cole asks for the fifteenth time. "Wouldn't you rather go someplace a little more . . . private?"

"Nope. This is it."

I look around at the field, which is currently being flooded by media, family, and a few rogue fans since we're not stopping anyone tonight.

We did it. After today's win, we're officially in the playoffs.

It has been a hell of a year. After a rocky start, it didn't take long for things to get back on track. I sobered up—for good this time. I started seeing Malcolm again and Lucy moved to Nashville with me. I meant what I said to her when I begged for forgiveness in Laurel Heights. I am committed on being the best man I know how to be. That includes therapy sessions, AA meetings, and anything else I can do to make sure I'm my best version of myself.

I'm trying to be the best brother. The best friend. The best teammate. I want to be a role model for the younger generation. More than any of those, I want to be the best forever for Lucy.

Am I there yet? Not even close, but every day I take another step. That's all you can ask of someone.

"She better say yes," Cole says as the intern who was tasked with holding on to the ring today sprints over to give it to me.

"Of course she's going to say yes. Why wouldn't she?"

"Let's see," Cole says as a group of fans attempt to push past him. "Maybe because you guys haven't been together for an entire year? Maybe because she wants to wait until your house is built? Or maybe she really doesn't love you like she says she does?"

I glare at Cole. "You're the worst future best man in the world."

"I'm just saying it's a possibility," he says as his eyes focus on something over my shoulder.

I glance back, and find my sister talking to Dexter.

"Oh shit," I say. "Does he not know about the rule not to fuck around with your quarterback's sister?"

"Maybe I need to remind him of that," Cole says, his voice dropping an octave.

I was over the moon for Lucy to move to Nashville, which she did as soon as we got back together.

What I didn't expect was for my sister to toss her bags into the moving truck and announce that she was coming too. I thought it was a joke until she showed up at my apartment and asked where she was going to sleep.

Our mother is not happy. I give her two years before she moves here as well.

"Not now, big guy," I say, holding him back as best I can. "As much as I'd love to see you scare a grown man until he wets himself, we have more important things to deal with. I need your tall ass to find Lucy for me."

Cole glares at Brenna and Dexter one more time before he starts looking for Lucy again. I figured she'd be here by now since it doesn't take that long to get from the wives' box to the field.

Wife.

The more I think about it, the more I like the idea of her becoming Mrs. Bryce Donald.

Luckily, Christmas fell on a weekday this year, allowing us to sneak up to Laurel Heights to spend Christmas with her family. When we were there, I was able to ask Mr. Valenti for his blessing. He said yes, but only if the Fury made the playoffs this year.

I'm still not sure if he was joking.

Either way, everything is exactly as it should be. Well, it will be in a few minutes.

"There she is," Cole says, pointing to the gate by the end zone. "Good luck."

He gives me a pat on the back and with one last, deep breath, I make my way to the love of my life.

"You did it!" she yells, running and jumping into my arms as I do my best to make sure the box in my hand doesn't press against her.

"We did," I say, giving her a kiss and lowering her back to the ground, quickly putting my right hand behind my back.

"You were amazing," she says. "I was keeping track of the other games today. It looks like you'll finish the regular season second in total passing yards but first in efficiency, which, to me, means more because quality over quantity, right?"

I laugh and lean in for another kiss. My girl will never not love math. Since she started attending games, she has found it to be her hobby to keep live updates of every quarterback in the league to see where I statistically rank against them. I think she's even made up new categories.

I love her so much.

"That's good to know," I say. "But I want to talk about something else."

She quirks a brow. "What else is there to talk about? It's a Sunday home game. You're going to go shower. Then you're going to go do your media interviews before coming home and eating pizza with me."

Yes, we already have a routine, and it's one I hope never goes away. It might not be Tripoli's pizza, but it will do.

And yes, I am trying to get Luciano and Celine to move down here and open a Lucine location. Plus, the guys in the Bachelor league really want to meet him after he won the league last season.

"Well yes, but I thought we could do one thing before that," I say as I get down on one knee.

"Oh my God," she says, covering her mouth as a hush falls around us.

"Many, many years ago I promised to ask you out on a date. I said that I'd wear a shirt with buttons and that you would wear a dress that drove me crazy. It took us a long time, but we finally got that date and many more after that. In that time, my love for you has grown in ways I didn't think possible. So now, I ask you today on another date. Except, maybe this time, I'll wear a tuxedo and you'll wear a white dress that will bring me to my knees? What do you say Lucy Valenti? Will you marry me?"

I have never heard this stadium silent before. Especially after a win. But I swear I could hear a pin drop.

That makes it hard to ignore that Lucy isn't saying anything. She's biting her bottom lip and blinking frantically to keep from crying, but those tears could be bad or good for all I know.

Shit. Was Cole right?

Just when I'm about to figure out how to save face, she says the best word I will ever hear.

"Yes," Lucy says, her head nodding frantically. "Yes, I will marry you."

The stadium erupts in cheers. With weak legs, I stand, take the ring out of the box, and slide it onto her finger.

It's perfect. A round solitaire diamond that can be seen all the way back in Laurel Heights.

What's even more perfect is the feel of Lucy's lips on mine as she jumps back into my arms.

Over the years, I've often felt like the king of the world. In high school when we won the state title. In college when we won the national championship. Hearing my name picked first in the draft. Hell, even throwing my first professional touchdown.

None of those feelings compare to this.

Nothing compares to the love Lucy and I share.

And nothing ever will.

EPILOGUE
LUCY

THREE YEARS LATER

THERE HAVE BEEN many times over the years when I have been proud of Bryce.

When he won the state title in high school. When his college career soared all the way to him being the top draft pick. When he battled his demons and came out the other side a better man.

None of those compare to tonight. When you watch your husband, the father of your unborn child and love of your life, win the championship and be named MVP in the process, it's a feeling like no other.

He did it. After years of hard work, tough times, near collapses, and a few missed opportunities here and there, he and the Fury can finally say they are the best in the league.

"Oh my God! They did it!" Brenna yells, nearly jumping on me as she gives me a hug. "Oh shit. Sorry. I'm just so excited I forgot that my nephew was there."

I laugh through the happy tears as I rest my hands on my very large stomach. "How could you forget? You already have three best-aunt-in-the-world shirts despite being his only aunt. You also organized the baby shower. How could you possibly forget that I'm about to have a baby?"

"I mean, can you blame me?" she asks, holding her hands in the air as she looks up at the confetti still raining from the rafters of the stadium. "I'm just . . . I'm just so proud of them, you know?"

I nod, fighting back another round of tears. "They really did it"

We link arms and watch our men, who are acting exactly like they should, as they hang out on the stage. Most of them have had their cell phones out the second the celebration started. They've already put on their league champion hats. Somehow, Dexter smuggled a bottle of champagne onto the stage and is dousing everyone with it.

In the middle of it all are Bryce and Cole, embracing like only best friends can. To think that they dreamed of this moment when they barely knew how to tie their cleats is almost unfathomable. They have been through so much together, and for a while, I didn't know if this dream would happen for them. Kind of hard to win a championship together when you aren't speaking.

Yet, here they are, celebrating this moment together, exactly how they should be.

"I'm going to go sneak on stage," Brenna says. "It's about time I show my man exactly how proud of him I am."

I laugh. "You go do that."

I look back to the stage, and Bryce has made his way behind Hunter, who is currently giving his speech as the youngest winning coach in league history. I'm too busy drinking in the moment happening behind him.

Bryce and Davis are in an embrace, and if I'm seeing things right, they both might be shedding tears. I don't blame them. If people only knew how much Davis has helped Bryce over the years, not only as a coach but also as a friend and mentor, they would realize what this moment means for them.

I look away and rest my hands back on my stomach as I make eye contact with Bethany. Neither of us say anything, yet we know exactly what each other are thinking. She's thanking me for coming back into Bryce's life, which coincided with the Fury's rise to the top of the league. I know this because she has told me it roughly a million times since I moved to Nashville.

I always play it off since no one woman is responsible for an entire team's turnaround.

Though, I have crunched the numbers, and the winning percentage of the team when I was in Bryce's life compared to when I wasn't is staggering.

"We'd now like to introduce, the most valuable player of tonight's game, quarterback Bryce Donald!" Coach Hunter announces.

The stadium erupts in cheers as Bryce steps up to the microphone, championship trophy in hand.

"There was a day I never thought this would happen. Hell, there were more than a few days. But here we are Nashville! At the top of the football world!"

The fans who made their way to Miami for the game go crazy in applause. As for me? It's all I can do to keep the tears at bay.

"I might be holding this MVP trophy, but one player isn't the team. I need to thank every single man who puts on the uniform with me every day. I'm not here without each one of you. I'd be remiss if I didn't give a special nod to Cole Campbell. My brother. My best friend. Who knew that what we dreamed of as kids would actually come true? And to my coaches. You never gave up on me, not even when I didn't give you any reason to believe in me. When you drafted me, I told you that we'd win a title. Here we are. Thank you. Thank you for everything. And last but not least, I need to thank my wife, who is the love of my life and the woman who is about to give me a gift greater than this trophy. I love you, Lulu. We did it baby."

The crowd goes crazy again as Bryce holds up the trophy one more time before exiting the stage. I'm in full-blown tears and thinking about the road he referred to. It was long and hard, but it was worth every trial we faced to get to where we are now. Still, sometimes I wonder if I'd do it all again if I knew this was the only way we'd end up together.

Actually, that's not even a thought. I would in a second. Bryce's love is worth that. Our love is worth that.

That's how I know he and I have that once-in-a-lifetime love from fairy tales.

"He did it," Mrs. Donald says, putting her arm around my shoulders. "He really did it."

I lean my head onto her shoulder as we watch Bryce finish his speech and exit the stage. I'm so glad that everyone we love is here tonight able to share in this moment.

My parents are even here somewhere too. Dad and Mr. Tripoli are likely trying to sneak autographs, and my mother is probably still talking to Guiliana. Luciano and Celine left before the game was over because Celine wasn't feeling her best.

That's what happens to us super pregnant women.

Yes, she's also pregnant.

Yes, we're due days apart.

Yes, our mothers are thrilled.

And secretly, so are we.

"There are my girls," Bryce says, finally making his way to me and his mom. He wraps her in a hug that, once again, makes the tears start flowing.

No one should be this emotional when they are this pregnant. It's just not fair.

"Hey, Lulu," he says, bringing me in for a kiss I feel all the way to my toes. I thought that, after a few years of marriage, this feeling would lessen. That I wouldn't immediately feel his presence the second he walked into the room.

I was wrong. They are stronger.

The butterflies will never go away.

"I am so proud of you," I say, wrapping my arms around his neck. "How does it feel to be the best?"

He leans in for one more kiss, and I swear if we weren't surrounded by thousands of people, I'd be having my way with him right now.

Pregnancy sex is no joke. It's the best.

"It's the second best feeling in the world."

I lift an eyebrow. "Only the second?"

"Yup," he says, picking me up to bring me in for yet another kiss. "Best day of my life was when you became my wife. Then this. Though, I'm pretty sure when this little guy comes, today is going to get bumped again."

He leans down to press a kiss to my stomach, and I'm pretty sure he says something to his unborn son, though I can't hear it. It's probably something about how this is going to be him in twenty-five years.

The man is dead set on our baby coming out of me already being able to throw twenty-yard passes.

I joke and say that he's going to be doing calculus in the delivery room.

"You ready to get out of here?" he says. "I have to do a few interviews then we can go."

"Sounds good," I say, taking his hand and turning to walk off the field. However, I don't get two steps before I feel something weird happening.

"What?" Bryce says, realizing I've stopped. "Lulu, what's the matter?"

I look back up to him, doing my best to stay calm.

"Want to ensure this day always stays number two? Then take me to the hospital. My water just broke."

EXTENDED EPILOGUE
BRYCE

I REMEMBER a certain moment from my childhood like it was yesterday. I was ten years old and I had just watched Cincinnati, the team I grew up rooting for, win the league championship. I was sitting in front of the television wearing my jersey that was two-sizes too big for me while holding my football like a doll.

My eyes were glued to the television as I watched their quarterback receive the Most Valuable Player trophy. He was celebrating as confetti rained around him. Then, like it was as natural as anything, he looked into the camera and told the world that he was now going to Disney World because he had won the championship.

I vowed to myself that one day I'd be just like him. I might have even practiced how I would say it a few times. Though I haven't done that since Brenna walked in on me practicing it in front of the mirror. She didn't let me live that down for a month.

I didn't get to say it tonight. I had to leave before I could. And I'm okay with that. In fact, I'm more than okay with that. Because tonight I'm becoming a father. And saying those words are a million times better than saying I'm going to see a mouse.

"You are never fucking touching me again! Ahhhhhh!"

Now those words? The ones that just came from my currently-in-labor wife as she squeezes my hand so hard that I think a few fingers might break? Well, I could go forever without hearing those again.

"You're doing great Lulu," I say, doing the best I can to reassure her. It's been four hours since her water broke minutes after we won the championship. I stifle a yawn, because yes, I might have played a football game tonight and had my body knocked around six ways from Sunday, but my wife is pushing out a person right now. I feel like saying that I'm tired might not go over well right now.

Lucy falls back into the pillows after another round of pushing. I take a cold cloth and wipe her brow.

"I hate that I can't do more for you right now," I say as I help her sit back up, knowing another round of pushing is coming soon.

"I hate you."

I can't help but laugh. "No you don't. Just like the nickname, you don't hate me at all."

"I wouldn't be so sure about that," she grits out as another contraction comes along.

"Okay, how about this," I say, trying to think of anything to help distract her mind.

"Let's do math."

"Math! After all these years *now* you want to do math? How about this equation? You plus your hand for the rest of your life equals. . ."

"I'm choosing to ignore those kinds of comments." I say as our nurse can't help but laugh. "Give me the math stats on babies being born?"

I know she knows them. She randomly drops them on me, usually when she's in the midst of reading some new baby or mom blog she finds online. She and Celine send them back and forth to each other every day. Brenna is even in on it and she's not pregnant. Well, not yet. I'm sure that day is coming soon.

Though I'd rather not think about that.

"No math today," our doctor says as he repositions himself. "One more push Lucy and your son is going to be here."

Her head falls back, her eyes filled with fright. "I don't know if I can."

I see a tear coming from her eye and I know the joking is over. For years, this woman was, and has been, my rock. What started as just calming words and a keen sense of knowing what I needed before I did has transformed into being the best wife and partner a man could ask for. She has helped me start my charity for high school athletes. She has created a home for us in Nashville. She is about to give me a child.

"Lucy Donald. You listen to me. You are the strongest woman I know. You have never let anything get the best of you. It's the final seconds of the game and we need one more big play. You can do it."

She takes a deep breath as I help her sit back up. "Leave it to you to give me a football analogy in labor."

"Did you expect anything else?"

"Absolutely not. Okay, let's do this. If he doesn't come out now, I'm going to start weighing the pros and cons to just leaving him in there forever."

This gets her another round of laughter from the delivery staff.

"No need Lucy. I see the head. One big push."

She looks up at me, a mixture of fear and determination in her eyes.

"Ready?" I ask.

She nods. "Ready."

Lucy

"THERE HE IS!"

My mother drops the arm full of stuffed animals she was carrying and races over to the bassinet where her grandson is peacefully sleeping. All my dad can do is shake his head as he bends over to pick them up.

"Nice to see you too Mom."

"Oh Lucia!" She stops and turns at my hospital bed to give me a chaste kiss on the cheek. "How are you feeling? How is he?"

I laugh, because I know she is just excited. She has been wanting a grandchild since . . . well, since before my ill-fated engagement to Luciano. The woman has waited long enough.

"He's wonderful."

"No, he's perfect," Bryce says, standing up from his spot on the couch in my delivery suite to stand next to where our son is sleeping.

"Damn right he's perfect. He's my nephew." Brenna walks in the room, followed by Pamela and Cole.

"Language Brenna," Pamela scolds as she walks over and stands on the other side of the baby.

"Oh he doesn't know what I'm saying," she says, taking a seat on the couch. "Plus, from what I've been told by my brother, the first word this little guy heard was—"

I shoot a look over to Brenna, begging her to stop talking. The last thing I need to hear right now from my mother is my use of profanities. Especially after the whirlwind last two days we've had. I don't even feel like I've slept, though I have dozed in and out every time there is even a remote amount of silence. Then there's Bryce, who I know is a walking zombie right now. But the man is determined to stay awake as long as I am.

"How was the celebration after the game?" Bryce asks Cole, who looks adorably out of place holding a baby balloon and a stuffed duck.

"Wouldn't know," he says. "Had my own celebration to go to."

"Yeah you did."

Brenna's words cause Bryce to fake gag, which makes us all laugh. "Don't want to hear about it," Bryce says, shaking his head. I can't help but laugh. Mainly because I called this all along. My husband just wouldn't believe me.

"Enough you guys," my mom chimes in. "You've held out long enough. Tell us the name of my grandchild."

Bryce comes over to my bed, sitting next to me and immediately reaching for my hand. We never intended to keep the name a secret when we found out we were pregnant. However, during one Sunday night dinner when the topic of baby names came up, everyone seemed to have an opinion on what we should name our son, as well as what Luciano and Celine should name their daughter. It was quickly decided that to make sure no one was disappointed, that we weren't going to tell anyone. Not even Brenna and Cole.

They were pissed.

"Gabriel Nicholas Donald. We're going to call him Gabe."

A chorus of oohs and aahs fill the room. Thankfully, no one states an objection. Which the answer would have been too damn bad. I love the name and I'm too tired to argue with anyone.

Our little man was born at three twenty-one in the morning, five hours after Bryce won the biggest game of his career.

Much to Bryce's chagrin he was not holding a football when he was born.

Much to my pleasure I can tell he already has his father's eyes.

"I love it," Mom says, leaning down and placing a kiss on Gabe's head. The sight brings a tear to my eye. Though I'm not sure if that's the emotion of the day or if I'm just so tired that anything is going to make me cry. "Oh I can't wait to tell Guiliana!"

"Speaking of," I turn to Bryce. "Where are Luciano and Celine? I thought they would have at least called?"

All Bryce does is smile. "Well, if I tell you that, it will ruin the surprise."

Before he can get another word out, Luciano comes walking into the room, pushing Celine, and a tiny baby wrapped in pink in her arms, in a wheelchair.

"No way!" I yell. "How? When?"

"After the game. Apparently a few hours after you," Celine says, handing the baby to Luciano.

Luciano clears his throat, though I feel like it's more out of emotion than anything. "Donald family, I'd like to introduce you to Gabriella Marie Tripoli."

A silence hits the room before everyone, well everyone except Luciano and Celine, start hysterically laughing.

This is what we get for not telling anyone our names.

"Gabriel and Gabriella," Bryce says, taking our son out of his bassinet to stand next to Luciano. "Oh you two, are we going to have stories to tell you when you grow up."

I can't contain my tears as I look at the sight in front of me. But who can blame me? Seeing Bryce and Luciano, holding our children, is too much to handle. Now I know where my mom was coming from all those years ago. I can already see the wedding. But before that, I see years of birthday parties and playdates and friendships developing. I take a quick glance over to Celine and I can tell she's thinking the same thing.

Let's just hope that when the time comes, and they make their decisions about who they love and how they want to live their lives, it will not end up going down in family history as an event that could have been sold on Pay-Per-View.

"Why the thinking face?" Bryce asks as he sits back down on the bed with me, Gabe still cradled in his arms.

"Sometimes it's hard to believe how we ended up here."

He places a kiss on my temple. One I can't help but lean into. "It wasn't easy was it?"

I shake my head. It hasn't. Even since we got married, things haven't always been smooth sailing. But the difference now is we know life with and without each other. And we know a life together is worth fighting for.

"Would you do it again?" he asks. "Would you put up with me being a complete dipshit for years knowing we'd end up here?"

I don't even have to think as I reach for my son, bringing him into me.

"Every time." I say, "Without question."

OFF LIMITS

NASHVILLE FURY: BOOK 4

PROLOGUE
COLE

SENIOR YEAR OF COLLEGE

MOST COLLEGE GUYS would give up a kidney to be where I'm at tonight.

Then again, I'm not most college guys.

I'm two short months from graduating from Clemson with honors. The professional football draft is in a few weeks, and despite battling through a knee injury this past season, I'm still projected to go in the second round. I can see the light at the end of the tunnel. I've worked my ass off these past four years; I've studied hard, never missed a class or a practice. I kept my nose to the ground, didn't get in trouble, and kept the partying to a minimum.

Don't get me wrong, I had my fun. But I was smart about it. Small gatherings. Safe places. Drinking with trusted people I knew wouldn't plaster my face on social media. I stayed far away from the party scene that usually included frat bros, bad music, and drinks made in plastic tubs.

Until tonight.

Because for the life of me, I can't say no to Brenna Donald. Even when she asks me to take her to a fraternity party.

"I don't wanna leave!" Brenna yells as she stumbles out of the fraternity house. I'm pretty sure she'd be eating pavement right now if I wasn't holding her up.

"Considering you can't stand up right now, I feel like it's time for us to go."

"You're no fun." Her slurred words shouldn't make me laugh, but they do. "Why aren't you fun, Cole?"

"I'm fun."

"Then why did you make me leave? I was 'bout to dance. Didn't you want to dance? Do you like to dance? I bet you're a good dancer."

I am, though she doesn't need to know that. Then again, she's so drunk right now I could bust out the Worm right here and she wouldn't remember a thing.

"We left because you're drunk. And despite what you might think, that's not my idea of a good time."

I don't know why I'm saying all of this like she can have a conversation right now. The girl is shitfaced, and I'm still not sure how it happened. I tried to watch her. Hell, at one point I tried to figure out a way to attach myself to her. She doesn't go to school here. She doesn't know who to trust—or who to avoid. She's my best friend's twin sister, for fuck's sake. Infuriating, yes, but I sure as shit wasn't about to let someone take advantage of her.

But then I got stopped by a group of guys who wanted to talk to me about my standing in the draft, and she snuck off. Next thing I knew, she was on the dance floor, a guy standing on a chair pouring a bottle of something down her throat.

I should have known that you can only keep Brenna Donald on a leash so long. The girl has a wild streak a mile long.

"What's a time good?"

I stop and look at Brenna, because in no way was that English.

"Are you asking me what's a good time?"

She nods. "Yup. What's a good time according to Cole Campbell? Let me guess. Football. It's always football with you guys."

She's not completely wrong. Football has consumed my life since I was six years old. But I'm more than the game. Just not many people know that.

"I like to do more than just play football."

I shake my head because again, why am I having this conversation? Besides the fact that Brenna is so drunk I can't believe she's only mixed up a handful of words, why do I care that she knows that I'm more than just a meathead football player? It's Brenna. The girl I've known since childhood. The girl I nicknamed "Trouble," because she was. And still is.

In third grade, I was upset that Bryce and I weren't in the same class. But Brenna was there and sat by me all year. She said if I couldn't sit by one Donald, might as well sit by the other. When we were in high school, I remember her mouthing "good luck" before every game. And after we won, she'd always give me a thumbs up from the crowd. I looked for that thumbs up every time. She never forgot.

And she was always the cheerleader who made me treat bags or painted a sign for me.

Bryce might be my best friend, but Brenna is right up there. She has always been a part of my life, and always will be.

It's kind of comical, considering I'm the always-serious football player, and she's the popular wild child. We have very little in common. Yet, every time she's around, she has a way of putting a smile on my face.

Even right now, when she's three sheets to the wind.

"I like to draw."

My words stop both of us: Me because I can't believe I said them. Her because when I stopped walking, so did she. At this point I'm basically carrying her.

"You do?" Her big blue eyes look up at me, and for just a second, I get lost in them. Have I ever noticed how beautiful they are? They're the color of the sky on a perfect summer morning at the lake?

"I mean, I dabble," I say, all of a sudden feeling self-conscious.

"What do you draw?"

"Mostly landscapes. Nature. That kind of stuff."

I want to smack my mouth shut. Did I really just admit that to her? No one knows that. Hell, Bryce knows everything about me, but he doesn't know that. What kind of voodoo magic does this woman possess?

Granted, I've probably asked myself that question at least twenty times since she showed up on our doorstep yesterday—unannounced—looking for a couch to crash on for the weekend. What were Bryce and I supposed to do? Tell her she couldn't stay with us after driving from our small town in Southwest Ohio all the way to South Carolina?

Then today she begged Bryce and me to go with her to this party. How she got invited I still don't know. Then again, Brenna makes herself known wherever she goes. I'd guess she was getting coffee this morning, and before she knew it, she had an invitation to every party on campus this weekend.

"I bet they are beau—"

I don't know what startles me the most, Brenna not finishing her sentence or how she's pushing me off her with a force that rivaled a defensive lineman. For someone who is barely five-foot-four, the girl has some strength behind her.

"Brenna! What are you doing?"

She doesn't answer me as she staggers toward someone's shrubs. I hear the sound of retching as Brenna hunches over in some poor person's yard.

"Brenna!" I run over to her and quickly pull her hair back off her neck. "Hey…it's okay. Get it out."

I try to comfort her the best I can over the next ten minutes. Every time she thinks she's done, another wave hits. Eventually, she stands up, and I don't know whether to have pity on her or crack up laughing.

Her makeup is all over her face, and she has a little bit of puke on her shirt. Her hair looks like it's been styled by a tornado. Yet somehow, she's still fucking beautiful. I don't know if I realized how gorgeous she was before tonight.

"Fuck!" Brenna yells, as she slaps my hands away from her.

"What's the matter?"

"I puked on my shirt!"

"It's okay," I say. "We're just a few blocks from the apartment. We'll get you cleaned up."

"No!" she yells. "It smells."

Before I know it, Brenna is pulling up her shirt and tossing it over her head.

And she isn't wearing a bra.

"Brenna!" I tear my eyes away from her chest and run over to her, wrapping her in my arms. I ignore how soft her skin feels—and how I just got an eyeful of the most perfect set of tits I have ever seen.

She wiggles away from me and holds her hands up in the air. "I'm free! Come on! Let's race home!"

She starts running…well, her idea of running after just puking for ten minutes and still not being able to walk in a straight line. "Brenna! Stop! You have to put on a shirt."

"Says who? Are you the shirt police?"

Before I can respond, the worst sound I could ever hear stops me in my tracks—the whoop-whoop of the actual police, flashing their red and blue lights as Brenna faces them, topless and doing the Running Man.

"What is going on here?" the officer asks as he gets out of his car. "Ma'am, can you please put on a shirt?"

Brenna shakes her head. "I don't have one. It has puke on it."

The officer takes a few more steps toward her. I do as well.

"Ma'am, are you drunk?"

She looks at the cop, then at me, then back to the cop. "I am. I am drunk. But it's fine. Don't need to worry about me, occifer. This guy isn't fun, but he's taking care of me."

The cop doesn't look amused. "Ma'am, if you don't put a shirt on right now, I will be forced to take you in for indecent exposure."

"That won't be necessary," I say, hurrying and pulling my T-shirt off. It might look like a nightgown on her, but at least she'll be covered. "Here, Brenna, put this on."

She takes the shirt from me, but instead of putting it on and shutting up, she acts like it's a rope, lassos it over her head, and chucks it back to me.

"No!" she yells. "How come when I'm topless it's indecent exposure and when he is it's just hot? This is sexist! So fuck this! Fuck you! And fuck the patriarchy!"

Oh. My. God.

"Ma'am, put your hands behind your back. I'm taking you in."

Like hell he is. Before I know it, I'm in front of the cop, blocking him from Brenna. "Look, man, she's just drunk. I live a block away. Let me take her home."

"Sir, please move out of the way, or I'll have to arrest you as well."

"For what?" I demand, my anger spiking.

"I'll figure it out later. Both of you, in the car."

Before I know it, he has both of us handcuffed and sitting in the back of his cruiser. Neither of us have a shirt on, though he did pull out a blanket from his trunk to cover Brenna.

And for the millionth time tonight all I can think of is *how the fuck did I end up here?*

"Hey," Brenna says. When I look over at her, she looks more sober than she has all night. But she doesn't look worried. In fact, it looks like she's about to start cracking up at any second.

"This isn't funny," I say. "I'm two weeks from the draft. I can't get arrested now."

"You aren't going to get arrested," she says with confidence. "All Officer Prude is going to do is give us a warning. Maybe I'll get a ticket for the boobs. Relax, Campbell, everything is going to be fine."

Our eyes stay locked as we sit in the back of the cop car. And for maybe the first time in my life, I don't look at her like she's my best friend's sister. Or like the Brenna I knew in high school.

No, this is a woman whose brown hair and blue eyes are making me forget how to breathe. Whose boldness makes me crazy. Who I want to protect more than anything at this moment. She's bold. Beautiful. A little crazy. And apparently, quite the feminist.

How have I never noticed these things about her? How have I never thought of her as anything more than Bryce's sister?

I let my head hit the back of the seat as one thought runs over and over through my head. It's not concern that I might get arrested. Or that some website could pick this up and my draft stock could tank.

No, right now I'm having an epiphany in the back of a cop cruiser: I'm in love with my best friend's sister.

So, no, Brenna, everything is not going to be okay.

1

BRENNA

THREE YEARS LATER

"NOPE. TOO SLUTTY."

I turn to look at Lucy with a questioning eye. "What do you mean *too slutty*? We're going to dinner then dancing. Of course it's going to be a little slutty."

My best friend, who is also my soon-to-be sister-in-law, sits up from her space on my bed, tilting her head as if she's analyzing every inch of fabric of my dress. Of which, I'll admit, there aren't really that many.

"I don't know. I know you want to be sexy, but I think it's the whole no-back thing for me. It just puts it over the top. Plus, this is a first date, Brenna; don't you want to leave him wanting more?"

I let out a defeated sigh. "Yeah, you're right. But then what do you suggest?" I walk back into my closet, examining every piece of clothing I have, including the eight other dresses I've tried on, which are now beginning to make a pile on my floor. "Dexter is going to be here in a half hour, and I'm running out of dresses."

I don't know why I'm freaking out over what to wear. Yes, it's a first date. But I'm a first date professional at this point. Maybe it's because Dexter is football famous? I know people are going to recognize him. He's one of the more social members of the Nashville Fury, so his picture is always on social media at some club or bar. Maybe it's that? I don't know...but I do know if I don't find a dress in a few minutes I'm either canceling or going nude. In which case, I might as well wear the slutty dress.

"What about the blue one? With the one sleeve?" Lucy says. "You look great in blue."

I sift through my clothes, wishing that I had used some sort of system when I moved in here. Then again, I was just so happy to have found a place I could afford—and out of my brother's apartment—I wasn't thinking about closet organization. I was just thinking of a good night's sleep without having to hear my brother make my best friend pray to gods I didn't know she believed in.

I find the blue dress and slip off the slutty one. I don't even have to look in the mirror to know this one is going to be the winner. It's a tight one-sleeved royal blue dress just a few shades darker than my eyes. The fabric has some shiny thread weaved through it that makes it jazzy without being over the top.

I love it.

I reach up and grab my nude heels as I make my way back to my bedroom, where I take a seat on my bed next to Lucy. "I should let you make all the decisions in my life. You're usually right. It would save me a whole lot of trouble."

"If I made all your decisions for you, you wouldn't be needing this dress tonight, because you wouldn't be going out with Dexter."

My brow creases as I look over to Lucy. She won't meet my gaze. Apparently something on my pillow is far more interesting.

"Is this because of the whole birthday clusterfuck?" I ask as I get up and sit at my vanity to finish my makeup. "You know that it wasn't Dexter's fault."

"I know, and it's not that," Lucy says. "That was all your brother being an idiot. But I choose not to think about that day."

I lean in closer to the mirror because somehow that will make my mascara go on cleaner. "Then what's the problem?"

"He's a manwhore and a player, and you deserve better than that."

I switch eyes and try to conceal the fact that I know Lucy is right. I've been choosing to ignore the gossip, but yes, I know Dexter's reputation as the team playboy. Still, I'm of the belief that you have to see something with your own eyes to truly draw a conclusion.

"Maybe the rumors are just that," I say. "Who am I to judge someone before they've had a chance to defend themselves?"

"You realize I've seen him in action, right? This isn't some tabloid rumor. This is me, your best friend, telling you that he's not for you."

I shrug Lucy off as I apply my lipstick. I know she's not a fan of Dexter, but this is the first guy who has asked me out since I moved to Nashville. So what if he has a few red flags? Who doesn't these days? Plus, this can't be any worse than any of the dates I would have had back when I lived in Ohio. I mean, that bar is set so low that if he came in under that he'd have to dig a tunnel.

"And I appreciate your warning, but I'm a big girl. Plus, Dexter passed the arm test. You know I have to go out with him just on that alone."

It's almost as if I can hear Lucy's eyes rolling. She hates the arm test. She thinks it's one of the most ridiculous ways that I judge if I want to go out with a man.

I think it's science. And if there is one thing I know, it's science.

Some women have a thing for asses.

Some women get their hearts and lady parts all tingly from the sight of a good smile.

Me? It's all in the arms. As in, I want to be able to look at them and know for a fact the man could pick me up and pin me against a wall without breaking a sweat.

Needless to say, Dexter passed the test with flying colors.

"You know who else passes the arm test?"

I turn to look at her and send her a glare. "Don't even say it."

"What?" she says with mock innocence. "I'm just saying, Cole's arms are quite…large."

"How many times do I have to tell you? Cole is Cole. He's basically my brother. His arms don't count."

"But he's not your brother," Lucy says. "Are you telling me you've *never* checked his arms out? If you can honestly say you haven't, then I'll never bring him up again."

I don't make eye contact with Lucy as I get up and walk to my closet to locate the clutch purse I want to take tonight. Because she's right. I have.

Not recently. It was years ago. In college. In the back of a cop car. And yes, for a second I had the flash of a fantasy where Cole lifted me up with ease. As if I weighed no more than a feather as he pressed me against the wall and kissed me.

But then the cop slammed the car door shut, and I came to my senses. Well, almost to my senses. I was pretty out of it at the time.

"Why aren't you looking at me?" Lucy says as I emerge from the closet. "Is it because you *have* fantasized about Cole and you can't lie to me?"

I sit back down on the bed. "Fine. I have. Once. Years ago. But it doesn't matter. His arms don't count."

Lucy raises an eyebrow. "What's that supposed to mean?"

"It means that even if he passed the arm test and every other one I could think of, it's Cole. My brother's best friend. I've known him since we were kids. It would just be weird. Plus, you also fail to consider that it needs to be a two-way street, and Cole Campbell absolutely would never go out with me."

Lucy just shrugs. "You never know."

"Oh, I know. I've been the annoying sister since we were six. Something like that doesn't change." I say as my phone vibrates with a text message. "That's Dexter. He's downstairs."

Lucy starts to make her way off my bed. "He's not coming up to get you? We will file that in the red flag column."

"He probably couldn't find parking," I say as I grab a jacket and my clutch. "Thank you for coming over and helping me."

We walk downstairs together. "I hope it goes well. I hope I'm wrong about him. But please be careful. I don't want you to get hurt."

We exit my ground-floor apartment, careful to walk around the huge puddle that has been growing since this rain started last week.

No one tells you how much it rains in Nashville in the spring. I stop for a moment to give Lucy a hug. "I'm a big girl. I can take care of myself. But I appreciate you."

We turn toward the parking lot, and right in front of me, in all of his flashy glory, is Dexter. He's standing next to some sports car that I'm sure is worth double my teaching salary. He's wearing all black and more gold jewelry than I own. And then there are the jeweled sunglasses, which I don't get. It's dark out.

"Hey sweet stuff. You ready to kick it?"

I have a very bad feeling about this...

"Please call me every hour for a status update," Lucy whispers. "Or if you need a ride home. Or anything."

I nod and give her another hug before I make my way to the car.

"You look good enough to eat," he says, opening the door for me. Well, at least he did that. "I have a whole night ready for us. Just wait until the crew at the club gets a load of you."

The crew? The club? What the hell have I got myself into?

I should run. Run back up the stairs right now, and put on my sweats, and catch up on the latest Turkish soap opera I'm binging. Those fuckers are addicting.

But instead, I take a deep breath, get into his car, and try to breathe through the smell of his cologne.

It's one of those that should smell good because it costs a fortune but actually smells like three-day-old takeout food.

"You ready?"

I nod as Dexter puts the car in gear. I wish I could recapture my earlier optimism, but it's too late to back out. Plus, it's just one date. How bad can it be?

2

____

COLE

I NEVER UNDERSTOOD why anyone would mock people who play video games.

I can't speak for everyone, but for me, it's a way of detaching from reality. It gives me something to concentrate on and lets the things rolling around in my head go away, even if it's just for a few hours. Some people read. Some do crafts or projects. I used to draw, but I never have the time to do it anymore. So now, I choose to blow people up in virtual worlds.

And lately, I'd much rather be in a virtual world than the real one.

"And that's how we do it!" Bryce yells, ceremoniously flipping his controller onto the couch as we successfully get through another level. He even adds a little victory dance for good measure. It's as bad as his touchdown dance.

"If this is how you celebrate moving to the next level on a video game, then I don't want to see you if we ever win the league championship."

"Not 'if,' my friend," Bryce says as he tips his can of Dr Pepper toward me. "When. *When* we win the title."

I tip my can to him and sit back on my couch as Bryce navigates to the next level of our game.

"Thanks for letting me hang out tonight," Bryce says.

I set down my drink and grab my controller. "I didn't have much of a choice when you showed up at my door, barged in, and grabbed the second controller before saying hello."

"Yes, you did," Bryce says before taking another drink of sugary goodness. Yes, we both know these are all sugar and crap for us. But Bryce is going on five months sober, and it's the offseason. The occasional Dr Pepper won't kill us. "You could have kicked me out at any time. But you didn't. Because that's what best friends do."

"True," I say as we start the next level. "By the way, why are you here tonight? Lucy already tired of you? She hasn't been living with you that long. I figured it would be at least a year before she had her fill."

"Not even a little bit," Bryce says with a smile. "Things couldn't be going better."

"Then why, my friend, did you take the elevator down three floors to come hang out with the likes of me tonight?"

"Can't a guy want to hang out and play video games with his best friend?"

I shoot him a look that clearly says I see through his bullshit. "He can. But since his fiancée moved in with him, he doesn't anymore. So spill."

"She's at Brenna's," Bryce says as we start fighting our opponent. "She had a date tonight. Lucy went over for moral support."

It takes every ounce of self-control in my body to not crush the can in my hand, but I manage not to. It takes an equal amount of strength to keep my face even. Actually, that's a lie. I'm so practiced at not having a reaction to hearing about Brenna's dating escapades, I could win the World Series of Poker.

I wish I wasn't.

It used to be easier. Before Brenna moved to Nashville, I only occasionally had to hear about Brenna and her quest for Mr. Right. But now that she lives in Nashville? It's constant. I thought it would get better after she moved out of Bryce's place and into her own. It hasn't. If anything, it's worse.

It's one of the reasons why virtual worlds are much better than the real world these days.

So here I am, pretending not to give a shit she is out with some loser while also beating myself up about the fact that I even give a fuck at all what she's doing.

I fucking hate being in love with my best friend's sister.

"So who's the guy?" I ask. I hate that I need to know, but if I don't ask my imagination will run wild.

"That's the thing," Bryce says. "Neither she nor Lucy would tell me."

That's interesting. But I can't tell him it is. "Probably not worth the mention."

I go back to playing, hoping that's the end of this conversation. Then the game suddenly pauses, and I realize it's not.

Lucky me.

"I mean why wouldn't they tell me? What's the big secret?"

"Maybe, and hear me on this one, it's none of your business?"

Bryce shoots a look at me like I've grown a second head. "What do you mean none of my business? She's my twin sister! Of course it's my business. Don't you care who your sister dates?"

I put down my controller and turn to Bryce, who clearly can't see beyond his ego right now. "For one: My sister is eight years older than me and married with three kids. I think she's fine. And second, did you care this much about who she dated when she was back living in Laurel Heights? Why do you suddenly give a shit? It's Brenna's life. Let her be."

Those last two sentences are part of my mantra when it comes to Brenna Donald. Every time I hear about her and another failed date, or about how she just wishes she could find a love like Bryce and Lucy's, I tell myself that I need to let her be. That I need to not let it concern me.

Because it can't. I can't be in love with my best friend's sister. I've been trying to fall out of love with her every day since I realized it three years ago. I've tried everything. I've tried going celibate. I've tried to fuck her out of my system with random women. I even tried seriously dating one. I've tried punishing myself by snapping a rubber band on my wrist every time I thought of her—that just left me with a really red wrist.

I've even sometimes wondered what it would be like if we were together. If she felt the same way about me. That train of thought leads me down a road where I imagine holding her during quiet nights in; her running up to me after a game and jumping into my arms; and of course, imagining what it would be like if she were to be in my bed.

But that train of thought only ends in disaster. Because I don't see a world where Bryce would be okay with me dating his sister. Especially after this past year, when he has made it his mission to be the involved and protective brother he never was before.

And if that wasn't enough, there's the unwritten and unspoken rule of professional football: Don't fuck your teammates' sister. Or the coach's daughter. Or pretty much anyone related to anyone who steps foot in the locker room with you.

No matter how I examine this, I'm fucked. And not in a good way.

"I just want her to be happy," Bryce says, pulling me from the Brenna rabbit hole I just went down. "Plus, I'm trying to be a better brother. For so many years—"

"You were a selfish asshole?"

Bryce pretends to throw his controller at me. I don't even flinch.

"I was going to say that I was preoccupied with football and life. I'm just trying to make up for it now."

He's not completely wrong. Though I would say the way I described Bryce would be more accurate.

"I'm sure they didn't tell you for a good reason. Maybe it's someone you know? Maybe he's a teammate?"

I don't know why I brought that up, but I guess since we're already on the topic, this isn't the worst way to gauge his reaction. Better than me randomly bringing it up. Plus, this is as close as I'm ever going to get to asking him what he would think if I asked Brenna out.

"A teammate?" he yells. "Which teammate?"

I hold up my hands in defense. "I was just giving a hypothetical."

"Well then, I hypothetically would kick any of their asses if they took Brenna out. Who would even think of doing that? Don't they know the rules?"

I shrug. "Some of the guys might not care about the rules."

"Well then, if they don't care about the rules, then they won't care about me making their lives hell. There is not one single team member who is good enough for Brenna."

Ouch, that kind of stings. "Not even me?"

This makes him laugh. "You? You and Brenna? Cole, seriously. I know you're trying to distract me from whoever the hell she's out with, but you don't need to go that far. You and Brenna! Ha! She's like your sister. That's fucking hilarious."

I guess I have my answer.

"But, speaking of you and Brenna," Bryce says. "I did want to talk to you about something."

"What's up?"

I can't even begin to imagine where this might be going. Besides the fact that we are best friends and play on the same football team, we live in the same building. We see each other literally every day. We text or talk multiple times a day. What on earth could he want to talk about that we haven't talked about already?

"I wanted to talk to you about the wedding."

Now it's my turn to pause the game. "If this is your grand way of asking me to be your best man, I kind of assumed I already was so you can save the mushy stuff."

Bryce shakes his head. "It's not, but what if it was? Were you going to rob me of that moment? That moment that two best friends only share once in a lifetime?"

Now it's my turn to pretend to throw a controller at him. "Don't make it weird."

"Anyway," Bryce says. "Yes, you are my best man. And now that it's official, I wanted to tell you that Lucy and I set a date."

"Great. When should I plan on showing up in the tux?"

"April sixth."

I have to blink a few times, because no way did he just say the date I thought he did. "April sixth? As in the April that's a month away?"

Bryce nods. "That is correct."

"Okay, and I ask this in a completely supportive way, is Lucy pregnant?"

He shakes his head. "No she's not pregnant. If that were the case I don't think I'd be here because I'm pretty sure her parents would have killed me already."

That's true. Lucy's family is a bit scary. "Then what's the rush?"

Bryce sits back, turning the game and the television off. "Because we're ready to start our life together. We've waited so long for this. Seven years, dude. Do you know how long that is to wait to be with the woman you love?"

Maybe not seven years, but I know better than he thinks.

"All right then," I say. "One month. I'm guessing that means you're going to need some help getting this shindig off the ground?"

Bryce nods. "I've told Lucy to hire a wedding planner, but she refuses. She thinks that between the four of us we can get this all done. And whatever my future wife wants, I'm bound and determined to give her. So, wedding mode activated. Also, get ready to spend a lot of time with Brenna. I have a feeling Lucy is about to put you two to work."

I pick up my can of Dr Pepper and chug the remnants. This time I do crush it in my hand. Thankfully, Bryce doesn't seem to think anything of it.

Me and Brenna. Together. Doing wedding things.

Me and Brenna. Walking down an aisle together. Dancing in front of friends and family.

Fuck. Maybe I need to start wearing the rubber band again.

3

BRENNA

I HAVE BEEN out on a lot of bad dates. In fact, I could probably write a book. It would for sure be a best seller and likely optioned for a movie. And a real one; not one of those crappy ones starring a former child star no one remembers.

What makes my bad dates different from those of others? I give nicknames.

There's Mr. Forgetful. Not only did he claim to forget what restaurant we were meeting at for dinner, he also conveniently forgot his wallet after running up a two-hundred dollar bar tab.

Then there was The Magician. He thought he was the next Criss Angel and wanted to test some tricks out on me over drinks. I kept wishing he would make me disappear, but no luck.

The best worst date was by far The Italian Stallion. I really thought that guy had potential. He was a resident at a hospital in Cincinnati. He was smart, good looking, and super close with his family. And he had the cutest little dog.

Who he talked to. In Italian. While we were having sex.

The list goes on, and tonight, we have a new entry.

"So you know I'm the highest paid wide receiver in the league?" Dexter says as he casually sips on a glass of champagne poured from the chilled bottle that he insisted on ordering despite me telling him I don't drink champagne. Guess he's not driving me home, then.

"Good for you," I say, not knowing how else to respond. Though the smart ass in me wants to say, *"Well that's great. You still make a million less a year than my brother."*

"That's how I can afford fancy restaurants like this."

I don't know what I'm supposed to say. Thanks? I mean, yeah, it's a nice restaurant, and the steak I ate was great, but I would have been just as happy at a restaurant where I didn't think I'd need to sell a kidney just to afford a side salad.

"So, Dexter, you're from Indiana, right? How have you made the transition to the South? I can't speak for Bryce, but for me it's been quite the culture shock."

He sets down his glass of champagne and leans back on his chair like he owns the place. "Baby, I didn't need to get adjusted. I owned this town the second I was drafted."

It takes everything in me not roll my eyes as Dexter goes on to tell me about how many places he can get into and all of the perks he has around Nashville. It makes me want to vomit.

I take the opportunity to think about what I will name Dexter in the *Brenna Donald's Failed Dating Chronicles*. The obvious choice is The Football Player since that is his profession. And, even though I've grown up around football players, he's the first one I've ever gone out with. A few asked me out over the years, but it felt weird going out with one of my brother's teammates. I didn't want it to cause friction when the relationship inevitably failed.

But for some reason, I gave Dexter a chance. Maybe it's because I'm still getting used to Nashville. Maybe it's because I've been feeling a little lonely. Maybe it's because I was blinded by his good looks and those very nice arms. He seemed like a nice enough guy.

Then he showed up spewing the doucheness, and I honestly have to wonder if this is the same guy who asked me out.

Oh. Maybe I could name him The Douche. Though to be fair, I could have named many men that over the years. I'll just stick with The Football Player.

I slyly check my phone to see what time it is and notice I also have a text from Lucy. Though I don't know why I'm trying to be stealth about it. For one, Dexter has checked his phone multiple times tonight. Second, I doubt he would notice. I've just finished listening to a list of all the country music stars he's met so far, and now he's counting all the restaurants or clubs he can get into with just one phone call.

Lucy: Regretting it yet?

I put my phone back down because I don't want to admit she was right. Though the playboy aspect hasn't come out yet, he said something about wanting to go to a club after this. I'm guessing it's only a matter of time before his female entourage shows up.

I look back up at Dexter, and he's staring at me like he's waiting for something. Shit, how much of his long-winded answer did I miss?

"I'm sorry. What was that you said?"

He signals for the waitress to come over and hands her his credit card. At least I didn't have to pay.

Is it bad when that is the highlight of the date?

"I was just asking you if you were ready to head to the club. I know it's early, but I like to make sure my VIP area is set up before my crew comes through."

I pick up my phone and notice that it's already ten-thirty.

"This is early?"

My question was sincere, but apparently to Dexter, this is hilarious. "Baby Girl! You got jokes. Yes, it's early. Are you telling me you're one of those old people who go to bed at eleven? You're young! Live it up!"

"I'm not in bed by eleven," I say defiantly. Though I don't go on to tell him that by eleven I'm on the couch. In my pajamas. With my latest binge on the television and my latest knitting project on my lap.

As we both stand from our table, I notice that most of the champagne is still in the bottle, thank God. The last thing I want is an awkward interaction about drunk driving with this guy.

"So answer me this," Dexter says. "When was the last time you seriously went out and partied? Like had a night out where the drinks kept coming and the night never seemed to end?"

"I…" I trail off because I don't know how to answer that question.

Shit… Am I the oldest twenty-five-year-old on the planet? When did this happen? I'm Brenna freaking Donald. I was the cheerleader who shotgunned beer in her uniform after football games. I'm the one who has almost been arrested more times than I'll ever admit. I'm the one who once organized a senior prank so legendary that the cops in Laurel Heights have to sit with the senior class each year and explain to them why it's not a good idea to allow livestock inside a high school.

When did I become this old lady? I'm the girl who drove to Clemson on a whim just because I heard about a few good parties. When was the last time I even went out, let alone got drunk?

Well, that ends tonight. This might be one of the worst dates I've ever been on, but I'm going to get something good out of it.

I'm going to get my groove back. Or something like that.

"All right, Dexter," I say as I stand up, grabbing my purse and righting my shoulders. "Let's do this."

4

———

COLE

SIX MISSED CALLS. Three text messages.

All from Brenna.

I shoot up out of my bed and throw on my glasses to see what the fuck is going on. It's only then I notice that it's just after one-thirty in the morning. What the fuck is Brenna doing calling me this late?

> Brenna: Are you up?
>
> Brenna: I'm stuck. No one is answering.
>
> Brenna: I don't like champagne. Shouldn't I like champagne? All girls like champagne, don't they?

I hurry and pull up her number, ignoring whatever the hell that last text was. Shit, she was on a date tonight. Is she with him? And who is him? Are they both drunk? The more the phone rings, the angrier I get.

"Cole!"

I can barely hear her. She must be at some club because all I hear is shitty bass and a lot of people yelling.

"Brenna, go to a place where I can hear you."

"Cole!"

"Yes, Brenna. Can you walk outside or to a patio so it's a little quieter?"

"Cole, did you know that there are different kinds of champagne?"

I get out of bed because I have a feeling I know what I'm about to do. "I did know that."

"Well, I didn't. Turns out, I don't like any of them. And, they don't get better the more you drink. Dexter told me it did. But he lied. He's a liar."

I stop mid-step. "Dexter? Is that who you're out with?"

The background finally gets a little quieter. It's still loud, but at least I can hear her now.

"Yeah. He asked me out a few weeks ago."

And that is the answer to the million-dollar question of why Brenna and Lucy wouldn't tell Bryce or me who her date was. And when Bryce finds out, he's going to fucking kill him.

"Where are you? What did you mean when you said you were stuck?"

"Oh, that."

I wait for a few seconds for her to continue, but she doesn't. My guess is she's either so drunk she doesn't know how to speak or she's the kind of drunk where she has the attention span of a gnat.

My guess is the latter.

"Brenna? Where are you?"

"I'm at Fire Lights. It's Dustin Wild's new place. It's sooooo cool. The bathrooms have women in them who will fix your makeup! Mabel did such a good job on mine."

I hurry up and throw on a pair of joggers and a T-shirt. "Brenna, were you trying to leave? Is that why you called me?"

"Yeah," she says, and if I can hear her right, she's a little defeated by that. "I thought I could be the fun Brenna, like I used to be. But I'm not. I'm not fun Brenna. I'm boring Brenna. I'm tired. I want to go home. Dexter won't take me home."

I'm grabbing my keys and out the door before she finishes that last sentence. "Meet me outside in ten minutes. I'm coming to get you."

She doesn't say anything for a second, and all I can think is the worst. Did she pass out? How much did she have to drink? Did someone spike her drink with anything? God help the motherfucker if that happened. He'd be dead, and I wouldn't even care.

"Cole?"

I let out a sigh of relief as I turn on the ignition to my Jeep. "Yeah, Brenna?"

"You're the best friend ever."

I let out another breath as I pull out of the parking garage of my building and head down Broadway.

Best friend. Yup. That's me.

I'M an idiot for thinking that she was actually going to be outside when I arrived. Or that she would answer her phone again. Granted, it took me more than the ten minutes I told her to get down here. But I'm willing to bet she wasn't here then, either.

Luckily for me, there's a spot on the side of the building for me to park, and I happen to know Sid, the bouncer working the door — he also does security for the Fury. Thank fuck, because I don't have the patience tonight for dealing with some 'roided up clown who thinks his dick is big because he's a bouncer in Nashville.

"Where is Dexter's table?" I ask, pushing past the people in line.

Sid must see the panic in my eyes as he points to the elevator. "Third floor. Use the staff elevator. Stairs have been packed all night."

I give him a quick nod as I hop into the elevator. Though I know this is the fastest way up, and I'm grateful to avoid dealing with drunks, it feels like I'm waiting forever for the doors to open.

Now that I'm not moving, I have five seconds to process what is going on. Fucking Dexter. Out of all the guys on the Fury, *he's* who she had to pick to go out with? He is all kinds of wrong for her. And I'm not just saying that because the girl drives me crazy seven ways from Sunday.

But Dexter is the actual worst. She had to know Bryce and I would forbid her from seeing him; that's why she was so secretive about tonight. Yes, Dexter is my teammate. Yes, I put my body on the line for him every week. But that doesn't mean I like the guy. He's a pompous asshat manwhore who likes to show off his money and toys. He prides himself on how many women he's slept with. If I had a nickel for every time he came into the locker room and talked about his "pussy-filled" night, I'd be able to buy my mom another new car.

I've tried on more than a few occasions to get to know him. I thought maybe it was just a front he was putting on. You know, trying to show off in front of his teammates. It's not a front. It's not a facade. That's him. I have to fight back the urge to punch him every time his mouth opens.

Tonight will be another night of exercising restraint. Apparently, he doesn't care about the bro code of football. Bold move, considering just a few months ago Bryce hated him. And now he's out with Brenna?

That boy must have a fucking death wish.

The doors to the elevator open, and my eyes quickly do a scan of the room. This must be the non-country music floor, judging by the music the DJ is blaring. There's a bar to the left, dance floor straight ahead, and as I look to my right, a section with a bunch of roped-off couches.

I don't have to see anyone to know that's where Dexter is at. I make a beeline that way, looking for anyone I might know. It doesn't take me long to see Dexter, flanked on either side by women who are definitely not Brenna. As I get a few steps closer to the roped-off area, I see her. *Passed out on a couch.*

"Brenna!" I shout as I step over the ropes to get to her. I have one foot over when someone who must feel like getting in a fight tonight puts his hand on my arm.

"You aren't on the list."

I turn to look at the guy, who's wearing a shirt that says "Security." He's big. Not as big as my six-foot-four, three hundred and fifteen pounds, but to most people, he would come off as intimidating.

I'm not most people.

"I'm here to get my friend. She's the one passed out on the couch that no one seems to give a fuck about," I say, pointing to Brenna.

"Hey! Cole!" Dexter says as he slides up next to the security guard. "What you doing here, man? Come on in. He's good."

I shrug off the security guard as I take the five short steps it takes to get me to Brenna.

"Oh shit! She passed out?" Dexter says, standing over my shoulder as I lean down to make sure she's okay. "I didn't even realize she was still here."

I shoot a look up to Dexter that is meant to kill. "How do you not fucking know if she's here or not? Didn't you bring her?"

He just shrugs. Asshole. "Yeah, but I hadn't seen her in a minute so I figured she dipped out. I had...other things to attend to."

He looks back at two women, who are subtly waving to him.

"You're fucking something else," I say as I kneel down to try and wake Brenna up.

"What's that supposed to mean?"

I turn back to look at him. This guy really doesn't get it. "You were here with Brenna. You were on a date with her. I'm guessing by the text she managed to make to me that you got her stupid drunk and what—you just left her cause she wasn't going to fuck you? What kind of fucking man does that?"

The man rolls his eyes at me. Fuck, I want to punch him so bad. "Don't be so fucking dramatic, Campbell. Not my fault she can't handle her booze. She's fine."

I want to fire back at him, but out of the corner of my eye I see Brenna start to stir.

"Cole?"

I turn my attention back to her, brushing the hair off her forehead. "Hey, Trouble. It's me."

She tries to sit up, but immediately groans and falls back down. I quickly reach for her, catching her just in time.

"Watch it there," I say, adjusting my hold on her so I can pick her up. "How about we get you out of here?"

She nods...or at least she tries to. It looks a little like her head is going to fall off every time it goes back. "That sounds good. Can we go get pizza?"

I laugh. "Sure, we can get pizza."

I put her arms around my neck and pick her up off the couch. As we begin to walk out of the VIP area, I see Dexter, looking bored since everyone else is watching me and Brenna. I stop in front of him because he needs to hear one more thing.

"If I find out there is anything in her system other than alcohol, you better fucking run. Or demand a trade. Either way, I will make your life a living hell, and that's if I choose to let you live."

He does his best to hide any fear, but the swallow he just took makes me know he heard me loud and clear.

"Dexter!"

I almost drop Brenna because I thought she was asleep. Apparently not. One arm is still behind my neck but the other arm is pointing toward Dexter.

"Yeah?" he says, trying to seem bored.

"You are a really shitty date. And your contract isn't even that big. I bet your dick isn't either. Let's get pizza!"

All I hear are "oohs" and "oh shits!" from the crowd that has gathered as I step back over the rope and head back to the elevator.

I might not be happy about having to come here, but at least the night ended on a high note.

And the assurance I never need to worry about Brenna going out with Dexter again.

5
———————

BRENNA

I take that back—I hate the sunlight hitting my face right now. I hate Dexter. I hate champagne. I hate whoever invented hangovers. I hate the thunderstorm that just woke me up.

I probably hate more things, but those are the top three—shit, four—things right now. Stupid hangover.

What I don't hate is this pillow. Or these sheets. Why do they feel so soft? How have I never realized my sheets are this soft before?

And why do they smell like the best cologne I have ever inhaled in my whole life?

I slowly open my eyes and quickly realize that I'm not in my apartment. Then I remember: I called Cole last night. And not only am I in his room and sleeping in his bed, but by the looks of the T-shirt that I'm currently swimming in, I somehow ended up in his clothes.

What the fuck happened last night?

"Good morning, Trouble," Cole says as I pull the sheets up, trying to hide whatever I can from him.

"I'm going to need you to take that volume down to like a three," I say, rubbing the sleep away from my eyes.

"I figured by now you'd be immune to hangovers," Cole says as he takes a seat on the edge of the bed. "But I got you water and aspirin just in case."

"I'm not as young as I once was," I grumble, holding out my hands for the cure. "Which is what got me in this mess in the first place."

Cole lifts an eyebrow. "Dexter wasn't the one who got you in this mess?"

I swallow the aspirin and take another pull of the water because damn is my mouth dry. "He wasn't exactly part of the solution. But you of all people should have realized last night had Brenna Donald written all over it."

"Well there was no sign of police presence nor was there a riot started, so I wasn't sure."

I shoot a glare Cole's way. "If I had the strength, I'd throw a pillow at you."

This only makes him laugh. "And I'm sure it would do damage."

I shift a little, sitting against his headboard. "Anyway. I was out with Dexter. It was horrible. I hated every second of it, and I was counting down the seconds until we were done with dinner so I could go home."

I can't help but notice that Cole smiles a little bit. I'm glad he finds such pleasure in my bad dating luck.

"Quit smiling."

That only makes it grow bigger. "I'm not."

Cole lays down on the bed, propping his head up with his rather large, rather girthy arm.

Don't look at his arms, Brenna. Those are off-limit arms. Even though they are sexy as hell.

"Anyway," I say, giving myself a shake to clear any dangerous thoughts from my brain. "Dexter made some sort of comment about me being the oldest twenty-five-year-old in Nashville. And for some reason, it rubbed me the wrong way. I don't want to be old! I want to be young and fun and go dancing until the sun comes up."

"But do you, though? Is that what you really want?"

I hesitate for a moment. "I thought I did. When I moved to

Nashville, I had these grand ideas. There's so much more to do here than in Laurel Heights, and I wanted to do it all. I wanted to learn to line dance. I wanted to go to a different honky-tonk and hear live music every night. Try new restaurants. I've heard all about this hot chicken, but I've never had it. I want to meet interesting people from all over. Date men who didn't already know I was Bryce Donald's sister. I wanted to do everything I couldn't do in Laurel Heights."

"But?"

I slump down a little further into the bed. "But now I'm not sure."

"You know," Cole says in his wise-beyond-his-years tone. At least that's what Bryce calls it when Cole's about to give one of his speeches on life. "People can change. And that's okay. Look at your brother. He changed. It took work, but he's a better person. Maybe your change just came more naturally. But just because you want to be in bed before midnight doesn't mean you're boring."

Now it's my turn to give him the questioning brow. "Really? You think a night of takeout pizza, a glass of wine, me knitting while watching a foreign soap opera is exciting?"

"I think it sounds like a perfect night."

I don't know if it's from the hangover or not, but all of a sudden I feel a shiver run down my back. Has he always smoldered before? It's…intense. I've never been looked at like that before. By anyone. It's…I don't know how to describe it, but I'm pretty sure I need to put on a thicker shirt because it is doing something to my body.

"Can I ask you something?" I say, needing to change this conversation.

"Anything."

I look down then back up at Cole. "How did I end up in one of your shirts? I remember calling you to come get me, but frankly, after that everything is blank."

The question seems to snap Cole out of the intense reverie, thank goodness. I don't know how much longer I could take that.

"Well, after I picked you up—literally—I didn't want to take you back to your place and leave you alone. You were passed out, and while I didn't think anyone slipped you anything, I wanted to be sure. So I brought you back here. As for the shirt, you announced you couldn't sleep in your dress because it would get wrinkled, and took it upon yourself to take it off."

My eyes grow about three sizes. "I did what? Oh my God, I'm so embarrassed. Then again, it wouldn't be the first time I've done that in front of you."

He shakes his head. "Don't be. I quickly turned away, found you a T-shirt and left the room. I didn't see anything Bryce would kick my ass for."

"I'm sorry. And thank you. For everything. Last night was definitely not one of my finer showings."

"I'm not sure about that," he says. "Before we left the club you did tell Dexter that he had a small dick. That was entertaining."

"I did not," I moaned, burying my head into the comforter. "That's it. I'm never drinking again."

"Sure…" Cole says, though his tone clearly doesn't buy it. "Now, my turn. Why did you go out with Dexter in the first place? You had to know his reputation."

I let out a long sigh. This might be more painful to admit than anything else we've talked about this morning. "Because he's the only one who's asked since I moved here. And he seemed like a nice guy when we first met. And while it might not have gone great, I did get to cross 'go on a date with a football player' off my dating Bingo card."

This gets me a laugh. "You know not all football players are like that."

"Well I don't plan on finding out," I say. "No more football players. Or celebrities, for that matter. No one who has an income that is newsworthy. From now on, just normal guys with normal jobs who want to do normal things at normal times of the night."

Cole doesn't respond—not that I expected him to—and it stuns me a bit when he just suddenly pops up off the bed and heads to his dresser. He pulls out a pair of shorts and tosses them to me on the bed.

"You should get dressed. I'll take you home."

I blink a few times, thrown from the sudden shift in mood. I want to ask if I said something or did something, but I don't have the chance. Before I can even get a word out, Cole slams the bedroom door so hard I feel an air gust when it closes.

What the hell was that?

6

———

BRENNA

"NO, no, Lucia. Too much skin. You need something more traditional."

I can't help but laugh as Mrs. Valenti tells her daughter what she thinks of the wedding dress she just came out to show us. Like mother, like daughter.

I think it's gorgeous. A little revealing? Sure. But compared to some of the dresses I've seen in this shop, Lucy looks like a nun right now.

"Mom, it's not bad," Lucy says, turning right and then to the left to see all angles of the dress. "What do you guys think?"

I look at the rest of the entourage gathered today at the wedding boutique in Nashville. Everyone is wrinkling their noses.

"It's just not you," I say honestly. "I thought you wanted something more on the traditional end of modern?"

She nods then looks back at the room. "I do, but my consultant insisted I try this on. I didn't have the heart to tell her no."

I signal for her to go back to the room. "Tell her to go back to the stockroom, and if she brings you another dress you didn't pick, come get me. I'll make sure she knows who's in charge."

Lucy smiles and walks back to the dressing room. I love my best friend, and when it comes to certain things, she can push back her shoulders and take control. Then there are the times when she wants to please everyone and doesn't stand up for herself. That's when I come in and remind her that shit won't fly.

"This champagne is delicious," Mrs. Valenti says. "Brenna, why don't you have a glass?"

I shake my head. "No thank you, Mrs. Valenti. I'm not a champagne kind of girl."

Celine, Lucy's other bridesmaid and wife of her former fiancée, takes a sip of hers, which quickly becomes a full-on gulp. "How can you not be a champagne girl? It's so delicious. Even this cheaper kind."

"That's because you were born in France. Don't they feed that to babies in the hospital?"

She laughs at my joke. "No, silly. They waited until we were at least three."

We all laugh and sit back as we wait for Lucy to come out in her next dress. As I look around at the women gathered, I can't help but smile at everyone who traveled here from Laurel Heights. And it wasn't just a simple drive a few hours down the highway. Storms have been nearly flooding Nashville for the past week. But that didn't stop her mom, Celine, and her mom's best friend, Guiliana—who is also her ex-fiancée's mother—from driving down here.

It could definitely be awkward, especially if you knew the history between these women. And the fights. And the name calling.

But everyone has aired out their laundry, and even if they hadn't, I'd make sure they were on their best behavior. I know Lucy has been looking forward to this day since Bryce asked her to marry him. She hasn't said much about the wedding, but I saw the bridal magazines when I was living with them, and I'm on Pinterest enough to know that she has been pinning dress after dress on her board.

My best friend is in full bride mode, and I couldn't be happier for her.

"So, Brenna," Mrs. Valenti says. "Will we be seeing you with a special someone at the wedding?"

I nearly choke on the sip of water I was taking. "Unfortunately, no. I think I'll be at the singles' table."

"Oh we can't have that!" Celine says, putting down her flute of champagne. "The wedding is still a few weeks away. That's still plenty of time to find you a date."

"She could have a date, but she doesn't want to look and see what's right in front of her," Lucy says as she walks out of the fitting room. "What do we think of this one?"

We all fall silent in awe of the beauty in front of us. *This.* This is the dress for Lucy. The long, lace sleeves don't look conservative on her at all. Maybe it's because they are stemming from a sweeping low neckline that almost gives it an off-the-shoulder look. And the rest of the dress? The lace fits her like a glove.

She looks like a princess. And Bryce is going to lose his mind when he sees her in this.

"That's it," I say, standing up to get a closer look. "This is your dress."

"Oh, Lucia," Mrs. Valenti says with a sniffle. When I glance back, she's dabbing at her eyes, Guiliana hugging her close with one arm. The two women are looking at Lucy just like mother figures should at this moment. Then there is Celine, who's crying harder than any of us.

"It's just so beautiful," Celine says. "You're going to be the most gorgeous of brides."

"Is this really it?" Lucy says, examining the dress again. "I mean, I think it is?"

I give a nod to the consultant, who must be reading my mind as she heads over to the veils. She brings back the one I had my eye on the whole time. It has a subtle tiara that spills into a beautiful lace that looks like it was cut from the same material as her dress.

"Oh my," Lucy says, holding back tears as the consultant places it on her head. As she turns to look at herself in the mirror, everyone is a crying mess.

Our girl looks perfect.

"This is it," Lucy says, a smile coming across her face that I have only seen a few times in her life, and all of those moments have been because of my brother. "This is my wedding dress."

Everyone jumps up and starts clapping, including the consultant, who realizes she's about to get a hell of a commission on this dress. We cause such a commotion that another sales woman peeks out from the dressing room next to us. I might not have noticed her except for her fire-red hair. She shoots us a look like we're out of line. *Whatever, lady.*

No one is going to put a damper on this day. Lucy said yes to the dress!

After the commotion dies down, Lucy goes back with the consultant to pay for a dress I'll never be able to afford in my life as the rest of us sit back down.

"So what was Lucy saying about how you could have a date to the wedding?" Celine asks. "Are you playing…what's the phrase…hard to get?"

I shoot Celine a look, but apparently it must get lost in translation because she's looking at me like she didn't just open a can of worms I'm not interested in eating. "Lucy is insistent that our friend Cole has a thing for me. She's been not-so-subtly trying to push me toward him since I moved here."

"Cole is such a nice young man," Mrs. Valenti says. "You could do worse, Brenna."

I know that's the truth, but I don't admit that out loud. Instead, I don't say anything, choosing at that moment to get up and pretend to peruse the bridesmaids' dresses, even though Celine and I already picked ours out.

Cole is a nice guy. I mean, would most men leave their house in the middle of the night to pick up a drunk friend who couldn't figure out how to order an Uber? Not many I know. And he could have taken me home that night and left me to fend for myself. But he didn't. He took me back to his place to make sure I was okay. And I would assume most guys were lying about not looking while I changed clothes, but somehow I know he's not. He's seen them before; he could have seen them again.

I hate how much I've thought about him and that night since it happened last week. I haven't told Lucy about it. If I did, she would only ramp up her push on getting us together. I definitely haven't told her that I've slept in his T-shirt every night since, either.

For comfort. It's comfortable. That's it.

"Will this Cole be bringing a date to the wedding?" Celine asks.

"No, he isn't," Lucy announces. How has she timed her entrances so well today? "Which is why he and Brenna should go together. I mean, it only makes sense for the best man and the maid of honor to go together."

I shoot her a look. "It's not going to happen."

"Why?" Lucy asks as we all stand to start making our exit, dress in hand. "Tell me one good reason why."

"Because, I'm done dating."

This makes everyone stop in their tracks. "You're done dating?" Lucy echoes.

"Yes," I reply. "After my last bad date, I've decided I need a break. No more dates. No more setups. I'm deleting the dating apps. I'd rather sit at home on a Friday than go on another horrible date with a guy who isn't worth my time."

Now, this is something I had been thinking about all week, but until this moment, I hadn't made the actual decision to quit dating. But as these words come out of my mouth, I regret none of them.

I'm done. For now, at least. I'm going to focus on me. I'm going to explore Nashville how I want to. I'm going to be the best maid of honor I can for Lucy and Bryce. I'm going to be the best seventh grade science teacher I can be. Yes. That's it. This is my time. And I'm not going to let some random guy I meet on an app, who only says the right things for five seconds, ruin this part of my life. Even if all of these beautiful dresses surrounding me are making me ache for the time that it's finally my turn.

My turn will come. It's just not my time yet. And I'm okay with that.

"Whatever you say," Lucy says as we walk out of the door. "But if I catch you checking out Cole's arms tomorrow while we're at the cake tasting, you owe me twenty dollars."

I reach out my hand. It's going to be like taking candy from a baby. "You've got yourself a deal."

7

———

COLE

WHEN I AGREED to be Bryce's best man, I thought I knew what I was getting into. Throw a bachelor party. Keep him alive during it. Make sure he gets down the aisle, and don't lose the rings. That was all I signed up for.

I did not sign up for this.

With her.

"Err my God, they have to put this on the menu," Brenna says, despite her mouth being half-filled with whatever flavor cake she is trying now. "Cole, you have to try this."

I want to say that I don't *have* to do anything. Then again, if I was really standing by that mantra, I wouldn't be here.

"Sure," I say, trying not to come off as grumpy as I'm feeling. I try to take the fork from Brenna, but instead she holds it up for me as if she's going to feed me.

God, I hate everything.

Except this cake. I can't deny that this is really fucking good.

"Definitely a winner," I say as I turn away from Brenna to wipe my mouth.

"I'll add it to the yes list." Brenna writes down the flavor on her notepad. "Ready for the next one?"

I nod and Brenna grabs the next piece of cake, which looks like some sort of all-chocolate concoction. I'm guessing it's going to go on the list, too, if the last five flavors are any indication. By the count of the samples still in front of me, I imagine we'll be adding at least ten more flavors to that list before we're done.

I sigh inwardly. When Lucy and Bryce invited us to the cake tasting, I just thought we'd be another vote if they didn't know what they liked. What I didn't realize was that the wedding venue provides all of the services in-house. So while Lucy and Bryce are in the back with the chef talking about the menu, Brenna and I are on solo duty to pick the five flavors needed for the cake.

Normally this wouldn't bother me too much. I've become quite the pro at being in the same room with Brenna and keeping my cool. But after the drunken club night…I don't know. Something shifted in me. Maybe it was when she said she wouldn't date an athlete. Or the fact that I can still smell her perfume on my pillow, no matter how many times I wash the damn thing. Either way, I'm in a piss-poor mood, and it looks like this is going to take all day.

"So what have you been doing since it's the off season?" she asks before taking a bite of the chocolate cake.

I shrug my shoulders. "Not much."

"Don't go into too much detail there. It might lead to conversation."

"What do you want me to do? Name all the video games I'm playing or walk you through my daily workouts?"

"Geez," she says, passing me the cake. "What's up your ass today?"

"Nothing. I just don't feel like talking."

We sit in silence through the next three pieces of cake. I don't even tell her audibly if I like it or not. I just give a thumbs up or thumbs down.

Fuck, I really am an asshole. I don't want to be an asshole to her, but apparently that's my default setting when I'm trying to hide the fact that I want to kiss away the little dab of icing on her mouth. I mean, how do you act around someone you can't stop thinking about when you know the feelings aren't reciprocated? And who do I talk to about it? I wish I knew. But since I don't have any of those answers or people, I'll just be an asshole.

"What do you think of that one?" Brenna asks of the cake she just passed over to me.

I barely look at the piece as I cut off a piece and stuff it in my mouth, chewing mechanically. "It's fine."

"Okay, what the hell gives?" Brenna asks loudly. It nearly makes me jump out of my seat. "No way did you like that piece."

I give her a scowl. "How do you know what I like or dislike?"

"Because—" She leans over the table and grabs the plate, holding it up to my face. "This has coconut on top. You hate coconut. So that means you're so out of it you didn't taste it, or you've had a stroke you didn't tell me about."

I look down at the cake. Yup, sure as shit, there are coconut shavings on top of the frosting. And unless I took the world's smallest bite, I would have had to have tasted a few. And she's right. I despise coconut. It tastes like tanning lotion. Fuck, I really am out of it.

"Okay, Campbell, what's the deal?" Brenna puts her fork down and leans on the table. "Talk to me. Are you okay? I'm used to you being a bit surly, but this is a lot, even for you. What's going on?"

"It's nothing," I lie, because no way can I tell her the truth. "Just didn't sleep very well."

Actually, that's not far off base. The thought of her has kept me up every night since she stayed at my place. Hell, if I'm honest, she's kept me up most nights for the past three years.

"Bullshit," she says.

"It's not."

"It is," she says with confidence. "Only one thing can make a person this angry and out of it at the same time. So, who is she?"

This takes me off guard. "What do you mean, 'who is she?'"

"I mean that only a woman—or a man, if I were the one acting like a mega bitch today— can cause this kind of grumpy mood. So tell me. Who is this woman who is making you all angry-bear, and what can I do to help?"

It would help if you weren't my best friend's sister so I could shoot my shot. It would also be great if you quit wearing leggings that hug every inch of your curves.

"Nothing," I lie again. "Don't worry about it."

"So it is a girl!" she says excitedly as she stands up and walks around the table to sit beside me. "Tell me who she is."

Fuck. Fuck. Fuck. I'm not a good liar. I never have been. It's why I keep saying the word "nothing." It's the only thing I can safely pull off. Plus, the truth is always the best.

Except for now. The truth is definitely not the way to go here.

"Fine. Her name is Jessica."

Shit. What the hell did I just do? I should have come up with a random name. Instead, I dropped the name of the last girl I dated. Though I don't take complete blame for it being on my mind. She texted me out of the blue earlier today, wanting to get coffee.

I haven't replied yet.

I also don't know if "dated" is the best term. I took her out three times and slept with her once in one of my many failed attempts to get Brenna out of my head. I never told anyone about her, though I almost had to when Bryce found her underwear in a couch cushion last year.

She's a nice girl. She has a good job, and if I brought her back to Laurel Heights, my mom would be over the moon about her.

Unfortunately, she's not Brenna. And while my head knows I should have tried harder to make it work with Jessica, my heart wouldn't let me. When I broke it off, she didn't take it very well. She kept calling and texting me, asking me to reconsider. Eventually she gave up. Needless to say, I was shocked when I saw her number on my phone this morning.

Brenna moves a little closer. "There. Was that so hard? Now, tell me what's the problem? Let's fix this. We have a lot more cake to try, and I'm not about to do it with you being all grumpy pants."

I take a drink of the water while deciding what I want to disclose. "We went out a few times last year."

"Oh! So an ex?"

"In a way," I say. "She texted me to get coffee this morning. That's it."

"That's not all of it," Brenna says. "I can tell. Do you want to call her again? Is she seeing someone? Did it end badly? I need details if I'm going to help you here."

Ugh, why won't she drop it?

"Things just kind of fizzled," I say.

"Well then you should definitely call her."

"And why would you say that?"

Brenna shrugs. "Because, I can read between the girl lines, and she's still totally into you. Maybe you two just weren't in the right space the last time. I mean, what could a dinner hurt?"

I try to say something, but nothing comes out. Because...maybe I should. I mean, it has been a while since I've been out. And it's not like Brenna is going to come flying into my arms anytime soon.

I need to get over her. I need to actually try to move on because just waiting for these feelings to pass isn't working. They aren't going to go away if I'm sitting alone every night on my couch playing Halo.

"Fine, I'll give her a call."

"Great!" Brenna says loudly. Does she not have an internal volume control today?

"Yeah, great," I repeat, trying to make myself believe it.

Brenna passes me another piece of cake. "Oh! I meant to ask you. Are you free to help me move a few boxes next week?"

I give her a confused look. "Didn't we just move you to your apartment? Why are we moving stuff again?"

"Bryce didn't tell you?" Brenna shakes her head as she passes me a piece of what looks like carrot cake. "My apartment and the complex had massive water damage from the storm last week. We've been told to find alternate living arrangements for at least the next month. So I'm staying with Bryce and Lucy. I should be there at least through the wedding. So get ready to see my smiling face every day! I have a feeling that every minute we're not doing something, Lucy will be putting us to work."

Fucking lovely.

Last time Brenna lived with Bryce and Lucy, it was during the season, so I wasn't around much. Now? I have a feeling I'm never going to be able to shake her.

Brenna goes back to trying cake while I try to decide whether texting Jessica back is something I really want to do.

Maybe Brenna is right. Maybe this time will be different. Maybe this time we'll hit it off, and I'll look back to this phase of my life as just that: the Brenna phase.

I guess there's only one way to find out.

8

______

BRENNA

"OH, BRYCE! YES...YES! RIGHT THERE!"

"Fuck, Lucy! You feel so fucking good."

"I'm going to...ahhh!"

I take the pillow and bring it back over my head. At the minimum, it will muffle the sounds of my best friend and *my brother* having sex. At the worst it will suffocate me. I don't hate that option right now.

It has been four nights of this. I didn't know people did it *every* night. I mean, I knew they were very active...and loud. But this has been on a whole new level. This morning, after Lucy's screams woke me up in the middle of the night from a melatonin-driven slumber, I asked her, as nonchalantly as I could, generally how active she and my brother are. Because I don't remember it being this bad when I lived with them a few months back.

The difference? Bryce was in the middle of the season. Many nights, he was either tired or on the road.

But now that we're in the middle of the off season, and the two love birds are in pre-wedding bliss? It's like living with humping bunnies.

I've tried everything. Headphones worked, but they were so uncomfortable I couldn't sleep. I tried drugs, hoping they would knock me out. They did, but not enough. I even tried moving from the bedroom I was staying in that shared a wall with them to the living room, hoping a little distance would help. It didn't. My future sister-in-law is quite the screamer.

It has gotten so bad that I fell asleep during my planning period today at school. And worse? The kids didn't wake me up when they came into the room. I slept for the first twenty minutes of class before someone dropped a book that shot me straight up out of my chair. The kids thought it was hilarious. When I asked them to be cool about it, somehow they conned me into bringing them pizza on Friday for their silence.

Middle schoolers are ruthless.

"Bryce! Again? Oh! *Oh!!!*"

I sit straight up on the couch once I realize that tonight is going to be a multi-round performance.

"I can't do this anymore," I say to myself, gathering my phone, pillow, and blanket. "Nope. Fuck this shit. I'm out."

Without a second thought, I leave Bryce's penthouse condo and take the elevator down three floors. It might be one-thirty in the morning, and it might be bold to think that Cole won't have company over, or if he's even home or awake, but I don't care. I can't. I'm at my wits' end, and if I have to hear one more Lucy orgasm, I might rip my ears off.

I pound on the door, which I know is rude for the middle of the night. Luckily, he answers it rather quickly.

"Brenna? What are you doing here?"

Cole barely has the door open as I push my way inside. "I'm getting away from the sex noises. My brother is a moaner. Lucy is a screamer. I can't unhear that. I'm sleeping on your couch."

"Wait. You're what?"

I drop my things on his sectional and turn to look at him, something I neglected to do when I barged in here. He was clearly in bed. If his gravelly voice and confusion didn't give that away, the fact that he's only in a pair of boxer briefs right now confirms it.

Holy hell. Cole is big...everywhere. I mean, I've known the man my whole life, and he's always been the biggest person I know. You knew the kid was going to be a professional offensive lineman when he was five-foot-five and a hundred and twenty pounds at ten years old.

But seeing Cole like this? I have to force a swallow and make myself not look at his arms. Or his chest that begs to be used for a pillow. Or any other part of him that is more on display than normal. I believe I read last year that he's over six foot and three hundred pounds. The man is big, burly, and towers over me and my five-foot-four self. Add in the adorable glasses that I didn't know he wore and his look of confusion, and I kind of want to wrap my arms around him and give him a big hug. And if I get lost in those big arms as they are holding me, then so be it.

Shit. Where did that come from? Lack of sleep. Has to be the lack of sleep.

"Hello? Earth to Brenna? Want to explain again what you're doing here?"

I shake my head; I hope I wasn't staring with my mouth open. "You know that I've been staying at Bryce's."

He huffs. "Yeah, I vaguely remember something about that."

I don't know why he said it like that, but I'm too tired to care. "Well, apparently my brother's off season cardio workout is the *horizontal* kind. I can't take it anymore. I haven't slept all week. Can I please stay here tonight?"

I know I barged in here without warning, but Cole isn't saying anything. I really didn't think it was that big of a request. He has a couch that isn't being used. I'd like to use it. But he isn't saying anything. Instead, he's just staring at me. And not because he's confused at my request. It's like he can't take his eyes off me.

"Cole? Can I stay?"

"Is that my shirt?"

I look down, a little thrown by his question. "Yeah, I guess it is."

"You're wearing my shirt?"

I suddenly feel very…conspicuous. I'm also now realizing that I don't have a bra on. And Cole's shirt is white. And very comfortable.

Which is why I'm wearing it. No other reason. Not that it still vaguely smells like him. Just the comfort.

"Yeah," I say, quickly crossing my arms over my chest. "It's comfortable."

"That's… I'm glad," he says. "That it's comfortable, I mean."

Neither of us say anything for I don't know how long. Which is bad, because that gives me a chance to look at Cole again. Why does he look so good right now? It's not like I ever thought Cole was ugly; I guess I just haven't really looked at him in a long time. He has a strong jawline, but because of his size, there's a little roundness to it. His blue eyes are behind glasses, but for some reason, I'm seeing them as clear as ever. Then there is his body, which is just big. *Everywhere.*

Shit. Stop, stop, stop. This is a consequence of my lack of sleep. That's it. I've never been this sleep deprived, and that's the only sensible answer. The only one I can accept.

I also need to get this conversation back on track, or I'm going to start picturing him without the boxer briefs.

"So is it okay?" I ask.

"Okay what?"

"Okay if I sleep here?"

He gives his head a shake. "Yeah. Of course."

I turn to make my way to his couch, which right now looks like the best bed I've ever slept on. I lean down to situate my blanket and pillow, only to realize Cole has moved right next to me.

"You can go back to bed," I say. "I'm sorry I woke you, but thank you. Thank you so much. You're a lifesaver."

"Are you sure you're okay?" he asks. "Why don't you take my bed? I can sleep out here."

"No," I say, even though memories of his soft sheets and fluffy blankets start dancing in my head. "This is plenty. I don't want to put you out any more than I already am."

"Are you sure? I don't mind. It might make up for the nights of sleeplessness."

This man… God, how is he still single? Here I am, barging into his place in the middle of the night, and not only does he let me in, but he's willing to give up his bed? Guys like this don't exist anymore. At least, I didn't think they did. Especially ones who look like him.

Stop it. Stop it right now.

I shake my head and reach for his hand. I don't know why I do, but it feels right at this moment. And I'm going to blame my exhaustion for the zing I feel when I give his hand a squeeze. "I'll be just fine out here. But how about this? You let me keep the shirt, and you keep your bed?"

This gets me a smile, one that relaxes me from my head to my toes. "Sounds good. Night, Trouble."

Now it's my turn to smile. "Good night, Cole."

9
___

COLE

GOOD NEWS: Brenna looks like she finally got a good night's sleep.

Bad news: She was the only one in this apartment who did.

I tried. God, I tried. I tossed and turned all night. But every time I closed my eyes, all I saw was Brenna in my shirt. Then I thought what it would be like if she was sitting on me, straddling my legs as I slowly took said shirt off her.

There is something about seeing a woman in your clothes that is the biggest turn on. Add to it her crazy, messy hair and her sleepy blue eyes, and there was no way I was going to be sleeping a wink.

"Good morning," she says over her shoulder as I make my way to the kitchen. She's still in my shirt, which I was prepared for, considering I didn't see her bring a bag last night. What I wasn't prepared for was to see it slowly riding up her legs as she tries, but fails, to reach for something in my cupboards.

"Do you need help?" I ask as I walk into the kitchen.

She doesn't look back at me. Instead, she continues to try to extend her reach because she's a hard-headed woman who has always refused to ask for help. "No. I almost…got it…"

I laugh as I walk behind her, easily grabbing the to-go mug she was reaching for. I really must be tired, because I do this without thinking about the fact that she is trapped between me and the counter. The remnants of her perfume hit my senses and nearly knock me on my ass. I know I've been close to her more than a few times recently, but this feels different. I'm so close that all I'd need to do is lower my head ever so slightly, and I'd be able to place a kiss on her shoulder. So close that if I don't step away soon, she's going to feel every inch of how happy I am to have her here.

"Here you go," I say, handing her the travel mug before taking a step back. "Did you get some sleep?"

"Thankfully, yes," she says. "Do you mind if I get some juice for the road?"

"Not at all," I say as she makes her way to the refrigerator. "You still don't drink coffee?"

She shakes her head. "If there was a week that was going to change that, it would have been this one. But I held out. And I'm going to continue to be strong. Because that's where you come in."

I was about to start making myself some coffee, but I have a feeling I better sit down for this. "What do you mean, this is where I come in?"

Brenna takes a seat next to me at my kitchen island. Her eyes are already pleading. I know that look. The last time she gave it to me was in college when she asked me to go with her to that party and we ended up in a squad car together.

"So, I had an idea. And you absolutely can tell me no."

I don't have a good feeling about this. "Why do I already want to say no?"

"Well, you can. But let me at least ask first," she begins, then pauses to take a deep breath. "My apartment manager called me yesterday. The damage is worse than they thought. They originally said four weeks, but now it's going to be closer to six to eight."

"Okay…"

"And, well, I love my brother and Lucy. You know that. But if I have to listen to them bang one more time it's going to drive me to join a convent."

Oh hell, I think I know where this is going.

"What are you asking, Brenna?"

"I mean, you have a spare bedroom. I know there's not a bed in it, but there could be. Or you have a couch. A really nice couch that's actually bigger than my bed. And I'll pay for groceries. And cook meals. And anything else. Just please, let me stay here so I don't have to go back to the sex den."

I was afraid that was what she was going to ask.

I want to say no. I should say no. I need to say no. No matter how many ways I look at this, saying no is the best thing to do for everyone involved. I told myself I was going to do everything I could to get over these fucking feelings I've had for her. Hell, I even took Brenna's advice and called Jessica. I made a commitment to myself that I was going to get over her. How can I do that if we're living together?

"I don't know, Brenna," I begin, trying to figure out the nicest way to say no without letting her know the real reason she can't stay here. "I just don't think—"

"Please, Cole," she says as she stands and wraps her arms around me. "Please, Cole, I'm begging you. Please let me stay with you."

Ah, fuck me.

"HEY HEY, ROOMIE!"

Brenna sets her purse and bag down, only to go back into the hallway. This time when she comes back, she's rolling in two huge suitcases and another bag over her shoulder.

"How long are you staying for again?" I ask, setting down my game controller.

"Don't judge me. Then again, you should see how much I left behind," she says, dropping her bag before falling down on the couch. "So what did you do today?"

"You're looking at it," I say, nodding to the controller. Wow, I'm getting really good at this lying thing. "Welcome to the off season."

"You don't just play video games all day, do you?"

I shake my head. "No. I work out. Sometimes I have appearances.

Sunday is grocery day. But today was an off day, so I took full advantage. How was your day?"

Brenna tells me about her day, and the pizza she had to buy as hush money for one of her classes. I hate how normal this feels. How we can just slide into conversation like this. I don't want to slide into conversation with her. I want it to be awkward and forced so my brain can rationalize not talking to her. And not doing other things with her.

But no, it has to be smooth. It has to feel as natural as breathing.

This is going to be the worst six to eight weeks of my life.

"So, is it time to figure how all of this is going to work out?" I ask.

Brenna nods. "Yes. If we're going to live together, then we need to be on the same page. And I'm going to say this now, do not go out of your way for me. I'm already so grateful that you said yes."

Everything happened so fast this morning that Brenna and I really didn't get a chance to go over how this is going to work logistically before she had to go to school. In fact, she left so quickly that I almost convinced myself that I had imagined the whole thing.

It wasn't a dream. It was real.

Brenna Donald is moving in with me.

When that hit me earlier today, I knew what I needed to do.

"I can sleep on the couch," she says. "I was more than comfortable last night, and that way you don't have to get a bed for your spare room."

"Well, I wish you would have said something earlier," I say, a smile I can't control growing on my face.

"What did you do?" she says, looking around like something is going to pop out and scare her.

I nod back to the guest room. "Go take a look."

She pops off the couch and nearly sprints back to the bedroom. I'm a few steps behind her when she stops and stares at the guest room, which is now furnished with a brand new bed and dressers.

"Cole..." Her voice is nearly a whisper. "You didn't. No. This is too much."

I shrug. "I needed to furnish it anyway. Now my parents have a place to sleep when they come to visit. It's no big deal."

She turns to look at me, and I think if I look hard enough, I can see tears forming. "It's a huge deal."

She takes two steps before wrapping me in her arms, hugging me with all of her petite might. I smile, hugging her back.

"I'm glad you like it," I say.

"I love it," she says as she slowly pulls away. "Thank you."

We step in the room so she can get a closer look. "Dressers are all yours. And the closet. I only have a few things in there, so consider this your space."

"I don't know what to say," she says, looking around in awe.

"You don't need to say anything. Though, speaking of saying things, have you told Bryce and Lucy?"

She nods. "I did when I went to grab my suitcases. Lucy felt bad. Bryce seemed a little *too* happy. I have a feeling he was putting on a show to make me as uncomfortable as possible."

"Sounds about right."

"Yeah, well, what are brothers for? And speaking of, he did say that if I were staying with anyone, he's glad it's you. Something about protecting family or something."

Well, that makes me feel like a piece of shit. If he only knew what I really thought about Brenna. Or what I was thinking about today when I was buying this bed.

Stop. Stop it now. No more. You're done.

"I'm glad to help," I say, turning to leave the room.

"Cole, wait, there's one more thing."

I turn back to her, noticing that she looks nervous.

"Everything okay?"

"Yeah," she says as she starts twiddling her fingers. "It's just this isn't an easy conversation, but I want to make sure you know that I'm totally cool with it."

I tilt my head, not sure what she's talking about. "What's that?"

"Your dating and sex life. What should I be prepared for?"

If I had a drink, I would have spit it out. Instead, I start choking on saliva because *wow*. I was not expecting that. "Excuse me?"

Brenna shrugs. "You're a grown man. I don't know what kind of life you lead. And I'm just saying that if something happens, just let me know, and I can make myself scarce. I know no girl wants to come home and see another girl on the couch. Or across the hall."

I don't even know what to say. "Don't worry. Nothing like that will happen."

Brenna quirks a brow. "Didn't you set up a date with Jessica?"

Shit, she's right. How did I almost forget about that? Clearly, this is a sign I do need to start getting over Brenna if I forgot about a date I made literally days ago.

"Yeah, that's not until next week," I say. "But don't worry. I won't bring her back here. We're just going to get dinner and drinks."

Brenna wags her eyebrows. "That's how it always starts."

"Are you trying to insinuate that I put out on the first date?"

"Why, Cole Campbell! I was insinuating nothing of the sort," Brenna says with a thick— and fake—Southern accent. "I've heard you are a perfect gentleman when it comes to courtin' the ladies."

"Courtin' the ladies?"

Brenna shrugs. "It just felt right."

"You're crazy, you know that?"

"So I've been told," Brenna says, jumping onto the bed. "But seriously, just give me a heads up if things escalate, and I'll make myself scarce. I'd hate to put a damper on your personal life."

Oh, Brenna.... if you only knew.

10

———

BRENNA

Cole gives me a confused look as he clasps his watch. "Snazzy pants?"

Yup. Snazzy pants. That's what I said. Did I mean to say it? Nope. Have I suddenly become oddly nervous around Cole? Have random things started spewing out of my mouth? Yup.

It started the day after I moved in when he asked me if Italian was okay for dinner. I responded with a five-minute speech about the proper rankings of pasta noodles and why angel hair is supreme.

I don't know why I reacted like that. It was a simple question. Then again, he was in gym shorts, without a shirt, and sweaty from a workout. That sight alone would be enough to make any woman's brain go to mush. Hence, the pasta rant.

Now tonight with *snazzy pants*? That's completely different. He's completely clothed. But he looks just as good as he did the other day. What is it about a man in a dress shirt with the cuffs rolled up that makes a woman want to pull her panties down?

"Well, if you were Lucy, I'd be calling you a 'hot mama' or 'hot piece of ass.'"

Why am I still talking? I just need to stop talking.

He laughs as he sprays on a bit of cologne. Thank goodness he's not asking me to speak right now because I don't know if I could. I'm currently wondering how you feel a smell in your lady parts, because I definitely am.

And it's freaking me out.

I've always had a love-hate relationship with cologne. I'm of the firm belief that you can tell a lot about a man by whatever he wears. One of my first boyfriends, back in high school, used to drown himself in some sort of knock-off of a name brand. I'm sure it would shock no one to learn that he became a fraternity president.

Dexter's might have been the worst I have ever smelled. I want to vomit just thinking about that scent.

Then there's Cole. It's woodsy, but with a sweetness. Kind of like him. He's this big, bad offensive lineman who gets paid millions of dollars to mow down men just as big as he is. But when you get to know him, he's a sweetheart.

A sweetheart who bought me a bed when I asked to move in. Who covered me up with a blanket the other night when I fell asleep on the couch.

Who gets my juice ready in a to-go cup and puts it in the refrigerator the night before so all I need to do is grab it and go in the morning.

I inhale the addicting scent, which takes me back to the morning I woke up in his bed. I might not remember much about that drunken night, but I'll never forget his smell. I was sad when it finally faded from his shirt.

Maybe I can sneak back in here later and give it a little spray. That wouldn't be creepy, right?

"So do you need something or are you just going to stand here and stare at me?" Cole asks.

"I wasn't staring," I say quickly, even though I absolutely was. "I was just wondering if you needed any help for your date tonight. Need any pointers? Where are you taking her?"

Again, why am I still talking? I had an out. I should have taken it. Now I get to hear about Cole's date.

Which I'm not in the least bit jealous about *at all*.

"And why would I ask you?" Cole says, walking past me toward the living room. "Aren't you the same person who just a few short weeks ago declared from the rooftops that you were done dating? Doesn't exactly strike me as a person I'd want to take dating advice from."

Well, I guess I'm in it now. Might as well go with it.

"See! That's where you're wrong," I say as I follow him out to the living room.

Cole sits down and gives me a questioning look as he slips on one of his shoes. "Okay, now I'm intrigued."

I take a seat on the part of the sectional that I quickly claimed as mine. "I have been on so many bad dates that I can identify a good date in the blink of an eye. Also, I know all the red flags, so I can spot those a mile away."

He thinks about that, slipping on his other shoe. "Somehow, that actually makes sense."

"I'm not just a pretty face," I say, sitting back. "So, tell me, what's on the agenda tonight?"

"We're going to go to dinner at the new sushi place in The Gulch. Then I thought maybe we'd get a few drinks."

I nod. "Sounds safe enough. Cool area to spend an evening. Appropriate first date protocol. Or, I guess this would be a second first date?"

He shrugs, standing up from the chair. "I remember she said before that she liked sushi, so I thought she'd enjoy that."

Of course Cole would remember a detail like that. "Bonus points, Campbell."

"Thanks. I forgot my wallet in my room. I'm going to go grab that and then head out."

I wave him away. "You do you! I'm just going to sit here and boot up my binge for the night while I wait on the pizza to be delivered."

"Are you watching another one of those crazy-ass Turkish soap operas?"

"Don't hate!" I yell. "And don't think I didn't notice that you were trying to sneak peeks of it last night..."

"I plead the fifth."

I laugh as I fire up the show and get situated for a night of leisure on the couch. Usually I don't think to do that, but I'm not going to have Cole here to bring me my knitting when I forget it in my room and don't feel like getting up.

He's really too sweet.

I knew living with Cole would be a breeze, but I didn't realize how quickly we'd fall into a routine. I know I told him I'd do the cooking, but he hasn't held me to it. Sometimes I'll make dinner, sometimes he does. After we eat, I sit on the couch and grade papers while he plays his video games or watches TV. Occasionally we've done wedding projects while talking about anything and everything. And despite his denial, he has watched my Turkish soap operas. In return, I've watched more hours of ESPN than I can count. He hasn't asked me how to knit yet, but I'm waiting for the day. Each night when I break out my yarn, I feel him taking more and more of an interest.

If I could just control my spewing of random words or rankings of pasta, I'd say this setup was pretty much perfect.

The apartment buzzer alerting us that someone is downstairs scares me for a second, but then I remember I ordered a pizza. I spring from my spot on the couch and hit the enter button without even asking who it is. I open the door before walking over to the table to grab my tip money for the delivery person. When I come back, I don't see anyone with a pizza. Instead, I'm staring at a redhead who looks quite confused.

"Can I help you?" I ask.

"Is Cole here?"

"Jessica?" Cole says from a few feet behind me. "What are you doing here?"

I look back and forth a few times before stepping out of the way so *Jessica* can enter the apartment, which she does without a formal invitation.

Red flag number one.

Also, why does she look familiar?

"I know we said we would meet at the restaurant, but I figured since I had to drive past your building to get there, I'd just come here first. Though I didn't know you had…company."

And this is why I said I would make myself scarce if Cole was dating. I know how this has to look to her. Then again, he would have had to know said company was coming.

Red flag number two.

"Hi, I'm Brenna," I say, extending my hand for a shake. She just stands there so I quickly pull my hand away. "I'm staying here with Cole for a few weeks. In the spare bedroom. My brother is one of his teammates. He lives upstairs. He and his fiancée have a lot of sex, so I'm staying here. But don't worry, there is no sex happening here. Because Cole and I have known each other for years. Since we were kids. Nothing but friendship in this apartment!"

I really just need to not talk. At least this time it wasn't Cole who threw me for a loop.

No, it was Jessica, who is stunningly gorgeous. She has long, red hair that flows over her toned shoulders in perfect waves. She's wearing a fitted red dress that shows every one of her perfect curves. And *wow*. I usually don't look straight at a woman's breasts, but it's kind of hard not to with Jessica. Especially in that dress. I almost want to ask if they are going to pop out, but even I know better.

To take my eyes away from the girls, I quickly look to her shoes. If I put those on, I'd probably fall over like a baby giraffe. But on her? She looks like a runway model. She's giving me vibes of that hot secretary from "Mad Men" who made every straight woman in the world question their sexuality.

Judging by the look she's giving me, pin-up model Jessica isn't a fan of my ramble. Or me. Maybe both. Without saying another word to me, she takes another step into the apartment, reaching out her hand for Cole.

"Can we go? I can't wait to try that new place. Should we just take one car since I'm here?"

Oh, I know this trick. Usually it's the guy trying to pull it so that way he can be in control of when the date stops and starts. Ballsy move for Jessica. But hey, men these days like a strong woman who knows what she wants. And clearly Jessica knows what she wants.

Maybe Cole is into that? I honestly have no clue what he's into. But the longer she's here, the more I hope he isn't it.

"See you later," Cole says as he leads her out the door.

"Have a nice time!"

I tried to genuinely mean that one. It's the polite thing to say. And I'm not a mean person. I do hope they have a nice time.

Even if the thought of them kissing is making my skin crawl.

***

"BRENNA? WHAT ARE YOU—?"

I don't wait for an invitation. Just call me Jessica. I barge right into her and Bryce's penthouse apartment.

Because I can. I'm the sister. And the best friend. And the woman who is currently experiencing a *very* unexpected emotion.

"Just seeing what my bestie and my brother are doing. No plans? It's Friday night!" I take a seat on the couch as Bryce appears in the living room. "Want to watch a movie? I have pizza downstairs. I can bring it up."

"I think that is my cue to head out," Bryce says, placing a kiss on Lucy's forehead. "You two girls have a fun night. Or whatever."

Bryce exits the penthouse, and Lucy takes a seat next to me.

"Where's Bryce going?"

"The rings are ready, and he is insisting on picking them up to make sure they are exactly what he asked for," Lucy says. "If there is one aspect of the wedding he has taken an interest in, it's the rings. So I've let him have it. It's one less thing for me to worry about, and I'm sure if I saw the price tag, I'd panic. It's better this way."

"Well, good for Bryce. And good for me that you could use some company!"

Lucy quirks a brow at me. "What's the deal? You haven't been up here since you moved in with Cole. What gives?"

I pick up the remote, suddenly very focused on finding something to watch. "He has a date tonight."

Lucy rips the controller out of my hand and turns the television off. "He has a what? With who? How can you be okay with this? I'm not okay with this!"

Not the reaction I was expecting. "Her name is Jessica. They apparently dated last year. She texted him a few weeks ago, and he agreed to give it another shot. And what do you mean *how could I let this happen?* I encouraged it. I told him it would be good for him. You know, get out of the house and all that."

"I can't believe it," Lucy says, standing up and starting to pace.

"What can't you believe? He's a good guy. A great guy, actually. If there is anyone in this world who shouldn't be single, it's Cole. He's made of boyfriend material. This is a good thing. And! And, she looks like Jessica Rabbit's twin. Well, her name is Jessica. Her twin probably wouldn't be named Jessica. So I guess she looks like Jessica Rabbit. I mean, good for Cole, am I right? Did I just say a lot of words?"

Lucy just stares at me.

"What?" I mean for it to sound normal, but for some reason it reaches a high pitch I'm not familiar with. "I'm happy for him. He's been grumpy lately. Nothing gets a man out of a grump funk than some good ol' fashioned hanky panky. And if her actions so far are saying anything, Cole can have as much of the hanky and the panky as he wants tonight."

I want to mean the words I just said, but the more I talk, the more I taste the bile in my mouth. And why is my stomach all twisty? Probably because the thought of Cole having sex is gross. You know, since he's basically my brother.

My hot brother with big arms who smells like sex. Okay, maybe I should stop thinking of him as my brother...

Lucy is now sitting back with her arms crossed. She gives me the exact look my mother used to give me when I did or said something stupid. "Seriously?"

"What? Just what? I know you want to say something, so say it."

"Ok, I'll say it. I think you came up here to vent about Cole being out on a date because it bothers you more than you want to admit."

"Pshh," I say, waving my hand in the air as my stomach simultaneously drops from her words. "I'm fine with Cole on a date. Didn't you hear the part where I pushed him to do this? Why would I do that if I cared if he was out with another woman?"

Wow, if I really listened, that almost sounded believable.

"Because," Lucy says. "You haven't realized you like him. Or you're just realizing it, and it's hitting you like a ton of bricks."

I forgot how smart my future sister-in-law is. And how she knows me better than anyone.

Because she's right: I'm crazy jealous because I think I like him, but I'm not sure if I like him, but I'm pretty sure I like him... but I can't like him.

"What makes you say that?" I say unconvincingly.

"Because every time I bring Cole and you up in the sense of a relationship, you get super defensive. Perhaps a little *too* defensive."

Ugh, I need another friend who knows me less. I also need to make her believe I'm fine with this. Because if I can convince her, then maybe these pesky feelings will go away.

Because I can't like Cole. I really, really can't.

"Okay Miss I Know Brenna So Well," I begin. "What can I do to make you believe that I'm completely fine with Cole being on a date?"

Lucy gets a devilish smile on her face. "Okay, I'm going to ask you a series of Cole-related questions, and if you say no to all, I will drop this forever. Hell, I'll go out with whoever this chick is and invite her to my wedding."

"You have yourself a deal."

"Okay, question number one—and remember, you have to be honest," Lucy says, taking a second to ponder whatever bullshit question she's going to throw at me. "Have you given Cole the arm test in the last three months?"

Maybe this quiz isn't as easy as I thought. "Yes, but in my defense, every guy I meet gets that test."

"Fine, but did he pass?"

I shake my head. "Again, not fair. You've seen his arms. They are tree trunks. Next."

Okay. I'm fine. If that's the only question she forces a yes out of me for, then I'm fine.

"Question number two: At any point tonight when thinking of Cole out with Jessica, did you feel the urge to punch a wall?"

"No," I say with certainty. I didn't want to punch a wall. I wanted to puke and scream into a pillow. Totally different.

Lucy eyes me like she's trying to tell if I'm bullshitting or not. "Okay, question three: Pretending he's not where he is at this physical moment, if Cole asked you out on an official date, would you say yes?"

I shake my head, take a big swallow, and say the biggest lie of my life.

"No."

Fuck, that physically hurt to say. Because if Cole were not who he was, I'd go out with him in a heartbeat. I think we would have a nice time. We'd laugh over dinner. Maybe people-watch at the bar, which always provides good entertainment, especially in Nashville. Or maybe the date would be a little simpler. Maybe we'd go mini-golfing and get ice cream. Maybe he'd come up behind me and pretend to show me how to putt. Maybe we'd hold hands as we walked, just talking about whatever comes up.

Now I really want to puke, because all of those sound amazing. And not just the activities; also the man I pictured doing them with.

My roommate. My brother's best friend.

"You said no, so I'm going to keep my word," Lucy says. "But I'm going to protest that I don't think you meant that last one."

I don't say anything, opting instead to just lie down with my head in her lap. "Do you mind if I stay here tonight? I don't want to be there, you know, just in case."

"Of course." Lucy gives me a little squeeze before putting a blanket over me. "And just because I know you're a liar and you're finally starting to realize that you're actually crazy about the guy, I'll make sure Bryce and I don't have sex tonight."

At some point I fell asleep, but I woke up at least three times in the night. No, not because of Bryce and Lucy. She kept her word. No, I couldn't sleep because of the mental movie playing in my mind. It was of me the next morning, making my way back downstairs, only to open the door and see Jessica in one of Cole's shirts. She's making him breakfast and wearing a smile a woman only wears after the best sex of her life.

Fuck...this is bad. So bad. Because Lucy is one-thousand-percent right— I'm up to my eyeballs crazy about Cole. And I have no idea what I'm going to do about it.

11

———

COLE

GROWING UP, Bryce and I always had this dream that one day we were going to live next door to each other. We'd build houses on a big piece of property, our wives would be best friends, and our kids would grow up closer than family. Yes, I know it sounds like a weird thing for boys to even talk about, but that was our dream. It still is. One of the first things we did when we both got drafted by Nashville was figure out where we would eventually build our houses.

But in all those years, we've never been out on a double date together. Why tonight is the first, I'm not sure, but Lucy was insistent on meeting Jessica. I couldn't tell her no even though I was ninety-nine-percent sure this second attempt with Jessica wasn't going to work out. We've been out nearly every night since our first date, and with each date, I become more and more sure she's not it for me.

She's…a lot. I don't mind a woman being what society would call high maintenance, but Jessica takes it to another level. I asked her the other night if she wanted to grab a late-night bite, and she said yes, but she needed two hours to get ready. It was already nine o'clock, so I told her we'd take a raincheck. I mean, we were going to a diner, not the Four Seasons.

Then there is her Instagram. She's obsessed with it. If she's not posting on it, she's talking about it. On our first date, she made me take no less than a hundred pictures of her standing outside the restaurant.

She called me an Instagram Boyfriend in Training.

I didn't like the sound of that whatsoever.

But I'm trying to keep an open mind. Maybe this is just how women are, and I'm being too harsh. So I agreed to the double date, hoping it would help me see if this was a me thing or not.

But now we're sitting across the table from Bryce and Lucy, and the more Jessica talks, the more sure I am that this isn't a me thing. At all.

"So Jessica, how did you and our boy meet?" Bryce asks. "If it's an embarrassing story, I won't hold it against you. Him? Probably."

"Oh it's nothing like that," she says, flipping her red hair over her shoulder. Something I found sexy at first, but now that I know she does it incessantly, the act has lost its luster. "We actually met at the grocery store. I don't know if you knew this, but Cole goes to the grocery store at the same time every week. And, crazy enough, so do I! I kept seeing him over and over at the deli, and one day I just pulled up my big girl pants and went over and said hi. The rest is history. This is, of course, after I drooled over him for months during football season. I had a bit of a crush."

She leans into me, wrapping her arms around my bicep as she leans her head on my shoulder. She's acting like she just retold the plot to the greatest love story ever told. What she doesn't know is that after I broke up with her last year, I had to change grocery stores. Which sucked. I failed to remember that when I gave this a second chance.

"That's so nice," Lucy says. "It's crazy where people meet each other nowadays."

"Tell me about it," Jessica says. "I hear about different places all the time. I'm the general manager at Eva's Bridal. You should just hear the stories we learn about how couples meet."

Lucy's eyes go wide. "You work at Eva's? That's where I got my dress!"

"What a small world!" Jessica says, giving the table a slap for extra measure.

"It is," Lucy says. "I was just in there a few weeks ago. I can't believe I found my dress on the first shopping trip. And thank goodness, because the wedding is next week and I needed a miracle."

"And it is beautiful on you," Jessica says. "That lace! My gosh, it's going to be gorgeous. Bryce, just wait until you see her. She's going to blow your socks off."

This all gets three very confused looks shot her way.

"How would you know that?" Lucy asks. And good, because I was wondering that too.

"Oh…well…I was at the salon during your appointment, actually. I was with another client. I happened to sneak a peek. I mean, how could I forget a bride as beautiful as you?"

We let it go, because it does make sense. I look across the table and can tell that Lucy's brain is working overtime. Something isn't sitting right. Bryce teases her that he can sometimes see the hamster wheel spinning in her brain. I now know what he means.

"I can't wait to see it," Bryce says, cutting the awkward silence. "But no more wedding talk. It's been a crazy month getting ready, and tonight is the first night we've taken a break from it."

"Well, anything I can do to be of help, please let me know," Jessica says. "I mean, it *is* kind of my thing. So anything I can do, even the day of, I'd be happy to help. I mean, since I'll be there anyway, I might as well make myself useful!"

The awkward silence returns as her last words hang in the air. Now I'm the one with the hamster wheel going. Did I invite her to the wedding? I don't think I did. I have a pretty good memory, and I feel like I would remember that. And if I did, then I didn't tell Lucy, because that's the look she's giving me right now.

"Who needs refills? Everyone? Great!" Lucy says, standing up from her stool at our high-top table. "Cole, how about you help me carry?"

Lucy gives me a look that screams "follow me now" so I do as I'm nonverbally told. But not before Jessica looks up at me, silently asking me to give her a kiss.

I do, but only because I'm scared that if I don't, I'll accidentally forget I proposed to her.

"So, Jessica," Lucy begins as we wait for a bartender. "She's…"

"A lot?"

"That's one way of putting it." Lucy sits on the barstool, so I do the same. Though she has always been Bryce's girl, I've always felt a connection with her. Maybe because we are the only two people in the world who get the fucked-up mind and world that is Bryce Donald, we share some sort of connection ourselves. "Now, I'm going to say this, and I'm being completely honest. If you want to bring her as your date, that's fine. I'm not mad. You can bring whoever you want and I'll completely support you, but—"

I cut her off. "Lucy, I didn't invite her. In fact, I never even mentioned when it was. And she never told me that she saw you in the store. All I said was that my best friends were getting married, and I was the best man. I don't even think I mentioned your names."

"Oh," Lucy says as she puts back on her thinking face. "Well, I mean, the engagement has been on social media. She seems like an Instagram type of girl."

"Oh she is." I look back at the table, and she's proving my point for me, turning her phone six different ways as she takes a selfie. Bryce is watching with a look of incredulity. I might laugh if I didn't have to go back to the table and sit with her.

"Well maybe she saw it there?" Lucy says. "And if she did see us at the bridal store, then she might have put everything together."

"Isn't that kind of…" I trail off, knowing what word I want to use but I'm not sure if it's the right context, or a bit too harsh.

"Stalkerish? Yes. It's screaming stalker vibes."

"That's what I thought."

"Actually," I say as the lightbulb all of a sudden turns on in my brain. "She texted me the day after the dress fitting."

"She did?" Lucy asks. "How do you remember that?"

"Because I was telling Brenna about her the day of the cake testing, which was the day after you guys went dress shopping. Do you think she messaged me out of the blue because she saw you at the store?"

"Would she know who I am?"

I nod. "Oh yeah. She's a huge Fury fan. Between that and her Instagram obsession, she would absolutely recognize you if she saw you in public."

"Do you think she messaged you because she saw me and was like, 'Hey, I miss that guy?'"

I shrug. "I have no idea. I'm starting to think there's a lot about Jessica that I don't know, and I'm not sure if I want to."

"Well then you have a choice to make," Lucy says. "She obviously thinks she's coming to the wedding. You have to either suck it up and bring her, or somehow tell her that she's not coming."

I let out a groan because both of those options sound horrible. Then I look back to the table where she is still in selfie mode. I can only imagine how many pictures she'd make me take at the wedding.

I look back to Lucy, who has just put in our drink orders. "Can we try and not bring it up when we go back to the table? I'll talk to her about it in private tonight."

Lucy nods. "I can do that."

"Thanks," I say. "Also, can I ask you something?"

"Of course," she says, turning more to face me. "I know you're technically Bryce's friend. Bros before hoes and all that stuff. But I want you to know that I consider you one of my best friends, and if there's anything you need or want to tell me, or just get off your chest, I'm here for you. And your secret, whatever it may be, will be safe with me."

Shit. Does she know? No. She can't. But the way she's looking at me, the way her eyes are trying to say something, makes me worry she knows.

But that's not what I need to talk to her about. At least, not yet.

"So the reason I wanted you guys to come out tonight was for you to give me your opinion on Jessica."

"My opinion?"

"Yes, your opinion." I reach over and take the beer the bartender just put down and take a pull. "I don't date much. And if I'm going to settle down, I want someone that will fit in with us. It's kind of a must. And I…I don't think she is. But I was worried I wasn't giving her a fair chance. I just need to know if you think my instincts are correct—that she's just not it."

Lucy places her hand on top of mine and gives it a few pats.

"I'm going to ask you three questions, and if you answer yes to any of them, I say stick it out. If not, then I think you know what you need to do."

I nod. "All right, shoot."

"One: is she the first thing you think of when you wake up in the morning?"

I'm silent, which we both know is a big old no.

"All right then. Now, number two: when she invited herself to my wedding, were you excited?"

Again silence. Again a no. Actually, that response was more under the shocked and appalled category.

"And last but not least: is Jessica the only woman you've thought about in a romantic way since you two started seeing each other?"

I'm silent again, and judging by the look Lucy's giving me right now, she knows exactly why. And exactly who.

Damn, she knows.

"I think you know your answer," Lucy says. "And, I know it's none of my business, and I'm not even sure if I'm on the right track here, but I think I am. If that woman you thought about happened to be the sister of a certain best friend, don't give up. In fact, I'd say it's a great time to shoot a shot."

My eyes go wide. "Really? What makes you say that?"

Lucy just smiles. "Best friend intuition. Now, let's get back to the table. And please, don't break up with Jessica now. I have a feeling she'd cause a scene, and I don't have the energy for that tonight."

12

BRENNA

"BRENNA? YOU HOME?"

Cole's voice almost makes me inhale the mask I'm currently putting on my face.

"Cole? What are you doing here?"

"Well, I do live here," he says, his voice getting closer. "I wanted to see… What are you doing?"

I turn to face him, my face covered in green slime. "A face mask."

He lets out a laugh, even though I can see he's trying to not laugh at me. "A face mask?"

"Yes!" I defend, crossing my arms. "The wedding is this weekend. I thought I'd pamper myself a bit and do a facemask. You know, remove all of those toxins and stuff."

Cole lifts an eyebrow. "Toxins and stuff?"

"Yes. Toxins and stuff." I let out a breath and tighten my robe a bit. Because yes, I just realized I'm only in a robe right now. And apparently still saying random things in his presence.

"What are you doing home? No hot date with your girlfriend tonight?"

I don't know why I'm bringing it up because the last thing I want to hear about is Cole and Jessica and their perfect dinner dates.

Not that I've been tracking their dates. It's just a little hard when she posts every single thing they do on Instagram.

Not that I'm following her. I'm not.

Fine. I am because I have a serious problem. I'm at least doing it under a fake account I created. So I'm not technically spying on them. Becky Cane is. Hey, the name worked on my fake ID in college, might as well bring her back for a second round.

"She's not my girlfriend. She might have been, but she's not anymore," Cole says. "Anyway, I'm ordering Chinese food and going to watch that new dragon show that I'm seeing everywhere. Want to join me?"

I blink a few times, because did I just hear what I think I just heard? They broke up? When did this happen? How did this happen? There is so much information I need to know. Actually, now that I think about it, this does now explain why Jessica posted a black and white profile selfie captioned by Taylor Swift lyrics.

"Brenna?"

"Yeah?" I say quickly, coming back to the present.

"What do you want to eat?"

"Um, yeah, lo mein and dumplings. Oh! And get some sweet and sour chicken. And maybe some crab Rangoon, but only if you'll help me eat it."

"That it? Maybe also a number five just in case?"

I open my mouth to protest before I realize Cole is teasing. His smile is small, but it's making me feel some big things.

"I think I'll be good," I say.

"All right, I'll go put in the order," he says. "Take your time here. I'd hate to interrupt the ridding of toxins and stuff."

"Shut up," I say as I close the door. All I hear is his laughter as he walks away from the bathroom.

Laughter I've missed hearing.

And not just the laughter, but him. I've missed him. So much.

Since he and Jessica reconnected, we've barely seen each other, mostly because I've made myself scarce. Now that I've quit denying the little voice in my head that always whispered about my feelings for him, I can't be in the same room with him without babbling like a lunatic.

So I figured out how I could limit my time as best as possible. I started going to school early to avoid any morning run-ins with him. There was a two-hour window between when I would get home and when Jessica would drag him off somewhere. I started spending that time using the apartment complex's gym.

Okay, fine. I would go to the gym and pretend to use the elliptical until he left. That's when I head back upstairs to start my nightly cycle of depression, knowing that I'm in his place, in his space, but he's with her.

The only comfort I had was that she never spent the night. And as far as I know, he never spent the night with her.

But now if they're not together, does this mean things will go back to normal?

I can answer my own question: no. Because pre-Jessica, I still believed that Cole was just my friend. Now I don't know how to act around him because when I see him, I want to climb him like a tree.

I wash the mask off my face and head back to my room. Pre-Jessica, I wouldn't have given two thoughts about what to wear for a quiet night in with Cole. Hell, most of the time it would have been a ratty T-shirt and a pair of oversized sweatpants. Do I wear that now so it seems like nothing has changed? Do I put on cute clothes? Do I put makeup back on? Would he notice one way or the other?

God, this sucks.

I wish I could text Lucy about this. But I can't. For one, I haven't admitted to her that she's right. Yes, she knows she is, but I'm not ready for the full "I told you so" speech. Also, it's the night before rehearsal dinner, and she and Bryce are having a quiet night, just the two of them.

Deciding to not overthink it, I grab a clean T-shirt and a pair of leggings then head back to the bathroom, where I give my hair a fluff and put on a minimal amount of makeup.

"Breathe," I quietly say to myself in the mirror. "It's just Cole. You've known him forever. Nothing is weird. Be natural. Be cool."

I let myself take one more deep breath before I head to the living room.

"Just in time," he says as he unpacks the unholy amount of Chinese food we ordered. "You get the drinks. I'll fire up the television."

Neither of us say anything for the first half hour of the show. I don't know why he isn't talking. Me? I'm trying to figure out what they're saying in their dragon language.

I'm also trying to ignore how freaking good Cole smells.

Do I try and talk? What would I say? I've never questioned talking to Cole about anything, and now all of a sudden I'm at a loss for words.

So I continue to not say anything. Instead, I lean down to grab an egg roll and accidentally bump arms with Cole, who is doing the same thing.

"Sorry," we both say at the same time, followed by awkward laughter.

"Is this weird?" I ask, because please let it not just be me.

He nods. "A little. When did it get weird between us?"

There are two answers to this question. I'm going to give just one. "I have a feeling it started about the same time I suggested you set up a date with Jessica."

Cole lets out a sigh. "Well that isn't going to be a problem anymore," he says.

"So what happened between you two?" I ask nonchalantly.

Cole grabs the remote and presses pause. "She's a nice girl. And she means well. But she isn't for me. She's a bit… intense. About a lot of things. She also kind of invited herself to Bryce and Lucy's wedding without asking me. That was the final straw."

My jaw drops. "No she didn't!"

He laughs. "She did. In front of Bryce and Lucy. When I asked her about it later that night, she said she just assumed I'd be taking her since we were an official couple and that she didn't know why it was a big deal."

"Oh…"

"Yeah. I had been thinking about ending things, but I didn't know if I was being too quick to judge. But that kind of sent me over the edge."

"I'm sorry," I say. "How'd she take it?"

Cole takes out his phone and tosses it to me. "You tell me."

I open up his text messages and holy shit… Jessica is not doing okay. And I'm talking more than playing sad song lyrics and eating ice cream. If I were Cole, I'd be worried about his tires.

> Jessica: So that's it? We're done? Just like that?
>
> Jessica: I can't believe you are breaking up with me. You're overreacting about the wedding thing. Let me explain.
>
> Jessica: I just wanted to go to the wedding with you. Don't you know how great for my career it would be if I was at their wedding? I even bought a new dress because I thought you'd like it and you'd finally want to be with me. Why don't you want to take me? Was I not good enough for you? I love you Cole! Why don't you love me?

"Wow. Love? Cole, I'm like, kind of worried about her," I say.

He looks over to see where I'm at. "Yes, at that point I did feel bad. But keep reading. The crazy is about to come out."

> Jessica: Do you know where I was last week when I couldn't see you? I was getting a tattoo. With your initials. It was going to be a surprise…

Oh shit…

> Jessica: Is there someone else? That's it. It's that roommate isn't it? I knew from the second I walked into your place she was more than what she said she was.

"Whoa! What did I do?"

Cole laughs. "Apparently you existed."

> Jessica: I mean, she's not even that pretty. And she's short. Does she even have a body underneath those T-shirts and sweatpants? I guarantee she doesn't have these.

"My eyes!" I yell as I toss the phone back to Cole. I suspected that Jessica's boobs were probably stellar compared to my barely B cups. But I really didn't need to see them for confirmation.

"Oh shit," Cole says. "I meant to delete that."

"Sure you did," I say, reaching for my dumplings. "Well, I'm sorry that it didn't work out. And, you know, for existing. But I think you dodged a bullet. She doesn't sound like a very nice person."

There. That was very diplomatic of me. Because what I wanted to say was, "Bitch, I'll fucking fight you in my sweatpants and your fake tits and red weave won't be able to help you."

But I didn't. I was nice. So two points for me.

"She definitely had two sides to her," Cole says. "Oh, and I don't agree with her."

"About what?"

"I happen to love your sweatpants."

Well, shit. I don't know if it's because it's coming from Cole, or I'm just not used to flattery, but that is the nicest and sexiest thing any man has ever said to me.

"Thanks," I say, suddenly feeling shy.

"You're welcome," he says. "I'm just glad I got out before it went any further. I can only imagine what she would have been like in the season."

"Likely accusing you of having different women in each city on the schedule."

"Or showing up at every hotel."

"You have a point. Though you can't say the woman wasn't head over heels for you."

Cole shakes his head. "True. Too bad she didn't check many of the boxes."

Well, now I'm intrigued. And also likely building myself up for heartache. But I don't see another time when this door will be open. So here goes literally *everything*.

"What are your boxes?"

Cole takes one of his hands and rakes it through his hair. "You want to know my boxes?"

"I do," I say, my courage amping up. "What would make Cole Campbell want to take a girl to his best friend's wedding?"

This makes him smile. "Well, she'd have to be smart. Funny. Someone not afraid to take a risk here and there. Someone who likes to go out but also embraces a night in on the couch. Someone who isn't afraid to speak her mind but also knows when to stop and listen to people. And she'd have to love football. Maybe a former cheerleader so she knows the basics of the game."

I nod, liking where this is going. "That's a good start."

"She'd have to get along with my family and friends. I can't imagine being with someone who doesn't fit seamlessly into my life. Oh, and she has to like kids."

I'm trying not to get my hopes up that he's talking about me, but I can't ignore the way his gaze is fixed on me as he's saying these words. His eyes are a piercing blue, and when they are looking at you, you feel like you're the only person in the world. And holy shit are they looking at me right now. I'm pretty sure a circus could be going on behind me and he wouldn't notice.

I swallow the growing lump in my throat. "Anything else?"

Cole inches closer to me and just with that little movement, I swear the temperature rises twenty degrees. His fingers are playing with a loose strand of my hair, and I'm ready to melt into a puddle on the ground.

"I'd love for her to have brown hair. Maybe be about a foot shorter than me so I could always help her reach stuff in the cabinets."

I lean into his hand, aching to feel his touch. "It's hard being short."

He smiles. "I'm sure it is. Oh, and she'd have to have the most beautiful blue eyes I've ever seen."

I bite my lip, aching to know what he's going to say or do next. "I'm a fan of blue eyes too."

Cole cuts the space between us down to nothing. His hand that was once just barely touching me is now fully holding onto my head, ready to bring me into him at any moment. His other hand is carefully tracing the line of my jaw. Up and down. Methodically. Like he's trying to memorize me.

"Brenna," he begins, letting his one hand drop down to hold mine. "Jessica was right about one thing." "Yeah?"

"You are more than just my friend. You're more than my temporary roommate. You're… well, I want you to be… what I'm trying to say is…"

I've always lived by the motto that if I want something, I have to go after it. Take it. I think that a person should do everything in their power to manifest their desire into existence. Because if they don't do it, no one else will.

So that's what I do. I put my hands on each side of Cole's face, and I kiss him. I kiss him because I know words can sometimes be hard. I know sometimes emotions are so big you don't know how to express them.

Plus, he's saying everything I'm thinking. Why not meet him in the middle?

Cole quickly follows my lead, lifting me up with ease so I'm on his lap. Now that I'm here, I never want to be anywhere else.

In all my twenty-five years, I never even had a glimmer of a thought about what kissing Cole would be like. That is, until three weeks ago. Since then it's practically all I've been thinking about.

Would it be weird? I mean, the man has been like a second brother to me my entire life. Or would it be the best thing that has ever happened to me?

Well, now I know. And oh my God, it's the latter.

Our tongues are meeting in a perfect balance of give and take. His lips are soft and perfect as they begin trailing away from my lips and around my neck. And when he gives one last kiss on my forehead, I am melted into a sentimental puddle.

"So," he begins, brushing a hair away from my face with the gentlest of touches. "I don't have a date for the wedding this weekend."

I can't help but smile. "Actually, neither do I."

"Well, then. Would you like to be my date?"

I smile, giving him one more small kiss. "I would absolutely love to."

We share a smile before Cole leans back in. Only this time, he takes me back, pressing me into the couch. Cole is a big guy, and he's doing his best to keep his weight off me as he starts exploring with his mouth, but I want it. It's almost as if I *need* it.

I wrap my leg around his, wanting to feel him closer. He responds. He gently covers me a little more, and I can't help but gently roll my hips into him. His mouth feels too good. His touch feels too tender.

I don't want to rush this, but I also can't say no. And judging how Cole's kisses are becoming harder, I think he feels the same way.

I want to say stop, but how do you say no to the best feeling you've ever felt?

I start to wrap my legs around his body when the sound of his cell phone takes me away from the moment. But not for long, because Cole is kissing my body on top of my clothes, and I'm five seconds away from just telling him to rip them off.

But I don't. Because his phone goes off again. And again. And again.

I swear to God, someone better be dying.

"I guess I need to get that," Cole says reluctantly.

"You have five seconds," I say, already missing his lips.

He pushes himself up just enough to reach his cell phone. Just seconds into opening the screen, his eyes go wide, and he blinks so frantically I'm concerned he has something in his eye.

"What is it?" I ask, sitting up to see. And when he turns his phone so I can read the messages, I now understand the problem. Because I wouldn't have believed this if I didn't see it with my own two eyes.

Jessica: I miss you.

Jessica: If you take me back you won't regret it. I'll make you the happiest man ever.

Jessica: Just imagine this in your bed every night.

Jessica: Image...

"Oh my God!" I yell, squinting my eyes shut and putting my hands over my face for good measure. "How did she even put herself in that position?"

Cole furiously shakes his head. "I don't know but it's safe to say I need to block her number."

We look at each other, and I don't know why, but we both start laughing. Uncontrollably. It takes us a few minutes to calm down, and by the time we do, Cole has brought me back to his lap.

"I believe, before we were rudely interrupted, we were in the middle of something," I say.

Cole nods. "I do believe you're correct."

I'll never admit this, but Jessica's texts did serve a purpose that night. It slowed us down. Calmed us a bit. Instead of continuing wherever we were going, we spend the rest of the night slowly and lazily kissing, wrapped in each other's arms. I don't know exactly when we fell asleep, but I do know that it was the best sleep I've had in weeks.

I also now know there is nothing, and I mean nothing, like kissing Cole Campbell.

13

———

COLE

The words seem like the right ones for a best man to ask the groom. They are also words that, at one point, I thought I'd never get the chance to say.

Bryce grins at me as we walk toward the altar, Luciano, Bryce's other groomsman, just behind us.

"I've never been more ready for anything in my life."

"It's a day that has always been meant to happen," Luciano says. "Now, let's go get you married."

I have to admit, this place is beautiful. It's at a historic house-turned-winery. The trees give the perfect amount of shade and almost serve as a barrier to the outside world. The white chairs are a stark contrast to the green surroundings. Between the trees and the flowers blooming, it's like Bryce and Lucy are getting married in a secret garden.

It's the perfect place for two of my best friends to finally start the next chapter of their story.

I hear the string quartet Lucy was able to find from one of the universities as we take our place at the front of the gathering. I double check my pocket to make sure I have the rings, which I do. I also feel the little piece of paper I found in my jacket when I put it on this afternoon. Somehow, Brenna snuck into the groom's room when we weren't there and slipped it in.

Remember to save me a dance. I'm the brunette in the gold dress. <3 Brenna

I've read it so many times now I've committed it to memory. Bryce nearly busted me reading it, but I somehow was able to convince him it was a note from the wedding planner telling us what time to be ready for pictures. He believed it. He's so happy today that I doubt he can think about anything else. Nothing's going to ruin his mood.

Except the news of Brenna and I. That could do it. For one, we've had one night together, and that was spent not talking. Sue me, but when the girl of your dreams won't stop kissing you, you let her. At some point, we fell asleep together on the couch, her little body curled up into mine.

It was perfect.

If I got my way, we would have spent all day yesterday continuing the kissing, and if I was lucky, maybe more. But the wedding craziness began bright and early. She had a mountain of things to do with Lucy, and I was on "keep Bryce busy" duty. And because of old traditions, Bryce spent the night at my place last night, and Brenna stayed with Lucy.

I love Bryce, but he is not the Donald I want to spend the night with.

Because of all of that, Brenna and I really haven't had a chance to talk about what we are, or what any of this is for us. So, until we are on the same page, and know that it's worth telling people, we are going to keep this between us.

We also know that telling Bryce won't be easy, and neither of us are about to do that at his wedding.

So for now this is a secret. But I don't mind. She's worth it.

"Here we go," Luciano whispers as the music changes.

The three of us straighten our shoulders as Bryce's mom is escorted down the aisle by one of our Fury teammates. Next is Mrs.

Valenti, who is escorted by one of her nephews. Then comes Celine, and I don't have to look back to know that Luciano is beaming right now. Funny to think this was supposed to be him and Lucy at one point.

I can't let my mind linger on that for too long, because right behind Celine is Brenna, and everyone else just fades away.

I knew she was wearing a gold dress, but she wouldn't let me see it. The thin straps show off shoulders that I want to put my mouth on immediately. The neckline has a small scoop to it, not showing off anything, but teasing nonetheless. The dress is long and hugs every curve of her body. Her hair is wavy, sitting perfectly just below her shoulders.

She's a vision. I can't stop staring at her.

"You need to blink," Luciano whispers to me. "Or your eyes might fall out of your head."

I do as he says, realizing that if he is noticing I'm staring at Brenna, likely others are as well. That lasts a whole three seconds before I see Brenna give me a wink before she moves to stand in her spot.

I hear the music start to play for Lucy, but my mind is elsewhere. All of a sudden I can't get the vision out of my head of Brenna walking up the aisle in a white dress. She's glowing like an angel as she walks toward me. She's on Bryce's arm as he gives her away. That is, before he gives me one of his ridiculous man hugs before going to stand behind me as my best man.

Fuck…I have it bad. I mean, I knew I did, but if all it takes is a few looks and one night of making out on a couch to make me feel like this… I'm done for when it comes to Brenna Donald.

"RIGHT HERE…ONE, TWO, THREE!"

I look at the camera for the umpteenth photo we've taken today. I never knew the bridal party was in so many of the photos. I also didn't realize that the normal, tough guy football player no-smile look wasn't appropriate for wedding photos. I wasn't trying to look angry, but apparently I was. Brenna whispered to me around picture twenty-five that if I tried to smile, she'd make it worth my while later.

I'm nothing if not goal-oriented.

"Okay, I think we're good out here," the photographer says as she scrolls back through her photos. "Bridal party, I hereby cut you loose. You can head to the cocktail hour. Bride and groom, let's head to the gazebo."

"You guys behave yourselves," Bryce says. "Don't get too drunk."

"We will be on our best behavior," Brenna says. "Now go take some more pictures with your wife."

Bryce looks at Lucy, smiling from ear to ear. "Wife. I like it."

The two of them walk toward the gazebo while Luciano and Celine waste no time heading to cocktail hour. I don't move, hoping that Brenna has the same idea as I do.

"I don't know about you, but I've never been one to be on my best behavior."

I smile as Brenna slips her arms around my waist. I quickly look to make sure we're alone as I turn around. We are. So I do what I've been dying to do all day—wrap Brenna into my arms and kiss the living hell out of her.

"Well then," she says when I release her lips. "And here I thought I was the troublemaker, out of the two of us."

"Oh, there's so much for you to learn about me," I say, walking over to one of the chairs, where I promptly sit and bring Brenna to my lap.

She puts her hands around my neck. "I can't wait."

"Want to know what I can't wait for?"

"What's that?"

I lean in and quickly place a kiss on her shoulder. "The day when we don't have to hide."

"I know," she says, tipping her forehead so it's touching mine. "But this is for the best. At least for now."

She's right. It was the decision we came to, and it's the right one. Plus, Bryce and Lucy will be gone for two weeks on their honeymoon.

That gives us fourteen days to make sure this is the real deal and to come up with a plan.

"At least I'll get to dance with you tonight," she says.

"I'm going to warn you, I'm a pretty good dancer," I say.

"Oh really? You've got moves?"

"More than you are prepared for."

Our lips connect again, and I know we shouldn't be doing this out in the open, but fuck, I can't help myself. She tastes too good. Her lips are too soft. Her body feels too right on mine. Unfortunately, our kiss doesn't get too deep, as we are interrupted by someone awkwardly clearing their throat, which immediately sends Brenna shooting right off my lap.

"Oh geez," Luciano says as Brenna tries to straighten her dress. "I'm so sorry."

"We...uh..." Brenna stutters before looking at me then back to Luciano. "It's not..."

This just makes him laugh. "Oh, Brenna, don't try to tell me what I didn't see. Plus, your man here was nearly drooling as you walked down the aisle."

I stand up and button my jacket, ignoring the drool comment. "What's up?"

"There's a woman at the reception asking for you. I told her you'd be there soon, but she wasn't happy with that answer and demanded I go get you. I feel like she also asks to speak to managers a lot. For the sake of not causing an incident, and also to escape her, I figured I'd come find you."

I give Brenna a bemused look because I have no idea who that could be. "Thanks, man. We'll be on our way."

"No problem," Luciano says. "And what I just saw? I didn't see anything. But I also think it's great. I also get why you're not saying anything. Your secret is safe with me."

"Thanks," I say as the three of us begin walking to the reception area. "We appreciate it. We're just waiting for the right time."

"No problem. I've been on the opposite side of having to deliver Bryce Donald news he might not like. I get it."

"Thanks, Luciano," Brenna says, giving him a quick hug. "Now, who in the heck is Demanding Debbie?"

We walk into the winery where the reception is being held and before Luciano can even point in her direction, I see exactly who he's talking about.

What the fuck is Jessica doing here?

"Are you kidding me?" Brenna says, though her voice is not as quiet as I think she thinks it is. "What in the actual wedding crasher hell is she doing here?"

Good question. "Let me go talk to her. See if I can get her out of here without a commotion."

I start walking away but feel Brenna next to me. "What are you doing?"

She looks up at me like I'm the crazy one. "You think I'm about to let you go over there and deal with a potential bunny boiler by yourself? Nope. Not happening."

"Bunny boiler?"

"*Fatal Attraction*. We'll put it on our movie list."

The fact that Brenna is having a seemingly normal conversation with me as she's shooting daggers with her eyes at Jessica is both impressive and slightly terrifying. However, it's not nearly as scary as Jessica turning toward us wearing a smile on her face like the damn Joker.

"There you are!" she says, quickly wrapping her arms around my neck to hug me. A hug I do not reciprocate.

"Jessica, what are you doing here?" I say, quickly removing her hands from me.

"I'm your date, silly," she says, turning to grab her flute of champagne. "Sorry I didn't make the ceremony. But I'm here now. Where are our seats?"

I turn to look at Brenna, who seems just as baffled as I am. Does Jessica not remember me breaking up with her? Is she choosing to ignore it? How do I handle this? Put a three-hundred-pound defensive tackle in my face, and I know exactly what to do. A redhead who won't accept a break up? No clue.

"We don't have seats, Jessica," I say as gently as I can. "You aren't my date. We broke up. Do you remember?"

In a reaction I wasn't expecting, she starts laughing. It has a shrill sound to it. It's kind of creepy. "Oh, silly. You didn't mean that. It was just a lovers' quarrel."

I blink a few times, because...*wow*. I'm speechless. I turn to look at Brenna for help, but all she's doing is mouthing the word "lovers."

She's going to pay for that later.

"Anyway," Jessica continues. "Where are we sitting? At the front table or maybe with the players and their girlfriends? I should start meeting them, you know. Before the season starts."

"Oh my God, what aren't you understanding?" Brenna whisper-yells. "Do you not realize that he broke up with you?"

Jessica's eyes get narrow as she focuses on Brenna. "I don't know what you're talking about, Breanne. Now, go be a dear and get some drinks for us. We're going to go and take a few pictures for my Instagram. I saw a beautiful gazebo while I was walking in!"

"Oh, hell no!" Brenna yells. Yeah, I knew the whisper yelling wasn't going to last. "One, I'm not your waitress. And two, you don't belong here. You weren't invited. He broke up with you. Get over it. Take your wannabe Ariel ass and get the fuck out of my brother's wedding before we call security."

I grab Brenna's hand, meaning to pull her back. Involuntarily, we link hands, which Jessica sees. How do I know this? It's the moment her face turns as red as her hair.

"I knew it was you!" Jessica shrieks, which definitely draws eyes. "No man lives with a woman and is just friends with her. You're the reason he left me! What do you have that I don't? I love him! I—"

"Whoa!" Bryce yells, coming in out of nowhere. "What seems to be the problem here?"

"Oh nothing!" Luciano says, running up next to me and separating Brenna and Jessica. "Just a little disagreement. Nothing to worry about."

"What are you doing here?" Lucy says to Jessica.

"What am I doing here?" Jessica yells, stepping back from Luciano.

Every person in the venue has turned to see what is going on. "I thought he loved me! I thought we were going to get married. I'm meant to be a football player's wife! But no! He dumped me! And for her! She moved into his home and seduced him! She ruined my life!"

Jessica starts walking in Brenna's direction but Luciano and I each take an arm, holding her back. I'm also not sure about this, but I could swear Brenna is smiling right now.

Yeah, Trouble is grinning like it's her birthday.

"Oh, Jessica," Brenna coos, clearly stirring the pot. "I did nothing. This is all you. But maybe try wearing a pair of sweatpants sometimes. I've heard he likes them."

"You bitch!"

Jessica flails between Luciano and me, but stops at the sight of two security guards.

"Let's go, ma'am."

"What in the fuck?" Bryce says as we watch the security guards guide Jessica away. "I knew she was crazy, but Brenna breaking you two up? She really is a nut."

"Yup," I say, taking a deep breath to regain composure. "Freaking hilarious."

As if nothing happened, everyone goes back to what they were doing five minutes ago.

Except me and Brenna. We just stand there staring at each other.

"Did that really just happen?" I ask.

"Yeah," she says. "I can't believe she showed up."

"I can't believe you egged her on like that."

Brenna shrugs as she takes a glass of wine from one of the waiters. "It's almost like you haven't known me my whole life."

I take a step closer to her so only she can hear what I'm about to say. "You know there are about three things that you said that you're going to have to pay for later?"

She smiles at me and ever so sneakily grazes her hand against my chest. "Only three? I must be slipping. Now let's go have some fun. Because ding dong, the crazy bitch is gone."

14

———————

BRENNA

WHEN YOU'RE twenty-five and single, the wedding scene starts becoming repetitive. Especially if you've been to as many as I have in the past few years.

You go. You eat a meal that's either a chicken dish that just tried too hard or a steak that's overcooked. Sometimes you'll get a pasta plate you can stomach, but that's only because you know you need the carbs to help soak up the liquor you're about to drink. You drink watered-down vodka sodas, dance to one Bruno Mars song after another, and if you're lucky, the bride skips the bouquet toss. By the end of the night, you hopefully have a good buzz, start dancing a little more provocatively because the music has changed once the grandparents leave, and before you know it, you're singing "Don't Stop Believing" in a circle before being told that you don't have to go home, but you can't stay here.

Oh, and of course, when you're single, you skip the slow dances.

This is the recipe for every wedding.

Except for tonight.

I don't know if it's because I'm in the wedding party, or if it's because my brother and my best friend are finally starting their life together, or if because I've already snuck off twice tonight to kiss Cole, but this is the best wedding I've ever attended.

And that's not even counting the Jessica incident. That was just a bonus.

"Hey girl, why you sitting here all alone?"

My eyes go wide as I take in a whiff of a cologne I never wanted to smell again.

"Dexter," I say as he takes an uninvited seat next to me. "How are you?"

"Doin' my thing. How you been? You haven't hit me up in a while."

No shit, Sherlock. Is he that dumb? Did he think I'd actually call him again? Does he not remember me yelling at him about his small dick? What is it tonight with people forgetting being rejected?

"I'm...okay," I say, frantically looking for anyone I know to get me out of this conversation. "Are you having fun?"

"Not really," he says, leaning in closer. Oh God, that cologne is horrible. "Not many single ladies here tonight. I was hoping you'd join me on the dance floor and turn my night around."

"She won't be doing that."

For a mammoth of a man, Cole can be quite stealthy.

"Campbell," Dexter says, standing up. Though that doesn't do much; Cole still towers over him. "I believe the lady can speak for herself."

"You're right, I can," I say, standing up and immediately looping my arm around Cole's. "And I believe they just called the wedding party to the dance floor. Have a good time tonight, Dexter. Maybe go try the champagne. I hear if you keep drinking it, you'll eventually like it."

Cole and I walk to the dance floor, where Luciano and Celine, along with Bryce, Lucy and all of the parents, are already dancing. To play it cool, Cole and I keep our distance while dancing, even though every part of me wants to lay my head on his shoulder and let the words and melody of Etta James flow through me.

"Thank you for saving me from Dexter," I say.

"I don't care that he's my teammate, I hate that guy."

"No, you don't," I say, inching closer to him. "But thank you for saving me."

"Yes I do," he says, pulling me in even closer and bringing our joined hands over his heart. "Have I told you how beautiful you look?"

"Only ten times."

I look up at Cole, who is smiling down at me in a way I don't think I've ever seen before. His smile is soft and genuine. From a man who is always so serious, this smile hits me straight in the heart. His thumb is slowly making small brushes on the small of my back, but I feel like he's touching me all over.

How have I known this man for as long as I have and not seen what is right in front of me? I was so stubborn for so long, telling myself that he was just my brother's best friend.

Well, that ends now. I don't care how long I've known him or how long it has taken me to get here, no man has *ever* looked at me this way. And I'm not going to give that up no matter what anyone thinks.

Because *I* think there is something special here. Something I've been chasing my whole life.

And it was right in front of me the whole time.

"Cole?"

"Yeah?"

I want to ask him when we can take off, or at least find a dark corner so I can kiss him the way I'm aching to right now, but we're interrupted by the couple of the evening.

Assholes.

"Whoa there!" Bryce yells. "Getting a little too close to my sister."

We both quickly step back, not realizing that at some point, we drifted so close together you could barely slide a piece of paper between us. And that the music has changed to some sort of upbeat group dance.

"Sorry," Cole says.

"It's okay, I know you didn't mean anything by it. I mean, you probably hate me already for making you dance with my sister all night."

"It's been torture," he deadpans.

"I figured as much. Anyway, come on, we're going to get a team photo."

Lucy walks over and grabs my hand. "Good. You boys head that way. I need Brenna's assistance in the ladies room."

Bryce grabs Cole while Lucy takes my hand and whisks us in opposite directions. I look back, trying to get one more glimpse of Cole. To my surprise, he's also looking back. And just before he's out of range, he sends me a wink, which hits me just as hard as that small smile did just a few minutes earlier.

"I'm waiting," Lucy singsongs as we enter the ladies room.

"For what?" I ask, hoping she's not going down the conversation path I think she is. "Because I'm waiting for a lot. Fat-free pizza. A woman president. All the streaming services in one convenient location."

"Don't be a smartass," Lucy says as she signals for me to sit on the couch in the ladies' room. "Are you ready to admit that I'm right and you have a thing for Cole?"

"I know you're the bride, and this is your day, but have you had a little too much to drink?"

"I've had two sips of champagne so cut the crap. I saw you two. You were trying to hide it, but you can't hide it from me. I know both of you too well. It melted my heart. It also made me want to jump up and down and cheer. So just say it, are you and Cole together?"

I don't say anything, because I have no idea how I want to play this. On one hand, this is Lucy. My best friend. The woman who has been there for me every day for the past five years. She's also now my sister. My family. She knows me better most days than I know myself. So of course I want to tell her every little detail about how crazy I am over this man.

The only problem is that Cole and I promised that we were going to tell Bryce together. We also want to make sure this is real before we do. No sense in poking the bear if he doesn't need poked.

He's going to freak out when he finds out. And we don't know in what way. And even though I love her and trust her implicitly, I don't want her to have to lie to her new husband. She shouldn't have to do that.

"No," I say, because, in some sort of weird justification in my mind, we aren't. At least, we haven't said it out loud.

Lucy gives me a look that screams that she clearly doesn't believe me. "So you're going to tell me with a straight face that there is nothing going on between you two? No flirting? No touches? Nothing."

I swallow because *shit*—I could justify the last lie. So I do the one thing I can think to do.

I grab her hand and start tugging her toward the door.

"How about we get you back to your reception?" My plan almost works until I open the door and see Cole. Waiting for me outside the ladies' room.

Lucy looks back and forth between the two of us, and even though we haven't been caught doing anything, I feel guilty as hell. Judging by the fact Cole is staring at the floor, he does too.

She *so* knows.

"All right you two, listen here," Lucy says in her best mom voice. "I don't know what exactly this is or what you two are doing. But I know enough to know that I freaking called this a year ago. I can tell. I know a guilty look when I see it. My husband might be a little dense on the subject, but you can't fool me."

"Lucy—"

"Stop!" she says, putting her hand up and stopping whatever Cole was about to say. "Let me get this out. What I was going to say was since you two are both stubborn mules and won't say words out loud for God knows what reason, I'm going to pretend I don't know that you two haven't been giving each other the googly eyes all night."

"Tha—"

"But!" Lucy says, cutting me off this time. "I won't lie to him. I won't tell him, but if he asks, I'm not going to lie."

"Thank you." I say. "We just—"

"No!" Lucy shushes me. "The less I know the less I eventually have to admit. So this conversation is going to stop right now."

I attack Lucy in a hug, fighting back tears. She's really the best.

"Thank you," I say. "We just need some time to figure a few things out."

"I know," she says. "Can I now say I was right?"

I step back, unknowingly into the waiting arm of Cole, who brings me into his side. "Yeah. Yeah, you can."

15

———

COLE

ONE OF THE most memorable games Bryce and I played in college was a six-overtime nail biter that ended with us winning by running one of the craziest plays we ever drew up. It was a nearly five-hour game from which I never thought I'd emotionally, or physically, recover.

Somehow, I'm even more drained right now after Lucy and Bryce's wedding than I was after that marathon of a game.

"How could one day make you so tired?" I ask, quickly unlacing these uncomfortable shoes and kicking them somewhere they hopefully get lost forever.

"High heels are the devil, likely invented by a man, and I hope this pair in particular burn in hell," Brenna chimes in, throwing said high heels across the room before falling back into my chest.

I wrap my arms around her as she nuzzles into me. This. This is the moment I've been wanting all day. Just to be able to sit back, relax, and get lost in the feeling of my girl in my arms.

Hell, if we never move from right here, I'd die a happy man.

"I can't believe they're finally married," I say as my fingers gently stroke up and down her arm.

"I can't believe your crazy ex-girlfriend showed up."

I let out a groan, which only makes Brenna laugh. "Can we please never talk about that again?"

"Oh, I don't think so," Brenna says while she gets up and situates herself across my lap. "I don't think we're going to forget that one for a very long time."

"Well then, maybe I can distract you."

I wrap my arms around her center and bring her to me, pressing my lips against hers. Yes, we were able to sneak a few of these in during the day today, but it still feels like too long since I've kissed her the way I want to. Our tongues meet as I slowly lay her back on the couch, careful not to put all of my body weight on her. Which is hard as hell when one of her legs begins to wrap around me, pulling me closer.

"Brenna." I don't mean for that to come out as a groan, but I can't help it. The woman is not only trying to wrap herself around me like a vine, she's also kissing a spot on my neck that I didn't realize had a direct line to my dick.

"What?" Her reply comes out as innocent, but there is nothing innocent about this woman.

"If you don't stop that now, I can't promise I'm going to behave myself."

"Who said anything about behaving?"

Oh this woman...I've known for years she was nothing but trouble. I just didn't know how much I loved trouble until right now.

I jump off the couch and scoop her up into my arms. She's nothing but giggles as I hurry down the hall to my bedroom.

"What's so funny?"

"Someone's in a hurry."

Does she not know that I've been waiting for this moment for three fucking years? Three years of dreaming. Three years of waiting. Three years of trying to make myself believe there was someone else out there for me *not* named Brenna Donald.

It was all for nothing. It's her. It's always been her. It will always be her.

I gently place her down on the bed, but I don't follow. Not yet, at least. Because while I would love nothing more but to get lost in this woman until the sun comes up, I have to make sure she knows where I'm at.

"Is something wrong?" she asks.

I stand up next to the bed, keeping her hands in mine. "No, but, before we go on, we need to make sure we're on the same page."

She gives me a confused look. "About?"

"This. You know what this means, right?"

She nods, but right now, I need more than that.

"I need you to say it, Brenna. I need you to know that once this happens, there's no going back. At least not for me. This? You and me? I'm all in. I've waited so long for this. For you. For the chance of an *us*. I don't know what the future holds, but I know damn sure that if this happens right now, the future—our future—begins right now. So what do you say, Trouble? You in?"

I let out a breath as the last words come out. I don't know where all of that came from. I'm not that guy. I'm not the guy who puts his heart on the table or wears his emotions on his sleeve. Apparently when it comes to Brenna, all the rules are out the fucking window.

Just when I begin to panic because she hasn't answered me yet, she slowly raises herself to her knees and cups my face in her hands, begging me with her eyes to look at her. As if I could look anywhere else right now.

"I'm all in. On one condition."

Shit, at this point she could ask me for the stars, and I'd figure out a way to get them for her. "Anything."

"That you'll catch me when I fall. Because while you've been waiting, I've been searching. I didn't know I was looking for you. But I was looking. I just didn't know I was looking in the wrong places. And now that I've found it—found you—I feel myself falling. I feel myself falling hard. And I'm scared. I'm scared in the best way possible. So, all I ask is that you catch me."

"Sweetheart," I say, picking her up so she is now standing in front of me. "That is one thing you will never have to worry about."

I lean down and bring her lips to mine, sealing our words with a kiss. I know there is still a lot to figure out. Frankly, that part terrifies me. But that's not tonight's worry. All I'm going to think about tonight is the fact that the woman of my dreams is here with me, and she wants this as much as I do.

The kiss starts slow but quickly speeds up. Brenna's hands are frantically trying to undo the buttons of my dress shirt and the knot in my tie. Our tongues are searching and begging for more while my hands begin to lower the thin straps of her dress.

The second they are off, it only takes one little push to make the gold dress fall to her feet. I stop the kiss, but only because I am fucking stunned to find her completely naked.

"Are you meaning to tell me that all day you've had nothing on underneath this?"

She shrugs, a devilish smile gracing her beautiful mouth. "I was hopeful you'd like this surprise."

"You are fucking trouble," I groan. "And I fucking love trouble."

I hear nothing but sweet giggles as I pick her up and take the two steps necessary to lie her back on the bed. And as much as I'd love to lie next to her and kiss every inch of smooth skin before me, that can wait.

I rip my tie off and toss it to the side as I lower myself to my knees. Like she can read my mind, Brenna slowly opens her legs for me. I have to remember to breathe when I see her lying in front of me. I always knew she was gorgeous. Hell, I've had to look at her every day of my life and keep my hands—and thoughts—to myself. But now? Now that she's lying here and giving herself to me like this? I don't have words.

"God, you are so fucking beautiful," I say before gently placing a kiss just above her knee. Her skin is just as soft as I imagined as I slowly kiss my way up to my desired destination.

"Fuck," I groan before letting myself take a long, slow lick around her wetness. I've barely touched her, and she's already soaked.

"Cole."

My name on her tongue does something to me that I've never felt before. Every cell in me leaps at the sound. It also spurs me on because

I want to hear it again. I want to hear it every day for the rest of my life.

I grab her legs and throw them over my shoulders, diving into her pussy like this is about to be my last supper. My sudden change in pace makes her stiffen for just a second, but the second my tongue hits her clit, I feel her relax back into the bed.

Good. Let her relax. That gives me the ability to take what I please. To savor every drop. I've thought about this moment no less than a thousand times, and I'm not about to let a second go to waste.

There's only one problem. My brain and my heart want me to take my time. But my cock? The one that's hard as a rock right now and somehow growing harder with Brenna running her hands through my hair? It wants more.

And now.

"More," Brenna says, apparently in agreement with my dick. "I need more, Cole."

What the lady wants, the lady gets.

I pick up my pace, letting my tongue work in circles as I push a finger inside her. Her hips begin to press into my face, which only heightens my excitement. I insert a second, letting them explore for just the right spot as I suck on her clit.

"Yes!" she yells, her hands now all but pulling my hair out as my fingers work in tandem with my mouth. It's only a few more seconds of this before she explodes for me, her body shaking as I give one more kiss to her drenched center before slowly bringing her down.

Fuck. That was... I don't have words. I'm also not sure I have any hair, either.

I don't care, though. Let her pull. Let her yank. Hell, let her leave bald spots on my head. They'd be a badge of honor. I've never felt like this before. And I never want to go back to a time when I didn't know what a true win feels like.

16

———————

BRENNA

EVERY INCH of my body is sore. My feet are aching. Hell, even my lips are swollen and chapped.

And I've never felt better and more relaxed in my entire life.

I'm going to name it the Cole Campbell Effect.

Because holy hell does that man have an effect on me.

I haven't opened my eyes yet, because I haven't fully committed this feeling to memory, and I want to remember this until I'm old and gray. His pillows and sheets are just as soft as they were last time I was here. The scent of his cologne—the one that drives me crazy in the best way possible—is hitting all the right senses.

But the best part? His arms around me, holding me like I might run away.

Not a chance in hell.

"You really need to quit doing that," Cole says, his voice a low and gravelly mumble in my ear.

"Doing what?"

He releases one arm from his hold on me, sliding it over to give one of my cheeks a good squeeze. Because yes, my ass might or might not have been rubbing against his growing erection.

"This. You know what you're doing, and it's not fair."

I don't open my eyes, but that doesn't stop the smile forming on my face. "I have no idea what you're talking about."

I have no warning before those strong arms lift me, pulling me up and over his body so I'm straddling him.

How did he do that?

And can he do it again?

"No idea what you're doing?" he asks as I feel his now hard dick nestled between my legs.

"How was I supposed to know you'd be so easy to wake up in the morning?"

I lean down, needing to feel his lips on mine. I don't remember when we fell asleep, but I do know that it was just about the perfect night.

"Mmmm, good morning to you," he says, locking his hands behind me. "Did you get any sleep?"

I place my hands under my chin, which Cole doesn't seem to mind. "A little."

Cole yawns. "Me too."

"Want me to put on clothes and let you get some sleep?"

His hands slide down from my back to my ass, his hands cupping one cheek in each. "Don't you fucking dare."

For being a big guy, Cole is surprisingly agile. And quick. That is just one of the many ways this man surprised me last night.

And now, apparently, this morning.

Cole quickly rolls me over and completely covers me while also kissing me like we didn't just spend all night tangled in each other. I don't mind, though; being buried under Cole is my new favorite place to be.

"What are you doing?" he asks, breaking the kiss that I thought was going very well.

"Huh?" I'm not even being coy. I'm genuinely confused.

"You keep doing that," he says, signaling to his arms. "I don't mind. It's just not something I'm used to."

I look at where he signaled, and apparently without even thinking, I've let my hands wander up his arms before taking hold of his biceps.

I can't help it. All I can imagine is them pinning me down. Or against a wall. Or holding me down as we sneak in a quickie someplace we shouldn't.

The possibilities are endless.

Arm test? He doesn't even need one. He's like the arm test cheat code.

"Is this the point where I admit my first semi-embarrassing thing to you?"

This gets me a soft laugh before a quick kiss on the nose. "I doubt it's embarrassing, whatever it is."

"You say that now." I take a breath, though I don't let go. "I kind of have a thing for arms."

He lifts an eyebrow. "Arms?"

"Yes. Specifically biceps."

"Really?"

I shrug. "What can I say? It's my thing."

"And you find mine…"

I bite my bottom lip, giving his arm one more squeeze. "They are one of my favorite parts of you."

"Oh really," he says, leaning in to kiss my neck. "What else do you like about me?"

This playful side of Cole was not one I expected. If you know Cole, you know him as serious. An old soul in a twenty-something body. The "dad" of the Nashville Fury because he's always the one who makes sure that business is handled.

Then there's this Cole. The playful one. The tender one, who opened his heart to me last night. The one who is willing to fight a steep battle for us to be together.

I like that I'm the only one who knows this Cole. I hate that it took me so long to get here, but now that I am, I'm not going to take it for granted.

"Well, let's see," I say, letting my hands begin to explore. "I like your lips."

He moves his way up my neck to give me a kiss. "Well, that's good, because mine like yours too."

"I like your butt."

This makes him laugh. "My butt?"

"Hell yeah," I say, reaching around giving each cheek a squeeze. "I like that my man has some cake."

"Your man?"

I didn't even think about those words when I said them. But now that I have, I don't regret it.

"Is that a problem?"

"Not at all," he says as he begins to smile. God, I love it when he smiles. He doesn't do it a lot. In fact, I grew up thinking he didn't know how. So when he does? It melts me every single time. "You have no idea how long I've wanted to hear those words out of your mouth."

Oh now I'm curious. "How long?"

He shakes his head. "Nope. Not admitting that."

"Why," I say, wrapping my legs around his, trying to entice him a bit. "If you tell me, I promise you'll be rewarded."

Cole moves off me slightly, propping his head up with his arm. His other hand is gently stroking the outline of my face and if I wasn't so invested in this topic, I'd probably fall back asleep.

"The night we almost got arrested."

My eyes go wide. "In Clemson?"

He lets out a sigh. "Yes. In Clemson."

I can't believe this. That was just over three years ago. "Was this before or after I puked in the bushes? Or after the cop let us go because he had to go break up a party?"

"After the bushes, before releasing us," he says, pulling me in closer to him. "I took you out that night to make sure you were safe. I never expected it to be the night I realized that you were it for me."

I bite my lip, because it's all I can do to keep the tears at bay. That night seems like a lifetime ago. All these years and not a word?

"Why didn't you ever say anything?"

"Because… I don't know. At first I thought it would pass. I was off to the league and you were back in Laurel Heights. I thought it was just a crush and I'd get over it. Interesting fact, you are not that easy to get over."

"I don't know what to say." And that's the truth. I had no clue.

"Don't say anything," he says, placing a small kiss on my forehead. "We're here now."

"Yeah. But now I'm going to beat myself up thinking about all the time I was an oblivious idiot."

"Hey," he says, bringing me back on top of him. "I didn't want you to know. I wasn't ready. I was scared, and if I'm going to be honest, I still am. I think we both know what we have to figure out the second we leave the bubble that is this room. All I know is that you? Here? In my bed with me? Me getting to hold you and kiss you and call you mine? I don't care if I waited ten years for this. I'm here now. And this is the moment our future begins."

My lips are on Cole's the second he says that last word. For one, that was the most romantic thing I've ever heard in my entire life, and two, if I don't kiss him immediately I'm pretty sure I'm going to start crying.

Because who says that? Who truly means things like that?

Cole. That's who.

I feel him grow hard again underneath me, which only makes my kisses more furious. Am I sore from last night? Yes. Is that going to stop me from having this man again? Hell no.

"You sure?" he asks, as if he was reading my mind. That or he was picking up on the signals I was clearly giving as I was rubbing my bare pussy against his cock.

"Mmmhmm," I mumble, letting my mouth trail across his jawbone over to his ear. I found a spot just underneath his neck that I think is his kryptonite.

"You really are nothing but trouble," he says, reaching over to his nightstand to grab a condom.

I take it from his hand as I sit up on him. I love being on top of him like this. He's so big and commanding in stature. But when I'm like this, and he's looking up at me with that fire in his eyes? I feel like the most powerful, beautiful, sexual being on the planet.

I rip the condom open with my teeth as I slide just far enough back to be able to roll it on to him. "I thought you said you liked trouble."

With my last stroke, he flips me over, pinning my arms above my head. "I'm starting to think I like it a little too much."

I wrap my legs around his, silently pleading him to enter me. "Show me."

He enters me with one thrust, which nearly takes my breath away. Maybe one day I'll get used to his size, but it won't be today. Secretly I hope I never do, because this man fills me like I never have been filled before.

Last night Cole took his time. And it was perfect. Exactly what a first time together should be. I felt adored and cherished and had orgasms that made me see stars.

But right now? Now I don't want to be slow and sweet. I want him to fuck me so hard I feel him inside me the rest of the day. And judging by the way he's still holding my hands down while his thrusts are getting harder, he wants that, too.

"Fuck me, Cole," I say, wrapping my legs tighter around him. "Show me what kind of trouble I can be."

My attempt at dirty talk does the trick, because I see the second the fire turns up a notch in his eyes.

He lets go of my hands, but that's only so he can bring my legs up to his shoulders. Which, holy shit... That angle is hitting something that I didn't know existed.

"Yes." I let the word spill out of my mouth because no matter what he asked me right now, that would be my answer. His thrusts are the perfect blend of hard and fast. But I want more. I need more.

I let my hands trace up my torso until I reach my breasts. I watch Cole as he watches me play with myself, his eyes literally now burning.

"Fucking trouble," he groans, his thrusts becoming faster. "Is that how you want to play it?"

I nod, giving each nipple one last twist. "Show me what you got."

I feel like this whole time I've been playing with fire. That Cole is a spark that's one splash of gasoline away from becoming an inferno. Apparently, those words I just said are all the gas he needs to explode, because before I know it I'm on all fours and Cole is fucking me like a man on a mission.

And his mission is to make me scream.

He's about to get his wish. I can barely hold myself up, but I meet him thrust for thrust. I feel my orgasm building, and I am so close. Judging by the way he's gripping my hips, he's not too far behind either.

"Brenna," he groans.

"Yes, Cole!" I scream. I don't mean to, but the second I opened my mouth, he hits the spot that sends me over the edge. My arms give out, and I sink back into the bed as I feel him push into me one more time. It's not long before he joins me, his big body covering me as we lie there in sated bliss.

Cole quickly tosses the condom into the trash next to the bed as he brings me into his arms, kissing me any place he can reach. How do we go from fucking to cuddling in five seconds? And how is it absolutely perfect?

Because it's Cole. The man of many layers. The man who one minute is the tough, badass football player and the next minute the teddy bear. The man who can go from grump to comedian at the drop of a dime.

The man I have a feeling I'm already falling for...way too fast.

17

———

COLE

"SO ARE we going to talk about it?"

Brenna doesn't acknowledge my words. Instead, she just keeps trying to get a glass on the top shelf that she knows she can't reach.

I walk up behind her, forcing myself to ignore her nakedness under my T-shirt, and easily grab it for her.

"You could just ask for help."

"But what if you aren't here one day and I need it?" she asks. "I have to be able to do it for myself."

"Has anyone told you that you're stubborn?"

She just shrugs as she takes the glass, rises up on her tiptoes to give me a kiss on the chin, which is the highest she can reach without me leaning down. "I like to say I'm independent."

"Sure, we'll go with that."

Brenna heads to the refrigerator to pour herself some juice. And I don't know what else she's trying to get, but it requires her bending over. The little minx is trying to distract me so we don't have to talk about the topic we know we have to.

"That's not going to work," I say as I take a seat at the kitchen island. But I might be lying.

She turns back to look at me, but doesn't bother standing up. "Whatever do you mean?"

"Do you really think tempting me with your bare ass is going to distract from the fact that we need to talk about the Bryce situation?"

She lets out a defeated sigh and closes the refrigerator. "A girl could hope."

"Come on," I say, standing back up. "The quicker we do this, the quicker you can get back to seducing me."

"Fine," she says, making her way to the living room and snuggling into "her" spot. I take a seat next to her and reach for her hand. I know if I get any closer we won't talk about a damn thing. But I can't not touch her. Now that I have, I can't imagine not touching her at every chance I get. "Do we think he has any idea?"

I shake my head. "He didn't give me any sort of hint yesterday that he did. And that's even after Lucy gave us her lecture. Your brother is clueless."

"Which is probably going to make things worse when we do tell him."

I let out a sigh, because yeah, this is not going to be easy. "Not only is he going to be pissed that you're my girlfriend, but the fact that I kept it a secret is going to only add fuel to his fire."

Brenna smiles and bites her lip in that cute way she does.

"What are you smiling at?"

"You called me your girlfriend."

Leave it to Brenna to turn a serious conversation into a moment where all I want to do is scoop her up and kiss the hell out of her. "Don't distract me."

"What? It was a significant moment. I wanted to make sure we properly acknowledged it."

I lean in and give her a kiss, though I fight the urge to start outright making out with her on the couch. "There. We've acknowledged it."

"Fine," she groans. "And you're right. Bryce is going to flip for many reasons. The problem is, I don't know what is going to set him off more. Since I moved here and he got sober, he has really tried to be more involved in my life. Which is great, but he tends to take it overboard. So when you combine that with the fact that his sister and his best friend are together, and that we hooked up behind his back, he's going to blow a gasket. Add on to that that you're his teammate and it's going to freak him the fuck out."

"You're right. He has this weird stance about the unwritten rules of football. And of course number one is don't fuck a teammate's sister." I let out a defeated sigh and throw my head back. "Is there any way we tell him this without him blowing up?"

"I doubt it," Brenna says. "You saw how he reacted yesterday at the wedding when we danced with each other. He didn't even think it was feasible. It's so far off his radar I don't think he's even comprehended it."

"He hasn't," I add. "One time I tried to hypothetically bring up the idea of you and me. He had no clue I was fishing for information. It was the night you were out with Dexter. He told me that not one teammate was good enough for you. I asked if I was. He all but laughed in my face."

"What an idiot," she says, now moving so that she is snuggled into my side. I quickly wrap my arms around her, loving the feel of her back to my front. "Well I hope you know, however we tell him, he's going to have to get over it. I'm my own woman. And you are a grown man who can see whoever he wants. Yes, it might take some getting used to, but he's going to have to suck it up. He might rule the football field, but he doesn't rule our lives."

God, I could kiss the hell out of her right now. "I couldn't agree more."

She turns to look up at me. "I hear a 'but' coming…"

"But we still need to find a way to gently tell him and try to minimize the damage as much as possible."

"You're right," she says, grabbing my arms and wrapping them tighter around her. "Any ideas on how to do that?"

"Not a clue," I say.

We sit in silence for a few minutes, both of us trying to figure out how to do this with the smallest amount of blood and the fewest casualties.

"What if we do it in private? Have him and Lucy over for dinner one night and just tell him?"

"No. Private means he could throw and break stuff. Which then leaves a public setting?"

Now it's my turn to shake my head. "Less chance of him causing a scene, but more of a risk of all of this coming out in social media. With our luck, someone would be ready there with a camera."

Brenna wiggles her way out of my hold, only to climb onto my lap. "How about this: We have two weeks before they get back from their honeymoon. The only people who know are Luciano, and now probably Celine, and they won't tell. So let's take these two weeks and figure us out while also taking our time to make sure we tell Bryce in the best way possible. That way, we know exactly what we're fighting for. He can't argue with us if we show him just how much we're both in this."

Two weeks. While I don't need time to know that she's it for me, I get what she's saying. If we sit Bryce down and tell him all the ways we work, backed by actual time spent together, maybe he'd be a little more willing to see things from our perspective.

Or maybe not. Either way, it's better than any other idea we've had.

"Two weeks, huh?" I say, pulling her a bit closer.

"Yup," she says. "So, what should we do with that time?"

I smile. "I have an idea."

"And what would that be?"

I pick her up, only to lay her back down on the couch. "First, I'm going to kiss you for a very long time. Then tonight, I'm taking you out on your last first date."

She raises her eyebrows. "Confident much?"

"Oh Brenna," I say, kissing my way across her neck. "You have no idea how confident I am."

18

BRENNA

WHERE IS Lucy when I need her?

Oh, right. On her honeymoon. With my brother. So even if I wanted to call her to properly freak the fuck out about tonight, I can't.

And oh boy, do I need to.

I usually have a solid panic before any date. And those are with men with whom I have little to no hope that things will go past the first date.

But this is Cole. COLE. Cole Campbell. Yes, I know we've already slept together. Yes, I know that he has seen me naked from every angle. But when it comes to a date, there is so much more to it than just sex. This is the time where we really find out if we're good together beyond the bedroom.

Believe me, we have that part covered.

And that's just one of the problems. Here's another one: normally before a date, I'd spread out every piece of clothing I own across my bedroom and overanalyze every outfit, all in an effort to find the perfect thing to wear.

Can I still do that? Sure. I mean, I did. It just feels a little different knowing the man you're trying to impress is right across the hall. And

I don't know how much I can impress when I was told to wear something "comfortable and warm."

Considering my feet are still hurting from being in heels all day yesterday, I'm completely okay with that request.

I give myself one final look in the standup mirror I had to buy because—shocker—Cole does not own a mirror besides the one over the sink in the bathroom. I frown down at my outfit. I think I like it. Cute sweater that I can still get away with despite it being spring, paired with leggings and short booties. I kept my makeup natural and my hair straight.

Is this the look of a girl who potentially might be going out on her last first date? Who knows. But the thought of it being a possibility makes me smile in a way I don't remember smiling before.

Maybe this is another part of the Cole Campbell Effect.

"Here we go," I say to myself as I exit my bedroom. Cole isn't in his room, but I can smell his cologne lingering in the hall. I follow it like a trail of breadcrumbs to the living room, where I find him sitting on the arm of his chair.

How dare this man tell me to "keep it comfortable" while he has the audacity to sit there and look like a whole meal. He's wearing a white button down with the sleeves rolled up. If that arm porn wasn't enough, the jeans he's wearing hug every muscle of his tree trunk thighs but would never be considered tight or skinny jeans. His hair is styled, which he only does on special occasions, and then there's the cologne. The scent that I would follow to the ends of the earth.

Before I can get a word out, probably because my jaw is on the floor, Cole takes the few steps he needs to be only inches from me. His hand gently pushes my hair behind my ear before he brings me in for one of the sweetest kisses I've ever received in my life.

"You look amazing," he says.

"Not too shabby yourself."

"I was going for snazzy."

I laugh, remembering back to that night just a few weeks ago. Was it really that short a time ago? "Well, snazzy has been achieved."

"Good," he says, taking my hand and walking me to the door. "You ready?"

"I am. Can I ask where we're going?"

He shakes his head. "You'll find out soon enough."

We take the few steps we need to get to the elevator. But when it opens, I get my first surprise of the night.

"We're going up?" I ask as Cole pushes the button to go to the roof. "I didn't know we had access."

"Most people don't," he says, a sly smile forming on his handsome face. "Then again, most people don't hook up the building manager with Fury tickets for every home game."

"I like it," I say, stepping in front of him just so I can wrap my arms around his waist. I gave up trying to go around his neck. I barely reach his shoulders. "What other tricks do you have up your sleeve?"

He leans down, giving me a quick kiss on my forehead. "Just wait and see."

It doesn't take long for the elevator to make its way to the roof. In all the months I've lived here, either with Bryce or Cole, I've never been up here.

Though I doubt it looks like this on normal nights. The entire roof is strung with white bulb lights, giving it a soft glow as we look out over Nashville.

"Cole," I whisper, awestruck.

"Just wait," he says, guiding me toward the north edge of the building. When we get a few steps closer, it takes every ounce of willpower in me not to stop and cry. Because before me is a red and white checkered picnic blanket, a cooler, and enough takeout boxes to feed the Fury. It looks like something out of a Hallmark movie.

"What is all this? I ask.

"Well, I thought I could take you out for dinner, but I'm a bit selfish, and I wasn't ready to share you with the public yet. Then I remembered you saying you hadn't tried hot chicken yet. And I'm sorry, but if you're going to call Nashville home, you need a go-to chicken place. It will make our takeout nights much easier. So, I took the liberty of ordering chicken from five different places around town. That way you can try each and see what you like."

Okay, now I'm going to cry. Over fried chicken.

Who does this? Who remembers a specific detail in a lengthy rant that happened more than a month ago and turns it into a storybook first date?

This man. That's who.

"Thank you," I say, wrapping my arms around him and hugging him as hard as I can. "This is perfect."

"Good," he says. "Now, let's dig in. It's time to make you an official Nashville resident."

"TOO HOT! TOO HOT!"

Cole laughs as I grope desperately for a napkin to spit my mouthful of chicken lava into. I should have known his choices would be too hot for me. Early into this process, I decided I was a mild-to-medium kind of girl. But then Cole dared me to try a piece of his.

I don't turn down dares.

Damn my stubborn streak.

"You okay?" he asks, handing me a little glass of milk.

"How in the world do you eat that stuff?"

Cole puffs out his chest. "'Cause I'm a man."

I playfully roll my eyes. "Oh yeah. My big strong man likes his chicken *super* spicy."

"I'll show you a big strong man."

I can't help but giggle as Cole, from a seated position, picks me up in one motion and brings me across the blanket to his lap. I don't mind. In fact, this is probably my new favorite seat in the world. It's pretty much the only time I get to wrap my arms around his neck.

"Have I told you thank you for tonight?"

He kisses me softly. "Only about twenty times."

"Well then let me make it twenty-one."

I can still taste the spices from that crazy chicken on his lips, but right now, it's my favorite flavor. This night has been nothing short of perfect. And if it really is my last first date, what a way to go.

We talk. We laugh. We eat more chicken than I thought was humanly possible. I learn that just because I'm okay with medium spice at one restaurant doesn't mean I'll be able to take the medium spice at another.

The best part, though? It doesn't feel like a first date. First dates are so awkward. You're asking canned questions in hopes of finding anything you have in common with the other person. But with Cole, I already know him. I know about his family and his career. I know he will dip *anything* in ranch dressing but thinks mayo is the grossest condiment on the planet. I know he loves country music, and he would love nothing more than one day to live in a house that has a ton of land so he could get a few horses.

Of course, this would need to be next to Bryce. Ever since they were kids they've had this crazy idea of living next door to each other. Back then I thought it was stupid. Now the idea of maybe one day living with Cole in a house next to my brother and my best friend… Well, that's the stuff fantasies are made of.

The conversation of already knowing each other hasn't been just one way. Instead of a random guy asking me about being a science teacher, he asked me about the experiment that I did with the kids last week where we turned random fruits and vegetables into batteries. I didn't have to put on this grand show. I could just be me.

Best. Date. Ever.

"How did you put this all together?" I ask. "This screams Lucy but I doubt she came home from Italy to help you with this."

"Honestly, she was my first thought," Cole says. "Then I remembered that Coach McAvoy's sister was a party planner. So I called in a few favors."

I look around the roof for probably the hundredth time tonight. Each time I see something different. Like now, I didn't realize that if you look up at the lights, it almost creates this sense of being under a lit pergola.

"I still can't believe you did all this," I whisper.

"Hey," he says, taking my jaw in his fingers and bringing my head around so I'm looking him in the eye. "Do you know how many bad dates I've had to hear about you going on, either from you or your brother?"

I laugh, because holy shit, I had no idea this poor man was painfully enduring my dating stories while trying to bury his own feelings. "Probably too many."

"You are right. Too many. So you must be crazy if you think I was going to put myself in that category."

I tilt my head, because though this is the best first date in the history of first dates, he's getting off too easy. The man needs to work a bit. "Well aren't you cocky? You think you can roll out a super romantic picnic and feed me so much food I end up in a coma and then you aren't lumped in with the rest?"

My words spark that fire in his eye, which is exactly what I was hoping for.

"Fine. If I'm there, then no need for dessert."

My ears perk up. "Dessert?"

"Yup," I can tell he's trying to hold in his laughter, but I give him credit for keeping up the character. "But if I'm just another bad first date, then I guess we can call it a night."

He might be able to hold character, but I can't. "What was for dessert? You can't tease me with dessert then tell me no."

I give him a playful pouty lip, which apparently does the trick as he reaches behind his back and pulls out a small, perfectly plated chocolate cake.

"This is for you," he says.

"What about you?"

He leans in to give me the cake, which also leaves him inches away from my lips.

"You. You are *my* dessert."

I don't know if it was his low tone, or knowing what's coming, but all of a sudden my body is on fire.

"Maybe I can reconsider where you are in the standings."

He lifts me up and lays me down on the blanket. "That's what I thought."

Yup.

Best. Date. Ever.

19

COLE

NO ONE in my life has ever described me as happy.

Grumpy? Sometimes. Serious? Without a doubt. Twenty-five going on sixty? I can say "get off my lawn" with the best of them.

So color me shocked today when not one but *five* of my teammates asked me what was wrong. Every one of them said I was smiling too much.

"Seriously, Campbell, what the fuck?"

This is coming from veteran tight end Wes Taylor. And I must be really smiling because this guy is the epitome of get in, do your job, and get out. After ten years in the league, he's all about just handling his business. He generally keeps to himself and rarely socializes with the younger guys. Except me. And that's probably because I barely socialize with the younger guys, and those guys are my age. This might be only my fourth year in the league, but I've been told I have the personality of a jaded veteran.

"I don't know what you mean."

We're walking back toward the locker room, both of us just having finished up our workouts.

"I think you do know what I mean, but I'm not going to push you. If you wanted to talk about something, you would."

"Thank you," I say, tossing my towel into my locker.

"But that doesn't mean I can't ask the question of who she is. Because only a woman puts a smile like that on a man. And whoever she is, I'm going to guess things are going *very* well."

I shoot a look at him, hoping I'm not giving myself away. I've never really needed a poker face. You don't need one when you don't usually talk or have anything to give away.

"Again, don't know what you mean."

I quickly grab a towel and shower shoes and head toward the showers. But before I get too far, Wes grabs my arm. "Hey. I'm just messin' with you. If you don't want to talk about her, I get it. If you want to ever, I'm here. I just want to say I'm happy for you, because that whole smiling thing looks good on you."

I give him a pat on the back. "Thanks, man. See you next week?"

"Sure thing. Have a good Easter."

I hurry and jump into the shower, hoping no one else stops me for smiling. Until today I never realized how rarely I did it. Don't get me wrong, it's not like I have been living in a state of depression for the past three seasons. But when I'm in the Fury facilities, I'm here to do a job. I'm an offensive lineman. I protect Bryce, I make room for the running backs to run, and I always have my fellow linemen's backs. That's my job. There is nothing I take more seriously.

Football has been my life since I was six years old. I remember that first game like it was yesterday. Bryce was the quarterback, and at that time, I was playing center. Apparently, I was the only one who understood how to snap the ball. Even then we were setting records. Well, at least that's what our coaches told us. I doubt they keep six-year-old football stats, even in a town as football-crazed as Laurel Heights.

I don't think I'll ever forget that first game, though. We were tied as the game wound down. We had the ball at the twenty-yard line, and when you're six, the end zone seems like a mile away. I snapped the ball to Bryce, recorded the first pancake block of my young football career, and Bryce went on to throw the game-winning touchdown. I was so excited I ran into the end zone and, for the first of many times in our career, picked Bryce up and twirled him around.

It was a great day.

Though now that I'm thinking about it, a new memory of that day is coming to light. As soon as I put Bryce to the ground I looked over to my right, and there she was. Brenna. Shit, I forgot that she was a Little Tigers cheerleader. But now that I think about it, I'm seeing her clear as day, jumping and yelling for us as we won our first game. I don't know if she was looking at me, but I was definitely looking at her.

And I remember smiling.

Shit, I had it bad for her even then. I just didn't know it.

I flip off the shower and head back to my locker, doing my best to keep a straight face. Enough guys were at the wedding that it would just be my luck for someone to connect the dots. Especially Dexter.

The only problem is my no-smile plan goes out the window when I see a text from Brenna as soon as I make it back to my locker.

> Brenna: Let the countdown begin: Two hours until a four-day weekend. I wonder what we can get into with four uninterrupted days. =)

Just as I'm about to text her back, my phone rings. And thank goodness I look instead of just assuming it's Brenna.

"Hey Mom," I say, switching the speaker to my AirPods so I can finish getting dressed.

"Hey, baby boy," she says. "How is everything? Catch me up. How was the wedding?"

My mom was devastated when she found out the date of Bryce and Lucy's wedding. She has loved Bryce like a son for so long, and she wanted to be there when he and Lucy finally got married. Unfortunately, the wedding fell right in the middle of my parents' thirtieth-anniversary vacation. They had saved for this for years— even though I could have paid for it in cash without batting an eye, and offered to. So, as much as my parents love Bryce, nothing was going to keep them from seeing the Caribbean.

"It was good," I say, slipping into my clothes to head out of the facility.

"That's it? Your best friend of twenty-plus years gets married and all you have to say is that it was good?"

"What do you want me to say, Mom?"

"I don't know. Make me feel like I was there. I mean, Lucy looked beautiful. And Brenna? Goodness. That dress was just perfect for her."

I make my way out of the facility and into my Jeep. "How do you know what Lucy and Brenna looked like?"

"Facebook, silly. I might not have been there in the flesh, but I made sure to look at every picture so I could make it feel like I was."

Fucking Facebook. Mom has been on me for years to get an account. I'm still holding out.

"Well then if you saw the pictures, what else can I tell you?"

"Maybe you can tell me why you were dancing so close with Brenna Donald when just a few weeks ago I heard through the grapevine you were dating some girl named Jessica?"

Thank God I haven't started driving yet, because I'm pretty sure I would have wrecked the car after hearing her say that.

"Mom, what are you talking about?"

"Which part?"

"Um...both?"

I swear I can hear her roll her eyes through the Bluetooth as I turn the car on. "Well, the Brenna thing was easy. Anyone with two eyes and an up-to-date glasses prescription could see that one. Hell, your granddaddy could probably see it, cataracts, and all. You love that girl, and we'll get back to that later."

Note to self: Find pictures of Brenna and me at the reception and make sure Bryce does not see them before we talk to him.

"As for the Jessica thing," Mom continues, "we have a Facebook group for families of Fury players. All of a sudden one day we get a request from this girl named Jessica, claiming she is your girlfriend. I had my suspicions, but she sent me a friend request and told me all about her and you. And I know you're not very comfortable telling me about your relationships, which I'm used to. I figured you'd tell me on your own time. At first, she was nice. Then… I don't know, Cole. I hope you're done with her, because I think she's a few McNuggets short of a Happy Meal."

This makes me laugh. "That she is, Mom. And don't worry. I broke up with her."

"Good. I'll make sure she's blocked from the group. And this works out great, because now you can bring Brenna home with you for Easter this weekend!"

I hadn't planned on going home for the holiday, especially now that Brenna and I are together. She has four days off, and I planned on spending at least three of them naked.

"Mom, I'm not sure…"

"About what? Seeing your family that you haven't seen since Christmas? Or is it a problem with Brenna? Does she not want to see her mama? *Is* there something going on between you two? Is there something wrong between you two? What are you not sure about?"

There is no guilt trip like the guilt trip of a mother. Thorough *and* unrelenting.

As much as I'd like to keep Brenna to myself this weekend, it has been a while since either of us were in Laurel Heights. Maybe she would like to see her mom? I know she didn't get to spend a lot of time with her around the wedding. And though I'll never admit this to my mother, it would be nice to bring a girl home as my girlfriend. Maybe telling Mom would be a good way to test the waters of how people will react to us being together?

"Fine. We'll drive up tomorrow."

"Good," Mom says. "But I have to know one thing first."

"What's that, Mom?"

"Is Brenna coming here as Bryce's sister? Or as something more?"

Fuck, there goes my stupid smile again. I can't stop it.

"Something more."

I think I hear my mom smiling. "Well, that's just wonderful. We'll see you tomorrow. Drive safe."

"Will do."

I pull up to the stop light and use the Bluetooth to send a text to

Brenna. I have a feeling if I wait any longer, I won't be the one informing her that we are about to take a road trip home.

> Cole: Change of weekend plans. How about a weekend trip to Laurel Heights?

The light doesn't even change colors before I get a reply.

> Brenna: I like the sound of that. Let's go meet the parents =)

20

———

BRENNA

Cole gives me the side eye as he pulls off the highway that puts us on the road leading to Laurel Heights.

"You know exactly where we are. You've made this trip dozens of times. So why the question and why in the world is your knee bouncing like that?"

I look down to see that I am, in fact, bouncing my knee like an amped toddler getting ready to run out to see their Christmas presents. I didn't even realize I was doing it.

"I feel dumb even thinking it," I admit.

"Nothing you can say right now will make me think that."

I let out a sigh. "Fine. I'm nervous."

This gets me another side eye. "Nervous? About what?"

Does he really not get it? I swear...men. "Meeting your parents!"

Cole starts to laugh, but sees the glare I give him and wisely sucks it up. "Okay, I want to get this right. You, Brenna Donald, the most extroverted and daring person I've ever met, is nervous about seeing, not meeting, people you have known for more than twenty years?"

I let my head fall back against the headrest. "I knew you wouldn't get it. And I know it sounds ridiculous. But this is totally different.

They aren't just Susan and Jeff anymore. They are Mr. and Mrs. Campbell, the parents of my boyfriend. I'm not just the little girl who is coming over because I tagged along with my brother. Or the cheerleader who had to leave you your game day treat bag. I'm the girl who is corrupting their son."

"Hey, I'm not complaining about the corruption. And you always gave me the best treats."

"Focus, Campbell!" I yell, turning in my seat to face him. "And this isn't about just me. You have to meet my mother, as my boyfriend!"

I didn't expect calm, cool, and always-focused Cole to be as worried as I am, but I didn't expect him to laugh. And this time he doesn't hold it back.

Asshole. That will cost him later.

"It's not funny," I say.

Cole reaches over the console to take my hand in his. "Brenna. Your mother loves me. She always has."

"But as Bryce's best friend. Not as my boyfriend."

He brings my hand up to his mouth, kissing each of my knuckles. "You need to relax. My parents are over the moon about this. I could hear my mom smiling from Nashville. Dad might even hug you. And your mom? She will be just fine."

This takes me back. "I don't think your dad has said two words to me in my entire life."

"Now you know where I get it from."

I smile a little, but that doesn't erase the worry. "I can't believe we're doing this. What if people see us? You know how the gossip mill is around here. News of us together would literally set the Laurel Heights Facebook page on fire. What if someone tells Bryce before we have a chance to? What if our parents think this is a bad idea and we have to break up? What if—"

"Hey," Cole says, giving my hand a squeeze. "Where's all this coming from?"

I take a deep breath, hoping that Cole doesn't freak out when I say this. "Do you think this is a mistake?"

He doesn't answer for a second, which I don't blame him.

"What part? Us?"

I shrug. "I don't know. Maybe? It was one thing when we were in the cocoon of your apartment. It was just us and it was perfect. But now? Thinking about how many people this affects? Bryce and Lucy. Our families. They've been friends forever. Is this going to make it weird? What if it doesn't work out and all of a sudden our moms can't go to book club together?"

"Well, then they'll just have to find somewhere else to go to drink while pretending to read."

"I'm serious, Cole. I'm scared."

Cole slows the Jeep down and pulls over to the side of the road. He unbuckles his seat belt and does the same for me so we can turn to look at each other.

"Where is this fear coming from? That's not the Brenna I know. The Brenna I know isn't scared of anything."

"You're wrong. I'm also scared of spiders."

"Don't deflect. Tell me. What are you scared of? If it's going to Laurel Heights, I'll turn right around and tell Mom I got sick."

I shake my head. "No. I want to see everyone. I might have moved, but sometimes I miss it."

"Then what is it? Tell me. You know you can tell me anything."

I look into his crystal blue eyes, and they are filled with nothing but concern—and maybe something more. And the something more has me scared shitless.

"This? This trip? This makes us real. Once we do this, we can't go back. And that makes me scared. I'm scared because this relationship isn't just about you and me. I'm scared because this feels more right than anything I've ever had. And I'm scared because you're the first thing in my life I'm afraid of losing."

Cole doesn't say anything. He doesn't need to. Instead he brings my face to his and kisses me with every bit of emotion and comfort he has in his body. It relaxes me. It lights a fire in me. It doubles down on the fact that I'm justified in being scared, because I never want to know what living without him would be like.

"I'm scared too," he says, keeping my face in his hold. "I'm scared that one day I'm going to wake up and find out that this was nothing more than the best dream I've ever had. But want to know what else I know?"

"What's that?" I ask, fighting back tears.

"I know that you're worth fighting for. That *we're* worth fighting for. And if our parents disapprove, then we figure it out. We'll make them approve. Because you? Me? Us? We're too good to go down without a fight."

I let out a big breath. "You're right."

This makes him smile. "Damn right I am."

"Okay, Campbell," I say, sitting back and re-buckling my seat belt. "Let's go see your parents."

"BRENNA, I hope you saved room for some strawberry pie."

My stomach gurgles in protest. Or in desire. Mrs. Campbell's strawberry pie is legendary.

"Maybe in a minute," I say. "Or twenty."

I put my hand over my stomach and look down at my plate. I haven't eaten that much in… I honestly don't know how long. We might be from Southwest Ohio, but Cole's mom is from Mississippi, and her Southern cooking, and Southern sayings, have stuck with her even though she's lived in Ohio for nearly thirty years. We had pork chops, twice-baked potatoes, green beans, and corn. There might have been more; I'm not sure. All I know is that I'm going to need to be rolled out of here.

I'm just glad I wore leggings.

"Mom, it was delicious," Cole says as he starts picking up the plates around the table.

"I had to cook your favorites. I didn't know when I'd get to see you again."

He leans down and gives his mom a kiss on the cheek before taking her plate. "Your guilt trip is noted for the record."

I can't help but smile as I watch Cole interact with his parents.

Adding to the many layers that make up Cole Campbell is the way he acts at home. With his mom, he is polite and loving. With his dad he is both of those things, but with a more formal delivery. This house is filled with love. I can feel it all around me.

Either that or it's the hug Mrs. Campbell gave me the second I walked into the house. I'm pretty sure Cole got some of his strength from his mama. The woman's hug was like a vise.

"Mrs. Campbell?" I ask, which only gets met with a stern look.

"Brenna, I told you to call me Susan. You have always called me Susan. I don't know why tonight you've decided not to."

Well, I can't tell her that reason. That reason is because I feel like if I call her Mrs. Campbell it will somehow be my way of saying sorry for the dirty yet delicious things her son does to me on a daily basis.

"I'm sorry. Susan."

"There, that's better. Now what do you need, my dear?"

"I was just going to ask if I could use the restroom."

"Girl," she says, tossing down her napkin. "Do you think you need to ask here? We're family. Just get up and go. You remember where it is?"

This makes me smile. "Yes. I do. Thank you."

I get up and walk up the few stairs in their split-level home to the restroom. Did I need to use it? Yes. But I also had a secret motive for coming up here. For some reason, I've wanted to see Cole's old room. I used to come up here a lot when I was in high school. It was tradition for the cheerleaders to drop in to the football players' houses and leave them treat bags. I always got Cole. I made sure of it. He was my brother's best friend, and I felt it was my duty.

Or maybe I felt something even back then? Who knows. All I knew was that over my dead body was that slut bag Moriah Marks going to give him treats. She used to say that if she were his cheerleader, she would leave more than candy on his bed.

Hell no.

I walk in, and it's exactly how I remember it. Football trophies line his dressers. There's a picture of him and Bryce when they were six, after they won their first of many league championships. It's right next to the one of the two of them the night they won the state championship in high school. Gosh, I remember that night. I was so proud of both of them. I had Bryce's number painted on one cheek and Cole's painted on the other. I remember after the game just trying to get through the fans and students who rushed the field after we won. Finally, I got a glimpse of Cole, and I gave him two thumbs up like I always did after a win.

If I only knew then what I know now, I would have done so much more. I would have rushed the field and rushed straight toward him. I would have jumped into his arms and given him the biggest hug and kiss I could muster. I would have told him how proud I was of him.

I probably would have told him something else back then. The words that have been rolling in my brain a lot lately, but I'm just not ready yet.

Soon. But not yet.

My eyes keep traveling around the room, and I can't help but notice a few drawings hanging up. Were those always there? I don't remember those from high school, but then again, I probably wasn't paying attention.

"He doesn't draw like he used to," Susan says, leaning against the door jam. "He was always so talented."

"I never knew he could draw like this. I knew he used to, but I never saw anything."

"Oh yes," she says as she signals for me to have a seat on the bed as she takes one herself. "He was always getting picked for art fairs at school as a kid. I think it was his way of giving his brain and body a break when the football got to be too much."

"Why did he give it up? I've never seen him draw, or even doodle."

"You know how kids are," Susan says. "Even when you're the biggest kid in the school, it doesn't mean you're immune to teasing."

When—not if—I find out who teased him for being able to draw, I will throat punch that person at the next reunion.

"Thank you again for having me," I say, not wanting an uncomfortable silence to take over.

Susan takes my hand between both of hers and gives it a pat. "Oh,

Brenna, don't you know how long I've waited for you to come through that door holding my boy's hand?"

I'm pretty sure my eyes grow two inches. "Excuse me?"

"Call it a mother's intuition, or maybe it was just hoping on hope, but whenever I thought about my baby settling down, it was always you who I pictured next to him."

Well, this is interesting news. "Can I ask why? It's not like we ever even flirted with each other back in high school."

"Oh, Brenna…" Susan trails off for a second, but then I realize she's looking at a picture on the wall I hadn't seen. It's Cole and Bryce in their uniforms. And right in the middle is me, smiling from ear to ear in my cheerleading uniform, my bow as big as my head. We are no more than eight in this picture. "I couldn't have asked for a better friend for my boy than Bryce. Was he a pain in the ass sometimes? Yes. But I knew from the moment those two played their first football game together that they were more than friends. They were brothers."

"They were," I say, knowing that's exactly how my mom and I feel about the two of them.

"But then there was you. It would have been easy to think of you as the little sister Cole never had, but there was one time, gosh, I don't even know why I remember this, but you guys were maybe ten years old. We were at the football fields, like always, and a boy came up behind you and pulled your ponytail."

I laugh, because even though I haven't thought about that in years, I do remember what she's talking about. "I was so mad."

"You were. I remember sitting back with your mama, both of us wondering how you were going to handle it."

"I was ready to punch him in the junk."

"That was our bet," Susan says with a laugh. "But you didn't need to."

I smile, the memory flooding back. "I didn't."

"Nope. Because my son was there in five seconds, lifting that poor boy off the ground by his shirt collar."

"I think I remember worrying he was going to pee himself."

"We all did. I remember thinking to myself that it was nice Cole did that for you. That it was a brotherly reaction."

I tilt my head, wondering where she's going with this. "I have a feeling there's a *but* coming."

"You're right. Because as soon as he dropped that pipsqueak, you ran up to my boy and jumped in his arms, giving him the biggest hug I had ever seen. You looked at him like he was your hero. And then when he put you down, that's when I knew. He wasn't looking at you like a sister. Nope, my boy had just rescued his princess."

I feel the tears welling up in my eyes. "Susan…"

She shakes her head. "I know neither of you realized it at the time, but that's when I looked at your mama and just knew in my heart we were going to be family someday. I know it took you both some time to get here, but I'm just glad you both made it."

I don't have any more words. Instead, I throw my arms around her neck, hugging her just as tight as she hugged me earlier.

"Thank you," I say, though I don't know what exactly I'm thanking her for.

"No, my dear. Thank you. Thank you for loving my baby."

"What are you two doing? Why are you both crying? I can't take you both crying." Cole's horrified voice cuts through the tears and makes both of us laugh.

"Don't you worry about us," Susan says as she stands up. "I'll leave you two alone."

She turns and gives me a wink as she walks out the door.

"Everything okay?" Cole asks, sitting on the bed where his mom just was. "What did she say to you?"

I shake my head and put my head on his shoulder. "Just shared some history with me, and reminded me of a few things."

This gives him pause. "History?"

"Yup. And guess what?"

"What's that?"

I turn and press a kiss to his shoulder. "I'm not scared anymore."

21

———————

BRENNA

Cole: What do you mean you haven't told her?

Brenna: I just haven't found the right moment.

Cole: You've been with her all day!

Brenna: I know. We're going to dinner now. I'll tell her then.

Cole: Do you want me to come with you? I've been with my sister and her crazy kids all day. I could use a break.

Brenna: No. They never get to see Uncle Cole. Go be the funcle.

Cole: We're going to see them tomorrow for Easter. I can come. No problem.

Brenna: While it would be nice for you to be here for backup, we're going out to eat at Celine and Luciano's place. I don't want the rumor mill to start up before we've told who we need to tell.

> Cole: I get it. I miss you. But you got this. Call
> me if you need backup.

> Brenna: Will do <3

I SLIP my phone into my purse as my mom comes back from the restroom at Lucine. I haven't been here since it first opened. I'm so glad for Luciano and Celine that it's just as busy tonight as it was opening night more than a year ago.

"So what looks good?" Mom asks as she opens her menu. "Did you order the pizza bread for the appetizer?"

"Yes, Mom," I say—like I'd forget that. Luciano's family owns the best pizza place in Southwest Ohio, Tripoli's. Also known as "what the Donald family has eaten for dinner every Sunday for nearly twenty years." When Luciano opened this place, he put Tripoli's pizza on the menu as an appetizer. It's a must-get.

"Good," she says, putting down her menu. "I'm so glad you came home this weekend. It has been too long since we've spent time together, just us."

We reach for each other's hands and give them a squeeze. "I know. And sorry I haven't been home more."

She waves me off. "No. I understand. You're starting a new life in Nashville. I can't expect you to be home every weekend just because of me."

"I know," I say, still feeling guilty. I hate that it's just Mom up here. Yes, she has her friends. Yes, she's still working so that keeps her busy. But knowing that Bryce and I are both away still stabs at my heart. "So what is new in Laurel Heights?"

"Ha. You're funny," she says. "You know nothing in this town has changed. But enough about here. Tell me about you. How are your students? Are you making friends? Maybe...I don't know... seeing anyone?"

A waitress comes to our table, and we put in our order. Her timing couldn't be more perfect. This now gives me a minute or two to decide how I want to enter this conversation.

Because it's now or never.

"Actually, Mom, I am seeing someone."

"Really?" she says, taking a sip of her water. "You didn't bring anyone to the wedding. Is this new?"

"Well, he was at the wedding. Though at the time, yes, it was very new."

She tilts her head. "I'm not following."

I suck in a breath, because here it goes.

"Cole. Cole and I are dating."

Mom doesn't say anything for what feels like minutes. I don't know if that's because she's processing what I just said or because the pizza bread was delivered to the table.

"Mom?" I ask, because her silence is killing me. "Do you have anything to say? You're freaking me out."

She shakes her head a bit, as if coming back to reality. "Oh, Brenna. Of course I'm happy for you. And I'm sorry if it sounded like I wasn't. It just…well, it took me by surprise."

"Believe me, no one was more surprised about how I felt than me."

"Wow," she says, like she's still processing. "I saw you two dancing at the wedding, and I thought for a second that you two looked cozy together. But I didn't think anything of it. Because it's Cole. And you."

"I know," I say. "Believe me, when I first realized I had feelings for him, I freaked out too. I mean, this is the guy who has been just as much a part of this family as anyone over the years."

"Can I ask when this started?"

I go on to tell Mom about the last few months as we munch on pizza bread. I tell her about my apartment flood, and I couldn't live with Lucy and Bryce. Though I kindly blame that on the wedding instead of the truth that my brother was loud during sex. He owes me one for that. I go on to say that I don't know exactly when it happened, but over the time spent we together, I started to realize he's more than just my brother's best friend, or the guy I've known since I had baby teeth. That he's Cole. And that every day I'm with him is better than the one before.

"Oh Brenna," she says, taking my hands in hers. "I guess now I do owe Susan a pie because she has been saying for years you two should be together."

"You can tell her that tomorrow over Easter dinner. She's invited both of us over."

"That would be lovely," she says. "So, since you said that this happened around the time of the wedding, and since I'm also just hearing about this, I'm going to go on a limb and say that your brother does not know yet."

I shake my head. "No. We didn't want to take away from the wedding, and we were still trying to figure out if this was real or not. No sense in telling him if it was just something that was going to pass by in a few days."

"And I'm guessing that it didn't pass."

I shake my head. "Not even a little bit."

Mom sits back against the backrest of the booth. "How do you plan on telling him?"

"That's the million-dollar question."

As our food gets delivered, my phone buzzes with a text.

Cole: Okay, I know you said you have this, but I don't feel right about you taking the bullet alone. Plus, I know your mom misses me. I'm on my way. Save me some pizza bread.

I can't help but smile as I dive into my bowl of shrimp Alfredo.

"If he makes you smile like that, then no way could your brother be mad."

I set down my fork and dab a napkin at my lips. "He's on his way."

"Oh good!" Mom says. "I barely got to see him at the wedding. I wondered why. Now I know. You must have been keeping him occupied."

I laugh as she wiggles her eyebrows. "Mom!"

"He's a very handsome man, Brenna. You have nothing to be ashamed about."

I feel the blush heating my cheeks. I was barely ready for this conversation. I'm definitely not ready to share details of my sex life with my mother.

I'll never be ready for that.

"I'm happy for you, Brenna, I really am," she pauses to take a sip of water. And I have a feeling I know why she did. "But, I still worry about how your brother is going to react. You know he doesn't take sudden news well."

A baritone voice answers her. "No, he doesn't. How about we send him up here so you can set him straight?"

I turn to see Cole standing next to the booth, looking just as handsome as ever in a fitted T-shirt and jeans. I also feel my heart melt just a little when I see the bouquet of flowers he's holding.

"Oh, Cole!" Mom says, leaping up from her seat to give him a hug. "How have you been?"

"No complaints at all, Mrs. Donald. Here, these are for you." He steps back slightly to give her the flowers before taking a seat next to me. I'm now thankful for the small amount of privacy we get from a booth. At least I can hold his hand under the table without the whole restaurant catching on.

"You didn't have to do that," she says, placing them down on the table.

He winks. "I didn't know what I'd be walking into, so I figured they couldn't hurt."

Mom just smiles at the two of us. "I'm so happy for you two. I couldn't ask for a better man for my baby girl."

"Can you make sure you tell Bryce that?" I say. "In those exact words."

Mom waves her hands in the air, as if dismissing the notion. "Bryce is stubborn. We all know this. And he's not great with change."

"Tell me about it," I mumble.

"He's going to feel like you both lied to him," Mom continues. "And though that's technically the truth, I understand why you both did it. Yes, he'll need some time to adjust. But if you show him that you're both committed to this relationship, and that it's more than just a fling, he'll have no choice but to come around."

"I don't know about that," Cole says. "He told me once that not one of his friends or teammates were good enough for Brenna. And when I brought up the idea of me, he all but fell over laughing."

Mom shakes her head, almost as if she can't believe it. "Oh, that boy. Such a dramatic. I always said if he didn't get into football, he would have been a great actor."

We all laugh at that idea. "We want to tell him," I continue. "We just don't know the best way. Any advice?"

Mom sits back into the booth. "I don't know if there is a best way, and unfortunately there might only be one way."

"And that is?"

"Rip the Band-Aid off. Don't drag it out. And don't expect his first reaction to be his last. Give him time to process."

We look at each other and nod. "That makes sense. Thanks, Mom."

"No problem. But there's one more piece to the puzzle."

"What's that?"

"Make sure Lucy knows and is ready to deal with the fall out. And buy her some wine. She'll need it."

22

COLE

"WHERE ARE WE GOING?"

Brenna points to the left from the passenger seat. "Turn here, then just follow the road."

I do as she says, though I have my suspicions about where she is asking me to drive her. "You know, if you wanted to make out with me, we could have just gone to my bedroom and pretended to take a nap."

"One: You know your nieces and nephew would not leave us alone long enough for any sort of kissing time. And two, who said anything about making out?"

"Are you not taking me back to Lake Laurel?"

"Yes, but what does that have to do with making out?"

I turn the car where she directs and head back to the spot that I only know exists because it's where Bryce used to come to clear his mind. It's also where he and Lucy used to go to get away from, well, everything. What they did there, I can only suspect. Though I do know that every time I saw him after a trip here his lips looked like they were just sucked by a vacuum.

"I guess I assumed that it was a Donald thing to come here for some privacy."

"Ew, gross," Brenna says, a visible shiver going up her spine. "I was more of a Heights Park fan. But no, we're not here because of that. Come on, follow me."

She gets out of the Jeep before I can even have a chance to go open her door. Hell, she's almost at a full-on sprint as she heads to a small, deserted picnic area. I mean, it makes sense given that it's Easter Sunday. But it's kind of eerie being the only ones here.

No, eerie isn't the right word. It's peaceful. Serene. Someone could get lost in their thoughts out here.

"Come on, Campbell!" Brenna yells, stopping at a picnic table. "You're getting slow in the off season."

"Excuse me for not sprinting for a race I didn't know I was in."

She shoots me a look for my sarcastic comment. "I'm going to let that one slide, but I should clue you in. You're with a Donald now. Everything is a competition. Now get over here. I have a surprise for you."

I can't help but smile as I make my way to the picnic table. I don't know if it's because I'm thinking of a lifetime of little competitions with this woman or the fact that somehow she's surprising me out of the blue. Maybe both.

"Okay, Trouble. What's up your sleeve?"

"Well," she begins as she starts pulling notebooks out of her bag, "I noticed something when I went into your room the other day."

"That my mom needs to take down the shrine she's made to me in there?"

She shakes her head. "No. I love that. Especially because there's a picture of me. What I was going to say was that I completely forgot you used to draw."

I feel a blush heating on my face. "That was a long time ago."

"I know. In my opinion, it's been too long." Brenna holds out the notebooks to me. When I take a closer look at them, I realize they aren't just normal notebooks. No, they are drawing and sketching books. And not only that—she also has an assortment of art pencils for me.

"What's all this?"

"I know they aren't the really good ones, but it was the best I could find on the fly. But I remember you telling me that you loved to draw, but that no one knew about it."

"You remembered that? I told you that when you were drunk in Clemson."

"I remember more of that night than you think," she says with a wink. "Anyway, seeing those pictures, I was blown away by how talented you are. And even if no one ever sees them, being teased years ago by asshole kids because they were likely jealous of you is no reason to let this talent go to waste. You're amazing at it. So, consider this your first step of picking back up an old hobby."

I'm not much of a crier. In fact, I can remember twice in my life when I ever cried.

This is very close to becoming number three.

"I don't know what to say."

Brenna puts her hand on top of mine. "You don't need to say anything. Just make me a promise."

"Anything."

"Draw one for me. I want something to look at in my classroom every day that will make me smile."

I set the drawings down and reach for Brenna. She immediately meets my hands and lets me pull her into me. Like it's the most natural thing in the world, she sits on my lap, looping her hands around my neck before bringing her lips to mine. We take our time savoring each other. Seeing family this weekend has been great, don't get me wrong. But that means we've only been able to steal a few moments with each other. I haven't been able to kiss her like this, slow and steady, where our lips and tongues are in no rush to take what they want.

"This is the best present I've ever gotten," I say as I push a strand of loose hair behind her ear. "Thank you."

"You are very welcome," she says, giving me one more small kiss. "Do you want to try them out? I thought this would be a good view for you to capture the sunset."

My hand travels down, only to go back up her shirt. I give her breast a squeeze, which immediately makes her squirm.

"I have a better idea."

"COLE! WE CAN'T DO THIS!"

I pull my Jeep up to a tucked-away corner in Heights Park. "You said you were a Heights Park kinda gal. So here we are."

"Yeah, ten years ago," she says. "What if someone sees us?"

Brenna looks around for the people she thinks are going to see us, but she's not going to find anything. The park is completely empty.

"What happened to the girl I used to call Trouble?"

She shoots me a look. "You called me that an hour ago."

"Well, an hour ago I thought you were. Apparently, the rumors are true, the once-fearless wild child Brenna Donald has lost her spunk."

I see the moment the challenge enters her eyes. There's my girl. Yes, I'm crazy about the woman she has become. I love our nights alone when we're being lazy on the couch. I can see myself marrying the school teacher and spending weeknights with her grading papers and her wearing my jersey on Sundays. But a part of me has always wondered what it would be like to be with the wild child...the girl I first fell for all those years ago. She might not come out often, but I know she's still there.

"How dare you challenge my spunk," she says as she takes off her seatbelt and turns to me.

"I'm just saying," I say, pushing my seat back. "I call it like I see it."

"You play dirty, Campbell," she says, situating herself on her knees.

"I don't know what you mean?"

"You know exactly what you're doing," she whispers in my ear, her hand grazing over my cock through my jeans.

"I don't," I say, trying not to groan as she continues to stroke me. "I was a good kid. I never came up here like you troublemakers."

Brenna unzips the fly on my jeans and releases the button. It only takes a little adjusting to push down my jeans and boxer briefs to let my aching cock spring free. Brenna's hand is on it as soon as it does. Fuck, it feels so good. Her touch is so warm compared to the cool bite in the spring air.

"I guess it's true what they say then," Brenna says, adjusting herself so her mouth is now inches away from my dick. "You good boys should always watch out for us bad girls. We're nothing but trouble."

The second her mouth is on me I nearly explode. I have to take the deepest breath of my life to not come then and there. But fuck, she feels so good. Too good. Her mouth is working in tandem with her hand. There is never a point where some part of my dick isn't being felt or tasted. And her tongue? I don't know what she's doing at my tip, but I never want her to stop doing that.

I sweep her hair off her face, which gives me a fantastic view of her working every inch of me. "Yes, Brenna. God, you feel so good."

My words must hit the right chord because her tempo increases. She's like a woman possessed right now, and I can't stop staring at her. She's so fucking gorgeous. So fucking sexy.

So fucking mine.

I knew it before, but today has cemented it. I can't imagine her not in my life. I can't imagine her being with another man. I can't imagine not spending every day of the rest of my life with her.

She's it for me. And fuck anyone, especially my best friend, if he's going to tell me otherwise.

I gently bring her head back, surprising her, because I'm pretty sure my girl was about to make me see stars.

"What are you doing? I wasn't done."

I lean over and scoop her off her seat. Thank the fucking heavens she's wearing a dress today, so it only takes me a few seconds to hike it up and slip her panties to the side.

"I need to be inside of you. Right fucking now."

I lean over to the glove compartment to grab a condom, but Brenna puts her hand on my arm.

"No," she says, shaking her head. "I'm clean and get the shot. I don't want anything between us, Cole."

"Are you sure? I'm clean, too. We have to get regular checks. And I've never. Not with anyone."

She reaches down and lines my cock up to her center. Fuck, I can already tell I'm barely going to last.

"I trust you."

Those might not be the three words I've been fighting back, but they are the best three words I could hear at this moment. The second she lowers herself onto me, I crash my lips to hers. It's either that or scream so loud that everyone in town will know what we're doing.

Fuck, if I thought her mouth was warm before, that was nothing. She's so fucking hot. So fucking wet.

And now, without a doubt, mine.

My lips work down the side of her neck and across the top of her chest. My hands are working her tits through the fabric of her dress. There might not be any skin to skin, but the way her hips are answering every time I pinch her nipple, the effect is still there.

"You feel so good," she says, her hips working up and down to take every inch of me.

"Too good," I pant. "Not sure how long I'm going to last."

Brenna leans in to me. Our bodies are now flush as our hips continue to meet at a frantic pace. "Let go for me. Let me feel you inside of me."

Her words go straight to my cock. And I might want to do exactly that, but not without taking her with me.

"Lean back. Come with me."

She does as I ask, and my fingers begin to work in tandem with my cock. The inside and outside stimulation must be too much because in a matter of seconds, my girl stills on top of me a second before I feel her explode on my cock.

"Brenna!" I yell, because it's too much for me, too. I bring her chest into mine as our orgasms rip through us, holding her tight as we ride the wave together.

Fuck, that was intense. And judging by Brenna's heaving chest, and the fact that she is shaking in my arms, it was something special for her, too.

When we both come back to earth, I slowly lift her up off me, though I don't let her go. No, I'm not ready to quite yet.

"You're mine, you know that, right?" I whisper in her ear, leaving small kisses along her neck.

"Good," she replies. "Because I'm not going anywhere."

23

———

BRENNA

"OKAY, let's practice what we're going to do one more time."

I think I hear Cole groan, but I choose to ignore it. He can pout all he wants, but tonight is important.

Tonight we're telling Bryce.

We didn't pounce on him and Lucy the second they got home from their honeymoon. Granted, we were still in Laurel Heights when they got back, so they had a few days without us. But Cole and I both know we won't be able to hide it from him, so it's best to do what Mom suggested— rip off the bandage of denial and tell him tonight.

"We're not going to bring it up right away," Cole says. "We're going to talk normal. Eat dinner, then bring it up."

"Correct," I say as we step onto the elevator to take us up to Bryce and Lucy's. "I'm going to take Lucy into the kitchen to get us all drinks, and you're going to begin bringing up the conversation."

"And then when you come back you're going to sit next to me. I'll either hold your hand or touch you in some way, and then I'll tell him, gently, that we have been seeing each other. That it's getting serious, and we wanted him to know."

"Then when he asks how long it's been going on?"

"We'll be honest and say the wedding, but we didn't want to get in the way of his day or honeymoon."

"And when he starts going insane?"

"We let Lucy handle him."

"Perfect," I say, letting out a relieving breath. "I have a good feeling about this."

Cole leans down and gives me a small kiss. "You really are a glass-half-full girl, aren't you?"

"I am," I say, returning the kiss. "But let's be real. Tonight's glass is going to be full at all times. That's the other part of the plan."

Cole holds up a six-pack of Dr Pepper. "Cheers to that."

The elevator stops and opens, bringing us face-to-face with Bryce's door. I might have been confident thirty seconds ago, but now that we're here, that confidence is draining fast.

"We got this," he says, giving my hand a squeeze.

I look up at him and give him a wink. "It's you and me. Of course we do."

I hear us each take one last deep breath before Cole knocks on Bryce's door. Cole lets go of my hand, and I miss the contact instantly. But it's necessary, because after tonight, we'll never need to sneak around again.

"There are my two favorite people!" Bryce yells as he swings open the door.

"Hello, brother," I say, giving him a hug and a kiss on the cheek. "How was the honeymoon?"

"Perfect in every way," he says, walking over to Cole to give him their weird man-hug-slap thing. "Come in. Dinner was just dropped off."

Cole and I make eye contact and give each other a nod. He sneaks in a wink, which nearly makes me giggle, but I hold strong.

"There she is!" Cole says as he sees Lucy walking toward the dining area carrying plates. He takes them from her, sets them down on the table, and wraps her in a big bear hug.

"I've missed you too, Cole," she says, giving his chest a pat as he lets go of her. "Have you been holding down the fort while we've been away?"

"I have," he says as he turns his eyes to me. "I've been holding it down pretty good, if I do say so myself."

My eyes go wide and I hurry and look at Bryce to see if he caught onto that little innuendo. Luckily, and predictably, Bryce is in his own world, playing with something on the television.

"Brenna, can you help me bring the rest of the food out?" Lucy says as she not-so-subtly summons me to the kitchen.

I don't say anything, though I do shoot Cole a "you better watch it" look before I head back to the kitchen. Though the second I step foot in it, maybe I need to be telling Lucy to chill out, judging by the way she's bouncing up and down.

"Are you okay?" I ask. "Did you come back with some sort of weird European disease?"

"Oh my gosh!" she squeals, running into me for a hug. "You two are so damn adorable together. Which I knew all along. Ahh! This is so great."

"Shhh!" I whisper-yell. "You're going to blow it."

"Well then you two better quit giving each other the fuck-me eyes," she says as she goes into the refrigerator to pull out the wine for us. "I mean, you can't help the 'we had sex an hour ago' energy. He's smiling, which—let's be real—Cole isn't exactly a smiley guy. And you? I think you're floating on air. Which, by the way, is a very good look on you."

I smile, because it does feel like I'm floating. "I'm so happy, Lucy. It's… I don't even know how to put it in words."

She smiles and gives my hand a squeeze. "That's when you know you have it. When you have all of the words, yet none of the words can do justice to what you're feeling."

My best friend is so damn smart. "So, I wanted to give you a heads up. We're telling Bryce tonight."

Lucy nods. "I think that's a good idea. He's in a good mood from the honeymoon. And even if he resists at first, how can he hold out when he sees how in love you two are with each other?"

"Whoa, love?" I say. "I never said love."

Lucy picks up a few containers of whatever she ordered and gives me a wink. "You didn't need to."

"WHO'S READY FOR DESSERT?"

All three of our stomachs lurch at the sound of Bryce's question.

"How can you even think about dessert after what we just ate?" I ask. Cartons of empty Chinese food litter the table at Bryce and Lucy's. I think Lucy ordered one of everything. And there isn't a noodle or grain of rice to spare.

"Fine," he says as she stands up to start clearing the table. "I just figured we'd want a little something to snack on as we looked at wedding photos!"

"How do you have wedding pictures already?" Cole asks. "I thought those took months to get ready?"

"These are just proofs, but we couldn't wait any longer," he says. "Now, you two grab a seat. Lucy and I will clean up and bring out drinks and snacks. It's picture time!"

Cole and I do as Bryce asks and take a seat on his couch, panic both shooting through our eyes.

"This wasn't part of the plan," I whisper.

"I know," Cole grumbles. "Leave it to Bryce to get as excited about wedding photos as he does about game film. I guarantee we are going to break down and analyze every photo."

"Shit! What if photos are there of us?"

His eyes grow wide. "The ones my mom saw..."

"Exactly," I say. "What if they are there and he puts the puzzle together?"

"Then that's how we tell him. That's our Plan B." Cole reaches for my hands and gives them a squeeze. "And if he doesn't then we're on to Plan C."

"What's Plan C?"

He shrugs. "Run."

"Personally, I'm waiting to see if the photographer got any of Cole's crazy ex trying to crash the wedding."

Bryce's comment startles us so much we nearly leap back from each other like two teenagers who just got caught making out. "Yeah," I say, trying to cover our reaction up. "That would be hilarious."

"No," Bryce says, firing up the television. "The hilarious thing was that she thought you were the reason Cole dumped her."

Lucy gives me a sympathetic look as she takes a seat next to Bryce.

"Why would it be so crazy?" I ask. I mean, he brought it up. "I'm living with Cole. We've known each other for years. It wasn't a preposterous assumption on her part."

Bryce looks at me, then at Cole, then back to me. "Yes, it was. You're basically family. So for one, it's gross to even think about. And two, there's the code."

The fucking code. I hate the fucking code.

"Is that really a thing?" I ask. "Or something that football players believe in that doesn't exist. Like a weird superstition?"

"The code is sacred," Bryce says, pushing the final buttons to connect the computer to the television. "You don't date a teammate's sister. Nothing good ever comes from it. The relationships rarely work, and all they do is cause drama in the locker room. It's just better to never have them."

I don't even look at the pictures as Bryce goes through each and every one of them. How can I, when all I can do is replay what Bryce just said on a loop?

I don't want to be that person. I don't want to be the person who causes drama. I just want to be with Cole and have my brother be on board with it. Is that too much to ask?

"Oh, look!" Bryce says. "Here's a picture of the bridal party dance."

I look up and immediately push back the tears. The photographer has a wide shot of the dance floor, letting us see every couple dancing. Bryce and Lucy are looking at each other like they are the only two in the room. Celine and Luciano are blissfully smiling at each other. Then there's me and Cole. I'm guessing this had to be toward the end of the song, because my head is on his chest, and he's holding me like he's never going to let me go.

"Everyone looks so happy," Lucy says, laying her head on Bryce's shoulder.

"They do," Bryce agrees. "Except Cole and Brenna. I'm pretty sure he's trying to figure out a way to move her head from his body."

"Actually," Cole says. "That's not at all what I was thinking. Not even in the slightest."

Bryce gives him a questioning look. Lucy pops her head up suddenly from Bryce. I stop breathing.

Holy shit, here we go...

"Dude, why are you all of a sudden so serious?"

I don't know if Bryce means to, but the television screen changes to the next photo. It's of the same dance, only this time, the photo is just of Cole and me. My head is still on his chest. My eyes are closed. He's holding my right hand against his heart as his other hand is completely around my waist. His eyes are also closed.

We both look so peaceful. Like nothing in the world that could ruin this moment for us.

Bryce looks at the television then looks back to Cole.

"Dude. What the fuck?"

In a move I wasn't expecting, Cole reaches over and takes my hand in his, linking our fingers together.

And that's all we need to say.

Because before I know it, Bryce is jumping over a coffee table and punching Cole in the face.

24

COLE

ONE PUNCH. I always knew in my heart of hearts that when Bryce found out, I'd give him one punch. I figured it was fair since I was doing things with his sister that no brother should ever have to imagine.

And I have to give my best friend credit; I didn't know he could throw a fist like that.

"Bryce!" Lucy yells as she does her best to pull him off me. "What are you doing?"

I stand up and put a little bit of distance between us. "It's okay, Lucy."

Brenna comes over and looks at my eye, which is going to surely have one hell of a shiner there tomorrow. Again, if it wasn't this situation, and I wasn't on the receiving end, I'd be pretty impressed with Bryce.

"No, it's not!" Brenna yells. "Bryce, I know this is a shock and might be hitting you out of left field, but that's no reason to punch him."

"A shock?" he yells. "A shock would be telling me the Fury got sold to the highest bidder. This? This... I can't even fucking *think* right now I'm so mad."

I look at Brenna, who is currently fighting back tears. I know we talked about his reactions, and this was one of them. But I don't think either of us knew how much worse it would be in person.

"Let's all sit down and try to relax," Lucy says, coming out of nowhere with two bags of frozen vegetables for me and Bryce. "We're all adults, and I think it would be wise of us to remember that right now."

Brenna and I sit down, and after Lucy gives his sleeve a tug, so does Bryce. None of us say anything for minutes. It is, without a doubt, the most uncomfortable stretch of silence I've ever experienced. But hell if I'm going to be the one who says something. Bryce is the one with the problem right now.

"How long?"

His question is so muffled I barely heard him. "Right before the wedding," I answer. "The reason we didn't tell you was because we didn't want anything to take away from your day."

"Bullshit," he says, pointing to the picture still on the screen. "That's not the face of two people who started fucking days before. So how long?"

"Sorry that we don't fit your timeline standards, brother, but Cole is telling you the truth," Brenna says. "We kissed the night before the rehearsal dinner. That was the first time anything happened between us."

Bryce looks at me, then to Brenna, then back to me again. "Brenna? Lucy? Can you excuse Cole and me? I want to talk to him. Just the two of us."

"Absolutely not," Brenna says as she stands up, almost daring to get in Bryce's face. "Whatever you want to say to him you can say in front of me."

I put a hand on her arm, bringing her back to me. "It's okay."

She looks between the two of us. "This is our fight. Together."

"I know," I say, standing up and kissing her forehead. "But let me take this round."

"Get a room!" Bryce roars. "Let me talk to my *supposed* best friend!"

Lucy steps in front of him, and I can tell she's trying to stay calm.

"You're allowed to be angry. You're allowed to have your feelings. But just remember, anything you're about to say to him, you can't take back. Do you understand?"

I've always called Lucy the Bryce Whisperer. She was the only one who was ever able to bring him back when he hit his low points. And apparently, she's the only one from stopping him from grabbing a kitchen knife and stabbing me.

"I'm fine, Lulu," he says. "I just want to chat with Cole."

Brenna grabs her purse and gives me a kiss on the cheek before she and Lucy leave the apartment. We both sit back down. I hold the frozen vegetables to my eye as he holds his against his knuckles. I plan on telling him anything he wants to know, but fuck if I know at this point what he's the most upset about.

That's the problem with being Bryce Donald's best friend. On the field? The man can handle pressure and blitzing defenses like it's nothing. Real life? That's never been his strong suit. He has trouble processing a lot of things at once. So something like this? I knew it was going to throw him.

I guess I just didn't realize how much.

"I'm going to ask you again," Bryce says. "How long? And not that you've been together. How long have you had feelings for my sister?"

I sit back in the chair and take the veggies off my eye. "That I can remember? Senior year at Clemson. That's when I first realized it."

"But?"

Figures my best friend could hear the unsaid word. "But now that we've been together, I think it was a long time before that. It was just—she was Brenna. She was your sister. That's what I thought it was. Now that we're together? I think it's always been her."

"That's it, though!" Bryce yells, standing up so he can start pacing. "She's a sister to you. Or at least she should be. You've known her as long as you've known me. This just... It isn't right."

"Or," I say, also standing up, which I don't know is a smart move on my part, but I'm going with it. "Maybe that's why it *is* right. I've known her forever. She knows me. We fit. There was no weird first date chatter. Hell, my mother was already picking our wedding invitations."

"Wait!" Bryce yells. "Your mom knows?"

I swallow, because here's the second low blow of the night. "Yes. And so does yours."

"Fucking wonderful!" Bryce yells, throwing the bag of vegetables against the wall. "Am I the last one to fucking know?"

"Yes, but not by design," I say. "We really weren't going to tell anyone. Then Luciano caught us at the wedding. And Lucy caught on, 'cause she's Lucy and you can't get anything past her. As for our families? Mom invited us home for Easter, and she just knew. We also talked to your mom so there were no secrets between our families. This wasn't done on purpose. It's just kind of how the hand played."

Daggers. That's what are shooting out of Bryce's eyes now.

"I'm sorry," I say.

"For what?" he asks. "For which of all of betrayals are you sorry for? Or is this some half-assed blanket apology?"

"Bryce, listen."

"No, Cole. *You* listen." He stops his pacing, which might be more frightening than wondering if he's going to punch me again. "You're my best friend. And, in a matter of minutes, I not only find out that you are fucking my sister, but that you also lied to me about it, and lied to me for years about having feelings for her. Then, to top it off, you tell me that everyone in my life knew except me, and you want me to listen? Fuck that, Cole. I've listened enough for one night."

"I understand," I say. "Please know though, we didn't mean to hurt you."

"Good fucking job on that one," he says.

I take the few steps I need toward his door but turn back to look at him. He's slumped down on the couch, his head resting on his fists. Usually this would be the time I'd try to coax him out of it. I'd try to help him figure out what's going on in that brain of his. And if I couldn't do it, I'd send in Lucy.

Thank God he'll have her tonight.

"One more thing," I say as I open the door. "I know this is a lot. But whenever you're ready to talk more, or to ask questions, or to figure out whatever you need to figure out, I'm here. But also know this. I love her, Bryce. She's not a fling, and I'm not just another guy. This isn't the fuck buddy of the week. I'd die before I let something happen to her. I promise to protect her at all costs. No matter who it is, that's who you should want for your sister."

Bryce looks up to me, his eyes more sad than I've seen in a very long time. The last time he looked like this involved Lucy, Luciano, and the worst months of his life. "You said that to me once. That you'd protect me. Funny how you end up being the one stabbing me in the back."

"Bryce—"

"Leave, Cole. Just fucking leave."

Realizing that this isn't going anywhere, I do what he asks and shut the door behind me.

25

______

BRENNA

"WAS THAT A GOOD IDEA?"

That is the eighth time Lucy has asked that question since we left the penthouse and came back down to Cole's apartment. Also known as the Neutral Zone.

"I mean, it's been a half hour," I say, setting down freshly refilled wine glasses for the two of us. "Either they are hugging it out, into the fifth round of their boxing match, or they are not speaking and uncomfortably staring at each other."

If I were a betting woman, my money would be on the last option. I would be utterly shocked if Bryce came around to the idea of Cole and me after one conversation. And while I'm sure Bryce felt better after getting in that punch, he's smart enough not to try to actually go rounds with a man who has six inches and more than a hundred pounds on him.

"Well, at least you get to stay here," Lucy says. "I have to go to the lion's den and admit that I knew about you two."

"Ah but there is the hypocritical difference when it comes to my brother," I say, tipping my wine glass to hers. "You are Lucy. His Lulu. You can do no wrong. You will be forgiven the fastest in this whole debacle. Yes, he might pout for a night. Maybe get a little angry when you have to rein him in, but you two aren't going to bed tonight fighting."

"I don't know," Lucy says. "He was pretty mad. Then again, if I knew what he was really angriest about, maybe we could end this sooner rather than later."

"Everything. He's mad about everything."

I don't even hear the door open as Cole walks through. His eye is already swollen, and he looks mentally exhausted, but he seems otherwise unharmed.

"Hey," I say, running into his outstretched arms. "Everything okay?"

He leans down and kisses the top of my head. "I guess that depends on what your definition of okay is."

We walk back to the couch together as Lucy brings him over a bottle of water. "I'm so sorry, Cole," Lucy says. "I really thought he'd handle it better."

Cole shakes his head. "You have nothing to apologize for. In fact, I'll apologize to you because he knows now that you knew before him. So for that, I'm sorry for whatever you're about to endure."

She leans over and gives both of us a hug. "Don't worry about me. I've learned how to handle an angry Bryce Donald."

"Thank you," I say as I get up to walk her to the door. "I'll text you tomorrow."

"You better."

I start to turn away, but Lucy grabs my arm. "Just so you know, my idiot husband might be against this right now. But me? I'm in. I'm all in. I always had a feeling about you two. And I couldn't be happier. I know this will all work out. Just give it time."

I bring my best friend in for the hug of her life. "Thank you," I whisper. "Now please go work your magic on your husband."

She gives me one more squeeze before letting go. "I'll do my best."

I shut the door as Lucy heads back up the elevator. "Well, we did it."

Cole lets out a humorless laugh. "Something like that."

"Can I get you anything? Your eye doesn't look so great."

He shakes his head and reaches out his hands. "All I need right now is my girl in my arms."

I smile, because that I can do. I walk back over to him and climb on his lap, him cradling me like he's holding a baby. Which sometimes I feel like he is, considering he's a full foot taller than me. "So, we told him."

This makes him laugh. "Yeah, we did."

"Should I ask how it went?"

"Well, I didn't come back with another bruise."

"If that's the best thing that happened, then I don't know if we should consider that a win."

Cole brings me in a little tighter. "There wasn't going to be a win tonight."

"Yeah, I know." I sigh. "I love my brother, but wow, he does not process news and change well."

"He never has," Cole said. "I told him when he was ready to talk, or to ask any more questions, that I'd be here. That the ball is in his court."

"That's good," I say. "I just wish I knew what he was the most mad about."

"I don't even think he knows."

I let out a frustrated breath as Cole and I sit in silence for the next few minutes. On one hand, I feel the weight off my shoulders now that Bryce knows. No more sneaking around. No more asking people we love to keep this secret. Cole and I can now really begin our relationship with nothing between us.

On the other hand, Bryce took this way worse than I thought. Did I think he was going to get mad? Yes. But I never expected him to punch Cole. Or to have such rage in his eyes.

"Did anything you say to him get through?"

I can feel Cole shrug. "I'm not sure. I told him everything he asked. I apologized that we kept it from him, and that others found out before him."

"Oh, I'm sure he loved that."

"It definitely cranked up the rage factor," Cole says. "But I also told him that when he calmed down to remember that this isn't just a fling."

I feel my eyes welling up with tears as I look up at Cole. "It's not a fling for me, either."

"I know this is still new," he says. "I know we've not had the most conventional start to a relationship. Hell, the majority of our relationship has been spent in this apartment. But I need you to know that I love you. I love you, Brenna Donald. I've loved you since you nearly got me arrested in college. Hell, I think I might have loved you long before that. Whatever happens with Bryce, I don't care. Because that's how much I love you. I know you might—"

I cut him off, putting two fingers on his lips. "My turn."

He gives me a small smile as I remove my fingers from his lips. "You're right. This isn't normal. We're not normal. But that's what I love about us. I love that I didn't have to get to know you by playing twenty questions. I love that you knew me in my awkward stage. And in my crazy stage. And in my even crazier stage. I love that I know I can call your mom right now and she will give me every incriminating baby picture that exists of you."

"She would. She likes you better than me."

I can't help but smile at that. "I love everything about us. And I love you, Cole Campbell. Yes, you might have known it first, but I got here eventually. And I'm going to spend my life making sure you know every day how much I love you."

Cole brings our mouths together and...wow. That's all I can say. I've always known Cole doesn't wear his heart on his sleeve. But what he doesn't say he tells me in other ways. Like this kiss. If a kiss could talk, it would say that we're in this for the long haul. That no matter what's thrown our way, it doesn't matter. We love each other. And that's going to be enough.

It has to be.

And I don't care if my brother has a problem with this. No one, not even the mighty Bryce Donald, is going to come between us.

Because a love like this? This isn't normal. Which is what makes it perfect.

26

COLE

I REMEMBER my draft night like it was yesterday, not three years ago.

Since I wasn't projected to go in the first round because of a knee injury I suffered senior year, I wasn't invited to the live event. Which was fine by me. I was content watching my name being called in my childhood home with my family surrounding me.

But a part of me wondered what it would have been like to be at the event on draft night. What it must have been like to be someone like Bryce, who had the red carpet rolled out for him as the eventual top pick.

Well, now that the draft is being held in Nashville, I'm here as part of the pomp and circumstance, and I can safely say I'm just fine with how my draft experience went. Yes, you can feel the energy and adrenaline from the fans lining the streets and the cameras and the lights. Yes, it's a pretty cool feeling knowing that in just a few short hours, football players' lives are about to change forever.

I'm still glad I got to do it in sweatpants while sitting on my parents' couch.

"This is insane," Brenna says, her eyes wide as she takes in the production set and the draft stage, which is situated at the end of

Broadway in downtown Nashville. "I didn't know they closed the streets for anything other than country concerts."

"I mean, it kind of is." I nod to the stage, where someone is entertaining the crowd, singing what sounds like a Luke Coombs cover. Leave it to Nashville to throw in a concert between the sports.

Brenna turns to me and fixes my jacket. "Are you sure you're okay to do this?"

"For the twentieth time, I'm fine," I say, taking her hands because I know for a fact nothing is wrong with my jacket. "It's just a television interview."

"But it's with Bryce," she says. "Speaking of, where is that brother of mine?"

We both look around, but neither of us see him. Since the draft is in Nashville this year, a bunch of Fury players are doing television hits and interviews. My agent, Dean, who also represents Bryce, thought it would be a good segment to put the two of us on camera together to talk about our draft experiences. Even though we've told our story a billion times, apparently people never get tired of hearing about the two guys who have played every level of football together since they first laced up their cleats.

Then again, it would require Bryce to be here.

"He'll be here," I say. "He might not be talking to us, but he knows better than to skip out on a media engagement. Dean and Coach McAvoy would have his ass."

"Whose ass am I having?"

Dean Braxton pops through the curtain that shelters us from the crowd gathering next to the stage. Because he's always in agent mode, he's wearing a full suit and tie, cell phone in hand. I swear the man never takes a day off.

"No one's," I say. "Bryce is running a few minutes late is all."

"No worries," Dean says, turning to Brenna and extending his hand. "I don't believe we've ever officially met. Dean Braxton, agent to this guy, your brother, and another twenty Fury players."

Brenna returns the gesture. "Brenna. Nice to finally meet you."

Dean looks at Brenna, then to me, then back to Brenna. "So the rumors are true? You two are an item?"

"Rumors?" I say, all of a sudden feeling protective. "What are you hearing?"

Brenna puts a hand on my chest, instantly calming me down. "Easy, Papa Bear. All Dean means is that he heard that we are together, and he's now seeing it for himself." She turns to face Dean with an apologetic smile. "You'll have to excuse him. Because my brother is a jackass and isn't taking this well, my boyfriend here is under the assumption that everyone is going to have the same reaction."

Dean holds his hands up in defense. "Hey, I'm happy for you two. As long as Bryce doesn't do anything stupid, everything in my world is A-Okay."

As if he was waiting to hear his name, Bryce approaches us from around the stage, Lucy at his side. The three of us are staring at him, waiting to see his reaction. I know Dean is worried this is going to push him off the ledge again. I don't blame him. Considering his history, it makes sense.

As for Brenna and I? Neither of us know what to expect. We told him to sit on the news for a few days. That was a week ago. I never thought he would be butt hurt for this long. Then again, I should have known this was Bryce Donald we are talking about. The man has a flair for the dramatic.

"Dean," Bryce says as the two shake hands. "How long until we're on?"

Okay then, Bryce is going to go with the strictly business route today.

"I'm not sure. Let me go find a producer, and we'll get you two mic'd up."

Dean walks away, leaving the four of us alone. Staring at each other in awkward silence.

"So, how've you guys been?" Brenna says.

"Fine," Lucy replies. "Just getting situated. How about you?"

"Well—"

Brenna starts to answer, but Bryce cuts her off.

"This is really what we're going to do? Make small talk like we're fucking strangers?"

"Really?" I say, now just angry. "You're the reason we're all walking on eggshells. So you don't get to snap at us when this is your fault."

"My fault?" Bryce looks genuinely shocked. "I'm not the one who decided to start fucking around behind my back."

"Oh my God, Bryce! Why are you so dramatic?" Brenna says. "How many times do we need to tell you—"

"Hey!" Dean yells, startling all of us. "I don't know if you realize how loud y'all are, but I'd tone it down unless you want to be front-page news on the gossip sites."

We all take a step back and hang our heads.

"Better," Dean says, handing Bryce and I wireless mics. "Now here's how it's going to go. They want Bryce first for a segment. Bryce, they are just going to talk to you about your draft year. What it was like being the top pick. All that shit. They have promised me they aren't going to bring up the mental health year. After they break, Cole, you'll join him on stage. You'll tell the story y'all have told a hundred times. Deal?"

Bryce and I look at each other and nod our heads.

"Good," Dean continues. "Now, I don't give a flying fuck who is dating who and who feels what way about it. That is a *you* problem that shouldn't have to be a *me* problem. So you two go up on that stage and act like the two best friends you are. If one of you acts like something is off, it will only stir the pot. So put this shit aside for ten minutes, deal?"

I look at Bryce, who refuses to make eye contact with me. "I'm fine."

Bryce doesn't say anything for a second, until Lucy elbows him in the stomach. "Fine."

"Good. Now, Bryce"—Dean gives him a push on stage—"Go make everyone fall in love with you even more."

Bryce enters the stage and I see the minute he puts on his media face. He learned it early. People knew Bryce was going to be special before he played one snap of varsity football. He was doing newspaper interviews in middle school.

As for me? I was just the guy who blocked for him. Offensive linemen don't make headlines. We're just the guys who do our jobs so the quarterbacks can get the glory.

And I'm fine with that. Even now, when he's pissing me off, I'm still okay with that. He's my best friend. I've laid my life on the line for him, both physically and metaphorically, for twenty years.

Which is what infuriates me the most about how he's acting. I've been there for him through everything—through his college decision, through his ups and downs with Lucy, through the drinking and the women. Apparently, this is the thanks I get.

"If you need me to say anything to him, let me know," Dean says to me as I continue to watch Bryce on stage.

"Thanks," I say. "I don't know why he's acting like this."

"It's Bryce. Do we ever know?"

It's funny because it's true. "What do you need, Dean?"

He turns to look at me like I'm nuts. "What? Can't an agent stand next to his client and just take in the moment."

I raise an eyebrow. "He can, but he doesn't. So what's up?"

"You're a smart one, Campbell," Dean says. "Which is part of the reason why the Fury wants to offer you a contract that is going to make your head explode."

Now both eyebrows are up. "Contract? I mean, I know this is the last year of mine, but I didn't think we'd start negotiating this early."

"It's informal," Dean says. "The Fury just want me, and you, to know they are going to be serious when it comes time to sit down and nail this out. The way the front office was talking, I'd expect to see somewhere around twenty-three a year."

Now my jaw is on the ground. "Twenty-three? As in million?"

Dean smiles. "Per year. Probably six years. It would make you the highest paid lineman in the league. I just wanted to let you know that's your future, if you want it."

I have to blink a few times, because I'm trying to imagine what that kind of money would even look like.

It means paying off every bill my parents have. It means my nieces and nephews are going to be set for college or whatever the hell they want to do with their lives.

Then I catch Brenna out of the corner of my eye. I know Dean was talking about my professional and financial future, but she's the only future I care about.

I'm going to build us our dream home. I'm going to give her the wedding and honeymoon of her dreams. She'll want for nothing. She's going to have everything she's ever wanted or dared to ask for.

"You staring at me?" she says as she makes her way to me.

"What if I was?"

"You know it's rude to stare," she says as she fixes my jacket one more time.

"What if I wasn't staring?"

"Then what were you doing?"

I take both of her hands in mine. "I'm looking at the future."

This gets me a smile. "And what does this future look like?"

Dean signals that I'm about to be up, so I lean down and give her a quick kiss on the forehead. "It looks perfect."

27

———

BRENNA

"I FEEL like I'm in high school."

I look over to Lucy, wondering what in the world she's talking about. "What do you mean? You never snuck around in high school."

Lucy's blush takes over her face. "Well, I mean this is what I guess it would be like. The most sneaking around I did was when your brother would ask me to stay up past my curfew."

"You rebel."

We both laugh as we take sips of our margaritas. There is nothing quite like a girls' day filled with shopping, laughs, tacos, and margaritas. If this were any other day, I'd file this under a perfectly lovely day with my best friend.

Instead we've nicknamed it "Operation Hard Head." As in, my brother is being a hard head. And that's the nice way of putting it.

Why did we have to give a code name to our girls' day? Because my brother still isn't talking to me or his best friend. Lucy and I talk, but only through discreet text messages. I wanted to run up to her last week at the draft interviews and give her a big hug because I miss her. It was then we decided we needed a day all to ourselves.

"So, we've not talked about it long enough."

Lucy shakes her head at my statement. "Nope. A little longer. For just a little longer I want to pretend everything is fine and this a normal day. So, right now, I'm going to sip on this delicious margarita, and you're going to gush about Cole to me the way you've been dying to for weeks."

I laugh a little at her enthusiastic denial. "Who said I've been wanting to gush?"

Lucy raises an eyebrow while simultaneously taking a drink. "Because you never stop smiling, and that says a lot when it comes to you. And, even though it's in the eighties today, you are, for some reason, wearing a turtleneck. Want to tell me what that's about?"

I feel the blush coming over my cheeks. "Cole might have been a little extra…*bitey*…last night."

Lucy lets out a shriek that I'm pretty sure the whole restaurant heard. "Cole is a biter?"

I shake my head. "No. He likes to kiss. And nibble. And last night it just got a little much. And that might or might not have had to do with the fact we were having sex in the parking garage."

"Brenna Donald!"

I shrug, while reaching for my glass. "I have found that I might not be wild in the ways of my past, but there is something about Cole that makes me feel a little…daring."

"Daring how?"

I smile and lean in, because this has to be whispered. "We might or might not like to have sex in places we're not supposed to."

"Brenna Marie Donald!"

I shrug, leaning back into the booth. "What can I say? Roofs. Jeeps. On the open road. We like to keep it spicy."

She furiously shakes her head. "I'm never going to be able to look at Cole now."

"Good," I say. "Now you understand how I feel knowing the kind of sex noises my brother makes."

"Fair," Lucy says in defeat. "So let's review: Cole passes the arm test. He also passes other tests I didn't know you had. Now, for the biggest question of them all, what, my dear Brenna, have you nicknamed him?"

This catches me off guard because I honestly hadn't thought about it. Maybe because other guys have been so bad so quick, the only thing to get me through the date was to figure out what I was going to nickname them for future stories. But with Cole? A nickname hadn't even crossed my mind.

"Can I sound cheesy?" I ask.

Lucy smiles. "The cheesier the better."

"Now don't laugh."

"I would never."

"He's Mr. Perfect."

In any other situation, I would vomit in my mouth if someone said that to me about a guy. Hell, I'm fighting back the urge just listening to myself. But it's true. The man is perfect. And yes, I know we're still in the honeymoon stage where everything is new and great. But even when things settle down and become normal, I can't imagine him not being perfect.

Because he's perfect for me.

"That is..." Lucy says, fighting back tears. "The sweetest thing I have ever heard you say. Which means now more than ever we have to get your brother to get his head out of his ass."

"Ugh," I moan. "Why is he my brother? Why not your husband?"

"Because I'm slightly still mad at him. Therefore he's your brother. He can be my husband later when he clues in."

I let out a sigh of disappointment. "I really didn't think he'd be mad for this long."

"Well," Lucy begins, then stops to take a healthy sip of her margarita. "I have at least got out of him the why."

"Really?" I nearly yell, but I don't care. This has been what has bothered me the most. "Please tell me. At least then we can know what to focus on so we can get past this."

"Well, that might be easier said than done."

"Go on..."

"So at the end of the day, it's a little bit of everything. He does think it's weird that you two are dating, and admits that he could get over that with time. He also said that he might put in a no PDA policy."

"That's fair," I say. "I know how weird it is when I see you two kiss, and we've only been friends since college."

"Exactly. So he has admitted to me, though the stubborn ass won't say it to the two of you, that the physical part will be an adjustment for him. The bigger thing for him is that he feels you both lied to him."

I sink into the booth a little bit. "I mean, he's right. But it wasn't this great conspiracy theory."

"And therein lies the disagreement."

I quirk an eyebrow. "I'm not following."

"In Bryce's head, Cole has been lying to him for years."

"Well, by that way of thinking, I should be mad at Cole too because he didn't tell me either."

"That's neither here nor there," Lucy says. "All that matters, at least to Bryce, is that he feels that his best friend lied to him and that it was ongoing."

"Cole won't apologize. In his mind, Bryce thinking that this was some massive conspiracy is unreasonable."

Ugh, I feel like both sides have a point and the answer is somewhere in the gray. And the problem is, both Bryce and Cole are very literal people. They prefer answers in black and white. In their minds, gray isn't an option.

Which sucks because this whole situation is fifty shades of gray.

And not in the kinky way.

"I hate this, Luce. For the first time in my life, I'm in a relationship that I want to shout from the rooftops about. This should be perfect. We should be the happiest couple of couples in Nashville. Two best friends dating other best friends. We should be double dating and having dinners with each other. We should be making silly videos on ForU where people get jealous of how amazing we are at being couples. This just sucks."

Lucy nearly slams down her drink. "Brenna! That's it!"

Now I'm confused. "What's it? The videos? I mean, it could be fun, but I doubt I could get Cole to do viral couple challenges."

"No—actually, if you could, that would be hilarious—but that's not what I'm talking about."

"Then please tell me what made you slam your drink down so hard it shook the whole restaurant?"

"A double date."

Hmm… I might have just said it in passing, but I like where this could go. "Continue…"

Lucy sits up straight like she's about to give a presentation. "Bryce used to always give Cole shit about not having a girlfriend because that meant they could never double date."

"Well, I mean, you guys did get to go out with him and Jessica."

Lucy rolls her eyes. "Don't remind me."

I laugh. "She was a bit crazy."

"Off her rocker, but that's not the point. What if we convince both of them to go on a double date? Something super casual. Let them let loose so they can remember their friendship. Maybe, just maybe, it will melt some of the frost, and we can start making our way back to peaceful times."

My smile grows wider with every word that comes out of Lucy's mouth. "That, my dear Lucy, is why you are the smart one out of our bunch. Absolutely brilliant. Do you have anything in mind?"

Lucy nods. "Of course I do. But let me make sure I can get Bryce on board. I don't want to lie to him; that would only put me on his shit list. He has to be willing to come for this to work."

"That's fair," I say. "And how are you going to get him to agree to this?"

Lucy's smile becomes devious. "Let's just say if he says no, I'm about to have a long string of headaches that come on just as we're about to go to bed every night."

I hold my glass. "Lucy Donald. You are a genius."

She clinks her glass with mine. "Some call it a genius. Some call it desperate times calling for desperate measures. Now, let's get our hard-headed men back together."

28

———

COLE

I chuckle and shake my head at how excited Brenna gets when I get a strike. It almost makes me want to do a little victory dance.

Almost.

"Lucky."

I hear Bryce mumble from the other side of the seating area. If we were on good terms, I'd throw back some remark about how I'm going to get lucky with his sister later. But I know my audience, and now is not the time for that joke.

I'm starting to wonder if it ever will be.

"No luck needed," Brenna says. "Just admit it. Cole and I are better bowlers than you two."

"Hell no," Bryce says, not an ounce of humor in his voice. "Give me the damn ball."

Bryce stomps up to the lane, ball in hand and flings it down the lane straight into the gutter. Now, Bryce is not a good bowler. Yes, the man who gets paid millions of dollars to throw a football to a moving target has trouble rolling a ball sixty feet to attempt to knock down ten stationary pins. However, every other time we've been bowling, it's usually been with teammates in some sort of team-building scenario. His terrible bowling has always served as a good joke among the guys. And he's leaned into it.

Not tonight. Tonight he wants to beat me. Decimate me.

He forgets that in high school, I was an all-state bowler and have rolled four perfect games in my life already.

And maybe if I were in a more generous mood, I'd take it easy on him. But considering he has barely looked my way tonight, I'm not.

"Maybe bowling wasn't the best idea," Lucy whispers from across the way.

"No, it was a good idea," Brenna says. "Nothing opens the lines of communication more than a little competition."

I give the girls credit; they are trying. They can both see how hard this is on everyone. If I thought Bryce was at all coming around, maybe I'd put in an effort. But as far as I see it, I'm not about to go killing myself for him when he would rather pout in a corner.

"Order number ten, your food is ready at the pickup window. Order number ten!"

"That's us!" Brenna yells, jumping up from her seat. "Lucy, why don't you come help me carry it?"

Lucy looks back and forth between me and Bryce. "Sure! I'd be glad to."

The girls leave, letting the two of us sit there in silence.

"I forgot how good you were at bowling," Bryce mumbles.

"And I forgot how much you stink."

For the first time in weeks, my best friend cracks a smile. "God couldn't have made me a good bowler too. It just would have made me too powerful."

I chuckle. "Yeah. That must have been it."

The silence falls back on us, though it doesn't feel as awkward as it did just minutes ago. Maybe this whole bowling/date night was a good idea?

"So how is married life?" I ask, hating how the small talk sounds, but not knowing what else to say.

"Great," Bryce says. "I mean, not much has changed. We started to look at property down in Franklin."

I can't hide the shocked expression on my face. "Wow. Already?"

He shrugs. "Yeah. I mean, it will take a while for the house to get built. Might as well get a move on it since we know that's where we want to be."

I swallow the response I want to say—which is "gee, thanks for including me." I mean, if we're still going to build next to each other, I should have been a part of that. But apparently I'm not a part of those plans anymore.

"Good for you," I choke out, looking to see if Brenna and Lucy are on their way back. Sneaky women are nowhere to be seen.

"You know they did that on purpose, right?"

I look back to Bryce. "Of course I do. But hey, at least they are trying to get the ball moving."

"What's that supposed to mean?" he asks.

Really? Is he that self-absorbed? "It means that I have tried to reach out to you to talk. The girls put this whole night together to at least try to break some ice. Then there's you, playing the Bryce Donald pity-me card. Well, guess what, buddy? It doesn't work on me. And you should know that after all the shit we've been through. I'm not going to fall for your woe-is-me, feel-bad-for me act."

"At least I'm not playing the holier-than-thou card."

"Excuse me?" He can't be serious.

"You're acting like you're innocent in all of this. You aren't, buddy. Not by a long shot."

I can't believe what I'm hearing. "Do you think I'm apologizing just to say the words? I know I did you wrong. And I've been trying to apologize for weeks, but you won't listen to me."

"What are you apologizing for?"

Bryce's question throws me. "What do you mean?"

"It means, what exactly are you apologizing for?" Bryce asks. "Sleeping with my sister? Breaking the bro code of not only friendship, but of a locker room? The sneaking around? Or the fact that you've been lying to me for years? Which one, Cole? Or is that one 'I'm sorry' supposed to make up for it all?"

Wow. I didn't realize I committed so many cardinal rules just by wanting to be with Brenna. "I don't even know where to begin with all that."

Bryce leans back, extending his arms out on the chairs at the alley. "Wherever you want to. I mean, you do that anyway, might as well continue."

"First of all," I say, trying my best to keep my voice and tone low. "It would be good to remind you that your sister is an adult. It's not like I kidnapped her and made her fall in love with me."

"Love?" He says it in almost a laughing tone.

"Yes, Bryce. Love. I love her. She loves me. I've told you this isn't just sex. Do you think we'd risk all of this for just sex?"

Bryce throws his hands in the air. "How the hell should I know? It seems that you did to start with."

"Are you going to be reasonable and try to listen to me or are you going to have a snarky comeback for everything?"

"Fine," he says, though I think he barely means it. "Go on."

"As for the sneaking around? It was three days. And the other part of it was when you were on your honeymoon. How can we sneak around when you were out of the fucking country?"

"Oh, well, then that brings up another point," Bryce says, now leaning toward me. "How about the fact that I was the last one to know? That's fucking nice."

"Get over it, man," I say. "It wasn't on purpose. In fact, everyone we told we specifically asked to keep to themselves because we wanted you to hear this from us. We didn't want to sneak around. We didn't want this to be weird. We wanted nights like tonight, you know, except without the fact that we are five seconds from punching each other."

This makes Bryce laugh, but not in the humor-filled way. "You have an excuse or a reason for everything. Yet in all of this, I still haven't heard an actual 'I'm sorry.'"

This man is going to be the death of me. "What do you want me to be sorry for? Just tell me so we can get on with our lives!"

Bryce just shakes his head. "We've been friends for twenty years. Twenty years of blood, sweat, and tears. Twenty years of sharing things with each other that will go to the grave. You were my brother in more ways than I thought was fathomable. Then I find out one day that you've been lying to me for seven years. And not just about something little. Something that affected us both. That's a hard pill to swallow, Cole."

"I'm sorry, Bryce. I'm sorry that's how you see it," I truly mean those words, even if he doesn't believe me. "I honestly never thought that's how you would see it. Because in my mind, I wasn't lying to you. If anything, I was trying to stop myself from feeling it. Do you know how many nights of sleep I lost because I felt like the worst friend in the world for wishing that I was with Brenna? How many events I skipped out because I knew she would be there, and it would be too much for me to handle? How many nights I drank myself stupid because I knew she was with another man? So you might see it as lying, but to me it wasn't that. If anything, I was trying like hell to make it so I was lying to myself."

I look back and I see the girls standing next to the seats, food in hand. By the looks on their faces, they heard at least my last rant. I know Brenna did. The tear escaping her eye gives her away.

"Hey," I say, standing up, taking the food from her hold, setting it down before I wrap her in my arms. As soon as I do, her one tear turns into many. "Shh. Don't cry. It's in the past."

I look back at Bryce, Brenna still in my arms. This. This has to be his turning point. Can't he see it as I can? That every step of the way I thought about him and our friendship?

"Can we call this?" I ask. "I'm tired of fighting. I'm tired of consoling. I'm tired of apologizing. Can't we start this over? Can't this *be* over?"

We all look at Bryce, who is just staring at Brenna in my arms. She's unsuccessfully fighting back her tears, but she hasn't let go of me. Can't he see what he's doing to us? To his own sister?

"I'm sorry," he says, walking toward Lucy and taking her hand. "But I'm not ready. Lucy, let's go."

She drops the tray of food she's holding as she lets Bryce lead her away. She turns back to mouth that she's sorry, which I know she is. I can't imagine being her right now, being torn like this.

"I thought that was going to be it," Brenna says.

I kiss the top of her head and squeeze her tighter against me. "So did I, Trouble. So did I."

29

———

BRENNA

THE ONE THING I always loved about my relationship with my brother was that we had what many twins have—the intuition. The twin brain sharing.

Except now. Now I don't know what the hell is going on in that thick skull of his.

Which is why I'm marching up to his apartment now and demanding that he tell me, once and for all, what the hell his problem is.

"Bryce!" I yell, pounding on his door. "Open up! I know you're in there!"

I hear him grumbling before he swings the door open. "Geez. What the hell, Bren?"

I walk through without waiting for a formal invitation. "Funny, that was the question I was about to ask you."

It's been three days since the blowup at the bowling alley, and I've decided I've had enough. Cole is sitting back doing nothing, as if he and Bryce are playing a silent game of chicken. But not me. Nope. I'm taking action.

"If Cole sent you up here, tell him it's no use," Bryce says.

"Cole didn't send me here," I say. "In fact, if he knew I was up here right now he'd probably tell me not to waste my breath. Too bad for him I'm a hard-headed woman, and I don't give up that easily."

Bryce walks to his oversized couch and takes a seat. "What do you want me to say, Brenna?"

I go and sit next to him. "I want you to quit acting like a jerk. I want you to actually try to be happy for us. I want you to stop acting like the whole world was out to get you."

He smiles. "Is that it?"

I shake my head. "No. My list is very, very long. But that's where we're going to start."

Bryce leans back, looks up at the ceiling and lets out a deep breath. Which is fine. Let him gather his thoughts. I have no place to be and all the time in the world.

Especially for something this important.

"I can't get over that he has been harboring something for you for years. Years! And he didn't tell me. Or you."

"Why does that bother you so much?" I ask, genuinely curious. "Don't you see he didn't tell you because he tried to put you and your friendship first? And think of it, what would you have said?"

"Huh?"

"What would you have said? He told me he first knew after I came down and visited y'all at Clemson your senior year. What would you have done if he had said, 'Bryce. I think I'm in love with your sister.'"

"I—" Bryce starts to speak, but quickly stops. "I don't know what I would have said."

"Neither do I, but I guarantee it wouldn't have been anything good."

He laughs. "Probably not."

"If I were to guess, you would have gone on and on about that bro code—that, by the way, is not a real thing."

"It is so."

"It's a convenient excuse for you to be mad."

"It's real."

"Okay then," I say sarcastically. "Whatever you need to tell yourself to sleep at night. But back to the point, if he would have told you then, don't act like you would have been 'Great! Let me set you up with my sister!' Because we both know you wouldn't have, so quit acting like you would have reacted differently if you had known."

Bryce nods, but doesn't say anything. Which in my book right now is a win.

"So tell me. Just you and me. What's the real reason? Is it really the lying? Is it something else? Because I miss my brother, and I know Cole hasn't said it, but he misses you too. And frankly, I'm not very good at Call of Duty, so I need you two to kiss and make up."

Bryce almost smiles before shutting it back down. "I just feel like this was slapped in my face and everyone else in the world had time to process it."

I nod. "That's valid."

"I mean, Cole had years. You—well, I don't know about you, and I'm not sure I want to. There's still some brother waters that I'm not sure how to navigate here."

I let out a little sigh, my shoulders starting to relax, because the more he keeps talking, the more he sounds like my brother.

"I mean, Mom knew. Luciano and Celine knew. Hell, even crazy Jessica knew. And it was right in front of my face, and I didn't see it."

"In your defense, you were kind of staring at your wife."

This gets me a smile. "I was. But I feel like I should have realized that for years my best friend was in love with my sister."

"So you missed some signs? So what? You're here now. You're in the know."

"Yes but…"

"But what?"

"Never mind," he says, trailing off. "It's not important."

I don't know whether or not to press right now. I feel like if I do, it's only a matter of time before I step on a wire. So I'm just going to sit back and let Bryce navigate this conversation. Which is why it makes me jump a little when I feel Bryce's hand on mine. Bryce and I are close, don't get me wrong. And I know since he quit drinking and started seeing a therapist consistently, one of his main goals is to be more present for his friends and family. But this? His whole reaction to me and Cole? This feels like I'm entering a new sibling territory of protectiveness.

"This wasn't how it was supposed to be," he says.

"What do you mean?" I ask.

"I just…it wasn't supposed to be like this. We had plans."

"Yes, I know," I groan. "You know it's not normal for two men to plan to build houses next door to each other?"

This gets me a smile. "I mean, it just makes sense that if we want to raise our boys to play football together then we should live next door to each other. How else are they supposed to practice together?"

"And didn't you always bug him about finding a girlfriend so you guys could double?"

He rolls his eyes at that one. "Yeah, but I didn't mean my sister."

"Well then you should have been more specific."

"I tried," he said. "But he didn't listen."

Now I'm smiling. "No, he didn't. Not at all."

We sit in silence for a minute or two, and for the first time in weeks, I feel the air is a little lighter. That I might have made a breakthrough.

"I'm sorry I've been acting like this, but you know I don't process things in normal ways," Bryce says.

"If that isn't the truest thing I've heard today…"

"I get what you're saying. I know I need to get over it. And I'm close. I promise I am. But I need some time alone to process it all."

I nod. "That's okay. I'm okay with that. As long as I know we're going in the right direction."

He wraps me in his arms and gives me a tight side hug. "Lucy and I have been talking about going away for a bit. Get out of town before the season starts."

"Didn't you two just go on a honeymoon?"

"Yeah, and that was nice. But we're going to go home for a few weeks. Maybe take a trip with Luciano and Celine. Maybe another few weeks just the two of us. Give me that time, and I promise when I come back, I'll be in a better place, and I can talk to Cole with a better head on my shoulders."

I give him another tight squeeze. Progress. It's not the end, but I see the light at the end of the tunnel. And I'll take it.

"You go do what you need to do," I say. "We'll be here. Always."

30

BRENNA

KEY TURN IN: Check.

Equipment inventory: Check.

All of my fun science posters that I insist the kids love, even if they pretend they are corny, off my walls: Check.

Another year teaching science to seventh graders: Check.

I throw up my arms in victory as I walk out of school for the last time this year. Technically, yesterday was our last day with students. Today was the teachers' last day. Summer vacation is here.

And boy, do I need it.

Don't get me wrong, I couldn't have asked for a better first year at this school. But no matter where you teach, middle schoolers are exhausting. Add on to it the drama with Bryce, who has also been acting like a twelve-year old boy, and it's safe to say I'm going to relish every second of this summer break.

Maybe I can even convince Cole to take a vacation with me. Somewhere warm. With a beach. Where we can have drinks with little umbrellas, soak up the sun during the day and soak up each other at night.

Yes, that's going to happen.

I smile thinking about our hypothetical vacation as I make my way to my car. I'm so in my head thinking about bikini shopping that I almost don't realize my six-foot-four hunk of a man leaning against my car.

Holding a bouquet of flowers.

"What are you doing here?"

He hands me the flowers, but, of course, not before pulling me in for a kiss that is borderline inappropriate for a school parking lot.

"It's your last day of school. I wanted to surprise you."

I look around to make sure we're not being watched before I jump into his arms, kissing him again. I find it funny that I once used to give men the arm test. Like anyone else's could ever compare to Cole's. Especially when he's holding me like I weigh nothing.

"How about," I whisper in his ear, while also leaving small little kisses on his neck, "we go home, I put on a little something that I've been waiting to surprise you with, and we celebrate the end of the school year with orgasms?"

This gets me a chuckle, which wasn't exactly the reaction I was looking for.

"While that does sound good, I thought we'd celebrate in a different way."

I bring my eyes back to his. I love his eyes so much. They are the clearest and brightest blue I've ever seen. Yes, I have blue eyes, but nothing like his.

I wonder what our kids' eyes would look like? I've never thought about that before. A little girl with our shared brown hair and his crystal blues? Or maybe a little boy with blue-gray like mine? I can see both so clearly. The four of us at a little league football game. Cole coaching on the sidelines while I get the cheerleaders ready. Our son geared up while our little girl jumps up and down with her pom-poms.

It's the most perfect thing I've ever dreamed about.

"Earth to Brenna. Did you hear any of that?"

I shake my head, coming back to the present. "Sorry. I was daydreaming."

Instead of being annoyed, Cole just smiles. "Well, then you're really going to be surprised, because I'm not going to tell you again what's in store for the rest of the night."

Now this surprises me. "The night?"

"Yup," he says, slowly putting me down. "Brenna Donald, your summer of fun begins right now."

"WHAT ARE WE DOING HERE?"

My body doesn't know whether to cringe or smile as we pull up to Fire Lights. On one hand, this was the scene from my awful date with Dexter. On the other hand, Cole had to come pick me up that night. It was the first night I spent in his bed, even if it was without him. It was the night I became addicted to his smell and comfy pillows.

"You're not very good at surprises, are you?" Cole jokes as he gets out of his Jeep. He comes around to my side to open my door before giving his keys to the valet.

"I'm a curious person."

Cole takes my hand and leads me toward the door. There is a line around the block of anxious people waiting to get in, but all he does is nod to the bouncer, who unclicks the velvet rope to let us through.

Well, isn't that fancy.

When we walk inside, the sound of live music overtakes my body. I don't remember having this experience when I came here with Dexter. Then again, he hauled me so fast up to the third floor, I don't even know if this was going on. But now that I'm here, I want to take in every second of it.

I let go of Cole's hand as I wander to the stage. I've always loved live music. There is just something about the energy in the room that is different from anything else. Take this band right now: They are no one anyone would recognize, but that isn't stopping them from treating this like they are headlining at Madison Square Garden. They are playing like tonight is finally the night some Nashville hot-shot producer is going to change their lives forever.

Also, this lead singer is belting the hell out of this Carrie Underwood cover, and I am here for it.

I'm swaying to the music, singing right along with her, when I feel Cole's arms snake around my waist. He doesn't say anything. Instead, he just stands and dances with me. I rest my head against his chest, loving every second about this moment. Our bodies are swaying to the beat, changing tempos with each song. I must say, this band is damn good. Either that or I'm just a sucker for 2000s country covers.

"Are you having fun?" Cole asks, his mouth right next to my ear.

I nod as I turn to him, his hands still firmly around my waist. "How did you know this is exactly what I needed?"

"Can I just say I know you that well?"

"You can, but even you aren't this good."

"Oh, but I am," he says, taking my hand and leading me toward the elevator. It opens and we quickly step in as he hits the button for the second floor. "I know how stressed you've been, so I wanted to give you a night that you didn't have to think about anything. Then, I remembered one conversation when you said that, more than anything, you wanted to experience Nashville. You wanted the food, and—"

"The music and the line dancing," I say, finishing his sentence.

Cole smiles as the elevator opens. "So, we crossed off the food on our first date. I knew no matter what there would be a band here, so that checks off the music. So now, there is only one more thing to do."

I look around and it's like every video I see on ForU of line dancing bars. Guys and girls mixed in together, somehow all knowing what to do at the same time. It's fascinating to watch.

"Oh my gosh, Cole!" I squeal, jumping quickly to give him a quick kiss. "This is amazing."

We take a few more steps toward the floor when the song changes to a pop song that for some reason has taken over line dancing culture. At least, that's what I gather from videos I watch. I mean, I can't blame them, the song is catchy as hell, even if it is sung by a redheaded guitarist who is usually known for his ballads.

"Oh I love this one!" I squeal. "I'm going to go out and try!"

I don't wait for Cole as I make my way onto the floor. For one, I'm too excited to try this dance in person. Second, Cole isn't a dance kind of guy. At the wedding I never saw him on the dance floor except when we had to dance together.

So color me shocked when he follows me onto the floor. And not only does he follow me, he jumps right into the dance like he made up the damn thing.

"What are you doing?"

Cole gives me a sexy smirk as his feet and body move effortlessly with the music. "What does it look like I'm doing?"

I'm frozen as I watch his feet move to the beat of the song. He's doing it perfectly. Believe me, I have watched no less than a hundred videos of people doing this dance. Yes, I will admit I have found a few of the men doing it hot as they hit every step to the beat. But watching Cole move like his body is in perfect sync with the music as he holds eye contact with me? It is by far the sexiest thing I have ever seen in my life.

I start moving my feet, though I have no idea if I'm doing it right. I can't possibly concentrate right now. "How did I not know you could dance like this? I feel like I should have known this."

He smiles again, but doesn't answer me right away. Instead, he waits until after the signature part of the dance where everyone jumps three times on a specific beat.

"I'm a man of many talents," he says.

"Obviously," I say, my feet now finding the rhythm and pattern of steps. Before I know it, Cole and I are in perfect unison. We even improvise a bit, changing the direction so we can look at each other. This isn't supposed to be a partner dance, but somehow we've made it one. Our eyes are locked as our feet continue to move to the music. I swear my body is on fire right now. Between the way Cole's body is moving and the way he's looking at me, I'm about ready to fuck him in the middle of this dance floor.

The song changes to a slow one, but instead of walking off the floor, Cole takes my hand in his, pulls me closer, and dips me so low I think I'm about to fall. But I know I'm not. Cole would never let that happen.

Ever.

The last time we were here, I trusted him to carry me to safety.

Little did I know then that he was carrying me to our future.

"Can I ask for one more thing?" I beg as he brings me back upright.

"Anything."

"Take me home."

31

———

COLE

I barely have the door closed before Brenna is furiously trying to undo the button of my jeans. In her defense, she at least listened to my request not to undo them in the Jeep during the ten-minute ride back to the apartment—or do anything else that would make me recite football stats from 1994 in my head.

What I have in mind for her is going to take a lot longer than ten minutes. And I can't be wasting precious restraint on whatever her naughty mouth had in mind.

"It's cute you think you're in charge," I say as I take both of her hands in mine and place them above her head. "But I'm not done with your surprises yet."

She bites her lip, which drives me absolutely insane. I don't know why. Then again, everything this woman does drives me crazy in the best possible way.

"Now, you have to be tired of wearing these pants all day," I say as I lower myself to my knees. I slip off her shoes before slowly unbuttoning her jeans, which, by the way her hips are moving, is driving her crazy.

Good. Exactly how I want her.

I slowly slide her jeans and panties down her legs. She steps out of each leg with ease, leaving her hands exactly where I told her to. Brenna might be as independent and hard-headed as they come, but in the bedroom, my girl is nothing if not obedient.

"Cole," she moans. I know that tone. She wants more.

Who am I to keep my girl from having anything?

I waste no more time, taking one leg and resting it on my shoulder, giving me perfect access to bury my face in her sweet pussy, sucking on her clit like my life depends on it.

I hear Brenna gasp, her hands all of a sudden tugging on my hair. Yes, I know I told her to leave them up, but I'll allow this. She doesn't know this, but I love it when she does that. The feel of the pull lets me know how much she loves my mouth on her. If anything, it makes me want to give her more.

And I do. I continue to suck, my tongue getting in on the action, flicking the swollen bundle of nerves as her hips begin to move circles on my face.

"Fuck, Cole!" she cries out, her one knee starting to wobble.

I know I should lay her down, let her enjoy this without having to keep standing. But I have a better idea.

My other hand scoops up her other knee so she's now sitting on my shoulders, the only thing holding her up is the door and my hands holding onto her for dear life. I feel her relax into my hold. Good. Because I am a man on a mission and like hell am I going to stop now.

She doesn't have much time to relax before my tongue starts working overtime. I'm a strong guy, but I don't know how long I can hold her here. Not because it's too much, but because with every second I taste her sweetness, it gets harder for me to concentrate. She's like a drug. I can't get enough of her. I crave her daily. And when I get a fix like this? All I want is to taste every drop I can get.

Brenna's grip tightens on my hair just as her legs begin to squeeze around me. "I'm close, Cole. I'm so close."

Her words send me into overdrive. My mouth is sucking and nipping while my tongue is flicking furiously on her clit. I know the combination is working because I am one nibble away from Brenna ripping half of my hair out.

"Yes!" she yells just as I feel her pussy begin to contract. My tongue slowly begins to ease its feast on her before I lay her back down on the ground.

I can't help but stare at her. God, she's beautiful. Her hair is a mess. Her face has a beautiful flush. The top she's wearing is now completely wrinkled and somehow missing a button. Her breathing is heavy, and I think she could pass out right here.

She has never looked more beautiful than she does right now.

I lean down to kiss her, knowing she'll be able to taste herself on me. She knows it too, as her fingers slide through my hair, bringing me in even closer to her.

"I love you," I say, brushing a loose strand of hair away from her face. "I love you so fucking much."

"I love you too," she says. "But you know what would make me love you even more?"

"What's that?"

"If you were to take me to our bedroom and let me show you how much today meant to me."

I don't know if it was the words "our bedroom" or knowing that when Brenna wants to be in charge in the bedroom I'm never disappointed, but I don't waste a second. I jump up from the ground and pick her up like she's nothing more than a lap dog. This, of course, makes her giggle as I all but run to our room, which is only twenty feet away, and nearly jump onto the bed with her in my arms.

"Anxious, are we?" she asks as she gently pushes me to my back.

"For you? Always."

I lay back and smile as she finishes the work on my pants she started the second we walked in the door. She then straddles my legs to get a better angle to work on the buttons of my shirt.

"Do you know how many places I wanted you to fuck me tonight?"

I smile, because even though I have an idea, I want to hear her dirty little mind and mouth at work. "How many?"

"Well—" She begins slipping the shirt over my shoulders. I sit up just enough to take it off, and of course steal a kiss. "I considered going down on you in the school parking lot when you surprised me there, but I figured I'd probably lose my job."

"We wouldn't want that now, would we?"

She shakes her head as she lifts her top off over her head and tosses it to the side. "Then there was at dinner. I figured there I could sneak under the table. It was a dark restaurant. No one would have noticed."

My hands trail up her smooth stomach to her perfect tits, which are covered by the sexiest lace bra I have ever seen. "I like that restaurant. Probably best we don't get kicked out for public indecency."

"That's what I thought too," she said, her hands trailing behind her back and quickly undoing her bra. "Then there was the club. I know we could have done it there."

"I'm sure I could have bribed my security guard friends to clear us a dark corner."

Her back arches as I start pinching her nipples. I know she wants to be in charge now, and I want to let her be, but fuck, if she doesn't hurry this up I can't promise that I'm not going to flip her over just so I can suck her tits for as long as I want.

"I bet they could have," she says, taking my cock in her hand and stroking it. "But as much as I love being adventurous, tonight is just about us. Because, Cole Campbell, I'm not sure if you realize this, but I love the hell out of you."

That's it. That's all I can take. I flip her over and cover her body with mine in point two seconds. Before she even realizes what I've done, my mouth is on her, kissing her like I've never kissed her before.

We don't say another word. Our mouths are too busy taking what they want. Without separating, I line up my dick to her core and slowly press in, filling her inch by inch as our mouths and hands touch each other everywhere and anywhere.

"Cole!" she yells as I push all the way in. "You feel so good."

"Not as good as you," I say, meaning every word. Her warmth

surrounds me, and as much as I'd love to take my time and savor every moment of this, I can't. I'm too worked up. She's right. We've had a whole day of flirting and foreplay. It's more than time.

I scoop her up off the bed and bring her to my lap.

"What are you doing?" she asks.

I take each of her tits in my hands, giving them a squeeze as I quickly suck the nipple of each one. "Seeing what I missed earlier?"

She raises her brow. "Earlier?"

"Earlier," I say, continuing to slowly work my dick inside her. "Show me how you would have let me fuck you at the club."

The fire in her eyes is immediate. "Really?"

I nod. "You heard me. Tell me how you wanted to be fucked. What kind of bad girl was Brenna ready to be tonight?"

She gives me a hard kiss and bites on my bottom lip just hard enough to send a shot of electricity straight to my dick as she climbs off me. She walks backward toward my wall, never taking her eyes off me, even as she turns to the wall and puts her hands against it.

"What are you waiting for?" she asks, slowly bending over.

It takes me three steps to get to her. I press one hand down on the small of her back as my other hand guides my dick back to where it's aching to be. She's so wet it's no problem sliding into her, and I know this was my idea, but it's taking every ounce of energy I have to hold myself up.

"Fuck, Brenna," I say, letting my hands wrap around her stomach, traveling up to her tits. I take one in each hand as I take her from behind, twisting her nipples as I begin to pick up my pace.

She meets me thrust for thrust. Her hands are the only thing keeping her from hitting her head against the wall. I take my hands and bring them up higher, holding her away from the wall.

"I got you, baby," I say. "I got you."

Her back is arched, and it only takes a few more thrusts before I feel her start to contract around me. Furiously, I pick up my pace, wanting to give this to her more than I want to take my next breath. It doesn't take long before her body freezes, nearly collapsing back into the wall.

"Fuck!" I yell, my balls tightening the second I feel her orgasm begin. I don't know how we both don't fall to the floor in that second. Somehow, we hold each other up and clumsily stumble back to the bed.

"That was…" I begin, though I don't know how to finish it.

Brenna turns to look at me. She looks thoroughly fucked—flushed and fucking beautiful. "That was us. And I wouldn't have it any other way."

32

BRENNA

I HAD SO many plans for Cole and I this summer. We were going to go on vacation. Go and visit our parents. Have lazy days by the pool. Go to the huge country music festival that takes over Nashville for a week in June.

Finally get Bryce and Cole talking again.

We did three of those things. We had plenty of lazy days by the pool. We made it to the country festival for one night. We got tickets in the Fury's suite and had it all to ourselves.

We made the most of it.

Twice.

We also made it back to Laurel Heights, and I don't know if it was a good or bad thing, but we missed Bryce and Lucy being there. It has officially been more than two months since Bryce and Cole have said a word to each other. They have never gone that long without speaking. Hell, before this fight they used to text more than teenage girls.

But now the summer is over—at least for the guys it is. Camp opens tomorrow, and it's officially football season again.

Which means tonight is the night. Lucy and I have it all planned out. If we need to, we're going to lock them in a room together until they kiss and make up.

We refuse to let them go to camp without speaking.

"You didn't have to go all out," Cole says as I put the final plate down at the dining table. "It's just Bryce and Lucy."

"Exactly, it's Bryce and Lucy," I say, straightening the centerpiece I picked up the other day. "Maybe if he sees how much this place has become ours, he'll realize this is for real between us, and he needs to suck it up and get over it."

"Speaking of ours," Cole says, tossing me a letter. "This came for you today from your apartment complex."

I take the letter and rip it open.

"What does it say?"

I hold up a finger as I quickly scan the letter. "It says that the renovations are finally done."

"Took them long enough."

"They also say that they realize since it took weeks longer than expected, that if we need out of our leases because of agreements we had to make, we have until the end of the week without being penalized."

I look up at Cole, who is doing a very bad job of containing his smile.

"What are you smiling at?" I ask, putting the letter on the table.

He reaches for me, and as always, I give him my hand so he can pull me into him. "I mean, I did buy you a bed."

I chuckle. "You mean the one I don't use?"

"And you've overtaken my closet. Seems silly to move all of those clothes back to your apartment when we both know that you are going to miss my sheets and pillows too much to not stay here every night."

I smile, because he's one-thousand-percent right. "This is true."

"So I think you should call your landlord and tell him that you won't be needing that apartment anymore."

I'm pretty sure my smile right now could light up Nashville during a power outage. "Are you sure?"

"Am I sure?" he asks, picking me up so we're eye level. "This coming from the woman who barged in here in the middle of the night and never left?"

"Hey! I gave you an option."

He tilts his head, giving me the "you're out of your mind" look. I get this look often. "As if I could have said no."

"I'm so glad you didn't."

I lean in to kiss him. I meant for it to be a small one. But like many kisses with us, it quickly grows deeper. My fingers start traveling up to play with his hair, which is usually my signal for let's-go-sneak-in-a-quickie, when I hear my phone alerting me to a text message. I unwillingly separate from him only to see the worst possible message on my phone.

> Lucy: Plan is off. I can't get him to come. I'm so sorry.

"What the fuck?"

I scan the text message again because there's no way I read what I just read.

"What's going on?" Cole asks.

I nearly throw my phone at the wall. "It's Lucy. She can't get Bryce to come. I'm so mad I could scream!"

I start pacing around the dining room mumbling swear words I didn't even know I could string together. It takes all the restraint in my body to not pick up one of these plates and hurl it against the wall.

But I don't. Because the only thing that needs bashed into a wall is Bryce's head.

"That's it, I'm going up there," I say as I start marching to the door. Somehow Cole gets in front of me and cuts me off, slamming the door shut as soon as I open it.

"You are not going up there," he says.

"Like hell I'm not!"

I try to maneuver around Cole, but it's impossible. He's just too damn big. First time I've ever said *that* about him.

"Brenna, you aren't going to get anywhere talking to him this mad. Now, go sit down on the couch and take a second to breathe."

I let out a huff but do as Cole asks. "Why is my brother so fucking ridiculous? I knew he was going to be weird about this, but we are going on *three months* of him being a fucking toddler. And camp is opening tomorrow, and if you two aren't speaking what does that mean for the team? This is all sorts of fucked up, and all because Bryce can't get his head out of ass."

Cole doesn't say anything as he sits next to me, which in this situation kind of surprises me. I mean, I wasn't expecting a "Brenna you're the smartest woman in the world" response, but a "you're right" would be nice.

Instead, he just sits there. Silent.

"Don't you think he's acting ridiculous?" I ask again.

Cole puts his hands together as he rests his elbows on his knees. He's looking at the floor, and all of a sudden I get this feeling in my stomach that I'm not going to like what I'm about to hear.

"I think he's acting like Bryce."

"What's that supposed to mean?"

Cole sits back up and turns to face me. "It means I get why he's acting like this. I didn't before, but I do now. Especially now that he's had time but still isn't ready to talk."

I shake my head, because now I feel like I'm in Crazyville: Population Brenna. "You're taking his side?"

"I'm not taking his side. I'm just saying I get it. I get him."

"And you're saying I don't?"

"I'm not saying that," Cole says. He lets out a breath, which I'm pretty sure is his way of trying to figure out how to calm me down. "What I'm saying is that yes, he's your brother, but he's been more than that to me for years. I know him better than anyone. Hell, there are things about him that Lucy doesn't know but I do. And if there's something that I'm sure of, it's that sudden shifts in his life? That is something that your brother is shit at. Hell, look at how long it took him to figure things out with Lucy. Or how far off the rails he went when he found out she was engaged? Brenna, I'm pretty sure the only reason he isn't in the bottom of a bottle right now over us is because of Lucy. So, I get it. I get that he needs his time."

"But he promised!" I yell. "He promised after this summer he'd come back and be ready. He promised me, Cole."

I can't hold back the tears anymore as I fall into Cole's arms, letting months of frustration, anger, and sadness flow out of me. I cry because I want Bryce to be okay with this. I cry because I hate that because Cole and I found each other, it means that the man I love doesn't have his best friend anymore. I cry because I just want things to be how I know they can, and I don't know how to get them there.

"I hate this," I say through tears. "I hate that it's like this."

Cole kisses my head and squeezes me a little tighter. "I do too. I never thought I'd say this, but I miss him. I just got him back from whatever the hell the last two years were, and now he's gone again."

This makes me cry all over again. "How do we fix this? Because right now, I don't see a way we can be together and have my brother be okay with it."

"No," Cole says, bringing me to his lap so he can look me in the eye. "Don't even think like that. I love you, Brenna Donald. I love you so much it fucking hurts. And yes, it hurts that my best friend is taking longer than I'd like to get to a space where he's okay with it, but we just have to let him take his time. When he's ready, he'll be ready. But you and me? Sorry, baby, you're stuck with me."

I want to smile, but I can't shake one nagging thing off my mind. "What if he doesn't come around?"

Cole takes my face in his hands and brings me in for a long kiss on my forehead. I close my eyes and let the feel of his lips soothe every part of me that hurts right now.

"He will. Just give him time."

33

———

COLE

I LOVE PLAYING FOOTBALL. I don't know what I would have done with my life if this wasn't my career. And knowing that, I will never take for granted a single day of the job I get to do for these few years of my life.

But training camp can suck my left nut.

"How do I forget every year how bad the first day sucks?" Wes asks as we finally make it back to our lockers after what might be the longest training camp day I've ever experienced.

"I mean, you've only had twenty training camps," I joke. "Maybe they are starting to meld together in that old man brain of yours."

"Watch it now," he says, grabbing a towel. "And it's only been ten."

We laugh as we both sit and take a breath. The locker room is silent except for muscle-weary groans and occasional swear words. We've just wrapped up our second session of the day, and I don't know what is up with Coach McAvoy, but he wasn't messing around today, first team practice of the season or not.

I look up for just a second, and like the world is trying to remind me that I'm not speaking to my best friend, Bryce walks past me to get to his locker. I nod my head at him, but it's only returned with an icy glare.

"What the fuck is up with you two?" Wes asks.

I shake my head. "There isn't enough time or beer to cover that."

He tosses me a towel. "Well, I don't have the beer, but I bet the story could make the time in the ice bath go quicker."

I nod and stand as we walk to the training room, where multiple ice baths are waiting for the team. They might sting, and I might never get used to the cold, but I can't deny that they do wonders for my body after a hard day of practice.

"So tell me," Wes says, easing into his tub. "Why is the Fury's favorite bromance seemingly on the outs? What did you do? Sleep with his sister?"

I don't answer because I'm not quite sure how to say yes to what Wes thought was clearly a joke. Apparently, by the look on my face, I don't need to.

"No, you fucking didn't!" he says. "Dude, what were you thinking?"

I shake my head. "No, it's not like that."

"Did you not sleep with his sister?"

"Well, yeah. But it's more than that," I say as I submerge myself in the icy hell. "We're dating. She just officially moved in with me."

"Wow. Congrats. That's a huge step. Wait! Was she the reason you were all smiles this summer?"

"Yeah. It was her," I say. "And I still want to be excited, but it's hard when everything else seems to be shit right now."

"I mean, how bad is it?"

For the next five minutes I fill Wes in on the events since the wedding, which he was unable to attend. I try my best to not paint Bryce in a bad light — he's still this team's quarterback, and the last thing I want to do is divide the locker room. Plus, if he's refusing to talk to me, I'm sure players will start picking up on it sooner or later. Wes just happened to be the first.

"Fuck," he says after I catch him up. "He's not speaking to you at all?"

All I can do is shrug. "Nope. Brenna and I tried to have him and Lucy over for dinner last night to try and clear some air, but he refused to come over."

"Shit, that sucks," he says. "I wish I had some great words of wisdom."

"You don't? Isn't that your role as our team's elder statesman?"

Wes tosses a towel at me, which I easily avoid. "Listen, just because I was playing in the league before your balls dropped doesn't mean I have all the answers. Hell, I'm dealing with enough crazy in my own house."

"Really? Everything okay?"

Wes shrugs. "I don't know. As you so nicely pointed out, I'm getting up there in years. I brought it up to my wife in the off season that there aren't going to be too many more of these. I have three years left in my contract and when that's up, I'm done."

"You? Retire?"

Wes nods. "Yeah, my body can't go through this for many more years. But when I bring up the R-word to the wife, she freaks out. Asks me what kind of job I'm going to get if I'm not making millions a year. As she so kindly put it, she has become used to a certain lifestyle."

My eyes go wide. "Wow. She said that?"

"More or less. But enough about me and my crazy wife. You and Bryce. We have to fix this. I don't know if you realize this, but if you two aren't talking, that could create some serious problems on the field. And in the locker room."

"I know, I just wish I knew what to do."

"I wish I could help," Wes says as he starts to stand up from the ice bath. "You broke the pro-football locker room bro code. Which I think is a load of shit, but I know others don't. Clearly, Bryce falls into that camp."

I stand up and step out of the bath, quickly grabbing a towel to dry off. "Bryce is a very black-and-white person. He's always had trouble seeing the gray area in anything. So in his mind, we betrayed him."

"I get that," Wes says as we start making our way back to the locker room. "But on the other hand, if I had a friend like you, I couldn't pick a better guy for my sister to be with."

"Thanks man. That's…"

He holds up his hand, clearly not wanting me to get too emotional about this. "I'm just saying, there are bad men in the world. You aren't one of them."

As if on cue, Dexter struts into the locker room. I still can't believe Brenna even went on one date with this ass hat.

I need the hell out of here. I need to go home and fall into bed with Brenna next to me. Maybe if I'm lucky she'll do that head scratch thing that puts me to sleep instantly.

My girl has magic fingers.

"How is Mr. Cole Campbell doing?" Dexter says, stopping at my locker. "How was your summer?"

I give a skeptical eye to Dexter. The question seems innocent enough, but this man rarely talks to me. He has his crew—the young guys who like to party and flash the kind of money they make. Yes, I'm only a year older than him, but that's not my scene, never has been.

"What do you want, Dexter?" I ask. "You've never once asked how my day is going."

"Can't a teammate care about another?" he asks, clutching his chest in mock pain. "Just asking how your off season went."

I know what he's fishing for, but I don't want to cause a scene.

"It was fine."

He pretends to be shocked by that answer just as Bryce walks behind him. "Just fine? Damn. If I were with the dime piece known as Brenna Donald, I'd hope my summer was more than fine."

I feel the temperature of my blood starting to go up. I can also feel Bryce staring at me, obviously having heard what Dexter said. And I'm sure that's exactly why Dexter said it.

Play it cool, Campbell. Don't give anyone any reason to blow this up.

"We had a great summer," I say as I finish getting dressed. "Now if you'll excuse me, it's been a long day."

Dexter puts his hand on my chest. I swear if we weren't in our locker room right now, I'd be forcefully removing it myself. "Listen, I just want to clear the air."

What is he talking about?

"Clear the air about what?"

"You know," he says, clearly liking that an audience is starting to form. "My history with your girl. I know it can be weird being teammates who have both...you know."

Apparently, this man woke up today and chose violence.

"There will be no—what did you say, weirdness?—because there was nothing between you and Brenna. You went out on one shitty date and I had to come rescue her."

"Excuse me, *what?*" Bryce yells, jumping in the middle, looking back and forth between us. "Brenna did what?"

Now I don't know if Dexter seriously didn't realize this or if he's just a decent actor, but he seems shocked by Bryce's reaction. "You didn't know? Yeah, man. Me and your sister were hot for a second."

"Oh for fuck's sake, no you weren't," I yell over a still-stunned Bryce. "You got her drunk off her ass, and she still proceeded to tear you down a peg. If that's what counts as hot on your dates, then you clearly need some help in the female department."

"You got her *what?*" Bryce yells, though Dexter seems to be ignoring him.

"I don't need no fucking help," Dexter says, trying to step closer to me. "Believe me, ask your girl. She'll tell you."

That's it. He can egg me on all he wants, but I refuse to let him make shit up about Brenna just because of his ego. "She'll tell me what? You two didn't do shit, so quit acting like you did. And if you're mad that she picked me over you, that's something you and your therapist need to work on. How about you go buy another sports car? I'm sure that will help."

Dexter lets out an annoyed breath. "Whatever. That bitch ain't worth—"

He doesn't get a chance to finish that sentence. I push Bryce out of the way and load my fist back. I'm inches from hitting his smug face before I feel multiple people holding me back.

"Get the fuck out of here," I say. "And I swear on my grandmother's grave, if I ever hear you say one fucking word about Brenna again, no one will dare try and stop me."

Dexter points to me then looks over at Bryce. "This the kind of guy you want with your sister?"

Bryce doesn't answer this, but takes a few steps into the locker room, where we have now accumulated quite the audience. "Has anyone else here gone out with or done anything with my sister that I need to know about?"

I look back at Wes, who was the one who came to grab me, and nod that he can let me go. I take a look around the room, filled with my teammates, who are all wide-eyed and slack-jawed at the events of the last few minutes. None of them is going to say anything to Bryce. Hell, Brenna could have dated the entire defensive line right now and no one would say a damn word.

Bryce looks back to me and Dexter. "See? These are true teammates. They know the code. And this? This pissing match between the two of you? This is why the rule is in place. You don't date, screw, or do anything with a teammate's sister. It never leads anywhere good."

"Whatever," Dexter says, now seemingly bored with this conversation. He tries to step away, but I don't think he really understands me yet.

"Listen here and listen good," I begin as I step in front of him. "This will be the last time you ever say her name. You see her? You don't look at her. You don't say hello. You pretend she's a stranger. Got it?"

"Or what? What are you going to do? Coach McAvoy will fine your ass if you hit me."

I step a little closer, which allows me to look down at him since I have a few inches on him.

"Let him. Hell, he can have my whole damn check. It would be worth it."

"Whatever, man. I ain't scared of you."

"I would be if I were you."

The words shock me because, yup, my ears didn't play tricks on me. They came from Bryce, who I didn't realize was standing next to us.

"Walk away, Dexter," Bryce continues. "If you ever want me to throw you another pass again you'll listen to what this man says. And considering I know you have a performance clause in your contract, it would be best for everyone if you took Campbell's advice."

Dexter looks back and forth between the two of us before turning away like a kid who didn't get his way. Good. Let him go.

I turn to Bryce. "Thanks, man."

The look he gives back to me sends a chill down my spine. Hell, it's colder than the ice bath.

"Are you happy now?" Bryce says.

I tilt my head in confusion. "What are you talking about?"

"This," he says, waving his hand around the locker room. "This is your fault. I hope it's worth it."

And before I can say anything else, he walks away.

34

BRENNA

"ARE you sure it's okay we're here together?"

I look over my shoulder to Lucy, who looks as nervous as I've ever seen her. "Why wouldn't it be okay?"

"I don't know," she says as we walk toward the practice field at the Fury's training facility. "Bryce said things got pretty heated this week. I don't want him to see us together and have it set something in motion."

"Oh please," I say. "If my brother is also going to try and tell me who I can and can't be friends with, then we might as well just throw in the towel. He can get over it. You're my best friend. The men we love play on the same team. It's the first open practice we can go to, so guess what, we're going. Together. And if he doesn't like it, he can suck an egg."

"You're right," Lucy says as we show our passes to the security guard. "Let's just go in and have a nice night and pretend that everything is great and right in the world."

"Sounds like a plan."

Pretending is as close as we're going to get right now. It has been a week since the near-fight in the locker room, and things aren't getting any better according to Cole. Each night he comes home looking more and more drained, and I know it's not just his body getting used to the rigors of the season again. He's mentally exhausted. I don't blame him.

"I hate this, you know," I say as we make our way to the seats.

"Everyone does," Lucy says. "Bryce said that when he and Cole are in the locker room at the same time, everyone just stops talking."

"Cole said that too. He even overheard a few of the defensive guys asking each other if they were on Team Bryce or Team Cole."

Lucy's shoulders slump. "This is horrible. What if this goes on through the season?"

"I don't know if it can," I reply. "I don't know why, but I feel like the volcano is about to erupt."

Lucy nods. "I completely agree."

Lucy and I take our seats in the impromptu Fury family section just as the teams start to run out onto the field from the locker room. Today's practice is the first that's open to the public, which means it's also the first time the families can come watch. Normally, a night like this would give me all the warm fuzzies. Dads bringing their sons and daughters to come watch the players, fans getting excited about the upcoming season, kids of players watching their dads in awe and amazement. But unfortunately for me and Lucy, all we can do is hope that our guys get through another day without killing each other.

We both put on fake smiles as we watch wives and girlfriends of players come up and take their seats. No, we don't have assigned seats, but everywhere we go, we seem to all gravitate toward each other. Probably because we want to be as far away from the fans as possible.

We appreciate them, but they are a tad crazy.

"Hey, Lucy! Brenna!"

We both wave as Sadie, Coach McAvoy's wife, and Bethany, who's married to Coach Davis, come up the stairs and make their way toward us. Bethany is carrying Charlotte, who I believe is now about eighteen months old. Her hair is dark like her dad's, but I'm guessing by the all-pink Fury outfit she is wearing that she is one-hundred-percent just like her mama.

Then there is Sadie, who just looks like she's carrying a basketball under her shirt.

"Let me help you," I say, standing up and offering her a hand.

"Thanks," she says, taking it before she plops down onto a bleacher seat. "I didn't realize how hard these stairs would be."

"I told you," Bethany says, sitting next to her and arranging Charlotte on her lap. "Everything is hard when you're about to pop."

"When are you due?" Lucy asks. "I thought you said at the wedding he was due before camp started."

"He was," Sadie says, her eyes all of a sudden looking angry. "Because of course, we tried to plan a child around football season. Then the doctor said he got the date wrong, and that he was a week off. Now on top of that, the little guy is two days late."

"Oh no," Lucy and I say in unison.

"Oh no is right," Sadie says. "I'm hoping that since this boy is the product of Hunter and me, that he would want to come watch football practice and be so jealous he'll decide it's time to vacate."

Bethany shoots her a look like she's insane. "Yup. That's exactly how it works."

"Oh shut it, Miss-I-had-my-baby-three-weeks-early," Sadie says.

Bethany just shrugs. "Hey, at least your baby daddy will be there when he's born."

"Davis ended up making it. Barely. But he was there."

Bethany laughs. "Let's not replay that night."

The two sisters continue to joke back and forth as the guys warm up on the field. Lucy and I look at each other, and as if we're thinking the same thing, grab each other's hand and give it a squeeze.

This should be us. Laughing and sharing inside jokes. Holding each other's kids, not just because the other needs help but because the child desperately wants their aunt to hold them. To have husbands who are best friends, so we could live our lives together as the family not only of blood but of choice.

That's what we should be having right now. Not senseless fighting that is going on for so long at this point I think we're forgetting what even started it.

I hurry up and brush the stray tear that has somehow leaked from my eye. But unfortunately, Sadie sees it and grabs my free hand.

"Hey," she says, giving my hand a squeeze. "Everything is going to be okay."

"You know?" I ask.

Both Sadie and Bethany nod. "Yeah," Sadie says. "The guys might think they're being sly about it, but the coaches know. Between us, they are trying to stay out of it and let them work it out."

"By the way, Brenna, you and Cole are just adorable," Bethany says. "The picture on Instagram of you two at Country Fest? It's everything."

"Thanks," I say, all of a sudden feeling a little bashful. Or because I'm remembering what we did about a half hour after that picture was taken.

"I knew you two were together at the wedding," Sadie says. "I love you both and think you're a great couple, but you were shit at hiding it. I called it then. Hunter didn't believe me. I won twenty bucks and a week of foot massages."

I laugh. "Glad to help. I just wish I could help fix this with Bryce and Cole."

Sadie looks out to the field where the offensive players and the defensive players have split now and are running individual drills. "I wish I had an answer, because believe me, Hunter wants it to end. He wants to let them work it out, but he's about two practices away from locking them in a room together."

"We wanted to try that," Lucy says. "Bryce wouldn't come."

"Doesn't surprise me," Sadie says. "Bryce is an emotional guy. I mean, look at everything he's had to learn to overcome the last few years. And now everything he's known is different. Not saying he shouldn't get over it, because he needs to, but for years it's been him and Cole. Now it's not. And I think that scares him."

"It does," Lucy says. "Even if he won't admit it."

"Then why can't they talk about it?" I demand. "I feel like if they just sat down and fucking talked this would all be over."

"Ah, and that's where you try and apply logic," Bethany says. "They are men. Logic does not exist."

Lucy and I can't help but laugh at that. Because it's the damn truth. "I had hoped by now this would be said and done," I say. "Because at this point, if it were a relationship, I'd tell them they'd either need to fight or fuck."

As the words are coming out of my mouth, I see a whirlwind of commotion on the field. Arms are flying. Guys are trying to hold their teammates back.

And not just any teammates—Cole and Bryce.

"Holy shit!" Bethany yells, pointing to the field where Cole and Bryce are now inches away from each other.

"Looks like they chose to fight." Sadie says, holding her belly as she stands to get a better view. "Bryce does know that Cole has a hundred pounds on him, right?"

I don't answer Sadie because I can't. I'm frozen. I want to go down and break this up, but I can't move.

Which is why I get to watch in real time as Bryce reaches back and punches Cole straight in the face. Again.

35

COLE

~~ TEN MINUTES EARLIER ~~

"OFFENSE, break for water. Make it quick! Two-minute drills when we're back!"

The offense runs over to grab a quick drink before the big show: the offense versus the defense in a game-like simulation.

"Everyone ready?" Bryce asks.

Most of the offensive guys nod or give him some sort of acknowledgment. I just continue to drink my water. I'm not about to say something that will ruffle his panties. Especially in front of fans.

"What about you, Campbell?" Bryce says. "You ready?"

I look at him, wondering why he's calling me out like this. "Of course, I am. You know I'm always prepared."

"How the hell am I supposed to know?" he asks. "I thought I knew you, but apparently, I never did. So, since it's your job to make sure I don't get my clock cleaned, I just want to make sure you're ready."

I want to roll my eyes because for one, he doesn't get hit in practice. The shiny red practice jersey he wears makes sure of that. And two, why the fuck is he starting shit in front of everyone? This isn't the time nor the place. Not in front of teammates. And certainly not in front of fans.

"I'm ready," I say, wanting to put an end to this. "Let's get out there."

Everyone must get the tone of my voice because the rest of our teammates start to disperse and head back to the field. But not Bryce.

"The girls are here," Bryce says, nodding toward the stands.

I turn to look at them, and I can't help but smile. They are each wearing Fury clothing and smiling at something Sadie, Coach McAvoy's wife, is saying. Coach Davis's wife is next to her. They all look happy. Content.

Like they should.

"I'm glad they can at least figure this out," I say, though that probably wasn't the best thing to say if I'm trying to diffuse this conversation.

"They shouldn't need to," Bryce says.

"That I can agree with," I say. "Because this shouldn't be an issue."

"Just the opposite," he says. "It shouldn't be an issue because it should have never had to be one. You started it. You chased after Brenna. It's a thing because of you."

That's it. I'm done. I'm fucking done. I've held this in for months now. I've tried to be reasonable with him. I've tried to take into consideration his past and how I know he copes with things. But now he's just being a child, and I'm fucking done with it.

"Why is what I did so fucking wrong?" I ask. "And don't give me that locker room, bro code bullshit. That has been a convenient excuse for you this entire time, but that's all it is. So tell me, honestly, what the fuck is your problem with me dating Brenna?"

"You really want to know?"

"Yes. Fucking tell me."

"Brenna has never had great taste in men," he begins. "Probably has something to do with our dad, but I'm not a shrink. And she picks horrible guys. Guys that don't deserve her. She's an amazing woman who deserves an amazing life. Not a life where her husband is on the road half the year with groupies surrounding him. Not a life where she has to come in second to a guy's career. She deserves better. She deserves better than you or any other guy on this team."

I feel my blood start to boil.

"Fuck you, Bryce. Just fuck all the way off."

His eyes go wide. "Excuse me?"

"You heard me. I said fuck off." Apparently, the rest of the team heard me because we're starting to gather an audience. "Fuck you for thinking that I'm the kind of guy who would cheat on Brenna—or any woman for that matter—with some cleat chaser. What does that say about our friendship that you would even think that?"

"Can you blame me? You've never been in a long-term relationship. How do I know how you'll act on the road? Or that you'll give my sister the life she deserves?"

I step closer to him, because he needs to hear this loud and clear. "I have been your best friend for twenty fucking years. I have protected you from linemen and life. I have stuck up for you when your sorry ass didn't deserve it. I picked your head out of toilets. I made sure you weren't dead in ditches. And you think that I would hurt not just anyone, but the woman I love? If you really think that then we were never really friends."

"We must not have been, because a true friend wouldn't have put us in this situation."

I feel my fists balling at my sides. "You're ridiculous. And a fucking hypocrite."

"A hypocrite? How so?"

I take another step toward him because I want to make sure he hears this nice and clear. "Take a look in the mirror, Bryce. Everything you said? It's the pot calling the kettle black. So by your logic, you're not good enough for Lucy either. Oh wait, we always knew that one."

I expected the punch Bryce threw at me when we first told him about us.

But this one? This one I didn't see coming.

Even though I should have with that last dig.

I feel the punch before I can react to it—a right uppercut right to my jaw.

That is when all hell breaks loose.

Teammates can't get to me fast enough as I dive for Bryce, driving him to the ground. I'm on top of him and before I can even consider whether or not this is a good idea, I punch him square in the face. I cock my arm back again, ready to deliver another one, but feel at least three sets of hands pulling me from him. At the same time, a group of guys are lifting Bryce off the ground as Coach McAvoy and Coach Davis come between us.

"What the hell is going on?" Coach McAvoy yells. "Both of you, in my office. Now."

We stare at each other for another few seconds before we shake off the teammates holding us back. We all start walking to the office, which is probably a good thing. If we weren't escorted, I might be up for round two.

"Sit your asses down," Coach McAvoy says. "I knew things were off between you two but fighting? What in the hell is going on?"

Neither of us say anything. Or look at each other.

"So it's going to be like that, huh?" Coach McAvoy says. "Do you know how bad this is? How could you do that? In front of fans and media, no less!"

That I will speak up on. "I'm sorry, Coach. We shouldn't have let our personal issues interfere with the team."

Bryce huffs. "If you really thought that you wouldn't be fucking my sister."

I snap out of my chair, because apparently he wants me to break the other side of his nose.

"Sit down!" Coach Davis yells, which I do, reluctantly. "My God. You two are the last ones I ever thought would be in this situation. Fighting at practice? Dividing the locker room? We hoped that you two would work it out like men, but apparently not."

"I don't even know what to do," Coach McAvoy says. "You two have put us in a real shitty position. You understand that, right?"

"Yes, sir," we both say in unison. I know it's not the appropriate time, but this reminds me of back in high school when Bryce and I orchestrated a prank on the freshmen. Our high school coach pulled us into the office and read us the riot act. I wish I could smile back at the memory.

"We're going to have to put out media statements. I'd ask you both to not do any interviews for the time being, do you understand?"

I nod. Out of the corner of my eye I see Bryce do the same.

"Second, we need to figure out what's next. You two are to stay away from the facilities and from camp until further notice."

"Coach!" Bryce says. "It's camp. We have to be at camp."

Coach McAvoy stands up from behind his desk. "Well, you should have thought of that before you cold-cocked your left tackle. We'll have meetings with both of you and then we'll figure out the best thing to do moving forward."

"Yes, sir."

We both try to stand, but Coach immediately waves his hands down at us. "No. You are not leaving together. I can't risk another blow up. Donald, I see your wife in the locker room. Go to your locker. Get your things and leave out of the back. Don't talk to one reporter, do you hear me?"

"Yes sir," Bryce says, giving me one more glare before he leaves the office, Coach Davis following him. That doesn't surprise me. The two have a bond after the last few years. Maybe he's the one who can get through to him.

"Put some ice on your chin," Coach McAvoy says.

I nod. "He got me good."

"You know I lost twenty bucks to my wife because of you?"

I look at my coach curiously. "Excuse me?"

He sits back down. "She bet me twenty bucks at the wedding that you and Bryce's sister were together. I said no way. No way would Campbell risk his friendship with Bryce. Turns out I was wrong."

I want to laugh, but it hurts. Shit, Bryce got me good. "Yeah, you were."

"Is she worth it?"

I look over at the locker room, where Brenna is standing, doing her best to hold back tears. "She's worth every punch."

Coach McAvoy nods. "All right. Then let's fix this."

36

———

COLE

IT TOOK FOREVER to get home.

Even worse, I was by myself because Brenna drove her and Lucy to the practice.

Coach McAvoy made me wait more than an hour after Bryce left before he released me, so I told Brenna to go home. No sense in her staying.

Though now as I open the door to our apartment, maybe I shouldn't have done that. Because all I see before anything else, is the sight of suitcases.

"Brenna?" I say, closing the door and dropping my keys. "Breanna, where are you?"

She doesn't answer, but I hear a sniffle come from the guest room. "Brenna?"

When I walk into the guest room, she's sitting in the middle of a pile of clothes, holding onto one of my white T-shirts, tears falling down her beautiful face. In two steps I'm sitting next to her, bringing her into my arms, kissing the top of her head. Anything to give her any sort of comfort.

"This wasn't how it was supposed to be," she says through heavy tears. "This wasn't how it was supposed to be at all."

"I know," I say, rocking her back and forth. "This isn't how I imagined it."

"We were supposed to be a family. You, me, Bryce, and Lucy. It was supposed to be the four of us. We were supposed to go to dinners together and concerts. Go back to Laurel Heights and finally bring all of our families together like they should have always been. Bryce and you should be looking at properties together so you could build your houses, and Lucy and I were supposed to not comment about how ridiculously excited you two were about it. But it's never going to happen, is it?"

I don't say anything, because I don't want to lie to her. A month ago? I probably would have said that everything is going to be just fine, because I honestly thought that. Now? Now my hope is dwindling day by day.

"Brenna," I say, already regretting the words that are about to come out of my mouth. "Why are there suitcases in the living room?"

"Because," she says, but not before a huge wave of tears hits. "Because I need to leave."

My heart sinks to my stomach in an instant. "What do you mean *leave*? For the weekend?"

She shakes her head against me. "I need to go back to Laurel Heights. For good."

My heart continues to free fall out of my body. "For good? You can't leave."

"I have to, Cole," she says, trying to pull away from me, but I won't let her. No. I just have to hold on to her. If I don't let her go she can't leave.

Because she can't. She can't leave me.

"Why are you saying that? You can't."

She pushes again, and I reluctantly let her go. "I have to. I've thought about this every way I can. And the only way for everything to be okay again is if I'm not here. I'm the problem, so I'm taking myself out of the equation."

"Okay," I say, taking a deep breath. "We can do long distance. That's doable in the season. If you go back to Laurel Heights maybe

Bryce not seeing us together every day will help him ease into this. Then you can come back when he's had a little more time."

Brenna shakes her head. "No, Cole... I need to leave. And we need—"

"No!" I yell, cutting her off. "Don't you dare say what I think you're about to."

"Cole, let me—"

"No!" I yell as I jump to my feet. I begin to pace in circles because no, I'm not even going to acknowledge what I think she was about to say. "Brenna, he'll get over it. He has to."

"No, he doesn't. And if tonight is any indicator, he never will," she says. "Seeing you two tonight? Fighting? Punching each other? It broke my heart. Not for us, but for you two."

"Don't worry about us."

"No, Cole, I can't. I can't *not* worry about you two. I never had a best friend growing up. I had a lot of friends. I was never lonely. I always had someone to sit with at lunch or go to the mall with. But I never had that person. I never had a Bryce until I met Lucy. And I know that because I watched you two grow up, and I was jealous of you. I was so envious of what you two had. And you didn't care that it wasn't normal for guys to be that close. You two ran with it."

"Maybe we shouldn't have."

Brenna shakes her head. "No, it was beautiful. You two have the kind of friendship everyone should have. And look where it got you. You two made a pact to get to this level of your careers together, and you're here. You're playing professional football together. If I were to go back in time and tell the seven-year-old versions of you two that you made it... I'd give anything to see those little faces."

I reach for her hands and pull her off the ground. "Do it. Go back and tell them. And tell a young me that the feeling he has when his best friend's sister comes over, that it's actually a crush. And not to pull her pigtails."

This gets her to laugh a little through her tears. "You and my brother have dreamed of this your entire lives. There has never been a day when this wasn't the end goal. And I'm not going to ruin it. I'm

not going to be the reason you two don't fulfill the dream. I can't do it.
I *won't* do it."

"Brenna," I say, though nothing else comes out. I just reach for her
and bring her in, hugging her to my chest where I'm pretty sure she
can't breathe.

"This is going to be for the best, Cole," Brenna says into my shirt. "I
know it hurts now, but it won't forever."

I shake my head. "You're wrong. Because I don't know if you
realize this, but I'm head over heels, crazy in love with you. This? Us?
It's worth more than football. It's worth more than a pipe dream of a
kid from Ohio. It's worth more than anything in this world. Don't you
think that? Isn't our love worth more than that?"

I feel her lips against my chest before she steps away. "I love you
too. That's why I'm doing this. Because I love you. I love you so much
that I can't be the one who stands in the way of what you were meant
to do. I won't stand in the way of destiny."

"What I was meant to do is love you. That's what I was meant
to do."

She shakes her head. "No, Cole. I wasn't the Donald that you were
destined for. You and Bryce still have the football world to conquer.
But I want you to know… I will never forget this. I was done dating
before you. I had given up. I thought that finding someone just wasn't
in the cards for me. But how you loved me? How you opened me up
to love you? It's something I'll never forget. And I'll always love you,
Cole. I just— I can't be selfish. I can't let this continue when it's
tearing up our lives."

"Selfish!" I yell. "You're not the selfish one. Your prick of a brother
is the one who is being selfish. Don't you see, you leaving means he
wins."

"But if I stay, everyone loses."

Brenna walks to the closet and grabs another handful of clothes.
"I still have my apartment for another week. I'm going to go sleep
there tonight. I'll come by tomorrow and grab the rest of my
things."

I'm frozen as I watch her pack her bag. This can't be it. This can't be the end. This isn't how it's supposed to go. I'm not done yet. I'm not done loving her yet.

She is supposed to be it for me. My end game. The reason my jaw fucking hurts and the reason my heart beats.

She exits the room, and I follow behind her.

"There has to be another way," I say.

She turns to look at me, nothing but sadness in her eyes. "There isn't, Cole. I have thought about this from every angle, and in every angle someone gets hurt."

"So you're choosing to hurt us? To hurt me? Is that it?"

Her tears start falling again. "I don't want to choose anyone. Don't you see I hate this? But what do you want me to do? I won't sit back and watch you and my brother destroy everything you've worked for. I won't do it."

"I won't let you go without a fight."

It takes me two steps to cut the distance between us. Before she can object, I kiss her hard. I kiss her with desperation. She doesn't resist as her hands cling to my shirt, pulling me closer. My hands are gripping her head because she needs to feel how much this is killing me. Tears are spilling from both of us as we kiss each other with every bit of grief and love in us.

Eventually we stop, though neither of us loosens our hold.

"There has to be another way," I say. "I'll find another way."

She shakes her head, slowly letting go of my shirt. "I wish there was."

And with that she backs away, grabs her suitcase and keys, and walks out of my apartment.

She doesn't look back. She doesn't say anything else.

She just leaves me. Standing in the middle of my apartment. Heartbroken and empty.

I don't know how long I stand there. Eventually I end up sitting down on my couch, though I have no memory of physically doing it.

I look down, sure that I'll see blood leaking from my chest. But I don't. All I see is that damn blanket that Brenna loves. I'm sure if I bring it to my nose I'll smell her sweet scent. How many nights did we sit here, her wrapped up in this thing while she snuggled into me? Those were the perfect moments. When it was just the two of us. None of the bullshit from the world.

No. This isn't over. It can't be. I'm not done holding her. I'm not done loving her. I'm supposed to marry her. We're supposed to have kids and dogs and memories for the rest of our lives.

Then it hits me. She didn't see another way—but I do.

I pull my cell phone out of my pocket and dial the only number that can fix this problem.

"Hello? Cole?" Dean says. "Are you okay? I was going to call you. Did you and Bryce really get into a fist fight at practice tonight?"

"Dean, when is my contract up?"

Judging by my agent's silence, that wasn't the question he was planning on getting from me tonight. "Excuse me, what did you ask?"

"My contract," I repeat. "When is it up?"

"Um, technically the end of the season. But the Fury wants you to renew before then. Remember the number they floated around? They are serious about it. Why do you ask?"

"Call around. See who needs a left tackle. I want a trade. Maybe see if Cincinnati is in the market. But no matter what, I want out."

"A trade?" Dean asks. "Cole, have you thought this through? You remember how much money the Fury is offering you, right?"

I look at the door that just shut. The one that isn't opening back up. And I look at the blanket, the one that I'm going to have to burn if she doesn't come back.

"I have. And it's not about the money. Hell, I'll take a pay cut. Do whatever it is you need to do. Get me out of Nashville. Immediately."

37

―――

BRENNA

COLD AND EMPTY. Those are the perfect two words to describe the last eighteen hours.

That was my heart when I walked out of Cole's apartment. That was *my* apartment when I walked into it for the first time in months.

And today, as I make my way back up to the place where I found true love for the first time, it's what I'm feeling.

Nothing but emptiness.

"Stay strong, Brenna. This is what you have to do."

I take one last deep breath as I open the door. Cole sent me a message that he had to go meet with the Fury, so he'd be gone for the next few hours. Thank goodness he's not here. Leaving him last night was the hardest thing I've ever had to do. I don't think I could do it twice.

I managed to stop crying about an hour ago, but as soon as I open the door, the waterworks hit me all over again.

Because there in the middle of the living room are the rest of my suitcases, all packed. The blanket I used every day is lying on top of one. And propped up on one is a letter next to a single red rose.

Trouble,

It took me all night, but I understand why you think you have to do this. Do I like it? No. Do I agree with it? No. But I understand it. Because what you are doing is why I love you so much. Because you are the most selfless person I know. So you go. For now. But just promise me that you won't give up on us. That you won't forget me. Remember how I said there had to be another way? Well I'm working on it. So go to Laurel Heights. See your mom. But know this. I'm coming to get you. Because we're not done yet.
Love you forever,
Cole

"Where are you going?"

Bryce's voice startles me as I finish reading the note. What is he doing here?

"What does it look like?" I say with a bite as I push back the tears. "I'm leaving."

"Good," he says, entering like he owns the place. I bristle. "I know you thought you loved him Brenna, but really this is for the best."

Oh, that's it. I'm done. I'm so fucking done with him. Maybe I'll punch him too. And mine won't come with a league fine.

"Look at me!" I yell as I step in front of him. "Does this look like someone who is happy with the decision she's made?"

"What do you mean?" he asks. "You're just going back to your apartment. Don't act like it's the end of the world."

"No, you dumbass! I'm leaving Nashville. I gave up my apartment. I'm moving back home. I can't do this. I can't be here anymore."

"You're what?" he asks. "You're moving back home?"

Is he really that dense? "Yes Bryce. I'm moving back home."

I march into the bathroom to make sure I didn't forget to grab anything last night. Like a puppy, Bryce follows. "Are you and Cole done?"

"Yup. I broke up with him last night," I say, tearing through drawers. "Thanks for that, by the way. First healthy and real relationship of my life and you shit on it every chance you got because for some reason it's an inconvenience to you. I'll remember everything you did for me these past few months at Christmas."

Bryce takes a few steps toward me and tries to put a comforting hand on my shoulder. I shew it away immediately.

"Brenna, I know you don't see it now, but this is for the best," he says. "You'll see that I'm right."

I turn to him, hoping he can see the anger and near-hatred in my eyes. "What am I supposed to be seeing, Bryce? Tell me. What in the world was so bad about us that you insisted on making our lives hell every day for the past few months?"

"You know."

"No, actually I don't," I say, pushing past him and heading back to the living room. "Because your story has changed sixteen times. First it was the so-called lying."

Bryce's eyes go wide. "Are you really going to tell me you didn't lie to me?"

"It was for two days before the wedding when we didn't even know what was going on with us. As soon as you got back we told you. How did we lie?"

"You didn't. Cole did. For the years that he had a thing for you."

"And how would that have played out? I can picture it now," I say, stepping to the side so I can play both of these roles. "Cole: Bryce. I have a thing for your sister." I step to the other side. "Bryce: Hell yeah man! Let me set you up!"

Bryce stares at me, not happy with my dramatics. "We won't know how I would have reacted. I never had the chance."

"Well then let's go with a situation that's a little fresher," I say. "What was this bullshit I heard last night that you don't want Cole with me because of the fact that he *might* cheat on me? Seriously? Do you have that little faith in the man?"

"You don't know what it's like being on the road."

"Do you know something I don't?" I ask. "Is Cole going from city to city picking up every woman who waits outside of your hotels? I thought Dexter was the manwhore of the team."

Bryce shakes his head. "Oh, and we need to talk about that."

"No, we don't. Stay focused. Have you ever seen Cole hook up with a cleat chaser?"

"No."

"Then why all of a sudden was his dick going to get bored and need to nail a woman in every city?"

"I just—"

I hold up my hands for him to stop. "You just nothing. You are grasping at straws. You have been for months, and you still are. So level with me, Bryce. Be honest with me once and for all: why the hell does this bother you so much? Especially because I distinctly remember hearing you say repeatedly last year that you couldn't wait for Cole to find someone. Well, he did. So was it me? Was I not the right pick? What was wrong with me?"

"No, that's not it."

"Then what is it, Bryce? I can't figure it out. Please, help me understand your madness!"

He takes a deep breath before answering. "It's not me I'm worried about. Or Cole," he says. "It's you."

"No," I say, shaking my head. "No, it's not. Because if it was about me you would have found a way to be okay with this. You would have seen how much I love this man. You would have tried harder because you would have seen that I'd marry him tomorrow if I could. But I'm not. And you want to know why? Because this hasn't been about me or Cole. It's been about you."

"Don't put words in my mouth, Brenna."

"Then do me the courtesy of telling me the truth. Because I'm over this. I'm so fucking over this."

He doesn't say anything, so I start to walk to the suitcases. I grab them and turn to leave when I hear Bryce whisper something that I almost don't catch.

"What did you say?" I ask.

I turn to look at him and for the first time in months, I see a true sadness in his eyes. "You just changed everything."

Is he serious right now? "What does it change? Tell me? And is that change so bad when it's two people who you supposedly care about being happy together?"

"I don't know," he stumbles. "I don't know how to put it into words."

I am five seconds away from slapping him silly. "Please, Bryce. Make me understand. Because right now? Right now, I'm leaving my life that I thought I was starting to build. I'm leaving the man I love. I'm leaving my best friend. I'm leaving my pain in the ass brother who, even though I hate him right now, I still love. Want to know why? Because I won't sit back and be the reason people are miserable. I refuse to be the Yoko in this situation. So even though you can't put into words what is so wrong with this, you'll still get your way. I hope you're happy."

Bryce gives his hair a tug while letting out a frustrated breath. "You threw things for a loop! I wasn't ready."

I just shrug, because at this point I'm done. I'm tired. And this conversation isn't helping anything.

"Well, now you don't have to be. You don't have to be ready for change. You can go exactly back to how things were before. You, Lucy, and Cole will be here, and I'll be alone in Laurel Heights. You two will get to live out your childhood dreams while I go back to teach and see the same people I've seen every day for twenty-five years. One day, you'll win a championship together. Cole will find someone else to love that will meet your ridiculous notion of who he's supposed to be with, and you can build your houses next to each other like you always wanted to. Just don't invite me over for holidays. I can't be there and see the life that I thought I was going to live."

"Brenna…"

I shake my head and hold my hand up. "No, Bryce. No more. Just let me leave. I'm sorry I caused so much trouble. But I promise, I won't be trouble anymore."

And with that I grab my suitcases, the blanket, and of course, the note and flower, and walk out of Cole's apartment.

Only this time, it's forever.

38

———

COLE

"BRENNA, please call me back. I just want to make sure you're okay. And I miss you. Please, just call me."

I hang up the phone and throw it across the room. I think I hear a shatter. Ask me if I fucking care at this point.

It's been three days since the incident. Bryce and I are supposed to go back to practice tomorrow—we were suspended for two days and fined—but I'm still holding out hope that Dean can make some sort of magic work and get me traded so I can get the fuck out of here. The problem is that this isn't the peak trade window, so many teams have already filled their rosters. Or at least, that's what he's telling me.

All I know is that if I have to go back out on that field tomorrow I can't be sure what I'm going to do if provoked. My plan is to keep my head down, do my job, and get the hell out of there. I sure as hell am not going to interact with Bryce. If I do, there aren't enough team members to hold me back.

She's gone because of him. And he couldn't give a flying fuck.

I flip on a video game but I barely get five minutes in before I turn it off. I can't pay attention. I can't do anything. I've tried to draw, play video games… Hell, I even tried just getting stupid drunk. Nothing worked. Nothing took the pain away. Nothing helped me sleep.

I'm miserable. And I don't know how to make it go away.

I stand up to get my phone, suddenly realizing that if I do get traded, Dean is going to need to call me to tell me, when the door to my apartment flies open.

"You asked for a fucking trade?"

I look over to see Bryce in my doorway, looking confused and upset. I also realize that we're alone, so there will be no witnesses if I do, in fact, decide to kill him.

"None of your fucking business what I asked for," I say, picking up my phone. Cracked my screen but otherwise seems to be fine. "Get out."

"How could you ask for a trade?"

I step back and actually take a look at him, because there's no way he's this stupid. But by the look he's giving me—confusion laced in with a little panic—yup, he must be.

"Gee, let's see. The woman I love won't be with me in this city because she thinks she's ruining everyone's life around her. So I did the only thing I could to get her back, and that's to play in a city, and on a team, where she doesn't have to worry about upsetting her toddler of a brother every day."

"Cole, you can't get traded," he says, taking a few more steps inside. "You can't break us up."

Holy shit, he is that stupid.

"Are you kidding me? What on earth makes you think I want to play one more fucking second of football with you?"

"Because that's what we do."

I shake my head. "Not anymore. You ruined that. You've ruined everything. Get out of my house. Get out of my fucking life."

I stand up to go grab a beer from the kitchen, only to realize that I've drunk them all. When I come back out to the living room Bryce is sitting on my chair, head between his hands.

"How did things get this fucked up?" he mumbles as he pulls at his hair.

"That better be a rhetorical question," I say as I take a seat on the couch, leaving a good six feet between us. Probably a safe distance.

For now. "Because all you have to do to find the answer is look in the fucking mirror."

He looks up at me, and for the first time in months, I see the guy who has been my best friend for twenty years. Not the angry asshole he's been passing for. "This is what I was afraid of. Since the moment you and Brenna told me about you two, this is what I was afraid of. Only in that scenario, it wasn't my fault. But now it is. Everything is fucked up."

I blink a few times because now I'm confused. "What are you talking about?"

"You and Brenna breaking up," Bryce says, falling back into the chair.

Holy shit, is he really saying now all of this has been built on a hypothetical that he has blown out of proportion?

"Let me get this straight. All of this, the whole time. All it has been is you worrying about something that might or might not happen?"

He shrugs. "Not my finest moment."

I stand up and start pacing in circles. I'm going to fucking kill him. No, I can't do that. Brenna would never forgive me.

Except maybe after I tell her why. Then she might be mad she didn't get to help.

"Okay, you better fucking explain everything. And I'm talking everything. Because I'm a miserable bastard right now and it is all your fault."

Bryce takes a breath before beginning. "Lucy for years has been hinting at you and Brenna getting together. I didn't think she was serious. For one, you never gave me any inclination that you were interested. And two, it was Brenna. I figured she was like a little sister to you."

"I thought that for a long time," I admit. "Then I held it in even longer so that those feelings were a lot deeper."

Bryce nods. "So when you told me that you two were together, and not only that, but you had been keeping it from me for years? That stung, man. And cross my heart—that was why I was so pissed at first."

That I can understand. "I get it, man. You don't do well with things being thrown at you. We knew that. But we didn't want to hide it from you, either. I don't know if there was a right move there."

"I'm not sure either," Bryce says. "And I swear to you, at first, that was the issue."

"Then what happened?" I ask. "What happened from the time you promised Brenna you would take time to process it and when you came back even more against it? And for reasons that frankly are a bunch of bullshit and you know it."

"The football bro code is sacred," he says tenuously.

I shoot him a glare. "I've punched you once this week. Don't think I won't do it again."

"Fine," he says. "I tried to come to grips with it. Every day when Lucy and I were gone, I sat back and thought about you and Brenna together. Not like in *that* way. That's gross and frankly makes me want to vomit. But I tried to think about you two together. And us together. And you know what my fucked-up brain kept going back to?"

I shake my head.

"It kept going back to the what-if."

"The what-if?" I ask, a little confused. "What what-if, exactly?"

"Everything," he says. "What if you two break up? What if you two get married but then get divorced? If you allow your brain to go down that road, it never ends. And that's all I could think. And then what happens to us? You and me? To me and Brenna? To Lucy and Brenna? All I could think of was the absolute worst, so I thought that if you two ended it before you began, we could save ourselves the future hurt that would be ten times worse."

I feel my blood temperature rising second by second. "You motherfucker."

We both stand, because I am two seconds from punching him again when I somehow stop myself. I slowly lower my arm, but need to get out this anger. My hands land on the nearby lamp and I grip it and sling it across the room.

"I fucked up," Bryce says.

"You think?" I scream. "How dare you! And for what? On maybes?

Fuck, Bryce! Maybe I could get hit by a car today. Maybe I could tear my ACL again and be done playing football forever. You can maybe yourself to fucking death! God, how could you do this?"

"I thought I was doing the right thing. That at the end of the day, this is what was best," he says. "Then I saw Brenna the day she left. The hurt in her eyes. Fuck, Cole, I hated every second of knowing that I was the reason she was doing what she was doing. But I thought that it was temporary pain that would pass."

"Who gave you the right to play God in our lives?" I ask. "What made you the keeper of our decisions? Or the verifier of feelings?"

Bryce shrugs. "I don't know. But I realized when she was leaving that I fucked up. Bad."

"What gave it away?" I deadpan.

"She said something that hit me deep. She said that one day, when everything goes back to normal, when we finally built our houses next to each other, and you were married and moved on, to not invite her to anything. Because she didn't want to see our lives without her."

"It would never happen," I say through gritted teeth. "At least not for me. You don't move on from the love of your life."

Bryce nods. "That stuck with me. Then today, when I overheard Dean and Coach McAvoy talking about a trade for you, that's when it really hit me. You really do love her."

I stare at the other lamp, my fist flexing. "No shit, you fuckhead! It took that to make you realize that I was serious about her?"

"I mean, I knew," Bryce stumbles. "But yeah. That's when it hit me."

"Listen here and listen good," I say, doing my best to stay calm. "I love your sister more than anything. More than football. More than you. More than our silly dreams and plans that we made when we were kids. More than anything. I'll do anything. I'll quit today. I'll go play in California. I don't care, if it means I get to spend the rest of my life with her. She's all that matters."

"Fuck," Bryce groans. "I'm sorry. I'm sorry for everything."

"Thank you," I say, because hell, at least he fucking said it. "I'm sorry I hit you."

He waves me off. "I deserved it. I said some pretty fucked-up things."

I shoot him a look. "You think?"

"I know," he says. "But I really need to apologize for one specific one."

"And that would be?"

"That you weren't good enough for her," he says, nothing but remorse in his eyes. "I love my sister. And I love you. And frankly, you're the only man on this earth good enough for her."

I extend my hand, and when I do, he takes it and immediately we pull each other into a bro hug. There's a lot of back slapping. There might be a tear.

Both of us will deny that until the end of time.

"I need to get her back," I say.

"Well then good thing we have another day off practice," Bryce says, holding up the keys to his truck.

"We do?"

He tosses them to me. "I worked it out with Coach. Let's go bring our girl back."

39

———————

BRENNA

WHEN I WAS A KID, I remember watching a movie where the heroine and her children had to move back in with her mom after her husband suddenly left her. She didn't get out of bed for days. She didn't eat. She barely showered or left her room.

I always remember wondering how someone could do that. Just not care.

I get it now.

Because I don't. I don't care.

It's been four days since I showed up on my mother's doorstep, heartbroken and alone. She didn't even bat an eyelash as she opened her door and just hugged me.

It was the best hug ever. Well, not as good as Cole's hugs. But it would have to do.

I turned off my phone the second day I was here. I couldn't stand to see Cole's name pop up. I want to talk to him. I want to hear his voice. I want him to call me Trouble and tell me that everything was somehow going to be okay.

But I can't. I can't get my hopes up like that. It's easier to go no contact.

Thank goodness it's summer, and I don't have to go to work. Fuck… work. Technically I still work for the school in Nashville. Is my position in Laurel Heights even available? I never even thought about all of that.

Oh well, that's future Brenna's problem. Right now, I'm going to just lie here, under the covers, and hope that when I wake up from the nap I'm about to take, that this is all one big bad dream.

"Brenna?"

I ignore my mom and her knocking on my bedroom door. Usually when I do this, she just walks away, which is what I'm hoping she'll do. But for some reason, she decides to sit on my bed, which I only know because I feel the mattress move.

"Brenna, sweetie, you have to get up," she says, rubbing my back through the comforter.

"I really don't," I reply. No sense in pretending I'm asleep.

"Sweetie, Lucy is here."

Now that makes me pop out of my cocoon. I lower the blanket, just enough so my face is now showing. "Lucy's here?"

Mom nods. "Yeah. She wants to see you, but she didn't know if you were up for it. I told her I'd make sure you were."

I sit up slowly, knowing that I'm going to be lightheaded when I do. That's what happens when you stay horizontal for twenty hours of the day. "Why is she here?"

"I'm not sure," Mom says, pushing back one of many loose strands of hair behind my ear. "How about you talk to her?"

"Fine," I say. "She can come in."

"You act like I wasn't coming in regardless of your answer," Lucy says as she steps into view of my open door.

"Nice to see you, too."

Mom gives my leg a pat, and she nods at Lucy as she leaves, shutting the door behind her.

Lucy looks at me and pushes back yet another strand of hair. "You're one Ben and Jerry's tub of ice cream away from being a stereotype."

"You're hilarious," I say. "What are you doing here?"

"You turned off your phone," she says with a sigh. "I was worried about you. I hated knowing that you were here alone."

"Thanks," I say. "I had to turn off the phone. Cole kept calling and texting. All I want to do is talk to him, but I know that it will only hurt more. Turning it off was my safeguard."

"I get it," she says. "I've been there."

"What did you do?" I ask. "When you thought it was over for you and Bryce?"

"Oh sweetie, your situation and mine are apples and oranges. With me and Bryce, I'd had it. I was done. I finally reached my wit's end. Was I sad? Of course. But I knew I had to wait for him to come around. It had to be him. And until then, I just had to keep pushing on. But for you? I don't know how you did what you did. You broke your own heart because you thought it was the best for everyone else. I don't know many people who would do that."

"Well, I can safely say I don't recommend it," I say. "It's literally the worst."

Lucy chuckles. "So I take it with your phone off and you living in this bed that you haven't heard the Cole news?"

I jerk upright. "No. What news? Is he okay?"

"Yes, he's fine," Lucy says as she reaches for my hand. "He asked for a trade."

Now this news is waking me up.

"A trade! Why would he do that? That's not what was supposed to happen!"

"I'm not sure," Lucy says, ducking away from me as I scramble to get out of bed. "All I know is that he called Dean after you left and said to make it happen."

"No!" I yell, grabbing a clean T-shirt and leggings from one of my suitcases. "I didn't leave just to have him go to another team. I left so he and Bryce could do what they were meant to do. They can't do that if he's not in Nashville."

I frantically look for a towel but can't seem to find one. I need to shower. I need to get my shit together. And then I need to get a hold of Cole.

When I find what I'm looking for, I catch a glimpse of Lucy, still sitting on my bed. She's wearing a smile that screams "I knew it."

"What?" I ask. "Why are you looking at me like that?"

She just laughs and shakes her head. "You and your brother. You think you're not alike at all. But that couldn't be farther from the truth."

I shake my head. "What in the hell are you talking about?"

"You'll find out soon enough," she says with a smile. "Get showered. Brush your hair. When you're ready, we're going to figure all of this out. Once and for all."

I CAN'T LIE, I feel like a whole new woman when I step out of the shower. Probably because I had the water temperature set to scalding and I let the hot water burn away every emotion in my body, along with the top layer of my skin.

Lucy isn't in my room when I get back there, but I don't think anything of it. Instead, I take my time to grab clothes that match and run a brush through my wet hair before making my way downstairs. I hear Lucy's voice, which means my mom probably has her wrapped up into some conversation about a visitation schedule for her and Bryce to come back to Laurel Heights. Or for when she can come to Nashville.

Mom misses us really bad.

But what I don't expect to hear are two male voices. And even though I'm hearing them clear as day, it doesn't hit me until I turn the corner into the living room that Bryce and Cole are here.

Together.

"What's going on?" I ask, almost afraid to step into the room.

"Hey there, Trouble," Cole says soothingly, standing up and walking toward me. I'm too stunned to shy away from the kiss he presses to my cheek. Or to fully realize that Bryce isn't making some sort of obnoxious comment.

I look to Lucy, who is sitting next to Bryce with a huge smile on her face. "Lucy? What is happening? I thought you were here alone."

She nods and signals for me to have a seat. "We thought it was better if you were under the impression it was just me."

"We?" I ask, looking at everyone in the room. "When did we become a we? The last I heard there was a me, a him, and a you two."

This makes everyone laugh. Great. I'm now the resident comedian. "While I'm very glad we can find some laughter at my confusion, is anyone going to tell me what the hell is going on?"

Cole comes and sits next to me, taking my hand in both of his. I hate that it immediately relaxes me. I know it's only been a few days, but I have missed this man so much. "I think your brother is going to take it from here."

I look over to Bryce, who is currently looking at Lucy. All she does is nod at him, but I feel like that one gesture just spoke a thousand words.

"I need to start by saying how sorry I am. It might be the first time I'm saying it, but it won't be the last."

"I… I don't know what to say." It's true. I'm speechless right now.

"That's okay. Because you don't need to say anything. I, on the other hand, will need to apologize to you and Cole for many, many years."

I look over to Cole, who is smiling peacefully. And not his forced smile—his real one that I usually only see when it's the two of us.

"I've already apologized to Cole. And we had a five-hour drive here to iron out any other things that happened in what I've decided to call The Lost Months of Cole and Bryce."

"He's being very dramatic about all of this," Cole says in my ear, but loud enough for Bryce to throw a pillow at him.

"Can you blame me? I fucked up. I fucked up royally, and I almost lost not only my best friend but my sister in the process."

I'm pretty sure my jaw is on the floor. I look at Cole, then to Lucy, back to Cole before looking at Bryce. "Are you saying what I think you're saying?"

Bryce nods. "You asked me the other day what the real reason was for why I was so against you two, and I deflected. I knew it, but I was embarrassed to admit it."

Well, now I need to know. "And? What was it?"

Bryce looks at Cole. "Do I have to say it again?"

"You know the ground rules," Cole says. "You fucked this up. You unfuck it."

"I didn't completely fuck it up!"

Lucy gives him a smack against the arm. "Yes, you did. Fix it. Now."

"Fine," he says. I swear this man would jump off a bridge if she said to. "I was scared that if you two didn't work, it would drive a wedge between us. No one would talk. Everything would be a mess. I thought if it ended before it began, we could go back to the status quo."

I start to stand up, because I really want to slap my brother upside the head right now. Luckily for him, Cole brings me back to the couch. "Easy there, Trouble. Believe me, he's already got an earful from me. And his wife."

Lucy nods. "I got you, girl."

I look to Bryce, whose contrite expression speaks to his guilt. He does seem to finally understand the hell he caused. "I have so many questions," I murmur.

"I know," Bryce says. "And I'll answer every one of them. But right now, I need you to know that I'm sorry. For everything."

I stand up, and this time Cole doesn't stop me. I hold out my arms, and Bryce does the same. Now that I think about it, his reasoning is classic Bryce. I don't know why I didn't see it before. He was scared to lose Cole. His constant. The one thing and person who has never wavered from his life.

"Thank you for the apology," I say as we let go. "Does that mean…?"

I turn back to face Cole, trying not to get my hopes up. He's standing up, holding his hand out for me.

I take it. I'll always take it.

"I know you left because you thought it was the best thing for us.

Hell, I requested a trade for the same reason. But there is only one right answer—only one thing that feels absolutely right—and it's you coming back to Nashville with me. With us. Like it was always supposed to be."

He doesn't need to say anything else. I jump into his arms, wrapping my legs around his waist and kiss him. God, do I kiss him. I know it has been less than a week, but I feel like it's been an eternity.

He's right, this is the only right thing. But it could be in Nashville or Laurel Heights. Hell, it could be in China or in New York; home is him. He's my home.

Forever.

"Okay, that's enough," Bryce says. "I said I was okay with this, but I'm still not okay with...*that.*"

Cole and I laugh as he gives me one more kiss before putting me down. But I don't let go of him. Nope, that's not happening for a long time.

40

COLE

I lift up my glass and give Brenna's leg a squeeze with my free hand, as we all raise our glasses for Bryce's upcoming words of wisdom.

Lord knows what he's about to say. But unlike a few months ago, I know it's going to be filled with love and kindness. And probably a little gloating.

"Here's to the four of us," Bryce says, looking first at Lucy then to Brenna and I. "I know I was scared of this. I know I almost made sure this didn't happen, but I'm so glad it did. And I'm so glad that everything is now working out exactly how we planned."

"Here, here!" we all say, clinking our glasses around the table at the steakhouse where we chose to celebrate.

I take my hand away from Brenna's leg and put it around her chair. Yup, this is it. This is how it's supposed to be.

We won our season opener today over Milwaukee. Bryce threw for more than three hundred yards and four touchdowns. He wasn't sacked once—a point of pride for me. The locker room has settled down since our blowup over the summer. Hell, even Dexter has backed off. Then again, rumor has it he is actually seeing someone, so that could have something to do with it.

And best of all? Earlier this week both Bryce and I renegotiated our contracts—we'll both be in Nashville for the next ten years.

"I'd also like to make a toast," Brenna says. "To making Nashville our forever home. And for Bryce and Lucy to build the bigger house so Mom eventually lives with them."

"Hell, no!" he says while the rest of us laugh. "She can have her own house. We can afford it. I'm not living with Mom."

The first thing Bryce and I did after finalizing our contracts, and making sure that we are going to be taken care of financially for a very long time, was head out to look at land to build our houses. We've talked about it forever, and the time is finally here. Somehow, we found a parcel of land about a half hour south of Nashville with plenty of space for all of us. And yes, there's even space for an in-law house.

Because that's what I will be calling it. As long as Brenna says what I think she'll say tonight.

"So do you guys want to hear the gossip that came from the wives' suite tonight?" Brenna asks.

"Brenna, we are grown men who play professional football," I begin.

"Which obviously means yes," Bryce finishes. "Now spill."

Lucy laughs. "So, we're all sitting there, fawning over Sadie's baby, when we hear a commotion outside the suite."

"Commotion?" I ask. "What kind of commotion happens on the suite level?"

Brenna wags her eyebrows. "The kind that happens when a certain someone's ex-girlfriend tries to get into the suite, claiming that she has the right to be there."

I look at Bryce, who is clearly just as confused as I am. "Ex...?" My eyes widen as I stare at Brenna. "No. She didn't!"

"Oh, but she did," Brenna says. "But that's not even the best part."

Bryce's eyes go wide. "There's a best part?"

"Yup," Lucy says. "Jessica didn't try to get in there because of Cole.

Oh no, she has a new man now who apparently forgot to leave a credential for her."

I rack my brain, trying to think of anyone who… No way.

"Dexter!" I nearly yell.

Brenna and Lucy both nod. "And she didn't get in because he forgot," Lucy explains. "So my guess right now is that he's getting his ass reamed out by our favorite crazy redhead."

"Oh, this is too good," Bryce says. "Gee, Cole, now you'll get to see your ex all the time! Hey, maybe we can triple date!"

"No!" Brenna and I both yell at the same time. This gets a laugh out of the whole table.

"Do you ever wonder what might have happened if you took a different path?" Lucy asks.

Brenna tilts her head. "For anything specific or just in general?"

"I don't know," she says. "Take, for example, Cole and Jessica, which is what made me think of it. What if they would have worked out? What if her crazy was Cole's cup of tea? Or what if she was nice and normal? Then we'd be here right now with her and not you."

"Thanks for that," Brenna says dryly. "But I see what you're saying. What if I never went to Clemson that weekend to visit Bryce and Cole?"

She turns to look at me, and I bring her in, giving her a kiss on the temple. "I don't think that one counts."

She turns to look at me. "Why's that?"

I didn't know how I was going to do this tonight, but I don't see a better opening. I'll have to buy Lucy something real nice for inadvertently opening this up for me.

"Because," I say, turning in my chair to face her better. "Brenna Donald, I would have fallen in love with you at another time. I don't know when. I don't know where. But I know more than I know my own name that our love is too strong and too right to not have happened. So yes, I realized it in the back of a cop car, but I knew it long before then. And I'll know it for as long as I live."

I hear Lucy gasp as I step out of my seat and go down on one knee. Bryce knew this was going to happen sometime tonight, so he's already recording. And then there's Brenna—hands over her mouth, tears flowing down her cheeks.

I take her hand in mine and breathe in the biggest breath of my life. "Brenna, for years I was in love with the idea of you. The fantasy. But now? After being with you these last five months? I can't imagine my life without you. You are every dream come true. Every day I get to spend with you is better than the one before."

I pause for a second to open the ring box. Somehow my hands aren't shaking, even though I feel like my entire body is.

"Brenna Marie Donald, will you do me the honor of my life and be my wife?"

She doesn't say anything. Instead, she leaps out of her seat and jumps in my arms, wrapping around me like a spider monkey.

"Can I take that as a yes?"

I hear laughter in the background as Brenna looks back up at me and kisses me hard and fast. "Yes, Cole Campbell. I will marry you."

"She said yes!" Bryce yells, which in turn gets the entire restaurant in on the celebration.

I stand up, Brenna still in my arms, as we embrace in the moment. When I finally put her down so I can put the ring on her finger, she doesn't let me go.

Good. I'm never letting her go either.

"Holy shit!" Bryce yells, putting down his cell phone. "We're going to be actual brothers!"

Lucy gives him a confused look. "Did you never think of that?"

"I mean, I did, but it really just hit me! This is the best day ever!"

Brenna and I laugh at Bryce's antics, while Lucy just shakes her head.

When the commotion settles down, Brenna signals for me to come down a bit so she can whisper something to me.

"Did you pay the check?" she asks.

I raise an eyebrow. "Why do you ask?"

Her eyes all of a sudden become heated. "Because as a now-engaged woman, I would like to have sex with my fiancé *very soon* while wearing only this ring. So, if we're not out of here in ten minutes, we're going into the bathroom, and I don't care who hears."

I take her chin in my fingers and kiss her again. I know she's serious as a heart attack right now, and it wouldn't be the first time we hit up a restaurant bathroom.

But tonight? Tonight is for her and me only.

EPILOGUE
BRENNA

TWO YEARS LATER

AFTER EVERY GAME in high school, I'd always make sure to find Cole in the crowd and give him a thumbs up.

Tonight he is getting so much more than that.

That's what happens when you win the league championship for the first time in your career.

"Oh my God! They did it!" I yell as I run and jump on Lucy, giving her a huge hug. Then I remember that I probably shouldn't have done that. "Oh, shit. Sorry! I'm just so excited I forgot that my favorite nephew was in there."

Lucy rests her hands on her stomach as what I'm guessing are happy tears pour from her eyes. "How could you forget? You already have three best-aunt-in-the-world shirts despite being his only aunt. You also organized the baby shower. How could you possibly forget that I'm about to have a baby?"

"I mean, can you blame me?" I say, holding our hands together in the air as the confetti still pours down from the rafters of the stadium. "I'm just... I'm just so proud of them, you know?"

Lucy nods, fighting back another round of tears. "They really did it."

We link arms as we watch Bryce and Cole on stage together, embracing the way only best friends can. The sight brings tears to my eyes, though there could be several reasons for that tonight.

The two of them have dreamed about this for so long. I remember growing up hearing them in Bryce's room, practicing in the mirror how each of them would say that since they just won the championship, they were going to Disney World. And tonight, Bryce will get to say it as he's been named the game's MVP.

Though, if I had a vote, the MVP would obviously go to Cole. I've learned a lot about football over the past few years, and I know Bryce can't do what he does without a good offensive line. And considering that Bryce wasn't sacked once tonight and threw for nearly four-hundred yards, I'd say my man and his line were of the utmost value.

"I'm going to sneak on stage," I say. "It's about time I show my man exactly how proud of him I am."

Lucy laughs at me. "You go do that."

I give her one more quick hug before making my way to where all the Fury players are currently gathered in celebration. Most of the guys have their phones out, recording every second of this amazing win. Everyone already has on their league championship hats. I laugh as I watch Dexter dance around the stage, spraying everyone with a bottle of champagne.

Champagne and Dexter... I can laugh about it now. That fateful date seems like so long ago, but it was really only two years. Amazing how much can happen in that time.

Dexter and Jessica dated and got married. And got divorced. I actually think they got divorced before our gift arrived at their home. Then again, I never got a thank you note. I don't know why. I figured she'd love the sheet and blanket set made from sweatpants material.

Bryce and Lucy are doing as well as ever and are weeks away from welcoming their first son. They are all moved into the new home that they built in Franklin, complete with a practice football field in the backyard.

And yes, our house is right next to theirs. They have the practice field. We have the custom gym and game room, which is actually like a mini movie theater. Lucy and I didn't even try and talk them out of it. We knew it was a lost cause. But at least they built us a she-shed that is big enough to fit every Fury wife and girlfriend for book club.

Smart men.

I say hi to Sadie, Bethany, and a few of the other wives and girlfriends as I make my way to the stage. I hear the announcer ask Bryce to come to the microphone to give his MVP speech, so I hurry and pull out my phone, needing to get this on video.

"There was a day I never thought this would happen," he begins. "Hell, there were more than a few days. But here we are, Nashville! At the top of the football world!"

I join the fans who made their way to Miami in screaming and applause. Bryce actually has to signal for the fans to quiet down so he can continue.

"I might be holding this MVP trophy, but one player isn't the team. I need to thank every single man who puts on the uniform with me every day. I'm not here without each one of you. I'd be remiss if I didn't give a special nod to Cole Campbell. My brother. My best friend. Who knew that what we dreamed of as kids would actually come true? And to my coaches...."

Bryce's speech continues, but I'm interrupted by a pair of hands snaking around my waist.

"We fucking did it, Trouble."

I turn around and leap into Cole's arms. Before I can make sure he doesn't drop me, my mouth is on his, kissing the living crap out of him.

"I must say," he says as I come up for air, "this is much better than two thumbs up."

"I thought so," I say as he gently puts me down. "Though I must say that I miss painting your number on my face."

"I don't know," he says, holding up my left hand. "I like this a lot better."

I smile as I look at my wedding ring. It's nearly been a year since we said "I do." In classic Cole and Brenna fashion, the wedding was filled with love, laughter, and chaos. I thought then that it was the best day of my life.

Though today might give it a run for its money.

"I'm so proud of you," I say. "I always knew you could do this."

"It doesn't feel real yet," he says, catching a glimpse at Bryce, who is waving to the crowd as he wraps up his speech.

"What does it feel like?"

"I can't describe it," he says. "Like I'm floating. Like nothing can go wrong. Like I'm at the top of the mountain, and somehow, if I jump, I'll be okay. I don't know how this night can get any better."

This is it. Not that I'm worried that he'll take this news badly, but why not keep pouring the good, even if unexpected, news coming?

"I bet you it can," I say.

He quirks a brow. "How so? And don't suggest locker room sex. I'm not going to get fined again for that one."

I shake my head and laugh. Yeah, we might have got caught, but the orgasm was worth it. "No. Though we could check another city off the list?"

Now I get both eyebrows raised. "I'll bring you back here for vacation. Now, what's the news?"

I reach into my purse and bring out a little treat bag. It's reminiscent of the ones I used to give him in high school before any big game.

"A treat bag?" he asks, clearly confused. "Aren't I supposed to get this before the game?"

I shake my head. "Not this treat."

He opens the bag and it takes him a second to realize what I put in there.

A baby Fury jersey with his number on it and a positive pregnancy test.

"Brenna…" he says through a breath, though nothing follows.

"You're going to be a daddy, Cole Campbell."

He doesn't say another word. He just drops the shirt and test and picks me up, swinging me around while peppering kisses on my face.

I laugh as he puts me down. I don't think I've ever seen him this excited over anything.

"I'm going to be a dad," he says, almost in a whisper.

I nod. "You're going to be the best dad."

He cups my face in his hands, bringing me in for another kiss. "I love you so much."

"I love you, too."

Both of us just stand there for a few minutes, soaking everything in. And for me? I'm not just soaking in tonight, or when I found out I was pregnant last week. No, for me? I'm soaking in all the years and everything it took to get here.

All the little league and high school football games.

The trip to Clemson, when I just wanted to party and instead started on a path I didn't even know about.

The perfect storm of Cole and Bryce getting drafted to the same team, allowing them to live young dreams that some might have thought impossible.

The actual storm that led to my apartment building being flooded, which forced me to eventually move in with Cole.

Bryce and Lucy's wedding.

The fallout.

The love.

The almost never.

And now…the happily ever after.

BONUS CONTENT

*A day in the life of your favorite Nashville Fury couples before the
championship parade. It's as chaotic, and hilarious, as you might expect.*

1

____

HUNTER

"DADDY! DADDY! WAKE UP! PARADE TIME!"

I barely have my eyes open before I feel a thirty-pound cannonball —also known as my son Camden—land on my chest. He is, in a shock to no one, very excited for the championship parade today.

"It's not time yet, buddy." I let out a yawn as I hold up the covers so he can burrow underneath them with me like usual. Except today he doesn't. Apparently when there's a parade, my three-year-old would rather use the bed as a trampoline.

"Nope. Mommy said to get up."

I look over to the clock to see that it's six in the morning. I doubt Sadie said those words. I told her last night I was going to try to sleep in. She patted my arm, curled up with her pregnancy pillow, and told me that I was cute if I thought that. I thought she was being her classic, sarcastic self.

Maybe I was wrong. Did she know that Camden was going to treat today like Christmas morning?

I've been going nonstop since the Nashville Fury won the league championship for the first time in franchise history. It also made me the youngest head coach to ever win the title. Apparently, that gets even non-football people interested. Along with the normal interviews on ESPN, the morning shows, and *The Tonight Show*, I've done interviews on YouTube channels, a few podcasts, and even with that online site that tells you what kind of fruit you are based on their non-scientific quiz.

I'm a cherry.

I think the only journalist who hasn't interviewed me in the past three days—four if you include the day of the championship game—is my wife. And that's only because *U.S. Daily* asked her to prose a "day in her life as a football wife on the biggest day of his life" piece.

Was it the biggest day of my life? I mean, it's up there. But can I compare this to the day Sadie and I got married? Or the day Camden was born? I mean, it's big, don't get me wrong, and I'll remember it for the rest of my life. But it will always trail marrying the love of my life and the day Camden was born.

The first because I've never been so happy. The second because I was simultaneously happy while also terrified.

"What are you smiling about?"

I sit up in bed to see Sadie standing against the doorframe. She's wearing a pair of flannel pajama pants and a very large Fury T-shirt. She's holding her pregnant stomach, which I think has doubled in size over the past few weeks.

Even after five years of marriage, I'm still borderline obsessed with this woman.

"The day Camden was born."

Sadie lets out a groan as she half walks, half waddles over to the bed. She's only six months along, but she's nearly as big as she was when she delivered Cam. I have a feeling my wife is growing a Division I volleyball player in there.

"You know I don't like talking about that day." Sadie sits between my legs, leaning her back against my front. I wrap my arms around her, my hands immediately going to her stomach.

"Actually," I say as I press a kiss against her temple, "I feel like it's good to bring it up now so we don't have a repeat performance when Carli arrives."

"I kick you out of the room *one time* and I never hear the end of it."

I laugh, and eventually Sadie joins in as we both remember that fateful day. And when I say day, I mean a literal day.

Camden's labor went on for twenty-three hours, from two o'clock on a Friday until our boy finally made his way into the world on Saturday at one-fifteen in the afternoon.

Davis was pissed because he had Friday in the baby pool. I was pissed because I felt so helpless. Sadie was pissed because I—and I quote from her—"knocked her up and ruined her life the day I laid eyes on her at the sandwich shop." At some point she also said that everything was my fault, she was never having sex with me again, and she was going to call a divorce lawyer. That was all *before* she kicked me out of the room.

"You know what I did when I left the room?" I ask.

"Do I want to know?"

"Probably not. But I have a feeling we're past the threat of divorce if I come clean."

"That depends," she says. "I heard Wes Taylor had a good one. I could call him up."

I just hear a shriek of giggle as I roll her over on the bed, sprinkling kisses all over her face, being careful to watch her stomach.

"You would never," I say as I lift up her T-shirt so I can start kissing her chest.

"Depends on what you did."

Just as I'm about to deflect from actually telling her—this is supposed to be a happy day and I'm not about to bring up the fact that I left the hospital to go grab a burger and a milkshake—Camden comes barging into the room and jumps on the bed.

"Mommy! Daddy! Parade Day!"

"You're not off the hook," Sadie whispers as she adjusts herself just in time for Camden to leap in between us.

All I can do is smile and watch the two loves of my life have a morning snuggle session. We do this a lot. We've learned that morning sex is out the door when you have a three-year-old who mastered child-proof door handles a year ago. And who are we to argue when our son wants to spend his mornings with us? Even though I don't like to think about it, I know these mornings aren't going to last forever. So I'm going to take every one I can get.

"Mommy?"

"Yeah, buddy?"

"You said you were getting Daddy up."

"Yeah she did."

Sadie shoots me a death glare as the inuendo goes right over my son's oblivious head. "I did say that Cam."

"So why in bed?"

I start to say something, but I get another look that says to think about my actions if I ever want to see my wife naked again.

I do, so I keep my mouth shut.

"Because," Sadie begins—she's dragging out the word, which means she has no idea what to say to Cam—so I jump in.

"Because it's parade day, and parade day means we get to stay in bed even longer!"

By the looks of Camden's wrinkled nose, my son isn't believing a single word coming out of my mouth.

"Nope. Parade! Balloons! Football!"

Camden leaps to his feet and starts jumping up and down on the bed in excitement. I can't blame him. It's parade day. The Fury are the champs. I have the best life I could ever have imagined.

It's crazy to think this day is here because of one fateful day six years ago. I had a feeling that getting hired by the Nashville Fury had the potential to change my life, but never in my wildest dreams did I imagine this. I never thought I'd meet a woman who'd change my life in so many ways. I never imagined I could have it all—work, family, love.

But I do. It's in front of me in the form of my beautiful wife, my amazing son and my daughter who I know is going to complete us in a way we don't even know yet.

And it's all because Sadie and I knew all those years ago that love was worth the risk.

2

DAVIS

I carefully nudge Bethany out of the way so I can lift Charlotte out of her car seat. Yes, I know she's four and can pretty much do this on her own. But sometimes a dad needs to still be a dad and not let his baby girl grow up.

I turn around to see my wife standing with her arms crossed and her hip popped. "Really?"

"What?"

"This," Bethany says as she waves her hand up and down as I hold Charlotte. "Four days ago I tell you I'm pregnant, and you're already taking over everything? I can lift my daughter out of her car seat."

"That's not what this is."

That's exactly what this is. That whole part of being a dad was just my cover story.

"Bullshit."

"Mama! Bad word!"

I hold in my snicker as my daughter calls her mom out. Mostly because it was Bethany's idea to start a swear jar to try to get me to stop cussing as much.

"Sorry, sweetheart," Bethany says. "But Daddy is being a word that would make me put more money in the jar, and I'd like him to quit acting like that."

Before I can rebut, I feel a set of small hands grabbing onto my face and doing their darndest to turn it toward her.

"Daddy. Don't be a bad word."

I laugh and give my little girl a kiss on the forehead. "Sorry, baby."

"It's okay."

I lean in to give her one more kiss but Charlotte all of a sudden starts wiggling like crazy trying to get out of my hold.

"Magnolia!"

I turn around to see Wes Taylor's family—including his six-year-old daughter, whom Charlotte is mildly obsessed with—getting out of their SUV a few spots down from us at the Fury practice facility. It's parade day, and we're all meeting here before heading to the start.

When I asked Charlotte if she wanted to come today, her answer was simply, "Is Magnolia going?" When I said I didn't know, she demanded I text Wes for confirmation.

"Be careful," I call as she sprints toward her best friend. I give Wes a wave, which he returns with a thumbs-up. I've learned that's the universal dad code for "I got your kid."

I'm grateful. Because I need a few minutes alone with my wife.

I come up to Bethany from behind, snaking my arms around her waist as she leans into the car to get her bag. "I'm sorry, Princess."

She stands back up, leaning into me as I place a few kisses on her neck. "You know I'm not going to break if I lift our child?"

"I know," I say as my hands find their way to her stomach. No one would know from just looking that Bethany is pregnant. Hell, we haven't even had time to go to the doctor to confirm it. Though the thirty pregnancy tests she has taken in the past three days all say that we are, so we're pretty confident.

"Then why are you already acting like I'm made of glass?"

"Because," I say as I turn her around. "You're my wife. The mother of my children. The love of my damn life. And if I can make your life easier during this pregnancy, I'm going to do it. And I know you're going to argue with me, and you're going to fight me, because that's what you do and it's also a reason I love you, but you're just going to have to get over it."

Before I met Bethany, I never saw myself being a husband, let alone a father. I had my mom and sisters to take care of. And they needed me. There wasn't enough of me to go around to also take on a family of my own.

I can't believe I ever thought that. Because I can't imagine my life without Bethany and Charlotte. They are my world. And my wife? She's everything. Every night when I kiss her goodnight and bring her into my arms, I say a little thank you to whoever is listening that we found our way to each other. That somehow my life led me to Nashville, and to the Fury, and eventually to Bethany.

So yeah, if she wants to fight me about being a helicopter husband over the next eight months, let her. She's not going to win.

Which is why I'm shocked as all hell that Bethany doesn't say anything back. She doesn't issue a smart-ass remark or tell me that I'm being a Neanderthal. Which is out of character.

Instead she just kisses me. And not just the little peck that she gives me to shut me up. This is a kiss that makes me consider putting her back in the car and driving back to our house and telling Wes that he's watching my kid for a few hours.

"What was that for?" I ask as we reluctantly pull away from each other.

"You being you," she says, her fingers beginning to toy with the hairs at my nape. "I forgot what expectant-father Davis is like."

I smile. "Is he that different from regular Davis?"

"Not really. Maybe a little more on the alpha side. Which isn't a bad thing."

"So why did you say you forgot?"

Bethany smiles. "Because with expecting-father Davis comes expecting-mother Bethany. And she is very…*very*…turned on by that dial-up in the alpha category."

I feel myself instantly harden. That's right before I say twenty words in my head that would have me putting money in the swear jar.

I squeeze her in even tighter. "You can't say things like when we're about to be surrounded by my entire team and the entire city."

"Davis," she begins, her voice dropping down to a whisper. "We got here an hour early. Charlotte is with Wes and Magnolia. And, if I remember correctly, you have an office with blinds and a door that locks."

She doesn't have to say another word. I take her hand and we make a beeline into the facility.

We pass a few players and families who have arrived early. I don't even look for my kid. I just have one goal in mind right now, and it has nothing to do with the fact we've just won the biggest prize in professional football.

Because there's no greater honor is this life than being Bethany's husband.

3

BRYCE

Lucy looks up at me, our son latched onto her. "What I need is for you to go to the parade and be with your team. But since you insist on being no more than two feet away from me at all times, I guess you can get me some water."

"You got it."

I nearly sprint to our kitchen as I put some ice and water into Lucy's oversized tumbler and grab her a snack, just in case. I've learned in my years as a husband that even if my wife hasn't asked for snacks, it's always a good idea to have snacks. Especially my pregnant —and now postpartum—wife. Keeping her fed I feel like can only help my cause.

"Here you go, Lulu." I put the snack and tumbler on the coffee table as I sit down next to her. I can't help but stare as she breastfeeds our son, Gabriel. This isn't the first time I've watched her do this since he was born four days ago. It surely won't be the last. It's fascinating to watch and think about how my wife—and all women—are fucking warriors. They grow humans and push them out of their bodies, then create food for them out of thin air. It's still baffling to me, and I was there and watched it happen. Lucy was a rock star. Even if she did threaten to never let me have sex with her again.

"You're being creepy again."

Lucy doesn't turn toward me, instead keeping her eyes down on Gabe as he starts to fall asleep while suckling.

"I can't help it. It's beautiful."

Little man finally lets go, and she slowly brings him to her knee to burp him. "You know you can go. I'm not going to be mad."

I look over to the television where the cameras are showing thousands of Nashville Fury fans lining the streets of downtown Nashville as they wait for the parade to begin. The parade I've chosen not to attend.

"And I told you, this is where I want to be."

It's true. Since the moment Gabe made his entrance into the world, I haven't wanted to leave their sides. Every news and sports media outlet in the world has wanted to interview me, and my agent has asked them all to respect my privacy as we get settled into our new routine. Because this birth wasn't what we planned for.

Correction: It wasn't what I planned for. Lucy, on the other hand? She had four birth plans, covering every imaginable scenario. Which was a good thing. The plan enacted was the one just in case she went into labor at the game. Which is why we brought her OB/GYN along with us. And when I say we, I mean *she* made sure he could come, and I was in charge of getting him a ticket.

Teamwork. It makes the birthing dream work.

And this teamwork is why her birth, despite it being away from Nashville, went as smoothly as possible. We did stay an extra day so the baby was more than ready to fly home on the Fury's plane. I told them I'd charter a private flight, but I was told by team ownership, as well as Coach McAvoy, that it was the least they could do.

I really don't know a better team to spend my career with. Which I am. I'm in the middle of my second contract, but barring catastrophe, both parties have agreed that I'm here for life.

And there's nowhere else I'd rather be.

Which is why I want to be here, in my house, with Lucy and Gabe.

There will be more championships if I have anything to say or do about it. Which means there will be more parades. But this time? Now? With my wife and our newborn baby? These are moments I'm never getting back. Which is why I told the coaches, Cole, and the rest of the team that I wasn't going to be there today. Everyone understood and were supportive.

Except my wife. She's been trying to kick me out all morning.

Lucy gently puts Gabe into his bassinet and comes back on the couch. "See that over there? That's our son going down for his third out of six naps today. Want to know what he's going to do in between those naps?"

"Why do I feel like we're back in high school, and you're quizzing me for a test I didn't know I had to study for?"

"Because I am. But I need you to answer. Do you know what he's doing in between those times?"

I stop and think, because the answer is eating. But is there more? Was this in a part of the parenting book I accidentally skipped?

"Eating, Bryce," Lucy says. "He'll be eating. That's all he does. Bonus question. Do you know what I want to do today?"

Oh shit. This wasn't in the book. "I don't know, and I don't want to say the wrong thing, so I'm just going to skip this question."

Lucy shakes her head, a small laugh accompanying it, as she scoots closer to me. "I'm going to shower. And I'm going to nap. I might even think about doing a load of laundry that isn't baby related. That's what I want to do today, Bryce. I want to bathe myself and I want to sleep. And I want you to be with your teammates and celebrate the thing that you've worked your entire life for."

"I know you do," I begin, hoping I can get her to see my side. "But I don't want you alone. What if you need something? Or something does happen? Or you need help with anything?"

"That's when I call my parents *from the in-law suite on our property.* This is one of the reasons they're here, Bryce. To help. And because they're overbearing parents who are happy to finally have a grandchild."

"I know," I say, not happy that my wife is making valid points. I hate when she does that. "It's just…"

I trail off, not exactly knowing how I want to put this next part. Lucy reaches over and takes my hand in hers. "Just tell me, Bryce."

Here it goes. "I put football before you too much in my life. I still am baffled every day that you and I made it, because I was an idiot for so long. I don't want our son to know that kind of life or hurt. I hate that you know it. I just don't want to start his life by making the same stupid mistakes as I did in the past."

Lucy slowly makes her way to my lap, placing her arms around my neck. "This is different, Bryce. I know from the outside it looks the same, but it's different."

"How? I'd literally be leaving my child, who isn't even a week old, to go be with my teammates. Tell me how that's different."

"Because this time you know it," she says. "I know you think about the past, and you still beat yourself up about it. But just by acknowledging that you don't want it to be the same is already putting you on the path of being different."

"But—"

Lucy shakes her head. "No buts. Bryce Donald, you earned this day. You and Cole and the rest of the team worked your asses off for years to get to this moment. You should celebrate it. You should be with your friends, and the family that is the Fury, and bask in this moment for what it is. You guys made history. You made history. Now go take that bow that you deserve."

This woman. Will she ever cease to amaze me?

"I want you there with me."

She nods and gives me a soft kiss. "I know. I'll be there for the next one. We'll make sure to plan for a spring baby."

My eyes go wide at just the thought of Lucy pregnant again. "Another baby?"

Lucy kisses me again but adds a playful slap to my chest this time before she slides off my lap. "Not if you don't get out of this house right now and let me sleep. Go to the parade. Have fun. Don't let Dexter talk you into anything stupid."

4

COLE

"TROUBLE, for the love of our unborn child, hurry up. The parade is about to start, and I swear if we miss one more thing today…"

"Keep your pants on, Campbell," Brenna says as she takes her time applying her lipstick in the passenger side mirror. It's like she thinks that we have all the time in the world and the parade isn't minutes from starting.

"That's why we're going to be late," I say with a huff. "Because you couldn't keep your pants on."

She shoots me a look. "Are you really complaining that I wanted to have sex? Because I don't think it was a complaint I heard come out of your mouth when I—"

"Just stop," I say. "And no, I'm not complaining."

"Glad we cleared that up," she says. "Who would complain that their wife was so horny that she just needed one more fix before we left?"

"I just don't like being late," I say. "And we're very close to *not being in the parade at all* if you don't hurry up."

"Calm down, I'm done," she says as she flips the mirror back up. "But I should warn you. I've heard that pregnancy hormones are out of control. Lucy said that she and Bryce did it every day."

"Stop," I say. "He's my best friend, but I don't want to hear about him and Lucy like that."

"Oh, shut it. He's my brother, and I can handle it." Brenna starts to open her door to get out of the Jeep. Fuck that. Doesn't she know by now that in this vehicle, she doesn't touch a door handle? I leap out of my side and sprint around as she's beginning to step down. Luckily, I get there just in time to step in front of her, effectively blocking her in.

"What are you doing?"

"Getting out of the Jeep because someone—that's you—is freaking out that the parade is going to start without us."

"When are you going to learn?"

"Cole, I am perfectly capable of opening a door and stepping down onto solid ground."

I lean in closer, making sure she can hear every word. "You are. But you're carrying my child."

"I am."

"And if you think that for the next eight months, I'm *not* going to basically be carrying you around and doing everything for you? Well, you have another think coming, wife."

Brenna leans in for a quick, but deep, kiss before slowly pulling back. "You better watch it, Campbell. You keep talking like that and we're going to be so late it will be next season."

I give her another quick kiss before lifting her up and setting her on the ground, closing the door behind her.

"Let's go, Trouble."

I take Brenna's hand in mine as we make our way to the double-decker busses that are going to be carrying us through the streets of downtown Nashville as we celebrate our championship win.

We were supposed to all meet at the facility, but I knew that wasn't going to happen once I saw a naked Brenna approaching me in our bedroom, so I texted Coach McAvoy and Davis letting them know we'd just meet them at the parade start. I know as one of the captains that I shouldn't be late and not participating with the team, but I don't feel that bad. Especially when I can still feel my wife bouncing on my cock like she was riding a mechanical bull.

"Get that smirk off your face," Brenna says. "Unless you want your whole team to know why we're late."

"I'm not smirking," I say, though I know I was. "Plus, no one will realize it. Most of these guys have been drunk since Sunday night. I doubt they'll even notice we're late, let alone why."

"Dude! Wipe that 'I just fucked my wife' face off your ugly mug and get up here!"

I look up and roll my eyes at Dexter, who's currently shirtless—even though it's thirty degrees—and holding a champagne bottle. This is what he's done for the past seventy-two hours. I haven't been out and about with the guys—I'd rather celebrate with my wife—but I've seen the pictures. And the group chats.

The man has been on a shirtless bender and shows no signs of stopping.

"Okay, you know it's bad when Dexter is calling you out from twenty feet away," Brenna says.

"He's full of shit," I say as we step onto the bus. "He's just being his normal pain in the ass self."

Before either of us can decide if Dexter knew or was just being Dexter, we're bombarded by hugs, high-fives, and selfies as we make our way to the top of the bus. The team went out and celebrated Sunday night after the game, but I opted to go back to the hotel with Brenna. Yes, I just won the biggest game of my life, but my wife announced we were having a baby. I'd much rather celebrate with her.

Plus, Bryce wasn't there, since he was on his way to the hospital with Lucy. It didn't feel right celebrating the thing we had dreamed of our entire lives without him.

"There he is!"

I smile as Wes, who just had possibly the best final game of any player in history, comes over to me, a beer in his hand. He's followed closely by his new girlfriend, Betsy, who I've heard from Brenna is "the tits" and so much better than his ex-wife.

"You're late!"

I laugh at Wes, who has clearly already had a few. "Yeah. A few things came up this morning."

"Yeah they did," Betsy says, wiggling her eyebrows. "Well, here. Time for you two to catch up."

Betsy hands both of us cans of beer, and I feel Brenna freeze next to me. Shit, we didn't even think of what to say when someone offered Brenna a drink.

"No, thanks," Brenna says, waving it away. "I'm driving later."

Betsy tilts her head. "You know the Fury has Lyft on call for all of us just in case?"

"Oh…yeah. Um…"

Brenna looks up at me, clearly scrambling for what to say. Before either of us can come up with another lame excuse, Betsy is squealing and pointing at Brenna's stomach.

"Are you? Oh my God, you are!"

"Shh," Brenna says, trying to calm Betsy down. "Yes, I'm pregnant. But it's early, and we're not telling anyone."

"Congrats, man," Wes says as he gives me a classic, football-style man hug. "You're going to be a great father."

"Thanks, man. I figured if Bryce can do it, so can I."

"Wait, what?"

The four of us turn to Bethany, who just walked past us, bottle of water in hand. "Who's preggo?"

"What do you mean?" I say, doing my best to deflect.

"Oh, shut it. I get supersonic hearing when I'm pregnant, and I need to know who I'm suffering for the next eight months with."

I smile as I look over to Brenna, who's slowly raising her hand. "That would be me."

"This is amazing!" Bethany runs over to Brenna, arms wide open. "Thank God I have a preggo partner. This will make the next eight months so much less miserable."

"Excuse me?" Coach Davis says as he makes his way to us. "Who are you going through what with, and why is it not me?"

"Brenna!" Bethany says, pointing to my wife, who is all smiles right now. "Apparently you and your captain over here celebrated a playoff win by knocking up your wives."

I look over to my coach, who is looking back at me with a mixture of happiness and slight embarrassment. I should know; that's how Brenna makes me feel most days.

"Congratulations," I say to Coach Davis as we shake hands. "Here's hoping they're born on a Wednesday."

This makes Davis laugh. "If I know anything about babies, it's that they come whenever they damn well please. Speaking of, how are Bryce and Lucy?"

I smile and pull my phone out to show him a picture of the Fury's brand-new dad. "Mom, baby, and Dad are all doing well. They made it home last night."

"Our boy did good," he says. "Through everything."

I nod. "I knew he would."

I look over to Brenna, who, even though she's Bryce's twin, doesn't look much like him, thank God. Except their eyes. Their eyes are the same. It makes me wonder if our child is going to have those signature Donald gray eyes? Or blue like me? Will they be crazy like their mother? Or more even-keeled like me?

Oh my God. Are we going to have twins? How did I not think about this before I went and married a twin?

"Hey," Brenna says. "Why haven't you blinked in the past thirty seconds?"

"I just had the realization that we could have twins, and I could have a little Bryce and Brenna at the same time, and I don't know if I can handle that. I handled it once. I can't do it again."

This makes her laugh as the bus picks up a little speed. "Don't worry, Campbell. We got this."

"What if we don't?"

Brenna shrugs. "We have Lucy. That's normally served us well in the past."

I laugh. "True. I wish she and Bryce could be here today."

"Me too. But they're where they should be."

"I mean, if you don't want me here, I guess I can leave."

I slowly turn around to see my best friend and brother-in-law standing in front of me, sporting Fury gear from head to toe and holding his MVP trophy.

"What the fuck are you doing here?" We come in for a hug, and I give him an extra squeeze for good measure. "I thought you were going to skip out today."

I let him go as he and Brenna embrace. "She kicked me out. Sorry, you two are stuck with me today."

"Dammit." I grab my wallet out of my back pocket and pull out a twenty to hand to Brenna.

"What's that?" Bryce asks.

Brenna smiles as she waves the money around. "We had a bet as to when Lucy would kick you out. I called today. Your brother-in-law here was convinced you'd make it a week."

"Thanks, man," Bryce says, patting me on the shoulder. "I tried."

"I know you did."

The three of us smile as we find our way to the edge of the bus so we can see the crowd as the parade begins. The streets are packed with fans as far as the eye can see, waving signs of support. Music is blaring over the screams and cheers.

It's everything I hoped it would be.

And now it's exactly how it should be, because Bryce is here next to me.

"We did it," he says. "We fucking did it."

"We sure did. Just two kids from smalltown Ohio."

Bryce and I share a knowing look. I have a feeling we're both currently playing back the highlights of our football lives. Pee wee and high school games, when we thought we were the kings of the world. College and the early years of the Fury. The ups. The downs. The moments we never thought we'd come back from. The times we did.

It's all led to this.

Me. Bryce. And Brenna, who is currently FaceTiming Lucy so she can be here with us. Standing on a championship float, celebrating everything we all worked for.

Family.

Football.
Love.
That's what it's all about.

This is officially (at least for this generation) the end of the Nashville Fury series. No matter whether I come back and write more in the future, or this is the end of the road for our favorite football team, I love what this series did for me. And I hope you loved it just as much.

That being said...

Wes Taylor, the veteran tight end who made appearances throughout the book, is kicking off the next series set in the small town of Rolling Hills in The One I Want. His football career is about to come to an end when he all of a sudden finds himself as a single dad. His world is rocked. Especially when he hires the nanny...

CHELLE SLOAN READING LIST

All titles available with Kindle Unlimited

NASHVILLE FURY SERIES

Off the Record

Off Track

Off Season

Off Limits

NASHVILLE FURY WORLD

Off the Market at Christmas

The Swiping Game (Free)

Off Guard (Free)

The One I Crave (Free)

LOVE ONLINE SERIES

Thirst Trap

Match Maker

Run Run Rudolph

ROLLING HILLS

The One I Want

The One I Need

The One I Love (Coming January 2024)

The One I Hate (Coming 2024)

THE SALVATION SOCIETY

Reformation: A Salvation Society Novel

ABOUT THE AUTHOR

Known for her witty sense of humor, Chelle Sloan is a former sports editor who recently completed her Masters in Journalism. She's now putting that to good use—one happily ever after at a time.

An Ohio native, she's fiercely loyal to Cleveland sports, is the owner of way too many — yet not enough — tumblers and will be a New Kids on the Block fan until the day she dies. She does her best writing at Starbucks, or anywhere that's not her house. Oh, and yes, you probably saw her on TikTok.

As for her own happily every after? Maybe one day...

Stay up to date with all things Chelle & join the VIP Squad!